The Wild Cards Series

Wild Cards

Aces High

Jokers Wild

Aces Abroad

Down and Dirty

Ace in the Hole

Dead Man's Hand

One-Eyed Jacks

Jokertown Shuffle

Double Solitaire

Dealer's Choice

Turn of the Cards

Card Sharks

Marked Cards

Black Trump

Deuces Down

Death Draws Five

Inside Straight

Busted Flush

Suicide Kings

Fort Freak

Lowball

A WILD CARDS MOSAIC NOVEL

LOWBALL

A WILD CARDS MOSAIC NOVEL

LOWBALL

Edited by
George R. R. Martin
&
Melinda M. Snodgrass

Written by

Michael Cassutt | David Anthony Durham

Melinda M. Snodgrass | Mary Anne Mohanraj

David D. Levine | Walter Jon Williams

Carrie Vaughn | Ian Tregillis

TOR®

A TOM DOHERTY ASSOCIATES BOOK

New York

LOWBALL

Copyright © 2014 by George R. R. Martin and the Wild Cards Trust

All rights reserved.

A Tor Book
Published by Tom Doherty Associates, LLC
175 Fifth Avenue
New York, NY 10010

www.tor-forge.com

Tor® is a registered trademark of Tom Doherty Associates, LLC.

The Library of Congress Cataloging-in-Publication Data is available upon request.

ISBN 978-0-7653-3195-3 (hardcover)
ISBN 978-1-4299-5641-3 (e-book)

Tor books may be purchased for educational, business, or promotional use.
For information on bulk purchases, please contact Macmillan Corporate
and Premium Sales Department at 1-800-221-7945, extension 5442,
or write specialmarkets@macmillan.com.

First Edition: November 2014

Printed in the United States of America

0 9 8 7 6 5 4 3 2 1

For Fred Ragsdale

A WILD CARDS MOSAIC NOVEL

LOWBALL

The Big Bleed

by Michael Cassutt

Part One

Prologue

SINCE HE WAS ELEVEN, when the terrible thing happened, he had been called Chahina instead of Hasan. Chahina was a most unusual name for a Berber boy, but fitting, translating loosely as "Wheels" or "Transport." At the age of eleven, Hasan had been brutally transformed into a joker who resembled a small motor truck.

His body had doubled in size and mass—during the feverish transformation he had eaten enough food for ten Hasans—becoming cube-like, with a swale on his back and a hunched, neckless formation where his head and shoulders used to be.

His hands and feet had become horny pistons with flat, circular "hands" that cracked off every few months—or, he learned, with wear—yet remained a part of him, like bracelets around a girl's wrist. Chahina learned that if he locked his four piston-like appendages just so, the free-rolling circular "hands" could act like . . . well, like wheels.

Wheels that allowed him to move down a city street or a dusty Moroccan highway much like a truck, with one obvious difference.

Chahina used his back legs to propel himself forward, giving him the appearance of a truck with a broken suspension as he swayed from side to side—

"Ah," said one of his customers, a burly Dutch weapons smuggler named Kuipers, seeing Chahina in action for the first time, "you are like Hans Brinker!"

Chahina's lack of comprehension must have been clear, even on his grille-like face.

"A skater," Kuipers had said. And, looking like a demented clown, had mimed the side-to-side motion of a boy on blades on ice.

Hans Brinker? Chahina wasn't sure . . . but from that day on he referred to his movements as "slip skating."

And, over the past eleven years, he had slip-skated his way to a decent career as a transporter of illegal substances, contraband, and, yes, weapons, from one point to another, usually at odd hours in great secrecy, frequently on less-traveled routes. His ability to combine stealthy movement with common sense won him many fans in the criminal underworld of northern Africa and southern Europe, so much so that when one of his primary customers expanded his operations to the United States, Chahina was "invited" to come along, traveling as—what else?—Deck ballast on a freighter.

Once he had adjusted to the rigors of life in New York and environs as an illegal joker immigrant, Chahina had grown to appreciate the relative ease of his new smuggler's life. Roads were better. Law enforcement was usually more predictable and honest (Chahina did not break speed limits, and so never got stopped).

And there were no hijackers! Chahina's time in America had been lucrative; the future was promising.

But on the evening of Monday, May 7, 2012, he made a mistake.

Chahina frequently looked down on human drivers and their vehicles, finding them an inferior breed, each half useless without the other. He, after all, was both brains and automotive brawn.

But there were times he wished he had a bit of navigation help, so he would have avoided that wrong turn coming north out of Tewksbury, where 519 and Old Turnpike overlapped: he had wasted ten minutes going west on OT when he should have continued north.

Normally this slight detour wouldn't have been a problem, but Chahina had a deadline: by eight P.M. he was to deliver his cargo to the customer on the edge of Stephens State Park. . . . The address did not appear to be either a commercial property or a residential one, but rather an open field.

In order to make up lost time, Chahina broke his self-imposed rule about speed limits, a risky move because in order to go faster, he had to make more exaggerated slip skates.

He noted the startled reactions of a pair of oncoming drivers, but knew from experience they would simply assume he was some foreign-model truck with unusually sleek, rounded lines. And possibly an intoxicated operator.

(One thing that night trips forced on Chahina was the addition of "headlights," in his case, literally: he had to strap lamps to the outside rim of each eye for basic illumination, and to ensure that he looked like a truck to other vehicles. There was no quicker way to draw attention from highway patrol than to be racing down a rural road with no lights. . . .)

What Chahina hated most was what he'd been driving through almost every day for the past two months . . . and that was rain.

First of all, it was simply uncomfortable. Chahina's transformation to joker had left him looking like a vehicle—and naked, which was a shocking situation for a boy who had never worn any garment more revealing than a T-shirt and long pants in public. His older brother Tariq had helped him sew canvas "trousers" that covered his nether regions and looked, to other eyes, like the fabric enclosing the cargo beds of real trucks. Chahina had improved on this early solution, however, fabricating better-fitting and vari-colored "trousers" to suit any environment. Tonight's, for example, were plain gray.

But they weren't waterproof, and Chahina slip-skated along with the uncomfortable feeling that he had just sat in a puddle while rain spattered his neck and back.

Worse yet, the rain made it more difficult to see. And it almost destroyed traction. (His "hands" and "feet" had none of the radial grooving found in tires.)

The rain had started fifteen minutes after he'd left Staten Island, before he even crossed the Goethals Bridge from Staten Island into New Jersey.

It never got heavy—but it didn't take much to make things uncomfortable for Chahina.

Fortunately, his load was just two dozen plastic containers. A little moisture wouldn't hurt them.

Safely out of Hackettstown now, just passing Bilby, the developments gave way to old farms and woods.

What little traffic willing to brave the rain vanished with the loss of daylight. Wheels took a breath and skated harder. He knew he was pushing both speed limit and energy reserves—why hadn't he eaten more? His roommates were always teasing him about what he consumed, and how much. . . .

Suddenly there was a man lying in the road—!

Wheels rode right over him. It was much like the impact on a suburban speed bump . . . if the bump squished like a human body.

And it *hurt*. Calloused as they were, his wheels were essentially bare hands and feet. Hitting that body was like stubbing your toe on a curb.

He lost traction, lost control, skidding and sliding like a drunk on an icy sidewalk until he hit a left turn a hundred yards farther up the highway—

And slammed into a ditch backed by trees.

The impact flattened his nose. He had not felt such pain since the time—pre-wild card—that Tariq had punched him for stealing a candy bar.

He was so stunned he wasn't sure how long he sat there, head down, rear high, leaning to his right. With darkness, it was impossible for him to measure time. Had it been a few seconds? Minutes?

He sure hoped it wasn't an hour.

Extricating himself from the ditch took patience. He was like a football player with a cracked rib: every attempted movement was painful.

Eventually, however, he had himself upright . . . and had used his good left front "hand" to push himself out of the ditch far enough to let his back "feet" find traction.

It was only when he was finally upright, on the highway surface, that he realized he had lost one of the containers he carried. He couldn't see it anywhere; even if he could, he was not capable of picking it up and replacing it.

It was like losing a tooth—but likely to be far more painful, once he met his customers.

Well, Wheels had lost items before . . . had been beaten and otherwise mistreated. But he knew it was better to show up with nineteen of twenty items than to try to avoid the confrontation completely.

There was another matter, however.

Slowly, painfully, Wheels skated a dozen yards back down the highway, to where he had run over the body . . . there was little he could do to help the victim, assuming he lived. And now time was truly critical.

But Wheels had been maltreated so many times in his short life. He couldn't bear to just . . . skate away—

Suddenly there were lights far to the south . . . another vehicle!

Wheels did not want to answer questions, nor did he want to be seen anywhere near a body in the middle of a road.

He turned and slip-skated into the rainy night.

Those About to Die . . .

---

by David Anthony Durham

Part One

MARCUS FLUNG ASIDE THE manhole cover. He pulled himself partway through and leaned back to check his cell phone. There. Finally. He had bars again! It wasn't the only problem with living in the tunnels and sewers below Jokertown, but the fact that cell phone service was spotty was one of the most annoying.

One voice mail. One text.

The message was from a girl who had been sweating him. He didn't know why he'd ever given her his phone number. She was a nat. Kind of average looking, with flat blond hair and too much smile for her face. She had approached him at Drakes in the Bowery last week. Grabbing his arm, she admitted out of nowhere that she had a snake fetish. "I just love serpents. Venomous ones the most." She had made him horny, but not exactly in a good way.

He pressed delete.

The text was from Father Squid. Marcus smiled. It always amused him to imagine the good father texting. It couldn't have been easy for him to hit the little buttons, considering that his fingers had suckers all over them. The text read: RMBR PRCNT. 5PM.

"I'll be there," Marcus said. "Not that it's going to do any good."

Marcus liked the priest well enough, but the old guy tended to get worked up about things. He'd roped Marcus into helping him look for so-called missing jokers. A few days into the search, Marcus was beginning to feel like there wasn't anything to it. Sure, some guys had gone awol, but they weren't the sort of guys anyone was too upset to see vanish. Why the priest cared so much Marcus couldn't fathom.

Flipping the phone shut and slipping it into his chest pocket, Marcus rose out of the sewer hole. He was normal enough from the waist up. A young African-American man, well built, with muscles that cut distinct lines beneath his fitted T-shirt. Hair trimmed nice, like someone who cared about their look, thick gold loops in his ears. Below the waist, however, he was one long stretch of scaled serpentine muscle, ringed down the twenty feet of tapering length to his tail. His garish yellow and red and black rings flexed in a hypnotic fashion as he carved a weaving course forward.

He didn't stay earthbound long. He surged up into a narrow gap at the alley mouth, curving from one brick wall to the other, creating a weave of tension between the two. Once out of the shadows of Jokertown's urban canyon lands, the spring sun shone down. The heat of it poured power into Marcus's tail. He pulled his shades out and slipped them on. He knew he looked fly. A couple years ago he thought his life was over. Now, things looked and felt a whole lot different.

As he skimmed along the edge of a roof, a voice called up from the street below. "IBT! Hey, IBT!"

Marcus peered down at a plump woman in a black T-shirt.

"I'm your number one fan, baby. Check it." She directed two stubby fingers at her chest. The bright pink letters IBT stretched taut across her T-shirt. She clearly had more than two breasts pressing against the fabric.

The guy beside her jabbed toward him with a finger. "You da man, T!" he said, stomping the ground with an oversized foot.

Marcus waved. He peeled back from the edge and carried on. "You da man, T," he mimicked. "What's the deal with shortening everything?" he grumbled aloud. "'T' means he's calling me Tongue but being too lazy to even say the whole word. The name is Infamous Black Tongue," he announced to the sky, then thought, *And IBT's all right, I guess, if you're in a rush.*

He found it a little strange that it wasn't his tail that gave him his moniker, but he had gotten a lot of early press for the concussive power of his tongue to deliver venom. Made an impression, apparently.

That reminded him of something.

He cut away from his intended route long enough to perch looking down on the graffiti-scarred wall of a building facing an abandoned lot-cum-urban garden. The wall had been repainted in one massive mural, a tribute to Oddity, whose cloaked and masked shape dominated the scene. IBT featured in it, too. Down by the far end, he rose up on powerful coils, half engulfed by licks of flame. One hand stretched out toward Oddity to accept the keys the vigilante legends were offering him. The other hand was smashing the dirty cop Lu Long across his dragon snout.

Marcus cocked his head. Squinted. They'd done some good work since last he saw it. They had his tail down pretty well. The color pattern of his stripes was mixed up, but he doubted anybody but himself would notice. The only thing he didn't really like was his face. He looked too angry, too full of teeth-gritting rage. Father Squid had warned him that when he became a public figure his image wouldn't be his own anymore. Here was proof, sprayed large.

He hit the street just down from the precinct. In the half block he nodded in response to several greetings, received an overly enthusiastic high five from a lobster-like claw, and autographed a furry little boy's Yankees baseball cap. He tried to protest that he was an Orioles fan, and not a baseball player in any event. The boy was insistent, though.

Father Squid waited for him on the precinct steps. Though it was warm, the tall, broad-shouldered priest wore his thick robes, as usual. He stood with his hands tented together on his chest, as if in prayer. He almost looked tranquil, except for the way his fingers tapped out his impatience. "Have you any news, son?"

Marcus shook his head.

"No sightings?"

"Nope."

The priest leaned close, the scent of him salty and fishy. The tentacles that dangled from his face seemed to stretch toward Marcus, as if each of them was keen to touch good news. "What about that abandoned apartment?"

"I checked it out. No sign of Wartcake."

"Don't call him that. Simon Clarke is the name his parents gave him."

Marcus shrugged. "I know, but everybody calls him Wartcake. When I ask about Simon Clarke nobody knows who I'm talking about. So I always have to say Wartcake, and then they go, 'Oh, Wartcake, why didn't you say that in the first place?'" He met the priest's large, dark eyes. "I'm just saying."

Motion inside the precinct didn't exactly freeze when Marcus and Father Squid entered, but a hush fell across the room. One after another, pairs of eyes found Marcus and followed his progress toward the captain's office. Officer Napperson glared at him from behind his desk, looking like he was wishing him dead with just the force of his eyes. Another guy in uniform put his hand on his pistol, fingering the grip.

Father Squid strode with lumbering determination. Marcus kept his eyes on the priest's back. He tried to keep his slither cool, but the scrutiny made him nervous. He couldn't figure the cops out. Most of them treated him like a criminal they were itching to bust for something. That didn't stop them from using him, though. Officer Tang once gave him a tip about a guy the cops couldn't touch, some politician's brother who liked getting rough with joker hookers. Marcus had caught up with him one night and given him the scare of his life, enough to keep him out of Jokertown for good. He'd caught, venom tagged, and gift wrapped three perps who had been sparkling with Tinkerbill's pink aura. Ironic, considering that he'd spent a long evening tinkling like a fairy himself.

He'd even played dominoes in the park with Beastie a few Sundays.

None of that changed the chilly reception at the moment.

Deputy Inspector Thomas Jan Maseryk sat at his desk, head tilted down as he studied a stack of reports. He lined through something with a red pen, wrote a note.

Father Squid knocked on the doorjamb.

Without looking up, Maseryk said, "Hello, Father. The way you waft the scent of the seashore makes me hungry for cotton candy and foot-long hot dogs."

"There are two more missing," Father Squid said. "Two more, Captain. Do the disappearances merit your attention yet? If not, how many must vanish before you take notice?"

"We take all complaints serious—"

"You've yet to grasp that something is truly amiss here. Shall I name the vanished for you?"

The deputy inspector plucked up the page and deposited it in the tray at the corner of his desk. Exhaling, he leaned back and stretched. His deeply lined face was stern, his graying hair trimmed with military precision. "If you have anything to add to what you offered last time, see Detective Mc—"

"Khaled Mohamed," Father Squid cut in. He counted them on his suckered fingers. "Timepiece. Simon Clarke. Gregor. John the Pharaoh. These are not prominent people. They're loners, ruffians, users, abusers. All of them male. They may not be the pillars of our community, but they're still God's children. Maseryk, I won't allow you to ignore them."

The captain's face could've been carved in stone. "Unless someone made you mayor while I wasn't looking, I'll ask you to refrain from threatening me. As I said, Detective McTate will be—"

"I want a commitment from you personally."

"My work is my word." Peering around the priest, the deputy inspector nudged his chin at Marcus. "What's he got to do with all of this?"

"Marcus has been doing the work that the department hasn't. He's been combing the streets, day and night, looking for the missing, asking questions, trying to piece together some explanation."

"And?" Maseryk asked.

"I haven't found anything yet."

"Wonder why that is?" Maseryk ran his eyes over the reports again, as if bored of the conversation. "Maybe it's because a few drifters and grifters and petty criminals going missing is as everyday as apple pie. The fact these guys are gone isn't exactly a hardship for the community." He shot a hand up to stop Father Squid's response. "I'm not saying we're ignoring it. Just that there may be nothing to this. You want our full attention? Bring us something real. Some solid proof that anything at all is going on here. Without that, you're on a back burner. Good day, gentlemen."

Marcus wasn't exactly an adventurous eater, but the scent wafting from the Elephant Royale got his long stomach grumbling. The sprawling restaurant featured outdoor seating, which relieved Marcus. More space for the tail.

The owner, a Thai man named Chakri, greeted Father Squid with a wide grin and flurry of back patting. A slim man dressed smartly, the only sign of the virus in him were his eyes. They were two or three times larger than normal. Round and expressive, they sparkled a deep green, with flecks of gold that reflected the sunlight.

"You've had success with your search?" Chakri asked, as he seated the two jokers at one of the curbside tables.

"I'm afraid not," Father Squid said. "We've been on our own. Very little help from the police. We will continue our efforts, though."

Marcus curled his tail under him, trying to keep the tip of it out of the way of passersby.

"You a good man, Father," Chakri said. "I do this: I tell my people to keep a lookout. Deliverymen. Grocers. Shippers. They're out early, up late. They see something they tell me. I tell you."

"Thank you, Chakri," Father Squid said. "That could be very helpful."

"No bother. Now . . ." He blinked his large eyes, changing their color from green to vibrant crimson. "What would these good men like to eat?"

Having no idea, Marcus let the priest order for him. Soon, the two of them sipped large glasses of amazingly sweet tea. Marcus tentatively tried one of the fish cake appetizers. They didn't look like much, but man they were good!

Father Squid said, "For a long time I couldn't eat Thai food. Reminded me too much of . . ." He paused and cleared his throat. "Of things I didn't want to remember. That's before I met Chakri. His kind, generous nature is a balm. As is his cooking."

Marcus plucked up another fish cake. "You fought in Vietnam, didn't you? What was it like?"

Father Squid blew a long breath through the tentacles around his mouth. "It's not something I discuss. War is madness, Marcus. It takes men and makes them animals. Pray you never see it yourself."

Typical old guy thing to say, Marcus thought. Why did people who had experienced all sorts of wild stuff—war, drugs, crazy sex—always end up saying others shouldn't experience the same things themselves?

Marcus's cell phone vibrated like a rattlesnake's tail in his chest pocket. He glanced at it. "I should probably take this."

Father Squid motioned for him to do so.

"IBT, my man!"

Slate Carter. Talent agent. Marcus had never seen him, but he had to be white. No black guy would butcher street slang with such gusto.

"Waz up, G? You got that demo for me?"

Looking slightly embarrassed, Marcus twisted away from the table. "Hi, Slate. Um . . . no, it's not ready yet. I'm not sure it's such a good idea any—"

"Don't blaze out, bro! I explained it all to you already. You got the look, the initials, the street cred, the vigilante backstory. You even beat down a crooked cop! That's our first video, right there."

"But—"

"You know what I've done for NCMF, right?"

"Yeah," Marcus admitted. Of course he knew. Slate never failed to mention his most famous client.

NCMF was a rapping joker who happened to be the spitting image of an extinct early humanoid known as *Paranthropus boisei*. Nutcracker Man. Dude could drop some serious rhymes. His latest video was a concert reel, him stomping around the stage before a frenzied crowd, long arms pumping and swiping. The crowd would ask, "What's your name?" He would answer, "Nutcracker, Motherfucker!" His rapping style was all natural flow. It never sounded like he was rapping. He was just talking, cursing, shouting. Somehow it all came out fast and funky. "NCMF but I don't crack nuts! I crack butts. That's right, I crack butts. I tear them open like I'm going extinct!" He proceeded to simulate his buttcracking prowess with the backsides of a number of dancers. "I crack butts!"

"You and I are gonna blow that away," Slate promised. "You gonna explode like Jiffy Pop! Shoot me that demo and we'll make it happen. You feel me?"

Marcus did. He was a twenty-year-old virgin, after all. Visions of bottles of Krug spurting fizz over bikini-clad dancers, SUVs bouncing and chants of "Gz Up, Hoes Down" . . . well, such things did have a certain appeal. He had conceded only one problem. A big one. He'd just never managed to actually say it to Slate.

Snapping his phone closed, Marcus muttered a curse.

Father Squid asked, with a raised eyebrow, "Something amiss?"

"That was an agent."

"What sort of agent?"

"Talent. He represents musicians. Rappers mostly. He reps Nutcracker M—" Marcus caught himself. "Well, that . . . guy, with that song. You might've heard it."

Father Squid frowned. "That one . . ."

"Anyway, Slate is legit. He thinks I could be a rap star. Blow up like . . . Jiffy Pop."

"I didn't know you were a musician."

"Neither did I." Marcus cut his eyes up at the priest's face, and then took a sip of his iced tea. "I mean, I'm not. Slate keeps asking for a demo, but . . . I can't rap. I tried. I got videos on my cell phone, but, man . . . I suck."

"I can't say that I'm disappointed to hear that."

"He's just after me 'cause I got a tight image, you know?"

"You have a measure of fame. With it comes responsibility. You understand that, right?"

"Yeah, you talk about it all the time."

The father dropped one of his heavy hands on Marcus's shoulder, the suckers on his palm squeezing. "I remind you because I care. Because I see a life of great promise ahead of you. I doubt very much that rapping would be fulfilling your potential. Marcus, if your card hadn't turned, where would you be now?"

"In college, I guess."

"Then you should be there now. The fact that you're a joker need not change that."

Marcus shifted uncomfortably. He couldn't imagine slithering across the quad of some campus, all the nat students staring at his tail. It might have been his future once, but college didn't seem possible anymore.

"Perhaps we can use your celebrity status for something other than making vulgar music," Father Squid said. "And you can do something other than dispensing vigilante justice. You do much good. I won't deny that. But where is the line? What happens when you err? When you hurt an innocent by mistake? What happens if you lose the bits of yourself that are kinder than your fists and muscles?"

The main dishes arrived.

The priest stuffed a napkin under his tentacled chin. After thanking the waitress, he continued, "Your life need not be defined only by the physical abilities the wild card has given you. That's why I'm going to set up a college fund in your honor. I think quite a few people would be willing to contribute to that."

Marcus hid the wave of emotion that rolled over him by digging in to his curry dish. Part of it was fear. Fear of wanting to strive for something that nats strove for. Fear of failing, of all the eyes that would watch him, critical and cold. Part of it was surprise that anyone would want to invest in his future that way. His parents didn't. Nobody in his old life did.

Father Squid chuckled. "I should have warned you it was spicy."

"Yeah," Marcus said, wiping at the moisture in his eyes, "spicy. It's almost got me crying."

The Big Bleed

Part Two

"DID THAT HURT?"

Jamal Norwood stared in pain and horror at the wound on his left forearm. Pain because, yes, it hurt to have the extra-large needle jabbed into his arm, to feel the blood being sucked into the giant, toy-like syringe. Even the withdrawal was slow and jagged. What, this guy couldn't have used a new needle? Or a small one?

"Yes!" Jamal couldn't help sounding surprised at his frank answer, and a bit ashamed of himself. The grunting, high-pitched squeal hardly matched the image of a buff former movie stuntman turned SCARE agent.

The doctor, a centaur in a lab coat, frowned. "Sorry," he said. His name was Finn and he came highly recommended, not that Jamal had done much in the way of due diligence. He had needed a quick, quiet consult . . . and the Jokertown Clinic seemed to be the best place.

Now, of course, with the crude, industrial-sized instruments, Jamal was revising his opinion. "It's not your fault, Doctor," he said, rubbing his arm. No, it was entirely Jamal's problem. Hence the terror: he was Stuntman! His whole ace power was bouncing back from damage that would have severely injured, or killed, another human being, nat, ace, or joker.

And quickly! Being dropped from a forty-story building and flattened? Stuntman would bounce back within hours.

In past experience, a pinprick would have closed as soon as the needle point touched his skin. In fact, Jamal couldn't remember the last time he'd had blood taken.

Or needed to.

"Hold on to this while I get something better," Dr. Finn said, placing a cotton ball on the wound and closing Jamal's arm on it.

Jamal wanted to tell the man no, no need.

But there was need: it felt as though his blood was gushing . . . it felt as though the cotton ball had already been soaked through.

What the hell was happening?

The spring of 2012 had been one of the warmest in New York history. When Jamal and the rest of the SCARE team arrived in late March for the presidential primary, they had expected a typical spring: cold, raw days interspersed with warm ones, rain, trees beginning to bloom.

Well, they found the rain, that was certain.

But the weather had been tropical . . . high temperatures, equally high humidity, and rain every day. New York streets, never in great shape in good years, were transformed into a collection of terrifying potholes and cracked pavement.

Jamal's immediate boss, Bathsheeba Fox, also known as the Midnight Angel, was a good Christian belle whose default setting was to accept "God's will" when it came to fouled-up situations. Jamal suspected that Sheeba felt glorified by the opportunity to protect the Holy Roller, the Reverend Thaddeus Wintergreen—the first ace to run for the presidency—from the increasing numbers of people who (in Jamal's opinion) quite understandably wanted this Mississippi shithead dead. Sheeba would gladly have called down her personal Sword of the Lord on any member of the SCARE task force who dared to offer a discouraging word. . . .

Yet even She Who Must Be Obeyed had stood in the rain yesterday, her signature leather outfit showing cracks from wear, her jet-black mane a sodden, tied-up mess, her minimal makeup smeared, as she looked up at the sky and said, "You know, this kind of sucks." Which summed up the whole New York tour . . . bad weather leading to ill temper all around. SCARE had assigned Jamal and Sheeba to provide coverage for Wintergreen. It didn't matter that the Roller had zero chance of winning—

Senators Obama and Lieberman and Attorney General Rodham were divvying up the delegates there. Known to millions from *American Hero* (that goddamn show again!), the Roller was drawing huge crowds wherever he went, and a goodly percentage of his fans resided on Homeland Security, Secret Service, and SCARE watch lists.

The Holy Roller detail had been a death march of long hours spent in grim factory gates, high school gymnasia, and an amazing number of cracker churches—more in the state of New York than Jamal would have believed. Each event required the SCARE team to engage in tedious "interfaces" with local police and sheriffs, plus the endless interviews, follow-ups, crowd scans.

It could have been worse, Jamal thought: he could have been assigned to cover one of the Republican candidates, but with Romney running away with the contest, SCARE's very own Mormon, Nephi Callendar, had come out of retirement to provide "interface" with that campaign—sparing Jamal Norwood and the others.

Even though they'd avoided involvement with the Republicans, a greater challenge loomed: the Liberty Party and its national standard-bearer, Duncan Towers, a blow-dried blowhard who made the Roller seem rational. So far Towers had been protected by the Secret Service and his own personal security force, but with the Dems moving on to California and what might yet prove to be a brokered convention, Sheeba's team had been ordered to stay in New York to provide "advance" work for Towers and Liberty.

Jamal devoutly hoped that the assignment would be a short one. He had joined SCARE because he was bored with Hollywood and determined to rehabilitate himself after the debacle of the first season of *American Hero*. What better way than to fight terrorists in the Middle East?

And that had been satisfying. But it was now five years in the past. . . .

Until the morning of May 8, 2012, he had a firm plan to resign from SCARE the day after the November election. He wanted to make more money; he wanted to enjoy his work again. (A friend had sent him a script titled *I Witness* that might work for television.) Jamal didn't particularly want to become the sole male lead of an action-adventure network series; that was a good way to make a lot of money and ruin your life. Nevertheless, going back to Hollywood and being thrown off tall buildings was a step up from a Sunday-night town meeting in Albany. And *I Witness* might wind up on cable . . . less money, but fewer episodes. The biggest

lure was that going back to Hollywood meant he could rebuild his relationship with Julia—

"Any ideas on what this might be?"

Finn shrugged. "Joker medicine is still the Wild West." Jamal let the
joker reference go uncorrected. "There's no reason to believe it's anything . . . dire at the moment."

"Wow, Doc, way to reassure a brother."

The words obviously stung. "Sorry," he said. "It's just . . ."

"We don't get a lot of aces in a place like this," Jamal said, sliding off
the table. "And at these prices, no wonder." The doc had obviously never
heard the old wheeze. Or maybe he was just freaked out by the unique
nature of Jamal's problem.

Either way, it was time to get out of here.

As a special agent for SCARE, Jamal could have taken his problem to a
facility higher up the scale than the Jokertown Clinic. Two things argued
against that move, however: a visit to, say, Columbia Medical or Johns
Hopkins or especially the New Mexico Institute would have surely come
to the attention of Sheeba and the higher-ups at SCARE. And Jamal Norwood wasn't eager for that.

Besides, Doc Finn and the Jokertown Clinic had more experience
dealing with wild card–related matters than anyone on the planet. They
were likely Jamal's best bet to find out what was wrong with him.

He had just received a promise from Finn for a follow-up report within
forty-eight hours when his phone beeped. Sheeba the Midnight Angel
herself. "Jamal," she said, her Southern accent and perpetual air of exas-
peration stretching two syllables to three, "where are you?"

"A personal errand," he snapped. "Does it make any difference why I'm
off duty for an hour? If you need me somewhere, now, I'm on my way."

"Yeah, well . . . we have a DHS incident in New Jersey. Some kind of
toxic spill."

"Why is that our mission?"

"They don't tell me why, Jamal, they just tell me. DHS is shorthanded
today. Tell me where you are and we'll pick you up on the way."

He improvised. He was still largely unable to visualize lower Manhattan—
had they been uptown, say, Seventy-second Street, it would have been

easier. But here? "Uh, corner of Essex and Delancey," he said, naming the only two major streets he knew.

"See you in ten minutes," Sheeba said.

Jamal grinned. It wouldn't be ten minutes. The Midnight Angel's metabolism ran hot, requiring at least half a dozen meals every day. (What would it be like when she hit menopause? he wondered. Would she slow down? Or would she blow up like a fat tick?) The moment she hit the street, she would see some food cart, and that would add ten minutes to the trip. And beat hell out of Sheeba's per diem.

Which would allow Jamal Norwood to find the corner of Delancey and Essex.

Jamal liked to run, as long as he was in gym gear, wearing sneakers and on grass or at the very least a track. Running down a hard and broken Manhattan sidewalk in suit and dress shoes was not only far from his idea of decent exercise, it was too damned slow, especially with the afternoon crowds.

It was also too damned public. He caught a startled double take of recognition on at least two faces, and heard one construction worker hollering, "Yo, Stuntman!"

He pretended not to notice. He kept hoping that his exposure on *American Hero* would fade. No luck, alas.

It took him thirteen minutes to reach the corner of Essex and Delancey from the Jokertown Clinic. And when he did—

He was on the northeast corner, about to cross with the light, when something flashed in his peripheral vision. A battered white van made a hard left headed south, so close to the corner that Jamal and the other pedestrians could feel the slipstream. "Shit goddammit!" a young man shouted.

Jamal glanced at him—a mistake. What he saw was an African-American joker, his upper half human-shaped, his nether regions more appropriate to a giant snake . . . if a giant snake adorned itself with rings of yellow, red, and black.

The social protocols required Jamal to say something. "Hey."

He hoped to disengage at that point, but it was too late. "Hey, you're Stuntman!"

Busted for the second time in a few minutes. *American Hero* had fattened Jamal's bank account, undeniably a good sign, and had led to his meeting Julia, a jury-is-still-out sign, but in most other ways had proved to be a disaster.

Especially when it came to anonymity. Working in Hollywood had exposed Jamal Norwood to the perks and the price of fame, and it had quickly become obvious that the price far outweighed the perks. "Guilty."

"Marcus!" the kid said, indicating himself. "What are you doing here, man?"

"Just . . . going from point A to point B." This joker wasn't likely to be satisfied with that, but it was all Jamal was offering. Maybe an autograph, if really pressed.

"Oh, wait," the kid said. "Yo, Father!"

Christ, now what? Jamal had barely formulated the thought when Father Squid appeared out of the crowd. Jamal realized that, in addition to cooking food and auto exhaust, he had been smelling the sea. Father Squid was the source: big, tentacle-faced, wearing a black cassock, he also reeked of brine. The good father turned to Jamal. "Stuntman himself! What are you doing here? Thought you were working as a secret agent or something."

"Something like that," Jamal said. "Protection for candidates."

The priest laughed long and loud. "Shielding the Holy Roller! What a task that must be!"

"Maybe that's why they don't know shit about anything going on in the streets," Marcus said.

"Charity, Marcus," the priest said.

Jamal was annoyed. "What's he talking about?"

One of Squid's tentacles uncurled in the direction of the nearest telephone pole. In addition to the usual long-past concert and job postings, the pole held three different homemade posters, the most prominent showing a joker named John the Pharaoh under the heading, *Have you seen him? Missing since May 1!*

"What's going on?" Jamal said.

"A bunch of jokers have disappeared," Marcus said. "I can't believe SCARE doesn't know about this."

"SCARE might," Jamal said. "My *team* doesn't."

"That sucks," Marcus said.

Squid placed a calming tentacle on Marcus's shoulder. "The local police aren't stepping up. We can hardly expect the Feds to do what Fort Freak won't."

"How many have there been?" Jamal said. After five years with SCARE, he was finding it easy to slip into an investigative role.

"At least half a dozen," Father Squid said.

"That's a big number," Jamal said, feeling alarmed. SCARE should know about this—

Suddenly Marcus started. "Who's that?"

A black Ford Explorer pulled up across the street. Jamal's phone buzzed.

"My team." He turned to the priest. "I'll make sure someone looks into this."

"You can reach me at Our Lady of Perpetual Misery."

"I know the place." As he turned to cross the street, he hoped he had gotten away without making too many promises. Squid and Marcus made him nervous.

He would not have believed that the sight of a black Ford Explorer with the Midnight Angel in the front seat would ever have made him happy.

Galahad in Blue

by Melinda M. Snodgrass

Part One

OFFICER FRANCIS XAVIER BLACK—known to his fellow officers as Franny—came whistling through the doors of New York's 5th Precinct ready to defend truth, justice, and the American Way in Jokertown. Only to be viciously elbowed by Bugeye Bronkowski.

The blow was so hard and so unexpected that it sent Franny stumbling into the chairs lining the walls of the waiting room. Mrs. Mallory reached up and stopped his tumble before he landed in her lap. Louise Mallory was a diminutive woman whose hulking joker son Davy ran with the Demon Princes. But Davy wasn't too bright, and he certainly wasn't very lucky. He was constantly getting arrested.

Franny righted himself and looked at Sergeant Homer Taylor, currently manning the front desk. But Wingman didn't say a word. Bugeye stomped through the gate and back into the precinct. "What's up his ass?" Franny asked Homer.

Wingman gave his drooping wings a shake that wouldn't have looked out of place on a dying bat. "Couldn't say," he said, in tones that indicated he knew exactly what had precipitated the assault.

Franny let it go and turned back to his rescuer. "Thank you, Mrs. Mallory, sorry I . . . stumbled. Here to bail out Davy?"

"Yes, that boy just keeps getting into hijinks."

"He does that."

"CO wants to see you in his office," Wingman grunted.

It was never a good thing when a patrolman was called into the brass's office. Franny's stomach became a small, hard knot against his spine. He wished he hadn't eaten such a big breakfast.

As he moved through the bullpen Franny became aware of the eyes. Everyone was staring at him. There were a few disgusted head shakes and several people looked pointedly away. *God, what have I done?*

Beastie, all seven feet of him, fur, horns, and claws, stumped up to him, and laid a hand on Franny's shoulder. The brown eyes gazing down at him were sorrowful and sympathetic. "Oh, Franny, dude."

Nothing else was forthcoming. Beastie mooched on. Franny made his way to Deputy Inspector Maseryk's office. At his knock the nat yelled a *come in.* Franny obeyed.

"Sir."

"Sit down, Black."

Franny took the proffered chair, but found himself perching on the edge as if preparing for flight.

"You took your lieutenant's exam."

"Yes, sir, I know I'm not technically eligible to be promoted, but I figured I could get in some practice."

"Well, you aced the damn thing." Maseryk's tone didn't make it sound like a compliment.

"Good?" Franny said diffidently. When there was no response he added an equally uncertain, "Thank you?"

"The damn brass down at One Police Plaza have decided in their infinite wisdom to promote you early."

Franny sank against the back of the chair. It was all becoming horribly clear. This was why Bugeye had hit him. Resentment curdled his gut—how was it apparently everybody in the precinct had known about this before *he* did? He gave voice to none of that however. "That seems . . . ill advised," he managed.

"To put it mildly."

"So, why—"

"Because we've been taking a beating over the corruption that's been uncovered in the two-oh."

"Oh."

"The damn press just won't let up so the brass decided to give them a new narrative. All about *famous captain's son steps up.*" His tone underscored the irony. "But a story about a flatfoot isn't news. A promotion, that's news . . . and fortunately the media vultures all have ADD. They'll stop writing about the two-oh and write about *you* until another scandal comes along."

Franny's first impulse was to refuse, to not be a hand puppet for the Puzzle Palace, as the plaza was sometimes called. Balanced against that was the drive to live up to his father's memory. To be not just a good cop, but maybe a great one. He had always wanted to make detective. His work thus far didn't involve much investigation. It involved a lot of intimidation and running after people. Plainclothes, no more walking a beat; that's when he realized he'd miss his beat and the people who depended on him—Mr. Wiley who ran the mask and cloak shop, Tina who managed the Starbucks, Jeff the bellman at the Jokertown Hyatt who spent most of his day out front carrying luggage and parking cars so he watched the world go by, and often reported what he saw to Bill and Franny.

Bill! Shit! How would his partner react to this?

He also had to acknowledge that he was ambitious. *You aced it.* The captain's words danced through his mind. Damn right he had. He'd gone to law school, passed the bar on the first try. No, he couldn't refuse. Franny stood and held out his hand. "Thank you, sir. I'm honored. I'll try to live up to your expectations."

"You've already failed in that regard. I thought you'd have the good sense to turn it down." Maseryk shuffled through papers. "Okay, I'm pairing you with Michael Stevens."

"But he's a nat too."

"I'm aware of that, but his partner just got transferred, and nobody else was willing to be broken up just to accommodate you. I'll fix it as soon as I can, but for right now you're with Stevens. Next, we've got a situation. Jokers have gone missing. Mostly loners, people without family or roots in the community. I think it's a tempest in a teapot. People like that drop off the radar all the time, but Father Squid is busting my ass over it, and we don't need another media feeding frenzy. So, as of now you're in charge of the joker investigation."

"Is Michael going to work with me on that?"

"No, Michael has a real case to investigate. Go find your desk."

"Yes, sir. Should I go home and change?"

"I wouldn't if I were you. Wait until tomorrow to rub their noses in it."

Franny slunk out of the office. Before he found his desk and new partner he went to find his old partner. Bill would be expecting him to join him on patrol . . . or not. Maybe Bill had gotten the word like everybody else.

He found the big Chinese-American officer in the locker room. Bill clipped his nightstick onto his belt, and turned when he heard Franny's footsteps. They looked at each other, each waiting for the other to speak. Bill slammed the locker door, and headed for the door. "I won't be going out with you today," Franny said.

"I heard," Bill said in a high-pitched, squeaky voice, so at odds with his massive form.

Since no congratulation had been uttered, Franny had at least hoped for noncommittal. Instead there was ice edging Bill's words. "Look, I didn't ask for this."

"Didn't turn it down either."

"Would you?"

"No, but I've got eleven years in on the force, not two. I've taken the lieutenant's exam three times. But you get promoted, and you're not even one of us."

"Yeah, I'm a nat. Why don't you just say it?"

"Not that, you moron."

"What then?"

"You're not Chinese."

"What?" Franny said, not following the logic at all.

"We've got jokers in this station. We've got aces, but we're on the edge of Chinatown, and only two of us are ethnic Chinese, and only a handful of us speak Chinese. How are you going to investigate crimes in my neighborhood when you can't even speak the language?"

"Get a translator."

Bill snorted. "Yeah, that's gonna work real well."

"Look, Bill—" But the big man turned his back on Franny and walked out of the locker room.

Back in the bullpen, Franny located his desk. It backed up to another desk, which belonged to Michael Stevens. The cops at the station loved to gossip and leer about Stevens—two live-in girlfriends and ace daughter. *And I can't even get a date,* Franny thought. SlimJim McTate gave him an encouraging smile and handed him a file. "Here's the list of missing jokers."

Franny had just started to look through them when he became aware of someone staring at him. He looked up to find Apsara Na Chiangmai standing at the side of his desk, smiling down at him. Apsara was the file clerk for the precinct, and the most beautiful girl Franny had ever seen. Dark hair hung to her curvaceous ass, and her oval face had skin as smooth and perfect as old ivory. He'd tried to ask her out back when he first started work at the Five, only to be turned down. It had been done with charm and a smile, but it had still been a shutdown. Now here she was. She drew in a deep breath, preparing to speak, which thrust her amazing rack almost into his face. "Detective Black, I wanted to offer you my congratulations," she said in fluting tones.

"Ah . . . oh . . . thanks."

"Would you like to ask me out?"

"Ummmm . . ."

Ties That Bind

---

by Mary Anne Mohanraj

Part One

DETECTIVE MICHAEL STEVENS WALKED into the Jokertown precinct and paused, blasted by noise that didn't help his pounding head. It had been a shitty day even before he came into work. Michael had woken with a raging hard-on, but he'd somehow slept through his alarm. Both of his girlfriends were already up and dressed, and his daughter was up too and hollering for her breakfast, so there was no chance of persuading one of the women to come back to bed, even if he hadn't been late. And then Minal had gotten distracted by Isai pissing all over the kitchen floor, so the eggs had gotten overcooked, and if there was one thing Michael hated, it was dry eggs. Also, piss on his kitchen floor. Isai was supposedly done with potty training, but sometimes, she got distracted. He'd finally escaped the family drama and taken the subway to work, jammed between a guy covered in spikes and a woman who smelled like rotted meat. Michael had entered into the precinct with a sigh of relief, only to be greeted by this wave of noise slamming at him, like a steel spike jackhammering on his head.

Not a wild card–powered wave, just the normal morning frenzy at Fort Freak. What you'd expect in a station where a handful of underfunded cops tried their damnedest to keep the peace in an increasingly strange and difficult borough of New York City. Perched on the front desk, where she had no business being, Apsara leaned over, making sure that the desk sergeant had a full view of her generous assets. Hey, sweetheart. Got something for me? Her voice loud enough to carry over the noise. Darcy the meter maid was just leaving the room, thankfully—he didn't need to hear her ranting about law and order and a civil society again.

Sure, that was why Michael had become a cop, to protect and serve. In the deepest parts of his soul, that desire was what pulled him through his days, the need to be a great cop, to prove himself. He'd grown up watching his folks struggle just to make ends meet; he'd promised himself that someday he'd have a job that was more than just a way to put food on the table and clothes on your back. Michael had never loved school, but he'd gritted his teeth and plowed through. He'd spent late nights over his books at the scarred Formica table in his mother's kitchen, while she cooked bi bim bop and they waited for his dad to come home from his second job. Michael's folks had skipped vacations, skipped meals, even skipped Sunday church sometimes because they were embarrassed by their threadbare clothes. Clothes they hadn't replaced because the money had gone to pay for Michael's grammar school uniforms, his high school books, his college application fees.

He owed them so much that it stuck in his throat, love and gratitude tangled up with resentment. Michael had been determined to pay them back for it, and eventually he had, at least a bit. When he'd made detective, the pay bump had been enough that he could finally put the down payment on a condo for them, and help them out every month with the mortgage. He'd worked as hard as he could to rise above, to be better than everyone else—a better student, a better cop, and now, a better detective. Michael Stevens was determined to be the best damn cop on the force. But unlike Darcy, he didn't need to talk about it all the time.

The door banged open and a kid scuttled in, shrieking. Really shrieking, in a voice pitched three octaves above normal. The hammering in Michael's head escalated along with it, and he fought the urge to cover his ears with his hands. That wouldn't look professional, but damn, if someone didn't shut that kid up—oh, thank God. Beastie had him, and was covering that horrible mouth with one warm furry paw. There were days when Michael wondered why he didn't just walk away from all the crazy here. He was a nat—untouched by the virus, at least so far. After the success they'd had a few years ago in taking down the Demon Princes, he could have transferred to any other city he wanted, left the freaks and weirdos behind to protect normal citizens instead. Michael could have risen through the ranks, become a captain, maybe more. He'd thought about going to D.C., applying to join the CIA or SCARE. But in the end he'd chosen to stay in Jokertown.

Michael slipped a hand into his jacket pocket to reassure himself that it was still there—yes. The visible manifestation of his reason for staying. A small red velvet box, holding a bit of captured sparkle—two of them, in fact. One box with two rings, for the two women who drove him crazy on a nightly basis. They were the ones who held him here—one joker girlfriend, one ace, both of them happy to share him, which was perhaps the strangest of all the strangenesses in his life. Minal, with tiny nipples that covered her torso, front and back—she looked ordinary enough when dressed, and walking the street, she could pass for normal. But her wild card burned within her, and just a brush against her torso was enough to set her simmering. No wonder she'd been such a popular hooker, back when she'd made her living walking the streets. Any other woman would have been insanely jealous. But his girlfriend Kavitha just smiled and dragged Minal off to bed, sometimes inviting him along. Maybe it was her ace powers that made Kavitha so self-confident?

When she danced, her brilliant illusions turned real enough to walk on, real enough to fight with. They'd learned that the hard way, two years ago, when their daughter had been kidnapped by a Jokertown gang. Kavitha had been a pacifist—she still was, in most ways. She did work for the Committee on occasion now, always stipulating that she would only use her powers for peaceful endeavors. But Kavitha had fought like a tiger that day, when their daughter was at risk. Michael didn't know if being an ace had anything to do with her welcoming attitude toward Minal; he was just grateful. In another city, their family would have garnered way too much attention. In Jokertown, Minal was just one freak among thousands, and their threesome was unconventional, but more the kind of thing that got you harassed by your buddies, rather than got you fired.

Besides, where else would they raise their ace daughter? Where else could Isai fly free when she transformed into a giant creature with the body of a lion, the head of an eagle, and a wingspan wider than six parked cars? Cleveland? Last year, Isai had started kindergarten, and had become the public school's problem for seven straight hours of the day—and somehow, the school had coped, which was a minor miracle in itself. Michael didn't know how they'd manage otherwise, with Minal finally in culinary school, and Kavitha performing most nights and leaving town periodically for the Committee's bizarre projects.

Michael had never asked for so much strangeness in his life—he'd just wanted a great, normal life. Solid career, beautiful wife, a couple of kids and a house of his own. That would have been plenty for him. But having found love, twice, how could he walk away? He was lucky, as the guys at the precinct kept reminding him. Today was a stunning May day, the prettiest they'd seen in months. The perfect day for a proposal, the back of his brain whispered. Michael was a half-black, half-Korean tough guy who'd fought his way up from the wrong side of town; he could handle a proposal. The question was, could he handle two?

"Hey, sweetie—you forgot something!" Minal had come up behind him, was tapping him on the shoulder and handing him an insulated bag. He felt his heart thump hard, once, at her wicked grin. That grin wasn't going to cure his headache, but if Michael could get half an hour alone with her, he was sure Minal would be able to help him out. Sadly, that wasn't going to happen anytime soon. The inevitable chorus of hoots and catcalls rose from the guys (and some of the gals).

"Hey, baby!"

"What'd you bring for me?"

"Something hot and sweet, I bet!"

"I need something spicy!"

Usually Minal would banter back, but today she was already late for her class. She smiled at the gang, dropped a kiss on Michael's cheek, and then was out the door again. She let the battered wood slam shut behind her, leaving him to face the music alone.

Michael knew how to handle this. It'd been two years since he'd come out to his old partner and the rest of the precinct about the threesome; he had this down. "Aw, you guys are just jealous," he said loudly. That quieted them down, because it was true. Not only due to the sexy bi babe whose curvy body had just walked out the door, but also due to the incredible scents rising out of the little carrier. The insulation might keep the rice and curry warm, but it wasn't nearly strong enough to keep the scent of Indonesian *rendang padang* trapped inside the bag.

Slow-cooked beef, simmered in coriander, curry leaves, ginger, cloves, lemongrass, coconut milk, and he wasn't sure what else, but he didn't care. Minal was taking a Southeast Asian class this semester, and Michael was grateful. Her curries were almost as good as his Korean mother's, and the rest of the precinct was jealous. Any cop knew that while it was nice to come home to some sweet loving after a long day, it was more important to keep your stomach well fed—that's what would keep you going when the night got long and crazy. Donuts could only carry a man so far.

Finally, his day was looking up.

He carried the food over to his desk, and almost dropped it when he saw Franny sitting across from him, at his partner Sally's desk. "Hi, Michael!" the kid said, his voice just a little too cheerful.

Two minutes later, Michael was in the captain's office, wondering how hard he'd have to beg to fix this. "Captain, please. You have got to be kidding me? The kid?" Just minutes ago, life had seemed so good. He'd been happy enough to propose, for God's sake. He was finally making some progress on his smuggling case, and he had a smart, sexy partner to work with him. Last week, Sally had taken down a mugger with a sneaky Jiu-Jitsu move that might not be academy-approved, but which was nonetheless impressive. And even though she was tough as hammered nails, Sally was also willing to flirt with the nerdy art insurer if it would get them a lead for their case. She had been the perfect partner—and now she was gone, and Michael was about to be thoroughly screwed. And not in a good way.

Maseryk frowned. "This isn't your decision, Michael. And it's not up for debate. Sally deserved that promotion to One Police Plaza, and I'm sorry for the short notice, but they needed her on something urgent. We'll throw her a racket at the bar Friday night; you can say your good-byes then. I'm promoting Black to be her replacement." He shrugged. "The truth is, the brass uptown dictated his promotion, and I don't like it any more than you do. The kid doesn't know shit. I've sidelined him on a dead-end case; you focus on that art ring you and Sally were handling."

"But sir—" Michael knew he was pushing, but he couldn't just let it go.

But Maseryk was already turning away, back to the mound of papers on his desk. "Enough, Michael. End of story. You can shut the door on your way out."

Michael just barely managed not to slam the damn door. He came perilously close, though, shutting it with a solid thud.

"Whee-oh! I remember that sound." His father was in the hallway, up on a ladder, fixing a light and grinning down at him. "What crawled up your ass, son?"

God, not this too, not today. When would the old man retire? "Dad. I don't need this right now."

His father peered down at him through thick glasses. "You mad 'cause the kid got promoted?"

"You know?" Shit. It would've been nice if the CO had told him first, instead of informing his dad the janitor. The old man should just retire—he was old enough now that his dark skin stood out shockingly against the pure white of his bushy eyebrows.

"Son, you know how fast gossip moves through this place. Everybody knows, and I can tell you that no one is happy about it. Poor kid."

Michael snapped out, "He's jumping the queue. He's too young. He's a goddamned smart aleck who is completely full of himself."

His father cackled. "Reminds me of someone else I know."

"We are nothing alike." That would have come out better if it hadn't sounded quite so whiny. Michael bit his tongue.

His father nodded serenely. "Yessir, whatever you say, sir. I know better than to argue with my superior officer."

There was nothing to say to that.

The old man continued, "When are you bringing those three pretty girls of yours over for dinner? I haven't seen my granddaughter in four whole days. Your mama was thinking Saturday would be nice. She's got plans for jambalaya, and she wants to teach Minnie the recipe."

Michael sighed. "Don't call her Minnie, Dad. You know that's not her name."

His father frowned. "I'll call her what I like; I'm old enough, and I've earned the right. She don't mind. When are you going to call her your wife, that's what I want to know. You ever gonna put rings on those gals' fingers?"

Not him too. It was bad enough listening to the voice in his own head. His parents had been harassing him to marry Kavitha, before Minal moved in—they'd been blessedly quiet on the subject for the past two years. But apparently, his grace period had ended. "I can't marry both of them, not legally." He wanted to, though. He was pretty sure.

The old man snorted. "Did I ask what you could do legally? Do you think we give a damn what the law says? Your mama is dying to throw a wedding for her only child, boy, and if you know what's good for you, you're not going to make her wait much longer." The old man hesitated, and then said, in a softer voice, "Her heart's been acting up again, you know."

Michael's own heart squeezed once, painfully. "I can't talk about this now, Dad." He had a case to solve. Now wasn't the time. He wasn't sure when it would be the right time. "We'll come for dinner, okay? Tell Mama." Maybe he'd propose this week; maybe he'd be bringing two fiancées to dinner on Saturday. Michael loved them, he did. But two wives? It wasn't the life he'd planned for.

His father shook his head. "All right. You be nice to that kid. The whole station's going to give him hell, he doesn't need to get it from his partner, too." Then he turned back to the light above their heads, leaving Michael to face the long walk back to his desk. No more Sally at the desk facing his; that was Francis Xavier Black's desk now.

Terrific.

The Big Bleed

Part Three

AFTER A TORTUROUS COMMUTE from Manhattan, Sheeba and Jamal had arrived at the spill site close to sundown, the worst possible time to conduct a visual investigation. *Too bad we aren't making a movie,* Jamal thought. It was the golden hour, that last bit of the day when directors and cinematographers preferred to film the kissing scene or something equally romantic.

Not that Stuntman had been involved in many such scenes. But he had frequently found his shooting days rearranged around the need to have the crew ready for golden hour. "Something funny happened here," Sheeba said, demonstrating her unfailing ability to state the obvious.

What was your first clue? Jamal wanted to ask, but didn't. Surely it couldn't have been the Warren Country Emergency Services unit parked halfway onto the shoulder of the two-lane asphalt road, and the crime scene tape delineating two squares—one large, one small—in the ditch.

The drive from Manhattan had taken twice as long as it should have. Sheeba Who Must Be Obeyed had elected to follow her Navstar, overruling the obsessive freak behind the wheel who kept insisting that it was taking them around three sides of a square. "Couldn't we have booked a helicopter?" Jamal said, only half joking.

"Unavailable," Sheeba snapped, meaning she had actually made the query.

The extra minutes they spent stuck in traffic allowed Sheeba to recount—largely for Jamal's benefit—the flurry of text messages, e-mailed maps, and other communications that resulted from one simple fact: sometime last night a vehicle had gone off this lonely New Jersey highway and spilled a container of ammonium nitrate.

"Why did it take so long?" Jamal had asked, not, he thought, unreasonably.

"No one found the container until noon today," Sheeba said. Her voice suggested that there was something lacking in the moral fiber of the residents of Warren County, New Jersey, that they would fail to note a container of dangerous material by the side of one of their roads.

Feeling a bit like an actor in a bad action movie, Jamal had felt compelled to persist: "And why are we chasing this and not DHS?"

"One of the locals said the whole thing felt joker-like."

"Some kind of keen perception?" Jamal said. "The smell, maybe—?"

"The crash site."

And so, yes, here they were, in the company of a pair of Warren County hazardous materials types, and Deputy Sheriff Mitch Delpino, a tall, hunched nat around forty who wore a gunslinger's mustache that clashed with his old hippie manner.

"It appears a vehicle went off the road here," Delpino said, spreading his hands and gesturing, as if the tracks could possibly have been mistaken for anything else.

"And it should have wound up nose-first in that ditch," Sheeba said. "It's pretty deep. How do you suppose it got out?" She turned to Delpino. "Any calls for tow trucks out here last night or this morning?"

Delpino glanced at Jamal, as if to say, *you poor bastard, having to work with this.* "Yes, we checked with all the services. No one got a call out here or anywhere near here in the past forty-eight hours."

Jamal said, "Officer, assuming this truck was carrying something illegal when it ran off the road, how likely is it, do you think, that it would call a legitimate service whose destination could be traced?"

Delpino allowed himself a smile so faint that only Jamal could see it. "Quite unlikely."

Jamal turned away and let his eyes adjust again. There was something odd about the tracks where they crossed the mud. "Any insights into what kind of tires were on this truck?" he said.

Delpino stepped forward like a grade schooler eager to recite. "These are not tire tracks," he said. "They are narrower than any commercial U.S. brand or any European one we know. And there's no tread."

"In fact, it looks as though they were thin and solid, like wheels on a kids' wagon," Jamal said. "It does sort of feel like a joker thing."

Ten yards off the road, its passage still obvious from crushed vegetation, a yellow plastic barrel sat upright in the weeds. "Was this how you found it?" Jamal said.

"It was on its side," Delpino said, which was a good thing: neither hazmat specialist seemed eager to talk. "It hit and rolled. You can't see it from here, but there's a small crack on one side. Some fluid spilled." He smiled. "Which we were able to identify as ammonium nitrate, which is why we called you. Well, DHS."

Sheeba reasserted command at that moment. "So strange truck rips along, loses a barrel, and then goes off the road? Seems wrong, somehow."

"How so?" Delpino said.

Sheeba's phone jingled. As she held up her finger, Jamal answered for her: "The logical sequence is, vehicle goes off the road first, spills its cargo . . . then gets out of ditch with no obvious help." She gestured at the crash site. "With all the rain, there would be tracks if another vehicle helped out the first one."

"So we have a mystery," Jamal said. "First step, though, is to secure that material."

"Where do you want it driven?" Delpino seemed eager to have this case off his plate as soon as possible.

"Let me check." Jamal reached for his phone. "They'll probably want us to cordon the place off. . . ."

Before he could make the call, however, Sheeba rejoined the conversation. "Get this," she said, clicking off her phone. "Highway 519 is already cordoned off between Bergen and Hackettstown. New Jersey Highway Patrol." Sheeba turned to Delpino. "What do you know about this?"

"Not a thing. Traffic here is light; the spill is minuscule. And we really don't have the authority—"

Jamal looked down the road. Several sets of headlights burned. "Looks like an accident scene." Christ, now he was stating the obvious. All these months with Sheeba must have affected him.

"What are the odds of two unrelated accidents at the same time on this stretch of road?" Sheeba asked. She turned to Delpino. "Do you know anything about this?"

"Not a thing. I got a call from dispatch just before noon and came straight here. Called in the haz-mat unit before one." Delpino hooked a thumb toward the haz-mat truck. "This is Warren County." He tilted an index finger toward the scene two hundred yards away. "One of those vehicles says 'New Jersey Highway Patrol.'"

"Shoot," Sheeba said, "not this again. Different jurisdictions."

Jamal said, "The bane of SCARE's existence. Wherever we go, we have to make sure the local PD and the highway patrol and the sheriffs are all in the same loop . . ."

Sheeba finished for him. ". . . and they never are!"

"Why don't I go?" he said. It would be informative, and would get him away from Sheeba as her blood sugar drove her to more frequent rages. He chose to walk. The cars weren't that far, he needed the exercise, and it saved him from a pointless discussion about being sure to bring the Explorer back. Maybe Sheeba suspected his eagerness to drive away and never look back.

Walking also allowed him to show up more or less unannounced, without adding that big movie moment of the black Explorer arriving at a crime scene.

Which is clearly what this was: a New Jersey State Police prowler half blocked the road, its flashing cherries clearly visible in the twilight. (Even in bright sunlight, the SCARE team would have seen them from the truck spill site, except that there was a small hill between the two locations.) A coroner's van was next to it.

The yellow chalk figure in the middle of the highway told Jamal much of what he needed to know: they had found a body. And, from the apparent height and shape—not that a chalk outline was remotely reliable—some kind of joker.

As Jamal approached, he saw and felt eyes turning toward him, especially those belonging to one of the New Jersey cops, a tall guy with his right arm in a sling.

Stopping an appropriate distance away, he hauled out his shield. "Special Agent Norwood, SCARE." As if the black suit didn't give him away.

"Gallo," he said, clearly not happy with Jamal's presence. "What brings SCARE to New Jersey?"

Jamal jerked his head back up the highway. "We've got a crime scene. Ah, Federal issues. Controlled substances." He quickly described the crash and the cargo. "And this might explain one problem we've found."

"You think they're related?" Gallo's whole manner suggested skepticism, but, then, he could barely see over the hill to the next site.

As patiently as possible, Jamal explained the mystery of the crash-spill sequence. Perhaps because he began to concentrate on crime scene matters, or possibly because he had already made it clear he didn't like a) Feds or b) aces or c) both, Gallo began to unbend. "We've got a DB here, male, joker approximately thirty years of age. Found here early this morning."

"Cause of death?"

"Now, that's an interesting question. First cut is, hit by a vehicle." Gallo nodded toward the coroner's unit. "But they say, not so fast. Indications are he was dead before that. Autopsy will tell us, I imagine."

"And the time?"

"That we've got: twenty hours ago, give or take a couple."

"But last night."

"No question."

"We don't have two crime scenes here. We have one in two parts."

"What do you want to do about it?"

Jamal thought about it. Have SCARE take it over? Their team numbered two and not only had to beg for any resources beyond an extra cell phone, but was at the mercy of DHS for its schedule: they would surely be detailed to a political event tomorrow. "Leave it where it is," he said. "We'll take custody of the ammonium nitrate. You figure out what happened with our dead joker." He reached for a business card and found one in the clip where he carried his driver's license and a single credit card.

Gallo took it, but didn't offer one of his own. Which was fine with Jamal. Then, possibly realizing that he had been less than helpful, he said, "Agent Norwood, you got any ideas what this might be?"

At that moment, rain began to fall.

"We get reports of wiretaps or signal intercepts about vital 'deliveries' about five times a week," Jamal said, wondering how long it would be before the gentle drops turned to a downpour. He could hardly expect Gallo to offer him a ride up the road. "They never amount to much."

"Until the day they do."

That sounded serious. "You heard anything?"

Gallo was shaking his head. "It is a little strange, though. Dead joker in the road, nasty shit spilled."

"Well, let us know if the autopsy turns up anything we need to know."

Gallo never turned back. Maybe he was eager to get in out of the rain, too.

Jamal retreated up the hill, back to the SCARE team. As he walked, he called Sheeba to report what he'd seen, trying to leave out Gallo's bored unhelpfulness. What else did he expect from the New Jersey State Police, anyway?

Naturally, Sheeba told him they were about to leave, could he hurry? Apparently coming to pick him up wasn't part of the plan. The instant he hung up and prepared to pick up his pace . . . with the Explorer and the Warren County team in sight . . . he suddenly felt weak, as if hit by a blindsided tackle.

He actually had to stop and bend over, trying to catch his breath. What the hell was happening to him? Blood loss, that was it. He had had blood taken—you were supposed to eat when that happened, or just take it easy.

The weak moment passed. It was only when he was feeling better and walking that he allowed himself to remember that the warning about weakness after blood work was for people who had been transfused . . . who had given a pint of their blood.

Not a few ccs.

Cry Wolf

by David D. Levine

GARY GLITCH SCURRIED ACROSS rooftops, the evening air cool on his face as he bounded from one roof to the next across alleys and streets, unnoticed by the people below.

If anyone had seen Gary, they might think he was strange-looking even for a joker. Four feet tall, with skinny arms and legs and huge ears, he resembled an animated sock monkey more than a human being. And if they should happen to see him leap twenty or thirty feet, landing with a muted clang on a fire escape or access ladder and continuing without pause, they might really start to wonder just what sort of creature he was.

Gary tried hard to keep that from happening.

Tar paper, concrete, and shingles flew past beneath his boots as he made his way quickly uptown, heading for the ritzy residential neighborhood north of Houston Street. The pickings were usually pretty good there on a weekday night.

Reaching a fancy apartment building where he'd often had good luck, Gary scrambled up the fire escape to the roof, then quivered on the parapet, peering down into an air shaft. There was a lesbian couple here who could be counted on for a good show. Alas, tonight their window was dark and silent.

Three more of Gary's usual perches yielded nothing, even after many long minutes of watching and listening. Finally, frustrated, he decided to take a bit of a risk. Dashing four long blocks to an apartment building on St. Marks Place, Gary crept quietly down the downspout to a ledge near an open rear window.

Gary didn't really like this spot. There was only one place where he could perch and see into the room, and it was illuminated by a streetlight and in full view of a dozen nearby apartments. But the view was worth the risk: the Trio were in full flagrante delicto.

The man—black and lanky—rocked enthusiastically behind the raised ass of the skinny brown woman, whose face was buried between the thighs of the other woman. The one whose entire torso was covered with writhing pink nipples. All around the three of them whirled a nimbus of light, gold and orange and red. It pulsed in time with their gasps and moans. Gary's throat went dry and his own breathing quickened, matching the rhythm of the three on the bed.

Then a slithering crunch came from above. So unusual was the sound that Gary pulled his attention away from the Trio.

Gary's eyes literally popped out of his head, extending a good three inches, as he saw just what had interrupted him.

A huge black snake-man was racing down the fire escape toward him, well-muscled arms reaching out to snatch him from his ledge. Twenty or thirty feet of black-and-yellow-striped snake tail extended behind his human upper body.

Gary shrieked and scrabbled away, barely avoiding the snake-man's grasp. Fingers clinging to the gaps between bricks, he scampered right up the wall.

But the snake was nearly as fast. "You've peeped your last, peeper!" he called as he climbed, his colorful snake body doubling back on itself.

Just before the snake could snatch him from the wall, Gary reached the parapet of the roof and clambered over it. But a loose bit of metal on the parapet's flashing caught his foot and he went down, falling face-first onto the tar paper. He lay stunned, expecting the snake to catch up with him at any moment.

"Freeze!" came a new voice, echoing up from the alley. "IBT, what the fuck?"

And the snake did not arrive.

Hauling himself to his feet, Gary risked a glance down into the alley. The black man from the Trio, still naked and glistening with sweat, was leaning out of the window Gary had just vacated, training a handgun nearly as impressive as his God-given equipment on the snake-man.

The snake put his hands up as ordered. "I'm on *your* side, man! I was on patrol, and I saw *that* little fucker peeping in your window!" He pointed right at Gary.

The man turned his attention to Gary, followed by his gun. Their eyes met over the gunsight. But then both of them were distracted by a lightning-fast motion.

Taking advantage of Mr. Trio's momentary diversion, the snake-man launched himself into the air. A moment later his whole coiled body landed with a meaty thud on the roof.

"Gotcha!" he cried, lunging inescapably at Gary.

Gary shrieked and vanished.

Back in his apartment, cartoonist Eddie Carmichael clutched his misshapen head and moaned. He preferred to bring his creations back to the apartment before erasing them; making them disappear where they were gave him a horrendous pain behind his eyes. But it was better than the alternative. If Gary had been killed—and the descending snake-man would certainly have smashed him to bits—Eddie would never be able to manifest him again.

Shivering with pain and adrenaline, Eddie took a Percocet and a sleeping pill and dragged himself into bed with his clothes on. But, despite the drugs, he lay awake for a long time.

He'd tried to quit peeping so many times. It was wrong and sick and twisted and disgusting, and someday it might get him into real trouble, but no matter how hard he tried he always started doing it again.

It was the only good thing the wild card virus had ever done for him.

The next morning Eddie was awakened by the bell of his cheap-ass landline telephone. "Hello?" he bleated, once he managed to get the receiver to his ear the right way around. The headache was still there.

"Eddie Carmichael?" A male voice, young and hesitant. "The artist?"

"Yeah . . ."

"This is Detective Black at the Fifth Precinct. We need a sketch artist right away. Are you available?"

"Uh, yeah." The response was automatic. As a freelance artist, he couldn't afford to turn down work, and forensic art paid well as contract assignments went. He hauled himself upright. It was ten minutes after eight in the morning. "I can be there by nine."

"Could you make it eight-thirty?"

"I'll do my best."

Eddie hung up the phone, then cursed with great sincerity as he hauled himself from the bed into his rolling desk chair, which he used to scoot himself to the bathroom.

Eddie's chair was the single most expensive thing in the whole apartment. It had seventeen different points of adjustment, and over the years he'd tweaked them all until the chair fit his twisted, asymmetrical body perfectly. It was the only place on Earth he could be truly comfortable.

The rest of the apartment, all three hundred and twenty square feet of it, was little more than an extension of the chair. He could roll from one side of it to the other with a good hard kick, all of the work surfaces and most of the storage were reachable from a seated position, and even his child-sized bed was higher than normal so he could lever himself in and out of the chair with a minimum of effort.

And then, of course, there were the drawings.

Every single square inch of vertical surface—walls, doors, cabinets, even some of the windows—was covered with Eddie's drawings in pencil, colored pencil, charcoal, and Sharpie. He added, subtracted, and rearranged them nearly every day, to reflect his latest work and current mood.

Not one of them had anything to do with the endless round of single-panel gags, greeting cards, advertisements, and other illustrations he did to pay the bills. Those lived only on the drawing board, and only long enough to satisfy the client. Once they'd been mailed off, he forgot them as quickly as possible.

The drawings on Eddie's walls were all of his own cast of characters. Twitchy little Gary Glitch; slick and sleazy Mister Nice Guy; The Gulloon, a bowling-pin-shaped gentle giant; voluptuous LaVerne VaVoom; hyperactive Zip the Hamster; and many more cavorted across every surface. They were crude in every sense of the word, executed quickly with Eddie's trademark shaky line and generally engaged in activities that would shock most people's sensibilities.

Sometimes he told himself that the sick, exploitative, sexist situations his characters got into were okay because they were only ink on paper. Just drawings, not hurting anyone. Sometimes he even believed it, a little.

None of Eddie's cast of characters had ever been or would ever be published. But in some ways they were all the family he had.

Eddie's mother had been killed by the same wild card virus outbreak that left him a joker. His father had died of a stroke—or the strain of caring for a hideous, deformed child as a single parent—just a few years later. But thanks to his cast of characters, one of the teachers in the group home had spotted and nurtured his artistic talent. Eventually his work brought him enough money to move out of the group home and live independently.

But independence for a freelance artist was always a precarious thing, and he really needed this paycheck if he was going to keep the wolf from the door. So once he had taken care of business in the bathroom and swallowed another Percocet, he gathered his tools and materials, threw on some clothing—keenly aware of the stink of his unwashed body—and hauled himself down the two flights to the street.

With his hunched, diminutive stature, Eddie's view of the heavy Canal Street pedestrian traffic was mostly butts and thighs. But he could still feel the pressure of eyes on the back of his neck, see the small children who pointed and gaped, hear the disparaging comments . . . he couldn't fail to know just what his fellow New Yorkers thought of him. Even his fellow jokers. Did they think the virus had left him deaf as well as ugly, malformed, and in constant pain?

Yes, ugly, even by Jokertown standards. Though he'd been hearing that Joker Pride crap for his whole life, he couldn't buy into the idea that "everyone is beautiful in their own way" applied to him. His head, one arm, more than half his torso, and both legs were hideous masses of deformed flesh, with lumpy pink skin like an old burn scar and tufts of black hair sprouting here and there. Even his bones had been warped and twisted by the virus into a parody of the normal human form.

And yes, despite his best efforts, he did have an odor. Thank you very much for noticing, ma'am. Was it his fault his warty, craggy, twisted body was so hard to keep clean? Bitch.

As if he needed a reminder of why he got all his groceries and other purchases delivered.

Grimly Eddie stumped onward. His right hand, the good one, gripped his four-footed cane, bearing more than half his weight on every other step. Every few minutes he paused to rest.

Finally he reached the station house, Fort Freak itself. Three labored steps up to the door, which opened even before he'd begun to fumble with his portfolio and cane. A massive pair of legs stepped aside, and a deep voice rumbled, "Morning, Eddie."

Eddie tipped back his hat and looked up at a furry face, the smile inviting despite its fearsome fangs. "Morning, Beastie." Beastie Bester was one of the few people in the precinct who didn't seem to mind Eddie's appearance.

"Haven't seen you in a while. What brings you in today?"

"Dunno. I got a call from a Detective Black." He shrugged. "It's work."

After signing in with the winged desk sergeant—and enduring the indignity of standing on a box to reach the desk—Eddie clipped a temporary badge to his lapel and waited. Officers in blue polyester bustled in and out, their belts crowded with guns and handcuffs and other cop equipment.

Daniel in the lions' den, Eddie thought, and loosened his tie.

The first time he'd come to the police station he hadn't slept a wink the night before. But he'd come anyway—no one knew what his characters got up to at night, and his fellow freelance artist Swash had insisted that the job was easy and the money good. And, indeed, he'd gotten nothing from his occasional forays into cop territory but a few modest paychecks and a paradoxical sense of civic pride. He could even boast that his work had helped to put away some very nasty characters.

If, that is, he had anyone to boast to.

"'Scuse me," said one of the cops, a shapely redheaded nat with a detective's badge clipped to the waistband of her skirt, and Eddie shuffled out of her way. But despite her surface politeness, as she pushed past he saw that her nose wrinkled in distaste. Eddie thought about what Mister Nice Guy might do with a redhead like her and a leather strap.

"Eddie Carmichael?" Eddie jerked his eyes up to see a pale nat in a cheap suit. "I'm Detective Black." He was young, even younger than Eddie, and had a soft voice that Eddie recognized from the earlier phone call. "You can call me Franny. This is my partner, Detective Stevens." Stevens was a tall, black nat in a dark suit. He was slim, with prominent ears . . .

Jesus Christ. It was Mr. Trio.

"Whoa," Franny said, catching Eddie's shoulder with one slim hand. "You okay?"

"Yeah, I . . ." He swallowed hard. "I just had a tough time getting here this morning." He wiped his face with his handkerchief. "I don't deal well with crowds."

"Maybe you should sit down."

Franny helped Eddie to a seat, then fetched him a paper cup of water. He took it with shaking hands, trying not to look at Stevens. "I'll be all right."

If the situation weren't so terrifying it would almost be laughable. Called in to sketch his own creation! But there was nothing, absolutely nothing, to connect him to Gary Glitch. As long as he kept calm and did his job—maybe not too good of a job, but not so bad as to attract attention—he could just collect his paycheck and that would be the end of it. The hardest part would be pretending that he'd never seen Stevens before.

No, the hardest part would be *not* drawing Gary Glitch as though he'd drawn the character ten thousand times before.

"What's the case?" Eddie asked, struggling to keep his voice level.

Franny shrugged. "Missing persons. Sort of."

"I, uh—oh?" Eddie fumbled with his portfolio and cane to cover his confusion and relief. "What do you mean 'sort of'?"

"It's not much of a case," Franny admitted.

"It's the best you deserve," Stevens muttered under his breath, so low that Franny couldn't have heard it. *Oh, really?*

"We aren't even really sure anyone has actually gone missing," Franny explained as he led Eddie through swinging doors and across the crowded, noisy wardroom, where too many desks were crammed together under harsh fluorescent lighting and a miasma of stale vending machine coffee. "Very few of the supposed missing persons are, you know, anyone that anyone would miss. But now we've got a witness—someone who claims he saw some of the missing jokers getting snatched off the street." They paused outside an interrogation room and looked through the one-way glass. "For all the good he does us."

Slumped in a plastic folding chair on the other side of the glass was one of the most pathetic-looking jokers Eddie had ever seen. His head resembled a wolf's—a mangy, flea-bitten, ragged-eared cur of a wolf. The fur was matted and patchy, with a lot of gray around the muzzle; the watery, red-rimmed eyes stared wearily at nothing; and the lolling tongue was coated with gray phlegm. The rest of him was essentially human, with a stained and tattered Knicks T-shirt stretched across a swollen beer gut. Dandruff and fallen gray hairs littered the shoulders of his filthy denim jacket.

Stevens crossed his arms on his chest. "His name's Lupo. Used to tend bar at some swank joint, he says, but that was a long time ago. Now he's just another denizen of No Fixed Abode."

"He was passed out behind a Dumpster," Franny continued, "and woke up just as the supposed kidnappers were leaving the scene. Didn't get a very good look at the perps, but maybe enough for a sketch."

Eddie was dubious. "I'll do what I can."

Franny sighed. "I sure hope so, or else this case is just going to fizzle out."

At the sound of the door, Lupo's head jerked up like a spastic puppet's, his eyes wide and feral. Eddie let the detective precede him into the room.

"It's just me, Lupo," Franny said.

Lupo's muzzle corrugated as Eddie entered, his eyes narrowing and his ears going back. Though the wolf-headed joker was no rose himself—he stank of garbage, cheap wine, and wet dog—his beer-can-sized muzzle probably gave him a keen sense of smell. "What's *that?*"

Love you too, Eddie thought.

"This is Eddie Carmichael, the forensic artist," Franny said. "He's going to draw some sketches of the men you saw last night."

With some reluctance Lupo pulled his eyes off of Eddie and stared pleadingly at the detectives. "I tol' you, it was dark. And I don' remember stuff so good anymore."

Stevens gave Lupo something that Eddie figured was supposed to be a reassuring smile. "Mr. Carmichael is a professional, Lupo. He'll help you to remember." He looked sidewise at Eddie, his hard glance saying *Right?*

Eddie froze for a moment, remembering those cold cop eyes looking over the barrel of a gun at him, then shook away the memory. "That's, uh, that's right."

"Well then." Stevens stood. "I'll leave you two to this oh-so-important case while I get back to some real detective work." He looked pointedly at Franny. "If you need any help . . . don't call me." And then, without a backward glance, he left.

Eddie swallowed, his heart rate slowing toward normal. There was something weird happening between the two detectives, but as far as Eddie was concerned, he felt like he'd dodged a bullet for the second time in twenty-four hours.

Hauling himself up into a chair, Eddie unzipped his portfolio. He pulled out a sketchpad, a fat black 6B pencil, and a battered three-ring binder of reference images, but to begin with he just laid them all flat on the table. "There's nothing magic about this process," he said, beginning a spiel he'd used a hundred times. But this time he was trying to calm himself as much as the witness. "I'm going to ask you some questions, but you'll be doing most of the talking. All right?"

Lupo's ears still lay flat against his head, but he nodded.

"So, just to begin with . . . how many of them were there?"

"Three, maybe four. They had this poor asshole with four legs all tied up carrying him toward a van. I only saw the front, couldn't get no plate—"

"Um, actually," Franny interrupted, "he doesn't need to know about the crime. That's my department."

Eddie nodded an acknowledgment at the detective, then returned his attention to Lupo. "All *I* want to know is what they looked like."

A wrinkle appeared between Lupo's eyebrows, and the pink tip of his tongue poked out. "Well, they were all guys . . . or really ugly women." He smirked. "This one big guy seemed to be ordering the other ones around."

"Tell me about him."

Lupo spread his hands like he was describing the fish that got away. "Big."

Eddie sighed. "*How* big? Six feet tall? Bigger?"

"I dunno. Six four, maybe?" The lupine joker squeezed his eyes shut and clapped his hands over them, bending his head down. "I used to be good at this," he muttered into the table's scarred Formica. "When I was tending bar at the Crystal Palace, I knew every regular customer. What they liked, how they tipped, everything."

The name of the bar struck Eddie like a lightning bolt. "You tended bar at the *Palace?*"

Franny just looked at Eddie. He was a nat, so he couldn't possibly understand how important the Crystal Palace was. Eddie himself could only dream of what the place had been like—he'd been only five when the place had burned in '88—but here was someone who'd actually worked there!

Lupo raised his muzzle from the table. "Yeah. I was the number two guy in the whole place—I was in charge whenever Elmo wasn't there."

Eddie felt as though he were in the presence of one of the Founding Fathers . . . or, at least, the decrepit, wasted shell of one. "Did you know . . . Chrysalis?"

Lupo's leer was an amazing thing, the long black lip curling up to reveal an impressive array of discolored fangs. "Yeah, I knew her." He sat up straighter, his eyes seeming to focus for once, though what they were focused *on* was something beyond the walls of the interrogation room. But after only a moment, he slumped in his chair again. "Not that she ever gave me the time of day."

For a moment Eddie actually felt sorry for the battered, alcoholic wolf-man. But then Franny cleared his throat meaningfully, and Eddie reasserted his professional demeanor. "So, the big guy, the one who was ordering the others around. Was he white? Black? Chinese?"

"Joker." Lupo nodded definitively. "His skin was kind of gray and slimy."

"All right." Eddie bit his lip. This would make his job easier in some ways, a lot harder in others. "How many eyes?"

They talked for half an hour before Eddie laid pencil to paper. It was always a good idea to get the subject thinking, forming a good strong image in their own mind, before beginning the actual sketch. He drew vertical and horizontal guidelines, dividing the page in equal fourths, then began to rough in the shape of the suspect's face. "You said his head was kind of narrow. Like this?"

"I dunno." Lupo stared uncertainly at the oval. "Maybe a little pointy on top."

"And the eyes, big and wide-set." He lightly sketched in a couple of ovals.

"Bigger. Wider."

Another half hour and the general proportions of the face were sketched in. The suspect was an ugly sonofabitch, no question, with no nose to speak of and a wide mouth full of pointy teeth. Now it was time to crack open the binder of reference images.

Most sketch artists used one of several standard reference books of facial features; some even used computer software. But in this, as in so many things, Jokertown was different. Eddie's binder, based on one Swash had loaned him when he was studying for his exams, included plenty of photos of actual jokers, but also animals, sea creatures . . . even plants, fungi, and rocks.

Eddie licked his thumb and flipped through the binder until he came to a page showing dozens of pairs of eyes. "Any of these look familiar?"

Lupo studied the page for a long time, tongue tip sticking out. "Could be any of 'em." He poked vaguely at one pair. "Those, I guess."

"Uh huh." Eddie's pencil scribbled in the eyes, big and black and dead, then began to sketch in the structures around them.

It went like that for a long time. Usually a sketching session would be over in less than two hours, but Lupo had gotten such a poor glimpse of the suspects, and his mind was so scattered and fogged by alcohol, that the process was slow and frustrating for both of them. Franny had excused himself before the first hour was up, asking Eddie to call him when he was done. Lupo slurped cup after cup of vending machine coffee; Eddie drank Coke.

Finally, some time in hour four, Lupo's replies to Eddie's questions had turned into little more than a mumbled yes or no, and Eddie's back, hip, and shoulder were screaming from hours in the cheap plastic chair. "All right," he said at last, tearing the final drawing from his sketchbook and tacking it to the wall. "Last chance. Is there anything in any of these drawings that does *not* match your memory of the suspects?"

There were three of them. The big guy, the leader, was a fish-faced joker, all eyes and teeth; the other two were nats. To Eddie the sketches all looked pretty generic—even Fish-Face could have been any of a hundred jokers Eddie had seen on the Bowery in the last year—but they were the best he could do with the information he'd been given. There may or may not have been a fourth snatcher, but Lupo's recollection of him was so hazy Eddie hadn't even attempted a sketch.

Eddie-the-commercial-artist itched to tear these preliminary sketches up and do finished, polished drawings. But Eddie-the-police-sketch-artist knew that composite drawing had its rules, and one of them was that whatever came out of the session with the witness had to be used as-is, with no subsequent cleanup, revision, or improvement.

"They're okay, I guess." Lupo scratched behind one ear, then shrugged. "I'll let you know if I remember anything else."

"Uh huh," Eddie grunted noncommittally, and used the phone on the wall to call Franny. He'd probably never see Lupo again; it might be months before he got another call from the police department. And the way his back and hip felt right now, he might wind up having to spend this whole paycheck on chiropractic. Maybe he should take his name off the list for police artist work?

But no, he realized . . . as frustrating as it was to work with random, unobservant idiots like wolf-boy here, and as humiliating and painful as it was to haul himself out of his comfortable little apartment, it did his heart good to help track down crooks.

It kind of balanced out his karma. He hoped.

A knock on the door, then Franny entered. "So . . . how did it go?"

Eddie gestured at the sketches tacked to the wall. "We got three of 'em, anyway. Lupo didn't get a good enough look at the fourth." *If there really was one*, he didn't say.

The detective looked over the sketches, then turned back to Eddie and Lupo. "These are great," he said. "I'm sure they'll be a big help."

"Thanks." Eddie began collecting his scattered reference materials, pencils, erasers, and sharpeners.

"So what happens now?" Lupo asked, not unreasonably.

Franny shrugged. "You're free to go. But you're a witness, so don't leave town. We'll leave a message at the White House if we need to contact you." Eddie knew the White House Hotel, one of the Bowery's few remaining classic flophouses. Fifty jokers sleeping on sagging beds in one big room.

"I thought I might, y'know, go into a safe house?"

The detective shook his head. "I'm sorry."

Lupo looked back and forth between Eddie and Franny, the whites showing all the way around his big brown doggy eyes. "I told you before, they might've seen me! I know what they look like, and they know it! As soon as I'm back on the street, they'll snatch me too!"

Franny spread his hands, palms up. "There's no budget for it."

Now Lupo was really panicking, ears laid flat against his head. "Can't I get *some* kind of police protection?"

Franny laid a hand on his shoulder. "I'm sorry, Lupo, really I am, but we just don't have the people for it. I can put in a request, but . . ." He shrugged. "Don't get your hopes up."

"Oh man . . ." Lupo put his head in his hands.

Eddie felt bad for the mangy wolf-man, but there was nothing he could do about it. He cleared his throat and held out his time card and pen to the detective.

"Oh. Sorry." He scrawled a signature across the bottom of the card. "Thanks, Eddie. You've been a big help."

"You're welcome." He leaned in closer to the young detective and spoke low. "Say . . . I know it's no business of mine, but is there something wrong between you and Detective Stevens?"

Franny swallowed, and at that moment he looked nearly as miserable as Lupo. "It's nothing you can help with. Thanks for your concern, though."

"Well, whatever it is, I'm sorry." Eddie struggled to his feet, taking one last look at the sketches on the wall. "I hope you get those guys soon."

"Me too."

◆

After the long day he'd had, Eddie wasn't even up to ordering dinner from the New Big Wang Chinese Restaurant down the street. He opened a can of soup and heated it up on his tiny two-burner stove, meticulously washing and stowing the pot, bowl, and spoon when he was done.

Then he rolled his chair over to the drawing table and began to work.

Sometimes he did four-panel strips, sometimes book-length stories. Tonight it was a single large panel, Mister Nice Guy disporting himself across the page with a collection of anonymous, pneumatic women. Eddie worked rapidly, sketching the characters' forms loosely in pencil before dipping his ink brush and bringing them to detailed black-and-white life.

One of the women resembled the redheaded detective from that morning, only with much larger breasts. Mister Nice Guy had her tied up. She smiled around a full mouth, looking up at him as he patted her head.

Eddie's fingers tightened on his brush and his mouth twisted into a sardonic grin as he detailed the woman's thumb-sized nipples.

After Eddie had finished the panel, cleaned his brushes, and taped the new pages up on the wall above his bed, he settled down in his chair with a small sketchpad and a black fine-point felt-tip.

Eddie tapped his fingertips together, pondering options and possibilities. Then he began to draw. With just a few quick lines, a familiar form began to take shape on the pad in his lap.

As Eddie sketched, something like white smoke began to swirl in the air, condensing and thickening, spiraling downward into a hazy bowling pin shape about seven feet tall. Bulbous arms and legs coalesced from the mist, a small head, an enormous cucumber schnoz.

Eddie looked up from his completed sketch of The Gulloon to see the same character looming over him in person, his big clodhopper boots pigeon-toed on the scuffed vinyl of Eddie's floor. He raised one hand and gave Eddie a little three-fingered wave. The Gulloon didn't talk.

Through The Gulloon's eyes Eddie saw himself, a hunched warty excrescence of a joker, but that didn't last long. The Gulloon turned away, clambered up onto the kitchenette counter, and squeezed through the finger's-width gap that was always left open at the bottom of the window. With an audible *pop* he reappeared on the other side, pausing a moment on the fire escape to mold himself back into his usual shape. Then he ambled down the fire escape ladder toward the street.

Eddie himself remained in his chair, conscious and aware, but he closed his eyes to block out the view of his apartment. It was easier that way.

The Gulloon wasn't a rooftop peeper like Gary Glitch; he liked to lurk in the shadows until he saw a pretty girl, then follow her home and look in her window. The big guy was surprisingly quiet on his feet. But tonight there was little foot traffic in Jokertown, and what there was all seemed to be heading in one direction. Curious, he joined in the flow.

Their destination was the Church of Jesus Christ, Joker, at the door of which Quasiman stood handing out flyers. The Gulloon took one. "HAVE YOU SEEN US?" it said, above a grid of sixteen photos. Every one of them was a joker.

The Gulloon, one of Eddie's first creations, was kind of funny-looking even for a joker . . . smooth and round and, frankly, cartoonish. But this crowd seemed preoccupied enough that he felt he could step out of the shadows without attracting too much attention. And, though he did get a few curious glances, no one in the crowd of winged, tentacled, and scaled jokers seemed too perturbed by his appearance. He entered and descended the stairs to the community hall.

The room was filling up fast. The Gulloon stood at the back of the crowd, between a bull-like man and an enormous joker who seemed to be made of gray rock, and edged back into the corner so nobody would touch him. The strange material that made up Eddie's characters' flesh and clothing felt kind of like Styrofoam, stiff and light and fragile.

As The Gulloon shifted around, peering around the heads of those even taller than himself, he spotted the snake-man—Infamous Black Tongue, that was what he was called—in the crowd. But though even the easygoing Gulloon tensed at the sight, Eddie reminded himself that the snake was just as welcome in the church as any other joker, and he had no reason to suspect The Gulloon of anything. Still, The Gulloon kept one eye on him as the crowd took their seats.

The murmuring crowd quieted as Father Squid rose and stood at the lectern. "Thank you for coming tonight," he said, the tentacles of his lower face quivering with each consonant. "As you know, Jokertown has been suffering a series of disappearances. It's said that some jokers have been snatched from the street. Others have simply vanished." He looked down at his hands, which rested on the lectern before him in a prayerful attitude. "Sadly, this is not unusual in our community. But the numbers are higher than usual, and many suspect that these disappearances are related."

Father Squid raised his head, and there was fire in his eyes. "We will not stand for this any longer." Though the joker priest was old, his muscles going to fat, Eddie didn't envy anyone who got in his way. "We will band together. We will be vigilant. And, if necessary, we will fight!" The crowd applauded. "Now, not all of us are fighters." A few in the crowd chuckled at that. "But all of us have a part to play. You have seen the flyers with the photos of the disappeared. If you have any information as to their whereabouts, or any clues as to what has become of them, call the number at the bottom. And if you should happen to observe a kidnapping in progress, or even anything vaguely suspicious, call the same number. Better to raise a false alarm than to let even one more joker vanish." He looked out sternly at his congregation, and a few "Amen"s were shouted. "We will now open the floor for testimony, remembrance, and ideas."

Joker after joker now took the podium, telling tearful stories about the vanished ones, or proposing strategies that seemed to Eddie completely ineffectual, or expressing fear and concern for their own lives. But The Gulloon kept his eye on Father Squid, who stood to one side with his still-powerful arms crossed above his substantial belly.

Eddie wasn't a religious man, and he wasn't a member of Father Squid's congregation. But he was a joker. And watching Father Squid standing there, looking over the crowd, he knew that the old pastor would do anything in his power to protect every joker in Jokertown.

Even him.

No matter how much of a worthless little shit he might be.

Eddie got an assignment from the J. Peterman catalog drawing men's shirts for their incredibly fussy art director—a royal pain, but the job paid really well.

He didn't peep at all; he didn't draw any salacious cartoons; he tried hard not to even have any impure thoughts. Instead, he drew a long, hallucinatory fantasy story involving Gary Glitch and Zip the Hamster on a cross-country road trip. But after a couple of days without peeping he woke up from a lucid, lurid dream of The Gulloon peering into basement windows, only to realize that it wasn't a dream. Eddie hustled his character back to the apartment and dispelled him immediately.

It was far from the first time he'd manifested his characters while sleeping. In fact, that was how he'd started. He hadn't realized the dreams of his characters wandering his own neighborhood had been the manifestation of a wild card talent until one of the other group home residents described a really strange-looking joker she'd seen peering in her window. But ever since he'd started peeping consciously it happened only rarely.

But now it was starting again. As Eddie stared at the spot on the floor where he'd dismissed the easygoing Gulloon, he wondered what Mister Nice Guy or LaVerne VaVoom might get up to if he couldn't keep control of them.

For that matter, what if they'd *already* gotten up to something? He didn't always remember his dreams.

He spent the rest of that night staring at the ceiling and worrying.

"Morning, Eddie," Beastie said, strolling up to the station house door. It was exactly eight in the morning and Eddie had been nervously shifting from foot to foot on the sidewalk for twenty minutes. If he'd been built for pacing, that's what he would have been doing. "So Lupo convinced Franny to call you in again?"

Eddie took off his hat to get a better look at Beastie's face. "No, I'm— I'm here as a concerned citizen. I was wondering if there had been any other sightings in the, uh, the monkey-faced Peeping Tom case."

Beastie shrugged. "Haven't heard of any such thing."

That was a relief, but something else Beastie had said nagged at Eddie's mind. "Wait, what was that about Lupo?"

Beastie rolled his eyes. "He's been in here every damn day, hoping for some kind of protection, but after a while he figured out that wasn't going to happen. Now he's telling anyone who will sit still that he's remembered more details about the snatchers and demanding another session with the sketch artist. Some of us are starting to wonder if he really saw anything in the first place."

Eddie considered the question. "I think he really did. He was a little fuzzy on the details, but I don't think he was making it up or hallucinating."

A rough, growling voice interrupted the conversation. "Oh, thank God you're here!" Eddie looked up to see Lupo running down the sidewalk toward him. Beastie spread his hands in a *see what I mean?* gesture. "I mean that, Eddie," Lupo panted as he came to an unsteady halt, hands on knees, before the station house steps. "I literally thank my Higher Power that you are here. I was beginning to think no one was listening to me."

Eddie shook his head. "I'm not here because I got called back for you. I don't think I've ever gotten called back on the same case. Memories fade with time. You have to get them when they're fresh."

"This *is* fresh, Eddie. I saw him again! The fourth snatcher!"

Eddie and Beastie looked at each other. "When?" Eddie asked.

"Just this morning."

"Really?" Beastie asked, not quite condescendingly. "The timing is awfully convenient."

Lupo raised a hand. "Swear to God." The raised palm was scrubbed and pink, though lines of dirt remained ground into its creases. "I saw him on Bond Street, just around the corner from my hotel." The whites showed all around his eyes. "They're looking for me, Eddie! They know I saw them, and now they're going to snatch me too!"

Beastie didn't seem convinced. "You're absolutely sure it was him?"

"Look, I know I haven't always been the most reliable witness. But my mind is much clearer now. I haven't touched a drop in two days." Lupo crouched down, bringing his head to Eddie's eye level. "You gotta give me another shot, Eddie."

"It's not my decision." Eddie looked to Beastie. "But for what it's worth . . . I believe him."

Lupo's heavy, lupine head swiveled between Eddie and Beastie. "I can give you a good description of the fourth snatcher now. Please." His big brown eyes were impossibly sad and soulful. "Please?"

Beastie sighed. "I'll pass the information up the line."

Lupo and Eddie sat on a hard bench outside the wardroom door while Beastie went in to talk with Franny. This wasn't exactly how Eddie had planned to spend the morning, but if he could get another few hours of composite sketch work out of it he wouldn't turn the money down. Anyway, pulling himself away from the desperate, pleading wolf-man would have seemed rude.

"I'm a new man, Eddie, I swear. You'll see. I was all messed up last time."

Eddie had to admit that Lupo was not only cleaner, he seemed more alert. And his voice, though still sounding a bit odd because of the shape of his mouth, wasn't at all slurred. "You're really serious about this."

"I've never been more serious in my life. There's nothing like the fear of getting snatched to make a man sit up and take notice of what's going on around him." He sighed. "Or what's going on inside him. I've made a mess of my life, I admit it. Maybe this is the wake-up call I've needed. I hope it isn't too late."

"It's never too late," Eddie said, though Lupo looked to be sixty or seventy . . . not an easy time of life to make a fresh start. "Even for people like us."

"People like us?"

Eddie winced, sure he'd crossed a line. Not even jokers liked to be equated with an ugly lump of flesh like him. "Sorry . . ."

"No, no, I'm not insulted. Just surprised to hear you say it. You're an artist, a professional . . . I figured you for an East Village type, not a J-town boy like me."

At that Eddie snorted. "Hardly. I live in an efficiency about a mile from here. Heart of Jokertown."

"No shit? Why haven't I seen you around the neighborhood?"

"I don't get out much." *Not in person, anyway.* Eddie cleared his throat. "I hear things, though. Rumors. Some kind of monkey-faced Peeping Tom, looking in windows at night. Maybe a whole gang of Peeping Toms. Have you heard about anything like that?"

"Not lately." Lupo's lip drew back, exposing yellowed fangs. "But two years ago . . . I was staying at my sister's place, and she came screaming out of her bedroom saying that some big-eared little bastard was on her fire escape watching her undress. I couldn't get the window open, but I got a look at the guy before he escaped." His hairy hands balled into fists. "I might be a joker, I might be an alcoholic, I might even have sold a few things that didn't exactly belong to me, but I'd never stoop that low. If I ever catch that little asshole . . ." He smacked a fist into the opposite hand,

and Eddie realized there was still some serious muscle under the ex-bartender's fat. "He'll be sorry."

Eddie was ashamed to admit that he had no idea which of the many women he'd peeped in on had been Lupo's sister. The incident didn't stand out from so many similar ones in his memory. "Sorry to hear about that," he said aloud.

"You wouldn't believe the shit that goes down in Jokertown." He blinked. "Or maybe you would. How long you lived here?"

"Almost ten years."

"So you never saw the Palace before the fire?"

"No. I've heard about it, though. Was it really as crazy as they say?"

"Crazier." He grinned, an evil thing full of yellow teeth. "One time I was damn near killed by a panda bear. A panda bear! In a bar! Where else but the Palace?"

He went on like that for a while, sharing fascinating anecdotes about people and places that were nearly legends to Eddie, until the wardroom door opened and Franny emerged. "Beastie tells me you saw the fourth snatcher?" he said to Lupo. He seemed half hopeful and half dubious.

"It's true! Swear to God!"

Franny didn't look convinced. He turned to Eddie. "You've been talking with him. Do you believe him?"

Eddie nodded. "I do, actually."

"Would you be willing to do a few more sketches?"

"Sure, if you're paying. But I don't have my stuff with me."

The detective set his jaw and did his best to look decisive. "All right. Come back in an hour and I'll try to find you an interrogation room."

After Franny left, Lupo said, "Thanks for standing up for me."

"You're welcome. And thanks for the stories."

The second session went much more smoothly than the first. Sober, Lupo turned out to be as keen an observer as he'd claimed to be, and in less than an hour they had a good sketch of the fourth snatcher, a hulking blond nat with a broken nose. Lupo also remembered some more details about the other two nats—one had a badly scarred ear, the other a tattoo on his left wrist that Franny identified as a Russian gang mark. "This will be very helpful," he said. "It might not hold up in court, but if we can use it to pull in a suspect, that's a start."

Behind the detective's back, Lupo gave Eddie a thumbs-up.

Eddie didn't even want to admit to himself how good that small gesture made him feel.

That night, instead of peeping, Eddie sent Mister Nice Guy out to prowl the streets on foot, peering at faces. Eddie had not been allowed to keep a copy of the sketches he'd made, but after so many hours with Lupo he knew the snatchers well, especially Fish-Face.

Mister Nice Guy had no trouble blending in with the street traffic in the shabby joker neighborhood near where the snatch had taken place. Pale and big-nosed he might be, but he was humanoid enough to pass for a joker as long as no one bumped into him.

It felt weird to just be walking around on the sidewalk like a normal person, not skulking and sneaking, and not the subject of stares and comments. By comparison with Eddie a cartoon character was normal, at least in Jokertown.

The people on the Jokertown streets at this hour were a mix of types, fashionable bohemians as well as drunks and thugs. A joker couple strolled down the sidewalk tentacle-in-pincer, their clear affection for each other making them cute. A trio of teenaged nats crept about, hesitant and frightened, pointing and giggling when they thought no one was looking. A muscular joker strode past them, heads high and chins up, his four-eyed glare forcing them to silence. But none of them resembled any of the snatchers.

As he walked, Eddie tried to think himself into the snatchers' shoes. Where might they have taken the struggling joker after tying him up? Where else might they be hanging out right now, preparing for another snatch? Were they even now closing in on Lupo, the only witness?

There were so many places to watch.

Fortunately, Eddie could be in more than one place at a time.

Back in the apartment, he opened his eyes and sketched up Zip the hyperactive hamster. A vibrating football-sized furball of nervous energy, Zip barely paused after being created, immediately bounding to the countertop and through the gap in the window. He tore across rooftops in the direction of the White House Hotel, hoping to catch Lupo there or nearby.

It took effort to maintain two characters at once, but it felt good, like the stretch he felt during an intense chiropractic session.

And he was doing it to help other people, for once. To try to catch the snatchers, prevent another snatch, protect his friend.

No. Protect an important witness.

No one could consider lumpy, ugly Eddie a friend.

Zip dashed through the night under a cloudless spring sky, the wind cool on his fur.

Saturday night. Eddie was out in force, with Mister Nice Guy barhopping and The Gulloon wandering back alleys. Gary Glitch was keeping an eye on Lupo, who sat on a bench in Chatham Square chatting with some of his buddies.

It had been three days that he'd been patrolling instead of peeping, staying up until two or three A.M. every night, but what sleep he'd gotten had been deep and dreamless. At night he felt alive, moving his characters around Jokertown like chess pieces, scanning and searching the crowds for the snatchers' faces.

Switching his attention among three different characters, all of them moving and active, was a challenge. Sometimes he realized that he'd left one standing stock-still, unobservant, defenseless. When he discovered these situations his heart pounded, but so far none of his characters had gotten into any serious trouble because of it.

It seemed that just about any kind of appearance or behavior was acceptable in Jokertown at night. If only it wasn't so hard for Eddie to move around, he might even . . .

Suddenly something tugged at his attention. It was Gary Glitch, hidden under a bush a few yards from Lupo's bench.

One of the passing faces seemed familiar. In fact, that same face had passed this spot a few times recently.

Eddie sent Gary scampering across the cold sidewalk, through the soft spring grasses, and up a tree to where he could get a better look at the burly, frowning pedestrian loitering on the far side of the park's play structure.

He seemed to be keeping a covert eye on Lupo as he paced the sidewalk behind the playground, sucking on a cigarette.

He was a nat, big and muscular, Caucasian with an ash-blond buzz cut.

He had a badly scarred ear.

Gary clambered down the tree and crept across the grass to another bush, just a few feet from the guy. He didn't *exactly* resemble the sketch that Eddie had made of the second snatcher, but then again he didn't exactly *not* resemble it. The sketch was pretty generic—it had been drawn while Lupo was still under the influence—and though the scarred ear was a strong identifier, in this part of town knife scars weren't that uncommon.

Eddie wasn't sure what to do.

There was little he *could* do, anyway. Eddie's characters didn't have a lot of physicality to them; they could make noise, maybe lift a few things as long as they weren't too heavy, but they were too fragile for fighting.

He'd keep an eye on the situation. Maybe if it seemed that Lupo were in danger he could have Gary shout a warning.

With another part of his attention, Eddie started Mister Nice Guy and The Gulloon moving toward Chatham Square. But neither of them was as fast as Gary; it would be half an hour or more before they arrived.

A burst of chat and laughter from Lupo's bench drew Gary's attention. Gary saw Lupo stand up, shaking hands and high-fiving his friends, then zip up his jacket and set off in the direction of the White House.

The muscular stranger took a drag on his cigarette, ground it out under his boot heel, and moved off in the same direction.

Keeping out of sight as much as possible, Gary followed.

As the stranger walked—loitering, in no visible hurry, but nonetheless managing to stay within a block of Lupo—he pulled out a phone and muttered a few words in what sounded like Russian. A few minutes later Gary saw him nod to another man across the street.

Fish-Face.

He wore a black leather jacket, scarred and torn at the elbows, and the streetlight gleamed on the silvery, slimy skin of his bald head. His eyes were big, black, and dead, exactly as Lupo had described, though Lupo had failed to mention the fin-like ears and had, if anything, underestimated the toothy horror of the fishy joker's mouth. He was bad news, no question.

Fish-Face and Scarred Ear stayed on opposite sides of the street, leap-frogging each other as they moved along in Lupo's wake. Lupo, oblivious, was enjoying the cool spring air, ambling along, stopping from time to time to chat with friends on the street. He had a lot of them.

Eddie didn't know what to do. The snatchers were big, strong, and probably experienced fighters, there were two of them, and they had the advantage of surprise. If Gary let Lupo know he was being tailed, whether quietly or by shouting, Eddie didn't doubt that Lupo would turn and try to fight them—and get himself snatched.

Could he defuse the situation by attracting the attention of pass-ersby? Hardly. It was nearly two in the morning, on a side street in the Bowery, and the few passersby were most likely as plastered as Lupo on a bad day.

Back in the apartment, Eddie opened his eyes and looked at the phone that sat near his bed. All he had to do was dial 9-1-1.

But Eddie's voice and phone number would be recorded, and sooner or later he'd have to explain how a crippled stay-at-home joker could be an eyewitness to a crime—a *potential* crime—more than a mile away.

Gary Glitch could pick up a pay phone, if he could find one, or dash into an all-night convenience store and raise the alarm. But Gary Glitch was wanted for peeping, and with his distinctive face and build Stevens would recognize him immediately. If Gary ever came to the attention of the police, Eddie might have to retire him permanently.

While Eddie fretted, Lupo continued to make his way home. He was now a block from his hotel; the two thugs following him were now on the same side of the street. Half a block behind Lupo and closing in fast, they were no longer making an effort to conceal themselves. Lupo was oblivi-ous, whistling an old disco tune as he strolled along.

If Eddie was reading the situation right, there probably wasn't much more than a minute before Lupo got snatched. Something had to be done, and fast.

Mister Nice Guy was just a couple blocks off, The Gulloon a bit far-ther away, but they were moving too slowly to offer assistance in time. Only Gary was close enough to do anything, and Lupo hated him.

Eddie had an idea, but it was going to be tricky.

As Mister Nice Guy hurried to meet up with the snatchers before they reached Lupo, The Gulloon lumbering along as quick as he could, Gary Glitch scrambled down a fire escape and dashed across the silent street to tug at Lupo's sleeve. "Hey, dog-breath!" he sneered. "Remember me?"

Lupo's hackles literally rose at the sight of the little cartoon. "You're that big-eared asshole who peeped in my sister's bedroom!" He raised a fist, murder in his eyes.

"Yeah, that's me!" Gary said with a smirk. "And I bet you can't catch me this time, either!" He turned and scrambled away, leading Lupo away from the two snatchers.

With an inarticulate growl, Lupo took off after him.

Two blocks away, Mister Nice Guy rounded a corner. He saw Gary running away, Lupo following him, and the two thugs running after Lupo.

Mister Nice Guy set off after the two goons. He wasn't as fast as Zip or Gary, but like them he was capable of inhuman feats. He lengthened his stride, his legs stretching to ten or twelve feet long as he hurried to catch up with the thugs. The pace was tiring but he wouldn't need to do it for long.

Gary scrambled on hands and feet down the cold gritty sidewalk. He could easily escape by scurrying up the side of some building, but if he did that Lupo would give up the chase and then get caught by the thugs. So Gary hurried along with frequent glances over his shoulder, fast but not too fast, carefully keeping himself in Lupo's sight. It was even more exhausting than running full-tilt.

Back in his apartment, Eddie sat in his chair with fists clenched and sweat running down his sides. With everyone moving so fast it was hard to keep track of who was where. Feet shuffling on the linoleum, he maneuvered his chair across the floor and pulled a New York street map from a shelf.

Meanwhile, The Gulloon plodded along. Eddie couldn't spare much attention for him so he just kept going in a straight line.

Loping with his impossible stride, Mister Nice Guy soon caught up to the two thugs. They didn't hear his cartoonish footfalls coming up behind them.

Three more giant steps and he was well past them.

Then he brought himself to a sudden boinging halt, extending one ten-foot leg across their path.

This was going to hurt. Eddie knew Mister Nice Guy's fragile material would crumble like paper under the impact of two thundering brutes, but he hoped it would stall them. He braced for the impact.

But as soon as he saw Mister Nice Guy's extended leg, Fish-Face shouted, and tried to stop himself. Big and strong though he was, Fish-Face's reflexes were merely human, and in trying to stop he stumbled and fell, tripping Scarred Ear in the process.

Mister Nice Guy pulled back his leg like a retracting tape measure, a fraction of a second before the thugs fell across the place where it had been.

"Gotcha!" cried Lupo.

Eddie jerked his attention back to Gary Glitch, who stood frozen like a scared rabbit in the wolf-man's path. Eddie had forgotten to keep him moving while Mister Nice Guy was dealing with the thugs. With a squeak Gary jumped up, barely dodging Lupo's grasp, and ran at top speed down the street.

But Eddie couldn't afford to ignore Mister Nice Guy for long . . . Fish-Face and Scarred Ear were disentangling themselves and in a moment they would be all over him.

That was exactly what Eddie wanted. He put Mister Nice Guy's thumb to his nose and blew an enormous raspberry.

Enraged, Fish-Face leaped up from the sidewalk. But his grasping hand closed on thin air as Mister Nice Guy swerved out of the way, his body curving into a parenthesis. Scarred Ear growled and tried to grab him in a bear hug, but he ducked that too, bending like a balloon animal.

The two snatchers weren't as dumb as they looked. They charged him simultaneously, from opposite directions. But Mister Nice Guy leaped straight up in the air at the last minute, grabbing onto the horizontal bar of a streetlight as the two thugs collided where he'd been.

That bought Eddie a moment to look in on his other characters. Gary was still running full-tilt with Lupo in hot pursuit, and The Gulloon was still plodding along, so far away from the action that he might as well be on another planet.

Eddie couldn't just keep his characters running forever. They might be cartoons, but they still tired . . . or maybe it was just Eddie who was getting tired. Either way, he had to find a place to stash Lupo pretty soon. The thugs had intercepted Lupo on the way to the White House, so they must know he roomed there. Fort Freak was too far away, and anyway the cops wouldn't take Lupo seriously.

There was only one place in New York City that Eddie knew was safe.

No. He couldn't possibly.

But he had to do *something*.

Eddie bit his lip and redirected Gary on a southbound trajectory.

Toward his own home.

Even as Gary ran, though, Eddie realized none of this would make any difference if the two snatchers lost interest in Mister Nice Guy and took off after Lupo again. Lupo wasn't that far ahead of them, and they could easily catch him before Gary reached Eddie's door.

Eddie returned his full attention to Mister Nice Guy, who was still hanging on the streetlight. Below him the two thugs had recovered their feet. But instead of either giving up on Mister Nice Guy or screaming at him, Fish-Face was just smiling up at him—the most disturbing toothy grin Eddie had ever seen. Meanwhile, the other thug was talking in Russian on his cell phone. What the hell?

Then Fish-Face reached out and grasped the lamppost in one gray, slimy hand.

And a horrible, juddering electric shock surged through the metal and into Mister Nice Guy.

Mister Nice Guy shrieked, his body vibrating and his bones becoming visible through his flesh. His hands clenched the lamppost in an uncontrollable spasm. The pain was incredible. Eddie gasped and curled up like a prawn in his rolling chair, and Gary and The Gulloon both collapsed where they were.

But pain was something Eddie dealt with every day. When the electric shock stopped, Eddie was still alive, still conscious, and still in control of all his creations.

And really pissed off.

Fish-Face seemed disappointed that Mister Nice Guy hadn't dropped off the lamppost like an overripe fruit. He reached for the post again.

Before he could touch it, Mister Nice Guy stretched out his arms, legs, and torso like a striking lizard's tongue, socking Fish-Face right in the jaw with both feet.

It wasn't much of an impact—it probably hurt Mister Nice Guy more than it did Fish-Face—but it was such a surprise and came from such an unexpected direction that it sent the joker tumbling over backward. Mister Nice Guy landed on the sidewalk beyond him, his extended legs coiling like springs, and bounced away into the night.

The other thug just stood there agog for a moment, until Fish-Face snarled something at him. He put the phone in his pocket and began running after the escaping cartoon.

Exhausted and stunned from the electric shock, Mister Nice Guy wobbled on his boinging, Slinky-like legs. But he couldn't slow down now. He headed north . . . back the way he'd come, and directly opposite the direction Gary was leading Lupo.

He risked a look over his shoulder. Both thugs were following him. Good.

Eddie switched his attention to Gary Glitch, who still lay where he'd fallen when Fish-Face had shocked Mister Nice Guy. Gary looked up from the pavement . . . to find headlights and a blaring horn bearing down on him. He yelped and scuttled away, fingernails tearing on the asphalt . . . reaching the curb just in time. But before he could catch his breath, Lupo was in the crosswalk and closing fast. Gary shook himself, looked around, and scrambled off toward Eddie's apartment as fast as he could.

Now Eddie, still dazed from the shock, was running *two* characters just fast enough to keep ahead of their pursuers. It was an incredible strain. Even with two fingers on his map he was having trouble keeping track of them. But he couldn't just make them vanish . . . he had to lead Lupo to his apartment, and at the same time he had to keep the two thugs as far away from him as possible for as long as possible.

God, he was tired.

By now Gary was only two blocks from Eddie's apartment door. He looked behind to make sure Lupo was still following.

Lupo was. But there was also someone following *him*, and gaining. A big blonde with a broken nose. The fourth snatcher.

How the hell—? But then Eddie remembered that the bald thug had made a phone call not long after Lupo had gotten away. Gary ran faster, hoping Lupo could keep up.

But even if he could . . . they were all heading straight for Eddie's home. He needed help, and fast. If only he had Zip in play . . . Could he handle four characters at once?

Eddie opened his eyes and reached for his sketchpad.

It wasn't easy drawing Zip while also keeping his other characters in motion. But finally the hyperactive little hamster coalesced into existence on Eddie's kitchen floor. He shook himself, then squeezed out through the window and shot off across the city toward Fort Freak. Zip had no criminal record, and with his speed he could plausibly claim to be a witness to the situation going down near Eddie's apartment.

Assuming he could make himself understood, and that the cops would listen to a football-sized manic hamster with a squeaky machine-gun voice. Eddie had to hope that Jokertown cops were prepared to handle a crime report from *anything*.

Then Eddie's attention was jerked back to Mister Nice Guy, as Scarred Ear picked him up by the neck. Fish-Face was there too, grinning a vicious, toothy grin. Electricity began to crackle . . .

. . . and The Gulloon, who'd been plodding along unattended this whole time, slammed into all three of them. He wasn't going very fast, and he didn't actually weigh very much, but he was *big,* and he sent the whole group tumbling like bowling pins.

Eddie took the opportunity to direct his attention to Zip, who had just arrived at Fort Freak. Even at this hour the station was brightly lit. Zip careened in the door, past the desk sergeant, and into the wardroom, looking for Beastie, or Stevens, or . . .

There! Detective Black!

"Franny!" Zip squeaked, waving his little paws. The detective looked around, his gaze passing well over the hamster's head. Zip stuck two fingers in his mouth and let out a piercing, almost supersonic whistle. "Down here, fuckhead!"

That got his attention.

"It's the snatchers!" Zip squeaked like a CD on fast-forward. "The snatchers! They're chasing Lupo! You have to come right away!" He gave Eddie's address.

And Mister Nice Guy looked up to find Fish-Face's heavy boot coming down toward his head.

Eddie swore and made both Mister Nice Guy and The Gulloon vanish. Clutching his head from the pain, he returned his attention to Gary Glitch and the wolf at his door.

Gary had just reached Eddie's apartment building. With a great effort he squeezed his way under the front door and collapsed, panting, inside.

Lupo came charging up. Seeing Gary through the glass, he pounded on the door with both fists. Eddie paused with his finger on the door buzzer. What the hell was he doing?

"You peeping asshole!" Lupo yelled, his voice muffled by the thick security glass. "I'm gonna get you if it's the last thing I . . ."

Behind Lupo, Gary saw the fourth kidnapper.

Eddie pressed the door buzzer and sent Gary scrambling away, up the steps.

Lupo snarled and snatched the door open, tearing after Gary.

Gary paused for just a moment on the first landing, looking back, hoping against hope . . .

. . . but the door, swinging gently closed on its hydraulics, did not click shut. A moment later it slammed open again, revealing the big nat. Lupo, hearing the noise behind him, turned.

And then the whole scene was flooded with red and blue lights and a voice on a bullhorn. "You! At the door! This is the police! Stop and put your hands up!"

The man stopped in the doorway. But he didn't put his hands up. Instead he turned and ran, vanishing into the night. "Halt!" cried the bullhorn. But the pounding footsteps kept going. The flashing lights followed.

All was quiet and still for a moment. Then Lupo turned back to Gary, who still stood stunned on the landing. The wolf-man's lips curled back and his fists clenched.

Eddie pressed the intercom button. "Forget about him, Lupo!" he shouted. "It's me you need to be talking with."

Lupo looked around, then noticed the intercom grille behind him. The door was still easing shut. "Eddie?"

"Yeah."

"You know this little fucker?" It hurt Eddie's already-throbbing head to hear Lupo's grating voice simultaneously through Gary's ears and, with an echoing delay, through the intercom.

"In a manner of speaking." Eddie swallowed. "Please, just listen to me."

Lupo gave Gary a vicious glare, but he stepped to the closing door and stopped it with one foot. "I'm listening."

"Look, the situation's kind of complicated and I'm not proud of it, but right now the important thing is this: the snatchers are real, and they're after you. But I . . . but my *friend* here"—he made Gary wave—"he led you away from them, while some of my other, uh, friends, distracted the thugs and called for help."

"How do I know *you* aren't in cahoots with the snatchers?"

"If I were, would I have given Franny those sketches that looked just like them?"

"Urr . . ." Lupo growled, looking uncertain.

As Gary looked down the stairs at Lupo, Eddie wondered what the hell he was doing. How could he let this alcoholic, wolfish joker into his own home? He might work with the police sometimes, but he wasn't a cop—he wasn't sworn to serve or protect anyone.

But still . . . saving Lupo from the snatchers had felt so good. He'd never dreamed that an ugly, twisted little joker like himself could have such a big impact on the world.

And Lupo was, if not a friend, at least someone who had treated Eddie like a human being. Eddie pushed the intercom button again. "I swear I am not a snatcher, Lupo. But the snatchers *are* still out there." He released the button, paused, swallowed, pushed it again. "If you come upstairs, I'll . . . I'll keep you safe for a while, until we can get this mess sorted out."

Lupo blinked, his big brown eyes shining in the vestibule's harsh fluorescent light. "You'd do that for me?"

"Yeah."

Lupo considered the idea for a bit, then stepped inside and let the door close behind him. "Okay."

Gary led Lupo up to Eddie's apartment. Lupo regarded the little cartoon with clear suspicion, but followed quietly, trudging heavily up the stairs. It was only now that Eddie realized just how exhausted Lupo must be after that long chase.

What a pair they were.

Finally the cartoon and the joker stood outside Eddie's door.

Eddie hesitated, the brass doorknob cold in his hand. He hadn't let another human being into his apartment in over five years.

He turned the knob.

Galahad in Blue

Part Two

APSARA SASHAYED INTO THE bullpen. Every male and even a few females paused to watch her progress. Everything was in motion, hips swaying, hair swinging, boobs bouncing. Last night that rack had been pressed against Franny's bare chest, the hair wrapped around him mirroring her arms' embrace. Franny was glad the desk hid his involuntary physical reaction. It was like being sixteen again. *Next*, he thought, *I'll break out, and my voice will start cracking.*

As she drew closer Franny could see the beautiful oval face was set in lines of worry and alarm, and the dark eyes were wide. Franny suppressed the desire to sigh. Looked as if her phi—otherwise known as her pissant wild card power—was giving her hell again. As soon as she got close enough for him to be able to see it, her dark eyes filled with tears. She was the only woman he'd ever met who could cry and stay beautiful. No red nose, no snot on the upper lip. Franny steeled himself for whatever crisis had arisen.

"Frank." Once they'd started dating she stopped calling him Franny. "I need to talk to you. Someplace private." Her voice trembled a bit, and cynicism gave way to actual alarm. Maybe something serious had happened.

He led her outside because there was no place in the cop shop that he would have considered truly private. They settled on a bus stop bench. Franny shifted to face her. "Okay, honey, what's wrong?"

"My parents," she wailed. "They're coming to visit."

Blinking in confusion Franny asked, "Isn't that a good thing? You said you really loved your folks."

She nodded vigorously, tears flying off her outrageous eyelashes. "I do, but I told them I was a cop."

"Well, you are sort of a cop. I mean, you work for the precinct."

"No, a real cop. A *decorated* cop. With a badge. And a uniform. And a gun."

Baffled, Franny stared at her for a few moments. "Why? Why would you do that?"

"Because they love me so much, and they're so proud of me, and I haven't done anything to earn that. If they find out I'm just a file clerk they'll put on a brave face, but they'll be so disappointed, and . . . and I just can't bear that." Her voice broke on a tiny little sob. Instinctively Franny gave her a hug and patted her on the back as she wept.

"Okay, I get the whole parent/child issue, I've got the famous cop father thing going on, but I'm not seeing how I come into this."

As if a spigot had been turned the tears ended. She straightened and took his hands in hers. "So, I rented a uniform from a costume store, and I took an old retired badge out of storage and I've asked for a few days off, and you could do the same and we could be partners, and take my folks along like they did when that Hollywood actor came to town last year," she ended in a rush.

Franny pulled his hands away and held them up palms out. "Whoa, whoa, whoa. First off, I can't take time off right now. I'm in enough trouble as it is, and I'm not going to put back on my uniform and go out on the street with an untrained file clerk and a pair of civilians. That's a good way to get *us* fired, and *all* of us hurt or worse. And didn't you sleep with that actor guy?" he added, jealousy making him resentful even though they hadn't been together back then.

"What if I did? I was with Moleka then, not you, so you shouldn't care."

"It's the pattern, Apsara, that's what bothers me."

The bus farted up and with a creaking of brakes came to a stop in front of them. Four jokers flopped, crawled, and hopped off. The doors stayed open, and then the driver yelled, "You gettin' on or not?" They shook their heads. "Then get off the damn bench!" The doors rattled shut and the bus pulled out, baptizing them with a blast of diesel fumes. Apsara and Franny retreated, coughing.

"So, you're not going to help me," she said once she caught her breath.

"If by help you, you mean play cops and robbers with you and your parents, then no, I'm not going to help you."

"Will you at least keep my secret?"

"Are you going to be prancing around in this uniform?"

"Yes." The word was defiant, an out-and-out challenge.

"You know it's a crime to impersonate a police officer," he said, still sparring, but more feebly now.

"I'm not going to arrest anybody. I'm just going to wear the uniform at dinner, and we'll stay away from Jokertown so no one will see us." She paused and looked up at him, big eyes pleading, the corners of her perfect lips drooping. "Please, Frank, let me make them proud."

"I don't know, and why do you need me along for this?"

"I need you to talk about all the cases I've solved. If you bring it up then it won't look like I'm bragging."

"And what cases would those be . . . exactly?"

"Well, there was The Stripper for starters, and you wouldn't be lying because I helped you catch that guy."

He didn't love the reminder. He had just started working at the precinct when he'd solved the case of the teenage ace whose power was to blow a kiss and have the clothes disappear off the object of his gallantry. Bruce Cordova. That was his name. Some of the guys at the precinct had thought it would be hilarious to have Bruce remove Franny's clothes day after day after day. It had been . . . for them.

And Apsara *had* helped catch The Stripper. She had been the luscious bait walking down the street. Franny had gotten only the smallest look at her attributes that day because he'd been busy arresting Bruce. Of course now he saw those attributes almost every night. He felt a stirring in his crotch. Apsara saw his boner forming. She gave a sly smile, and pressed up against him. "Please, Frank."

All his resistance collapsed. "Well, okay, but so help me God, if you try to act like a real cop . . ."

"Oh thank you, thank you. You are the *best* boyfriend." She rained kisses on his face. Franny finally caught her lips, and they shared a long deep kiss until the whistles and catcalls from passersby on the street drove them apart.

Road Kill

by Walter Jon Williams

GORDON WISHED HE HAD more time to examine the body. Not just to find out who killed the victim, but to find out how the joker was put together.

It looked as if there were extra attachment points on the biceps brachii, for example—the normal two on the scapula, plus another, stronger attachment to some kind of disk-like rotating bone, equipped with a nasty ten-centimeter spur, which seemed to float somehow off the head of the humerus. When the biceps contracted, not only would the forearm rise but the spur would rotate forward, as if aimed at an enemy. So if the joker raised his fists in a boxing stance, say, the spurs would roll forward, and he could impale an enemy by shouldering him in the clinch. Or he could grab an attacker and pull him close, and the very act would throw the enemy onto the spur.

And if the arms were relaxed, the spur would rotate backward to protect the head from a surprise attack from the sides or rear.

There were spurs on the knees as well, but these looked like an anatomically simple extension of the tibia. There were also some scars to suggest there had also been spurs on the heels, but these had been amputated at some point to allow the subject to walk normally.

Gordon thought that the wild card was sometimes capable of great beauty, even genius, in its adaptation of human anatomy; but it was also capable of forgetting that someone apparently designed as a street fighter might also need to walk.

Gordon would have liked to dissect the shoulder just to understand the mechanism. But that wasn't part of his job.

His job was ascertaining cause of death, here in his morgue annex in the basement of the Jokertown precinct, a room that smelled of antiseptic and plastic body bags and the bitter-cherry scent of death, where deformed bodies lay on steel tables coated in blue-gray porcelain, and where police officers paced as they drank coffee from paper cups and waited for information.

"So," said Detective Sergeant Gallo, "it was the hit-and-run did him in?"

Gallo stood a respectful distance from the body, by the door. He wanted to be in the room during the autopsy, but he didn't have a compulsion to stand right by and watch the pathologist at work. Maybe he didn't like corpses, Gordon thought, or maybe he'd seen so many that he was no longer interested.

Which was not something that could ever be said of Gordon.

"No," Gordon said. "He was dead by the time the vehicle hit him."

"The vehicle hit a corpse," Gallo said.

"The vehicle was pretty unusual," Gordon said. "It had slick tires—the prints on the victim's body and clothing were absolutely featureless, no tread marks at all." He looked at Gallo and blinked. "What uses slick tires besides a drag racer?"

Gallo shrugged. He was a tall, broad man, dark-haired, blue-eyed. His right arm was in a fluorescent red fiberglass cast and carried in a sling, and he wore a black leather jacket on the left arm and thrown over the shoulder on the right. His pistol was tucked into the sling for ease of access.

"Coulda been a drag racer, I suppose," he said. "Though it wasn't going very fast when it hit the victim. But if the vic died from the beating, there's no point in chasing down the driver."

"It wasn't the beating," Gordon said. "El Monstro didn't kill him."

Gallo was startled. "Who?"

"El Monstro."

Gallo was New Jersey State Police and not from New York, so he wouldn't have had a chance to meet El Monstro. Certainly the joker was hard to miss—nearly eight feet tall, horned, with chitinous armor plates covering most of his body—and plates on his knuckles as well, plates that left a very distinct imprint.

"His real name's José Luis Melo da Conceição Neto," Gordon said. "Brazilian kid, raised in Jokertown. I testified on his behalf about fourteen months ago, in an assault case." Gordon gestured with one hand at the distinctive bruising on the dead man's upper arms and torso. "El Monstro pretty clearly left these marks. Nobody else has fists like that."

Gallo reached for his notebook, juggled it one-handed for a moment, then put it on one of the counters that surrounded the room. "Can you give me that name again?"

Gordon did. "Neto isn't really part of the name," he said. "It just means 'grandson'—grandson of the original José Luis Melo da Conceição."

Gallo wasn't used to writing left-handed and it took some time to get the name down.

"He was a nice kid," Gordon said. "He'd be about nineteen now. Works a couple jobs, trying to support a disabled mother and get through NYU. I was able to show the court that he suffered at least half a dozen defensive injuries before he put his assailant in a coma with a single punch. The assailant had a history of violence and robbery, so El Monstro walked."

"He walked all the way to Warren County," Gallo said, "where he killed this other joker."

Gordon shook his head. "No," he said. "He didn't kill this John Doe."

Gallo's tone turned aggressive. "If the truck didn't kill him, and your El Monstro didn't beat him to death, what the hell did put his lights out?"

Gordon looked up from the body. "SCD," he said.

Gallo stared at him in disbelief. "Sudden cardiac death? You're telling me the John Doe had a heart attack?"

"Not a heart attack. Cardiac arrest caused by aortic valve stenosis." Gordon gestured toward the victim's heart, which was sitting in a plastic container on the counter. "His aortic valve narrowed to the point where the heart couldn't pump enough blood into the aorta, which caused the heart to pump faster and faster until it went into ventricular fibrillation, and then . . ." Gordon made a vague gesture. "Asystole, cardiogenic shock, loss of circulation, death. It happens pretty fast, sometimes within seconds."

"What caused the, ah, stenosis?"

"At his age, it was most likely congenital. Happens to men more often than women."

For the first time Gallo approached the body and looked at it thoughtfully. "So he got beat up by this El Monstro guy."

"The wounds were antemortem, though not very far in advance of death."

"And then the vic has SCD, and drops dead on the road, apparently, and was then hit by a drag racer?" The fingers of his left hand reached into his cast and scratched the fingers of his right. He looked up. "He can't have been pushed out of a car or something?"

"No drag marks. No skid marks." Gordon shrugged. "Lividity hadn't developed when the vehicle hit him, so he was run over less than twenty minutes after death."

Gallo shook his head. "This is the worst case of bad luck in all history," he said. He made a disgusted noise. "What was he doing on Route 519? Rural New Jersey, for cripe's sake!"

The victim wasn't, technically speaking, Gordon's business. New Jersey had its own forensic pathologists. But jokers weren't very common in northwest New Jersey, and when the body turned up beaten, run over, and naked except for an athletic supporter and a pair of Adidas training pants, it had been taken to Jokertown for an examination by a specialist in joker bodies.

By Otto Gordon, M.D., known to his colleagues as Gordon the Ghoul.

Gordon adjusted his glasses. "You sure there weren't any prizefights in the vicinity?" he asked. "Cage fights? He'd been through a beating."

"Nothing in that area but dairy farms. We didn't see any crowd leaving, any sign of anything unusual."

"Footprints? Tire tracks?"

"Zilch. And certainly no sign of anyone like El Monstro."

"Well." Gordon shrugged. "Let me stitch up the body, and you can take it home. I'll send you the report when it's done."

"And I'll liaise with NYPD to see if we can pick up this Monstro guy."

Gallo left to do his liaison work. Gordon closed the Y-shaped autopsy incision, made sure the plastic containers with the victim's organs were properly sealed and labeled, and then called his diener, Gaida Hanawi, to help shift the victim back into the body bag he'd arrived in.

Gallo returned along with the uniformed trooper who had driven him into the city from Warren County. Gaida and the uniform began wheeling the body out to the loading dock, past a couple local cops who looked at him in surprise. The trooper's sky-blue jacket with its gaudy yellow patches and the gold-striped black trousers were a considerable contrast to the more severe dark blue uniform of the NYPD.

"How'd you hurt your arm, anyway?" Gordon asked.

"Hit by a vehicle when I was trying to make an arrest," Gallo said. The uniformed trooper snickered.

"Shut up," Gallo told him.

"It was a skateboard," the trooper said. "The detective got hit by a kid on a skateboard, and now I have to drive him everywhere."

"Fuck you," Gallo said.

"Kid got away, too."

"Fuck you twice."

They went to the loading dock, and loaded John Doe onto the vehicle from the Jersey morgue. "I'll be glad to get out of here," the trooper said. "These jokers give me the creeps."

"Moriarity," Gallo said, in an exasperated tone. The trooper looked at him.

"What?"

Gallo rolled his eyes toward Gordon. The trooper looked skeptical, then turned to Gordon. "You're not a joker," he asked. "Are you, Doc?"

Gordon considered the question, and then gave a deliberate laugh, *heh heh heh*. "If only you knew," he said. He went back into the clinic, and as the door sighed closed behind him, he heard Gallo's growling voice. "Jesus Christ, Moriarity, the guy looks like a praying mantis on stilts, and you don't think he's a fucking joker!"

Gordon returned to the morgue and looked at himself in the mirror. Tall, thin, hunched, thick glasses beneath short sandy-brown hair. Praying mantis on stilts. That was a new one.

He returned to the morgue and found Detective Black waiting for him. Franny Black was dark-haired and ordinary-looking and young—too young for his job, or so Gordon had heard it said. He was the son of one of Fort Freak's legendary officers, and he had so much pull in the department that the NYPD had violated about a dozen of its own rules to jump him to detective way early.

This hadn't made him popular with his peers.

"Okay," Franny said. "Now you're done entertaining the folks from out of state, maybe you can do what you're actually being paid to do, which is work on stiffs from this side of the Hudson." He gave a snarl. "What about my Demon Prince body?"

Franny wasn't naturally this belligerent, or so Gordon thought—he was just talking tough in hopes of acquiring a respect that most of the cops around here weren't willing to give him. "The Jersey body might be yours, too," Gordon said. "Have you checked Father Squid's list of the missing?"

Franny's eyes flickered. "You have a copy of the list here?"

"No. Father Squid keeps dropping off handbills, Gaida keeps throwing them away. She likes a tidy lab." He cocked his head. "But," he said, and flapped a hand, "when a mysterious joker appears in Jersey, he had to have come from somewhere."

Franny seemed impatient. "Maybe," he said. "But how about the Demon Prince?"

Gordon indicated a body laid out on a gurney and covered with a sheet. He'd looked at it earlier and seen that its wild card deformities had made the banger uglier, but not necessarily tougher. "I only had a chance to give your victim a preliminary inspection," he said. "But it looks like the murder weapon was oval in cross-section, tapering to a point from a maximum width of about point seven five centimeters."

"Like a letter opener?" Franny asked.

"I'd suggest a rat-tail comb."

Franny frowned to himself. "Okay," he said.

"Your perpetrator is between five-four and five-six and left-handed. Female. Redhead. Wears Shalimar."

Franny for his notebook. "Shalimar," he repeated, and wrote it down.

"Your victim," Gordon said, "had recently eaten in a Southeast Asian restaurant—Vietnamese, Thai, something like that. Canvass the restaurants in the neighborhood, you'll probably find someone who's seen him with the redhead."

Franny looked puzzled. "I thought you said you'd only done a preliminary," he said. "You've already got stomach contents?"

Gordon shook his head. "No. I just smelled the nuoc mam on him—the fish sauce."

"Fish sauce." Scribbling in his notebook.

"High-quality stuff, too," Gordon said. "Made from squid, not from anchovy paste. I'd check the pricier restaurants first."

"Check." Gordon lifted the sheet, revealing the pale corpse with its tattoos and wild card callosities. "You can give it a whiff if you like. Check it out for yourself."

A spasm crossed Franny's face. "I'll trust you on that one, Doc."

"I'll let you know if I find anything else."

The subsequent autopsy revealed little but the bùn chả in the stomach and some gang tattoos, not surprising since the victim was a known member of the Demon Princes. The question for Franny was going to be whether the killing was gang-related, or something else—and since rat-tail combs were not a favored weapon of the Werewolves, Gordon suspected that the homicide was more in the nature of a personal dispute.

Gordon and Gaida zipped the body up into its bag, put the bag in the cooler, and then it was time to quit.

"I'm heading uptown tonight," Gaida said. She was a Lebanese immigrant, a joker, who wore her hair long to cover the scars where her bat wing–shaped ears had been surgically removed. "Going to take in *Don Giovanni* at Lincoln Center."

"Have a good time," Gordon said.

"You have plans for the weekend?"

"The usual." Gordon shrugged. "Working on my moon rocket."

The diener smiled. "Have a good time with that."

"Oh," Gordon said, "I will."

Gordon hadn't mentioned to Sergeant Gallo that he owned a house in New Jersey, a two-bedroom cabin in Gallo's own Warren County where Gordon went on weekends to conduct his rocket program. Though Gordon followed all precautions and did nothing illegal, it had to be admitted that he kept a very large store of fuel and explosives on his property, and he figured that the fewer people who knew about it, the better. Especially if the people in question were the authorities.

He took the train to Hackettstown and picked up his Volvo station wagon from the parking lot near the station. On the way to his cabin he found a nice fresh piece of roadkill, a raccoon that probably weighed twelve or fourteen pounds. It was a little lean after the long winter but would make a fine dinner, with cornbread-and-sausage stuffing and a red wine sauce. He picked up the raccoon with a pair of surgical gloves, dumped the body in a plastic bag, and put the bag in his trunk. Once he got to the cabin he put the raccoon in his refrigerator. He'd cook it the next day, when Steely Dan came by to help him make his rocket fuel.

The raccoon was boiling in salt water when Steely Dan arrived at mid-morning. Dan was, so far as Gordon knew, the only joker in Warren County, and he lived there because he had family in the area. Steely Dan was short, squat, ebon, smooth, and shiny, as if he were made of blackened, polished steel. He had no body hair, he was very strong, and his head was literally bullet-shaped. Children tended to think he was some kind of robot.

He'd been on *American Hero* in its fifth season, but had lasted only two episodes.

Dan worked at auto repair, and he brought useful skills to Gordon's rocket program. He had built the steel cells used to synthesize sodium perchlorate, and also scavenged lead diodes from an old auto battery, which would have been messy if the job had been left to Gordon. The synthesis of $NaClO_4$ was easy enough; but then any residual chlorides had to be chemically destroyed lest the subsequent addition of ammonium chloride turn the compound into a highly unstable chlorate. The oxidizer itself, ammonium perchlorate, was created through a process of double decomposition, then purified through recrystallization. And because NH_4ClO_4 could be absorbed through the skin, Gordon and Steely Dan both had to wear protection even though the danger to the thyroid was slight.

Gordon didn't know if Steely Dan even had a thyroid.

At the end of the long afternoon Gordon had a substantial quantity of ammonium perchlorate, a pure white powder that when mixed with aluminum powder and a few minor additives would form solid rocket fuel, the formula used by the Air Force in the boosters of their Hornet shuttle.

The operation was carried out in the old barn, amid the scent of musty old hay and rodent droppings. By the end of the afternoon, the ammonium perchlorate was safely transferred to steel drums, then pushed on a handcart to Gordon's storage facility, a prefabricated steel shed in the middle of a meadow, and surrounded by berms of earth pushed into place by a neighbor with a bulldozer. If anything unfortunate should befall the shed, the force of the explosion would go straight up, not out into the countryside.

Which was good, because of what Gordon kept there. The aluminum powder that would turn the ammonium perchlorate into flammable mixture. Kerosene. Tanks of oxygen. Syntin, which had driven the Russians' Sever boosters into space. Hydrazine and nitrogen tetroxide, which were not only explosive in combination but also highly toxic.

Gordon hadn't quite worked out what fuel he wanted to take him to orbit, so he was keeping his options open.

♥

The stuffed raccoon had been sizzling in the oven for two hours. Gordon sautéed new potatoes to serve with it, and he'd made a pesto of ramps, which were the only local vegetable available at this time of year; he served the pesto on linguine, with a sharp parmesan made by one of the local dairy farmers. With the meal Gordon offered a robust Australian shiraz, which Steely Dan preferred in a ten-ounce tumbler, with ice.

"Damn, man," Dan said, after tasting the raccoon. "That's amazing. It's kinda like pork, isn't it?" He had a half-comic strangled voice that contrasted with his formidable appearance.

"Tastes more like brisket to me," Gordon said. He lowered his face over the plate and inhaled the rich aroma.

"This is a first for me," Dan said. "If my family ever ate varmints, that was way before anyone can remember."

"I hate to let an animal go to waste. The whole license business is ridiculous." New Jersey required a license to prepare roadkill, which Gordon thought was simply weird. *Who thought of these things?* he wondered. And who would actually enforce such a law?

"So," Steely Dan said, counting on his fingers, "I've had squirrel here, and possum, and rabbit."

"Venison," Gordon pointed out. "There's a lot of roadkill venison out there."

Steely Dan jabbed at Gordon with his fork. "Is there anything you won't eat?"

"Rat. They can transmit Weil's disease—and believe me, you don't want that."

"I never heard of Weil's disease, but I believe you." Steely Dan took a generous swig of his shiraz.

Gordon chewed thoughtfully, and then remembered the previous day's autopsy. He looked at Steely Dan, and saw himself reflected in the joker's glossy skin. "Do you know any other wild cards living in this area?" he asked.

"Besides yourself?" Steely Dan said. And, at Gordon's blank expression, said, "You are a wild card, right?"

Gordon ignored the question and explained about the unknown joker found on the road nearby. Steely Dan was surprised.

"Just up 519 from here," Gordon said.

"That's weird," Steely Dan said.

"You haven't heard of any, say, sporting events involving wild cards?"

"In Warren County?" Steely Dan shook his bullet head. "Man, that's nuts."

"Murder isn't exactly the most rational act."

Steely Dan's smooth face contorted into an expression of amusement. "Unlike trying to shoot yourself into space," he said.

Gordon grinned. He raised his glass. "Ad astra," he said.

Gordon had been involved with amateur rocketry since he was in his early teens. He had been an Air Force brat, and every air base had a model rocketry club where Gordon could find like-minded peers. He and his friends had built rockets and explosives while consuming vast amounts of science fiction, mostly stuff that had been in the base library for years, if not decades.

Gordon remembered George O. Smith's *Mind Lords of Takis*, Leigh Brackett's *Journey to Alpha C*, Dick's *Radio Free Skait*, "Skait" being the secret, anagrammatical name of Takis, at least according to Philip K. Dick. All books that shared the common assumption that it was only a matter of time before Earth's scientists succeeded in duplicating Takisian starship technology, leading an unshackled humanity to spread into the galaxy. (Though in the Dick, it turned out that humans were grub-like creatures groping along on a burned-out planet, and all human history an illusion implanted by sinister Takisian telepaths.) All these renderings of smooth, efficient Takisian technology made rocketry seem a little quaint, but Gordon was willing to settle for what he could get, at least until someone handed him a starship.

In fact Gordon still belonged to an amateur rocket club, the American Rocket League, which had a big meeting in the Nevada desert every year to fire off boosters that required the participants to have a Federal explosives license, and which regularly climbed higher than fifty miles, right to the brink of space. Gordon was not alone in wanting to send himself into orbit. He liked to think he was farther along than most of them, however.

The fact was that Earth physicists had failed to decode Takisian technology, despite regular claims of breakthroughs that seemed loudest at every budget cycle. Ever since 1950 scientists had promised whole armadas of starships in ten or twenty years.

In the meantime the Air Force and its Space Command shared Earth orbit with an underfunded Russian program. Each operated as secretly as they could, each spied on the other, each put up thousands of communications and spy satellites, each may or may not have weaponized near-Earth orbit. There was no exploration of the Moon or Mars or any of the bodies that had held the imagination of early-twentieth-century writers. Everyone was waiting for his starship. No one got them.

It was beginning to look like the solar system might be all humanity ever got. And now it was the turn of Takisian starships to seem like a quaint, old-fashioned chimera, while rocket technology was beginning to seem like the most contemporary thing in all the world. With the military program in stagnation, it was civilians who were driving rocket innovation now. There was even a cash reward now, the Koopman X Prize, for the best, cheapest, and most practical design.

Gordon figured he was an underdog in the race, but then so were the Wright Brothers. So was Jetboy. Sometimes an underdog could surprise you.

Sunday was a cool, blustery day, with low clouds that scudded urgently along, dropping lashings of rain. Steely Dan picked Gordon up in his pickup truck for a run into Belvidere, where Gordon had a delivery waiting. This was a scaled-down version of an aerospike hybrid rocket engine, a working prototype of a larger design that had never been built. Gordon had bought the prototype when the subcontractor had gone out of business following the cancellation of the Air Force project.

Gordon was beginning to think that hybrid rockets were maybe the way to go. A hybrid had certain inefficiencies, but the aerospike design would more than make up for that. He'd have to work out a way to perform static tests with the new engine, some way that didn't involve setting his property on fire or blowing anything up. He'd have to build more berms, or maybe big trenches. And he'd have to get some HTPB, or make some. . . .

As windshield wipers slapped back and forth, Gordon and Steely Dan discussed the technical details on the ride to Belvidere. Around them the low mountains were green with new spring growth.

One of the nice things about living in rural New Jersey was that the lady who owned the express company was willing to open on a Sunday so that Gordon could collect his delivery. She even fired up her forklift in order to load the rocket engine on the back of Steely Dan's Dodge Ram. The engine came with a good deal of plumbing and electronics, and these were packaged separately, and Gordon and Steely Dan strapped the containers into place around the engine.

"You've got the plans, right?" Steely Dan muttered. "Even with a schematic this is going to be like working a jigsaw puzzle."

After the cargo was strapped in, Gordon bought Steely Dan lunch in a diner. People stared: they weren't used to jokers. This reminded Gordon of the dead joker who had been found nearby. "Let's go look where that victim was dropped," Gordon said.

He knew the place only approximately, but there wasn't anything to look at anyway—just as Gallo had said, there wasn't much around but dairy farms and woods and tree-covered ridges. Holsteins either endured the drizzle or clustered under shelter. Then a different sort of facility loomed into sight around a curve, and Steely Dan slowed without being told.

There were a series of long, low buildings, some of them new, some older and maybe repurposed from another use. There were spotlights on tall metal masts. Surrounding the compound were two forbidding twelve-foot chain-link fences, each topped by dense coils of razor wire.

The place looked more secure than some prisons Gordon had seen. "All it needs is a guard tower in each corner," Steely Dan said.

There was no sign out front, so the place wasn't an enterprise that sold to the public. A fifty-yard-long gravel drive stretched from the highway to the gates, and Gordon could see a small metal sign on the gate.

"Turn down here," Gordon said.

Steely Dan brought the truck to a halt at the driveway entrance. "You sure?" he asked.

"Yeah. What are they going to do, arrest us?"

"They could hit us with fucking baseball bats."

Gravel crunched under the Ram's tires as Steely Dan steered it toward the front gate. He brought the vehicle to a halt, and Gordon stepped out and regarded the facility.

Cold wind rustled up the back of his jacket. He heard dogs barking. There was a wet animal scent in the air. Gordon looked at the rusted sign on the front gate.

IDS
CANINE BREEDING
AND TRAINING FACILITY
UNIT #1

Gordon had no idea who or what IDS was. There was a rubber squeeze bulb hanging outside the gate, with a wire that led to the nearest building. Gordon squeezed the bulb, and he heard a metallic clatter from inside the building. A chorus of dog barks rose at the sound.

A door slammed behind him as Steely Dan left the pickup truck. His bullet head was shrunk in his jacket, and his eyes scanned uneasily back and forth.

"What are you gonna do?" he asked.

"I'm going to tell them I want a puppy," said Gordon.

"Yeah," Steely Dan said, "they're for sure gonna believe that."

A man came out of the building. He was tall and wore a scowl on his face. He seemed fit and wore green-and-brown camouflage fatigues with lace-up military boots. The only piece of apparel that didn't look government issue was a wide cowboy belt, with a buckle in the shape of a longhorn bull's head.

"Yeah," the man said. "You need something?"

Surprise rose in Gordon at the man's Eastern European accent. "You breed dogs, right?" Gordon said. "I was thinking of getting a dog."

The man didn't reply. His eyes moved from Gordon to Steely Dan, and then his expression turned thoughtful.

"You do sell dogs, right?" Gordon prompted.

The man's eyes didn't leave Steely Dan as he answered. "We breed and train dogs for the military, police, customs, and border guards," he said. "We only sell to government agencies."

"Oh," Gordon said. "Sorry to bother you."

The man pointed at Dan. "Wasn't he on the television? *American Hero?*"

"Yes, that's right."

The man raised a fist and made a muscle. "Very strong, yes?"

Gordon nodded. "Yes. Very strong."

The man said nothing more. Gordon and Steely Dan returned to the truck, backed out onto the highway, and headed for Gordon's cabin. The man stood behind the gate, watching them the entire way.

There was only one dead joker in the morgue on Monday morning, a straightforward shooting, and Gordon went upstairs to the squad room to deliver a copy of the autopsy to Harvey Kant, the detective in charge.

Kant was the most senior detective at the precinct and had been there at least forty years. If anyone had told him it was time to retire, he'd ignored the advice. Rumors were that he was holding something, or several somethings, over senior members of the department, and they'd decreed he could stay as long as he liked.

Kant was brown and scaled and looked like a heavily weathered dinosaur. He dressed in a frayed suit of polyester-blend gabardine and smelled strongly of cigars. He ignored the autopsy photos, glanced at the written report, then put both in their jacket and tossed it on his desk. Because he held a detective rank equivalent to lieutenant, most of the cops just called him "Lou."

"Nine millimeter," he said. "Fits the Sig found on the scene." He gave a sound like a cross between a snarl and a hacking cough. "Another goddamn drug shooting," he said. "I'm gonna be chasing my own ass for days on this one."

"Hey Doc!" Franny Black crossed the room smiling. He carried a tall clear plastic coffee go-cup from Café Mussolini down the street.

"I wanted to thank you about that description you gave me the other day," he said. "Redheaded woman, five six?"

"You found her?" Gordon asked.

"Sure did. She was hostess in the third Vietnamese restaurant I visited. And I'm glad you told me she was left-handed, because that was the hand I was watching when she drew the rat-tail comb out of her purse and tried to stab me."

"Glad you didn't end up on my slab," Gordon said.

"Yeah, Franny." The new speaker was the rail-thin Detective McTate, known as Slim Jim, who had followed Franny into the squad room. "You're lucky all around. The doc here gives you a perfect description of the perp, and you get credit for the bust."

Franny flushed. For a cop, Gordon thought, he flushed rather easily.

"How's the search for El Monstro coming along?" Gordon asked.

"El Monstro? He's vanished." Franny shrugged. "I don't know how a joker eight feet tall can just disappear, but that's what happened."

"The family?"

"His mother's in a wheelchair and doesn't speak English. The father's dead." Franny's eyes narrowed. "But the sister's hiding something."

"But not her brother?"

"Not in that little bitty apartment, no."

Kant eyed Franny's coffee. "What's that you're drinking, Fran?"

"Iced peppermint macchiato," Franny said in all innocence.

"Yeah." Kant nodded. "All us detective he-men like us our peppermint macchiatos."

Franny flushed a deeper shade, and he turned to Gordon. "Thanks, anyway," he said, and faded in the direction of the men's room.

Kant's lipless mouth stretched into a grin as he watched Franny's retreat, and then he looked at Gordon. "Sometimes the information you dig up is uncanny," he said. "Sometimes it's useless." He picked up the jacket with the weekend's homicide. "I mean, yeah, I know the guy was shot, thanks anyway. And sometimes . . ." He shook his head. "Remember when you told me that the perp was six feet six and armed with a club?"

Slim Jim was grinning. "I ain't heard this story," he said.

"I was lookin' for a fucking Neanderthal," Kant said.

"I didn't see the crime scene," Gordon explained. "Nobody told me about the—"

"About the ladder," Kant said. "The perp was four foot nine and killed the vic by dropping a bowling ball from a ladder."

Slim Jim guffawed.

"If I had seen the crime scene photos," Gordon said, "I would have seen the ladder."

"I spent ten days looking for the Terminator," Kant said, "and instead I was looking for a munchkin."

"If I don't have all the information," Gordon said, "I can't—"

He looked up and saw a group of uniformed officers coming into the squad room to report to Kant on a door-to-door survey of the area around the crime scene. Among them he recognized Dina Quattore, the telepathic ace attached to the K-9 unit.

Oh, he thought. *That would work.*

"You turned investigator now?" asked Dina Quattore. "Maybe I should buy you a freakin' Sherlock Holmes hat."

She was in Gordon's Volvo station wagon, heading toward the dog-breeding facility. Dina was a New York cop out of Fort Freak, a short, buxom woman with curly black hair. Gordon had talked her into joining him on her free afternoon, and she was out of uniform, dressed in jeans and a baggy nylon jacket that covered the pistol she wore on her hip.

"I just got curious about this place," Gordon said. "They claim they're a dog-training facility, but I think there may be other things going on in there."

"What kind of other things?" Dina asked.

"A joker was found dead near there."

"Uh-huh," Dina said. "Doc, it's the Sherlock Holmes hat for you."

Gordon was clearly stepping outside his sphere. Despite what might be seen on television, real-life forensic pathologists and profilers and crime scene investigators and other specialists did not actually confront suspects, participate in car chases, or get involved in shootouts. Gordon's job was to perform autopsies. Sometimes he'd be called to the scene, sometimes he'd testify at a trial, sometimes he'd hear about an arrest, and often he never ever found out about the disposition of a case. His focus was normally confined to the morgue.

But he couldn't help but notice that there were some unaccounted-for anomalies here in Warren County. The dead John Doe was one, and the IDS facility was another. Maybe the two belonged together.

He'd done research on IDS. They had no web page, no listed telephone number. They had a business license in New Jersey, with the address of the facility.

It wasn't even clear what IDS stood for.

"Also," Gordon said, "the man at the facility was a Russian or something."

Dina snickered. "I hope you give me my share of credit when you crack the spy ring."

"Just look at the place," Gordon said. "Tell me it's legit."

He slowed the Volvo to a crawl as they approached the compound. Dina looked out the window in silence as the buildings moved past. "Pull off the road once we're out of sight," she said, her voice suddenly serious.

"What are you getting?"

Dina shook her head. Her eyes were closed in concentration. Gordon drove on till the compound was hidden behind a stand of silver maple, then pulled onto the shoulder and parked. Dina led Gordon across a roadside ditch partly filled with water after the last rain. The humid, cool air was filled with the scent of spring flowers. Gordon and Dina walked slowly through the trees until they had a view of the IDS facility, and then Dina bent her head, her face set in an expression of fierce concentration.

Dina, Gordon knew, was a telepath. She could read the thoughts of others at a distance.

But not humans. Dina could only read dogs. That's why she worked with the K-9 unit. NYPD Public Relations called her "K-10." Everyone else called her Dina.

Water dripped down Gordon's collar as he waited. Then Dina straightened and shook her head. She tapped her nose. "You know what I'm smelling?" she asked. "Semtex."

"Plastic explosive."

Dina nodded toward the compound. "They're training bomb-sniffer dogs right this minute," she said. "Other dogs are being trained to find drugs." She shook her head. "Man, that chronic must be twenty years old, it's a miracle they're not training the dogs to find mold." She began walking back toward the car. "None of the dogs seem unhappy, and none are being mistreated. And if there are explosives and controlled substances used to train the dogs, that explains the high security." She looked at Gordon and laughed. "Sorry to destroy your detective fantasy."

Gordon shrugged. "It's better to know," he said. He opened the passenger door for her. "Dinner's on me," he said.

Dina started to get into the car, then hesitated. "No offense, Doc," she said, "but does that mean you're doing the cooking?"

Gordon blinked at her. "Sure."

Dina gave Gordon an uncomfortable look. "You know," she said, "my taste in food is pretty conventional, when all's said and done."

"Game is organic," Gordon said, "and it's lean. Free-range. It's better for you than anything you'll find in a supermarket."

A stubborn expression entered Dina's eyes. "Doc," she said, "I've eaten your chili."

Gordon surrendered. "I'll take you to a restaurant."

Dina's smile was brilliant. "Thanks."

He took her to a place in Belvidere with a view of the Delaware. He didn't know whether she was on a low-carb diet or whether her tastes in food were more like a dog's than those of a human; but Gordon watched Dina devour a fourteen-ounce rib eye while taking only a few bites of her salad and baked potato.

The conversation was pleasantly professional, ranging from weird crimes to weird autopsies. An older couple at a nearby table asked to be moved when Dina described a cadaver one of her dogs had found.

Gordon found himself enjoying Dina's company. She was a very attractive young woman, and he was far from immune to her allure.

Most men, he supposed, would be wondering what Dina looked like naked. Gordon had no such questions, for the simple reason that he already knew the answer. He'd seen more naked women, of every size and age and description, than the most accomplished seducer. There were no mysteries left—not even cause of death, because he always found that out.

That the vast majority of the women he met were dead put him at something of a social disadvantage with living females, but not as much as most people might think.

Beauty did not leave with death. The human body was a marvel of intricate design, the highly crafted product of millions of years of evolution. Contained within its morphology were membranes as delicate as a spider's web, a muscle as powerful and enduring as the heart, a structure as diffuse and ephemeral as the lymphoid system. The musculoskeletal system was a glory of complexity, the interaction between muscles and bone producing everything from a champion athlete to a shy girl's smile.

The human body was as varied and wonderful as the surface of a planet.

The wild card added to the wonder: sometimes its improvisations were brilliant, sometimes merely chaotic. It subverted every single cell—or enhanced it. Or both.

Gordon lived a fair percentage of his professional life in a constant state of awe.

After dinner Gordon joined Dina on the train back to New York.

"You know," she said, "everyone at the precinct thinks you're a joker."

He looked at her in surprise. "You think I'm not?"

"You've been around some of my dogs," Dina said. "They can usually smell a wild card—the metabolism's generally tweaked some way that causes the difference to come out the pores."

"I've noticed that myself," Gordon said.

"I think you're just—" She laughed. "Skinny and very tall."

Gordon nodded. "Good observation, there, Officer."

"And another thing," she said, tapping his arm. "You make a terrible Sherlock Holmes."

I guess, Gordon thought, *I'll have to settle for being Wernher von Braun.*

They left the train at Pennsylvania Station and ran into the usual Penn Station crowd: commuters, street people, and pimps waiting for the arrival of runaway teenagers from Minnesota. Gordon saw Dina to a cab. "Dinner again some time?" he said.

She smiled up at him. "I feel like I need a booster seat sitting across the table from you," she said.

He shrugged. "I'll have the waitress bring you one."

Dina nodded. "Okay. Give me a call."

Well, he thought as he watched her drive away, *that went well.*

There was a lot of yelling from Interrogation Room Two. A woman kept wailing, "He was a good boy!" and a man's voice was uttering threats against the city, the department, and probably everybody else.

Gordon looked around for Detective Kant and saw only Detective Van Tranh, the vibrating ace who failed utterly to rejoice in his nickname of "Dr. Dildo."

"Kant sent for me," Gordon said.

Tranh waved in the direction of the interrogation room. "Your Jersey John Doe got identified," he said. "He's one of the missing on Squid's list. Franny and the Lou are trying to calm the family down."

"And I'm supposed to help with that?"

"You're supposed to explain the medical evidence," Tranh said. "So far, the family isn't convinced."

Gordon stepped toward the door, then hesitated. "I should go back and get my autopsy report."

"Fran's got a copy."

"Okay." Gordon walked to the door, knocked, and entered the small room where Kant and Franny were being shouted at by the grieving family.

Gordon had met his share of bereaved couples over the years, but he had never encountered quite so much drama stuffed into two people. They were both broad and tall and took up a lot of space, and they made so much noise that they seemed to occupy the whole room. Mrs. Heffer cried, wailed, asked God to punish her, and kept insisting her son was a good boy. Mr. Heffer suspected conspiracy, refused to believe a thing he was told, and banged the table as he uttered threats. "My son did not have a heart attack!" he shouted as he kicked a chair. "He worked out all the time! He studied Brazilian Jiu-Jitsu!"

"It wasn't a heart attack," Gordon attempted. "It was sudden cardiac death."

Mr. Heffer beat himself on the chest with a fleshy fist. "My son did not have a heart attack!" he screamed.

"Aortic valve stenosis is not uncommon in young men—" Gordon began.

"Not uncommon," Mr. Heffer repeated scornfully. "What the hell does that mean? You're contradicting yourself already!"

"People were always making trouble for him!" Mrs. Heffer said. "Tommy was a good boy!"

Mr. Heffer waved a fist. "My son was kidnapped!" he said. "Why else would he be way the hell out in Jersey?"

Franny opened his notebook and readied his pen. "Do you know anyone who might want to kidnap Tom Junior?" he asked.

Heffer stared at him in utter scorn. "That's what you people are supposed to find out!" he said. He beat his chest again. "How the hell would I know who kidnapped him? Do I look like I hang around with kidnappers?"

"Kidnapped!" Mrs. Heffer burst into tears. "He was probably kidnapped by that communist from down the street."

"Communist?" Confusion swam into Franny's face. "What communist?"

"He runs the tobacco shop," Mrs. Heffer said. "He sells poison to the kids!"

"How do you know he's a communist?" Franny asked, and then they both began shouting at him.

Gordon decided to interrupt with the one fact that might be relevant. "Tom Junior didn't smoke," he pointed out. The lungs had been pink and healthy.

"Damn right Tommy didn't smoke!" Mr. Heffer said.

"He was a good boy!" Mrs. Heffer wailed.

Perhaps it was the mention of tobacco that spurred Harvey Kant's action. He drew a large cigar out of his gabardine jacket, snapped open his lighter, and brought the flame to the cigar's tip. He puffed noisily and with great satisfaction, blowing out clouds of smoke. Mrs. Heffer sneezed. "Hey!" said Mr. Heffer. He pointed at the No Smoking sign. "You can't do that in here!"

"I'm the lieutenant," Kant said. "I decide who smokes and who doesn't."

Within a few minutes Kant had succeeded in gassing the Heffers into silence, after which he gave them the information necessary to claim their son's body from the New Jersey morgue.

Mr. Heffer managed to summon an echo of his earlier belligerence. "Jersey!" he said. "What's my boy doing up there?"

"It's the Jersey cops' case," Kant said. "That's where he was found."

Heffer sneered. "Why in hell are we talking to you, then?" he said.

After the Heffers left, Gordon stood with Kant and Franny in the squad room. Gordon's head swam, though he couldn't tell whether it was from the cigar smoke or the Heffers' shouting.

Kant took a last draw on his cigar, then crushed the lit end against his scaly palm.

"Right," he said, and turned to Franny. "Tommy Heffer was kidnapped here and dumped in Jersey, the CO gave you this case, so liaise with the Jersey cops. Now—" He handed Franny the victim's file. "In spite of what the mom said about his being a good boy, the vic had some scrapes with the law—drunk and disorderly, fighting, vandalism. He was never formally charged with anything, so he doesn't have a record per se—but you can start by talking to the other kids who were arrested along with him."

"They're not kids. One of them is this guy Eel," Franny argued.

"I know you're the the big celebrity cop, but I'm the lieutenant." Kant grinned. "So talk to the kids."

A muscle in Franny's jaw moved. "Yes, sir," he said.

"Good boy." Another gesture with the cigar. "The vic studied Brazilian Jiu-Jitsu," Kant said. "And El Monstro was Brazilian. So there's a connection, maybe, at the Jiu-Jitsu school."

Franny looked dubious. "El Monstro was working at least two jobs as well as going to college," he said. "I doubt he had time to train in martial arts—especially as he didn't need to. Anyone attacking him would just bounce off. And Eddie said some of the guys sounded Russian."

"Check it anyway," said Kant.

Kant ambled back to his desk. Franny looked at the file folder in his hand, and his lips tightened. "Fran?" Gordon asked.

Franny jerked out of whatever thoughts were distracting him. "Yeah?"

"When you see the Jersey cops, could you not mention I have a house out in Warren County?"

"I didn't know you had a place out there. But sure, okay." Franny frowned. "Why?"

"I go out there to relax and work on my own stuff. I don't want to be the guy they call on weekends when their own medical examiner is drunk."

Which was true enough, though the shed full of rocket propellant had a lot more to do with why he preferred to remain invisible to his neighbors.

Franny nodded slowly. "Sure. That makes sense."

"Thanks. See you later."

Gordon returned to his basement morgue and finished helping Gaida bag the shooting victim, after which Gaida went to lunch and Gordon signed off on the last of the paperwork while gnawing on a log of homemade pemmican. He heard a knock on the door and looked up to see Dina Quattore. "Come in," he said.

Dina was in uniform, curly black hair sprouting from beneath her peaked cap. The radio at her hip hissed and squawked.

"Just wanted to let you know another stiff is on its way," she said. "Elderly street joker, walked in front of a bus while drunk, stoned, or otherwise impaired."

"Am I needed at the crime scene?"

"No. Plenty of witnesses to what happened."

"Okay." Gordon capped his pen and offered his plastic container of pemmican. "Care for some?"

Dina approached and peered at the dark brown pemmican logs. "What is it?"

"Pemmican."

"And what's that?"

"Ground venison," Gordon said, "rendered suet . . ."

"Wait a minute!" Dina yelped. "You're offering me a roadkill meat bar?"

"It also has dried fruit, nuts, and honey," Gordon pointed out. "Very nutritious. Everything your Mohawk warrior needs on the trail—good for quick energy, and you can store it for years."

"How many years has this—?" Dina began, then shook her head. "Never mind. I'll stick with the turkey sandwich I got at Mussolini's."

"Bring it and we'll have lunch, if you have the time."

Dina considered this. "You may not have the time, with the stiff coming."

Gordon shrugged. "The deceased won't be in a hurry."

"True that." Dina went upstairs to her locker, then returned with the plastic-wrapped sandwich and a can of Diet Pepsi. She parked herself on a plastic chair near the X-ray machine, then began to unwrap her sandwich. She looked at him from under the brim of her cap.

"Is it true what they say about you?" she asked.

"Depends," Gordon said. "What do they say?"

"That you build rockets?"

He hadn't realized any of the police officers actually knew that. Gaida, he thought, must have talked. Still, there was no reason to lie. "Yes," he said.

"How big?"

He preferred evasion. "Different sizes," he said.

"Gaida says you're going to shoot yourself to the moon," Dina said.

"Well," he said. "I'd need help." He told her about the Koopman Prize, and how anyone with a decent design was eligible. Dina chewed her turkey sandwich thoughtfully, then took a sip of her Pepsi. "I'm trying to figure you out, Doc," she said.

Gordon considered this. "I don't know that I'm particularly mysterious."

"You're not hidden," Dina said, "but I'm not sure how all the parts fit together."

Gordon had never considered himself as a collection of randomly ordered parts and had no answer to this. He took a bite of his pemmican and chewed.

Dina took off her cap and hung it from the X-ray machine. "You know," she said, "I think you're some kind of goofy romantic."

"Uhh—" Gordon began, uncertain. He had never categorized himself this way.

"Yeah!" Dina said, suddenly enthusiastic. "You cut up bodies as part of your crusade for justice! You want to plant the flag on another world!" She pointed at the pemmican. "And you recycle dead animals!"

Gordon blinked. "I usually autopsy them first."

She frowned. "Okay," she said. "That's disturbing."

"I learn stuff," he said.

He was about to object to being called a romantic and say that he was interested in the way jokers were put together in the same way that he was interested in the way rockets were put together—but then it occurred to him that if Dina thought of him as a romantic, that might say good things about her intentions toward him.

"Anyway," Dina said. "I'd like to see the rockets."

"Okay." Pressing his luck seemed a good idea. "This weekend?"

"I've got family stuff on Saturday," she said. "How about Sunday?"

"Sure."

"I can take the train out, and you can pick me up at the station. I'll see the rockets, and then you'll take me out to dinner."

"Great."

"At a restaurant," she added.

"If you like."

Gordon decided that being a romantic was working for him. Until the weekend, when he found that Steely Dan had gone missing.

"Another joker vanished," Franny said. He looked around Steely Dan's living room, his pen paused over his notebook without anything to write. "Another element in the series," he said. "And this time, the crime happens

in New Jersey. And you think that dog-training facility may have something to do with it?"

Gordon followed Franny as he prowled into Dan's kitchen, where a
half-eaten breakfast of eggs and sausage sat on the dinette next to a cold
cup of coffee. If there'd been a knock on the door while Dan was eating,
he'd have left his breakfast and walked to the door to open it . . . and then
what? A clout on the head, a jab with a Taser? Dan was strong, but his
skin only looked like blackened steel. He was as vulnerable to a weapon as
any nat.

"That Russian at the facility was very interested in Steely Dan," Gordon said. "Kept staring at him."

"Jokers get stared at," said Franny. "More in the sticks than anywhere,
I imagine." He frowned. "The Jersey cops looked into that place when
Tommy Heffer turned up there. But it's legit—they even sell their dogs to
the Jersey state cops."

"They could have a legitimate business on top of whatever it is they're
really up to," Gordon said.

"Maybe," Franny conceded. "But there's no grounds for a warrant."

"I suppose not," Gordon said.

If only Dina had sensed something.

And the weekend started so well, he thought. Normally Friday was one
of his busy days, for the simple reason that a lot of people got killed on
Thursday night. The reason the homicide rates jumped on Thursday was
that Friday was usually payday, and by Thursday people were starting to
run short of money.

The usual scenario ran something like this:

1. **Mommy wants to use the remaining money to buy Little
   Timmy's school lunch on Friday.**
2. **Daddy wants to use the money to buy beer.**

Therefore:

3. **Daddy beats Mommy to death, takes the money, and gets
   drunk.**

Unfortunately Daddy is usually unable to reason out the next couple
of steps, which are:

4. Daddy ends up in prison, and;
5. Little Timmy gets lost in the foster care system, which mightily increases the odds of Timmy becoming an angry sociopath who perpetuates the cycle of violence into the next generation.

The other high time for homicide was late Saturday night and early Sunday morning, where the motivation might also be money, but was usually sex and/or love.

However, on this particular week in May, the bliss of a beautiful spring seemed to have descended on New York, and all the Daddies had decided they didn't need the beer after all and taken all the Little Timmys of the city to the park to play catch, and Gordon was finished with his work by one in the afternoon. So he gave himself and Gaida the rest of the day off and took the train to Warren County, where he spent the rest of the afternoon loading model rockets with his homemade APCP and firing them into the mellow May sky.

On Saturday Steely Dan was scheduled to come round in the afternoon to help plot a static test facility for the aerospike engine, but he hadn't turned up. Gordon called his home and mobile with no result, then called the garage where he worked. His boss said he hadn't come in for work on Friday, and that he'd called Dan's cell phone without getting an answer.

Steely Dan lived in an old shiplap farmhouse that came with twenty acres of decaying apple orchard. Gordon drove there, found Dan's truck and car in the garage, and pounded on the door without result. That's when he called Franny Black, and Franny called the Jersey police, who still hadn't turned up.

New Jersey loved its jokers, that was clear.

Franny had found Dan's spare key under a rock in the garden, and he'd let the two of them inside. "No sign of violence," Franny said, prowling into Dan's bedroom. "Nothing obviously stolen. No sign of abduction at all."

Frustration flared in Gordon's nerves. "I can tell you one thing," he said. "Dan didn't do Brazilian Jiu-Jitsu."

"Christ." Franny rolled his eyes. "That lead went nowhere," he said. "Just like I told him it would."

"Any leads on El Monstro?"

Franny shook his head, and tapped the butt end of his pen against his jaw. "Jokers," Franny said. "Dogs. Jokers and dogs. Dogs and jokers." He waved a hand in frustration. "I don't get it."

"What I get about the Jersey cops," Gordon said, "is that they care more about the dogs than the jokers."

Franny hesitated, then put a hand on Gordon's arm. "I'll find your friend."

"Let's hope," Gordon said, "that he's not found stretched out on a road somewhere."

The Jersey police did eventually show up, but Gallo had the weekend off and wasn't among them, and Franny had to explain everything from the beginning. Gordon lacked the patience to hear it, so he went back to his cabin and for lack of anything better to do took one of his rockets out of the barn and put it on the launcher. He pressed the igniter into the solid fuel at the base of the rocket and connected it to the nine-volt battery and remote receiver. He then stepped to a safe distance, flicked the rocker switch on his remote control to ON, and saw the LEDs shift from Safety to Armed. He poised his thumb over the Fire button, looked at the rocket, made sure his binoculars were in his other hand, and pressed the button.

Gordon raised his binoculars to his eyes as the rocket flew straight and true for six or eight hundred meters, then ran out of fuel, popped its parachute, and drifted home to Earth.

He watched the launch without pleasure. After the rocket drifted silently to its meeting with the lush New Jersey meadow, Gordon stared at it for a long while, frustration building in his heart, and then he put the rocket gear back in the barn and carried his binoculars to the car. He drove to the grove of silver maples from which he and Dina had observed the IDS facility, parked, went into the woods, and settled down to observe the compound.

The NYPD would call Gordon's operation a "plant." Everyone else in the world called it a "stakeout."

Observation didn't reveal much. A trainer exercised half a dozen German shepherds on a dog run inside the compound. Both the dogs and the trainer seemed to be enjoying themselves. Occasionally Gordon saw people walking from one building to another. He was too far away to recognize any of them. He coped with the tedium by planning a more scientific investigation of the compound. He'd visit a spy store in Manhattan, he decided, buy some boom mikes, a video camera with a telephoto lens, a capacious hard drive capable of holding twenty-four hours' worth of images.

If Steely Dan's distinctive silhouette appeared on any of the video, or his distinctive strangled-puppet voice on audio, that would suffice for a warrant. Or so he imagined.

Gordon was working out the finer details of this fantasy when he heard a car slowing on the highway behind him. He turned and his heart gave a lurch as he saw a white panel van pulling up onto the highway shoulder behind his Volvo.

Moist earth squelched beneath his feet as he ducked behind a hackberry bush, then raised his binoculars. He could see only the dark silhouette of a driver behind the windscreen. The driver seemed to be peering around, looking for the Volvo's driver. Gordon huddled into himself on the far side of the hackberry.

After thirty seconds or so the driver gunned his engine, then pulled the van back onto the highway. Gordon watched as he drove past, then turned into the IDS facility.

I believe I have been busted, he thought. If the driver had got his license plate, they could have his ID in short order. He'd been in newspapers with one thing or another, and all they'd have to do to get his picture was Google his name.

Maybe Dina was right, and he really sucked as an investigator.

Sunday afternoon with Dina wasn't a success. The day was gray and overcast, with scattered showers, and Gordon was too distracted by Dan's disappearance to play host. Though Dina actually seemed interested in the rockets and the big aerospike engine sitting unassembled in the barn, Gordon himself couldn't raise his usual enthusiasm. As he loaded one of his bigger rockets with APCP, he told Dina about his plan to stake out the IDS facility, and asked what kind of cameras and detectors would be best.

"I'm not an expert on any of that stuff," Dina said. "You should ask some of the detectives back at Fort Freak—Kant or somebody. They're used to running plants."

"Franny Black is supposed to be in charge of the investigation."

"Little Mister Golden Drawers. The Spy from the Commissioner's Office." Her face gave a little twist of distaste, and then she gave the matter more thought. "It doesn't have to be you running the plant," she pointed out. "You don't need a warrant to surveil a place, or to point a shotgun mic out a window. Franny could do it legally." She cackled. "And the rest of the precinct would love it if he spent all his time out here."

Gordon nodded. "I'll talk to him."

Dina gave another laugh. "And if Franny weren't so wet behind the ears," she said, "he'd know that while he can't get a warrant to visit IDS to look for a missing joker, there are agencies who have a job inspecting places like IDS. There has to be some Jersey state agency who has the right to walk in and make sure the dogs aren't being abused." She thought for a moment, her eyes staring into space, and then she snapped her fingers. "Office of Animal Welfare," she said. "I've worked with them a couple times. I can make some calls for you."

"I'd appreciate that."

She looked at the rocket. "How far can that one go up?"

"A couple miles."

Dina was startled. "Seriously?"

"Sure. Three stages, it'll go high. I have to make sure there aren't any aircraft around."

Her eyes narrowed. "You got rockets bigger than that?"

"Sure. But I'm a lot more careful about firing them off. Some of them, I have to go to Nevada."

She grinned. "Area 51?"

He gave her a blank look. "Where?"

"Never mind."

"I go to Black Rock," Gordon said.

She smiled, shook her head. "That's great," she said.

Gordon had the feeling he'd just missed something.

He shouldered the five-foot-long rocket and they walked out into a meadow wet with spring showers and fragrant with the scent of wildflowers. Dina followed, carrying the launch rod that supported the rocket while it was on the ground. Gordon readied the rocket and connected the battery. After they retreated to a safe distance, Gordon listened for any approaching aircraft and heard nothing beyond the sough of the wind. He took the control out of his pocket, pressed the rocker switch to ON, watched the LEDs shift to Armed, and then handed the control to Dina.

"Be my guest," he said. "Just press the red button."

A delighted smile flashed across Dina's face. Gordon decided he liked the smile a lot. "Really?" she asked.

"Sure." He readied his binoculars.

Dina looked from the control to the rocket and back. "Do I do a countdown or anything?"

"You can do a countdown," Gordon said, "recite a poem, sing 'The Star-Spangled Banner.' Whatever you like."

"Three. Two. One." She flashed the smile again. "To the Moon!" She pushed the button and the rocket hissed upward.

The staging worked flawlessly, with no tip-off, and the first stage tumbled back to the ground while the second stage pierced the low cloud and disappeared. Even the hiss of rocket exhaust faded. There was a distant pop as the third stage separated and—Gordon trusted—ignited. The scent of burnt propellant tinged the odor of spring flowers. The second stage, trailing streamers, drifted down through the cloud layer and landed fifty feet away. And then the third stage arrowed down, aimed like a spear at the ground.

"Oh dear," Gordon said, and then the falling stage impaled the turf with the sound of a wet slap.

Gordon and Dina walked to the third stage, which had crumpled beyond repair. "Parachute failure," Gordon said.

"Maybe we'll make it to the Moon next time," said Dina.

"We'll send up a really big one," Gordon said. "I'll get Dan to come out and . . ." His voice trailed away as he remembered that Dan had gone missing.

Dina touched his arm. "We'll get him back," she said.

Gordon wasn't comforted. *Dogs and jokers*, he thought. *Jokers and dogs.*

Gordon decided to take Dina to dinner amid the bustle and excitement of Phillipsburg, the county's largest town. Because they were taking the train to New York and wouldn't be coming back, Gordon locked the cabin and closed the gate on the road as they left. Rain drummed down, and Gordon turned on the wipers.

"So there's something I've been meaning to ask," he said as he pulled from his rural route onto Highway 519. "Do you think you're a romantic?"

Dina was surprised. "Me?" she said. "I don't think so."

A burst of rain clattered on the roof. "With your skills," Gordon said, "you could be a dog trainer, or a dog whisperer, or whatever they're called. Or you could have a famous dog act and travel around the world putting on shows. But instead you wear a uniform and work in a dangerous part of town and catch criminals." He grinned at her. "Isn't that a romantic thing to do?" *At least as romantic,* he thought, as *cutting up dead bodies.*

Dina knit her brows in thought. "Those other jobs you mention," she said, "they don't come with pensions."

Gordon looked at her. "Are pensions romantic?"

She grinned. "I hope so," she said. "I plan on living happily ever after with mine." She waved a hand. "With the NYPD, I've got a pension, I've got a decent paycheck, and what I do isn't really dangerous—I just follow a dog around. The only problem I have is finding an apartment that'll let me keep dogs."

"You've got dogs of your own?"

"Yeah. Two rescue dogs. They were abused."

"Bring them next time you come," Gordon said. "They'll like the country."

She gave an unexpected scowl, and Gordon was startled at this reaction to his invitation; but then he decided she was thinking of the abuse her dogs had suffered. Then her head whipped around, and Gordon realized that they were passing the IDS facility, visible as a floodlit glow in the rain. "Stop!" she said urgently.

"What?"

"Stop. Now."

His mind whirling, Gordon slowed and pulled to the side of the road. Dina's eyes remained focused on the IDS compound. Her hand scrabbled for the door release.

"I've got to get closer," she muttered.

"Wait," Gordon said. "What's going on?"

But she was already out of the car, her jacket pulled over her head. Gordon set the parking brake, opened the door, and followed. Cold rain needled his scalp and spattered rainbows on his glasses. He blinked and pursued Dina's dark silhouette outlined by the floodlights.

She slowed and Gordon splashed up to her, his shoes half submerged in a puddle. Dina was hunched over, her jacket still pulled up over her head, both hands pressed to her forehead. Suddenly she straightened.

"They're in there!" she said. "The captives!"

Gordon's heart lurched in his chest. "What?" he said. He stared at her through glasses pebbled by rainfall. "How do you know?"

Dina made a frantic gesture, pointed at her head with both forefingers. "I'm seeing through a dog's eyes!" she said. "I'm looking right at them. Dan's in there with the others!"

"Others?" Gordon said.

Dina frantically started digging into her jacket pockets for her phone. "Gotta call Franny!" she said. "Get a warrant!"

Her words were buried beneath a torrent of barking. The chain-link fence rattled and bowed under the impact of heavy German shepherd bodies. And then Gordon was dazzled by a battery of floodlights switching on, brilliant halogen beams burning into his eyes . . .

"STAY WHERE YOU ARE," said an amplified voice. "YOU ARE TRES-PASSING."

"Fuck this," Dina muttered. She grabbed Gordon's arm. "Back to the car!"

She turned as electric motors rolled open the front gate and three dogs raced out, barking. Heart hammering, Gordon readied himself for a doomed sprint to the car. Dina spun again, gestured with the hand that had pulled the phone from her pocket. The dogs slowed, seemingly puzzled. Then two of them stopped and sat down on the wet ground. The third walked timidly up to Dina and sniffed her hand.

She was in telepathic contact with the dogs, Gordon realized.

"Can you control them?" he asked.

"Not control," she said. "But I can fill their minds with happy thoughts."

"Um, good," Gordon said. His limbs twitched, wanted to run. "What do we do now?"

"Go to the car. But slowly. You don't want to run, because that might activate the pack instinct to chase you down."

"Okay," Gordon said. He began easing backwards toward the Volvo. Dina moved with him.

Lightning sizzled overhead. In the sudden searing brilliance, Gordon saw two men walking out of the IDS gate. One of them had a rifle, the other a pistol. They moved forward onto the floodlit driveway. "You stop there!" one of them called. He was the man Gordon had spoken to earlier, and he wore a cowboy hat against the rain. He brandished his rifle. "We'll shoot!" he warned.

"Uh," Gordon said, uncertain. "Do we run now?"

He heard steel enter Dina's voice. "Not . . . just . . . yet," she said.

The dogs' ears pricked up, and they turned to look at the two advancing men. One of the dogs rose from its sitting position and took a few steps toward the two, and paused in a hunting posture, leaning forward, one forefoot raised.

"Nobody move!" said the man in the cowboy hat. He raised the rifle to his shoulder as he and his comrade advanced. Neither of them seemed to have noticed their dogs' uncharacteristic behavior. *Maybe,* Gordon thought, *Dina isn't filling their minds with happy thoughts any longer.*

All three dogs were on their feet now, moving low to the ground as they advanced on the two armed men. And then one of them gave a savage growl and hurled itself at the throat of the man with the rifle.

There was a shot that went nowhere and the man went down. The other two dogs were bounding to their prey, and the man with the pistol started shooting.

"Now we run!" Dina said, and she and Gordon both turned and began racing for the car. Dina's legs were a lot shorter, but she was fast, and pulled ahead.

There were more shots, followed by an agonized canine howl. Dina gasped and pitched forward onto her face.

Gordon's nerves gave a jolt. He splashed to a stop, turned, bent over Dina, looked for the bullet wound, asked if she was all right. Her eyes were open and staring. Her face was blank. He could hear her breathing heavily but there was no response.

Gordon shuddered as more shots cracked out. He gave a desperate glance in the direction of the gate, and through the rain beading his spectacles saw that both men were on the ground. Two dogs lay stretched out on the driveway, and one of the men wrestled with the third.

Gordon grabbed Dina by the jacket collar and began hauling her toward the car. He was all too aware that he was underweight and not very strong, and was thankful that she was so small. He was dragging her headfirst over the ground, and he realized he could injure her neck, so he tried to support her head with his forearms.

He was gasping for breath by the time he got her to the Volvo. He groped behind him for the door handle, found it, and swung the door open. The dome light flashed on, silhouetting them perfectly for any shooter taking aim. . . .

Actinic light flashed from the heavens. Thunder roared. Gordon took a deep breath, bent his knees, and heaved Dina's head and shoulders up onto the passenger seat. Hot pain shot through his back. He grabbed Dina's hips and tried to shove her center of gravity up into the car.

Normally he had help moving limp bodies around. Normally it was from slab to gurney, or gurney to slab. Normally he didn't have to wrestle someone into a bucket seat, or avoid slamming her into the stick shift or getting her jammed against the console.

"Give me some help here!" he told Dina. "Just pull yourself into the car!"

Dina's eyes stared blankly from her lolling head. He seized her feet and tried to shove them up into the Volvo.

A shot jolted Gordon's nerves, and he heard the bullet hit pavement nearby. Shoving the limp body was clearly not working, and Gordon dropped Dina's feet and ran around to the driver's side. He threw himself into the station wagon, grabbed Dina's collar with both hands, and tried to haul her toward him. Pain lanced through his back again as he heaved her over the central console. Her head hung in his lap in a swirl of wet, curly hair.

Another shot cracked out. There was an urgent bang somewhere in the car as the bullet struck home.

Gordon reached under Dina's shoulder and shoved the gearshift lever into drive, then stomped on the accelerator as he cranked the wheel hard over. The Volvo made a screaming U-turn on the highway, and Gordon steadied the vehicle as a flash of lightning showed him the way home.

The car's acceleration had swung the passenger door closed onto Dina's feet, which were still dangling out of the car. He switched the dome light off to make himself a poorer target, then put his fingers on Dina's throat. Her pulse was strong, just a little elevated. He could hear her respiration. He hadn't seen or felt any blood.

But there had been shots, and she'd collapsed. That was pretty good evidence that she'd been hit somewhere. He drove to his cabin, opened the gate on the road, drove through, and locked the gate behind him. He despaired of dragging Dina into the house, so he drove behind the house, unlocked the barn door, and drove into the barn.

At least he'd have a dry place to make an examination.

Gordon took some of the plastic sheeting he'd draped over his rocketry gear and laid it on the ground next to the passenger door. Then he pulled Dina out of the car and laid her on the sheet. He performed a careful examination and could find no wound.

He had a medical bag in the cabin in case there was an accident with rocketry material. He unlocked the cabin's rear door, fetched the bag, and returned.

Pulse stable. Blood pressure normal. Respiration normal. Pupils responded normally to light. There didn't seem to be anything wrong with Dina other than catatonia. Which, it had to be said, was really, really wrong.

She'd been in mental contact with the dogs, he thought. She'd been getting them to attack their trainers. And then the shooting had started. The dogs, he thought. The dogs had been shot, presumably killed. And Dina had been in their heads when that happened.

Maybe the shock had been too much.

He put the blood pressure cuff back in his bag, then touched her throat. The skin was chill and clammy. He should get some blankets and insulate Dina against hypothermia.

Then call an ambulance. Then call Franny and the state police and get a warrant and go crashing into IDS to free the captives. Officer down. It was one of those calls which would result in immediate action by the authorities. And Dina certainly was down.

He unlocked the rear door of the cabin and went into the hall closet for the scratchy wool trade blankets he kept there. Returning with the blankets under his arm, he saw headlights flash across the front windows.

Gordon walked across the darkened room to the living room window and peered past the drawn curtain. He saw a large panel van parked by his gate, and a man silhouetted against the headlights peering at the house.

Gordon's heart lurched. He remembered that one of the IDS people had seen his car when he'd surveilled the compound the previous day, that they probably had his license number and ID by now.

They might have recognized his car, even in the rain. They might have just come straight here. Gordon backed away from the curtain and went to the back door. He locked the door behind him and sprinted to the barn.

Dina was as he'd left her. He put a pair of blankets over her, and her head rolled as, for a moment, her eyes fluttered open and seemed to focus. "Doc . . . ?" she said in a hoarse whisper, and then her head fell back and her eyes closed again.

Gordon knelt and opened one eyelid. The pupil narrowed in the light, but it didn't focus. She'd lapsed into coma again.

Gordon's nerves leaped as he heard a roaring engine, followed by the crash of his gate going down in front of the panel van. He stood, looked down at Dina, looked at his car. It seemed futile to try to drag her into his car again, especially as all that he could hope for would be a car chase that he could well lose. He bent again, felt under the blanket, and took Dina's gun and holster from her belt. He looked at it for a moment as the faint scent of gun oil floated to him, and then he put the holster on his own belt, feeling foolish as he did it.

What was he going to do, start a Western gunfight? These were professional bad guys, kidnappers. They'd shoot him down.

He looked again at his car. He had to draw the pursuit away from the barn.

And he knew exactly where to take them.

He went to the steel cabinet where he kept rocketry supplies and opened it. He took a battery, a set of a half-dozen igniters, a wireless receiver, and his controller. Then he turned off the lights in the barn and got in his car. He put the rocketry gear on the passenger seat.

He waited till he heard a crash as the front door of the house went down, and then he started the Volvo, gunned the engine, and backed out of the barn in a storm of power. Gravel rattled against the car as he swung around, snapped on the lights, and put the transmission in drive. Gordon stomped the accelerator again, wove through a line of evergreen, and took off down the two-rut trail that led across the meadows.

He figured there was no way the bad guys could avoid seeing his departure.

He'd gone a quarter mile before he saw the lights of the van coming after him. Lightning illuminated the rolling terrain, helped him chart his course. The Volvo bucketed up and down as it leaped along the trail, brush beating on the grille, rocks cracking against the floorboards.

The station wagon slithered down a slope and hit what seemed to be a shallow pond between it and the next slope. The tail kicked out, and the wheels spun as Gordon tried to correct. Forward motion died in mere seconds. Gravel hammered against the rear panels as the wheels spun uselessly.

Gordon grabbed his rocket gear and bolted from the car. Rain drummed on his skull as he splashed through standing water and began to run up the nearest slope. Brush clawed at his legs.

The van crowned the slope behind him and dove toward his stalled car. Gordon panted for breath. The van splashed into the same lake as the Volvo and came to a halt, wheels spinning. Two men jumped out and charged the Volvo, finding no one inside.

A flash of lightning turned the scene into day as Gordon crowned the slope, and Gordon heard a pair of shouts as he was spotted. But the flash had illuminated something else—the berms that surrounded the shed filled with rocket fuel.

Gordon dragged himself forward. He dragged himself up the nearest berm, then ran down the steep slope and slammed to a tooth-clattering halt against the steel door of the shed. Breath heaved in and out of his lungs. He wasn't used to running. He wasn't used to panic, or to fighting, or being soaked to the skin.

Better use his brains then, he decided.

He fumbled at his belt for the key to the padlock on the door, then opened the lock and threw it over his shoulder. He tore open the door, ran inside, and reached for the tank that held the syntin, the Soviet liquid rocket fuel. He opened the valve and the fuel began to drain, filling the shack with a rich hydrocarbon scent. Gordon dropped an igniter into the fuel, put the battery on the concrete floor nearby, twisted wires around the terminals, and ran back into the open. He left the door invitingly ajar, ran around the building, and scrambled up the far berm. At the top he tripped and fell, and as he lay sprawled in the grass at the foot of the berm he heard an accented voice say, "He's in there!"

Gordon got to his feet and felt pain shoot through his right ankle. He lurched toward the grove of hawthorn at the far end of the meadow.

As he ran he looked at the remote control in his hand and pushed the rocker switch to ON. The LEDs flicked from Safety to Armed. He heard the door to the shed go booming back on its hinges as the intruders stormed inside, and he heaved in a sobbing breath and pressed the Fire button. He was faintly surprised to find that the berms worked exactly as they were supposed to.

"The perps were blown into their constituent atoms," Gordon told Dina two nights later. "The crime scene guys weren't able to find a single piece of remains."

Dina seemed impressed. "I have to say that once you make up your mind to do something," she said, "you're damned thorough."

"You'll have to speak up," Gordon said. "I'm still a little deaf."

The shed had exploded and then kept exploding, going on for several minutes at least. Gordon had watched from the shelter of the hawthorns as one blast after another rocked the peaceful meadow and sent flame reaching toward the low clouds overhead.

It had to be admitted that he'd put a lot of oxidizer in that shed.

For their dinner Gordon had taken her to Au Pied de Cochon, the New York incarnation of a well-known Parisian brasserie. The linen was crisp, the waitstaff efficient, and the tulip-shaped lights cast a fine mellow glow over the dining room with its dark wood paneling. The restaurant offered proteins in substantial quantities, which given Dina's carnivore instincts seemed appropriate.

"I hope you'll forgive me for not going with you to the hospital," Gordon said. "I didn't know how to fix you, and I wanted to be there when the captives were freed in case they needed a doctor."

Dina affected thought. "Maybe I'll forgive you," she said. "I'll have to think about it."

"I was there when you woke up," Gordon pointed out.

She'd come to herself about noon on Monday, demanding her clothes, meat protein, and her gun. No permanent harm seemed to have been done to her, and she could remember nothing of the time she'd been in a coma. "You were the first person I saw," said Dina. "You get points for that."

"At least the sight didn't send you back into a coma."

She laughed thinly.

"When the first cops turned up at the facility," Gordon said, "they saw three dogs shot dead in front of the gate and the corpse of a man who'd had his throat ripped out. It was an obvious crime scene, and they no longer needed a warrant to go in, but they felt a little leery of going in by themselves and called for backup, and while they waited Franny Black showed up with about half the detectives from Fort Freak." He grinned. "They were toting some serious firepower and a lot of attitude. Harvey Kant even had a tommy gun that must have dated from Lucky Luciano's day—which, by the way, made me wonder just how old Kant actually is. So our guys just brushed the Jersey cops aside and stormed the place."

Gordon laughed. "They were serious. For some reason they thought you were being held captive in there."

Dina's eyes narrowed. "Who gave them that idea?" she asked.

"They must have misinterpreted my phone call," Gordon said. His face was deadpan. "Our guys were too late. The compound had been emptied. At least three computers were carried away, but they did manage to pull up a few names off envelopes and bills. But they did find Steely Dan and two kidnapped Jokertown residents held in some kind of steel-lined underground cells in the rearmost building." He shook his head. "It was like some supervillain's headquarters from the movies."

"I'm surprised they didn't put them in dog cages," Dina said.

"Dog cages aren't strong enough for Dan or any other wild card with extra strength," Gordon said. "He would have ripped his way right out. The perps needed a custom facility."

"But what was it for?"

"Even the captives didn't know." All Steely Dan knew was that he'd gone to answer the door, and there had been a couple of guys there with stun guns. They'd tased him into helplessness, then bound him, thrown him in a van, and driven away.

"They were fed regularly. They weren't mistreated beyond being held against their will." He looked down at the gleaming tableware laid out on either side of his fine china plate. "The brass are thinking they were to be used to train dogs to kill people," he said, "but I've been thinking. Maybe they were being held for . . . medical experiments."

Dina gave a canine growl that came very close to raising the hairs on Gordon's neck. "That ain't right," she said.

"Maybe if we can ID the body, or if the latent fingerprints tell us anything . . ."

"That dead guy was Russian or something, right?" Dina said. "If he was a crook, maybe the Russians can tell us who he was."

"Maybe." Gordon spread his hands wide. "So now the Jersey cops are involved, and the NYPD, and the FBI because there was a kidnapping. And FBI and ATF are both investigating my shed, because they're half convinced I'm a terrorist."

"'Blown to constituent atoms,'" Dina quoted. "Where's their evidence?"

"Well," Gordon said dubiously, "there's the big rocket engine in the barn. They might make something of that, I suppose."

She gave a laugh. "At least you're not a joker. They'd put you with the Twisted Fists." He looked at her. She looked back at him, then frowned. "You aren't a joker, right?" she said.

The police at Fort Freak had every reason to think he was a joker, because there it was in his file, the fact he'd tested positive for the wild card. In fact he'd been struck by the virus on the island of Okinawa, where his Air Force father had been stationed. Gordon had been in the hospital, out of his mind with fever, vast tumors growing everywhere on his skin, his heart thundering as his blood pressure crashed into the basement . . .

American military hospitals come equipped for all sort of contingencies. They'd given him the trump, which in those days had only a thirty percent chance of success. And it had worked, reversing the chaotic wreckage the wild card was making of his body. He'd test positive for the rest of his life, but in fact he was a nat. A nat with his height, his weight, and his olfactory sense on the extreme edge of normal, but a nat nonetheless.

"Am I a joker?" he repeated. "No, I'm not."

She screwed up her face as she looked at him, as if she wasn't quite sure whether or not to believe him. Then she picked up the menu. "Maybe we'd better order." Dina frowned over the menu, which did not include an English translation. "Well," she said, "I know what *porc* means."

"*Cochon* also means pig," Gordon added helpfully.

"What's *panés*?"

"In breadcrumbs."

The waiter stepped forward with his smile and his pad. Gordon ordered calf's face for an appetizer, followed by pig's knuckle braised in spices. Dina had onion soup for a starter, followed by—her finger traced the words on the menu as she spoke them aloud—*queue, oreille, museau et pied de cochon panés,* the pork dish coated in breadcrumbs.

Gordon didn't tell her that she'd just ordered the ear, tail, snout, and foot of a pig. Foreign cookery, he thought, should come with its share of surprises.

If she didn't like it, he decided, he'd buy her a hot dog from a vendor. Or maybe two.

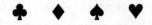

The Big Bleed

Part Four

"IT LOOKS LIKE OUR terror plot is stalling out," Jamal said.

They had returned to the Bleecker after a Holy Roller speech in Harlem, a mercifully brief and trouble-free event, if you ignored the reverend's disconnected ramblings and his signature "roll-up," which never failed to win laughs . . . and lose votes.

Roller had gone to ground, and the SCARE team had been released. Upon returning to their ops center, after a slow, nasty drive through the apparently never-ending rain, Jamal had found an update from the Analysis Team at Riker's.

"We didn't find ammonium nitrate?" Sheeba said, collapsing her tall frame into her desk chair. No matter what he thought of the Midnight Angel's leadership style or personal habits, these maneuvers still fascinated Jamal. It was like spying on a whooping crane or some other long-legged bird bending to snatch a fish from a lake . . . improbable, a bit awkward, but endlessly watchable.

Especially when you happened to be bored and exhausted—and eager for any kind of distraction. "Oh, it's am nitrate," Jamal said. "A dangerous amount, too."

"So, good for us, right?"

"No. The shipment doesn't connect. Homeland Sec has no lead on a source for it, and more to the point . . . no buyer. It's an orphan."

"Would they know every buyer or potential terrorist in and around New York City? I mean, look at our watch lists. . . ." They bore hundreds of names, Jamal knew.

"That's what took a few days. They did a big search and crosscheck, and found no one who seemed to be in the right place to get hold of the shipment."

"That still doesn't answer my question. What about the guy DHS *doesn't* know?"

"They've got an analysis staff that interfaces with every agency on the planet—"

Sheeba suddenly stood up—another impressive physical display. "Are you working for them or us? You're defending these guys and their lack of information!"

"I'm just telling *you* what they're telling *me*!"

Sheeba had started to pace. "Maybe I should call Billy Ray." Another surprise: on the infrequent occasions when Sheeba admitted that she spoke to her husband Billy Ray, aka Carnifex at SCARE HQ, she usually said "the home office" or "our nation's capital."

Never his name. Maybe Sheeba wanted to go home, too. Back to a normal life. Whatever that was, for aces. "We have other options," Jamal said. "New Jersey State Police were at the site. I do know that the body somehow wound up here in Manhattan, Fifth Precinct."

"I suppose we could call them," Sheeba said, clearly unenthusiastic about either.

"It's end of day and we'd just get run around," Jamal said, struggling to his feet. "Fort Freak's not far from here. Why don't I just go over there?"

Sheeba blinked. "Now. In the rain."

"I have an umbrella," he said. He glanced toward the window, and, not particularly caring about the truth, said, "And it's letting up."

And, what the hell, he might actually learn something at Fort Freak.

To his amusement, his ruse about the weather turned out to be true. The rain had let up, which allowed him to dangle the umbrella from its wrist strap . . . and use his free hand to hold his phone.

It was the end of the workday, when lower Manhattan's buildings released their daily captives. But Jamal found the sidewalks blessedly empty . . . perhaps the threat of additional downpours was keeping people inside. Even the traffic seemed lighter.

No matter—Jamal was free to walk and talk to Julia, the one activity in his day that gave him pleasure, even though it had become increasingly difficult to arrange of late.

Part of it was the time difference, of course. Jamal was three hours ahead. Then there was the SCARE schedule along with its mandatory group dinners.

The real problem, however, was Julia's schedule. If she was at the club, she was unavailable from nine P.M. Jamal's time until two or three in the morning—and those were the times he could talk.

She would sleep from five A.M. his time til early afternoon. Her physical situation required that amount of sleep.

So in the past couple of weeks they had taken to saying hello during a brief window between five and six P.M. New York time.

It was a hell of a way to run a relationship.

Not that it was like any relationship in Jamal's undistinguished history. He had had several long-term arrangements, including one that was headed toward marriage until Jamal booked a film shooting in Mexico, where the combination of insane hours, high stress, unnecessary amounts of tequila, and an actress named Mary-Margaret had contributed to some relationship-toxic behavior on Jamal's part.

Even his bad long-term relationships were a long way in the past . . . thank you again, SCARE. He wanted to keep this one alive. More precisely, he wanted to follow this one wherever it was going. But his first call went straight to voice mail, which was annoying.

Two blocks later—deeper into Jokertown now, where, given the surging population on the sidewalks, the freaks did not seem deterred by the nasty weather—Jamal tried again. Still nothing.

Julia never went anywhere without her phone. It was her one piece of essential gear. In the four months that they'd been seeing each other, she had never ignored two calls in a row. At worst, the second attempt resulted in a "Busy, call u in a few" text. Which she always did.

What could be wrong? Worse yet, what could he do about it?

"Something I can do for you?"

The Fifth Precinct desk sergeant—Sgt. Homer Taylor according to the oxidized nameplate—was a joker. On the short side, lighter-skinned than Jamal, as if that had mattered since 1946, with droopy wings shaped like those of a giant bat. He also possessed a bland, possibly even pleasant expression, so it was hard for Jamal to get a read on his tone. Was that a genuine question, or some kind of challenge?

Jamal elected to play it straight, displaying his badge. "Special Agent Norwood, SCARE."

Taylor's wings fluttered—a sign of recognition? The joker cop turned to the ancient assignment board. "Crash in New Jersey . . . we have a DB in New Jersey that belongs to our Detective Black." There was something in Sergeant Taylor's voice that Jamal could not quite identify . . . a hint of scorn, perhaps, or, to be charitable, possibly just amusement.

"Okay, I know this is risky, but is Detective Black available?"

Taylor shot him a look; his turn to wonder whether Jamal was zinging him. "Actually, not at this moment. If you'd like to leave a number—?"

Jamal was already sliding his card across Taylor's desk. "So, as we used to say in the 'hood, I'm SOL."

Taylor waggled the tiny piece of paper. "Right now. But I will personally see that he gets your name and number. Best I can do."

"There's no officer or sergeant who could talk to a Federal agent?"

"It's mid-shift, Mr. Norwood. If people can be on the street, that's where they are. And it's been a busy day in Jokertown. Detective Black will respond, just not this five minutes."

Jamal suddenly felt tired and angry, never a good combination. He turned away, suddenly unsure of his next move. Which allowed him to consider Fort Freak.

The ancient brownstone was like a police museum. The phones were thirty years old at least; even the rings sounded analog, not digital. Even weirder was the joker-heavy nature of the few staffers he could see, from a human-sized rat to a big tabby cat—

"Not one of these officers has any information for me."

Taylor sighed. He was big in girth—Bill Norwood would have called him a perfect lineman, except for the wings. "Normally, yes. But incidents in New Jersey are outside our jurisdiction. I understand it's a bit unusual for even Detective Black to be involved."

Jamal knew he was being slow-rolled, and fairly skillfully. "Thank you, sergeant," he said. As he turned away, his cell rang—Julia!

No. . . . "Is this Jamal Norwood?" a voice said. It took Jamal a moment to realize that it was Dr. Finn from Jokertown Clinic.

Jamal did not want to have a conversation inside Fort Freak, so he hustled out the front door. The instant he emerged he was assaulted by the gamy, fishy, and oily smell of the East River. How had he missed it earlier? Probably because the rains had cleared the air, however temporarily. "Hello, Doctor," he said, hoping his voice sounded stronger than it felt. "What's the word?"

"The best I can say, Mr. Norwood, is confusing."

"Help me out with that."

"I'm sorry." Jamal could easily imagine the joker medico pawing the carpet with his hooves. He himself was pacing, as if sheer movement could make a bad thing better. "You are showing symptoms of what, for lack of a better term, I would have to call a degenerative . . . situation."

"Is that better or worse than a disease?"

"It could be better. You could be suffering from the ace equivalent of an injury, even an allergy, that might be treatable."

"But I could also be suffering from, what, ALS? Parkinson's?"

"Those terms don't apply."

"But the analogy—"

"Fits, yes. What we need are more tests."

Standing in the lonely entrance to Fort Freak, with the drone of New York all around him, awash in the vibrations and smells of Jokertown . . . and feeling much as he had felt all his life . . . Jamal found it difficult to know what to say next. Beyond the initial churn of his stomach when he realized that Finn's message was not, *"Found it. Antibiotics for a week and you're good."*

"More tests . . . that's never good."

"Let's concentrate on the positive, Mr. Norwood. I would like to see you as soon as possible, however."

"I'll call your office first thing to set up an appointment," he said. "Thank you, Doctor." He hung up . . . and then, like the delayed blow of a tackle, it hit him.

He could die. Worse than that—if anything would qualify—he might fade away slowly, horribly, first losing mobility . . . then hands . . . bodily functions.

Finally unable to breathe, helpless. *No bounceback from that shit, right, Stuntman?* He really wanted to talk to Julia . . . why hadn't she called? Maybe it was best that she hadn't; they were hardly in a stable, long-term relationship. She didn't need to deal with this—not while it was so uncertain—

"Agent Norwood?"

Jamal turned. It took him a moment to remember that he was at Fort Freak . . . getting stiff-armed. Now, here was a good-looking young man, late twenties, in a white shirt and loosened tie, out of breath. "I'm Franny Black."

"Oh, Detective Black. Call me Jamal."

Franny held up Jamal's card. "Sergeant Taylor just gave me this. I'm glad I caught you."

If not for Finn's call, you wouldn't have. "What do you need?"

"What else? Information."

Ten minutes later, Jamal had heard enough bizarre information about missing jokers and phony dog-training academies in New Jersey that he had been able to wrap Finn's news into a small box and put it high on his mental shelf. "That must have been tough," he told Franny. "Having to tell the Heffers about their kid."

Franny sat back. They were at his desk in the corner of the second-floor squad room, a space so low rent it made SCARE's nasty hotel-room ops center seem state of the art. "It was. Especially because . . . I didn't have anything good to tell them. No reason. Nothing."

"So you don't get used to it."

"First time I've done it."

Jamal was surprised. "You're a detective!"

"Pretty much just happened. I only had a couple of years in uniform, and my partner usually took the lead . . . on everything."

"What's a nat doing at Fort Freak, anyway?"

"The more I think about it, the more it feels like unresolved father issues."

Jamal had to laugh. "Copy that."

"So what does SCARE want with my dead joker?"

Jamal hauled out a hard copy of the DHS report on the ammonium nitrate, and his own notes on the crash site. Franny nodded at the DHS paper, but sat up when he read Jamal's material. "This sounds familiar," he said. "The unusual wheel base, the lack of treads . . ." He turned to his crusty keyboard and fat old computer monitor.

"Is that thing steam-powered?" Jamal said.

"I'm lucky I have one at all." As he clicked through various documents, Franny nodded to the other desks in the squad room. Sure enough, Jamal realized: maybe a third of them had computers.

"How the hell do you catch anyone?"

"Sometimes they show up at the front door and beg to confess." Franny smiled, then turned the monitor so Jamal could see it. "Maybe this is your guy."

Jamal looked at the screen, which showed a page from a typical police profile of a suspect. A black-and-white picture showed what struck Jamal as the strangest-looking front end of a vehicle he'd ever seen. "His name's Chahina, aka Wheels. He's a joker built like, and apparently able to move like, a truck. Early twenties, new to our shores."

"What's Wheels done?"

"He's been stopped for an amazing number of moving violations in the boroughs and in New Jersey. All dismissed." Franny smiled. "For a truck driver, he seems to have a great lawyer."

"Really."

"It's the ACLU, apparently. Wheels keeps getting cited, the ACLU gets him off because they contend vehicular laws apply to vehicles, not—"

"Automotive jokers."

"It's a funny old world sometimes."

Jamal held up his phone. "Is there somewhere—?"

"Don't tell me you want to link this data? Or have me e-mail? You're in Fort Freak, Jamal." Franny pressed several keys. Across the room, a printer wound itself up. "But we can get you a hard copy of the file. We have indeed reached 1994 here."

"Looks as though he's worth talking to. Does it say where he lives?"

Franny clicked to a different page. "Where else? Jokertown."

Julia finally called. "Sorry, sorry, have I said I'm sorry?"

"I sense that you're feeling a bit apologetic."

It was four hours after Jamal met with Franny Black at Fort Freak. He had returned to the Bleecker and used the hotel's business center to scan the papers on Wheels, then e-mailed them to Sheeba before meeting her upstairs.

Dinner had been substantially more interesting, with Sheeba popping up from the table to talk to her husband Billy Ray in Washington, then to connect with other federal agencies in the New York area. Finding out that Wheels was a foreign joker just changed everything, but the excitement of the discovery had worn off for Jamal. Finn's news—or lack of good news—played like a heavy-metal bass line through his every thought.

Now Jamal was flat on his back, unable to sleep, counting the potential good days he had left to his life, when his phone buzzed.

"Did I tell you my parents were in town?"

"You did not." Julia was not a Los Angeles native: she had grown up in rural Idaho, which could not have been a treat for a joker girl.

"So you're off tonight?"

"Heck, no." One of Julia's many charms was her choice of profanity, which was so tame it could have come from a 1940s movie about hot rods and malt shops. "I just ducked into the office here. The folks did keep me busy earlier, though."

Jamal tried to picture them, but his brain conjured up the grim farmer and wife from *American Gothic,* so he judged that a fail. He wasn't even sure of their names. "Are they staying with you?"

"Oh, God, no." Julia laughed. And Jamal should have known better.

In a weak moment, in conversation with his mother, Maxine, Jamal had let it slip that he was "seeing" someone, and uttered her name, Julia Jackson.

But Maxine had pressed for information, as moms will. So Jamal had let it slip: "She's a joker."

Silence on the line. "She looks perfectly human," Jamal said.

"That's a relief," Mom had said, laughing. "I thought you were going to bring home a white girl."

Needless to say, the meeting had yet to take place.

Jamal hated that memory. It wasn't just that it demonstrated how tricky any relationship with Julia would be . . .

It also reminded him of his own problems on *American Hero,* the mess with Rustbelt.

Put it away!

Yes, Julia Jackson was a joker . . . the size of a Barbie doll . . . maybe a bit taller. ("All my friends kept wanting me to kiss their Kens, but he was just too short." "Did the word 'creepy' ever enter into that?" "Not then and not much since.")

Jamal had met her, he liked to say, "between Riyadh and New York," which suggested something out of a romantic novel—meeting on the QE2, perhaps—but was really only a joke: they had met when Jamal took leave in Los Angeles after the SCARE-up in the Middle East.

Whether it was the long absence, or some yet-to-be-understood sense of real accomplishment, he returned to his home city feeling like King Shit. Well, why not? He was fit, good-looking, well-spoken, well-dressed, and, best of all, famous.

Which was better than being rich, because everyone assumed famous people had money.

With his friends Brett and Roland, he had gone to Gulliver, a new club on Ventura Boulevard. "Can you believe this?" Roland had said. "Going out in the Valley!" Roland was an over-the-hill snob who lived in a new, retro-fitted tower in the heart of Hollywood. Jamal, who still had a condo even deeper into the Valley, had no such reservations. In the relatively short time since *American Hero,* Ventura Boulevard had sprouted all kinds of new restaurants and clubs, and Jamal was happy to sample them, especially since he had limited time at home.

And word was that Gulliver had exotic joker flavor to its staff or design. Since Brett was sure, at some point in the evening, to suggest a follow-up trip to a joker-staffed gentleman's club, Jamal hoped this place would satisfy his friend's urge, and allow them to experience the ideal night out: which meant staying in one place.

The first phase of any night out, ideal or less than, meant checking out the women who were entering or already present when the trio arrived at Gulliver.

"Thursday night is ladies' night," Roland kept saying.

"Meaning it's Jamal's night," Brett said. He was the white guy in the trio, a friend from high school. Like Jamal, he had been a good athlete who, thanks to lack of height, got no respect or opportunity. Unlike Jamal, he had not been hit by the wild card.

Of the three, Jamal was the most likely to come out of any club with a number, if not an actual woman on his arm. Jamal had realized long ago that he needed Roland and Brett, or two guys a lot like them, to make this happen. Women were warier around a man alone. . . .

The bar was filled with actress wannabes and some never-weres busy posing and chatting, along with any number of middle-aged hotties celebrating birthdays.

The only men in the place—aside from those obviously attached to various women—were huddled at the bar like nervous teenagers at a school dance. "I'm not seeing the joker angle," Brett said.

"Well, maybe you're not looking at it the right way," Jamal said. The interior of the place was done up like a medieval village, with "stone" walls, battlements, wooden chairs and tables . . . all of them scaled in such a way to make even Jamal feel like a giant.

Confirmation arrived in the form of the hostess, a beautiful blonde in some kind of medieval-style dress with a pretty-definitely-not-medieval-style hemline. She possessed flawless milky skin and had eyes so blue they were almost purple. As they say in Hollywood, she was actress pretty, not just girlfriend good-looking.

He would have been attracted to her in any case: any male who could fog a mirror would have. Her only flaw, if the word applied, was that she was about a foot and a half tall. "Dinner or bar?" she chirped. Her voice was pitched a little high, but no worse than Betty Boop.

Brett grinned, thinking he was perhaps forty percent cuter than he actually was. "Both."

"Any particular order? Or shall I surprise you?"

"Surprise us," Jamal said.

"This way." To Jamal's amazement, the tiny waitress hopped onto a ramp behind her podium, then fluttered across the floor. Of course: the inverse square law (which Jamal knew from the Tak World movies), which doomed giant aliens invading Earth to muscle failure and early death, worked in Julia's favor. She could practically fly . . . like a cartoon fairy.

Within seconds they were seated, giants in a Lilliputian village. Menus arrived via a joker doing a creditable impression of a troll. But Jamal and his friends were watching Julia flutter away. "I hope no one steps on her," Brett said.

The meal passed with the usual amount of chat and teasing, most of it aimed at Jamal and his adventures in Africa. When they had paid and were heading out, Julia called to them from her stand. "Don't tell me I scared you?"

"What are you talking about?" Jamal said.

Julia indicated a couch in the corner of the crowded library-bar. "It's been waiting for you for fifteen minutes."

"We already ate," Brett said.

"I know, darling," she said. "It was dinner first, then bar. Surely you remember."

"Actually," Jamal said, "we hadn't. But we do now."

And they proceeded to spend two more hours in Gulliver, having one of the most enjoyable evenings Jamal had had in years . . . laughing, meeting half a dozen new people, including four women. "A new low," Brett said, grinning. He had not only gotten a phone number, at one point Jamal had spotted him kissing a woman he had just met. . . .

"Julia's good," Roland said as they were leaving.

And so she was. But Jamal had not tried to get her number that night—indeed, had not considered it—even though Roland had noted his interest at beer round number three. "Jamal's got tone," he said. Roland liked military technology. "Tone" was a cockpit signal that told a fighter pilot he was locked onto a target.

"Get serious!" Brett had said. "You are . . . not a match." He made a face and pantomimed a big finger penis bumping up against his scrunched fist.

"Relationships aren't always about the act, my friend."

As they left, Jamal made sure to pass by the hostess station, where he was rewarded with a Julia smile, and: "Come back soon."

"We just might," Brett said.

"Not you, big boy," Julia said, her smile dazzling. "You seem nice," she said to Roland, and here she looked directly—eye to eye, thanks to the height of the podium—at Jamal. "I meant *you*."

He went back the next night . . . with Roland. And came away with Julia's number. "Call me between one and four," she had said.

And he had done that. They had talked for two hours, until Julia said, "Oh my God, you charming, distracting bastard, I've got to get ready for work."

They had spoken again the next day—and the next—and three more times, before seeing each other in person again.

When they did have their first actual date, to see some English movie about another star-crossed couple in love, Jamal had driven to Julia's address in Studio City. It was on a side street behind Republic Studios. In their first extended conversation, Julia had said she lived in a "treehouse."

It turned out to be the literal truth: the address drew Jamal to a tiny A-frame built into a notch of an ancient oak tree, six feet off the ground.

There was an access ramp winding around the trunk. And a rope. Jamal wondered again at Julia's strength: he was in shape and there was no way he could have climbed the equivalent height. . . .

She emerged and, mercifully, took the ramp. Jamal had wondered about the protocol of walking with Julia—let her go at her own speed, two of her steps for every one of his? Or—

"You may pick me up," she said. Which, most carefully, he did, allowing her to rest in the crook of his arm.

"Shouldn't you be calling this a dollhouse instead?"

She slapped him on the arm with surprising effect. "Don't start with the short jokes."

"A serious question, then." They were almost at Jamal's car.

"One serious question."

"Don't you worry about . . . ?"

"What?"

"Hawks."

Fortunately, she laughed. "I have Mace, baby! So don't get any ideas."

He had helped her into the passenger seat. "The belt—" Was as likely to crush her as protect her, he was about to say.

"It's okay."

"You've done this before."

"This is not my first date, correct." He had the car in motion when she said, "Not to get ahead of ourselves, but, sexual relations are likely to be nonstandard."

"Not a problem."

"So you say. Now."

"As you said, we're a little ahead of ourselves."

She smiled over at him. "I have some work-arounds."

The work-around turned out to be the phone.

It was just a natural extension of their soon-to-be-daily catch-ups, almost always between the hours of two and four Pacific Time, when they talked work, books, movies, people, SCARE, and sleep schedules and then—

What they would like to be doing with each other, to each other. How it would feel. How it would look. Taste.

It turned out to be surprisingly easy . . . and even more surprisingly, satisfying.

Which was the big reason why Jamal hated missing Julia's calls.

This one turned out to be a huge fizzle, however, mostly because Julia started it by saying, "How are *you* doing?"

Now was a perfect time, and Julia was the perfect person, for Jamal to unburden himself about his health problems. Instead, he offered a curt "Fine."

"Now I know something's wrong," she said.

"Work is what's wrong." This had the virtue of being true while avoiding her question.

"Tell me."

So he gave her the short version—his boredom with the campaign, his Sheeba fatigue, the ammonium nitrate shipment, joker truck mystery, how they were going to grab Wheels later tonight. "Isn't some of that, what do you call it, classified or special access?"

"Probably," he said. "If they're bugging us—"

"—Hah! We're already in jail!" They both laughed. And then she said, "They need me—"

"I know," he said. "Thanks—"

"Now listen," she said. "Because I was so hard to reach, you get a pass this time. You can lie by omission. But next time we talk—tomorrow—tell me what's *really* wrong, okay?"

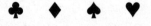

Galahad in Blue

Part Three

"PUT A FORK IN it and call it done," Captain Mendelberg said.

Franny stared down at the precinct's joker captain. Her bloodred eyes seemed to glare back, and her high-set, fin-like ears were waving slowly, the bright blood vessels in the lacy flesh as red as her eyes. She swiveled her chair around and turned her back on him. "We'll find something else for you to do."

"I assume you're talking about the missing joker file, ma'am," Franny said.

"Well, what else would I be talking about? The case is closed."

"Respectfully, I don't agree, ma'am."

"Oh, cut the crap, you sound like a fucking Boy Scout, or worse, a fag in some Brit movie. This case is closed. The perps were using the missing jokers like poodles to train their attack dogs. Gordon blew 'em up. End of story."

"They were Russian, ma'am."

"And the Russian mob isn't all over New Brighton?"

"None of the mob guys had ever heard of them."

"So, they were a new mob." A vein was pulsing in Mendelberg's temple.

"That doesn't make any sense. The bosses would have heard if someone was trying to move in."

"Do you know what this means, Black?" Mendelberg said and pointed at her ears. They were now motionless and stiffly upright.

"No, ma'am."

"It means I'm really pissed. The case is closed. Now get out."

Franny returned to his desk, stomach acid churning and an incipient headache lurking behind his eyes. He knew police forces were overworked and understaffed, and a simple explanation was a godsend, but this was malfeasance in his opinion. There were just too many unanswered questions. He was on thin enough ice with his promotion to keep pursuing this himself, but he knew someone who could. And who probably had better resources than he had.

He picked up the phone and called Jamal. It went right to voice mail. Franny returned the phone to its cradle, and sat drumming his fingers on his desk. Make another call and this time leave a message? If Captain Mendelberg found out, his ass was grass—a local cop calling in the Feds was one of the cardinal sins. He thought of the strained and frightened faces of the jokers they'd freed from the pens at that dog-training facility. Fuck it. They were wrong to close the investigation. He called Norwood's cell, and this time he left a message.

"This is Black over at the Fifth. I need your help with something."

He went back to the Warren County files.

He went to Mary's Lamb for lunch. Bill had introduced him to the restaurant when they'd walk the beat together. It only served breakfast, but the food was cheap, plentiful, and delicious—perfect for a cop on a budget, and it kept them in touch with the people they were protecting. A win all around. It was owned and operated, not surprisingly, by Mary, a joker whose true shape could only be guessed at because her large form was swathed in a cloak and she always wore a mask.

"Cherry almond muffins today, Franny," Mary said as she lumbered past. Her voice had a strange, burring rasp.

"Sounds great. Let me have a Denver omelet with a side of ham, and coffee too."

"You got it."

The coffee and muffins arrived. He broke open a pastry and it added its steam to the pennant floating over the coffee cup. The mingling odors of coffee and warm baked goods had his stomach grinding. Slathering the muffin with butter and jam, he leaned over to Tim at the next table, who was reading the *Jokertown Cry*.

"How'd the Jets do?" he asked, referring to Xavier Desmond High School's baseball team.

Tim tilted the paper so Franny could see the photo and the headline. "We're in the playoffs," he said with pride. The pale green cilia that filled his mouth quivered from the puffs of air carried with the mumbled words.

The plate of ham arrived, and he dug in. The bells over the door gave an agitated ring as it was pushed violently open. Franny, along with everyone, else looked up as the door banged into the wall.

Abigail Baker strode in. Her mouth was set in a tight line, and her brow furrowed. Franny reflexively checked to see if he had done something to piss off the girl, but since he hadn't seen her in months he couldn't think of anything. Of course, Abigail was just enough of a drama queen to have gotten upset about something that happened ages ago.

His mental trashing of the girl didn't help. Franny's heart still raced and his breath went shallow when he saw her. He reminded himself that he had a girlfriend now. An irritating girlfriend.

Could she be walking over to him? *Nah, it had to be somebody else on this end of the room.* He had had a crush on Abby from the first moment he'd seen her naked and angry on a Jokertown street, another victim of The Stripper.

She couldn't be walking over to him.

Liked her even when she insulted him.

Could she?

Liked her when she shot him down when he'd asked her out.

She was still coming his way.

Kept liking her even when she took up with that part-time small-time crook, Croyd Crenson.

Speculation ended when she pulled out the chair on the opposite side of the table and sat down.

"Hi," Franny began, then had to cough to clear the muffin crumb that had lodged in his throat.

She didn't waste time on social niceties. "I need your help," she said in her clipped British accent.

She needed his help? *Oh, holy shit.*

"Why aren't you asking your lowlife boyfriend?" his mouth said, before his brain engaged and thought better of it.

She reared back in her chair, and she flashed her eyes at him. "Are you not an officer of the law? Isn't it your *job* to bloody well help people?"

He discovered that shame had a funny taste. It laid on the back of his tongue and seemed to burn. "Uh, yeah. Sorry. So, this is official?"

Now she looked uncomfortable. Horribly uncomfortable. "Umm, not exactly."

Franny opened his mouth to make another smart-ass remark only to be completely unmanned when she started to cry. Soundlessly, shoulders shaking, tears sliding down her cheeks. Unlike Apsara she didn't cry beautifully. Her nose turned bright red. He thought she looked adorable.

He bounced out of his chair like he'd been shot from a catapult, came around the table, and knelt at her side. He slipped an arm around her heaving shoulders. "Oh, God, Abigail, Abby, I'm sorry. What's wrong and how can I help?"

Franny noted that the other patrons in the restaurant had politely looked away, engaged pointedly in conversations with their breakfast companions, or buried themselves in newspapers or e-readers. He was struck again by the courtesy and sensitivity of jokers. More than any other humans they understood the need for privacy and empathy to another's pain. "Come on," he said, lifting Abby out of the chair. "Let's take a walk."

"But you haven't finished your food," she sniffed.

"It's okay." He threw a twenty on the table and guided her out of the restaurant.

The sidewalk was filled with people, nats and jokers on their lunch hour. He tried to think of someplace private to talk. Only one thing came to mind. "Uh . . . look don't take this wrong, but my apartment is just a couple of blocks away." She just nodded. His arm was still around her shoulders, and Franny noticed she wasn't pulling away so he left it there. He looked down at the flash of multiple earrings climbing up the curve of her ear.

They climbed the four flights of stairs past the sounds of televisions, and a crying baby, and the smell of frying liver and onions. He really wished Mrs. Fortescue didn't make liver so often. He let Abigail into his apartment, and she stepped away, head turning as she inspected his space. Franny followed her gaze; touching on the small flat-screen TV and the Xbox. At the leather recliner facing said TV. At the TV tray off to one side of the chair. For art he had a framed print of a Fredric Remington painting, *The Stampede*. Franny decided the place looked tawdry and ordinary and like a sad, single guy lived here, which was the absolute truth. "You like cowboys?" Abigail asked.

"Well. Yeah. My dad had a huge collection of Louis L'Amour books. I read 'em all."

"Because he made you or because you wanted to?" Abigail asked.

"He died before I was born. I wanted to."

Her face was a study in embarrassment. "Oh. Sorry about that." Her fingers writhed through her hair, making it even more spiky and tousled. "My being rude, I mean. Sorry about your dad too. I mean, being dead and all. Oh, Christ, I'm making such a muddle of this."

"It's okay. It's not like I ever knew him to mourn him. I've actually got *two* chairs at the table in the kitchen. Want some coffee? Or tea?"

"Tea, please."

She followed him into the postage-stamp-sized kitchen, and settled at the tiny two-person table. He filled up two cups with water and stuck them in the microwave to boil.

While the mugs twirled like dancing partners Franny sat down across from her, and put on his best *you can trust me, I'm an officer of the law* expression. "So, what's wrong?"

"It's Croyd."

Great. Just great. She was going to talk about her boyfriend.

She gulped down another sob, cleared her throat, and composed herself. "He hasn't slept for weeks, he's cranked out of his mind, and . . ."

"I take it you're about to tell me the worst part," he said.

She sniffed. "He's got this barmy notion that this joker, I suppose it's actually two jokers because they're twins and they're not so much conjoined as they just share a lower body, anyway, Croyd thinks they're part of this gang that's been kidnapping people, and they're coming for him next. You see, he woke up a joker this time so he feels very threatened and fragile . . . emotionally fragile I mean because he's hideously strong, with skin like rock, and when he makes a fist his fingers disappear and they become like giant sledgehammers. . . ."

Franny pictured his soft nat body going up against *hideously strong* and *rock skin*, and *sledgehammers*. It was not a pretty picture. He rose abruptly, and dumped tea bags into the two mugs. Handed one to Abigail.

". . . He could really hurt someone if he had a mind to, and I'm afraid he does right now. Not that he would. He's usually very good about controlling his impulses, but when he hasn't slept . . ."

"Is there a point in here somewhere? Are we coming to it soon?" he asked.

Abigail's fingers twisted and knotted in her lap. She tore them apart and pressed her palms against her cheeks. "So, he's planning to kill them—him." The final words came out in a rush.

Now it was his turn to run his hands through his hair. "Jesus." He stood and started pacing. "Why didn't you report this at the precinct?"

"Because I don't want him arrested, and I don't want him to hurt anyone, and he's bound to fall asleep soon."

"You actually heard him say he was going to kill them?" She nodded. "So, what did you think *I* could do?"

"I thought maybe you could help me . . . put him to sleep. Or help me lock him up until he does fall asleep."

"In case you've forgotten—I'm a nat. No powers."

"Your colleagues at the precinct said you were very clever and—" She broke off abruptly and turned bright red.

"And what? What else do they say about me?"

"You mean it?"

"Yes."

"That you're an ambitious prick, and you'd knife anybody, even a friend, to get ahead."

That hurt. Enough to completely cancel out the grudging compliment. "I didn't want the promotion," Franny said, a refutation not to the woman in front of him, but to the universe at large.

"All right. And what does that have to do with the price of tea in China?" Abigail asked.

"Sorry, it's been . . . well never mind, I won't bore you with it." He gave himself time to think by draining the last of his tea, refilling his cup with water, and setting it back in the microwave. "Do you know where Croyd is holed up?"

"Yes."

"And do you know where I can find these jokers?"

"They're working as shills at Freakers trying to get hapless tourists in the door."

"Okay, I see two approaches. We help put Croyd to sleep, or we get the jokers out of town. Or maybe we do both, a two-pronged attack."

"I've tried dousing his food with sleeping pills, but I have to be careful because he's very paranoid right now, and the couple of times I succeeded it hasn't done a damn thing. And I'm out of pills. I got them when my mum came to visit and they only gave me thirty, and I used quite a few of them during *that* nightmare, so I only had about seven to use on Croyd, and I didn't want—"

He stopped the seemingly inexhaustible flow of words. "Maybe we need something stronger than sleeping pills."

Dr. Bradley Finn, head of the Jokertown Clinic, agreed to see them. Finn was a man in his fifties with silver-streaked blond hair, and a small paunch that pushed out the material of the Hawaiian shirt he wore beneath his white doctor's coat. The middle-age spread that was affecting the human torso wasn't echoed in the body of the palomino pony that made up the rest of the good doctor's form.

"Yep, you've got a problem," he said after hearing their story. "We've had occasions where we really, really needed Croyd to go the fuck to sleep, and we've tried everything, even horse tranquilizers. Nothing pharmaceutical works. His wild card decides when he's going to sleep, aided and abetted by Croyd."

"But that doesn't make any sense," Franny said. "How can he use speed to stay awake, but drugs can't put him to sleep?"

"Damned if I know," the doctor said. "Ask the virus."

Franny and Abigail exchanged looks. The doctor sensed their disappointment and her desperation. "Look, I've known Croyd for a long time, and I was able to put him to sleep back in the eighties—"

"How?" Abigail demanded.

"Brain entrainment and suggestion, but it takes time, and he was motivated. He'd promised some girl he wouldn't go out with her cranked."

Franny risked a glance at Abigail. Her face was set as she tried to hold back any reaction. "Problem is when he's in this state he's very paranoid—"

"No shit," Abigail interrupted the doctor.

"And this time he doesn't want to go to sleep because he feels threatened," Finn added.

"You're not telling us anything we don't already know," Franny said.

"Bear with me. In addition to being paranoid he's also very suggestible." A faraway expression crossed the doctor's face as he looked at a memory, and he gave a soft chuckle. He then gave himself a shake. "Point is, if you can get close enough to him you might be able to convince him to go to ground, or obsess about something else until the virus does put him to sleep."

"Thank you, Doctor." Franny stood and shook hands with the joker.

They walked out of the clinic accompanied by the sound of clashing bedpans, and the squeaking wheels on carts, moans and cries from patients, and incomprehensible gabble over the intercom. Franny felt like his clothes were absorbing the smells of alcohol, old coffee, overcooked peas, and sickness.

Outside he said, "I'm going to go talk to these jokers. You keep an eye on Croyd, and warn me if anything changes. Here's my card and my cell phone number."

Abigail started to walk away, then paused and looked back. "Thank you," she added softly.

The entrance to Freakers was between the spread legs of a neon multi-breasted joker woman. Standing at the entrance was the joker . . . jokers. Franny could see why Abby had been a bit vague. From the waist up they looked like two aging bodybuilders, but their torsos plunged into insanely wide hips set atop two pile-driver legs that culminated in extra-wide feet encased in black wingtips.

The torso on the right wore a T-shirt that read REPENT OR BURN! The one on the left screamed out BLOW ME! The man wearing the religious T-shirt also held a Bible in one hand. "Do not enter this den of iniquity!"

The twin with the goatee rolled his eyes. "Come right in. Feast your eyes, and grow a chubby—"

"Actually, I want to talk to you guys." He flashed his badge. "Detective Black."

"What? Why?" said Religious, suddenly dropping the bombastic tone.

Franny paused, realizing he needed to tread carefully here. If he named Croyd the twins might actually go to the cops, and that would upset Abby. He also realized he didn't even know their names, and he couldn't spin a tale when he so obviously had no idea who they were. He took out a notebook and pen.

"Full names," he rapped.

"Rick Dockstedder," said the twin with the goatee, and jerked his thumb at his brother. "He's Mick."

"Look, I've got a tip that you boys ruffled some feathers. Might be a good idea for you to get out of town for a couple of weeks until it blows over."

"Whose feathers?" Rick asked.

"We can't," Mick said. "Our mother's sick. She's at the Clinic, and her surgery is tomorrow."

"Ovarian cysts," Rick offered.

"Mention not the private, female parts of our mother," Mick cried.

Rick smacked his brother on the back of the head. "Jesus, you are such a tool."

"Take not the Lord's name—"

"And we gotta feed her cat," Rick interrupted the latest religious eruption from his twin.

"And she needs my prayers," Mick added, and shot his brother a smoldering look. That elicited another eye roll from Rick.

Franny toyed with arresting them on some trumped-up charge and putting them in protective custody, but there would be awkward questions from his superiors. What settled it was the knowledge that he'd want to be there if *his* mom was sick.

He temporized. "Well, just keep a close eye out. Maybe get off the streets and just spend your time at her apartment and the clinic."

"Who's after us?" Rick asked again.

Franny shook his head. "I'm not at liberty to say. It could compromise an informant and an investigation." He started to walk away.

"You sure you don't want to come in?" Rick called.

"I don't think so."

"Bless you, you are a good man, and your purity will surely be rewarded," Mick shouted.

Rick smacked his brother on the back of the head then gave Franny a sly smile. "It's roast beef special today. $8.99."

He had had to cut short his lunch, the price certainly recommended it, and the dancers were very . . . flexible.

The Big Bleed

Part Five

OPERATION RE-PO WHEELS COMMENCED far too early the next morning. That is, three A.M. Which figured: Jamal had left the planning to Sheeba. She was a big fan of special operations stories, where the raids always took place in the middle of the night, when the target was likely asleep or otherwise weakened. And the streets were emptier.

They gathered in their ops center, joined by a young FBI agent Jamal had never seen, a nat named Gunn—surely fodder for a million jokes ("Is your first name 'Lone'?")—who was a little pudgy, pale, and clearly from the accounting side of the Bureau.

"We'll have your unit and two of ours," he said, pointing to locations on the streets bracketing their target's residence. He smiled. "If Wheels rolls, we'll be ready for him." Gunn was also, as Jamal soon realized, one of the annoying compulsive punsters.

Sheeba had reverted to Big Sister mode, had brought coffee for all of them. Of course, she had probably stopped off at a Dunkin' Donuts to upload a dozen for herself.

Jamal took a sip, and regretted it. The coffee was nasty. They did have several key operational details to get straight before they got too close to their target.

Nevertheless, Sheeba's briefing was, well, brief: name, images of Wheels. Rap sheet vitals, mostly suggesting he wouldn't be armed. "How could he be?" Gunn said. "He hasn't got arms."

Sheeba had a question. "What about Fort Freak? Do we bring them in?"

"Speaking of knuckleheads," Gunn said.

Jamal quite agreed that Fort Freak was a collection of knuckleheads, but so was every other police department he'd worked with at SCARE. And, to be fair, not everyone at Fort Freak was equally useless: Francis Black had actually made this raid happen. "Actually, we should have."

"Doubt they'll be able to do much at three A.M.," Sheeba said.

"Or at any A.M.," Gunn said.

"I have to let Franny know," Jamal said. "Let me text him."

"He won't appreciate it at this hour."

"He'll be even more unhappy finding out we staged a raid in his precinct after it's done."

They finished up the basics: address, type of building, the likelihood that Wheels lived on the ground floor ("Thank God for small favors," Sheeba said). Rules of engagement. Where Wheels would be taken—the federal lockup on Rikers—and by whom (Jamal with the FBI team).

Gunn had already departed when Jamal asked, "How do we haul him in?"

"What do you mean?" Sheeba said. "We will have the wagon—"

"The guy is literally the size of a truck."

"I will, ah, remind them the moment we're done here."

"Yeah," Jamal said, "remind them to bring a flatbed and chains. Tell them to think King Kong."

Jamal and Sheeba grabbed their vests and weapons. As they were leaving, Jamal noted that one of the computers was live, Skyping. "Big husband is watching?"

"He's interested."

That was a surprise. Sheeba had been so skeptical of Wheels's value as a target that Jamal assumed that Billy Ray felt the same way. Maybe not.

Or maybe he was just afraid of having his team screw up.

Jamal had spent considerable time traveling into, out of, and around Manhattan wondering who lived in its buildings. The fancy Upper East Side towers held no mysteries, obviously: the rich, often the foreign rich. Upper West Side, yuppies, families, more diversity.

One thing they had in common? No jokers.

But everywhere else . . . the East Side near the FDR, Eighth Avenue and Fifty-second . . . in all those grim brick buildings with their tiny metal entrances, those windows above the awnings, the places where the smells of food from the restaurants below had to be overwhelming . . .

And in the worst places. The old tenements on the Lower East Side and TriBeCa and SoHo and Jokertown. Worker storage units, obviously, but Jamal had no idea what the workers looked like.

Well, tonight he would.

The Explorer glided down narrow streets wet and shiny enough for a Ridley Scott commercial. There were few inhabitants to be seen . . . the master of one all-night news kiosk, a skinny man who looked to be homeless who was nevertheless sweeping the sidewalk in front of a closed Le Pain Quotidien, an amazingly tall tranny hooker leaning against a door, a three-legged joker hobbling God knew where. . . .

None of them spoke for several minutes, not until the Explorer made the turn from Grand onto Ludlow. "Okay," Sheeba said, "we've got our warrants."

The phone buzzed in its dashboard mount. "FBI is on station." Sheeba pulled the Explorer to a spot in front of a fire hydrant, the only open one on either side of Ludlow Street. That moment, at least, felt like a movie production—

"Do we have to wear the jackets?" Jamal said. The last item they had to don were blue Windbreakers with the word SCARE written on the backs in huge yellow letters.

"Yes. That was the one thing Billy made me promise: wear the jackets!"

Wheels's building was a typical tenement, pre–World War II, six stories tall, decayed, soot-covered. "How many jokers you figure you'll find here?" Jamal heard himself ask. "And just how the hell are we supposed to get around back?"

Sheeba held up an iPad with an illuminated street map: it showed a narrow alley to the south of the actual address that ran to a courtyard of sorts in the back. It was so narrow that it wasn't visible from half a block away.

The alley was SCARE's route. The FBI would hit the front door. The backup team would stand off to the north, ready to move laterally, should Wheels slip the leash.

Sheeba closed the iPad and left it in the car. "Showtime," she said. "Isn't that what they say in Hollywood, Jamal?"

"We say 'action.'"

But the reminder was apt. He had not been able to shake the feeling that this was a movie . . . except that on movie sets, things moved slowly and deliberately. It wasn't unusual to spend six hours rigging and rehearsing a single stunt.

Now they were just walking quickly up a dark Jokertown street at three A.M. Up ahead, Jamal could see the three FBI agents approaching from the opposite direction.

Sheeba had her hand to her earpiece. "Turning into the alley," she said quietly.

And they did.

"Tight quarters," Jamal said. The alley was so narrow that Jamal felt as though he could have touched the walls merely by spreading his arms.

Sheeba was thinking the same. "How the hell does Wheels get in and out?"

"He sucks in his gut," Jamal said.

In the courtyard, forty feet away, the edge of an ancient garage door—the kind that opened like a vertical accordion, not a roll-up—glimmered in the yellow light from apartment windows. As they got closer, about to turn the corner, Jamal and the others could see a second door next to the first, and a single floor of truly ancient rooms above both. It was quiet enough that they could hear their shoes scraping on the broken pavement. No music. Then, a voice from around front: "Open up! FBI!" And the sound of a door being forced.

Still no response in the courtyard. "Which one is he in?" Jamal asked.

"One way to find out," Sheeba said, striding toward the first.

A siren started grinding from somewhere out on Ludlow. In seconds, it was a full howl. Sheeba stepped back, trying to talk loud enough to be heard by the FBI, but not so loud that she spooked Wheels. "What's going on?"

She listened. Then shook her head in disgust. "Fire station!"

Sure enough, a fire unit, siren blasting, cherries flashing, rolled south to north down Ludlow, rousing the neighborhood. Windows lit up in the apartment building, and much worse, in the garage unit. The right-hand garage door opened and—with no warning rev of an engine, and no lights—a vehicle emerged. It skewed into a right turn in the small courtyard, then executed a left into the alley.

Sheeba was in the courtyard and managed to skip out of the way. She held on to her radio, screaming, "He's in the wind!" Jamal started chasing the vehicle down the alley.

Reaching the street, Wheels pulled up short, obviously wanting to be sure he wasn't rushing into traffic. The hesitation allowed Jamal to jump for the truck bed.

Which, as it turned out, was like trying to mount a wild horse.

It was . . . alive, sweaty human flesh. Nothing to grab on to—and the smell! Like a locker room mixed with oil-stained garage. All Jamal could think to do was shout, "FBI! You're under arrest!" (He had enough presence of mind to know that SCARE would mean nothing.)

All this warning did was spur Wheels to motion. The joker managed to turn on four appendages, like a show horse in an arena, aiming left, facing directly at Gunn and his FBI partners.

Who had to dodge behind parking meters and between cars as Wheels picked his way down the sidewalk. Being flung from side to side, Jamal stretched his arms and legs, bracing himself against the "walls" of the "bed." Then Wheels hit the street and began a sickening rock-and-roll motion as he gained speed. Jamal could only think, *the son of a bitch is getting away—!*

But up ahead, a black Escalade pulled into the street, a blocking move by the second FBI team. "Give it up, man! We've got you!" Wheels didn't hear or didn't understand. He slewed into an impossible turn and tipped his right side toward the front of the Escalade. The joker managed to avoid hitting the FBI vehicle. Not so Jamal, who was flung into its grille. As he felt himself getting airborne, he dug his nails into Wheels's "bed," the equivalent of scratching a man's back.

The last sound Jamal heard before slamming into the Escalade was Wheels's anguished cry. Jamal bounced onto the street, landing on his side. He felt as though he'd been punched at the same time someone twisted his arm and kicked him in the leg.

There was no bounceback. Just Jamal Norwood half conscious, in horrifying pain.

Those About to Die . . .

Part Two

"ARE YOU SURE ABOUT this?" Marcus asked. He slithered along beside Father Squid, having to work at it to keep up with the furiously striding joker. "Meeting in the middle of the night and all? Don't sound right to me."

Under streetlights, into shadow and out, along parked cars and down alleys, the priest marched like a man on a mission. "We can't let this opportunity escape us," the priest said. "This could be the key to everything. It's the lead I've been praying for. God always responds to us, Marcus. Sometimes he even provides us the answers we seek."

The priest turned unexpectedly, heading east on Water Street. Marcus had to carve around and shift it to catch up. "Okay, but . . . who called and what did he say?"

"I don't know who he is, but he mentioned Chakri's name. Said he'd heard I was looking for information about the disappearances."

"You sure that's not been solved already? I mean, the dog-training—"

"Was a sideshow, Marcus! Breaking that up was a rare success on the part of the police, but not all of the missing were found at the kennel, and it hasn't stopped the disappearances. Two more went missing just this week. There remains something sinister at work."

Dryly, Marcus asked, "Which makes it a good idea to be going to meet some guy in the middle of the night?"

He knew he was pushing the skepticism, but he'd been hoping that the case was indeed closed. He'd had enough of this. Cruising around the city at night, looking for creeps nobody really wanted to find anyway, getting nowhere. There were other things he could doing.

He checked the time on his phone. 11:13. It wasn't actually that late. Early enough for a few good hours at Drakes. His thumb caressed the screen. He itched to replay the video greeting the snake-loving nat girl had sent him. She was persistent. He had decided to meet up with her there just before Father Squid had called him.

He thought to himself, *Option One—meet up with blond girl that did some very weird things with a garter snake in a video. Option Two—follow a fishy-smelling, tentacled joker priest on the wild-goose chase to meet some unknown dude.*

"If you had heard the man's voice," Father Squid was saying, "you'd have no doubts. He had reason to be nervous about reaching out, and yet he did so anyway. His line of work is not entirely legal."

"Great." Marcus put as much sarcasm into the word as he could.

"He runs a chop shop. He dices up stolen cars, gets new ones in every night. Earlier this evening a vehicle came in that wasn't stolen. It wasn't even new. It had little value, and yet the owner wanted it painted and detailed. Disguised."

"You think it's this van Lupo and Doctor Gordon saw?"

"Why else would someone go to an illegal establishment to have work done to an old vehicle?" He turned and set his dark eyes on Marcus. "We just need to confirm it. Then we call the police into action. They wanted tangible leads? We'll give it to them."

"Yeah, but the guy's not going to want the police anywhere near his chop shop."

"We're meeting him in the East River Park. He is taking great risks, as you must now see."

As they passed a fenced basketball court lively with late-night play, a lanky nine-foot-tall joker shouted, "Hey, IBT, ball's up!" He tossed a basketball over the high fence.

Marcus caught it. The court was crowded, jokers and nats mixed together, shirtless guys with cut abdomens, groups of girls milling around, bottles tilted in the air. Speakers boomed out the ubiquitous, deep-throated lyrics of Nutcracker Man's latest release. It was tempting. He'd never been much of a ball player before his card turned, but he had some skills now.

"This is no time for ball playing," Father Squid said. He snatched the ball away and spun around long enough to hurl the ball back over the high fence and right through the hoop. If the ring had had a net it would've whooshed. The priest acknowledged the impressed exclamations with a raised hand, but he kept moving.

Marcus tore his eyes away from the crowd. As they called after him, he followed the striding, hooded figure of the priest toward the dark shadows of the East River Park.

♥

"That's it," Father Squid said. "Just where he said he would be."

The van sat under a thick copse of trees on a dead end street in the park. As they got nearer, Marcus noticed a lone figure standing a little distance away, illuminated by a streetlamp just behind him. He could see him clearly, but kinda wished he couldn't. He was a thin man, naked except for a cloth wrap around his privates. His bald head and boney chest and pigeon-toed legs all glistened with a sticky-looking moisture. He ran one hand over his abdomen, streaking the sticky stuff. The man walked forward to meet them.

The name came out of Marcus's mouth all by itself. "Gandhi?"

"That supposed to be an insult?" Expecting a Hindi accent to complete the look, Marcus was disappointed. The guy's voice was pure Village, a bit nasally and dipped in sarcasm. "I'm no Gandhi. Just a joker, like you."

A gust of air blew in from behind him, draping a pungent medicinal scent over Marcus. He covered his nose with his hand. He'd heard of this guy. "Vaporlock," Marcus said, "you don't chop cars. Petty burglary's your deal, isn't it?"

The joker chose to ignore that. "I said for the kid to come by himself."

"I saw no reason to send Marcus alone," Father Squid answered. "I am a man of God. I am no danger to you. I could not, however, know that you were not a danger to us. I could not send the boy into harm's way alone."

"That's real like . . . fatherly of you, Father," the guy said. "Annoying, too." He rolled his eyes and said, as if speaking to someone other than the two jokers, "He was supposed to come alone. But no, there's two of them!"

"It doesn't matter," Marcus said. "Just show us the van!"

The guy chewed the corner of his mouth. "All right. Why the hell not?" He gestured toward the vehicle with a glistening finger. "That what you're looking for?"

It wasn't much to look at. A battered, off-white cargo van. Dent in the side, hubcaps missing, gang tags etched in the coating of grime on the back door, half a Yankees sticker on the bumper. New York plates. "Wait till you see what's inside," Vaporlock said.

Marcus's long stomach tensed with unease. He could've been at Drakes, getting stroked by an average-looking blond girl with a thing for shiny scales. Instead, he was about to look into the back of a parked van. Images from serial killer documentaries flooded his mind. Father Squid, however, sounded resolved as ever. "Open it." He crossed himself and glanced at Marcus. "Prepare yourself, son."

Vaporlock got a grip on the latch with one moist hand. His free hand slid up his chest, cupping a handful of gook. "It's nothing like what you're thinking." He yanked on the handle.

Inside was one of the ugliest jokers Marcus had ever seen.

Huge black eyes, tiny ears, no nose at all. The guy hissed, drawing his lips back from a bristle of needle-thin teeth. All of this supported on a muscle-bulging weightlifter's body. Before Father Squid could draw back, the joker punched him. The blow knocked the big priest's head back, but it wasn't the impact of the fist that really hurt him. It was the electric sizzle that accompanied it. Father Squid shook with convulsions. His eyes rolled back and he fell.

Before he hit the pavement, Vaporlock snapped his hand out and shoved the palmful of gook up Marcus's nose. The scent exploded in his head. His vision blurred. Tears sprang from his eyes. As he crumbled to the ground beside the priest, he heard the joker say, "Told you I was no Gandhi."

Ties That Bind

Part Two

THE RINGS WERE STILL in Michael's pocket days after he thought he'd be proposing. He walked in the door at home, exhausted and late for dinner, to be met with chaos. Happy chaos, for the most part—Kavitha had her latest show mix blasting, and was slowly twisting in the living room, sending out happy sparkles, rainbow coruscations. She must have just gotten back from the studio; she was still dressed for rehearsal, in a black leotard and long flowing skirt, her eyes darkened with kohl, her hair piled high, in elaborate braids. Kavitha looked gorgeous, like an Indian queen from a storybook, and once again, Michael wondered why she'd picked him. A woman that beautiful could have had her pick of guys—a doctor, a lawyer, a Wall Street trader. But instead Kavitha had gone for a skinny black cop. He should count his blessings. Isai was dancing around her mama and laughing, trying to catch the lights. Minal was, for a change, not at the stove—dinner was clearly over, with a clutter of dirty plates still on the dining table and the scent of curry lingering in the air—but was sprawled across the sofa instead, smiling and watching the show.

And, surprisingly, they had a guest.

Some guy was in the easy chair, his back to Michael, so that for a minute, Michael couldn't place him. Was it unenlightened of him, that for that minute, Michael's pulse rate quickened, and he felt a surge of possessiveness? A strange male in his territory, among his women. The adrenaline rushed through him—and then drained away a moment later, as the boy turned. It was only Sandip. What was he doing here?

"Brother!" the boy said, enthusiastically bounding out of his chair to wrap Michael in a hug. Michael hugged back, wincing a little.

Why did teenagers have so much energy? He was tempted to correct Sandip—after all, the kid was Kavitha's brother, not Michael's. But on the other hand, the boy was only jumping the gun a bit—if Michael ever actually managed to propose, then Sandip would be his brother, in law at least. Frightening thought. Did that mean he'd have to take on familial responsibility for this wild child? Kavitha smiled approvingly at him, still twisting in the center of the room, her body a long, lean poem of grace and beauty. His throat tightened. For her, okay. He could watch over Sandip. And he was honestly fond of the boy—Sandip had some of the same passion that Michael had felt at that age, the same need to prove himself. Although Sandip was more culturally directed, toward his own Tamil Sri Lankan people. Not the safest of passions.

"It's good to see you, man. What are you doing in town?" Michael hadn't seen Sandip in months—it only cost a couple hundred to fly down from Toronto, but that was a lot for a seventeen-year-old working odd jobs. "You finally checking out colleges?" Sandip was still living at home, and had decided to take a year off between high school and college; his parents weren't thrilled.

"Can't I come to visit my sister? See my adorable niece?" Sandip turned and stuck out his tongue at Isai, delighting her—she grinned and returned the gesture. In that moment, he looked closer to twelve than seventeen.

Kavitha slowed her spinning, long enough to say, "You know, I'd be happy to take you up to Columbia tomorrow. They have a great poli sci department." She smiled hopefully at her little brother.

Sandip groaned. "Aw, let it go, okay? I don't want to study politics, like some geek—I want to be in it, making shit happen."

Michael's pulse quickened. God, if the kid was getting involved with the Tamil separatists—that shit was dangerous. There were quite a few, up in Toronto; some people just couldn't accept that the war was over, like it or not. And yes, the Tamils back in Sri Lanka were getting treated like shit, again, but that wasn't a reason to return to the killing. On that subject, Michael and Kavitha were in complete agreement. But this hothead—the kid was just like Franny, wanting to skip the work, jump the queue. It wasn't right, and it wasn't fair. "You need to grow up, Sandip.

Go to college, learn something about how the world really works." Michael snapped the words, and laid a warning hand on Sandip's arm.

The boy hesitated, and for a moment, Michael thought he had managed to get through to him. But then Sandip's face hardened, and he shook off Michael's hand. "You're not my father, bro. And I'm not an American—you don't need to police me."

Damn it. He'd come on too strong, as if he were questioning a suspect. Michael gentled his tone. "Sandip, I wasn't trying to—"

Sandip flung up a warning hand. "Yeah, *machan*, I don't need this kind of crap from you. I just came here to get a meal, see my sister and my niece. Minal Acca, thanks for the food—it was delish. I gotta get going. Later."

"Sandip, wait!" But it was too late. The kid had already grabbed his leather jacket and was out the door, slamming it behind him.

Kavitha came to an abrupt stop in the middle of a spin, her eyes wide. "Michael. What the hell just happened? Where's Sandip going?" Minal was sitting up on the sofa now, and Isai came running up to Michael. He bent down and scooped her up into his arms, bending his head down to smell the sweet child scent of her. Almost five, and she still smelled like a baby, vanilla and cinnamon mixed together.

"Uncle Sandip went away?" Isai asked, her eyes wide and confused.

"He'll be back soon, sweetheart," Michael said, forcing a smile. "He just went for a walk."

Typical teenager—Sandip would probably walk the streets for hours, but he'd be back when he got hungry and tired enough. Isai snuggled down into his arms, reassured. Kavitha seemed less convinced, but she let it go for now. Tension still lingered in the air. Probably not the best time to break out two engagement rings. Besides, he was starving, and the food smelled great. Michael smothered a twinge of guilt. The kid would be fine.

They were in bed that night, the three of them, Isai safely asleep, when Sandip's call finally came. Michael had just shifted over to the middle of the bed, to take his turn for some extra attention. Minal's mouth was moving on his, her hands tangled in his tight black curls. Kavitha was sliding down the bed, her body slick with sweat. When they were together like this, warm and sweet and hot as hell, that's when Michael realized how lucky he was, how all he wanted was for this sweetness to go on forever. That was why he'd bought those rings in the first place. But today had been a rotten day, and right now, he couldn't think about getting married. Maybe later; proposing in bed could be romantic, right? But right now, all Michael wanted was to forget himself in their bodies for a while. Kavitha was just lowering her mouth onto him when the phone rang. Michael groaned.

"I'm sorry," Kavitha said. "When people call at this hour it's usually important . . . or bad." And she was up, rolling out of bed, picking up the handset and walking out of the room, still gloriously naked. Her tight dancer's ass lifting and releasing with every step.

"Sandip? Where the hell are you?" Michael was relieved the kid had finally called, but damn, his timing sucked.

Minal grinned at him sympathetically. "Don't worry, sweetheart. I think I can keep you occupied until she gets back." She rolled over so that her body was braced above his, and Michael slid his hands up her hips, feeling his dick get painfully hard. There, just above his fingertips, the nipples started. He'd tried to count them more than once, with fingers and lips, but he never got very far. Tonight would be no different. She was just lowering her lush body down to his when Kavitha started yelling from the hall. "What? What are you talking about? Sandip, don't be an idiot!"

Michael groaned, and reluctantly slid out from under Minal. Cop training—respond to trouble. There was a phone extension in the hall; five steps had him there, picking it up, hearing Sandip ranting. "I don't need school, I don't need Amma and Appa, I don't need you! I got a job, sis. I've got people who appreciate me and my skills!"

Kavitha spat out, "What skills?"

Sandip snapped, "Wouldn't you like to know? I'm not a little kid anymore. I can do shit."

What kind of mess was the kid getting involved in? Michael tried to intervene in the sibling shouting match. "Hey, no one doubts you have skills, Sandip. We just want you to come home." He'd come on too strong before; Michael tried to keep his voice calm and coaxing this time.

But to no avail—the kid was too far gone, practically screaming into the phone, "I'll come home when I'm ready! When I've proved myself. Then you'll see. You'll all see!"

Kavitha said, "Sandip, shut up and listen to me!"

"Go to hell, sis!" And then the click—they'd lost him. Well, that was a terrific end to a truly crappy day. Michael stood, naked in the hall, staring at an equally naked Kavitha. This night really hadn't gone the way he'd planned. Now what was he supposed to do? Wander the streets looking for his girlfriend's brother? The kid was almost an adult—surely he could manage in Jokertown for one night? Minal came out of the bedroom, wrapped in a blanket, and leaned against the doorway, her face worried.

"Was he calling on his cell?" Michael asked. They could track that at the station.

"No," Kavitha said, shaking her head. "His cheap phone doesn't work in the States. He must have used a pay phone."

Damn it. The kid could be anywhere. "Look, I'm sure he'll come back in the morning." He wasn't actually sure of that, not anymore.

"I have to call my parents," Kavitha said.

"Of course you do," Minal agreed. She came forward then, wrapped an arm around Kavitha and clumsily draped the blanket around both of them.

"I thought they weren't talking to you?" Michael asked tentatively. It was something they didn't talk about much.

Kavitha's face was stark, wiped clean of all expression. "They'll talk to me for this," she said flatly.

Michael groaned inwardly. It was going to be a long night. "I'll make you some tea." It was something to do, at least. He didn't know why it was that both women always wanted tea when they were upset, but after all this time, he'd learned that much, at least. Tea wasn't going to find the kid, but maybe it would give them the strength to start looking.

The Big Bleed

Part Six

"**WE CAUGHT HIM,**" **SHEEBA** said. "And he's singing."

"Good," Jamal croaked.

"But it's not what anyone expected." She went on to relate the details of an exotic smuggling and manufacturing cartel, only the product wasn't heroin or meth. "It's *food*."

"Get the fuck out of here."

"There's no need for that language. The product is illegal—endangered species used for entrées, magic mushrooms, other stuff that isn't supposed to be imported because it could get loose and wipe out indigenous plant life—"

Jamal tuned out at that point. The only relevant thing he heard was: "Everyone at HQ is happy with our results," implying that Carnifex had not been entirely enthusiastic about the mission—no surprise there. "And now that that's behind us—"

"That's it?" Jamal said. "No follow-up?" Jamal Norwood was sitting up in a bed at the Jokertown Clinic. He had been taken first to St. Vincent's, but the single attending there was over-burdened (there had been a bad fire several blocks away, with four people brought in suffering from burns and smoke inhalation), and claimed to know nothing about aces.

Loaded with painkillers, Jamal had waited, conscious or dozing, for four hours until an ambulance arrived to move him to Jokertown Clinic and Dr. Finn.

Who examined him yet again, and again just shook his head. "This obviously can't be considered part of your . . . syndrome."

"Is that anything like illness?"

The joker doc smiled. "We still don't know that whatever is . . . afflicting you doesn't have, say, an environmental trigger. So, no, syndrome, not illness."

"Not yet."

"Do you want to be ill, Mr. Norwood?"

"Have you added shrink to your job title?" Jamal had snapped. "Consider this a firm 'no.'"

Finn wanted to keep him for the day, for observation. And in truth, Jamal was not eager to be discharged. He was *finally* feeling bounceback, and was confident that he would be a hundred percent in a day . . . but he wanted that figure to be closer to sixty percent before he chanced the streets.

And told Julia. And his parents. Because each notification would be as good as telling the recipient that something was seriously wrong with Jamal Norwood—because his ace power should have put him back on his feet within the hour.

Not forty-eight.

The door hadn't even closed before Sheeba slid onto the corner of Jamal's bed and, assuming what must have been her idea of a motherly manner, said, "What's wrong, Jamal?"

He saw no benefit to denying the obvious: the Midnight Angel had worked with him for years. She knew how Stuntman was *supposed* to bounce back; she'd seen him hit harder. So he gave her the quick version.

"Why didn't you tell me? I can't let you back on active duty in this state, Jamal."

"Okay, Sheeba, two things." He was getting angry. "One, I'm not fit for duty today and could probably use another twenty-four hours off. Fine.

"But, two, I *am* bouncing back. A nat would be out of duty for months, maybe crippled for life. So whatever rules you're trying to access . . . they just don't apply." He smiled. "Don't make me charge you with discrimination."

Sheeba was so shocked she actually stood up and struggled for a response.

Jamal spared her. "I'm kidding," he said. "Really, really kidding."

But maybe he hadn't been kidding. He owed his whole SCARE career to his win on *American Hero* . . . and he owed that win to his confrontation with Wally Gunderson, the ace known as Rustbelt, a big, goofy, iron-skinned hoser from Minnesota, a world without African-Americans or anyone other than white Lutherans. Rusty had bugged Jamal from the moment he showed up at the *American Hero* house . . . he was too obviously trying to be nice, too simple. No one was really like that. No one outside of a group home, that is. And in one of the contests, with cameras rolling, Jamal was convinced he had heard Rusty come out with what he was really feeling, the words, "I'm gonna beat his black ass."

Or so he remembered it after all these years. It wasn't as though he had ever watched any footage of *American Hero* since the day it ended for him. . . .

Jamal had confronted him. Rusty had denied it, of course, but Jamal had been shaken . . . enough to lose. Days later, with what his mother would have called more charity, he realized it was possible Rusty had said "black ace." Which wasn't really objectionable, though whenever a white person threw "black" into a sentence, it was usually loaded—

"What do you want, then?" Sheeba was asking him. Jamal realized that he had her on the run—which was exactly where he wanted her.

"Look, let me see how I feel when they turn me loose. I'll tell you in the morning," he said.

She nodded, patted the bed while smiling wanly. "Just get better."

Jamal Norwood's wild card had turned his first year out of USC, when working as a junior stuntman on a bad movie. But there had been a harbinger.

It was a JV football game between Loyola and Cathedral. A Friday in early October, it was raining, cold, miserable. The moment he got off the bus, Jamal wanted nothing more than to have someone postpone the game.

No chance. Big Bill Norwood and every coach who ever lived said the same thing: football is violence and bad weather. (Jamal had Googled that quote later, and found that it wasn't complete. "Football was violence and bad weather *and* sex and rye." He still wondered what rye was.)

In spite of the mud and wet, the game turned out great, for Jamal.

He'd returned the opening kickoff sixty-five yards. He might have reached the end zone except that he slipped getting past the Cathedral kicker . . . and landed on his butt.

He had made four solid runs on that drive, only to see Trey Lackland, the QB, take the ball for the touchdown. On the second drive, however, Trey sent him on a deep post pattern. Jamal had shot out of the backfield around the right end, faked the safety toward the sideline, then cut into the middle. He could see the other safety heading toward him, but Trey's pass was already in the air . . . long, but Jamal had simply stuck out his right hand. The point of the football buried itself in his palm; his momentum allowed him to quickly draw the ball into his chest.

And he ran fifty yards into the end zone, untouched, his first receiving touchdown ever.

He was on his way to the best game of his life. On the sidelines, he glanced toward the stands. With the nasty weather, the crowd was sparse . . . it was easy to find Big Bill Norwood on his feet, cheering. Cheering in a way he had never done before tonight.

When Jamal returned to the field on offense, he was pumped, eager for another pass play, or even a run. True, Trey's lack of game sense had left the team with a field position right between the hash marks, which is to say on the most chewed-up part of the field (would it have killed him to run plays to the right or left, where there was grass?).

But Jamal was eighteen . . . he was fast and furious. He could make this work.

The call was a forty-two dive right, a handoff to Jamal with the idea that he would bust through a hole on the right side of the offensive line. Trey's handoff was clean, but the hole collapsed. In a third of a second, Jamal turned to his right, paralleling the line, planning to simply go around it. Easy if you're fast—

—but not if you're turning on mud. And get hit by a defensive end going one way through your left ankle, and a linebacker the other way above your left knee.

Jamal heard his knee crunch even before he felt the pain.

Which still managed to be instantaneous and over-powering. Jamal had hit the ground as the ball squirted out of his hands, recovered by Cathedral and returned for a touchdown . . . something he didn't learn for a day. Because he was howling in pain, trying to put his left leg in a position where it wouldn't hurt. Wouldn't be swollen. Would function again.

He was foolish enough to try to stand. He failed. By then Trey and Mosicki the trainer and one other player had reached him. They waited for a stretcher to carry him off. The diagnosis—several torn ligaments in his left knee, specifically the anterior cruciate, which allowed a runner to make cuts and sharp turns.

Surgery was recommended, though not for several weeks, until the swelling subsided enough for a doctor to determine the seriousness of the injury.

Basic recovery for a healthy eighteen-year-old male would have been six weeks. Jamal Norwood was running and making cuts again in three. Of course, the season had long ended. Over the rest of Jamal's senior year, there was some talk around the Norwood house about that surgery . . . but since basketball was out, and Jamal found no difficulty competing in the 100, the 200 and the 4x100 in track . . . it just went away.

It wasn't until five years later, once he had become Stuntman, that Jamal Norwood began to wonder if that injury had triggered his first bounceback.

Whatever. Now he was on the other side.

Jamal was still in the hospital gown, about to get dressed and get back to what was left of his life and career, when Detective F. X. Black appeared in the door. "How are you doing?"

"If I wasn't an ace, I'd be fine." Well, that was largely a lie. But since he didn't know anything for sure . . .

"When do you get released?"

"The moment you're gone."

"Hey, I can—" Franny hooked a thumb toward the door: *I can beat it out of here.*

Jamal waved that away. "It will only take a few minutes. Besides, there was something I needed to tell you."

Franny listened with growing amusement. Finally he said, "All this chasing around for some . . . magic mushrooms?"

"Not magic, just illegal. And not just mushrooms. All kinds of exotic foods. It's a huge deal to the Department of Agriculture." Jamal laughed at the image in his head. "I can just see *those* guys on a raid now, in their official Windbreakers with 'AG' written on the back. They probably wore green."

Franny shook his head. "Well, that's just fucking great. The big Wheels caper turns out to be about food, not bombers or kidnappers."

"It is, as we say in the law enforcement biz, a dry hole."

"Yeah, well, my hole just got reamed by one of my captains about my end of this little investigation. I am to forget the Warren County incidents forthwith and completely."

"Don't you still have a building—that dog-training joint?"

"You noticed that." He was as angry as Jamal had seen him. "According to everyone on the planet but you and me, there's no connection! These dead guys don't show up in any Fifth Precinct files, which means that they might as well not exist. Even if we had some info on any of them for any reason, they're not locals, which is about all we deal with. They're just . . . no-name hoods from another land, someone else's problem. Fuck." As he spoke, Franny had taken the file folder he carried, opened it up, and started dropping pages into Jamal's trash can, one by one.

"What's that?"

"My files on the hoods."

"Don't you archive those things?"

"I wasn't supposed to have them in the first place."

"Well, even so, throwing them away here isn't smart. . . ." Jamal had the folder fished out of the can and was presenting it to Franny before he realized: "You're not throwing it away. You want me to take it."

Franny smiled. "Thank you."

"Assuming I agree to spend five more minutes on this thing, which isn't automatic . . . what the hell do you want me to do?"

"Run the names through your database. SCARE must have access to FBI, DHS, CIA, Interpol, and, fuck, the Jetboy Junior Club, right?"

"Yes, but—"

"Look, maybe these three guys were just wannabe mobsters though they had a few kidnapped jokers stashed in cages. My captain has made up a story, but truthfully none of us have any idea why. And, naturally, my boss has made it clear that she doesn't want me proving her guess wrong and making her look bad, so I should just back off. That's bad enough. But just suppose, though, that they are deep-cover terrorists, the kind that always seem to bite us on the ass. They're dead, but they must have come from somewhere, must have been working with someone."

"I'll do what I can."

He woke, as usual, before his alarm. He had his right arm over his head . . . when had he started sleeping like that? He blinked. Oh yes, it was Wednesday. Tuesday he had spent in the Jokertown Clinic.

He had come home, spoken to Julia briefly—she was at work—and yet, in a few moments, managed to terrify her with a description of his symptoms.

Good work, Jamal. That conversation convinced him to defer the parental notification for a day or two.

Then, feeling as though he was probably seventy percent bouncedback, he had collapsed in bed.

Now, this morning, ten hours later, he couldn't seem to move. Not with any ease.

He fought the panic. *Listen to me, whatever you are! You are not a degenerative disease! You are only accumulated injuries!*

Okay, he told himself. *Whatever.* Maybe he was suffering from *something* (and when was that useless piece of shit Finn going to give him some good news?). Obviously it didn't help to have a vicious close encounter with a joker sized and shaped like a small truck—

Build yourself up. Bounce the fuck back.

Breathe. Stretch.

Take a moment and think. Listen to the city coming alive around you.

Where are you? Where have you been?

Where do you want to be?

He had a condo in Toluca Lake, so close to the Warner, Universal, and Disney studios that he could have walked there . . . and a short drive from Republic, Columbia, and Paramount. He hadn't seen it in two months. His parents were checking up on it, making sure there weren't letters jamming the mailbox, that the plants got watered.

He'd gotten so used to life on the road, to hotel rooms, the lonely breakfasts and nasty coffee, because he couldn't stand another buffet, the piled-up laundry, and the street roar, even on the twelfth floor. He wasn't entirely sure, but he believed that it was quiet at his condo. Maybe there was some freeway drone. Surely the planes taking off from Burbank Airport. . . .

What troubled Jamal was that he couldn't remember!

But that wasn't a sign of diminished capacity—he hoped, anyway. That was entirely due to living on the road for most of the past four years.

He took another breath. He seemed to be better.

Roll to your left . . . elevate with hands and arms, not your middle—

He was sitting up.

Then, miraculously, he was standing. Heading for the bathroom and feeling as though he were seventy years old.

Forty-five minutes later he had showered—and conducted a survey of the bruising on his legs and right side—shaved, and dressed. After a yogurt and cereal breakfast, with one cup of coffee, he was functional if nowhere near good. Maybe back to where he was last night. His phone carried no new messages from the Angel or anyone at SCARE. No surprise there; as far as they were concerned, he was off the grid. Nothing from Franny, either, which was nice: no "reminders."

Why not check out the cop's information? What else was he going to do with his time? He opened his laptop and set it on the foot of the bed. (The desk was the wrong height . . . he had developed a severe case of lower back pain using the computer in that position during his first week at Bleecker Towers.)

He logged in, going through the tedium of entering his password. (Clearing the cache was not only a habit, but a requirement). Then called up a multi-agency search, able to access the master DHS watch list, FBI and ICE and even Interpol.

While the page was loading, he opened the file Franny had given him—pages of standard police narrative as well as crime scene photos—and flipped to the list of names.

"Gornov, Dennis Timofeyevich." Thirty-six, Russian, from the sound of it, and from the ID photo. Blond, born to be a thug. Search.

New window: "Krekorian, Sev." Armenian. Twenty-seven.

"Rafikov, Zakir." That sounded Kazakh. Forty. New window.

God, these names. The African-American community had a few brain-twisters and Jamal was generally good at them . . . but today, especially, he kept having to look at his notes and re-type. Jamal's laptop wasn't new or fast, and the Wi-Fi connection in the Bleecker was iffy. So it took several moments for the database searches to turn up results. The wait was worth it. U.S. agencies and Interpol *all* had files on the men. All had made border crossings in questionable circumstances or with suspect associates. Jamal quickly noted one surprising commonality: All three were ex-KGB.

Suddenly Jamal felt sicker than he had since getting slammed by Wheels on that Jokertown street. This wasn't some random, small-time crime. When you found three Russian hoods, you were likely to find half a container ship filled with contraband, or de-stabilizing weapons. Or even a goddamned nuke.

And these clowns were kidnapping jokers. Why? Potential suicide bombers, maybe? People who could be blackmailed into doing bad things? Jamal fumed. This was important information—

—but not necessarily to SCARE, not yet. Especially with the team so concentrated on candidate protection . . . and the dismaying results of the search for Wheels so unrelated to terrorism. And tomorrow he'd be going back on Holy Roller detail.

He dialed Franny at Fort Freak.

Galahad in Blue

Part Four

IT WAS GOING TO suck to tell Father Squid that the precinct had closed the case on the missing jokers. Especially since Franny wasn't sure he was a good enough actor to cover his own misgivings about that decision. But it had to be done. The priest deserved that much respect. Franny also wanted to talk to the priest about Croyd. Maybe enlist his help. If anyone could get through to the paranoid ace it might be the man who embodied, at least in Franny's mind, the conscience of Jokertown.

He also figured a morning spent at mass wouldn't be amiss—he'd certainly been afflicted by impure thoughts about both Apsara and Abby, and a corrosive anger toward his fellow officers and his captain. He promised himself he'd go to confess on Saturday, but for now he could try to find some peace among the polished wood and the smell of incense. He still found it hard to look at the joker Jesus crucified on a DNA helix, but he'd never been all that comfortable with the nat Jesus on his cross.

He turned the corner and was startled to see a crowd spilling out of the church doors onto the sidewalk. He mentally reviewed the liturgical calendar, but couldn't think of any particular saint days or holidays that would have caused the crush. Some people spotted him and reacted.

"Oh thank God!"

"The police."

"Now we'll get some answers."

Franny pushed through the people. From inside he heard Quasiman's voice stretched with anxiety. "No Father! No Father!"

The hunchback stood in the center aisle twisting his fingers together and shaking his head so violently that the trail of drool that perpetually ran down his chin flew onto nearby people.

"What's going on?" Franny asked.

"Oh thank heavens." It was Mrs. Flannery, an energetic joker woman in her fifties who ran the altar guild with ruthless efficiency, and made certain the altar was always decorated with appropriate flowers. She was clutching a bouquet to her chest right now with her misshappen hands. "Officer Black, we can't find Father Squid. Poor Quasi is so upset, and he has a hard time talking at the best of times. I know Father thinks he's getting better but—"

"Mrs. Flannery, you need to focus. What do you mean you can't find Father Squid?"

"No bed. No sleep. No eat. No Father," Quasiman burst out. As Franny watched a portion of the joker/ace's left arm phased out and disappeared. He seemed unaware of the loss.

A gnawing pain settled into the pit of his stomach. "Show me," he ordered.

The entire crowd lurched into motion. Franny held up his hands. "No, if there's evidence we have to preserve it. Quasi, take me to the rectory. The rest of you stay here, and figure out when you saw Father Squid last."

Quasi lurched off with Franny following close behind. The priest's bedroom was spare and very orderly. Franny remembered that the man had been a soldier in Vietnam, and the room reflected that military background. It didn't take long to search and produced nothing. Father Squid's office showed the same organization. There were multiple versions of the Bible on the shelves and works by great religious teachers. The desk's surface held only a blotter, a notepad, and a pen holder. The notepad held a few notes that seemed to pertain to an upcoming sermon.

"Quasi, when did you last see Father Squid?" The joker stared at him and drooled, the saliva dripping onto the front of his T-shirt and forming a dark patch. Franny considered the last time Father Squid had come to the precinct. He had been with IBT. "Quasi, do you know where I can find IBT?" Drool. "Marcus." Drool. "Infamous Black Tongue?" Drool. "The big snake?"

There was a flicker of comprehension in the dull eyes. "With Father."

"Okay, when was that?"

But Quasi was gone. The office held only Franny and questions. As he walked back into the church Franny wondered if Quasi had gone to wherever his arm currently resided. Another time, another dimension, another galaxy . . . who knew? The hunchback, maybe, but he wasn't saying.

The parishioners had been busy in his absence. They were on cell phones, calling friends and relatives in Jokertown, and there was a small amount of information. A security guard had seen the priest and IBT either last night or the night before, but hadn't spoken to them, and had no idea where they were headed.

"Okay, all of you keep checking. And call me if you learn anything or if Father Squid returns." Franny headed to the precinct.

Maseryk was on duty so it meant Franny didn't get to march in, throw the missing joker file dramatically on the desk and announce, *"This case is no longer closed!"* For one thing he wasn't pissed at Maseryk the way he was at Mendelberg, and frankly the crew-cut captain intimidated him worse than Mendelberg.

Franny laid out the situation. Maseryk rubbed a hand wearily across his face. "Damn fool, I told him to back off, leave it to the professionals."

"Yeah, and the professionals closed it," Franny shot back, forgetting to be intimidated.

"Watch it," Maseryk warned. Franny folded his lips together. "The case is now active. Get on it. And find him. This is the kind of thing that can be like lighting a match in a tinderbox."

Franny returned to his desk. He felt a sense of grim satisfaction. Until he realized that he still was nowhere, no leads, and one of Jokertown's most revered citizens taken without a trace. Then he noticed Jamal had called. Maybe the SCARE agent would have something . . . .

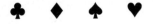

Those About to Die . . .

Part Three

MARCUS OPENED HIS EYES. For a moment he could see nothing but shapes behind a thick Vaseline-like coating. He blinked and rubbed at his eyes with his knuckles, trying to clear them.

"Awake finally," a voice said. "'Bout time."

The voice was strangely familiar, but he couldn't place it. He heard footsteps move away, a chair scrape, and a person exhale as he sat down. Marcus realized the sitting person had touched him. That's why he'd woken up. But it wasn't the same person who was speaking.

"You know you snore, right?" the voice continued. "There's operations that can fix that. Think about getting one if you ever get out of here. That's a big if, by the way."

Even before he could focus on him, Marcus knew that last line was said through a crooked grin. It didn't make sense, but he thought he knew who was speaking. "Asmodeus?"

"You remember me! I'm touched. I remember you too. Last time I saw you you were on the ground in an alley, twitching, drooling, two cops standing over you."

Marcus lifted up his T-shirt and scrubbed furiously at his eyes. When he looked up again, the world was oily, but he could see clearly enough. Asmodeus, the philosophizing general of the Demon Princes, paced a few yards away. He moved with the same cocky posture Marcus remembered. There was the crooked grin, the crown of short horns that ringed his head, the profusion of acne on his cheeks. His wardrobe had gone up a few notches. Gone were the pinstriped trousers, suspenders, and undershirt. Instead, he wore a shimmering maroon suit, with black shoes so sharp they looked like dagger points.

The seated man looked like a nat. He wore a wifebeater undershirt. It was not an attractive look considering his paunch, sagging breasts, and the black hairs bristling from his shoulders. His round face looked deeply bored. His jaw worked in a slow, bovine mastication of a piece of gum. He seemed to be staring at a spot on the wall.

The room provided no clues to what was going on. Sparse. Small. Simply furnished. He lay on a bed, though his long serpentine section spilled off onto the floor. He had no idea where he was. Last thing he remembered was . . . His gaze snapped back to Asmodeus. "Where's Father Squid?"

"He's here. Wasn't really meant to be. Bit of a fuck-up, if you ask me. Those numbnuts were supposed to pick you up, not Squiddy. Anyway, looks like he'll be staying. You'll see him soon. Before anything, though, you gotta sit through the talk."

"I'm not sitting through anything," Marcus said. Venom washed into his mouth like a surge of saliva. He drew himself upright and began to slide toward the door. Asmodeus moved to block him. Marcus snapped, "I'll take your fucking head of if you don't get out of my way."

"No, you won't," Asmodeus said. "Dmitri? Show Snake-boy why he's gonna sit and be good."

The bored man stopped chewing. He didn't look at Marcus, but his features tensed with concentration.

Not impressed, Marcus leaned forward, fists balled to knock the grin off Asmodeus's face. Before he could, he felt something crawl across the back of his neck. Tiny legs, sharp points that moved with the rhythm of a centipede. He tried to swat at it, but his hands wouldn't move.

"That's how it starts," Asmodeus said. "Wait, it gets better."

The creature cut into Marcus's flesh. He felt it saw on his skull, cutting a slice through his cranium from ear to ear. Marcus's whole being cried out to shout and writhe and fight, but he just stood, trembling. Something slipped fingers into the crease and wrenched the back of his skull away from his brain. Scorching breaths burned his skin as the lips of an unseen mouth pressed close, using the slit in his skull to speak into his head. It spoke a garbled language that made the air curdle. Marcus didn't understand, and yet he knew the horrors the mouth spoke because he could see them before him. The world melted around him, went dark and sinister. The voice spoke of the unmaking of the world. It spoke of rot and disease and misery. Marcus felt the speaker moving around into his center of vision. He felt the enormous bulk of it, and he knew that whatever he was about to see was horrible beyond imagining. Just seeing it would kill him. Would stop his heart. But the worst part was knowing that even with his heart stopped he would go on, and the horror would use him like a cat plays with her mouse. It would never end.

And then it did. It stopped. The speaker vanished. The dark, formless world disappeared. Marcus slumped forward, gasping.

Asmodeus's tongue played along the line of his teeth. "That's some fucked-up shit, isn't it? That little trip was courtesy of Dmitri." He tilted his head to indicate the other guy, who had resumed working on his gum, eyes vacant again. "That's what he does. He fucks with people's heads. Now that he's been in yours, he can visit you anytime he wants to. Doesn't even have to be in the same room as you. You step out of line, Dmitri here steps into your cranium and escorts you to hell."

Marcus slithered back onto his bed, leaned against the wall, eyes snapping between Asmodeus and Dmitri.

"Now, let's try it again," Asmodeus said. "Here's what you need to know. Listen carefully because I'm not gonna say it twice. You may be wondering where you are, and how and why you're here. The where part is irrelevant. You just are. Deal with it. Don't worry about how you are either. The why is a bit more of a thing. You're here because Baba Yaga wants you to be. This is all her baby. Because of her, you've been plucked from the streets of J-Town and offered a chance at fame and riches. All you have to do is beat the shit out of fuckers. That's all this is about. It's about tapping into that primal urge for violence. It's about being a man and proving it in the arena. You're gonna be a gladiator. Understand?"

"No," Marcus said.

"Don't worry," Asmodeus said, moving toward the door, "understanding is coming at you fast. Come on. Take a look at the compound. You better get something to eat, too." When Marcus glanced at the ace, he added, "Dmitri's not gonna fuck with you. Unless you act up."

As if dismissed by this, Dmitri stood, pulled out his iPhone, and began scrolling through his messages.

Leaving his room, Marcus's gaze turned upwards to the arching dome above the open space. Daylight shone through the material, bathing the green, garden-like space so completely that it almost seemed like they were outside. Insects buzzed among the flowering vines that ran up the rafters. Birds flitted about. Birdsong blended with the low, sinuous pipe music that floated on the air, exotic, meant to tempt and entrance. The scent of incense hung in the air.

It was almost beautiful, until he lowered his eyes and took in the tables and chairs, couches and plush rugs that crowded the main room. Amongst them, a motley collection of jokers lounged. Burly men. Dangerous-looking. Some of them were bandaged and bruised. Some played cards. A few watched baseball on a large flat-screen. Several browsed tables laden with food. One met his gaze, snarled. Judging by the growths all over his face and arms, he answered to the name Wartcake. Father Squid had called him Simon Clarke. They'd wanted to find the vanishing jokers. Now they had.

"This is the common area. Canteen. Bar. Place to hang out and shoot the shit. We're pretty much free to do whatever, until a bout."

A short-armed bartender mixed drinks at a bar. A small crowd gathered around it, talking, smoking. A gorgeous, nearly naked young nat woman started dancing to the accompaniment of cheers, her body all moving curves and lean arms and legs. Another climbed onto the lap of a grinning joker.

"We get treated well," Asmodeus said. "You could get some of that, too. Just bring it in the arena. Win, and get the crowd loving you and you'll get rewards, too."

Marcus caught sight of Father Squid. The priest moved slowly through cots of injured jokers, talking quietly with them as he checked their injuries. "This place can't hold us," he said, though his voice didn't carry the conviction of his words. "We're not staying long."

"Jailbreak, huh?" Asmodeus asked. His voice dripped with sarcasm. "Gladiator uprising? Shit, you really are clueless. My first day here a joker named Giles made a fuss. He started ranting, trying to wind us up, saying our power was in our numbers and we could smash this place if we wanted to."

"Sounds like the type of shit you used to spout," Marcus said.

Asmodeus grinned. "He was all right, but didn't quite have my gift for oratory. He got folks pumped. Dmitri could've taken him to hell, but this time Baba's thugs appeared. They dropped out of the ceiling all of a sudden. Had Giles strung between three Tasers, jerking and twitching, before anybody knew what was happening. They took him away. When they brought him back he wasn't Giles anymore. He wasn't even a man."

"What's that supposed to mean?"

"He came back as that." The joker leaned close to Marcus's shoulder and stretched his slim arm out to point.

For a moment Marcus didn't know what he meant. There was nothing where he was pointing but a weird-looking chair. He almost said as much, but the words caught in his throat. Something about the piece of furniture made his skin crawl. It was strangely organic, as if it were all made of one substance, stretched and morphed into shape.

"That chair is Giles. Don't ask me to explain how. We all just knew. When it first came . . ." Asmodeus lowered his voice, speaking with hushed reverence. ". . . it even looked like him. You could see him in there. He was twisted, changed, but he was still alive. We could see him breathing. We could see his eyes move. Sometimes, at night, I heard him pleading. Not really words, but, just sounds of anguish. He's dead now, but it was a long time in coming."

Marcus tried to think of something flippant, but there was nothing in Asmodeus's face to indicate he was joking. He looked at the empty chair. Maybe his mind was playing tricks on him, but he could almost see a kneeling man, tilted backwards, arms frozen in a rictus of agony.

"Baba Yaga's into some serious shit," Asmodeus said. "It's not like what Dmitri does. Some of it's for real. It's why you're gonna fight when she says fight."

Once More, for Old Times' Sake

by Carrie Vaughn

ANA CORTEZ WAS PLAYING hooky from work. She called in sick—first time ever, not counting the couple of times she'd ended up hospitalized *because* of work. On the phone with her boss, she sounded as pathetic and self-sacrificing as she could, saying that she couldn't possibly come in and risk infecting anybody else with whatever twenty-four-hour stomach bug was ravaging her system. She wasn't sure Lohengrin believed her, but she'd earned enough status over the last few years, he didn't question her. She *deserved* to play hooky.

What would she do with her day off? What any self-respecting New Yorker—transplanted, but still—would do: she went to a baseball game at Yankee Stadium. Not that she particularly liked baseball, but Kate would be on the field today, and Ana wasn't going to miss it for the world.

Except for the local favorites and the one or two who made the news in some scandal or other, Ana didn't know who any of the players were, didn't follow baseball at all, but she got caught up in the excitement anyway, cheering and shouting from her seat in the front row off third base.

The player who won the Home Run Derby, Yankee hitter Robinson Canó, was a local favorite, and the crowd stayed ramped up for the next event. The special charity exhibition was billed as a Pitching Derby—the major league's top pitchers took to the field, facing home plate and a radar gun, and pitched their fastest. 100 miles per hour. 101. 99. 102. The crowd lost it when Aroldis Chapman pitched 105—it had broken some kind of record, apparently. But the show wasn't over, and when the last pitcher in the lineup walked onto the field, an anticipatory hush fell.

The athletic young woman wore the tight-fitting white pants of a base-ball uniform and a baby-doll T-shirt, navy blue, with "Curveball" printed on the back. No number, no team affiliation, which was Kate all over these days. Curveball, the famous ace who could blow up buildings with her pitches, who'd quit the first season of *American Hero* to be a real-life hero, who'd then quit the Committee, because she didn't need anybody.

The crowd never got completely quiet as they murmured wondering observations and pointed at the newcomer. Ana leaned forward, trying to get a better look at her friend, who seemed small and alone as she crossed the diamond and reached the mound, tugging on her cap. She didn't face home plate like the others, but turned outward, to the one-ton pile of concrete blocks that had been trucked to the outfield.

Kate looked nervous, stepping on one foot, then another, digging the toes of her shoes into the dirt, pressing the baseball into her glove. Her ponytail twitched when she moved. Some traditionalists hadn't wanted her here—were appalled at the very idea of a woman on the pitcher's mound at venerable Yankee Stadium. But this was raising money for charity so they couldn't very well argue. Ana wondered how much harassment Kate had put up with behind the scenes. If she had, she'd channel her anger into her arm.

Ana's stomach clenched in shared anxiety, and she gripped the railing in front of her until her fingers hurt. Why did this feel like a battle, that Ana should be out on the field with her, backing her up? Like they'd fought together so many times before. Here, all Ana could do was watch. This wasn't a battle, this was supposed to be for fun. Gah. She touched the St. Barbara medallion she wore around her neck, tucked under her shirt. The action usually calmed her.

Finally, the ace pitcher settled, raised the ball and her glove to her chest, wound up, left leg drawn up, and let fly, her whole body stretching into the throw.

Sparks flared along her arm, and the ball vanished from her hand, fol-lowed by a crack of thunder, the *whump* of an explosion—and the pile of concrete was gone, just gone. Debris rained down over the field in a cloud of dust and gravel. The sound was like hail falling. The crowd sitting along the backfield screamed and ducked. Kate turned away, raising her arm to shelter her face.

Something weird had happened. Ana had seen Kate throw a thousand times, everything from a grain of rice to a bowling ball. She'd blown up cars and killed people with her projectiles. But she'd never erased a target like this.

Then the speed of the pitch flashed on the big board: 772 mph.

The announcer went crazy, his voice cracking as he screamed, ". . . that sound . . . the sonic boom of a *baseball*! Oh my God, I've never seen anything like it! Unbelievable!"

Kate had also put a sedan-sized crater in the outfield, but no one seemed to mind. The crowd's collective roar matched the noise of a tidal wave, and the major league players rushed out on the field to swarm Curveball. A pair of them lifted her to their shoulders, so she sailed above them. Her face held an expression of stark wonder. The screen at the backfield focused on her, her vast smile and bright eyes.

Ana clapped and screamed along with the rest of the crowd.

It took two hours for the stadium to clear out. Ana lingered, making her way toward home plate, where Kate was entertaining fans leaning over the boards to talk to her. Signing baseballs, posing for pictures. Ana arrived in time to catch one exchange with a girl, maybe twelve, a redhead in braids and a baseball cap of her own.

"I play softball," she said, handing Kate a ball to sign.

"You pitch?" Kate asked.

"Yeah, but not like you."

"Chapman doesn't pitch like me. I bet you're good enough."

The girl shrugged. "I don't know. We didn't win the season."

"Keep practicing. That's what it takes. Work hard. Okay?"

The girl left smiling.

Kate saw Ana hanging back as the last of her admirers left. Squealing, she pulled herself over the barrier and caught her up in a rib-squishing hug. Ana hugged back, laughing. They separated to get a better look at each other. Kate was still grinning, as well she should be, but Ana noticed the shadows under her eyes.

"I'm so glad you could make it," Kate said.

"Are you kidding? I wasn't going to miss it. You ready for the party?"

Kate sighed. "I need a couple more hours. They want a press conference and a photo op for the charity. We raised seventy-five grand." Her gaze brightened.

"That's so great. How about this—come over as soon as you can, and I'll have a chance to pick up a few more things and get the place cleaned up."

"You promised me a gallon of margaritas. Is that still on?"

"Oh, you know it. A gallon of margaritas, a pile of DVDs—and all the gossip on that new boy of yours."

Kate blushed, but her smile glowed. "You got it."

Ana had brought home the tequila, limes, salt, and a bag of ice already. Now, she went for approximately a metric ton of burritos from the excellent taquería around the corner from her apartment. They had to eat if they were going to keep up their strength for more margaritas.

The Lower East Side walk-up used to be her and Kate's apartment, back when Kate was still on the Committee, until she quit and went back to school in Oregon. That had been a couple of years ago now, and they didn't get to see each other very often these days.

Her apartment was on East Fifth Street, a few blocks off Jokertown, in a neighborhood that wasn't great but wasn't awful. Ana liked the place. It wasn't pretentious, and she could maintain some level of normality. Like go to the taquería without anyone giving her a hard time or snapping pictures. With her straight dark hair and stoutish frame, she wasn't as photogenic as Kate, but she'd had her own share of publicity as the Latin American Coordinator for the UN Committee on Extraordinary Interventions. She didn't much *feel* like a public figure most of the time. So she stayed in her unassuming neighborhood. The street food was better.

At her building's front door, she paused to find her key one-handed, when a voice hissed at her from the stairwell to the lower-level apartment.

"Ana! Ana, down here!" She looked over the railing.

The joker wore dark sunglasses and had his top two arms shoved into an oversized jacket. His middle two arms held it tight around his torso in some futile attempt at a disguise. He made his best effort to huddle in the shadows, away from the view of street level, but the guy was over seven feet tall and bulky: the world-famous drummer for the band Joker Plague.

"DB? What are you doing here?" she said.

He made a waving motion, hushing her. "Quiet! Get down here, will you?"

She swung around the railing, and Drummer Boy pulled her into the shelter of the stairwell, making her drop the bag of food. "Michael!"

"Shhh! Sorry. Here." With a fifth arm emerging from the bottom of the jacket, he picked up the bag and shoved it at her. The contents were probably mushed. Maybe they could have burrito casserole. "Ana, I need to talk to you, can I come in?"

"Couldn't you call?"

"*In person.* Come on, at least can we get off the street?"

She hadn't seen him in almost a year. Normally, she'd be happy to see him, and they tried to get together the rare times they happened to be in the same zip code at the same time. He'd gotten her tickets to a Joker Plague show awhile back, and she'd love to do something like that again. But she really wished he'd called. What she *didn't* want was him still hanging around when Kate arrived.

She spent too long thinking, and DB continued cajoling. "I'm passing through town, and I really need to talk to you but I'm trying to keep a low profile—"

She raised an eyebrow and gave him a skeptical look. With six arms and tympanic membranes covering his torso, Michael Vogali, aka Drummer Boy, could never keep a low profile. Ever.

"Michael, what do you want, really?" she said.

"Can I crash at your place? Just for a couple of days. Please?"

Three hundred sixty-five days in a year, and he picked this one to show up asking for a favor. He was a friend, she didn't want to say no, but this *couldn't* be happening. This . . . this was not going to end well.

She winced. "You don't have anyone else you can stay with? Don't you own an apartment on Central Park or something excessive like that?"

"Never did get around to it," he said. "Our recording studio's in LA."

"You can't stay at my place, it's *tiny.*"

"It's just for a couple of days—"

Exasperated, she blurted, "You can't because Kate's staying with me tonight."

He brightened. "She is? I haven't seen her in ages. Is she . . . I mean, is she okay and everything?"

She hadn't meant to say anything about Kate. "Are you *sure* you can't stay someplace else?"

"This isn't just about someplace to stay, we really do need to talk. And Kate . . . oh fuck, I didn't want to be the one to tell Kate, I was hoping you could do it after I'd talked to you—"

"What are you talking about?"

"Please, can we go inside?" He gave her a hangdog look that should have been ridiculous on a seven-foot-tall joker behemoth, but he managed to make himself endearing.

She rolled her eyes. "Okay. Fine. But Kate and I are still having our margarita night."

"Hey, that sounds like fun—"

"Michael!"

He raised his hands in a defensive pose and backed up a step. "No problem."

"Hold this." She handed him the burritos and found the key for the door. "Why didn't you just call me instead of camping out like a homeless person?"

"Because you'd be more likely to say yes if I just showed up on your doorstep?"

She growled and hit him on the side, generating a hollow echo through his torso.

"My walls are thin—you're going to have to cut down on the drumming."

"Sure, of course," he said, smacking a hollow beat as punctuation.

Oh yeah, was this going to end badly.

Kate and DB had quit the Committee at the same time, over the politicization of the group in the Middle East. Ana hadn't been there, but she'd gotten an earful when Kate called to tell her about it. She'd cried a bunch during that phone call—Ana might be the only person in the world who knew how torn up Kate had been over the whole thing. Ana had been stuck halfway around the world, on another mission for the Committee, and couldn't do a thing about it. DB had just been angry—he hadn't called Ana to vent. A bunch of the tabloids insisted that DB and Kate had run off together in some torrid romance, but that wasn't at all true. It was all getting to be old history, now. They'd moved on. Ana hoped they didn't revive the soap opera here tonight.

Kate's call from the downstairs intercom came an hour later, and Ana buzzed her in.

"I never thought they'd let me leave," Kate said, pushing into the apartment and dropping her bag by the door. "One more picture, they kept saying. Not like they didn't already have twenty million."

Ana stepped aside, closed the door behind her, and waited. Didn't take long.

DB stood from the sofa and sheepishly waved a couple of arms, while a third skittered a nervous beat that sounded like balloons popping. He'd taken off the oversized jacket and stood in all his shirtless, tattooed glory. "Hey, Kate."

Kate turned to Ana. "What's he doing here?"

DB stepped forward. "It's just for the night, I promise, I'm trying to keep a low profile—"

"I'm a pushover," Ana said, shrugging.

Kate glared, and Ana wasn't sure whom the glare was directed toward. "I hope you have those margaritas ready."

"Two pitchers, ready to go."

They headed into the kitchen, or rather the corner of the apartment that served as the kitchen. DB followed them, sidling along, as delicately as his body allowed. "So, hey, Kate. How you doing?" DB had been nursing a crush on Kate for years now. He wasn't any more subtle about it than he had been back on the set of the first season of *American Hero*. He'd gotten a little more polite, at least.

"I pitched past the sound barrier at Yankee Stadium today, how are you?"

"Um . . . hey, that's great. I think. I just happened to be in town, and, well, we really need to talk—"

Kate said, "Michael, Ana and I planned a night to chill out, with too much alcohol and a lot of TV and not thinking about anything. That's not going to change just because you're here, okay? I can't be mad about Ana letting you stay here. But can you just . . . leave us alone?"

DB sat back on the sofa, his arms folded together contritely.

Feeding everyone margaritas kept them quiet for a little while. Half an hour, maybe. The first DVD of the latest season of *Grey's Anatomy* was good for another hour or so, especially watching the episode where Meredith and Derek spent the whole time fighting over Derek's ethically questionable experiments using a new version of the trump virus on a collection of hideous joker patients. It was pretty awful.

DB chortled through the whole thing. "I wouldn't mind it so much if they actually used joker actors rather than nat actors with fucking rubber tentacles."

Ana agreed with him, but they had to have the rubber tentacles so they could take them off and declare them cured for five minutes before they melted in a hideous ooze of sudden-onset Black Queen.

But the episode finally ended, and in the quiet while Ana changed out DVDs, DB had to ruin it. "Okay, I know you're having your party and all, and I know I'm interrupting—"

Kate, nested on pillows on the floor in front of the TV, took a long drink of margarita and ignored him. Ana almost felt sorry for the guy. He was nice, usually; he'd take a bullet for his friends, and with their history that wasn't just a saying. But he was way too used to being the center of attention, and definitely wasn't used to being ignored by a couple of women.

"—but I really need to talk to you. This is serious. Seriously." The sofa creaked as he leaned forward, and half his hands drummed nervously.

Ana shushed him, got the DVD in and hit play, hoping that would shut him up. But Kate rolled over and glared. "Michael, what are you doing here? Isn't Joker Plague supposed to be on tour in . . . in Thailand or someplace?"

He brightened. "You've been keeping up with us—"

She glowered. "Crazy guess."

"The tour was last month. We're supposed to be recording the new album, but . . . I gotta tell you, it's not going well. I knew we were in trouble when all our songs started being about how tough it is being a band on tour. So I'm telling the guys, maybe we should take some time off, get back to our roots. Hang in Jokertown for a while—"

Kate turned back to the TV.

"—but never mind that. I was doing this signing in LA a week or so ago, and a fan brought me this . . . this *thing*. I think you really need to know that this is out there." He was serious—worried, even, reaching for something in the pocket of his oversized coat, draped over the back of the sofa.

The intercom buzzer at the front door went off.

Ana needed a minute to scramble up from the bed of cushions. Her first margarita was already making her wobbly. She really needed a vacation. . . .

"You expecting anyone?" Kate asked.

"No," Ana said, and hit the intercom button. "Hello?"

"Ana. It's John. John Fortune."

This had to be a joke. Someone had put him up to this. This was too . . . If it had happened to someone else, it would be funny.

"*What?*" Kate said. Both she and DB were staring at her. So yeah, they'd heard it.

She didn't want to argue. "I'll be right down," she said, and left before Kate and DB could say anything.

He was waiting at the front door, hands shoved in the pockets of a ratty army jacket. She couldn't say he looked particularly good at the moment. He was a slim, handsome man, with dark skin, pale hair, and a serious expression. The white lines of an asterisk-shaped scar painted his forehead. At the moment his hair was too long and uncombed, and he looked shadowed, gaunt, like he hadn't gotten enough food, sleep, or both.

"Hi," he said, his smile thin, halfhearted.

"John. Hi. What's the matter?"

"I need a favor." Oh, no, this was not happening. . . . He said, "Can I stay with you? Just a couple of nights."

Any other night . . . "This really isn't the best time. Can't you stay with your mom?"

He winced and rubbed his head. "I would, except she's trying to talk me into coming back to work for her on *American Hero*. And that . . . I can't do that. I'm avoiding her."

"No," she said. "You sure can't."

"I know I should have called ahead . . . but it's just a couple of nights, I promise."

Whatever else she was, Ana was not the kind of person who left a friend standing on the street. She held open the door. "Come on in. Um, I should probably warn you . . ."

Ana half expected Kate to be hiding in the bathroom, the only spot in the studio with a closable door and any modicum of privacy. But she was standing in the middle of the room, side by side with DB, waiting. Ana led John inside and softly closed the door.

John slouched, and his smile was strained. "Hi, Kate."

"Hi," she said, her tone flat. That was it.

"Well," DB drawled. "Look what the cat dragged in."

"Can it, Michael," Ana said. She drew herself up, hands on hips. She'd stared down diplomats from a dozen countries and addressed the UN Security Council. Surely she could lay down the law here. "You're all my friends and I'm not going to leave anybody stranded. But I would appreciate you all acting like grown-ups. You think you can do that?" Nobody said anything, so she assumed that was yes. "I'll heat up some food, we can have dinner. Like normal people." While she pulled food out of the fridge, she listened.

"How you doing?" John said.

"I'm okay," Kate answered. "You?"

He might have shrugged.

Ana hadn't been there when they broke up, but she knew it had been bad—Kate walking out while John was still in the hospital, recovering from having a joker parasite with delusions of grandeur ripped out of his forehead. John had gone from being a latent, to drawing a Black Queen, to having his father die to save his life, to having an ace power in the form of a scarab-beetle ace living inside him—to nathood. And then his girlfriend broke up with him.

But Ana had heard both sides of that story, and John had screwed up as well. He'd never trusted Kate. He kept assuming she would run off with someone else, someone with power—someone like DB. And he threw that in her face. She'd told him she loved him, and he never really believed her, so she walked. Now, Kate had her first real boyfriend in years. Ana wondered how John felt about that, if he even knew. He had to know—Kate was a celebrity, the pictures had been in the magazines.

They'd all met in the first season of *American Hero*—Ana, Kate, and DB as contestants, John working as a PA for his mother Peregrine, producer of the show and arguably the most famous wild carder of all time. Those days seemed dream-like, surreal. Part of some fun-house carnival ride that ultimately meant nothing. So much had happened since then, but that was where it all started. The show was still going strong, riding high in the ratings; Ana didn't pay attention.

DB paced, pounding a double beat on his torso.

"You in town for anything special?" John said to Kate, as if they were alone in the room.

"Yeah, charity pitching derby at the All-Star Game."

"Oh yeah? Cool."

"You?"

"I've been traveling, I guess. Here and there."

This was the most gratingly awkward conversation of all time. Ana wondered if she could fix it by feeding them more margaritas. She went to the kitchen to get started on that.

"I figured you'd be staying with your mom," Kate said.

John rolled his eyes. "I'd have to spend all night hearing about how I should go back to work for her on *American Hero*."

"Oh, *no*," Kate said, with genuine outrage.

The drumming and pacing stopped. "Hey, maybe you can get the Winged Wench to explain *this*. Unless *you* know where it came from."

He held out a DVD case, which he'd retrieved from his coat pocket. Poor quality, low production values, with a photocopied cover shoved behind cheap clear plastic. The title: AMERICAN *HERO UNCUT, VOL. I.*

John gave a long-suffering look at the ceiling. "My mother had nothing to do with that. *I* had nothing to do with that."

Kate yanked the DVD case out of DB's hand and stared at it. "What the hell is this?"

Ana drifted over to Kate's side, to study the case over her shoulder. The image on the front featured DB, all his arms wrapped around the svelte figure of Jade Blossom, another of the first season *American Hero* contestants. Naked Jade Blossom, Ana noted. Her state of undress was obvious even through the shadowed, unfocused quality of the picture. Uncut, indeed—unauthorized footage from the reality show's seemingly infinite number of cameras.

Somehow, Ana couldn't be entirely surprised that such a thing existed. What did surprise her was not stumbling on the footage online somewhere. Now that she knew it existed, she probably wouldn't be able to avoid it.

Kate gaped for a moment, then covered her mouth with her hands and spit laughter. "I'm sorry. It's not funny. But it *is*." She might have been having some kind of fit, doubled over, holding her gut. "Karma's a *bitch*!"

"Look at the back," DB said, making a turning motion with one of his hands. "*This* is what I've been trying to tell you."

When Kate turned the case over to look at the back, Ana almost turned away. The back showed three more pictures: two more of DB, captured in the moment with two entirely different contestants of the show. And one of Kate, her back to the camera, towel sliding off her shoulders as she stepped into the shower. The picture was a tease, of course. How much did the video actually show?

Ana couldn't tell if the red in Kate's cheeks was from alcohol or embarrassment. When Kate set her jaw and hefted the DVD case as if to throw it, all three of them reached for her, making halting noises. Glancing at them, Kate sighed, and merely tossed the DVD back to DB, without her ace power charging it. DB fumbled it out of a couple of hands before managing to catch it.

Kate said, "At least I can say there aren't any sex tapes of me. Unlike some people."

"You had your chance," DB muttered.

Kate glared. The TV played through the pause; two characters were making out in a hospital supply closet.

"Volume I," Ana said. "So how many of those are there?"

"Who the fuck knows?" DB said. "The guy wanted me to *sign* it for him."

"Whoever's doing these has to have access to the show's raw footage." She looked at John, inquiring.

He said, "Could be anyone with access to the editing process. Mom and Josh have a pack of lawyers working on it—you can imagine what it's doing to the *American Hero* brand. But there's not much they can do about it once the videos hit the web."

Ana went to the kitchen and stuck a plate of burritos in the microwave. Food. Food would make everything better. And more margaritas. If she could just get everyone commiserating over the shared trauma rather than making accusations, maybe she could salvage the party.

"I do *not* need this right now," Kate said, and started pacing. "Oh my God, I should tell Tyler . . . but if he doesn't know about it already maybe I shouldn't tell him. . . ."

"Who's Tyler?" DB said.

John smirked. "Haven't you heard? It's been all over *Aces!*. Kate's new boyfriend—she's dating nats now."

"John, don't be an asshole," Ana said. She'd had no intention of bringing this up while the love triangle from hell was in her five-hundred-square-foot apartment. She'd kill John for poking Kate like this.

Kate plowed on. "I told you then, I didn't break up with you because you lost your powers. I broke up with you because I couldn't keep . . . propping up your self-esteem. You kept making the whole thing about you."

"Wait a minute, boyfriend? What boyfriend? Who is this guy?" DB said.

Kate didn't answer, and Ana sure wasn't going to say anything.

DB continued. "No, really—we can settle this. Tyler, huh? I don't care if he's a nat or the king of Persia, I want to meet him. You know, just to make sure he's a nice guy."

"I can pick my own boyfriends, thank you very much," Kate said.

"Apparently not," DB said, pointing three arms at John.

Kate growled and cocked back her arm. Despite watching for it— hoping to minimize damage to the apartment—Ana hadn't seen whatever projectile she picked up; but then, Kate always kept a few marbles in her pocket, for whenever she lost her temper.

"Kate!" Ana yelled. "Cool it! No throwing in the house! Nobody uses *any* powers in the house! Got it?"

The ace pitcher froze, a static charge dancing around her hand. For their parts, John and DB had both ducked, because she kept turning back and forth between them, unable to decide who to target first.

Then her hand dropped. "You know what's real rich? That neither one of you can figure out why I won't go out with you." She stomped into the bathroom and slammed the door.

The microwave dinged, and Ana said, with false brightness, "Anyone want burritos?"

DB and John circled each other, but finally settled down, DB on the sofa and John on a chair in the kitchen. Ana shoved plates of food at them both, and miracle of miracles they ate. She decided against giving them any more margaritas, but took an extra-long drag on one herself before heading to the bathroom to knock on the door.

"You okay?" she said to Kate, angling herself away from the rest of the apartment, hoping the boys weren't listening even though she knew they were.

The door wasn't locked; Kate was sitting at the edge of the bathtub. Ana slipped in and closed the door. Leaned against it, just in case DB or John decided it was a good idea to try to sneak in.

Kate didn't look particularly angry or upset. She did look thoughtful, her brow furrowed and face scrunched up. Finally, she sighed. "It's better knowing it's out there than not knowing, right? I'm not really surprised, I guess. It's just . . . annoying."

Ana quirked a smile. "That's the worst thing you can come up with? Not murderous rage?"

"I'm too tired for murderous rage," Kate said.

"I'll kick them out. Say the word and they're gone," Ana said.

Kate sighed. "You can't kick them out. They're still friends. Let's go get some food."

They hugged, and Ana liked to think some of the tension went out of Kate's shoulders.

When they emerged from the bathroom, John was there, holding a glass full of margarita, which he offered to Kate. Giving him a thin smile, she took it.

DB was sitting contritely—as contritely as he could, anyway, slumping, his hands still in his lap—on the sofa. "I'm sorry. I wasn't trying to upset you—I just thought you should know that these are out there."

"No, it's okay. You're right. Better to find out from a friend than in some random interview."

"Do I even need to ask if there's any footage of me on those tapes?" Ana asked.

DB winced. "They got everybody with that shower cam."

She thought for a minute. "Would it be wrong of me to be insulted if I *didn't* show up on an *American Hero* bootleg sex tape?"

"I think you need another drink," John said. He'd produced a second glass from somewhere, and she was happy to take it.

They couldn't argue when they were eating. Ana was starting to be pleased with herself and her diplomatic skills. But, inevitably, conversation started again and circled back around. Wasn't anything Ana could do to stop it.

"So much for the hero part of the show," DB grumbled around a bite of burrito. "Not like it's been about anything but politics and sex scandals since the first season. Nobody's trying to save the world."

"I'm trying," Ana said softly. The margaritas were a warm flush through her system, making her talk more than she usually did. "Maybe it doesn't look like much from the outside, when I spend most of my time in an office, but I'm trying."

Kate frowned. "Seventy-five K for children's cancer research has to count for something."

"It does," John said, maybe too eagerly. "At least I think it does." She gave him a tight-lipped smile.

DB said, "You guys hear what happened to Joe Twitch?"

Joe Twitch, another first season veteran. Being on the show hadn't helped him out at all, and he hadn't saved anything in the end. After falling in with a very bad crowd, the ace had been gunned down in some messed-up police shoot-out.

"Yeah," Ana said, and the others nodded in grim agreement.

Kate shook her head. "Let's hear it for first season alumni. God, we're a mess."

They weren't, not really. Ana had her work, Kate had her charity fundraising. After leaving the Committee, John had done volunteer work overseas, and DB donated a chunk of his concert earnings to the International Red Cross and other refugee aid organizations. He didn't even publicize it. They were all trying, though it felt like spitting into the wind sometimes.

"You know who probably knows something about those videos?" DB said. "Bugsy. He's working for *Aces!* now, he knows everything. Right?" Bugsy, Jonathan Hive, another first season alumnus who now wrote for a tabloid. So maybe they weren't all on the side of angels.

"Not a bad idea," John said. "So who wants to actually call him?"

"We had a little talk awhile back," Kate said, not looking particularly pleased. "He wouldn't tell us even if he knew. But he's got his own problems going on, we don't need to bug him. Um. Sorry. No pun intended."

John smirked. "I'm sure you did talk to him, after that story he did on you and your new boyfriend."

"John!" Ana and Kate both declared, cutting off that track before it went further.

More eating. Ana wished for continued silence. The episode on the TV had wound down, and she wondered if she should turn the DVD back on, for a distraction. DB said to his plate, carefully, "I don't suppose you have that copy of the magazine with the story Bugsy did—"

Kate raised her fork to throw it.

"You really want to know where those bootleg DVDs are coming from?" Ana burst, interrupting. "Why not ask the guys selling them."

"And I suppose you know who that is?" DB said.

"Sure—there's one of those stalls on the Bowery, just a couple blocks from here. You know those creeps who sell bootlegs CDs and everything. I'm sure he's got some of these. Ask *him* where they're coming from."

DB shrugged. "Sounds good to me."

Ana suddenly wished she hadn't said anything, but everyone else embraced the plan. Plates and glasses went into the kitchen sink, leftovers went into the fridge, and DB shrugged on his overcoat.

"Aren't you hot in that?" Kate asked wonderingly.

"I'm incognito," he said, and Kate squeaked out a stifled, tipsy laugh.

In a very brief moment they were all on the stairs heading down and outside.

◆

Ana shouldn't have had that second margarita. Or was that third? Not that it mattered. This was a bad idea, drunk or sober. John caught her arm when she stumbled on the stairs, asked if she was okay. She was sure she was fine, really. Right?

After leaving Fifth, they walked a couple of blocks onto the Bowery. The street was busy—not late enough to have cleared out yet. The sky was dark, but headlights and streetlights and storefronts glared brightly. Some people marched, clearly on missions, to or from work or home or miscellaneous errands. Clumps of people moved together, laughing at each other, out for a night of fun. Like Ana and the others should have been, if they knew what was good for them. The Guatemalan woman who ran the mobile taquería that Ana liked leaned out the window of her truck and shouted in Spanish, and Ana answered, *bueno,* everything was just fine.

This close to Jokertown, no one looked twice at someone who had an extra limb or three or was covered with a layer of fur or scales. But people were looking at DB.

"That coat isn't doing *anything* to disguise you," Kate observed.

DB scowled.

Really, people were staring at all of them. And when people were staring at you in *Jokertown,* you knew you were in trouble.

She almost walked right past the row of storefronts and streetside booths, selling everything from knockoff handbags to cheap souvenirs. It was almost a carnival along this stretch. A guy playing guitar and singing on the corner of Bond had his hat out. Another block or two along the Bowery and you'd be in Jokertown's red light district. But this was where she'd seen the guy with the DVDs. Stopping to take stock, she glanced up the row, then pointed. "There it is."

The guy had wooden racks set up on folding tables, filled with CD and DVD cases that weren't fooling anyone. The covers showed the right images for all the latest hit movies, but they were obviously fourth-generation photocopies. The plastic was cheap, warped, already coming apart. The DVDs inside wouldn't be any more slick or reliable. Buyer beware.

The guy didn't do much business that Ana had ever seen. Downloading had replaced much of the pirate CD and DVD market, she imagined. But guys like this selling crap like this would probably never go away. Not everyone had a fancy computer.

The four of them lined up in front of the stall. The stall owner, or proprietor, or clerk, or whatever, blinked back at them with round, dark eyes. A joker, he had a bony fan of flesh sprouting from his shoulder blades, through a modified slit cut into his T-shirt. Leathery and wrinkled, they didn't look functional as wings, but who could tell.

"Hey, hey. Ana, right? Wha-what can I do for you? *Que pasa?*" His accent might have been Puerto Rican. His smile was strained.

She opened her mouth to say something, then completely forgot what it was she'd been about to say. Some accusation. Swearing, probably. This man was a criminal, she stood for truth and justice, she ought to do something about it. Shouldn't she?

"Where are they?" DB said, looming. The guy cringed, stammered, and DB grabbed the collar of his jacket and hauled him up. "I know you're selling them, where are they?"

"Michael, calm the hell down," Kate muttered, hanging off one of DB's arms.

Ana spotted a Joker Plague CD that might have been used or might have been a bootleg; she decided not to tell the drummer about it. Stepping in front of DB, subtly edging him away from the stall, Ana reminded herself that she was an international agent for good and found her voice again. "He's asking about special stuff that isn't in the racks, that you sell under the table. Right?"

The guy shrugged. A line of sweat dripped from his hairline. "Yeah, I got a lot of stuff. I mean, there's, you know, the triple X stuff—"

She shook her head. "No. Well, sort of. Outtakes from *American Hero*, bootleg behind-the-scenes stuff. I guess some of it's rated X. . . ." She winced.

His eyes widened, and Ana swore if he said something about her being too nice a girl for that sort of thing . . . "You *sure* you want to look at that stuff?" he asked instead. "All'a you. I mean you seem like nice kids, and I haven't watched any of it myself—I'd never do that, you know—but I hear it gets kind of rough."

DB grumbled, "Don't tell me about it—I was there for most of it, Bat Boy."

The joker cringed.

Ana made soothing gestures toward them both. "We want to find out where the videos are coming from—who's distributing them, who's making them. Who might have access to the footage, you know?"

"I don't know any of that—I just get the boxes of 'em from the wholesaler. I don't even look, you know?"

"You have to look—you already said you had some. Can we see what you've got?" Maybe some of the other DVD cases would have identifying information on them, unlike DB's copy.

The joker wore a skeptical frown, but he crouched to pull a cardboard box from under the table and started pawing through it. "I'm telling you, most of what I got's just porn, not from the show. You interested in any of that? I got a bunch of stuff here, ace on ace, ace on joker—"

"Just the *American Hero* stuff," Ana said. John was looking on, interested. DB and Kate were fidgeting, their patience stretching thin. DB pattered a riff on his torso that made people up and down the block look over. Why any of them had thought they could do this without drawing attention . . .

The stall owner pulled DVD cases out of the box and laid them out on his table. They were just as awful as Ana could have imagined, with all seasons of *American Hero* represented, most of the covers featuring particularly photogenic female contestants in various states of undress. And those were probably the least prurient covers of the bunch, because as promised he was selling a bunch of outright porn as well as other reality-based sensationalism.

"What's that?" DB said, grabbing a pair of cases out of the guy's hand. They all leaned in to get a better look.

Large, yellow capital letters, in a bullet-ridden font spelled *JOKER FIGHT CLUB VOL. III.* The image behind the words was murky, showing poorly lit figures moving in a blur. Two men—jokers, large ones, with abnormal muscles and bison-like bulk, one with horns growing from his shoulders, one with claws on his arms, beat on each other. The one who faced the camera had blood covering half his misshapen face. This didn't look staged. It didn't look like special effects.

"Where'd you get this?" Ana said.

"I don't know, they just turn up." He looked scared now, his hands shaking as he tried to grab the cases out of their hands.

She raised a brow at him, skeptical.

DB picked three or four more of the *Joker Fight Club* videos out of the batch. "How can you even sell this crap?" he said, disgusted.

"I gotta pay rent, just like everybody else. Those guys in the fights—they're paying rent, too, wanna bet? You're a joker, you know how it is."

"And what?" Ana said. "These just magically show up in a cardboard box so you can pay your rent? Where do you get them? Who sells them to you?"

He cringed away, but Ana didn't have any illusions that she was the one intimidating him. DB was looming, fury in his gaze.

The guy's vestigial wings flopped weakly against his back. "These ones, the fight club ones, they come from a couple of *hombres* in a white van. They drop 'em off every week or so. They just dropped these off this evening."

"Here?" Kate said. "They were here?" The ace turned to Ana. "You think maybe it's the same people doing the *American Hero* DVDs?"

Ana shrugged. "Worth finding out. Where'd they go?" She glared at the joker, who pointed down the street.

"East. Turned on Houston." Straight into Jokertown. Ana could think of a dozen scenarios where some lowlife gangsters in Jokertown had decided to go into video production and managed to snag the *American Hero* outtakes. Not to mention the other stuff. God, if there was a porn studio in Jokertown she didn't want to know about it. Who was she kidding, there probably was. Never mind.

"How long ago?"

"Hour, maybe?"

DB started shoving DVDs into his coat pockets with two hands. A third threw a couple of tens down on the table. "I'm buying the whole fucking mess," DB said. "Hand 'em over to my lawyers and let them have a crack."

"Wait, what—" The stall owner pawed at the money. "Who do you think you are?"

DB snarled at him in answer and stalked off. Ana, Kate, and John followed.

Ana thought the guy was lucky DB'd given him anything at all and not called the cops. The joker at the stall must have realized that because he didn't argue further. Not that anyone would argue with DB when he got into a mood like this.

Except for John, who should have known better. "So what, we're going to search Jokertown for a white delivery van? How does that make sense?"

"What do you suggest?"

"Exactly what you said, hand it over to the lawyers and let them sort it out."

"Because that's worked so well for you so far."

Ana walked with Kate, leaving the boys arguing in front of them. "Some party, huh?" she said, by way of apology.

Wonder of wonders, Kate smiled. "I'm hanging out with my friends. That was the point, right?"

"I wasn't sure wandering Jokertown at midnight was what you had in mind."

"We always joked about doing it when I was living down here but never got around to it. So, why not?"

"I think you wouldn't be saying this if we weren't quite as drunk as we are."

Kate giggled.

DB stalked ahead like a predator on the hunt; Ana hung back, looking down side streets and alleys. At one point DB stopped somebody—a round, rubbery walrus of a joker selling newspapers out of a cart. The guy looked half amused, half worried when DB demanded to know if he'd seen a van. Amazingly, the guy pointed a direction, turning them down another street off Houston and deeper into Jokertown. Probably just to get rid of the angry seven-foot-tall man in front of him.

Ana had paused to look down another side street when she saw it: *a* white van if not *the* white van. She could just make it out in the light from a streetlamp bleeding into the alley. The back doors were open, and two jokers were hauling a third into the back. The third guy, a huge, lumbering man with muscles layered on muscles, covered with ropy, elephantine skin, seemed to be sick. He wasn't standing on his own, and his head lolled to his shoulder. His friends were probably taking him to the hospital. She wondered if they needed help.

"Hey," Ana said. "Everything okay?"

The first two jokers—one of them slick-skinned with fishy eyes, the other with a second set of arms that were actually tentacles, or vegetative tendrils, or something green and sinewy—looked at her with round, shocky eyes. Instead of answering, they rushed, shoving their charge into the van and slamming the doors.

That was when she noticed the elephantine joker's hands were tied behind his back.

"Hey!" she yelled, while thinking that this was all about to go very wrong in a minute. "Hey, stop!"

DB and the others hand turned back to look at her. She shouted, "Somebody call the police!" She patted her pockets—she usually had her phone in her pocket, where was it?

Tires squealed, filling the alley with smoke and the stink of burning rubber, and the van roared backward, out of the alley, toward Ana. All she could do was stare.

Then she fell, yanked out of the way by three powerful arms, and she crashed against DB's bulk as he pulled her in to the brick wall of the adjacent building.

"Ana, Jesus, you okay?" he asked, propping her up while she regained her feet.

Meanwhile, the van screeched into the street and made an awkward turn before racing down Suffolk. A couple of other cars slammed on brakes and wrenched out of the way. Nobody crashed, but car horns blared.

"The van, those guys in the van, they grabbed someone, it's a kidnapping!"

Kate threw something. She must have had a whole handful of something, because half a dozen projectiles zipped past Anna, crashing into the retreating van with the pings of bullets. Something popped. The van kept moving, rocking on a blown tire.

DB ran after the van. Ana called for him to stop, but he didn't listen.

"Who are those guys?" John asked, joining her along with Kate.

Ana said, "I don't know, they just bundled some guy into the back of the van."

"Well, looks like a party," Kate said, and ran to follow DB.

John had his phone in hand, and Ana sighed with relief. "You call the cops?"

"On the way," he said. "Not sure what else I can do."

"You can help me keep Kate and DB from getting themselves killed."

She thought he might argue, but he snorted and took off running after the others.

Somehow, the van was still going, throwing off sparks from its naked rim; smoke poured out the exhaust. A couple of taxis swerved, tires screeching, but DB and Kate ignored the chaos. Kate cocked her arm back, threw another marble, but the projectile fell short and blew a crater in the street. DB's chest swelled, six hands beating a tangled rhythm along his torso, building, speeding, until he arched his back and let out a wave of sound, a sonic sledgehammer. Ana ducked and covered her ears.

The shock wave caught the van, which lifted off its back wheels, tipped, and tumbled to its side. There were screams, more screeching tires and confused taxis. People running, and Ana wondered how bad this was going to get, and what she could do about mitigating the collateral damage. Her instinct was to get to ground and build a wall—raise enough earth to cordon off the street, isolate the van, keep the kidnappers from escaping. And perpetrate a couple million dollars of damage to the city's infrastructure in the process. She could already hear the press conference after that. So, no. She felt suddenly useless.

She ran toward the van along with John, Kate, and DB. Sirens sounded in the distance. The driver's door was open, the fish-eyed joker driver hauling himself out with impossibly muscular arms. His whole body slithered, powerful and agile, springing to the side—now top—of the van. His huge mouth bared to show needle teeth. Bulging, lidless eyes rolled over his shoulder to look at his pursuers, then he jumped to the far side of the van and out of sight. Kate reached to the ground for a piece of debris and threw. Ana didn't see it land, but heard an explosion. A puff of smoke rose up from the next block. Kate and DB kept running. Ana and John stopped at the van.

"The other guy's unconscious," John said, looking in through the shattered windshield.

The back doors, crumpled and warped, had swung open. Ana looked inside to find two jokers, the elephantine guy and one other, equally muscular and tough-looking, hands and feet and tentacles tied up, mouths gagged. They'd flopped to the side of the van—now the bottom—unconscious. She hoped they were only unconscious.

The blaring sirens rounded the corner—two patrol cars fishtailing onto

Suffolk. "Freeze! Everybody freeze!" one of the cops yelled through a loudspeaker.

The guy in the passenger seat of the van, the joker with vines for an extra set of arms, had woken up. Bleeding from a gash in his head, he managed to crawl to the back of the van and wrestle Ana for the door. Shoving, he knocked her back. He was holding a gun.

"John!" Ana called, dodging to the front of the van to take cover. "Cops are here! Where are Kate and DB?"

John pointed down the street, around the next corner. They'd gone after the driver. Great.

The order came again. "You two! Freeze!"

A shot fired from the back of the van. Cursing came over the loudspeaker behind them, the gunman fired again, and the orders to freeze turned into orders to put the gun down. Ana figured the police had better things to do than go after her and her friends.

"Go!" Ana yelled at John, and they took off, turning onto the next street.

The desk job hadn't been kind to her stamina. Not that she'd ever been in great shape, but she used to do better than this. Two blocks of running and she was heaving. John was ahead of her and pulling away.

Ahead, he hesitated. Rounding the corner in her turn, Ana stumbled up against him in time to see DB go down, screaming. He'd grabbed the fish-eyed joker—who was tall, it turned out. DB only had a few inches on him. The six arms should have given him an advantage, but the joker had done something, let loose some crackling bolt of energy, sparking like a Van de Graaff generator. DB went limp and fell, and the joker fled.

Ana's heart skipped a few beats and she had to concentrate to get her legs moving again. She was afraid of what she'd find when she reached him. "Michael!" she called when she did get moving again, and dropped to the ground beside him. The big joker groaned. Alive, at least.

John yelled down the street, "Kate, stop!"

"I can catch him!"

"He'll kill you!"

"What do you care?"

A pause, and he yelled, "What do you mean, what do I care?"

"Find me something to throw, damn it!"

"Michael?" Ana asked, hand on his uppermost shoulder.

"Wha . . . happen . . ." An arm went to his forehead, and the other five flailed as if attempting to tread water.

"The guy zapped you. You okay?"

"Ung . . ." He rolled over and vomited.

Now that she had time to use her own phone, she fished it out of her jeans pocket. "I'll call an ambulance."

"No, no, I'm . . . shit, I feel like a truck hit me. Don't call an ambulance. Where's the fucker?" He slowly rolled over, propping himself on one hand, wiping his mouth with another. Ana tried to help him up when it looked like he was going to fall over, and grunted with the effort. Guy was *big*.

"You *sure* you're okay?"

Something blew up down the next street. An explosion, followed by a pattering of debris. "The hell?" DB asked. Leaning on Ana, he managed to climb to his feet. He was trembling, and the tympanic membranes on his torso hummed with a sympathetic vibration.

"I don't think you should go running after them."

"Bullshit, I've been through worse than this." He took off, limping.

Another explosion sounded. "Was that one of Kate's?" DB asked.

"Yeah," Ana said, sighing.

"Should I be worried about her or the other guy?"

Good question. "John's looking out for her."

"That loser can't do jack shit." He limped, winced, rotated a couple of sets of shoulders.

"Give him a break, Michael."

"Why should I? He had it all. Kate—the most beautiful, most amazing girl in the world—she picked him and he threw it back in her face. He broke her heart."

She'd done a pretty good job of breaking John's, too, but DB wouldn't listen to that. He might be okay with him and Kate not being together now. But he'd always regret the might-have-been that he'd lost.

That wasn't why Ana winced and looked away, trying to turn the expression into a smile. "I suppose I can always go for runner-up."

"What? Ana, hey, that's not what I—"

"There they are." Ana trotted ahead.

They found John and Kate standing on the next corner, peering around to an empty storefront on Orchard. Periodically, she hurled debris—broken glass, smashed soda cans—at the building. She'd just thrown a piece of brick, which landed with another blast, a shower of concrete. John handed her the next projectile. They argued.

"You really think I don't care if you live or die?"

"John, no, that's not what I meant."

"Then what did you mean? Is that what you think about me?"

"You always make these arguments about you, you know that?"

"What arguments? We haven't said a word to each other in over a year!"

Ana interrupted. "Where'd the fish guy go?"

"Kate's got him pinned down there," John said. Sure enough, the fish-eyed man lurked in the shadows of the shop's interior, hanging back from Kate's wall of destruction. Occasionally, he waved his gun and random shots fired, pinging off the brick wall above them. They ducked back behind the corner, except for Kate, who hurled another missile. Another chunk exploded out of the storefront across from them, but the joker was still there, moving back into the building, gun in hand.

"I'm calling the cops, telling them we're here," Ana said, punching the number into her phone.

DB huffed. "As long as you do all the talking when they get here. You're the diplomat."

She wasn't, really. More like a bureaucrat. Pencil pusher, desk jockey. Babysitter?

The joker tried to make a break for it again, creeping up to a broken doorway. Kate threw, and the guy stumbled back in a panic. "I should just go in there and take him down," DB grumbled. "Drum him out of there."

"And have him blast you again?" Ana said. "No. We wait for the cops."

"If he doesn't shoot us all first," Kate said. "I can't get to him as long as he keeps hiding. Maybe if I bring the whole building down on top of him . . ."

She'd already gotten a good start on that.

"Sure hope they have insurance," DB said. He was grinning.

"Are you actually enjoying this?" Ana said.

"Beats a press conference," he said, and she couldn't argue.

Kate glared. "Are you guys going to help or just stand there staring?"

"I thought I was helping," John said.

"That's not what I meant—"

"Kate—"

The gunfire from the storefront had stopped. The street had gone quiet; a car horn from a few blocks away echoed, and a distant police siren sounded. No fish-like movement flickered in the shadows of the broken glass and brick wall.

"Did you get him?" Ana asked.

"No," Kate said. "He's gone." She growled and threw the piece of glass at the nearby wall; it popped like a firecracker and left a mark like a bullet hole. They ducked as debris pattered around them.

Kate pointed at John. "*You* made me lose him."

"*I* made you—"

The siren rang out behind them now, and a squad car came through the intersection, barreled toward them, and screeched to a stop a few feet away. Ana's first impulse was to run. Which said a lot about the situation, didn't it?

"What the hell are you people doing?" The first cop who stepped out of the car might have been a joker, or a nat with an unfortunate set of features—bulging eyes, scraggly hair.

His partner was definitely a joker. Her shape was enough off the human norm to draw attention, though she ended up being more fascinating than ugly. She was barrel-chested, rib cage hinting at huge lung capacity and vast stamina. Below that she was wasp-waisted, and her legs were powerfully muscled. She was shaped like a greyhound, built for running. No getting away from her.

And she was pissed off. "No. Oh, no, not you guys. Goddamn ace vigilantes. I *hate* ace vigilantes."

Both John and DB responded, earnestly, "I'm not an ace." Kate punched John in the shoulder, and he glared at her.

The four of them stood shoulder to shoulder, regarding the two officers. They looked like kids caught fighting on the playground: gazes on their shoes, scuffing at the concrete. Kate had her arms tightly crossed, maybe to keep her from wanting to throw something.

"Is it one of you who called in a kidnapping?" the nat cop said.

Ana stepped forward. "Yeah. John called it in, but I'm the one who saw it. In an alley off Suffolk. There were two of them, the guy they pulled into the back of the van was unconscious—"

"Can you describe the driver of the van?" she asked.

"Gray, pale, bald. Big black eyes. Fishy, almost."

"And he's got some kind of badass electric shock," DB added. "Beat the *shit* out of me."

The joker cop—Michaelson, the name badge on her uniform read—scowled. "That would be the Eel. We've been on his tail for a while." She exchanged a look with her partner; neither seemed happy.

"So that really was a kidnapping?" Ana said. "I wasn't just imagining it."

"Don't give yourself a medal just yet," said the first cop—Bronkowski. "Which way did he go?"

Kate hitched a thumb over her shoulder, to the corner and the next street. "Saw him running that way. I almost had him until I got distracted." Again, she glared at John, who glared back.

Michaelson spoke into the radio at her shoulder, and a garbled answer came back. It must have made sense, because she nodded. "Right. I'm going to need you all to come down the station—"

"But we didn't do anything wrong!" DB grumbled.

"—just to make a statement. You think you can do that?"

Yes, they finally agreed. They could do that.

Michaelson's radio crackled again, and she replied. "Right, on our way." Turning back to them, she admonished, "Let us catch the bad guys, and you guys get yourselves to the precinct. Don't make me come after you."

With that, she and Bronkowski climbed back into the car. The spinning red and blue lights splashed across them as the car pulled away. Ana squinted and ducked away at their glare. Kate groaned. "So we're going to spend the rest of the night at a police station? Some party."

"All the best parties end that way," DB said, chuckling.

Ana sighed. "At least we did some good. I think." Some tiny amount of good. Assuming the kidnapping victims in the back of the van were okay.

"Kate," John said, his tone earnest, and Ana wanted to smack him before he said another word. Couldn't he just let it go? "I really do worry about you—"

"John—" Kate stopped herself, closed her eyes. Maybe counting to ten. "I know. But I'm fine. Really. Can we just go talk to the police now?" She started walking.

"I could really use another margarita," DB said, following her.

"Yeah," Ana said. That second pitcher still sat in the fridge. If only they could get to it before morning.

John stared after Kate. "It's not like I'm trying to annoy her. It just comes out that way."

"Maybe you should stop treating her like she's different. Like she's some sparkly fairy ice queen. You know?"

He pursed his lips, confused, which she took to mean that he didn't. "I just—"

"John, let it go." He only slouched a little before squaring his shoulders, settling his expression into something resembling calm as he walked off after the others. Ana needed her own moment to gather herself.

The sharp crack of a gunshot rang. Instantly, instinctively, Ana dropped to the concrete even as she looked for the source. The others had done likewise—they all had experience with getting shot at. Another shot fired— and DB roared, falling back, a spot of red bursting from the sleeve of his coat. *Shit.*

Ana saw the flash of shining gray skin in the streetlight at the opposite corner. The Eel, crouching in hiding, leveling his gun for another shot at the trio walking half a block ahead of Ana.

He'd targeted them because they were the dangerous ones; at least the ones who *looked* dangerous. People tended to glance right past Ana. Just as well.

She shouted a wordless warning, and one hand went to her St. Barbara medallion, which she clutched through her shirt. The other she spread flat on the pavement.

This wasn't like digging into bare soil, tilling a garden or drilling a well, actions that came as easily to her as touching air. The city was full of dirt, rock, soil, but it had a crust over it, concrete and steel, and she had to get past that to get to her power. She almost had to trick herself— technically, asphalt was earth, containing bits and fragments, if she could work past the tar and additives. Concrete *did* have a trace of soil in it.

She pushed, found the layer between the streets and sidewalks and tunnels underneath, found the substrate through which the city had insinuated its limbs and tendrils. Then, she *shoved*.

The street trembled with the sound of an earthquake. Pavement cracked, crumbled. A section of sidewalk rose on a pillar of earth, pressing upward from under the city itself—trapping the kidnapper on its peak. Debris rained down the sides, bits of concrete broke off and fell. The pillar climbed a full story high. The joker was trapped in the open, unable to flee, unable to move. He'd flattened himself to the broken sidewalk, gripping the edges, staring down with fearful eyes.

She could feel the city's infrastructure—pipes and conduits, straight concrete and steel running like veins through the earth—and avoid the obstacles, for the most part. Curl the earth around it, nudge it aside. As careful as she tried to be, a water main broke, and a geyser spewed from a crack in the street, spilling a river into the gutter.

Well, so much for minimizing damage. At least the joker was caught.

Except that he looked down to the crevice and the flood pouring out of it, gave a determined nod, and jumped.

It should have been a suicide move, except halfway down he changed, his body morphing. His clothing ripped and fell away as he elongated, his limbs shrinking, his head bulging. Now, he didn't just seem like some slimy sea creature, he was one, and he disappeared into the flooded crack in the pavement and into the sewer pipes. Gone.

"Damn, didn't see that coming," DB said.

The others had doubled back and now huddled in a crouch behind her, holding onto ground that had turned unstable. DB clamped a hand over a bloody wound on an upper shoulder. Seemed okay, otherwise. Ana sighed with relief.

"What did he think he was doing?" John said.

"Thought he could get the jump on us," Kate said. "Idiot."

"Doesn't matter, he still got away." Ana sighed.

DB looked at her. "You okay?"

Using her ace had burned the last of the tequila out of her system. Now, she was just tired. She brushed grit off her hands and sat back against the nearby wall.

Over the sound of gushing water, the wail of police sirens returned. This was going to take a little more explanation than last time. Perfect end to the night, really.

The patrol car arrived, splashing through the river of water now pouring down the street. It stopped, and the whippet-shaped Officer Michaelson stepped out, followed by her partner, Bronkowski. She regarded them, arms crossed. "Can't leave you clowns alone for a second, can I?" None of them had an answer to that, and she continued, "I'm going to need you all to come with me."

Ana looked to her friends, but they were all staring back at her like they expected her to do something. She sighed. "Officer, please, Michael's hurt—"

"Not *that* hurt . . ." he muttered.

"You want to argue with me, go right ahead, that'll give me an excuse to put cuffs on the whole lot of you."

"Bugsy would love that for *Aces!*," Kate muttered.

"At least someone would get something out of the night," Ana replied.

They could make a break for it. A couple of cops against the Committee. Well, the scattered remnants of the original Committee, at least. And Team Hearts of *American Hero*. The more Ana thought about it, the lamer it sounded.

Two more squad cars pulled up, more cops spilling out—some with guns drawn. Who were the bad guys again?

A big—monstrously big—joker, with fur and horns to boot, trotted toward them. "Rikki, Bugeye, you guys got a problem here?"

Michaelson smirked at the aces. "I don't know, do we?"

They didn't.

Ana at least talked Michaelson and Bronkowski into taking them to the Jokertown Clinic first, to get DB's arm looked at.

"Just another scar to add to the collection," he said. He had a gauze bandage taped over the wound. The bullet had just grazed him, and a nurse had cleaned it out and stopped the bleeding. He probably wouldn't even need stitches.

"You could have been killed," Ana muttered. Now that the adrenaline—and margaritas—had worn off, the danger was only now becoming apparent. They should have called the cops, and waited.

But no, then the two kidnapped jokers would be gone. Instead, they were lying on gurneys in the Jokertown Clinic emergency room, and they were going to be okay.

Daylight had started to press through the room's glass doors. The four of them sat in a row of worn plastic chairs in the emergency room waiting area, right where Michaelson told them to sit. The place smelled tired and antiseptic. Way too many sick and hurt people had moved through this room.

Michaelson and her partner had taken up position by the door. The muffled voice in her radio said something, and Michaelson relayed the information that the passenger in the van, the other joker, had been arrested. In the meantime, dawn had broken, and Ana really wanted to go home. When Kate smashed a hand against a wall, they all jumped."Sorry," she muttered, studying the crushed insect on her hand. "I thought it was Bugsy. It's just a fly."

Now Ana was convinced she heard a buzzing in her ear and looked around expecting to see one of the reporter's green wasps reconnoitering.

After what seemed like half the night, the whippet-looking cop—Officer Michaelson—came over, along with a plainclothes detective. Young guy, but grim-looking, with a set to his jaw that might have been there awhile.

"I'm Detective Francis Xavier Black," he said.

Ana stood, brushed off her clothes, offered her hand for him to shake. "Ana Cortez," she said. "These are—"

"Um, yeah, I know who you all are," he said, in a tone that indicated he was chagrined about the whole thing. "Rikki tells me you tore up half the Lower East Side playing vigilante."

And what was she supposed to say to that? Should she call a lawyer? And wouldn't Lohengrin love that. . . . The others looked at Ana, like they expected her to play diplomat. They expected her to throw herself on that grenade, and after she'd fed them all burritos and margaritas.

"Why do I have to do all the talking and herding cats and crap?" she said to them, pouting.

"Because you're good at it?" Kate said.

Ana blinked at her. Really? Well. Okay then. She straightened and matched Black's gaze squarely. She'd met the president for crying out loud, she could face him. "We called the police as soon as we realized something was wrong. You'll have to tell me where the line between concerned citizen and vigilante is."

"Or I could have a judge do it," Detective Black said, shrugging.

"Give me a break," Kate muttered, slumping back in her chair.

DB, easily the biggest guy in the room, drew himself up and thudded his chest. The sound reverberated through the floor. "We were only trying to help."

Ana said, "I saw someone get hauled into the back of the van—it looked like a kidnapping. I wasn't just going to sit by and watch. I wasn't wrong, was I? That really was a kidnapping."

"And what were you doing wandering around Jokertown at midnight?" he asked.

Like he couldn't believe she would do something like that. "It's a free country."

Black sighed, and Ana got the feeling he'd been awake and working for a very long time. He said, "You weren't imagining it. There've been a spate of kidnappings over the last few weeks. We haven't had a lot of luck tracking down the victims or perpetrators. Catching Rance is a big break." Rance must have been the other kidnapper, with the extra limbs.

"So we actually helped," John said, brightening.

"Yeah, well, don't think you need to *keep* helping."

"Look," Ana said. "I can help put the street back together. Free excavation services. Just let me know."

Black nodded, and Ana expected she'd be getting a phone call from the city before too long. Then he turned to DB. "You picked up some DVDs from a stall on the Bowery, right?"

"Yeah?"

"I'm going to need to take those into evidence, if you don't mind." He winced. Maybe afraid he was going to have to argue with DB, which would make anyone wince.

"Why?" DB said.

"Part of an ongoing investigation."

"Having to do with the kidnapping? What the hell is going on, really?"

He hesitated, as if debating how much he could share. "It's early yet, I'm afraid I can't discuss details. But getting those disks would really help." Ana nudged DB's shoulder, and the joker pulled DVDs out of his copious coat pockets without further prodding. He'd managed to stash a dozen or so.

"Thank you, Mr. Vogali, I really appreciate this," Black said. The detective sorted through them, looking at titles, and nodded in satisfaction. "You'll be free to go just as soon as you give statements to Officer Michaelson. Thanks again, and please—try to stay out of trouble. We really don't need any more paperwork." Offering a weary smile, he turned away.

Michaelson appeared with a stack of clipboards and forms. "You need to fill out reports and contact info. Are you willing to testify if this goes to court?"

Testifying in court seemed like the easy part at this point. At least Michaelson had stopped threatening to arrest them.

In the middle of filling out her statement, Ana's phone rang, and she fumbled in her pocket for it. Caller ID said Lohengrin. Great. She couldn't avoid this, only delay it, so she went ahead and answered. "Yeah?"

"Earth Witch," he said, his accent making the name sound lilting and exotic. "You're in the news this morning. What happened?"

Already? She groaned. "It's a very long story. Can I tell you later?"

Then DB's phone rang. Then John's. Then Kate's. The story must have hit the papers, the Internet, the morning talk shows, and everything in between, all at the same time. Ana caught sound bites of conversation.

From DB: "No, Marty, I'm fine. Everything's fine . . . what do you mean, doing something stupid? I didn't do anything stupid!"

From John: "Mom, I wasn't trying to cause trouble . . . can we talk about this later?"

And Kate: "I'm fine, Tyler, really. No . . . yes . . . yes, it was kind of stupid, but I'm not going to apologize. See you tonight?"

Lohengrin was still talking, and Ana didn't really care that she'd missed half of what he was saying. ". . . return to the office, right now."

She took a deep breath. "I'm sorry, could you repeat that? It's really loud in here."

"I've arranged a press conference in two hours. You need to state on the record that your actions last night were in no way associated with the UN, and the Committee is not operating on American soil. I need you here for a briefing. After the press conference, I'm sending you to Mexico while this clears up."

Oh, for God's sake. She really wanted to feel like she was doing good—but did there have to be quite so many hoops for her to jump through? She pressed her St. Barbara medallion through her shirt and concentrated on being polite.

"I'm at the Jokertown Clinic right now—"

"Are you hurt?" To his credit, he actually sounded concerned.

"No, I'm just tying up a few loose ends. I'll get there as soon as I can, but it might take a while."

"Two hours, Earth Witch."

She hung up.

DB finished his conversation next, clicked off his phone, and regarded Ana. "How much trouble are you in?"

"Don't ask," Ana said, frowning. "You?"

"That was my manager," DB said. "The record label's threatening legal action if I don't get back in the studio. I need to go to LA and sort it out."

"I guess getting sued makes recording another album not sound so bad?" Ana asked.

"For now. But I'm thinking it may be time to go indy. Don't tell anyone I said that."

"Just keep an eye out for Bugsy, yeah?" They both looked over their shoulders at that one.

The others had finished their calls and caught the last bit of the conversation. "LA, huh?" John said. "I'm heading that way, too, looks like. I have a job interview."

Kate's eyes grew wide. "Not for *American Hero*—"

"No. Mom's charitable foundation needs a new manager. I told her I'd only consider the job if I applied for it just like everyone else."

"Great," Kate said. "I think."

"Hey Ana, can I put you down as a reference?"

"Sure, but a letter from Lohengrin might sound more impressive," she said.

"I think I'd rather have one from a friend."

They looked at Kate next, with expectation. She blushed. "That was Tyler. Just, you know. Checking in."

Ana tensed, expecting a jab from one or the other of the guys, and Kate's defensive reaction. But it didn't happen.

"Cool," DB said thoughtfully, and that was that.

John looked down the row of them, and wonder of wonders, he was smiling. It had been a while, Ana realized.

"You guys have an hour before we all go flying off?" he said. "I want to show you something."

An hour after returning to Ana's flat to wash up and retrieve some cash, they ended up standing in a row, staring at the newest waxworks diorama at the Famous Bowery Wild Card Dime Museum.

They'd caused a scene at the ticket booth on the way in—how could they not? The four of them together, for the first time since before the famous press conference when Drummer Boy quit the Committee. Tourists snapped pictures on cell phones, and Ana cringed because the photo would be all over the Internet in seconds, and she'd get a million phone calls, and yet another summons to the office of Lohengrin to explain herself. But that didn't matter.

The joker at the ticket counter, a girl in her late teens with green scales and a sagging throat sac, wouldn't let them pay, no matter how much they argued about it. They finally let her give them tickets, but Ana shoved forty bucks into the donation bucket in the front lobby out of spite. Then John led them to a display that was so new it still had signs announcing its grand reveal. They'd stared at it for five minute before saying a word, when Michael declared what they were all thinking.

"That's fucked up," he said flatly.

They, or rather waxworks versions of them, battled the Righteous Djinn in Egypt. Seven feet of Drummer Boy stood in the back, mouth open in a scream, all six arms flexed, some mythological creature captured in sculpture. Curveball braced, as if on a pitcher's mound, her arm cocked back, ready to throw the stone she held. John Fortune held a commanding hand upraised; the smooth gem of Sekhmet was still imbedded in his forehead. And there was Earth Witch, her expression a calm contrast to the others, kneeling on the ground, lock of black hair falling over her face, pressing her hand down where a realistic-looking crack in the rock opened under her touch. The Djinn hovered above them all, laughing. His features were too plastic to make Ana think he was real. The wires suspending him from hidden rafters were visible. She could look at the image, detached, impassive, and not flash back to the scene as she remembered it, the sounds of screaming, blood soaking into sand, bullet ripping through her own gut. She didn't remember it hurting so much as she remembered falling, and fading as the world turned upside down around her. She pressed a hand to her side, where the scar lay under her shirt.

They were all there: Rusty, Bubbles, Bugsy, everyone who'd made the trip to Egypt to try and save the world. An "In Memoriam" section featured Simoon, Hardhat, King Cobalt. It all felt like it had happened to someone else, in another life.

Two different artists had worked on the figures, and one had clearly been less talented. The Drummer Boy figure was uncanny, every flexed muscle accurate, the rictus of his scream exact in its lines and tension. On the other hand, Earth Witch might have been positioned to be partially hidden because her face was unnaturally smooth, the bend of her body slightly awkward. Ana imagined that not too many people would notice, distracted by special effects: LEDs in Curveball's hand, John's forehead, and the Djinn's arms seemed to bring their powers to life. From hidden speakers, the sound of a desert sandstorm hissed. The smell of baking, sandy air came back to her, and Ana couldn't tell if her memory generated the sensation, or if the museum really was piping in the chalky, throat-tickling smell.

Kate tilted her head, her brow furrowed. "Are my boobs really that big?" The figure's chest bulged inside a too-tight white T-shirt.

"No," John said.

Everyone looked at him. Kate crossed her arms, and if she'd had any ace power at all in her gaze, John would have been flayed.

Ana laughed. Then laughed some more, hand clamped over her mouth, gut spasming in her effort to stop. They were probably thinking she was crazy. She'd had a lot of surreal things happen to her, even by the standards of wild card Manhattan. But this had to win the prize. "I'm sorry," she said, trying to catch her breath, hiccupping. "It's just . . . it's just . . . never mind."

They didn't have much time left and cruised quickly through the rest of the museum. The Great and Powerful Turtles' shells suspended in procession, the depictions of history that had been old before any of them were born. There was a curtained-off "Adults Only" exhibit, one of the classic dioramas that had been here for decades. John stopped there. "That's . . . yeah. That's the one on my dad. I'll pass."

Put it like that, Ana decided she'd pass, too. They all did.

Outside, the bright afternoon sun gave her a headache. She had to be at the UN in half an hour, when what she really wanted was a glass of water and sleep. But she didn't really want to leave the others. She wasn't ready for the night to be over—even though it was the middle of the next day.

John said, "This is going to sound really weird—but I'm glad we could do this. You know—get together."

"Drink some margaritas, fight a little crime," Kate said.

DB added, "Like what, 'Team Hearts catches muggers for old times' sake'? " He scoffed, but Kate bowed her head and smiled.

At least nobody died this time, Ana thought, but didn't say it. She didn't want to ruin the mood. "Maybe we can do it again sometime."

They exchanged phone numbers and called cabs. Having reached a compromise with his mother that didn't involve *American Hero,* John agreed to return home for a visit before moving on. DB's manager had arranged a flight back to LA. Everyone managed hugs. Even Kate and John, though theirs was fleeting. Still, if those two could be civil to each other, maybe world peace had a chance.

Before folding himself into his cab, DB leaned over Ana—his immense body filled her vision—rested a hand on her shoulder, and kissed her on the cheek. His other hands pattered a beat. Straightening, he smiled. She was shocked, and embarrassed to notice she was blushing red hot. "Call me next time you're in town?" she said.

"You bet."

His cab drove off, and Kate stared at Ana. "What was that about?"

She couldn't even make a guess.

Ana and Kate shared a cab. Kate would stay at the apartment—catching up on sleep, if she knew what was good for her—while Ana went to work to try to talk Lohengrin off the ceiling. Not likely she'd succeed, but she'd try. "I'm sorry the night didn't really go the way I planned it."

"Maybe not," Kate said, and her smile was bright. "Still, it was a hell of a party."

Ana couldn't argue with that.

Galahad in Blue

Part Five

HE HAD MET CURVEBALL and Drummer Boy. And he'd been a complete zero, a modern day Joe Friday, just the facts, ma'am. He could have done something to make an impression . . . but no. At least he'd managed to take custody of the DVDs that Drummer Boy had grabbed.

By the time he got back to the Five, Joe Rance, small-time hood with a lot of arrests and a lot of pleas, had already lawyered up. Franny studied the multi-limbed joker in his cell. "Has he said anything?" Franny asked Sergeant Vivian Choy.

"He asked for a lawyer and then clammed up. That's the problem with career criminals," she said. "They get arrested enough times and *we* end up teaching them how to beat an interrogation. You get anything from the aces?"

"Not a lot. They did have these." He showed her the DVDs. Franny jerked his head toward the multi-limbed joker. "Is his lawyer still around?"

"No, Flipper had a court date."

"Great. I'll leave a message, and meantime I'll check these out," Franny added, gesturing with the DVDs.

"Take the player out of Mendelberg's office and plug it in in the conference room. The one in there is a piece of shit."

"Thanks."

Once he had everything set up Franny loaded one of the fight club videos. The images of the screaming spectators were almost more revolting than the two jokers locked in combat in the ring below. Under the bright lights the blood seemed garish, almost fake. The people watching weren't rednecks in T-shirts and jeans. They wore tuxedoes and floor-length gowns. The lights glittered off diamonds and gold cuff links, and glistened in their sweat-damp faces. Discreetly attired waiters moved through the crowd carrying silver trays with champagne flutes.

Franny was too new in Jokertown to be able to identify many of the jokers who passed beneath the camera's unfeeling lens. If Father Squid were here, he would have known them. Franny decided to ask for help from Dr. Finn. Some of these people had probably passed through the clinic.

He picked up another DVD, the handwritten label read *And the Beat Goes Down*. Franny loaded it. Drummer Boy's broad back and hips pumped accompanied by harsh grunts, and a woman's shrill cries. At one point they rolled over placing the woman on top and Franny recognized Tiffani, one of the contestants from *American Hero*'s first season. Face flaming, Franny quickly ejected the DVD, feeling like a Peeping Tom. He picked up another one—*Bath Time* was the title. He watched Jade Blossom squeeze water down her back as she lolled in a bathtub. The next cut was of Curveball, one long shapely leg extended out of the water as she scrubbed down with a loofah. He kept watching that one. He tried another, and another. The disks were a mix of the fight club and sex tapes from *American Hero* featuring Drummer Boy fucking an astonishing number of the female contestants.

He stood and paced around the conference room table. Did the *American Hero* disks qualify as evidence? He knew he needed to watch the fight disks, but this stuff? His stuttering thoughts settled, and he picked up a fight club disk and a sex disk and compared the printing on the titles. It looked like the same hand had lettered both. So maybe the same cameraman? But it wasn't like he'd signed his work, so who would know? He needed to talk to somebody associated with the making of *American Hero*. He knew Peregrine had something to do with it.

The door to the conference slammed open, and Sergeant Taylor, who was normally on the desk, rushed in. His eyes were wide, and his usually drooping wings were fluttering with agitation.

"Detective! You're wanted! At the holding cells!"

"Why? What?"

"You can see faster than I can explain," Homer said.

Franny ran. There was a clot of people gathered around the door of Rance's cell. Franny pushed through them, and checked at the sight of Joe Rance slumped on the steel toilet, orange jumpsuit around his ankles.

Gordon the Ghoul knelt at the man's side holding one wrist. The extra, vine-like appendages between his waist and his real arms were blackened and wilted as if a fire had swept down those faux arms. Gordon climbed back to his feet and dusted off the knees of his slacks with an embroidered handkerchief.

"What happened?" Franny demanded of nobody and everybody.

"Somebody made him dead," the pathologist answered.

"Yes, thank you. I gathered that. How?"

Gordon rolled the body off the john, and inspected the blackened posterior. "Electrocuted. Got him right in the ass."

"God *damn* it!" Franny swung his fist at the wall, only to have it caught by a giant paw tipped with vicious claws.

"Don't," Beastie said. "You'll just hurt yourself."

"I never even got a chance to talk to him!" Franny took several deep breaths, fought for control. "Did he say anything? Anything at all?"

Head shakes all around.

"Should have let me squinch him down, and put him in the castle," Jessica Penniman said. Slender and delicate with flyaway blond hair, she didn't match anyone's idea of a cop.

Vivian Choy glared at her. "Hard to question a suspect when they can barely talk because their vocal cords are the size of threads."

"Harder when they're dead," Jennifer snapped back.

"Stop it," Franny ordered. Amazingly both women did.

Gordon motioned to a couple of orderlies, who entered the cell and loaded the body on a gurney. "I'll have the autopsy report for you tomorrow," the medical examiner said as the sad little parade passed by. "But I'm pretty confident I won't find anything more."

Franny went to his desk and began writing up the report. The death of a prisoner in custody would bring in internal affairs, and lawsuits would follow. He could just imagine the reaction of the precinct brass to this FUBAR.

Aside from the bureaucratic shit that was about to hit the fan, there were very real consequences for his case. This was the first real, clean break they'd had, and now the suspect was dead. He asked Bronkowski and Michaelson to stop by his desk to see if Rance had said anything to them during his arrest. Typically Bugeye refused, but Michaelson agreed. Unfortunately Rikki had nothing to add. "He was pretty woozy," she said, as she fidgeted in the chair next to his desk. "Look, if there's nothing else, I'm beat. My shift ended hours ago." She stood up, and stretched her whip-lean body. "Sorry Eel got away from us. If he hadn't, Rance would still be alive."

Franny sat, drumming his pen on his desk. It was a safe bet that Eel was behind the murder. Franny pictured the sewers beneath the city, a highway, albeit a disgusting one, for Eel. He could travel everywhere, enter anywhere. And Franny was the lead investigator on this case. He wondered if his home address was obtainable online? Probably, everything was. He pictured himself vulnerable, sitting on the toilet taking a crap. His sphincter tightened. Do they still sell chamber pots, he wondered? A bucket would work too. He resolved to stop at a hardware store before he went home that night.

He realized he had left the DVDs in the conference room when Homer had burst in. Franny went to collect them, and stood holding them for a long moment. All hell was about to break loose over this murder. He really didn't have time to call Peregrine right now. Could he ask Stevens? Would his supposed partner be willing to do that for him? Then Franny realized that he knew someone who had federal clout, and who had actually been on *American Hero*. He returned to his desk, and called Stuntman. The agent answered on the first ring with a terse, "Norwood."

"I confiscated some DVDs this morning," Franny began. "Some of them show my missing jokers fighting in a kind of gladiatorial arena, but others are from the first season of *American Hero,* and they're . . . well, let's just say somebody had pinhole cameras where there shouldn't have been cameras. What's clear is that the same person prepared both the fight club DVDs and these Contestants Gone Wild DVDs from *American Hero.*"

"Am *I* on any of these DVDs?" Norwood's voice was low and rather dangerous.

"Not that I saw. I just thought given that you were on the show you might have contacts."

"Why can't you do it?"

"I've got problems. A prisoner died while in custody." Franny wasn't going to say more, but he knew a shitstorm was about to break over his head, and he had a feeling he was going to get blamed for what had happened to Joe Rance. "One of the people kidnapping jokers. This could have broken the case. He could have told me where they were taking them. Where they are now! They're in that ring, and it's brutal. Some of them have to have died." Disgust at his own impotence choked off the words. Worse, Franny realized he'd shown weakness and admitted to police incompetence to a Fed. He waited for the inevitable insult.

Instead there was a long silence, and Norwood said quietly, "I'm sorry. I understand these are your people being taken. I'll talk to Michael Berman, he actually runs the show, see what I can find out."

"You'll let me know what you learn?" Franny asked.

"Absolutely."

"I'll make copies of the DVDs and send them over to you." Franny hung up.

It was late afternoon by the time he'd finished copying the DVDs and sent them to Norwood, finished his report, talked to internal affairs and Rance's public defender.

"Well, that's unfortunate," the joker lawyer wheezed asthmatically. "Rance told me he was open to making a deal in exchange for immunity."

That little tidbit added to Franny's sense of despair and the stunning headache that had settled behind his eyes. He realized it was nearly six P.M., and he'd had nothing to eat since the night before. He started out in search of dinner, only to be waylaid by Apsara. "Remember, tomorrow night, Starfields, eight o'clock. Dinner with my parents. They're looking forward to meeting you. And wear your dress uniform."

"That's just for funerals and parades," he said, his headache intensifying.

"They don't know that, and you look very handsome when you wear it." She started away with that swaying dancing gait.

But Franny had had it. Three long strides and he caught her by the upper arm. "No." He pulled her aside and said in a low voice, "I'm going along with this for your sake, but I don't like it, and I'm not going to act like a clown."

Tears welled up in her eyes and trembled on the ends of her lashes.

"Forget it, Apsara, the tears won't work. And what does your phi think of all this?" It was low of him, but it had the desired effect.

"You're right," she whispered. "Be yourself, Frank."

"I could recommend the same to you," he growled.

Those About to Die . . .

Part Four

THE DOOR SWUNG OPEN and the guard prodded him forward and he slid out onto the smooth floor of a small arena. He blinked under the bright lights, barely able to make out the ranks of expectant faces that ringed him. They stared at him from behind a wall of thick glass. Above it, a crosshatch of netting enclosed the space. Whatever this was, he was trapped in it.

The guard shoved him forward, and then retreated back through the door. It closed, trapping Marcus in the oval. *This can't be happening*, he thought.

He'd told himself that again and again since he'd woken up in that small room with Asmodeus and Dmitri. He'd said it several times to Father Squid as they talked. The priest—kindly, grave, the membranes of his eyes sliding closed and then opening again—had assured him that it was, in fact, happening. "We are trapped in a garden of evil," he had said. "Have courage, son."

Marcus gaped at the spectators. Men and women in suits and fancy dresses, champagne glasses in hand. Fat men grinned their pleasure. Beautiful women rubbed up next to them, bejeweled and gaudy. Some of them clapped. A few shouted at him, jeers or encouragement—he wasn't sure which.

Set apart from the others, a private box hung above the netting. An old couple inside of it. The woman looked like some ancient librarian with shockingly red hair. What the fuck was she doing here? The man was a twisted monstrosity in a wheelchair, with wires and tubes running all over him, connecting him to the machines that crowded behind him. Attendants hovered around him as if he might croak at any moment. He looked like he was close to it. His gaping mouth drooled. His face twitched. His palsied hands squeezed in on themselves. Head cocked to one side, eyes closed, breathing labored: he was a monster, a knotted deformity of a man.

Lining the wall at the back of the box was a row of big-shouldered men in black suits and dark sunglasses. They looked like some Hollywood versions of Russian gangsters on steroids. It went without saying that they were packing.

Who were these people? Why were they here and what did they want from him? Asmodeus may have explained it, but it still seemed mad and unreal.

A voice spoke over the commotion, announcing him. "IBT in his debut bout, ladies and gentlemen. Vigilante of Jokertown. Serpent of the sewers. Villain or hero? You be the judges. Place your bets."

This can't be happening.

The door at the other side of the oval swung open. Through it, Marcus saw a figure in silhouette. His heart hammered. The figure was like something dredged out of his childhood nightmares. It emerged into the light, a perversion of a centaur, horrific in a way that made Marcus's skin crawl. From his torso up he was humanoid, but beneath he merged into a bulbous, arachnid body, with eight long, segmented legs.

The announcer spoke over the new tumult of applause. "The Recluse, ladies and gentlemen. Reluctant combatant with a deadly sting. Veteran of three bouts. A battle of half men, the first ever such bout in the entire history of gladiatorial combat. Betting remains open until the first contact . . ."

The lights above the audience faded to black, leaving just the ring alight. The announcer spoke on, but Marcus stopped hearing him. He stopped hearing anything, or seeing anything but the spider-man. He watched him through ripples in the air, like heat waves. They distorted his vision, but they also brought waves of clarity. Crystal-clear images and understanding.

The spider-man circled to the left. The sharp tips of his legs skittered across the floor with audible clicks and scratches. At first, it looked like he was trying to run, searching for an exit. Marcus knew that was a ploy. The more he watched him, circling to stay away from him, the more he saw the man was sizing him up, testing him, trying to trick him. He kept saying something. Marcus saw his teeth gnashing together. He swayed crazily, his arms lashing at the air. His eyes flashed cold and savage, cut with highlight and shadow cast from the harsh lights.

He's insane, Marcus thought.

The guy kept up such a frantic scurrying that Marcus felt trapped, pressed up against the glass wall that hemmed him in. He bunched his coils beneath him, and hovered above them, looking for a way to attack. His tongue trembled in his mouth, venom-soaked and ready to dart out. But he couldn't get his aim set. The guy's upper body wouldn't stay still. He was trying to hypnotize him with the motion, confuse him.

This fucker wants to kill me.

Marcus surged at him, trying to get a good shot at the guy's face. His venom needed to hit skin, not the man's shell-encrusted legs or hairy underbody. Marcus shot, too early, poorly aimed. His tongue darted out a full ten feet. It nailed nothing but the air beside the spider-man's head. He snapped it back. He swung his momentum into a haymaker. His fist would have caught the man's jaw perfectly, but, before it did, one of those sectional legs clipped it at the wrist. The blow slammed Marcus's arm down onto the stone floor, yanking his body with it.

Marcus writhed on the floor, trying to wrench his arm free as his opponent's bulbous, hairy black torso loomed over him. He punched at the joker's underbelly with his free hand, slamming it again and again. It responded by pressing him down, rising and turning and pressing him down again. It was sickening. When it rose a third time Marcus caught sight of a jagged barb protruding from the underbelly. All the pressing and rising was just to keep him down while he moved into position to strike.

Marcus's flesh tore as he ripped his arm from under the leg that pinned it. His torso corkscrewed him out of there just as the barb slammed down against the stone that had been beneath him. He rose up so fast that his head spun. He saw a blurred image of the spider-man. The man's face craned up to follow him. Marcus took his shot.

His tongue impacted with the man's face with all the force he could muster. It hit hard as a fist, snapping the joker's head back. Marcus loosened the muscles so that his tongue lapped venom all over the man's cheeks, across his lips and into his nose. And then his tongue snapped back into his mouth. It only took a second.

The spider-man careened away. His legs skittered even more wildly as he clutched at his face with his hands, crying in delirious pain. Marcus followed him. He held his damaged arm snug to his body, but struck blow after blow with his other fist, punching from high up on his coils, fast, snake-like. He kept at it until the spider legs collapsed in a jumbled splay. The man fell unconscious on top of them. Marcus shouted for the fucker to get up and take more of a pounding.

The lights above the crowd flared. Where there had been darkness a moment before, the close-packed people reappeared. They rose to their feet applauding. They laughed and shouted and pumped the air with their fists. Their eyes were wild with glee.

The announcer's voice returned. "The Infamous Black Tongue, ladies and gentlemen! The Infamous Black Tongue! Now that was a show, wasn't it?"

Marcus's eyes settled on the elderly couple in the private box. They were the only two not caught up in the frenzy. This time, it was the woman who drew his attention. As horrible as the deformed man was, the woman was somehow more frightening. She stared back at Marcus, arms crossed, eyes hidden behind elaborate glasses, her red hair in a snug swirl atop her head. Her face betrayed no emotion that he could fathom. Compared to her, the screaming crowd looked positively sane.

"It's not your fault," Father Squid said. He sat across from Marcus, a table between them.

Marcus pushed morsels of egg around his plate with a fork. "So you keep telling me."

"I saw the entire fight. They made us all watch it in the common room. It was horrible, but the man in that arena was not you. It was a perversion of you. I can see that even if you cannot. Trust me." The priest managed to convey calming empathy through his eyes, and with the shape and movement of his dangling tentacles.

Marcus tried not to see it. "I trust you," he said, "but you shouldn't trust me. Not anymore. I would've killed that guy. I don't know why, but . . . I hated him. I still do."

"You would not have gone that far," Father Squid said. "It's this place. Somehow it turns men's natures, brings horrible things out of them. It's not your fault, though." The priest reached across the table and tried to place a sucker-covered palm on the young man's hand.

Marcus pulled away. "You haven't been in the arena. You don't know what it's like."

The older man pulled his hand back. "I will soon."

"What?"

"I have been matched to fight tomorrow night."

"Against who?"

"That I don't know."

"But they won't be able to make you fight. Not you!"

"They can put me in the arena, but I will strive not to give in."

"If anyone can resist it you can!" The thought buoyed Marcus like nothing else had. Father Squid would beat them by not fighting. He could see it: the priest standing with his arms crossed, proud and defiant, staring down that old lady. And if he could do that, maybe Marcus could too. "You can beat it."

The priest ducked his head, seeming unnerved by Marcus's sudden enthusiasm. "I will try, but I have violence in my past, Marcus. I fear it's not buried as deeply as I would like."

That evening, as he lay staring at the ceiling, his mind crowded with thoughts, his door cracked open. Of all the things he might have imagined would step through the door, the girl that slid into view wasn't one of them.

As far as he could tell she was a nat. A jaw-droppingly beautiful one. Beauty wafted in with her like a scent that he inhaled through his eyes. Fashion model–slim, firm and soft in the right places. She wore jeans so tight they looked like she'd been dipped into them. Her shirt opened all the way down the front, a gauzy-thin, semi-transparent material. He could just see the curves of her breasts. Her large eyes were spaced widely, but they were more striking for it. Icy blue, sparkling, they studied him with a frankness that set his heart racing.

"I am for you tonight," she said. "You must have fought well, yes?"

Marcus couldn't say a word.

She considered him for a long moment, and then asked, "Is your tongue really black?"

Marcus had never heard a sexier question.

Her name was Olena. She sat beside him on his bed. The threads in the stitching of her jeans sparkled gold when she moved. She was Ukrainian, from a city called Poltava. "You know it?"

Marcus pursed his lips, frowned as if he was trying to place Poltava.

"It's on the Vorskla," she said. Her accent reminded him of when his sister used to imitate Natasha Fatale from the *Rocky and Bullwinkle* cartoons. It would almost have been funny, except that she was too earnest, too beautiful, for him to possibly laugh at. "Is a river. Vorskla. You should know it." She punctuated this by stabbing out her small hand and slapping him on the shoulder. "You live in New York, yes?"

Marcus nodded. He almost specified Jokertown, but the name died on his tongue.

"Do you know famous persons?"

"Not really." Seeing disappointment in the way she bit the corner of her lip, he added, "I . . . I'm a little bit famous." He chose not to say "infamous."

"What makes you famous? Are you rapper?"

"Ah . . . no." He had no idea what to say. He was famous for beating up a crooked cop? For living in sewers? For roaming around at night looking for thugs? "Just for . . . getting in trouble."

This seemed to please her. She laughed and swayed into him. "You're bad boy, aren't you? I can tell you are!" Her head dipped coyly. For a moment her face was hidden behind a screen of her long black hair. Then she parted her hair with a hand, scooped it clear, and swiped it over her shoulder. "Show me your tongue."

Initially, Marcus refused, but she insisted. She seemed fascinated, first staring into this open mouth and then making him demonstrate his talent. She clapped with pleasure when he shot his tongue out and nailed the far wall.

"Is your 'little snake' as long as that?" she asked, sliding a hand over his torso.

Marcus felt an instant erection press against the scales of his groin.

She pulled her hand away and changed the subject. "Where would you take me in New York?"

An easy enough question, but it stumped him. Where would he take her?

"Not just your apartment," she cautioned. "Not just there. I need to see places. United Nations. Broadway. Liberty Statue. Where else?"

To his relief, she didn't make him answer the question. She went on talking about the places she wanted to see. Not just in New York, but at random points all across America. Marcus tried to listen, but he couldn't understand who or what she was. Where had she come from? How was it possible that she was sitting here on his bed chatting with him like it was the most normal thing in the world? Why was she speaking as if they had a future together, filled with voyages to amazing places? He wanted to know, but he didn't want to ask. Asking might kill whatever spell he was living in.

"Are you a good man?" she asked.

Marcus's stomach knotted. "I try to be."

"I know you are. I can see it in you. You won't hurt me, will you?"

"No, I would never—"

"Asmodeus is not a good man. He hurts me. He wins and then hurts me. I say I don't want to go to him but he always chooses me. That's not so good for me. A better thing is that you fight and win and have me. Be a monster at fighting. A monster for me. Then we will do things to make you happy. All the things you want. You know what I mean."

His face must've indicated that he didn't.

Olena slipped off the bed onto her knees, sliding her hands across his scales. She smiled and whispered, "I show you."

"We should be in there," El Monstro said, pointing at the screen. "Front-row seats, baby. Wanna see the blood splatter." He punctuated this by smacking one of his massive, plated fists into the palm of his other hand.

The Somali girl who was oiling his horns drew back to accommodate his movements. She was beautiful, brown-skinned and lithe. Marcus had never heard her speak a word. He wondered if she even understood English.

El Monstro had just sat down beside Marcus, saying winners should sit together, shouldn't they? Eight feet tall, plated, with an oddly benevolent smile: Marcus couldn't figure him out. He'd been in here longer than anyone but Asmodeus. He was thriving here, enjoying the violence and the raw pleasures it afforded him. At least, outwardly he was. At times, Marcus saw a timorous quiver beneath his arrogant facade, as if every now and then he forgot who or where he was. Or maybe it was that every now and then he remembered. Once, during a melancholy moment, he'd mumbled something about his mother. Marcus didn't hear what, and he didn't ask for him to repeat it.

Marcus pulled Olena tight against his body. She repositioned her arms around his neck, leaned in and nibbled his ear. He felt the room's lecherous eyes on her, and on the other girl. The jokers didn't even try to hide their lust. If it wasn't for Baba Yaga's rules and Dmitri's talent, Marcus was sure he'd be fighting them all off. El Monstro seemed to thrive on the jealous attention. Marcus didn't, but he couldn't miss seeing the fight. And he wanted Olena with him. It had only been one night, but he wanted her beside him forever and ever.

Everyone in the gladiator compound had gathered to watch Father Squid's first bout. Chairs and couches had been pulled together before a large-screen television. The buffet table lay ravished behind them. The mood was festive, edged with menace, but festive nonetheless. None of the spectators had to worry about their own lives tonight. That was on the priest and whomever he was going to fight. Nobody knew who that was yet—somebody brought in special for it, apparently.

"Look at them," El Monstro said, nudging Marcus's shoulder. "They're like wolves licking their chops. And they say we're the savages!"

The large screen panned across the expectant faces of the audience. Men and women, old and young, different races and features: they all shared the same expression. They looked possessed. Their noses flared as they breathed. Their eyes bulged. The sight of them made Marcus's skin crawl.

Asmodeus entered the room. He stood in the door a moment, staring at Marcus. Or . . . that's what he thought until the joker's eyes shifted and met Marcus's. He glared at him for a long moment, and then he moved into the group to take a seat. Before he met his eyes, Marcus realized, he'd been looking at Olena.

Onscreen, the camera shifted to one of the combatants. The joker shook out his muscle-bound shoulders, snapped his hands, and flexed his fingers. He shouted and stomped, his enormous eyes trembling with rage. Marcus tensed. The guy was hard not to recognize. Marcus had last seen him emerging from the white van.

"Ladies and gentlemen," the announcer intoned, "tonight's main event features two debut performances in our arena. Aleksei the Eel, a joker of incredible physical strength, a fighter just recently snatched from the mean city streets. Formidable—and horrible—to look upon. There's more to him than brawn. He's endowed with a high-voltage touch. Aleksei the Eel, ladies and gentlemen!"

Wartcake said, "That's how the ugly bastard caught me. Fucking shocked me." Others spoke up as well. It seemed that many of them had had run-ins with the Eel.

"Why's he in there?" John the Pharaoh asked.

Asmodeus answered. "He screwed up when he nabbed the squid. Was supposed to just get snake-boy, here. Add to that selling DVD's on the side, and wreckin' a van and slugging it out with a bunch of fucking aces. Baba Yaga ain't happy. She's teaching him a lesson."

Marcus didn't say anything. He just glared at the screen.

The announcer described the fighter facing him as an agent of righteous retribution, a killer who hides beneath the robes of a saint, a man with a past mired in unspeakable violence. "Some know him as a saint, but saint and sinner; what's the difference? Ladies and gentlemen, the Holy Redeemer!"

Father Squid appeared on the screen. He stood motionless, his arms slightly raised to either side, like a gunfighter awaiting the moment to draw. His gloved hands hung loose. His cloak draped him and covered his head, but the lights illuminated his face. The camera even drew in near enough to show the sway of the tentacles covering his mouth as he breathed. His expression was impossible to read.

It began abruptly. Bellowing, Aleksei barreled forward. Father Squid stayed immobile as the hulk charged. His head hung forward. It didn't even look like he saw the guy rushing toward him, not until the last minute. Just as Aleksei reached him, Father Squid shifted to one side, dodging Aleksei's headlong attack. It was a swift, efficient motion, just enough to send Aleksei stumbling into the wall beyond him. He bounced off it and whirled.

Father Squid strode away. His steps looked as heavy and ponderous as ever, but there was a grace to him that Marcus hadn't noticed before. The priest circled and shifted as if his body was remembering the motions for him. He kept Aleksei at arm's length, near enough to talk to. That's what he was doing. Marcus couldn't hear what he was saying, but he saw his tentacles shifting and flexing as he spoke.

He's going to do it, Marcus thought. Look how cool he is. How calm.

Gesturing with his arms, Father Squid made some argument that Aleksei kept trying to punch through. Aleksei shook his head savagely. He spit and hissed and pressed to get in striking range. "The squid's a coward," Wartcake said.

Marcus snapped, "He's no coward. He's just above this shit. He's not going to fight for those fuckers."

This got him a few jeers and insults, but mostly they all just watched the fight. Aleksei was all testosterone-pumped, muscle-bound rage. He threw wild, powerful punches, changeups that went from high to low, swinging wide or jabbing for the torso. His fists sparked with electricity. His ugly face contorted as he concentrated.

For his part, Father Squid moved with an uncanny precision. He backed and dodged, slipped his head to the side, twisted from the torso. No matter how he tried, Aleksei couldn't land a blow. Father Squid didn't move any faster, but it seemed he knew what his opponent was going to do just before he did it. He swatted the joker's punches away with sharp, karate-like motions, his body taking on stances Marcus had never imagined the old priest capable of. Once, he caught Aleksei's fist in his gloved hand. Judging by the way the big man scowled, Father Squid must've squeezed it painfully. Just for a moment, though, then he flung it away.

"Squid's getting pissed," El Monstro said.

Don't, Marcus said to himself. *Don't give in.*

Aleksei landed a punch in Father Squid's gut. The priest lurched over around it, and Aleksei slammed another fist into his temple. The electric force of it hurled Father Squid's body backwards. He rose just as Aleksei bore down on him. He snapped out a hand, catching Aleksei's arm at the wrist. He twisted around, keeping a grip on the arm while clipping the man's legs with his body and using his momentum to trip him. The joker flew heels over head. Father Squid planted his feet and pulled. The arm popped out of its socket. It was a sickly thing to watch, the unnatural way the body and arm moved in opposite directions. Father Squid let go and backed away. He looked horrified at what he'd done. He stared with bulbous eyes as Aleksei squirmed across the stadium floor, helpless.

"Finish him," Asmodeus said, mouth open, tongue sliding across his teeth.

Shaking his head, Father Squid stepped forward. He made soothing gestures with his hands. He reached out, and Marcus knew he was trying to position Aleksei to slip his arm back into its socket.

Yes, he thought. *Show them.*

He didn't get a chance to.

Aleksei transformed. In the blink of an eye, he became an eel. Eight thick, muscular, slimy feet of one. His jaws opened and he lunged up at the priest's face. Father Squid blocked with his forearm. The eel bit into it and thrashed, yanking the priest off his feet. The crowd went wild, roars so loud Marcus could hear them through both the television and through the actual walls themselves. He watched, unsure what to feel, his stomach tied in knots.

After a few frantic moments, Father Squid got the eel pinned beneath his thighs. He gripped the joker around the neck and banged his head on the floor. He banged it hard, over and over again.

Grimacing, Marcus shut his eyes.

Ties That Bind

Part Three

THE CONDO WAS NORMALLY quite roomy. One bedroom with a king-size bed for them, one bedroom for Isai, two large bathrooms, and a modern open-plan layout for the rest. It worked great for their family—or at least it had, until Kavitha's family showed up on their doorstep and moved in. Two parents, two sisters, and their husbands, all bunking on air mattresses in the living room. Glorious.

"He was here in New York, Michael," Kavitha's mother said in British-accented English. "That was where he called us from last. The phone records are clear."

"Yes, I know," Michael said, trying to be patient. Sandip's parents had hired an investigator when the kid had first gone missing, but the man had turned up nothing. So far, neither had Michael. It wasn't technically his jurisdiction, but he'd squeezed looking for Sandip into every free minute at work. You did that for family; the other cops understood and covered for him when they could. But phone records, bank records, Internet, nothing. Michael had walked the streets, checked his contacts, but with no luck. As if the kid had dropped off the planet. "I know Sandip was here in New York; we saw him then." Was he still here? Michael had no idea.

"So, I tell it to you again," she snapped, regal in her silver sari and hair in a perfect bun, despite four nights sleeping on the floor. "And you will listen!"

Michael could only nod in response. He didn't have a lot of moral ground to stand on, given his living situation, which Kavitha's parents were handling with a fierce lack of acknowledgment. They had barely spoken to their daughter for years, ever since she'd gotten pregnant by a black guy and decided to keep the kid. But for this, for their only son, they'd finally broken the silence with a vengeance. Family was the most important thing to Kavitha, Michael knew; it had broken her heart when they'd turned so cold. But she wouldn't betray them now, no matter how they'd treated her. It was one of the things Michael loved about her—he knew that no matter what, she would be loyal to family forever. Which loyalty now included him, Isai, and Minal. And as for her parents, Kavitha might never forgive them, but she'd still feed and house them until Sandip was safely found.

Now Michael stood in front of Kavitha's mother, trying to swallow his own anger at the kid who had driven the whole family to distraction by disappearing. He was probably running around with some gang, pretending to be a hero. But he couldn't say that to this tiny old woman, wrapped tightly in her shawl and shivering, clearly out of her mind with worry for her youngest child. When he found Sandip, he was going to strangle him. But he couldn't tell her that; what Michael said out loud was only, "Don't worry, Aunty." She frowned at him, and he wasn't sure if it was for the fatuous reassurance, or if she thought the "Aunty" impertinent. What was he supposed to call her? He couldn't use her name—he was sure she'd think that was rude. This whole situation was impossible. "I'm sure he's fine."

If Michael was honest with himself, he had to admit that he was worried about the kid too. It was only two years ago that his own daughter had disappeared. Just for a few hours, but he'd thought his heart would stop. If Sandip would just pick up the damn phone and call.

He couldn't spend all his time looking for the kid, not if he wanted to keep his job. Most of Michael's days were spent on the street, talking to contacts, trying to figure out how the art smugglers were getting their pieces into New York. He'd nailed down almost every other part of the case—he knew who was doing the smuggling, where the pieces were coming from, who was buying. The one thing missing was the point of connection, the person or place that moved pieces from thief-seller to buyer. As soon as Michael found that link, he'd be able to make an arrest. Not that anyone at the station would care—everyone's attention was focused on the missing jokers now. His punk partner was getting all the glory on what had turned out to be a much bigger case than anyone had expected. Michael glared across the desk at Franny, at just the wrong moment—the boy happened to look up, caught the glare, and then ducked his head back down, flushing.

Michael felt a surprising pang of guilt. He had been kind of hard on the kid; Franny wasn't that much older than Sandip. Children, all of them, playing at being men. And Franny had a massive stack of papers in front of him; that couldn't be fun.

"Hey—you want a hand with that?" Maybe it was time for a peace offering. They were supposed to be partners, and the truth was, it was Michael's job to watch over the kid, help him out.

But Franny just spat out a brusque, "I can handle it."

Not even a thanks in there. Fine. If Franny was determined to drown in paperwork, Michael didn't need to extend a helping hand. He already had one kid to rescue. When he got off this shift, he'd go hit the streets again. Someone had to know where Sandip had disappeared to. Jokertown wasn't big enough to hide a kid forever.

They'd canceled dinner with his parents last Saturday; this week, Minal had decided to invite Michael's parents over to their place instead. She said it was time the parents met, that since Kavitha's parents were here, they might as well take advantage. Get some good out of the situation. Neither Michael nor Kavitha were enthused about the idea, but Minal was insistent.

There wouldn't have been room to seat everyone, but Kavitha's sisters and their husbands had finally decamped this morning, pleading jobs and other commitments. Her middle sister was just getting to the uncomfortable stage of pregnancy, and had sounded relieved to go home and sleep in a real bed again, instead of bunking on an air mattress on the floor. Kavitha's father was making noises about work responsibilities as well, but so far, her mother had held firm. And so here they were, waiting uncomfortably for Michael's parents to arrive. Minal, busy in the kitchen, had banished everyone from her domain, and so they sat, awkwardly, in the living room. Thank God for Isai.

She had started part-shifting lately—just enough to sprout feathers on her head and arms, to turn her nose into a beak. Michael worried that her nose was turning more beak-like with every day, even when she wasn't shifted—if she transformed too often, would the changes become permanent? But try to tell a five-year-old not to do something fun; it was impossible. And no one had the heart to discipline Isai right now in any case.

"Ammama! I can't find the birdie!" She leaned against her grandmother on the sofa, book in hand. Isai's current obsession was hidden picture puzzles, and Kavitha's mother was remarkably good at them. She could find any hidden object with just a glance—she was equally good at finding dust. The one thing she couldn't find was her missing son.

The phone rang, shrill and loud. Had someone turned the ringer up? The sound made Michael's head ache. Kavitha jumped up and grabbed an extension. "Hello?" Hope in her voice—not that any of them really expected Sandip to call, but you never knew. But then she just walked away, out of the room, listening to whomever was on the other end of the line. Apparently not Sandip.

And then another ring—the doorbell. Michael's turn to jump up, this time to open the door. His mother bustled into the room, dripping rain from her coat. He turned to help her with it, but she ignored him, heading straight for Kavitha's mother, who had risen to greet her. His mother's wet bulk engulfed Maya in a huge embrace. "I am so sorry," she said, her voice thick with its Korean accent, but even thicker with sympathy. And Maya's stiff formality broke down completely; the tiny woman was sobbing now, in his mother's vast arms. Hugely muscled, from long hours over decades of wrestling wet clothes at her laundromat. Strong and warm, the kind of arms that could hold you up when you were drowning.

Michael's heart was aching now, along with his head, but Minal had been right to invite his parents here. His dad was slipping off his own coat, closing the door behind him. And even though Michael couldn't remember the last time he'd hugged his father, in this moment, it seemed natural to rest a hand on the old man's back, to feel the warmth of skin under the thin shirt, as he ushered his father into the room. Michael knew in that moment that if he were the one missing, even as a grown man, his dad wouldn't rest until he found him again. He had to work harder to find Sandip. Maybe after dinner, he'd go out again, talk to some more people.

Kavitha came out of the hall, the phone still in her hand, to see her mother straightening up out of his mother's embrace, tears still running down her face. Kavitha's face was stricken, and thank God for Isai, bewildered Isai, who asked loudly, "Is it crying time?" And his father scooped her up and leaned his head against hers, saying, "No, sweetheart, baby girl. Crying time is done for now. Now it's hugging time, okay? And as soon as your Mama Minnie tells us all that yummy-smelling food is ready, it's gonna be eating time. Sound good?"

Isai loudly agreed. Michael took his mother's wet coat that she was finally shrugging out of; Kavitha pulled herself together enough to explain that the studio had called to remind her that she only had one more week of rehearsal time before her show was due to start. She had to get back to work tomorrow morning, for at least a few hours. That started her father talking about business again; import/export problems, ever-higher taxes, lying and cheating employees. It was never pleasant listening to Kavitha's father complain about his work, and Michael caught Kavitha wincing at a few of the worst comments. But it was still a relief to talk about something normal, and at least his mother was happy to join in, commiserating on the travails of the small business owner.

Somehow, the mundane details carried them through to dinnertime, when Minal's food on the table and their faces around it seemed like a blessing. Michael had never expected to see his parents and Kavitha's together, not really. But they got along surprisingly well—Kavitha's mother even laughed at a few of his father's wry jokes. If they got married, maybe this would be normal, would happen often. That might actually be nice.

He just had to find Sandip first.

Galahad in Blue

Part Six

AS HE'D EXPECTED THERE had been a long, tense, and unpleasant conversation with Deputy Inspector Maseryk about the death of a prisoner while in custody. After it was over Franny returned to his desk and went through all his notes on the joker kidnappings. Another person had been reported missing. A schoolteacher named Philip Richardson. The kidnappers were no longer taking just the lost, the discarded, and forgotten.

His now almost constant headache was back, pounding in his temples and behind his eyes. He closed his eyes, but all he could see were images from the fight club DVDs. The blood, the fists, the contorted faces of the men fighting in that arena. There had to be something he'd overlooked, a thread that might lead to the taken.

Michael came in at one point. His eyes were sunken and he looked exhausted. Franny opened his mouth to ask if his partner was all right, but Michael seemed to just look right through him, and he walked past without even a grudging hello, and headed straight to Slim Jim's desk. Franny swallowed the words.

Adding to his misery was the fact that tonight he'd agreed to have dinner with Apsara and her parents. He'd started to head to the file room about ten times to cancel, but then he'd think about the shitstorm that would cause and he'd return to his desk unable to face one more person who was pissed at him. Apsara had wanted him to go with her to the Hyatt to collect her parents but Franny refused. He would meet them at the restaurant. That would give him another hour to work.

Norwood still hadn't called back. The agent probably wasn't going to follow up on the *American Hero* thing. Why would a fed do something to help a local? Franny's sense of being abused deepened. He decided he was being stupid and paranoid. Jamal had gotten him the info on the Russian thugs.

He slumped in his squeaking, broken-down chair. *So much* American Hero—*Curveball and Earth Witch and Drummer Boy, Peregrine's son, and of course Jamal, the first season winner, and the tapes . . .*

Various Wikis listed all the contestants who had actually made it onto the show. There were some jokers—the preponderance were aces, and why not? Hollywood liked attractive people, most jokers weren't very attractive. He watched an online video showing some of the humiliating tryouts. *Tryouts.* He checked his watch. It was only four o'clock on the West Coast. He called the studio that made *American Hero,* and after only a minimum amount of runaround he was connected with an efficient assistant who e-mailed him the full list of everyone who had ever auditioned for the show. He ran down the list. Nearly every one of the missing had auditioned for the show.

He put in another call to the SCARE agent. "Jamal, found another link with *American Hero.* Most of the victims auditioned for the show. There's got to be a connection. Please call me once you've talked to Berman."

Starfields was one of Manhattan's better restaurants, and it didn't hurt its caché that the owner, Hastet, was a real live alien, a woman from Takis. Actually she was now the only alien on Earth, since Dr. Tachyon had departed. The menu was eclectic and rather than the traditional large plates of food served in most American eateries, Hastet specialized in what Franny thought of as Takisian dim sum. Small plates, exotically spiced and unfailingly delicious. You ended up ordering a lot of them to fill up, and were presented with a large bill at the end of the meal. That wasn't something he was looking forward to. It was unworthy of him, but he was really hoping that Apsara's dad would pick up the check. Then he wondered if *he* ought to offer to buy dinner? Ugly thought.

Franny was waiting in the lobby when the elevator doors opened to reveal the trio. Apsara's mother was an older version of her daughter and just as beautiful. Her father was bald, with a slight paunch, but neither condition detracted from his strong, powerful features. Apsara looked adorable in her police uniform. Franny suppressed a sigh. He stepped forward to meet them, and felt gigantic. At five foot ten he towered over all three.

Introductions were made, hands were shaken, and they moved from the lobby into the restaurant proper. Franny paused for an instant before stepping in and scanned the people in the restaurant. He mentally assessed and dismissed the patrons as any kind of threat. He then took a good look at his surroundings. The ceiling was painted space-black and gold and silver stars twinkled against the dark background. Hastet herself, looking neat as a pin and dressed in traditional Takisian clothes, escorted them to a booth.

He'd read that at one time the waiters had dressed in colorful and flamboyant styles in imitation of Tachyon, but the Takisian doctor had been gone for almost two decades and that affectation had ended. Now the waiters wore black pants and white shirts with bow ties. Hastet supplied them with menus, while a waiter filled water glasses, and another shook out napkins and laid them in their laps.

Mrs. Chiangmai looked at him over the top of a menu and said in her softly accented voice, "Detective Black."

"Frank, please."

She inclined her head with the grace of a dancer. "Frank. Apsara has been telling us of some of her cases. They sound quite hair-raising. How dangerous is this for my daughter?"

Apsara cast him a pleading glance. He wasn't exactly sure what she wanted so he made a guess. "The truth, Mrs. Chiangmai, is that we almost never draw our guns, much less fire them. I'm not saying it can't be rough, but it's not normally life-threatening." The next glance was grateful. He'd guessed correctly.

"And what's your job like now that you've been promoted?" Mr. Chiangmai asked. "Apsara tells us you are one of the youngest people ever to make detective."

Because of politics, he thought, but he kept his remark as neutral as possible. "Less active. I mostly interview people now."

"Do you like it?" Apsara asked.

He thought about it. He knew he was supposed to, but he had made a discovery. "I liked walking a beat. Seeing my people. Hearing about their days. But this is the career path if you want to make captain."

"And you do," Mrs. Chiangmai said.

"My father was a captain. In fact, captain of the precinct where I work."

"A lot to live up to," Mr. Chiangmai said.

Uncomfortable, Franny looked away. The conversation swirled around him. Apsara spinning tales. He recognized them as recent cases handled by both detectives and uniformed officers in the 5th Precinct. With luck her parents would not know enough about protocol to tell she was fibbing, or not pause to wonder how she had taken part in so many arrests.

He lost interest in the conversation thread. Found himself thinking about Abigail. He'd promised her he'd help and he was no closer to a solution for the Croyd problem. Back when Abigail had first gotten involved with Croyd Franny had abused his position to look up the file on the man. A file that extended back into the 1950s.

Some of the old-timers in Jokertown claimed that Croyd had actually been around on Wild Card Day back in '46. The length and age of the file suggested it might be true. The crimes listed were mostly B&Es and larcenies. Then as the years had passed and Croyd had become a fixture in Jokertown a degree of sympathetic understanding for the man's plight had taken root in the minds of the officers of Fort Freak. Croyd's ace meant he really couldn't hold a job, and none of the crimes he committed were so very bad. Or so the argument went. But if Croyd acted on his threat and killed Mick and Rick there would be no turning a blind eye. Croyd would go to jail.

Franny again scanned the restaurant. Croyd could probably remember when the waitstaff were all dressed up like faux Tachyons. Hell, he probably remembered Tachyon himself. Remembered when Aces High, on the top floor of the Empire State Building, was the pinnacle of wild card chic. When the Astronomer and Fortunato had battled in the skies over Manhattan, the day Franny's father had died.

He's also very suggestible. Dr. Finn's words came back, and with it an idea. A crazy idea, but it was the first one Franny had that didn't involve him trying to subdue, handcuff, and keep Croyd locked up until the ace fell asleep.

"Uh huh," Franny said agreeably when the cadence of Apsara's voice indicated she'd asked him a question. From the puzzled look on her parents' faces it hadn't been the right response. "Would you excuse me a moment?"

Franny slipped out of the booth and went to the men's room. He washed his hands, splashed water on his face, and stood staring into the mirror. Would Abby think he was crazy or just stupid if he mentioned his idea for dealing with Croyd? He realized he did not want to sit through a meal while Apsara hosed her parents. They seemed nice, and he didn't want to be a part of it. He also wanted to go call Abby and put his plan in motion *right now*. And he had the perfect out. Duty called.

He returned to the table. "I just got a call about a case I'm working on," he explained. "I'm afraid I need to leave."

"We certainly understand when duty calls," Mr. Chiangmai said expansively. When the older man spoke the words aloud it almost embarrassed Franny into staying, but only almost.

It was also clear from Apsara's ice-dagger stare that she didn't.

"So, what do you think?" Franny asked Abigail after he had outlined his plan. Since Franny had bolted before eating they were seated in a booth at a burger joint. A french fry liberally coated with ketchup hung forgotten in Abby's hand.

"I think it's either completely mad, or madly genius."

"I'll need your help to pull it off."

"The theater's dark tonight, nobody around, and I don't think the director will mind if I borrow a few things from the costume department." She cocked her head in that way she had that reminded him of the cardinals that visited the bird-feeding station at his mother's house in Saratoga. "But rather than *ask* maybe we'll just assume it's okay."

"Better to ask forgiveness than permission?" Franny suggested.

"I like that. I think it shall become my motto."

They polished off their burgers. Abby reached for her purse. Franny held out a hand. "Let me get this."

She glared up at him from beneath her bangs. "This is *not* a date."

"Absolutely not," he hurriedly agreed. "But you're a starving artist, and I got a promotion."

"Well, all right then." He thought she looked relieved.

Three hours later, in the stairwell of a Chinatown apartment building Abby helped him into the costume they had "borrowed" from the Joker-town Rep. It had been used in a performance of *Cyrano*, and however chic it might have been in 1680 Franny knew he looked like an idiot.

Abby tugged the shirt ruffles from beneath the wide cuffs of the long paisley coat so they hung over his hands. The knee-high boots were too big, causing him to shuffle, which was probably appropriate given the shoulder-length gray wig Abby had provided. The coat and matching pan-taloons were both too small, which had him breathing in shallow gulps. The drooping feather in the musketeer's hat fell into his eyes, and he blew it away in irritation. Abby had her knuckles stuffed in her mouth trying to hold back giggles.

"Okay, ready?" Abby asked.

"No. If anybody sees me in this getup I'll . . . I'll . . ." Words failed him.

"Nonsense, you look . . . you look . . ." Giggles overcame her again.

"Yeah, that's what I thought," he said sourly.

They left the stairwell and went down the hall. Standing outside the apartment door they could hear both a television and a radio playing inside.

"Maybe he's asleep, and that's why both are on," he whispered.

Abigail shook her head. "Probably not, he tries to stay stimulated when he doesn't want to sleep," she whispered back. "Okay, good luck. He shouldn't see me here, or he'll know something is up."

"You'll rescue me if this goes pear-shaped, right?" Franny asked plain-tively as she hurried back toward the door leading to the stairwell.

She flashed him a smile and a thumbs-up. Franny gave himself a shake, faced the door, tried to take a deep breath, and palmed the pass key he'd obtained from the building super by flashing his badge. He tried not to think about how many laws he was breaking. He slid the key into the lock, opened the door, and swept into the room.

His first impression was that smells could have weight and heft. The room reeked of pizza, fried chicken, beer, and man sweat. A hulking figure, hollow-eyed, skin like bumpy rock, and dressed in baggy sweatpants and a T-shirt jumped out of a recliner and curled his fingers into fists. The individual digits vanished and the hands became solid, skin-colored sledge-hammers.

"Greetings!" Franny said. He swept off the feathered hat. "I am a Takisian anthropologist, and I have been sent on behalf of the Star League to seek your help in determining if Earth is ready to join our glorious hegemony." Croyd gaped at him. *Nobody would buy this bullshit.* Franny eyed the massive hands. Yep, he was going to die. Desperate, he plowed on. "We have determined that you are the human who can best accomplish this task as you move in circles both high and low."

A frown knotted Croyd's brow. "What does that mean?"

"Criminal and not criminal," Franny explained.

"Did Tachy send you?" Croyd asked.

"Uh . . . yes . . . yes, he did." Franny prayed that Croyd wouldn't ask for any details regarding the alien doctor.

Croyd turned away. "I can't. I gotta deal with these bastards who are kidnapping jokers." He paced the room, his footfalls heavy on the linoleum floor. "They're coming for me. But I'd be happy to do it after I kill these guys."

"Not necessary." Franny removed a small pocket recorder. "This device will not only record your interactions with the citizens of this world, but it will protect you from any kind of assault."

Sweat trickled through Franny's sideburns beneath the ridiculous wig. Given Franny's shitty luck Croyd would get mugged while carrying around the recorder. Then he would come find Franny and pound him into the ground like a tent peg. One the other hand Croyd looked like an Easter Island statue right now. No mugger in his right mind would assault that. But in Jokertown *right mind* was a sliding scale.

Croyd rubbed a now semi-normal-shaped hand across his face. The rasp like rock on rock could be heard even over the radio and television.

"Well, that's fine for *me*, but they'll take somebody else. Nope, I gotta kill them."

"No! You don't. They're not involved." Croyd turned back to face him, the eyes buried deep under that protruding brow line were suspicious.

"And how the hell would you know? I'm supposed to be the expert on this community. At least according to you."

"We've been monitoring Jokertown from space. They haven't taken anybody."

"If you can watch from space then why the hell do you need me?"

"We can't . . ." His brain felt like it was frantically picking up and then rejecting ideas. "Can't . . . hear what they say."

Amazingly Croyd bought it. He grunted. "Okay. So, what's in it for me?"

Frantically Franny considered. "First human . . . delegate to the League." He hoped it didn't sound as lame to Croyd as it did to him.

"I'd get to go into space?"

"Yes, on a spaceship." Franny winced.

Fortunately exhaustion and the level of drugs in his system made Croyd less discerning than the rock he resembled. "Cool," he said. He took the small recorder. "And this will really keep me safe?"

"Absolutely. Guaranteed. Just turn it on and walk around."

"Okay."

"And please, don't kill anyone while you're working for me. It would make it a lot harder for me to present you as a League delegate. Well, I must go."

Franny hurried to the door. "Hey," Croyd called. "How'd you get in?"

"Alien technology," Franny said, and fled. He knew he needed to get clear fast so he opted for the elevator rather than shuffling to the stairwell.

Thankfully there was nobody in the entryway. Franny dropped the key through the mail slot on the manager's door, left the building, and pulled out his cell phone to call Abby, and tell her where to meet him. He heard footsteps approaching, and he withdrew to the stairs leading down to the basement apartments.

"Hey, you!" came the never to be mistaken, high-pitched voice of his former partner Bill Chen. "Step out here where I can see you. What are you doing?" The powerful beam from a cop's flashlight blinded Franny.

Yes, Franny decided, he had the worst luck of any living human. Bill lived in Chinatown, and of course fate would put Franny in his path right as Bill was coming off duty. "Relax, Bill, it's me," Franny said, stepping out of the shadows, and pulling off the hat and wig.

A grin split the big face as Bill took in his appearance. "Halloween's not for months."

"Costume party."

"You know what you need? Some *bling*." And Bill unlimbered his nightstick, whistled, and pointed the stick at Franny. Franny tried to dodge, but the too-big boots tripped him up. An instant later he was surrounded by a pink glow shot through with stars and glitter.

"Tinkerbill! You *dick!*"

Abby turned up at that moment. Bill looked from her to Franny and back again. Gave a snort of laughter.

"You kids have a nice night," Bill said and sauntered away.

Those About to Die . . .

Part Five

MARCUS HAD A PRETTY good burn on. He was working his biceps, slow curls with the dumbbells. He looked down at the taut bulges of muscle, trying to focus, trying not to think about Father Squid, or Olena, or the fights, or Dmitri's mind trips. He wasn't having much success, but it was better to be doing something than lying on his cot. He didn't notice that Asmodeus had entered the workout room until he spoke.

"It's not all about muscle," Asmodeus said. He strolled toward Marcus, his slim, lanky body at ease. "I don't work out. Don't need to. Five bouts, me on top every time. Bet you wonder how I do it, don't ya?"

"Fuck you."

A tick of annoyance flashed across the joker's smug visage, gone just as quickly. "I thought Olena was taking care of that for you. But then again she's not yours anymore, is she?"

Marcus glared at him, hating the fact that his mouth even formed her name, hating the way he grinned and let the tip of his tongue show. He knew what was going to happen before he did it, but he couldn't help himself. He surged at Asmodeus, propelled by the long muscles of his tail. His weight-heavy fists swung up from his sides. He nearly smashed one of the dumbbells into the joker's spotty face.

"Dmitri!" Asmodeus called.

The name was enough to freeze him. The ace strolled into the room, looking bored as ever. He leaned against the wall. His dead eyes fixed on Marcus, though without a spark of genuine interest.

"Yeah, they sent me with Dmitri," Asmodeus said. He pulled up a stool and leaned back against it. "I'm not here to shoot the shit. Baba Yaga didn't much like the way you handled your last fight. She wants me to school you."

Resuming his curls, Marcus muttered, "I won, didn't I?"

No one could dispute that. The fight hadn't lasted more than a few minutes. The joker facing him looked like one of the ogres in that old animated version of *The Hobbit*. He had come at him with his massive mouth open, teeth like curved daggers. Marcus swiped his feet from under him with his tail. He pounced on his back while he was down and pounded his face into the floor. He could still hear the joker's teeth snapping on the floor and saw them spinning away, dragging thin tendrils of blood. He'd bashed his face to pulp and hadn't seen the guy since. Marcus wanted to feel more sorry about it than he did. It was wrong hurting someone like that. He knew that, but he didn't quite feel it. Part of him found beauty in the broken teeth, the thin lines of bloody spittle they left behind.

"Yeah, you fucked him up real good, but Baba Yaga wants us to fight. Not to kill each other. And you could've made more of a show of it. That's what I do. I string them along a bit before closing the deal. It was that shit with the audience that pissed her off, though."

It hadn't been enough to destroy the ogre. Marcus had been too enraged. He turned from beating on the guy to raging at the audience. He smashed into the glass. He bounced off of it and came back pounding and shouting. He thrust himself straight up and ripped and yanked at the webbing above the glass. He almost believed he could get through it. If he just tore hard enough, found a weakness. If he could've gotten through, he'd have ripped the spectators apart. He'd have torn at them, bit them, crushed them. Only when Dmitri entered his skull and dragged him into his own personal hell did he stop. It had been far worse than the first time.

When he came out of it, alone in his room—Olena nowhere to be seen—he'd nearly lost what sanity he had left.

"You do something like that again and Dmitri's gonna spend a long time in your head," Asmodeus said. "Bet. Just get your act together. Use your anger; don't let it use you. Master that, and you'll do all right. There, that's my charity work done." He stood. "I gotta go rest. Got a fight tonight.

When it's over . . ." He grinned. ". . . I'm heading to Poltava. Nothing like Ukranian pussy, is there?" He strolled away.

Marcus watched him go, feeling like each step he took away slammed another nail into his heart. Just as he reached the threshold, Marcus called out to him. "Hey! Who are you fighting?"

The joker spun on his heel, amusement—and challenge—in his eyes. "Why do you want to know?"

Marcus's knuckles were sore from the knocking. Strange how he could pound flesh without a problem, but something as simple as knocking on a door made him wince. It wasn't just the physical sensation that hurt.

"Father, it's me! I'm not leaving until you open up."

No response.

Behind him, life in the compound went on. Jokers lounging, tossing insults at each other, posturing. Girls. Drink. Amusements. In some ways it was all the same as when he'd first beheld the place. Things were changing, though, slowly, gradually, almost unnoticeably. The more they fought, the more the gladiators found the violence of the ring staying with them.

For Marcus, it was like a smell that clung to him. Sometimes he didn't notice; sometimes he caught the scent and his muscles tensed and his face went hard and any and everything seemed like an insult. He'd bashed Wartcake in the face with his tray at the buffet table and would've done more, had he not felt Dmitri's creeping touch coming over him. Afterward, he couldn't even remember what had angered him. More and more, the trigger didn't matter. Just the urge toward violence did.

Making it worse was that he didn't have Father Squid to turn to. The night of his fight the priest came back stunned, shaken to the core, shamefaced and silent. He'd stayed in his locked room ever since. Marcus had tried getting him out several times. He'd been refusing to eat or interact. Not even Dmitri's mind tricks seemed to affect him. He was beyond it all. Marcus had heard him praying. Once, he heard a repetitive thwack! thwack! thwack! He didn't want to imagine what that meant.

Leaning in to the door, he said, "You can't stay in there forever."

Nothing.

"You think you're the only one that feels like an animal?" Marcus snapped. "I got news for you. All of us feel that way! Some like it. I don't. But . . . I'm getting tired of fighting it. You know? It's hard. It's easier to give in." He paused, clenched his fist again and touched his knuckles to the wood. "What about all that stuff you said to me? How it wasn't my fault. How it was this place that drove me crazy. If that's true about me it's true about you, too."

There was a noise behind the door, a snuffling and murmur that he couldn't make out. It sounded like some sort of prayer.

Annoyed, Marcus said, "Whatever, Father. I'm getting on with it. Just so you know, I'm fighting tonight. Didn't even have to, but I want to. Yeah, I do. They took Olena from me. You probably think that's for the best, but you've never been in love."

The praying cut off abruptly.

"We got something. It's real. It's not like you think it is. She's the only truly good thing in this place, and they took her from me. If I don't do anything, Asmodeus is going to . . ." He couldn't get the words out. "I'm not gonna let that happen. That's why I'm fighting tonight—for her. What else do I have to fight for now?"

Out of words, Marcus felt the urgency drain away. He sighed and pushed himself away from the door. "Anyway, that's all I wanted to say. I'm going. Guess I'll see ya when I see ya."

He turned and made it only a few steps away before he heard the door open. Father Squid peered through the crack, his face haggard, streaked with tears. "Marcus . . . You're wrong about me. I did know love once. I would've done anything to keep her safe, or to punish the one that . . ." He cut off. He blinked and inhaled a long breath and said, "Come in, son. I'll tell you about it. I'll tell you about my Lizzie. And you can tell me about your Olena." He drew back, leaving the door open for the young man to enter.

◆

"Stupid move, kid," Asmodeus said. "Stupidest thing you've done yet."

The joker was slick on his feet. He moved as if sliding across ice, deceptive, graceful. In his skintight jeans and white T-shirt, he could've been a dancer in *West Side Story*. Only he wasn't singing.

Marcus pursued him. He slithered with a purposeful fluidity all his own. He wanted to pound him, to feel his fists thudding against his face.

Backing Asmodeus up to the ring wall, he snapped his tail around to one side, to keep him from fleeing to the left, and then he curved in from the right. He released his tongue. It shot from his mouth sopping wet with venom.

Asmodeus blocked it with the palm of his hand. The impact thwacked wetly, spraying his face and knocking his arm back. He spun away, shaking the sting out of it. Good luck with that, Marcus thought. His venom would work just the same. Skin contact. That's all it needed. Marcus kept his sinuous curve around the joker, waiting for him to weaken. He wanted to see his face register the venom, and then he would come on swinging, beat the crap out of him, and then end it.

Asmodeus looked at Marcus. There was no awareness of his impending doom on his face. He grinned and wiped the moisture from his forehead. "Your venom's crap," he said. "It's nothing to me but the stink of your breath. I've got a bit of reptile in me as well. I produce my own venom. Comes out in my semen." His grin widened. "The ladies love it. Olena more than most. Says my spunk lights a fire inside her."

Marcus lunged, swinging his fists with everything he had. Asmodeus tried to leap over his tail, but Marcus swiped his feet out from under him. As he fell, Marcus landed punches on the back of his head. It was sloppy, ugly fighting, but he kept at it, battering the joker until he was on his knees. Marcus grabbed him by the hair. He raised his head up, ready to drive him face-first into the floor.

Asmodeus began to convulse. Surprised, Marcus let him go. Maybe the venom was working now. On all fours, dry heaves racked the joker, making him look like a cat coughing up a hairball. As much as Marcus wanted to kill him, he wanted everyone to see how pathetic he was. He wanted Olena to see his humiliation.

Asmodeus, in one terrible cough, expelled something from his mouth. It hit the floor with a clank. He picked up the object, sprang to his feet, and slashed at Marcus's chest. A knife. The blade opened a slit from shoulder to shoulder. It wasn't deep. He punched at Asmodeus. The joker ducked under it and landed a jab on Marcus's chin. As he spun away, his knife sliced a gash to the bone on Marcus's forehead. It gushed blood.

Laughing, Asmodeus danced away. He gestured toward the audience, raising the knife and waving it about. "Here's my talent, kid," he shouted. "Give me enough time and I could cough up a samurai sword. That would be overkill in this situation."

The two engaged again. Asmodeus slashed and dodged, landing kicks every now and then. Marcus didn't want to risk his tongue, so he worked in close, pounding at him. He knew he was getting cut, but he didn't feel it. He could barely see, but it didn't matter. His own voice inside his head screamed at him to kill. It shouted and cursed and banged on his brain. The noise was incredible.

Asmodeus sank the blade into Marcus's tail. The pain of it threw him sideways. He couldn't see anything but blood, no matter how he tried to wipe his eyes free. In a moment of sheer panic, he realized he might lose. Ignoring the man's blade, Marcus grabbed blindly for him. He pulled him into an embrace, bashing his bloody head into Asmodeus's face. He pushed him down and wound his tail round and around him. Asmodeus thrashed and yelled, but Marcus got his arms pinned. His coils slid around him. He let go of him with his arms and just coiled and coiled, squeezed and squeezed and squeezed. . . .

When Marcus awoke, he thought, *I killed a man. That can never be undone.* Was he changed by it? He wasn't sure yet. He hadn't meant to kill him. Not really. He wasn't sure what he felt. In the arena everything was different. Outside the arena . . . well, it was getting harder to tell the difference. Even Father Squid had admitted as much. Thinking of the priest, a flush of shame warmed his face.

Olena sat on the edge of the bed. She was fully clothed, leaning forward with her head clutched in her hands. She must've sensed that he was awake. She didn't turn, but she said, "Baba Yaga makes a promise to you."

Reaching out, Marcus touched her back.

Olena snapped, "No! You can't touch me."

"Why?" Marcus sat up.

"Because of Asmodeus."

"I took care of him. He doesn't matter anymore."

"He does matter. Baba Yaga is mad. You weren't supposed to kill him."

"He had a knife! He was going to kill me. Everyone saw that. I was . . ." Marcus tried to believe his own words, but it was hard to get them out. ". . . defending myself."

"But you didn't have permission. She didn't say you could kill him. That made her mad. Oh, she was mad. You don't even know."

"So what? What do I care if she's mad at me? She's an old—"

Olena shot to her feet and turned to face him. "Stupid! She's not just mad at you. She's mad at me. She thinks I made you do it. I didn't. I didn't say to kill him!"

"Okay," Marcus said, trying to soothe her. "I'll tell her that. I'll say it's not your fault."

"You don't understand nothing. She was going to kill you, Marcus! I begged for your life. You don't know how I begged. She didn't listen to me, but the crowd—to them she listens. The crowd went crazy. They loved watching you kill. They want more. They'll pay so much. So much. Enough that Baba Yaga thinks again. She thinks of something better than killing you. I tell you how it is. She made a promise to you, and told me to tell it. That's why I'm here. To tell you." Looking through a tangle of black hair, Olena looked miserable. And beautiful. Beautiful like nothing Marcus had ever seen before. "She said you have one more fight. She said . . ."

When she hesitated, Marcus slipped his body forward and grasped her arms, gently. "What did she say?"

She pulled away from him. She struggled to get the rest of the sentence out. ". . . it must be a fight to the death. 'You and the other troublemaker,' she said. 'Why not put them against each other?' She will make big money from it. High rollers coming in from Moscow. Billionaires from China. Vietnam. They want to watch a big death match. Is the only way for you to live. Is the only way for me to live. But, Marcus, if you fight, and win, she'll let us both go. That's what she said."

Marcus didn't hesitate in answering. The words just came straight from his heart to his mouth. And that was it. He was committed.

The Big Bleed

Part Seven

"DIVERSIFIED CONTENT."

Going by her voice alone, the assistant was a young woman, no older than early twenties, filled with attitude. Or so it seemed to Jamal Norwood when he called Berman's office.

Jamal identified himself. "I'd like to speak to Mr. Berman."

"And you are?" There it was again! As if Jamal had interrupted her at curing cancer or, more likely, repairing her nail polish.

"Jamal Norwood, also known as Stuntman. Mr. Berman knows me."

The assistant sighed, as if the effort of doing her very basic job was some kind of imposition. "Hold on."

The waiting music turned out to be hundred-strings versions of past Berman television theme songs. Which suggested to Jamal that Diversified was more than just a vanity card, Berman, and an assistant—that it might be a real production company.

The former producer of *American Hero* had his office in the Brill Building on Forty-ninth and Broadway, just north of Times Square. The eleven-story structure had been home to various songwriters, Broadway impresarios, and jumped-up television producers for the past seventy years. Jamal's SCARE research turned up a fifth-floor office number belonging to a Diversified Content, a name that was a perfect fit for Berman's smarmy self-conceit.

A bit of shoe leather reconnaissance would have told Jamal whether or not it was a real operation—DC was listed as a company that had "under twenty" employees, which could mean nineteen, or one. One employee would be easy to deal with. A dozen or more and Jamal's off-the-books operation would be outed.

He had considered an ambush interview at Berman's Upper East Side condo, especially since getting that home address had been a greater challenge. (The condo was owned by another of the producer's endless supply of personal service entities.)

But ambushes were tough to accomplish when you were in a hurry and your window of available time was narrow. Yes, you could stake out the man's condo and catch him on his way to work, if you had that time—which Jamal didn't.

The other option was to hit him coming home—but that could just as easily have been ten P.M. after a business dinner as seven.

He didn't want to spend three or four hours lurking without payoff.

A quick cost-benefit analysis convinced Jamal to simply phone the man at Diversified. And here he was, on the speaker. "Jamal Fucking Norwood!"

Jamal wondered who else was in the office with him. "Do I have a new middle name?"

"That's been your middle name since 2007," he said, laughing. "To me."

"Oh, good, I was afraid this was going to be contentious," Jamal said.

"You knew it was dangerous when you called me," Berman said. "What's on your mind? Is this about your new gig? Gonna say good-bye to being a G-man?"

"What new gig?"

"I hear you're top of Cinemax's want list for *I Witness*."

Jamal was momentarily stunned to silence. It wasn't impossible that Berman would know about the script—scripts floated around Hollywood like dandelion puffballs. But even Jamal didn't know that the project had been set up at Cinemax . . . which made it slightly more attractive as an alternative to SCARE. Assuming Jamal was ever strong enough to be Stuntman again. "No," he said, hoping his voice projected more confidence than he felt, "I'm still working for the national interest."

"Schmuck. What's on your mind?"

"I need to ask you some questions. About an investigation."

Suddenly Berman was off speakerphone. "Did I miss your transfer to the IRS?"

"Would it speed things up if I said this was an audit?"

"Not a chance. You'd have to get in line for that." Jamal heard thumping on a desktop—Berman obviously turning the phone or re-arranging some item. "If it's not my money, it's what?"

"There are some DVDs floating around that are going to cause someone to go to jail. And they all tie back to *American Hero.*"

Jamal had the satisfaction of shutting Berman up for an entire ten seconds. "Well, then, it obviously behooves me to share what I know with law enforcement. When do you want to talk?"

"Let's start with right now."

"Let's revise that to two hours from now, my place."

"Okay." Berman rattled off an address that matched what Jamal had discovered.

Then, without a good-bye or even a parting shot, Berman was off the phone.

Which was good. Jamal needed to lie down for an hour. Of course, what he really needed was a shower to remove the taint of a conversation with Michael Berman.

The moment Jamal emerged from the cab at Berman's building, he was forced to make a further adjustment in his evaluation of the man's current success.

Berman's condo was in a building at 675 Madison Avenue, near Sixty-second a block east of Central Park. The building looked like an expensive hotel, the effect enhanced by its ground-floor tenant, a high-end English lingerie store. Jamal could easily picture Berman stopping on his way into or out of the building, window-shopping the models . . . possibly telephoning their agents while he smudged the window with his nose.

Jamal found the entrance, which was discreetly tucked to one side, and a doorman who granted him access to the elevators.

On this May evening, Michael Berman, creator and executive producer of *American Hero,* former CBS vice president of reality programming, current asshole for life, was still on the south side of forty—which, to Jamal Norwood, seemed impossible. He was one of those creatures that grew like mushrooms in Hollywood. More clever than smart, greedy to the point of idiocy, entirely lacking in moral standards, over-sexed, operating on the principle that what was theirs was theirs, what was yours was negotiable, possessing only a single useful skill . . . the ability to give an audience the things it wants.

Things that are bad for it. Empty calories. Heroin.

He opened the ornate door, and showed that the years had not been kind. True, he was wearing his Berman casual uniform of pressed jeans and tailored white dress shirt unbuttoned a button too far. But he had gained weight: his paunch strained the lower third of the shirt. And he had lost what little hair he had possessed in *American Hero* days. Then Berman had rarely been seen without a baseball cap.

"Boy," he said by way of greeting, "and I thought I looked like shit." Jamal knew that he had gained weight, too—thank you, hotel and restaurant food. And while there was no hair loss, he was moving slowly and looking sickly.

But then, strangely, Berman offered Jamal a hug.

"Checking for weapons?" Jamal said.

"Come on, man, we're foxhole buddies."

"From opposing armies."

Berman pointed an index finger at Jamal—his way of saying, *good one*. He indicated that Jamal should take a seat in the beautifully furnished living room, all white floors and rug, glass and white furnishings. "Something to drink or eat?"

"No thanks. On duty."

"That's it, remind me that I'm in a world of trouble."

"Since when do you need a reminder?"

Another finger, as Berman yelled, too loudly for the space, "Mollie, darling!"

Not unexpectedly, Berman wasn't alone.

"This is Mollie Steunenberg. Mollie, Jamal Norwood, the Stuntman. He's also an agent of SCARE, so be careful what you tell him."

Mollie offered her hand. She was a plump little redhead, maybe a year past twenty, wearing heels that were higher than absolutely necessary and a greenish summery dress that was so short as to be unappealing to anyone this side of a recent parolee. Someone had probably told Mollie that redheads should wear green. *Not that green, young lady.*

"Hey," she said, tiredly, nicely completing Jamal's mental portrait of Berman's bored assistant.

Berman flopped onto the couch. Jamal carefully lowered himself to the nearest chair. It felt good to sit.

"So, nasty DVDs," Berman said. "And you think I had something to do with them."

"The only thing every scene has in common is you."

Berman rocked his head from side to side, like a metronome. It was as obvious a tell as an eye blink from a nervous poker player. With Berman, it meant: I'm actually going to be honest. "Look around me, Jamal, and ask yourself this: what possible value would there be in my involvement in naughty outtakes from my shows? You don't get rich off stuff like that. And I'm rich."

Shit, Jamal realized, what if Berman wasn't the source? "If not you, then—"

Berman turned to the redhead. "Darling, who was I just complaining about five minutes before Agent Norwood called me?"

"You want the short list?"

"Don't fuck with daddy, baby." He was getting impatient.

"Joe Frank," she said.

"Joe Frank!" Berman said, turning to Jamal and gesturing, as if to say, *problem solved*.

"Okay, who's Joe Frank?"

"Mollie, tell Agent Norwood who Joe Frank is!" Berman smiled. "Because I can't fucking bear to talk about the cocksucker."

"Joe Frank," Mollie said, "is the cameraman Michael fired off *Jokers of New Jersey*."

"What the hell is that?"

Mollie answered without being prompted. "Our new History Channel series about jokers trying to make lives for themselves as waitresses or plumbers or truck drivers—"

"In New Jersey?" Jamal said, finishing for her, wondering what that had to do with history—and whether or not there was suddenly some connection to Wheels.

"Tell Agent Norwood why, darling." Suddenly Berman stood up. "No, better yet, *show* him."

Like a hostess turning letters on a game show, Mollie tottered over to the big-screen, high-def television and expertly called up a display that showed nine pictures-within-picture, each one a fixed camera within the *American Hero* house in the Hollywood hills that Jamal knew so well.

"As you may recall, Agent Norwood, our various reality series locations are filled with cameras, all capturing unique footage that is then brutally and skillfully edited to create the fine entertainment that American audiences have come to expect from Diversified Content. But there's always a lot left over. Hours and hours of footage, most of it tedious beyond belief." Here Berman smiled. "Some of it rather private and salacious."

Mollie aimed the remote, and one small picture filled the screen . . . Jamal Norwood emerging from the shower, naked and semi-erect. "Look away, Mollie," Berman said, smiling wickedly. "I wouldn't want your love for me to be affected by the sight of Agent Norwood in his . . . natural state."

Jamal was too ill to be embarrassed. He was also growing tired of this hound and horse show, though he was impressed that Berman had been sufficiently frightened that he'd created an actual pitch. "There's more to this than just aces gone wild," Jamal said. "These things are also snuff films."

Berman did his head tilt again. "I fired Joe Frank because we caught him copying raw files on *NJ2*, Jamal. I have no idea who else he was working for or had worked for. I just know that he was a cheap motherfucking sleaze." He smiled again. "And when I say that, you know it's bad."

Before Jamal could respond, Berman turned to Mollie. "Get Agent Norwood our file on Joe Fucking Frank, please." Then he stood up, terminating the interview.

At the door, Jamal accepted a thick letter-sized envelope from Mollie's hands. For an instant, he felt something tingly and life-affirming. He had been dismissing Mollie Steunenberg as a truck stop waitress who had probably slept her way into a job in New York and a tawdry relationship with Berman.

Nothing about her had changed . . . but Jamal decided that her freckled nose was actually rather appealing, that she had a pretty voice, and maybe that green wasn't wrong.

"Thanks, darling," Berman said, dismissing her.

He did watch her go, and worse yet, caught Jamal watching her totter and wriggle back into the living room. "Just for the record, I'm not sleeping with her," Berman said, using the most normal voice Jamal had ever heard from the man.

"So noted."

"Just in case you want to take a shot . . ."

"Thanks."

Then the old Berman was back, clapping him on the shoulder. "Hear much from Julia these days?"

Jamal blinked. For the second time today, Berman had managed to make it clear that he knew too much about Jamal's business. "We're in touch," he said, neutrally. "Do you know her?"

Berman made his *oh, come on* face. "I know everyone I need to know, right?" He sipped his drink. "Nice girl." Smirked. "Petite. Bit of a mouth on her."

"Never boring."

"I bet you really want to get back to Hollywood."

"It's crossed my mind," Jamal said. There was no point in trying to game Berman: the man possessed a freakish power of perception that could have qualified him for wild card status.

And Jamal suddenly wondered if Mollie Steunenberg didn't have a power, too.

Jamal needed the cab ride back to the Bleecker to gather his strength.

With what felt a lot like his dying breath, Jamal tapped the auto-dial for Franny. Thank God, he picked up. "I just left Berman," he said.

"And yet you live."

"Barely," he said, meaning it in a way that Franny couldn't know. He gave him the recap. "Consider the source, who happens to be a pathological liar . . . but the DVDs came from this Joe Frank individual. Berman was kind enough to give me his address and phone, in case I was motivated to contact him."

Franny gratefully thanked him for the information. "I'll handle this particular numbnuts."

"Let me know how it goes."

All he wanted to do was lie down.

Maybe forever.

But first a shower: he truly needed it now.

Galahad in Blue

Part Seven

THE GARROTE WAS DEEPLY embedded in the skin of Joe Frank's throat. Frank was an older man, maybe late fifties, early sixties with a face lined by the sun and years. Rivulets of blood filled the wrinkles on his turkey-like neck. His blackened swollen tongue protruded from between purpled lips, and his eyes were open and staring.

"Son of a bitch," Franny said.

The small apartment would have been pleasant if it hadn't been trashed. Cushions on the chairs and sofa had been ripped open, books and DVDs and a few VHS tapes were pulled off the bookcase.

The moment Jamal had provided him with the cameraman's name and address Franny had headed straight to SoHo to find a door that swung open at his first knock, and a body. It was only that unlocked door that had Franny inside. Joe Frank's murderer hadn't cared enough to close the door behind him, much less lock it. The man's contempt and confidence had saved Franny the trouble of a warrant. The only plus in this shit sandwich.

Franny called in the crime, and while he waited for criminalistics and an ambulance to arrive he donned gloves and began to search the apartment. He doubted he would find anything. The thoroughness of the search conducted by Frank's murderer extended to every room. In the kitchen every cabinet, cereal box, and canister had been emptied. In the bedroom the mattress lay on the floor looking like a gutted white whale. Every drawer, every article of clothing had been searched. In the bathroom Franny's shoes crunched on broken porcelain from the shattered toilet tank lid.

The evidence techs and a coroner arrived along with a detective from the 9th Precinct. He was not happy with Franny, and indicated that he found Franny's rather disjointed explanation of why he was even in Joe Frank's apartment to be less than compelling—though he didn't phrase it that way. What he said was far more terse, and expletive filled. He promised his captain would be calling Franny's captain.

Before he headed back to the 5th Franny swung by the street corner where the aces had confiscated the DVDs. He wasn't surprised when he found the bootleg DVD seller had vanished. Probably decided things had gotten too hot. Or he was dead too.

When Franny returned to the 5th Homer was quick to tell him that Captain Mendelberg wanted him in her office—pronto. "And she is *pissed.*" He drew out the word with obvious relish.

"What the fuck were you doing in SoHo?" she asked the moment Franny stepped into the office. Her ears were waving more than usual.

"Ummm, well, I had a tip."

"From who?"

Franny knew her eyes were always bloodred, but did they seem redder than usual? "Umm, Agent Norwood."

"And why, pray tell, are you taking tips from a Fed?"

So, he tried to explain. About *American Hero,* and the audition lists, and the DVDs, and how all of that led them to Berman, but the longer he talked the more convoluted and confusing it seemed even to him.

"So when Jamal . . . uh, Agent Norwood got this cameraman's name he did the right thing and turned it over to me . . . and . . . I . . . went . . . there . . ."

Mendelberg was staring at him. Kept staring at him. "Get out of here, and try to do some work that might actually result in us finding our missing citizens!"

"Yes, ma'am."

The fifth martini was going down a lot smoother than it had any business doing. Franny and Jamal sat in a booth at a cop watering hole just outside

Jokertown on its northern edge. "The Ninth is ruling it a home invasion," Franny muttered into his glass.

"Yeah, so many burglars carry a fucking garrote," Jamal said, and took another sip of his beer.

"Yeah."

"Dead end," Jamal said.

"Yeah," said Franny.

"I think that bastard knew he was dead when he sent us his way."

"He? Who? Huh?" The amount of alcohol he'd consumed was making it hard for Franny to untangle all the pronouns.

"Berman. I think he knew the cameraman was dead when he gave me his name," Jamal said.

"Throwing him under the bus."

"Exactly."

"But we can't prove it."

"I know. We can't prove a goddam thing."

Franny sat quietly for a moment, feeling the alcohol buzz through his bloodstream. "We know from the DVDs that the missing jokers are fighting in an arena . . . somewhere. And we know people are betting on the fights."

"Yeah. Like dog fights."

"Uh huh, but a really different crowd than you find at a dog fight. Tuxedos, fancy dresses, bling, but fancy bling—diamonds and rubies and emeralds and stuff." Franny's tongue felt thick. "Berman's a big Hollywood guy. He could be in that crowd. Instead he's providing them with the names and abilities of jokers—or so we think. So maybe he's working off something."

"People bet on *American Hero*," Jamal said thoughtfully. "How could we find out?"

"My undergraduate degree is in accounting," Franny said. "Then I went to law school—"

"And then you became a cop. You're an idiot."

"But lucky for us, an over-educated one."

Ties That Bind

Part Four

"KAVITHA! I NEED TO talk to you!" Minal was hollering down the hall, giving Michael a headache. This was not a great way to start the day. He stumbled out of bed, to hear Kavitha shouting back, "After rehearsal!" and disappearing out the door. God. She'd spent almost the entire day yesterday at the studio, and now she was gone so early? It wasn't even six A.M. yet. He wasn't even sure they turned on the AC in her building at this hour of the morning.

"Michael, I know you don't like dealing with money, but we have to talk about this," Minal said, walking up to him, frowning, hands balled on her hips. Finances always gave him a headache—maybe the residue of all those years of hearing his parents worry about money, about whether the laundromat would make enough to see it through another month. It had been such a relief when Minal, capable Minal, had taken over the family finances. "She spent way more than her discretionary budget allows for yesterday."

"Minal, that's not my problem. Take it up with Kavitha." Michael was relieved that it really wasn't his problem. He had enough to worry about. He was going to go back and re-check the docks for Sandip on his lunch break today; he'd thought of a few more places worth looking at.

Minal thumped him gently on the arm. "I tried to talk to her! You saw—she just ran away from me."

Maya Aunty came out of Isai's bedroom, the child rubbing sleepy eyes and holding her grandmother's hand. "What is the problem? Why all the shouting? I would be happy to give you children some money."

"No, no, Aunty," Minal said hastily. "We have plenty. It's just important to stick to a budget, you know? Kavitha has always had trouble with that, but we've been working on it—I thought we finally had an agreement. She was being so good, but now—"

"It's a difficult time," Maya Aunty said quietly. Isai let go of her hand and climbed up into Michael's arms for a good morning hug. He buried his face in her unruly hair and took a moment to enjoy the fierce embrace of his daughter. This part, he loved.

Minal sighed. "I know. She probably bought herself some new clothes to cheer herself up. Although I haven't noticed any shopping bags."

Isai slid down impatiently and went to give Minal the same monster hug treatment. Michael said, "Maybe she was embarrassed. She might have left them at the studio." It was sort of charming, actually—he could imagine Kavitha there, surreptitiously trying on clothes in front of the big glass mirrors. Something red and slinky would look so great on her, although that wasn't really her style. Maybe when all this was over, he would buy her something she could wear out to dinner, with his ring on her finger. He was pretty sure Minal already had plenty of slinky red dresses. Although it might be the better part of wisdom to get her a present too. A man didn't survive this long with two girlfriends without learning a few things.

Minal sighed in reluctant agreement. "I suppose we can talk about this later. C'mon, sweetie." She settled Isai more comfortably on her hip. "Time for morning potty and teeth brushing."

Morning potty was another thing Michael was happy to leave to Minal, along with the financial headaches. Right now, all he wanted was coffee. "Coffee, Aunty?" That, he could take care of.

Yesterday, Kavitha's mother had finally explicitly told Michael to call her Maya Aunty. It was a huge concession, and won only after her husband had decamped. He had tried to persuade her to come too, saying, "What is the point, *kunju*? The boy will come home when he wants to come home—it's not up to us."

She had responded, "You! You are the one who drove him away! Go, go now. I will stay, and make sure that he comes home."

And so Maya had stayed, moving into Isai's bedroom, giving them back their living room. A bit of breathing space, and even some grandmotherly babysitting—whatever her prejudices, Maya had been completely won over by her grandchild. And Isai, for her part, adored her new grandmother. It was endearing, if bizarre, to see the old woman crooning over her grandchild, singing old lullabies in Tamil while preening the girl's shape-shifted feathers.

So things were relatively quiet at home, and quieter at work too—no new snatches. There were reports of similar incidents overseas, but nothing in America recently. Yesterday, he'd found the final link in his smuggling case; it was all over, except for the paperwork. Michael was going to keep looking for Sandip, of course, but he was still hoping Sandip would find his own way home soon. Michael was almost ready to relax—until he was ambushed in his own home.

Maya dug into her dressing gown pocket. "I do not want coffee. I want to know, what is this?" she hissed, holding up a little red box, practically shoving it into Michael's nose.

"Where did you find that?" Michael whispered, with a glance down the hall, to where Minal was in the bathroom with Isai. The door was closed; she shouldn't hear anything, as long as he finished this quickly. Follow a question with a question, that's what he'd been taught—keep them on the defensive. Easy to say, hard to do, especially when your heart is racing.

"I wanted to wash your jackets and coats yesterday; winter is coming."

Not for months! "You don't need to do that, Aunty," Michael said, automatically.

She frowned. "If I don't, who will? At least that girl"—she always referred to Minal as *that girl*—"can cook, but none of you clean properly. You live in filth."

Michael was glad neither of the women were around to hear that—Minal would probably shrug and move on, but Kavitha would be hurt. She was just beginning to mend her relationship with her mother, but it was a fragile peace—she wasn't up to taking much in the way of criticism yet. Michael had had enough of conflict in the last month to last him a lifetime.

Yet here Maya came with more. "So what does this mean?" She flipped the box open, letting the two rings sparkle. One was a vintage ring, lots of tiny little diamonds in an intricate setting, for Kavitha, who loved old things. And the other was a single large-ish diamond, flanked by two tiny rubies—that one was for Minal; he'd thought she'd appreciate a flashy rock to show her old street friends. Neither ring was terribly expensive, but the best he could afford on a detective's salary.

"It should be obvious, I think," Michael said, striving for calm.

"For both of them?"

Quiet certainty, that was the tone to use. He needed to sound sure of himself, even if he wasn't. Maya would leap on weakness like a shark on its prey. "Yes."

She raised a diminutive eyebrow. "So what are you waiting for?"

"What?" He felt as if she'd just punched him with that tiny little hand.

"How long have these been sitting in your pocket?"

"Umm . . . a while?" Had it really been less than a month since Sally had gotten that promotion? The weeks with Black as his putative partner seemed endless.

Maya snapped, "A while? Do you know how far we could have gotten in planning the wedding in a while?"

Michael frowned, bewildered. "You mean—you're happy about this? You wouldn't mind if your daughter married a man who was also marrying someone else?" This was not the reaction he'd expected.

Maya frowned right back, and stepped even closer to him. He wanted to step back, but he was enough of a cop to stand his ground. He wasn't going to be pushed around by a little old lady, even if she was his almost-mother-in-law. Maya said, "It's not the marriage I would have chosen for her. But the important thing is that she get married. She is so old."

Michael winced. Another thing Kavitha didn't need to hear.

Maya continued, "Besides, the marriage is your affair. The wedding is mine. I will have to hurry if we want to reserve elephants for next summer. We cannot get them any earlier, I am quite sure."

"Elephants?" Michael felt as if she'd added a set of brass knuckles to the fist she was punching into his gut. Metaphorically.

She sighed. "Well, of course, elephants. In the old days, we would have had to go back to Sri Lanka for a proper wedding, but now, things are advanced. You can get anything you need here. The elephants, thali necklace, saris, saffron and jasmine, a priest willing to perform mixed marriages . . ."

"There isn't going to be a Hindu priest," Michael protested. His parents would freak out if the wedding wasn't Catholic. God, he hadn't even thought of that. But Maya just flipped her hands in his face.

"Details, details. You let me worry about that. Me and your mother—we'll sort it out. Don't worry about the money—we have plenty saved up. I was going to spend it on a luxury cruise, since I didn't think the girl would ever get married, but cruises can wait."

"Aunty—"

She stopped him, with a raised hand in front of his face. "Michael. Do you love them? Both of them?"

It was so strange—the last few weeks had been so crazy, there hadn't been any time for fun, or romance, or even sex. And he still couldn't really imagine the life to come, when he was married to two women, until death did them part. He was pretty sure that wasn't a wise choice for an ambitious man who wanted to go far with his career. But when she asked the question, Michael was surprised to find that none of that mattered. Because the answer was easy, it just slipped right out, grounded in a bone-deep certainty. "Yes."

Minal with her cooking and sexiness and the practical competence that got the four of them through their days; Kavitha with her beauty and grace, her passion for family and commitment to lofty ideals. Michael loved them both to death, so much that it was easier not to think about it. He wasn't sure a man should love a woman, especially two women, so much.

"So ask her, *kunju*," Maya said, her tone suddenly gentled. "Ask them both. Life is short, and unpredictable. You must take happiness where you can. If the past few weeks have taught me nothing else, they have taught me that." Her eyes were bright, but her voice was steady.

"I'm sure Sandip will turn up," Michael offered weakly. He wasn't sure of any such thing.

Maya just pushed the ring box into his hand, shook her head in that strange South Asian gesture that meant yes—no—and it's in the hands of the gods all at once, and turned away, her shoulders erect and unwavering.

God. Michael swore, if he had a dozen like her on the force, he'd clean up this dirty city in a month.

Just ask them. Okay. What the hell had he been waiting for?

Michael had thought about how to do it. He couldn't ask one of them first, and then the other—that would be too strange, and might lead to problems. It had to be both at once, and the only time he had alone with them both was at night, once Isai and Maya had gone to bed. But he'd also eventually realized that he couldn't ask them in bed—it would be too weird. Like saying "I love you" right after an orgasm—no one could take it seriously. So not in bed, but after Maya and Isai were asleep. Which meant during dishes, which they usually did at the very end of the day, after picking up the disaster of scattered toys. It wasn't the most romantic time ever, but it was the best he could do.

Usually Michael washed, Minal dried, and Kavitha put away. It was fast and efficient, but tonight Michael left Kavitha to wash the dishes and disappeared into the front hall. The box was waiting in his jacket pocket, the rings still safe inside. He took it in a hand that was suddenly shaking—it was funny; he'd faced down more than his share of bad guys, some of them with guns, some of them twisted by their wild cards into something scarier than a gun. Yet here he was, the big bad black cop, shaking.

Michael took a deep breath, steadied his hand, and then turned and walked back down the hall, into the kitchen. He'd left the room with everything calm; he came back in to find the women bent over the sink, snapping at each other in lowered voices, clearly angry, but also careful not to wake Kavitha's mother or the child.

"Are you serious?" Kavitha asked, her hands still furiously washing dishes. "You're going to abandon me now? We still have no idea where Sandip is." Her voice was sharper, more shrill, than Michael had ever heard it. He felt a pang of guilt that he wasn't looking harder for her brother. Although he had his doubts that the kid was even still in New York. Maybe he'd managed to cross the border, go back to Toronto, to hang with his friends. Wasn't that the sort of thing teenagers did?

Minal took a plate from her and rubbed it dry. "I'm not trying to abandon you. Gods, I know you're a performer, but do you have to be such a drama queen? Don't you think it would be easier, if I weren't here? Spring semester will be over in two more days—I can take the summer off, head out of town for a month or two. It won't be so crowded here; you won't be tripping over each other."

Kavitha said flatly, "You just don't want to deal with my mother anymore."

Minal sighed. "Look, I won't claim it's easy talking to her, especially when she so carefully avoids discussing our relationship. But it's not that. She's actually kind of sweet, in her own way. I just don't want to make her life harder right now."

"You think I do?" Kavitha's hands stilled in the soapy water of the sink.

"Oh, God. That's not what I was saying! Michael, will you tell her, please? Can you explain what I meant?" Minal turned to him, finally seeing the box in his outstretched hand. "Oh, shit."

Kavitha turned too, her open mouth abruptly closing. He didn't want to know what she'd been about to say. He didn't know what he ought to say. This wasn't how he'd pictured this going.

Well, he wasn't going to put the box away, not now. He popped it open, so the rings were visible, and slightly awkwardly slid to one knee in front of them. "Umm . . . I love you. I love you both. Will you marry me?"

Minal looked at Kavitha, then back at him. "You idiot. Your timing sucks. But yes, of course. Yes." She grinned widely, and reached a joyful hand out to Kavitha. "Sweetheart? Marry us?"

Kavitha swallowed, and took a step back, pressing up against the porcelain sink. It seemed like an endless awful time before she said, "I'm so sorry. I can't. No."

The Big Bleed

Part Eight

AFTER THE WORST TWENTY-FOUR hours he could remember, Jamal returned to his Bleecker Street room at eleven P.M. Tuesday night.

And found Sheeba waiting for him.

"The logical question," he said, panting as if he'd climbed the stairs rather than ridden the elevator, "is how the hell you got in here."

"I'm a federal agent? It gives a lot of leeway with hotel managers. And when that fails, I can fly. Remember. You should sit down."

The suggestion was unnecessary: Jamal had already collapsed in a chair.

"Here's where I also say, 'whassup?'" He barely managed his street black voice. "If this is an intervention, you should have my parents and my girlfriend, too."

"You've got a *girlfriend?*" She shook her head. "Jamal, you aren't well. You've been running off and not telling anybody where—"

"—On my own time."

She held up a hand. "No malfeasance is suggested."

"Christ, Sheeba, you've been in management too long—"

She bristled. Of course, Jamal had used "Christ" improperly. "I just want to help."

"While getting in my business."

"That seems unavoidable, since your business is our business."

"Well," Jamal said, "this wasn't really a sin of commission as much as omission. I'm tired of hiding it."

They had done Memorial Day duty with the Rodham campaign, then up early on Tuesday for Holy Roller—again; his appearances seemed to require double Secret Service and SCARE detachments—and no release from duty until ten that night.

With the late Wednesday, Jamal had been able to visit Dr. Finn at Jokertown Clinic—the doctor had asked him to come in Thursday the week before, but there had been no time. "You appear to be suffering from muscular deterioration."

"Do you know what or why or whether anything can be done?"

"No to all of those, at least provisionally."

Had he felt strong enough, he would have lunged across the desk at the doctor. "Mind if I ask what the fuck you have been doing?"

If Finn was disturbed by Jamal's vehemence, he didn't show it. He merely indicated the files spread out on his desk. "Eliminating other factors, mostly. Environmental, chemical—"

"So this is something in my wiring."

"It appears to be." The centaur paused, as if searching for something positive to offer. "You may be the first of your type."

"So after this kills me, it will be known as the Jamal Norwood Disease? Do I get to address the crowd at fucking Yankee Stadium, too?"

"Mr. Norwood, it is difficult and progressive, but not . . . dire." He cleared his throat. "I would advise you to take a much less . . . active role in your work, possibly go on leave. Help us with tests and conserve your energy."

There had been more, but Jamal could no longer remember it. It all added up to . . . telling the Angel everything that had happened to him.

By the end, Sheeba, bless her, was blinking back tears and reaching for Jamal's hand. "Oh my God, Jamal. This sounds awful."

"Try feeling it."

"We feel it," a man said from the bedroom doorway.

Carnifex himself entered. Jamal couldn't decide which annoyed him more: the fact that Billy Ray was part of this . . . or that he hadn't even thought to look and listen. "That was pretty sneaky."

Ray chose not to acknowledge the rebuke. "Here's the deal: you're on medical leave until further notice."

Jamal was looking at the floor, feeling nothing but relief as Ray continued: "I'm going to light a fire under our medical people and get you into Johns Hopkins. I can't believe you've been dicking around with the Jokertown Clinic all this time."

"They're sort of the world's specialists in folks like us."

"They give Band-Aids and aspirin to jokers, Norwood. They may have some sympathetic docs there, but that place is as far from a world-class research facility as you are from being a first-rate agent."

Typical Billy Ray: never pass up a chance to step on a subordinate.

He stood up. Sheeba did, too. "Jamal, is there anything you need tonight?"

"Sleep," he told her, quite truthfully. "It will be nice not to have to hit the road tomorrow."

Billy Ray and Sheeba had not mentioned it, but Jamal assumed that being on leave would mean loss of access. *So use it while you've got it.*

The first thing to do was follow up on a promise he'd made to Franny, to search the intel database for Joseph Frank—

Well, no. First thing was, open a beer and pour it into a glass.

Then repeat.

It didn't make him feel stronger, but he did feel *better.*

Then it was back to the computer, playing cyber sleuth. Jamal was surprised to find that, in the past fourteen months, Joseph Daniel Frank had made a number of exits from the USA and entrances to the Republic of Kazakhstan.

It further developed that Mr. Frank had been involved in a disturbance—a drunken dispute with a prostitute that resulted in a beating and an arrest (in Kazakhstan, likely the same thing)—three months ago.

In the city of Talas. Talas. Not Astana, the capital.

Talas, specifically at a casino-nightclub named Maxim's.

What was in Talas that would draw Michael Berman's cameraman there repeatedly over the past year-plus?

What would a real cyber sleuth do here? Well, since the one given was that Joe Frank, and by extension, Michael Berman, had to be involved in something illegal, Jamal ought to search for criminal enterprises or individuals that could be tied to the city of Talas, of course.

That turned out to be a rich vein. Kazakhstan was an oil producer, with oil producer–level corruption. Drugs, whores, counterfeiting, human trafficking, all on a significant scale—especially for a city with a population under fifty thousand.

Drilling down in each category, Jamal built up a list of names and links that he saved in another file. By the time he had gone through the primary areas of criminal activity, he realized one name showed up in all four: a party known as "Baba Yaga."

There was no file on Baba Yaga, just a name and a list of activities that filled a page. All agencies were on record as welcoming further details—

God bless those foreign crime lords. They were always coming up with cute names for themselves. Johnny Batts. The Vicar. Of course, Jamal himself was known as Stuntman and he worked with the Midnight Angel—

Whatever. The name "Baba Yaga" was familiar to Jamal from some childhood book or movie, so he called up Wikipedia for a refresher even as he pictured some slick-haired, black-eyed young thug out of *Scarface.*

Oh. It turned out that Baba Yaga was a witch or a hag. Didn't sound like the kind of name a young male hood would choose . . . unless that young male hood had a terrific sense of humor, which was not usually part of the ensemble.

Male or female, Scarface or hag, this Baba Yaga owned an establishment named Maxim's. Which happened to be the establishment where citizen Joseph Frank got in trouble with a hooker.

Jamal sat back. Detective Francis Xavier Black was going to find this useful. Which was a good thing, because Agent Jamal Norwood was down for the count, out of the game, on the disabled list.

Likely for the rest of his short life.

No Parking
Mon–Fri 7–9am 3–5pm
Except Buses
No Loading Except Authorized
Commercial Vehicles
Mon–Fri 9am–3pm Except Wednesday
With Pass—1 Hour Limit
Snow Emergency Route/No Parking
Odd Side During Snow Emer.
No Parking 3–5am March/November
No Standing Other Times

by Ian Tregillis

WALLY GUNDERSON SIGHED WHEN he saw the conglomeration of parking signs. They were bolted to a single streetlight, like a profusion of fungus on a steel tree. His steam-shovel jaw creaked up and down as he read each line to himself, trying to decipher Jokertown's byzantine parking regulations. He scratched his forehead. It sounded like a railroad spike dragged across an iron skillet.

No *standing?* What the heck did *that* mean?

The blare of a car horn broke his concentration. A hairy lizard leaned from a window of the delivery truck idling behind Wally's rusted and battered '76 Impala.

"Hey, Tin Man!" she yelled. "Move it!"

He glanced at his watch. *Crud.* He'd be late picking up Ghost again. The adoption committee got sore about stuff like that.

He didn't have time to cruise around for a different spot. But Wally

wasn't very good at parallel parking—it would take just as long shimmy-
ing the car back and forth to ease into the spot. Plus, he felt pretty badly
when he scraped the other cars. So he used a shortcut.

Wally hopped out of the Impala. The lizard lady lay on her horn. He
waved at her. Crouching alongside his car, he reached underneath to grip
the frame in one hand. He paid careful attention to his hands, knowing
from experience that if he wasn't careful he ran the risk of accidentally
rusting through the chassis. Then, after wrapping his other arm over the
trunk, he gave the car a solid shove.

It skidded sideways seven feet and slammed against the curb. It went
straight into the gap, but Wally overshot. The Impala bounced over the
curb, cracked against the parking meter, and scraped a Toyota on the re-
bound. The Toyota's car alarm shrieked. The parking meter toppled to the
sidewalk with a crash.

"Nuts," said Wally. "Not again." The delivery truck sped past him.

He surveyed the damage. The meter had been felled like a tree in high
winds, complete with a little clump of concrete at the base like the root
ball. The LCD window in the meter blinked nonsense patterns of static
hash before fading to black, like the last gasp of a dying robot. He couldn't
open the Impala's passenger door, which now sported a large dent. He'd
have to pound it back into shape later.

From the glove compartment, he fished out a notepad, pen, and roll of
duct tape. Wally scrawled a note of apology on the pad, tore off the sheet,
folded some money into the note, and taped the package to the broken
meter. Duct tape worked better than masking tape. This he'd learned
through trial and error.

People were staring. Wally gave a guilty shrug, then headed at a fast
walk toward the Jerusha Carter Childhood Development Institute. He
glanced at his watch again. The fast walk became a jog. The pounding of
his iron feet left a trail of cracks in the sidewalk.

Things would have been so much easier if he could take the subway.
But sometimes it got crowded, and when that happened people got shoved
up against him, and when that happened the seams and rivets of his iron
skin could hurt folks. Didn't matter how careful he was.

As he passed the Van Renssaeler Memorial Clinic, a flash of yellow
caught Wally's attention. He paused at the entrance to the Institute, his
hand resting on the door. A boxy three-wheeled cart turned the corner
a few blocks up. It was painted blue and white like a police car and had

a yellow strobe on top. The cart puttered along the row of parked cars. It eased to a stop alongside a Volkswagen. The driver strutted out, brandishing a ticket pad. A dishwater blond ponytail poked from the brim of her hat.

Wally sighed. "Aw, rats. Not her again."

Ghost hadn't yet finished her counseling session when he arrived. She sat cross-legged on the floor in one of the glassed-in side rooms along the courtyard, talking to one of the Institute's child psychologists. The doc saw Wally but kept her attention on Ghost. Wally's foster daughter didn't see him. He tiptoed away.

Ghost had resisted the counseling for quite a while; it had been a relief for all involved when she started engaging with the teachers and staff at the Institute. For the longest time she trusted only one adult, and that adult was Wally. He'd rescued her from the life of a child soldier in the People's Paradise of Africa, where she had been an experiment: infected, traumatized, brainwashed, trained to kill. But she was also a little girl who liked Legos, Dr. Seuss, and peanut-butter-and-mango sandwiches.

More and more, she was a little girl. But traces of the soldier remained. And probably always would.

A few of her classmates played in the courtyard. They shouted and waved at Wally. He knew most of them; he and Ghost had been coming here since before the Institute opened. There was little Cesar, whom he'd known as long as Ghost, and who faced similar counseling issues; Moto, the boy who exhaled searing gouts of flame when he got excited, or frightened, or a case of the hiccups; Allen, whose mother and father were both in jail; Jo, who always wore the top half of a cow costume and refused to say anything except "Moo" and "Dickwad." Some of the children had come from Africa, like Moto and Cesar, though not with Wally. Others had come to the Institute in the intervening years.

The world was full of troubled kids. But you couldn't save them all. Wally had learned that the hard way. No matter how much he wanted to, he couldn't forget the smell of the mass grave in Nyunzu, where his pen pal had been murdered. Failing Lucien was the worst thing he had ever done. The shame made Wally so sad and angry that sometimes he wanted to punch the whole world.

He swallowed the stone in his throat and waved to the kids. "Howdy," he said.

An immense baobab tree shaded the sandbox. Wally laid a hand on its bark. "Hi, you," he whispered. The surrounding building shielded the tree from wind, but sometimes it seemed as though the leaves rustled in response to his greeting. The baobab smelled of rain, and jungle, and a lost friend. It made Wally smile, but it also made him feel lonely. Sometimes it felt like his ribs were still shattered, pushing spurs of bone to pierce his heart. But he tried not to let it show.

Wally knelt in the sandbox. "So what kind of trouble are you guys getting into today?"

"Moo," said Jo. Her cotton cow ears flopped up and down. "Dickwad. Moo."

"She says she's glad you're back," said Cesar. "I'm moving to Brooklyn!" he added. "I'm going to have a room and my own bed and everything. And they even said I could have a birthday party! You'll come, right?"

"Heck yeah, pal. We wouldn't miss it for the world."

Moto sniffled. His tears wafted across the courtyard like smoke from an extinguished candle. Wally put an arm around him. The heat from his breath seeped into Wally's skin, conducting through the metal across his back and sides, to soothe an old surgery scar/weld. It felt good.

The poor kid didn't get many hugs. Wally also knew, from what Ghost told him, that Moto had been bounced from his third foster home. Another accidental bedroom fire. His foster parents lacked the patience to sleep in shifts.

"Hey," he said. "You know what Ghost asked me the other day? She asked if we could throw a party for your birthday. Would you like that?"

The sniffles trailed off. "Really?"

"Well sure, why not?"

Moto hugged him again. Wally made a mental note to buy another fire extinguisher.

When Wally sifted his fingers through the sand they came back covered with random phrases: "The joy a." "A rainbow it axe." "Shadow the the running barn to under." A few days earlier another foster parent had brought a set of refrigerator poetry magnets for the kids' message board. At least half of these were already scattered in the sand.

Wally didn't understand poetry. He didn't read much.

Allen saw the magnets stuck to his iron fingers and tossed the letter "H" at his chest. It stuck with a muted *click*. Wally could feel the tug of the magnet through his coveralls, like a faint buzzing in the rivets of his sternum.

"Gosh," he said. "That tickles."

Moto saw what Allen had done and flung a handful of magnets and sand at Wally's shoulder. He blinked the sand out of his eyes to see the letters "R," "G," and the word "cattle" stuck to his forearm. Moto covered his mouth when he giggled; little tongues of flame fluttered through his fingers. Then Jo got into the act. Wally lay sprawled in the sand while the kids climbed over him. Laughter and the stink of melted plastic filled the courtyard.

Wally had to pluck the magnets from his scalp a couple of times. They made his head feel funny, like he had a mild fever, or as if his brain were stuffed with cotton. The game went for a few more minutes until Ghost's session ended. Her therapist followed her into the courtyard.

"Moo," said Jo.

"Hi, Ghost," said Cesar.

"Huh," Ghost said, and shrugged.

The therapist beckoned to Wally. He rolled gently to his feet, careful not to pinch little fingers or toes under his bulk. He hugged Ghost just as gently, but more firmly.

"How was your day? I broke another parking meter."

She shrugged, and then became insubstantial to pull away from his hug. She floated to the sandbox, toes dangling an inch above the ground, before settling to earth alongside Allen. It had been a while since she'd been so withdrawn. Wally wondered if he'd find her standing over his bed in the middle of the night with a knife in her hands, like the haunted little girl he'd met in the jungle.

"Okey-dokey. You guys just hang out for a sec," said Wally. He followed the doctor into a cloister alongside the courtyard. "What's going on, Doc?"

The psychiatrist wore her hair pulled back, and the scarf around her neck matched her earrings. She looked fancy, like somebody on TV. Her name tag read "Dr. Miranda." She shook her head.

"Yerodin threatened a classmate with a pair of scissors today." Yerodin was Ghost's real name. All the adults at the Institute used it, but she hated it when Wally called her that.

"Awww, cripes," said Wally. He ran a hand over his face and added "new bedspread" to the mental shopping list, just under "fire extinguisher." "How come?"

"She's been acting up all week. Since we told the children that Mr. Richardson was ill."

Wally remembered Richardson. Ghost talked about him a lot. He taught math, and sometimes he gave the kids rides on his carapace. He could fit three or four of them on the flat of his back, between pairs of detachable legs. He kind of reminded Wally of Dr. Finn, except more like a bug than a horse. He also told really corny jokes, which Ghost loved.

"Well that's a bummer. What's he sick with?"

Dr. Miranda lowered her voice. "That's what we told the children, but he hasn't called in sick. N-nobody has seen him since last Friday."

Wally said, "She's been doing real good at home, you know. Real good."

"Well, she wasn't today. She still reverts to using sharp objects when she feels angry or frustrated."

"Okay. I'll have a talk with her." Wally frowned. "Will this affect the adoption?"

She started to answer, but then her face crumpled into a scowl a second before Jo started to bawl.

"DickWAAAD!"

Wally turned just in time to see Ghost, scissors in hand, stuffing a trophy in her pocket: a cotton cow ear from Jo's costume. The sobbing girl didn't pull away when Ghost pulled the second ear taut and opened the scissors.

Wally vaulted the cloister railing. He crossed the courtyard in one hard stride. But rather than pulling Ghost away, or lifting Jo out of reach, he gave the blades a gentle flick of his finger. They dissolved into a fine orange mist. Ghost floated away.

"Cripes, kid," he called after her.

Wally spent a few minutes consoling Jo. "Don't you worry. We'll fix your ears right up. You'll hear good as new, okay?" Wally couldn't sew. But maybe he and Ghost could learn together. That sounded like a good idea.

"Moo," said Jo between sniffles. "Moo . . . moo . . ."

Wally found Ghost with Dr. Miranda. Silently, they packed up her teddy-bear backpack, plastic bag of dry cereal, and Dr. Seuss book. The doctor gave Wally a Look as he led Ghost down the corridor. His feet left deep imprints in the carpet, but not as low as Jo probably felt.

He said, "That was a pretty crummy thing you did."

"I don't care," said Ghost. "She's dumb. I hate her."

"No you don't. She's your friend. Remember the time I forgot to pack your juice and she shared hers with you?"

"No."

"Really? I know a guy, an ace like us, and he can tell if somebody is lying or not. But when he does it to you, it feels like having a hundred spiders crawling all over your body." Ghost shrugged. She'd spent a lot of time in the jungle. Creepy-crawlies didn't bother her. "But they don't bite like normal spiders. No. You know why? Because . . . they . . . *tickle!*"

Wally reached for her, careful to miss as she squealed and danced away. She took his hand as they stepped outside. Good. Maybe she'd open up a little bit.

Ghost stopped to stare at the flashing lights when they reached the street. The meter maid's cart flanked Wally's dented Impala. She pointed at Wally's car, then at the parking meter, while two more police officers listened.

One of the cops was a petite woman. Her tag read "Officer Moloka." Her partner was a huge hairy guy who towered over Wally. With his wolf snout and long black claws, he looked like a drawing in one of Ghost's books.

"Uh-oh," said Wally.

The hairy guy, Officer Bester, nodded to him. "Hi, Rustbelt." Ghost giggled at his deep voice.

Most of the 5th Precinct knew Wally by sight. NYPD sometimes provided security for Committee events in the city. Wally didn't recognize the officers, but he waved anyway. "Howdy."

The meter maid wheeled on him, red-faced and sweating. "You! Why can't you park like a normal person?"

"I'm real sorry about that meter. Did you get my note?"

"Your note? This is—" She pointed at the broken meter so strenuously that she had to grab her hat with her other hand. "—destruction of city property!"

"Yeah. Those things aren't cheap, Rusty," said Officer Moloka.

"Sorry."

"Don't you know it's illegal . . ." The meter maid trailed off. "What is that on your face?"

Wally's fingertips scraped along his jaw and forehead. He found a blue plastic "E" stuck to his left ear, and the word "barrel" over his right eyebrow.

"You really want us to take him in, Darcy?" asked the furry cop.

The parking lady seemed ready to choke. Ghost hid behind Wally's legs. "He—the—it's—city property, and he's a repeat offender! This is how it starts, the death of the city. First it's jaywalking and littering, then it's people ramming parking meters just for fun, and then it's a short slide to lawless anarchy. This," she said, again gesticulating at the destroyed meter, "is the bellwether of the decline of a civil society!"

The policewoman sighed and crossed her arms. Her partner leaned over to look at Wally's license plates. "Diplomatic plates. If we issue a citation they'll just appeal and have it rescinded."

"He does this on purpose. He's hiding behind his job!"

"Oh. You mean them fancy plates? I didn't even want those," said Wally. "But Lohengrin insisted."

He was trying to agree, but that only seemed to make the meter maid—Darcy—more angry. Or, at least, the color of her face turned a darker red.

She said, "Do you see what I mean? Practically boasting about his ability to flout the law. And he does! Broken windshield, broken taillight, parking beyond the allotted length of time at a broken meter, destruction of city property."

"Write him up if you want," said Officer Moloka, "but we can't walk him down to the precinct. First, I don't want to be the one who has to explain to the chief why the UN is breathing on the mayor who's breathing on him. And second, he's got his kid with him." She winked at Ghost.

The meter maid flipped open her pad and clicked her pen. Officer Bester said, "Your funeral, Darcy."

"I'm doing my job." She started to fill out the ticket, paused, and waved her pen at the cops. "And I'm going to find that van, too."

"Whoa, whoa. No." Officer Moloka shook her head and waved her hands as if trying to fend off somebody with bad breath. "Those guys are dangerous. They won't balk at hurting a meter maid—"

"Parking enforcement officer!"

"—and they won't be intimidated by a parking ticket."

"Yeah," said Officer Bester. "If you see them, call the cops."

"I *am* a cop."

The other police officers waved good-bye to Ghost and returned to patrolling their beat. The hairy one turned around and made a face at Ghost. She giggled.

"I won't try to get out of this ticket," said Wally.

Darcy wrote out the citation, tore a carbon copy from her pad, took the magnet from Wally's hand, and used it to stick the ticket to his chest.

"You'd better not," she said. Wally waited until her cart puttered away to haul the Impala out of its parking spot. He really needed to learn how to parallel park.

"That was funny," Ghost said when the coast was clear.

The run-in with the parking lady caused Wally to forget all about Ghost's trouble at school until he saw the severed cotton cow ear on the floor alongside her bed when he tucked her in. Wally was too heavy to sit on the edge of her bed without causing her to flop onto the floor, so he knelt beside it. Ghost handed him *Green Eggs and Ham*.

"Read it, Wallywally. With voices," she said.

"Tell ya what. I'll read a little bit if you tell me about what happened at school today." He picked up the scrap from Jo's costume. "This wasn't very nice."

"I hate Jo. She's dumb."

"No you don't. Tomorrow you'll forget all about it and want to be pals again. But she won't forget it, because you hurt her feelings real bad. She'll remember you as a mean person. You should tell her you're sorry."

Ghost looked away. She went insubstantial, as she sometimes did when she wanted to run away from trouble. But she didn't float away through the ceiling. Good kid.

Wally asked, "Is this about Mr. Richardson?"

She rematerialized. "He's gone. He didn't say good-bye." Her voice broke; her accent grew thicker. She sounded much more like the girl she'd been when she first arrived in New York when she added, simply, "He was nice."

Ghost still didn't trust many adults, but she talked about Richardson from time to time. That counted for a lot.

Wally read to her. He did the voices.

Later, he took out the telephone book. Richardson, unfortunately, wasn't an unusual name. There were several Richardsons in and around Jokertown. But one of those had to be Ghost's teacher. A guy like that, if he worked in Jokertown he probably lived nearby, too.

It took half an hour to work his way down the list of telephone numbers. The first number he called belonged to a man—or a woman, it was hard to tell—whose voice sounded like two people speaking not quite in unison with each other. They (he? she?) didn't know any school-teachers. The second number rang fifteen times with no answer. When Wally called the third Richardson on the list, he got an earful from a lady whose telephone number was apparently quite close to that of a popular Chinese takeout place and who was pretty sensitive about wrong numbers. The fourth number belonged to Mr. Richardson-the-teacher's cousin, but she said she didn't keep in touch and hadn't spoken to him for a while. She gave Wally her cousin's telephone number, apologizing that it might be out of date. It was the number that rang without answer. Wally gave her his name and number and asked her to please have Mr. Richardson get in touch if she happened to hear from him.

Ghost floated through the wall from her bedroom just as he was hanging up. She mumbled to herself in a language Wally didn't understand; it was spoken only in the PPA. Her fingers curled as though clutching a knife hilt. He had to wake her because his hand passed through her shoulder when he tried to lead her back to her bedroom. She yawned. He carried her back to bed, wondering about her dreams.

It seemed part of Ghost would always dwell in the dark jungles of the Congo, in a land of mass graves and Leopard Men. Some wounds healed; some turned into scars.

She had enough of those. He wanted to be a good foster dad for her. That meant protecting her from new scars and new traumas when he could. He couldn't always be there; the world was a big place. You couldn't protect everybody all the time. But the way he saw it, this meant it was important to save Ghost from the little hurts of life when he could.

He thought about it while preparing for bed. He took a fresh pad of steel wool from the box under the bathroom sink. As he scrubbed himself, Wally decided it wouldn't take more than a couple of hours to stop by Richardson's place. He'd find him before picking up Ghost tomorrow.

He touched the photo of Jerusha Carter on his bedstand. It wasn't a real photo—he'd printed it from the *American Hero* web site. It was all he had. But it was something.

"Miss you," he said, and turned out the light.

On weekday mornings, Ghost took the subway to school with Miss Holmes, their neighbor across the hall. Miss Holmes was a bat-headed physical therapist who worked at Dr. Finn's clinic, next door to Ghost's school. Sometimes she let Ghost ride on her shoulders, and when she did Ghost practically disappeared between the enormous hairy ears.

Before they set off, Wally said, "Remember our talk last night? About Jo?"

Ghost looked down, scowling at the thin fuzz atop Miss Holmes's head. "Yes."

"You're a swell kid. See you later, gator."

"Not now cacadile!" Her English was pretty good, but sometimes Ghost had trouble remembering rhymes.

Wally stood in the hallway, watching and waving until they got in the elevator. Then he went back inside and called the Committee offices in the UN building up near Forty-second Street. He had plenty of vacation built up, so taking a day off was easy. They were happy as long as he wasn't running off to a remote corner of the world on a personal mission.

After copying Mr. Richardson's address from the phone book, he retrieved his fedora from the coat closet and headed out. The hat had been a gift, so it actually fit. And it looked snazzy. Wally had watched enough black-and-white films to know how detectives dressed. A good detective also knew where to go for information. Nero Wolfe had Archie, Nick Charles knew all sorts of guys . . . But Wally could do them both one better. He knew Jube.

Jokertown existed in a perpetual state of frenzy. It had been an exciting but difficult adjustment when Wally moved here, until he accepted that venturing outside the apartment inevitably meant navigating a scene of low-level chaos. The cacophony of traffic—idling delivery trucks, car horns, a siren in the distance—washed over him. Sometimes, when she was nearby, he could barely hear Miss Holmes's echolocation, like a high thin screech just at the edge of his hearing. He stepped into the street to make room for a lady pushing a walker and towing a little girl who floated like a balloon on a string tied to her mother's wrist. She gave him a grateful nod. He must have been getting better at it, because he didn't find himself dodging and jostling as many people as usual.

A sheen of thin, high clouds cast a faint haze across the sky. It was early June, so the garbage cans waiting for pickup along the sidewalks weren't quite as ripe as they would be in high summer. His stroll took him past the Italian bakery a couple streets down; he bought a bag of bombolone pastries dusted with powered sugar. They reminded him of eating beignets in New Orleans. He munched as he walked the few blocks to Jube's newspaper stand.

He could have driven, he supposed, but a good detective beat the pavement. A good detective had a feel for the streets and could read the city's mood through the soles of his feet. Weren't they were called gumshoes for a reason? He stuffed the wax paper from his breakfast into an overflowing garbage bin that smelled of sour milk. The odor faded, masked by the more pleasant scent of buttered popcorn as he approached the newspaper stand across the street.

"Howdy, Jube." He waved at the walrus sitting behind the counter.

"Wally Gunderson. You've been a stranger." The tusks made it sound like he was speaking around a mouthful of food. Or maybe it was the cigar doing that. "I ever tell you the one about the two Takisians who walked into a bar? The third one ducked."

Wally scratched his chin, trying to remember. "No, I don't think I've heard that one. How does the rest of it go?"

Jube blinked. His cigar paused in mid-roll from one corner of his mouth to the other. Little puffs of ash wafted down to dust his bright Hawaiian shirt with spots of gray. "You know what? Never mind. Anyway, you haven't been around much."

"Yeah. It's lots of work, raising a kid. Hardest thing I ever did."

Jube's stand normally did a brisk turn of business. He had a trickle of customers, but it wasn't busy as usual. Was it Wally's imagination, or were there fewer people on the streets? Jube made conversation while unwrapping a bundle of tabloids and making change for customers. "How is she?"

"So-so. She's pretty upset. One of her teachers stopping coming to school. I was kind of wondering if maybe you knew him? You know everybody around here."

Folds of blubber jiggled when Jube used a penknife to cut the twine on the bundle. He unwrapped the papers and plopped the pile on a corner of the counter.

"Not everybody," he said. "But could be I know him."

"Philip Richardson? He's the bug guy with six legs, kind of shaped like Dr. Finn, but not a horse. Kind of a strange-looking fella, but real nice."

Jube fell silent for a moment, that awkward kind of silence that people sometimes got when Wally said something. Then he said, " 'Strange-looking,' he says. Uh-huh. You do know this is Jokertown, right? Two fifty."

The last part he said to a translucent shadow in the shape of a woman; she was wrapped in what appeared to be twinkling Christmas lights. They chimed. Three one-dollar bills appeared on the counter, and then a tabloid floated up, folded itself, and disappeared into the silhouette. "Keep the change, Jube," said a whispery voice. The ethereal woman faded into the play of light and shadow on the street.

"Anyway, you ever seen him?"

"Sounds vaguely familiar. You sure he's missing?"

Wally told Jube about what they'd said at school.

Jube adjusted his hat (Wally thought it was called a porkchop hat, though he couldn't figure out why) and shook his head. "Guess they got another one. Getting so nobody's safe anymore."

"Who got another what?"

"The fight club. What else could it be?"

"The what club?"

For the second time in a few minutes, Jube just stared and blinked at him. He seemed to do that a lot. Wally wondered if it was a walrus thing.

"You know, the joker fight club? Videos, death matches. That one."

Something about what Jube said, or the way he said it, momentarily reminded Wally of the PPA. The humidity, the sting of rust eating his skin like slow acid, a line of rippling V's in the water as a crocodile cut across the river . . . *Death matches?*

He shook off the chill. "I don't read much."

Jube made a pained sound, a cross between a rumble and a sob. *Here it comes,* thought Wally. People always got real judgmental when he admitted that. Except Jerusha.

"Wally, Wally, Wally . . . You're killing me here. How can you say that to a poor newspaper vendor? 'Doesn't read,' he says. Gah."

"Sorry. Maybe you could fill me in a little bit?"

Jube asked, "You're not pulling my leg, are you?"

Wally shook his head. It didn't take long for Jube to fill him in on the basics. Learning about the cage match videos put Wally back in Africa again: the flapping of buzzards, the hum of mosquitos, the smell of quick-lime and rot as he excavated a mass grave . . . So many dead kids, black queens and jokers stacked like firewood.

"Wally? *Wally!*" The cigar stub came flying out of Jube's mouth. It left a trail of ash and slobber across the counter.

The front of his stand had crumpled. Wally looked down. His hands had curled into fists, each containing a chunk of wooden newsstand. *Rats.*

He said, "Hey, I'm real sorry about that."

Jube waved it off. He fished the cigar stub from between two stacks of newspapers and shoved it back into his mouth. "Don't worry about it. Occupational hazard, serving this community."

Wally barely heard him. He was thinking about Ghost, and Jo, and Cesar, and Moto, and Miss Holmes, and Allen, and Lucien . . . All the folks everywhere who couldn't defend themselves. He'd seen plenty of that working for the Committee. Guys like Mr. Richardson, decent folks just trying to get by. Dying, or forced to do horrible things, just because they were jokers.

Forced to fight and kill. Just like Ghost.

It wasn't fair. It wasn't right. The seed of an idea sprouted in the back of Wally's mind.

"How many of them videos are there?"

"Beats me." Jube shrugged. "I won't sell that filth."

"Who all have they taken?"

"Well, that's the question, isn't it? Some folks, like your kid's teacher, might disappear for any number of reasons. We'll never know unless somebody spots him in a video."

"Oh."

"But others . . . I hear they got Infamous Black Tongue. And you know Father Squid? He's missing, too."

"Gosh." Even Father Squid?

"Yeah, the creeps. Shining Moira, Charlie Six Tuppence, Nimble Dick, Morlock & Eloi, Glabrous Gladys . . ." Jube leaned forward, whispering, "I hear they even tried to snatch the Sleeper, but they botched it and now he's looking for them."

Looking for them. Wally's seedling idea grew.

"You wouldn't happen to know where folks are getting snatched, would you?"

"Not thinking of doing something stupid, are you?"

"I just want to see what's going on."

"These people are dangerous, Wally."

"I can be, too. Breaking stuff is just about the only thing I'm good at."

"You're not a killer."

"Don't have to be." Wally looked around, over both shoulders, as he said, a little loudly, "I'm a real good fighter, though. Pretty tough."

Jube sighed. "Yeah, I hear things. It's happening all over. But maybe, I don't know, this is just street talk, maybe there are some places that folks try to avoid these days." He gave Wally a rundown of the rumors.

"Thanks, Jube. This is swell of you." Wally bought a paper, tipped his hat, and turned to leave. He stopped. "Hey, by the way. Do you know where I can buy a fire extinguisher?"

Richardson lived in an apartment building on the north side of Joker-town. Kind of a long walk, but Wally was glad he chose not to drive. Every minute he spent outside was a better chance of getting snatched. He tried to look like a potential victim.

It was a tough sell. Few people thought it was a good idea to mug a guy made out of iron.

The way Wally figured it, if the fight club bums were snatching regular people from the street, they weren't accustomed to dealing with some-body who had lots of experience fighting for his own life, and defending others'. He'd be back by the time school let out this afternoon.

But just in case . . . He called the school, and left a message saying he might be late picking up Ghost. They arranged to have Miss Holmes bring her home.

A good private eye knew disguises, too. Wally decided that he'd be an old friend of Richardson's. What kind of person would be easy to snatch? He thought about this long and hard before deciding that maybe they belonged to a crossword puzzle club together. That seemed like a good fit for a schoolteacher. And maybe Richardson missed their last meeting, and so Wally was going to his house to collect his membership dues so that the club could buy more pencils. *Yeah,* thought Wally, *that's pretty good.* Mechanical pencils, really sharp ones, and separate clicky erasers. Crossword people probably went through lots of those. Oh, and news-paper subscriptions. Maybe they got a bulk discount or something. Jube could help with that.

It was a good fake identity. Lots of detail. The creeps running the fight club would probably get a kick out of snatching somebody real brainy like that.

He stopped to loiter on several street corners along the way, talking loudly to himself. "I'm nervous," he would say. "I don't like being out on the streets by myself," he would say. And then, with a sigh that he hoped conveyed both fear and weakness, he'd sum it all up: "I sure hope I don't get kidnapped."

There were no takers.

The walk to Richardson's apartment took Wally past Squisher's Base-ment, a joker-only place Jube had mentioned. It was situated under a clam bar, so Wally decided to stop in for an early lunch. The place had just opened but it smelled skunky, like bad beer, and fishy, like the bottom of a Styrofoam cooler after a long camping trip. The bartender stared at Wally through shafts of mustard-colored sunlight leaking in from the dingy windows at sidewalk level.

"Wow. Rustbelt? Never seen you in here before."

Wally shook his head. "You must have me confused with somebody else. I don't think that Rustbelt fella, whoever he is, wears a hat like mine. I'm just here to eat lunch and do the crossword puzzle. I'm real good at those."

Wally ate a mediocre hamburger, washing it down with a bottle of skunky beer while he pretended to do the puzzle. A few folks, regular customers, drifted in and out.

"Gosh," said Wally. "I'm having a hard time with the puzzle today. Probably because I'm so nervous about getting kidnapped."

He cast furtive glances around the room, checking to see if this projection of vulnerability caught undue attention from anybody. But most of the other customers seemed to ignore him. One fellow got up and shuffled to a table farther away. Wally found that promising. As his gaze followed the guy across the room—he made squelching sounds as he moved, and his body jiggled like a water balloon—he thought he might have glimpsed somebody staring right back at him. A big gray guy covered in round nodules of stone, sort of like a concrete wall frozen in mid-boil. But Wally spent another forty-five minutes writing random words in the crossword grid, and the stone man never looked once in his direction.

He wasn't far from Richardson's apartment when a yellow flash caught his eye again. A parking enforcement scooter idled alongside an expired meter.

Officer Darcy finished her ticket before he caught up with her. So he trotted down the street, waving and taking care not to dig gouges in the sun-softened asphalt with his hard feet. He made eye contact with her in the rearview mirror. Her cart puttered to a stop.

"Howdy," he said. "I just—"

She gave him a nasty look. "Save your breath. You're not getting out of those tickets."

"What? No, I—"

"But if you keep trying, I can cite you for interfering with a police officer in the course of carrying out her duties." She put the cart into gear and started rolling forward again. Wally walked alongside her. It was easy; she didn't go very fast.

"I didn't come over here to do any of that. I know I deserve those tickets. I just, well, I feel real bad about the whole thing. I wanted to say I'm sorry."

Darcy's cart jerked to a halt. The suspension creaked as it rocked back and forth. "What?"

"I know I'm real bad with parallel parking. I swear I don't break those meters on purpose, okay? And I'm going to talk to folks and get it straightened out with them fancy license plates. I never wanted 'em anyway."

Wally wasn't sure, but her eyes looked a little wider. Her lips made a little "o." Like she was frightened or surprised or something. He hoped this didn't count as interfering.

"Wow," said Darcy. "Nobody has ever apologized to me for getting a ticket before. Not once."

"Well, probably nobody breaks as much stuff as I do."

"That's true," she admitted. Wally strolled alongside while she studied meters. They had to wait for a giraffe-necked lady in a convertible to pull out of a parking spot.

Darcy squinted at Wally. The bridge of her nose crinkled up when she did that. "Are you wearing a fedora?"

"Yeah. Pretty nifty, huh? I saw it in a Humphrey Bogart movie."

"Nobody wears fedoras anymore. Not since forever."

"Private detectives do." Darcy twisted her lips in a little moue of doubt. "Anyway," said Wally, "I like hats. I used to have a really neat pith helmet, but I lost it."

"How'd you lose it?"

"Not sure," said Wally. "But I think it was the crocodile."

Darcy cocked her head. "You are very strange."

"I've heard that. Usually they use the term 'weirdo.' "

She snickered at that, but saw the look on his face and looked guilty. "Anyway, what's this about being a detective? We both know you work for the UN."

"Yeah," he said, "but I took the day off."

"Well, at least you're not driving. Or parking."

"Nah. A good detective pounds the pavement."

"And why, I ask entirely out of idle curiosity even though I'm sure to regret it, are you a detective today?"

Wally tapped the side of his nose with a finger. *Clang, bang.* "I'm working the case of the missing jokers," he said quietly.

"Do you know what the term 'vigilantism' means?"

"No. But it sounds like a real good crossword puzzle word. How do you spell it?"

"Are you for real?"

"What?"

They went down the street, crossed an intersection, and kept going. Darcy didn't say much. She was pretty focused. At one point, when they encountered a double-parked two-seater with its blinkers flashing, she muttered to herself, "Look at this clown. Why do people think that turning on their hazard lights will make them immune to tickets?"

Darcy opened up a little more when he asked her how she liked being in the police. It meant the world to her; he could tell. Justice meant a lot to her, too. Her eyes went a little wide when she said that word, "justice."

And she said it a lot. She had this whole long thing about justice and civil society and police as guardians of order. It was pretty interesting, though Wally didn't catch all of it, and it all came out in a smooth rush like she'd said it a hundred times. Secretly he was a little glad when she trailed off.

A white van eased past them on the narrow street. Darcy lifted her sunglasses to watch it. Her gaze followed as it rolled away.

"What's wrong?" She didn't answer, too busy squinting at the van as it dwindled in the distance. "You want me to stop that van? I can, you know."

For a second there, it looked like she was considering it. "Nah," she said.

The van turned a corner. She shrugged, put her sunglasses back on, and went back to work. Wally asked, "What was that all about?"

"Probably nothing," said Darcy. After a tired sigh, she said, "There's a van I kept citing. I'd written well over a dozen tickets. It was always illegally parked . . . double-parked, or blocking a hydrant, or in a loading zone . . ."

"Do they bust up parking meters?"

"No, they're not like you. You don't tear up your tickets and toss them on the ground." Veins pulsed in her neck and forehead. Just talking about it got her upset. "Once I found a pile of shredded tickets in the gutter."

"I guess you have to mail them, huh?"

Her voice went flat. "Can't. Fake plates. They're not in the system. No registration, no address. They even filed the VIN off the dash."

"That's strange."

"Illegal is what it is."

They crossed another street. Wally poked a finger under the brim of the fedora to scratch his forehead. He tried to think like a detective. It was hard.

"I guess I don't get it. Why go to all that trouble of having a made-up license plate just to avoid parking tickets? He could learn to park better and then he wouldn't get them in the first place. Or why even bother with the plates at all?"

Darcy's nose crinkled up again when she stared at him. "You're kidding, right?"

"No."

"It's not about the parking tickets, Wally. The plates look legit because they don't want to get pulled over. Probably because they don't want anybody to see what's in the van. I wouldn't be surprised if it belongs to the same people who are kidnapping jokers."

He stopped. "Really? That's super!" But then he thought about it a little more. This detective thing was hard. "Uh, I still don't get it."

Darcy sighed. "If they stop to grab someone, or drop something off, they have to do it when and where the opportunity arises. So they park illegally." She explained it patiently, and didn't make him feel dumb. He liked that.

This was great. He'd been on the case less than a day and already he'd made his first major break in the case. Granted, it was really Darcy who'd made the breakthrough, but Wally didn't mind. Good detectives always forged a relationship with the police. He'd managed that much.

"Wow. You found the kidnappers!" He frowned. "How come you haven't arrested them?"

"Last time I ticketed the van was before we recognized the probable connection to the fight club. Before those aces busted it up . . . and half of Jokertown." She shook her head, mumbling, "Right through my fingers . . . Could have stopped them way earlier . . . some police officer . . ."

All of a sudden, she looked really sad. Wally said, "You'll catch 'em."

"I'm not so sure. I followed it once, after I realized the plates were bogus."

"Oh yeah?"

"It turned down an alley. Narrow, dead end. But when I came around the corner, it was gone. Where the hell did it go? But people still keep disappearing so they must have gotten a new ride. I keep looking, but . . . ."

Darcy sounded so dejected that Wally tried to hide his disappointment. "Huh. Well, better luck next time."

She fell silent after that. Not entirely sure why he kept at it, other than that it seemed Darcy was pretty neat, Wally tagged along while she checked meters and wrote tickets. One guy who received a parking ticket got pretty steamed and called Darcy all sorts of mean things. Wally didn't like that at all and told him so. Darcy seemed even sadder after that, so he walked with her for another half mile, until she demanded that he buzz off and leave her alone. It was demeaning, she said. "Chauvinism masquerading as chivalry," is what she called it.

But she also said, "Thank you."

Mr. Richardson's place was a bust. Wally rang the bell a whole bunch, and circled the block about ten times, each circuit beginning and ending with Wally sitting on the stoop in case Richardson went out or came home. But Wally never saw him. No mysterious vans, either.

Each day, Wally visited another spot on Jube's list. Each day, in spite of his disguise, and much to his disappointment, he wasn't kidnapped. And Ghost grew more sullen with each day Mr. Richardson didn't return to school.

Wally had decided to pack it in for the afternoon, and was turning his thoughts to the weekend and fun places to visit with Ghost, when he noticed somebody following him. Well, not really following. More like keeping pace with him across the street. The big gray guy across the street paused every time Wally did. He hurried when Wally hurried; he dallied when Wally dallied. Wally pretended to start to cross the street before turning the corner instead. Behind him, the blare of a car horn told him somebody had darted through traffic. Wally stopped to study his reflection in a storefront window but it didn't work as well as it seemed to in the movies. He bought a hot dog from a jellyfish with a street cart, and took his time scooping relish and mustard on it. The other fellow drew steadily closer. He was covered in chunks of rock like a walking fireplace. Wally had eaten most of the hot dog before he recognized the guy from Squisher's Basement.

This is it! thought Wally. *They're coming for me.*

He tried to hide his excitement. It was difficult pretending to not notice as his kidnapper drew closer and closer. Wally concentrated on looking vulnerable.

"Gosh," he said aloud. "I don't feel so good. Maybe I'm coming down with something. I feel pretty weak."

But the stone guy never made his move. Was he waiting for the van to arrive? Wally walked slower and slower. He faked a couple of sneezes. Even that did no good. Finally, feeling impatient, he decided to pretend to be lost. He gazed up at a street sign and made a show of being confused. Then he looked around, as if needing directions.

"Gosh. Where am I?" he said.

The gray rock guy approached him. He held something that resembled a little digital voice recorder. It seemed pretty sinister, he decided. Wally wondered what that thing really was, and what it really did.

"Hey," said the rock guy. "Can I talk to you?"

It's working! thought Wally.

"Sure, fella. I hope you can help me. I'm pretty lost." Wally looked around. *Maybe it would be easier to kidnap me if we weren't out in the open.* "How about we step into that dark alley over there and talk?"

The stone man stopped dead in his tracks. "Oh, I'm not falling for that! I know who you are. And I won't let you take anybody else!"

"Hey, pal, I just want directions—"

The stone man punched Wally in the face with a boulder fist.

Sparks rained on the sidewalk as Wally stumbled backward, toppling a streetlight. It hurt like heck. The gray guy was strong. Wally shook his head, dazed, while the streetlight clanged to the ground and other people on the street quickly scattered.

"You can't hurt me!" yelled the other guy in a voice like an earthquake. With his other fist, the one that hadn't clobbered Wally, he waved the recorder in Wally's face. He jumped up and down, gibbering, "You can't even touch me!"

Uh oh. Had the kidnappers seen through Wally's disguise? If he was going to get taken to their secret hideout, he needed to impress them, make himself irresistible. He'd show them he could fight pretty well before letting the other guy win.

"No, please, I don't want to go with you," said Wally. He leaped to his feet, and blocked another punch with a wide sweep of his forearm. With his other fist he landed a jackhammer blow to the kidnapper's stomach. There was a loud *crack* and another burst of incandescent sparks like the dying embers of a Fourth of July firework. It knocked the wind from the other guy; his breath smelled like hot ash.

"Oof." The rock guy fell to one knee. He glanced at the recorder. "Lying alien bastard," he groaned. It crumpled in his fist, and then he sent the pieces whistling over the rooftops.

Wally wound up for a kick, but the other guy lunged. The tackle threw Wally against a mail truck. It crunched like a soda can and toppled over, blocking the street. They wrestled atop a mangled heap of metal and glass. Each punch and kick threw sparks like a Roman candle as iron scraped against stone. A chorus of shrieking car alarms echoed up and down the street.

"I know you're one of them! Following me everywhere, reporting everything I do," said the rock man. His eyes darted around really fast, like he had trouble keeping still. "Bribing my dentist, eavesdropping through my fillings! Poisoning my thoughts with fluoride!"

He kept up a steady stream of paranoid ranting, even as Wally slipped in a pair of incandescent jabs to the chin and chest. The kidnapper grabbed Wally by the shoulders and kept slamming him against the flattened truck until it felt like his rivets were coming loose.

Wally got a knee up. One hard flex sent the other guy skidding down the sidewalk with a fingernails-on-blackboard screech. He pulled free of the twisted wreckage of the mail truck and got to his feet just as the other guy wrenched a big blue mailbox from the sidewalk with the groan of tortured metal and popping of broken bolts. He swung it at Wally. Wally slapped the blow aside with an open palm. The mailbox exploded into a cloud of rust and fluttering envelopes. The bright orange rust eddied into his opponent's eyes. He flinched, coughing. Wally used the opening for a solid roundhouse to the jaw.

The kidnapper's head snapped around. The shower of sparks ignited a pile of mail.

The other guy kept twisting, and took advantage of the momentum from the blow to land a high spinning kick to Wally's ribs. It sent Wally sprawling across the street. He landed on a compact car. Pain lanced down his side from shoulder to hip. A shiny dent now creased his old surgery scar. He didn't feel like fighting much more.

"Oh, no," said Wally. "I'm feeling pretty woozy now." Which he was. It didn't require any acting to make a show of stumbling to his feet. His ears rang. The ringing turned into sirens.

The kidnapper ran away. Wally tried to give chase but tripped over the flattened mail truck.

He was still laying there when the police arrived.

It was a tight fit in the squad car, but this time they did take Wally to the precinct. The kidnapper was long gone, but they hauled Wally in on charges of disturbing the peace, destruction of city property, mail tampering, and reckless public endangerment. He wondered what would happen when the adoption committee heard about this. At least the police let him call Ghost's school, to arrange to have Miss Holmes take her home again.

The booking officer, whose name sounded like Squint or something like that, kept a large dollhouse on her desk. That seemed strange. She wasn't very interested in Wally's side of the story. She didn't appear to be listening at all until Wally mentioned that the whole thing happened because he was defending himself from one of the fight club kidnappers. And suddenly the police were *very* interested in Wally's story. Particularly in his description of the kidnapper. They put him in a room and left him waiting.

The room had two chairs, a wooden table, and a water cooler with a little tube of paper cones hung alongside it. A window with broken venetian blinds gave him a view of the station house. The precinct was a busy place. All sorts of people—uniformed officers, plainclothes detectives, lawyers in suits, criminals and suspects—passed back and forth outside the room. Wally even glimpsed Darcy at one point. He knocked on the glass and waved at her; she seemed disappointed, but not surprised, to see him.

Wally pressed a paper cone full of cold water against his bruises. It helped to numb the ache. He wondered what Ghost and Miss Holmes were eating for dinner. He drank the water, laid his head on the table, tried to ignore the rumbling in his stomach, and closed his eyes. He hadn't quite fallen asleep when a voice roused him.

"I'll be goddamned . . . Wally Gunderson."

The voice was vaguely familiar. Wally sat up. And then he blinked. There were two men in the doorway. One he recognized.

"Cripes," he said. "Stuntman?"

The man standing across the table wore a suit. Moving like a man in pain, he flipped open a thin leather case about the size of a wallet. "It's Agent Norwood now. I'm with SCARE. More or less."

Heart sinking, Wally stared at the badge. He couldn't remember what SCARE stood for but he knew it was a pretty big deal. "Gosh."

The other guy leaned across the table, extending a hand to Wally. He looked tired too, but in a different way from Stuntman. "Mr. Gunderson, I'm Detective Black." He glanced at Stuntman. "And shouldn't you be in bed?"

"Yes. But I've got to hear this story."

Stuntman closed the badge case hard enough that the breeze tickled Wally's face. He tucked it back into a breast pocket.

"Howdy." *Detective?* "Is this about the mail truck?"

The men shared a look. Stuntman rolled his eyes and shrugged.

"Uh, no," said the detective. "Agent Norwood is helping me investigate the Jokertown kidnappings."

From his suit pocket Stuntman produced a narrow notebook. The kind with a spiral wire along the top. Clicking a pen he pointed it at Wally. "I'm just dying to hear how *you* of all people got mixed up in this mess."

Wally told them about Ghost's teacher, his conversation with Jube, and his decision to infiltrate the fight club by letting himself get kidnapped.

"This is the most idiotic thing I've ever heard," Stuntman said.

The detective frowned at the agent, then said to Wally, "What you were trying was very dangerous, Mr. Gunderson. People are dying in that ring."

"That's why I'm doing it. Somebody has to stick up for them folks."

Stuntman rolled his eyes. "You're moderately famous, and apparently

well liked," he said, "for reasons I've never understood. Did it never occur to you that they might choose to avoid nabbing a minor celebrity?"

"Father Squid is way more famous than I am. Everybody in Jokertown
knows him."

Wally imagined he could hear the grinding of Stuntman's teeth.
"We're aware of that."

"And anyway," Wally continued, "I was undercover. With a special hat
and everything. So they didn't know who they were grabbing."

"You're made of metal and covered in rivets. What kind of disguise
did you think—"

"Tell us about this disguise," prompted the detective.

Wally explained the made-up crossword puzzle club, and how they
needed to find Mr. Richardson so that they could afford more pencils.

Stuntman laughed. It wasn't a friendly laugh. "You know, I used to
wonder if the rube thing was just an act. I'll never wonder again."

Detective Black shot another sharp look at Stuntman. "Please continue."

"No, wait," said Stuntman, struggling to get the laughter under control.
"Let me make sure I get this down." He clicked the pen again and jotted
something in his notebook. "Crossword puzzles. Genius."

"Zip it," Detective Black snapped. He turned back to Wally. "Keep going, Mr. Gunderson."

Wally did. When he got to the part about the botched kidnapping,
the detective sighed. He said, "Big gray guy? Covered in stone? Fists like
boulders?"

"Yep."

"Ranting and raving?"

"Uh huh."

The detective ran a hand over his face. To Stuntman, he said, "That
wasn't a kidnapper. That's Croyd Crenson."

Stuntman stood. He and the detective conferred in the corner, whispering. Wally caught the words "sleeper" and "Takisian." Stuntman came
back a moment later, and sat with a sigh of disgust. He glared at Wally,
shaking his head. Finally, he said, "I swear to God. You make hammers
look smart."

Wally said, "Well, I don't know about this Croyd fella, but he sure
seemed suspicious to me."

"Of course he did," said the detective. "He's blitzed out of his mind on speed." He shook Wally's hand again. "Thank you for your time, Mr. Gunderson, and please leave the police work to the police. You could get hurt." He walked out, muttering, "Paranoid delusions, fists like sledge-hammers, and now he's blaming *me*. Wonderful . . ."

Stuntman closed his notebook, and threaded the pen through the spirals. "Thanks for wasting our time."

"Can I ask you a question?"

"That is a question."

"I was just wondering if you ever get tired of always blaming other people when things don't go the way you want. I mean, that must be a pretty lonely way to live."

"What the hell are you talking about? I turned my short turn with celebrity into a good career." Stuntman spoke with a hollow pride that didn't touch his eyes. He still looked tired. "I was smart about it."

"I dunno. You still seem like a pretty angry guy."

"Holy shit. Did you just call me an angry black man? You, of all people?"

"No, I think you're a mean person who is also black." Wally remembered a conversation he'd had with Jerusha. It seemed like yesterday. They were piloting a boat down a river in Congo, and talking about their time on *American Hero*, which even then had seemed like a jillion years ago.

I didn't say that stuff.

I know, Wally. Everybody knows it.

"You never fooled anybody," said Wally.

Stuntman made another show of checking his watch. He yawned. "Let me know when you get near a point."

Wally thought about that. What was his point? He hadn't thought he had one; he was just curious, because it seemed like a crummy way to live. But then he realized maybe he did have something to say. "If you hadn't done what you did all those years ago, my life would be a lot different. Actually, maybe lots of lives would be different. Because of you I went to Egypt, and then so did some other folks, and that's how the Committee was formed. And then I got to know Jerusha and I met Ghost and now I'm adopting a kid and everything. I miss a lot of folks—" Wally struggled to force the words past the lump that always congealed in his throat when he thought about Jerusha. He thought about Darcy, too. "—And it hasn't fixed everything for everybody. But, I dunno, I think maybe my life would be a lot lonelier if not for you. So, thank you."

Stuntman stared at him as if he'd just grown another head. He stood. "We're finished here." He left without another word.

"You know what?" Wally called after him. "You're still a knuckle-head."

♦

"Gosh," said Wally to nobody in particular in his loudest speaking voice, "those joker kidnappings sure do worry me. I hope those cage match guys don't decide to make me fight because I'm so strong. I have a kid at home."

He pitched his voice so that it carried over the music; past the rotating stage where a bored-looking lady covered in goldfish scales half danced, half strutted around a fireman's pole; and even into the darkened corners where ladies danced privately for solitary drinkers.

Early afternoon at Freaker's was one of the most depressing things he'd ever witnessed in Jokertown. Nobody here looked particularly happy.

The bartender, a man with tattoos covering both his arms and most of his neck, wrapped a dirty dishtowel around the lid of a jar of pickled pearl onions. The tattoos shifted as he heaved on the jar.

"Do you need help with that? I'm pretty strong." Wally studied the room from the corners of his eyes, adding, "Strong enough to be a wres-tler or something, probably."

He gave Wally a Look. "Thanks, tough guy. I'll manage." The jar lid came loose with a wet sucking sound. Wally caught a whiff of vinegar.

"Can I have another beer please?" And then, to cover up the "please" he added, "I don't know how many I've had."

That wasn't true. He'd nursed that first bottle for an hour and a half. But he wanted the kidnappers to think he'd be easy to grab. He didn't like to drink alone. But it was important to blend in. All part of being a detective. Still, it was embarrassing, picking up Ghost from school with beer on his breath. Even worse when it was beer from a place where la-dies took their clothes off. He was glad his mom and dad couldn't see him now.

"Yeah," said the bartender. "That higher math is hard."

The bartender set another bottle in front of him. The crinkled edge of the bottle cap made a screeching sound against the pad of Wally's thumb as he flicked it off. The cap tinkled on the bar. The bottle foamed up.

One of the dancers sidled next to him. She leaned on the bar. She had a feline face, and wore a bikini that didn't cover very much.

"Neat trick," she said.

"Oh, sure. I do that lots. It didn't hurt or anything—" He looked around the room again to see if anybody was listening, which is how he noticed she had more lady parts than he assumed was normal. The rest came out in an embarrassed cough: "—Because my skin is so tough."

The dancer purred. *"Really?"*

She ran a finger down his arm; the purring got louder. "Tell me. Is your skin this hard all over?"

"Well, yeah. It's—" And then he realized she was doing that thing where somebody appeared to be talking about one thing but was actually talking about a totally different thing. Wally blushed so furiously that it actually hurt his face. She watched him, waiting for an answer, but he focused all of his attention on his beer. He took a swig, clutching the bottle so hard that it cracked. The dancer sighed, rolled her eyes at the bartender, and walked away.

The beer ran over his fingers. He flicked them dry, earning a dirty look from the guy sitting a couple barstools down. Wally hadn't seen him come up to the bar. Now his shirt was stippled with dark spots where flecks of foam had soaked into the fabric. Great.

"Oops. Sorry about that, fella."

The guy glared at him with huge iridescent eyes like those of a housefly. Wally said, "Here, I'll buy your next one."

The other guy shrugged. "Won't argue with that." He took a stool closer to Wally. Wally caught the bartender's eye and put another bottle on his tab. The dancer lady returned not long after that.

It was a long, embarrassing afternoon, and by the end of it Wally was no closer to finding the fight club.

Somebody knocked on their door just as Ghost was nodding off for the night. Wally placed the Dr. Seuss book he'd been reading to her on the bedside table next to the sippy cup of water, tiptoed to the door, and turned off the light. Another knock came while he stood just outside Ghost's bedroom, listening for the long slow breaths that told him she'd fallen into true sleep. Only when he was certain she'd stay asleep did he go to answer the door.

Darcy stood in the hallway. He didn't recognize her right away because she wasn't dressed like a police officer.

"Cripes," he said. "I mean, howdy."

She shrugged, more to herself than to him. She said, "Do you have a minute?"

Wally beckoned her inside. "I just put Ghost to bed," he said in a half whisper, "but we can talk in the kitchen."

Darcy shook her head. "I'm sort of in a hurry here." Wally paused. She said, in a rush, "I think I've found the fight club kidnappers. Do you want to come and help me catch them?"

Wally straightened up so quickly he nearly ripped the doorknob off the door. "Holy smokes, yes!"

It took another half hour before they were under way, and Darcy fidgeted the entire time. First, he had to put Ghost back to sleep, and then he had to go across the hall to speak with Miss Holmes. Wally didn't know what he would have done without her willingness to watch over Ghost. He made a mental note to buy her a cake or maybe cook a casserole for her to say thank you. He wondered if she liked eating Tater Tots. He knew a good recipe for Tater Tot casserole.

But eventually he and Darcy were under way. They took his car. She directed him west, to the very edge of Manhattan.

"How'd you find these guys?" he asked.

"I've been spending my off hours reviewing footage from traffic cameras."

"Gosh. I didn't even know that was a thing."

"It is a thing. But it took about two hundred hours before I found a pattern."

Holy cow. Two hundred hours? That was . . . Wally tried to do the math in his head, but he couldn't do that and drive at the same time. Anyway, it was a *lot* of days.

"Wow," he said. "That's pretty neat."

"It wasn't as fun as it sounds," she said. But she sat a little straighter, puffed up by the fact of his amazement. "You have no idea how many vans drive through this borough every day. But only one that can disappear and reappear. Turn here."

He did, saying, "I'm real happy to lend a hand. But I thought you weren't real keen on my acting like a detective. You had the fancy word for it. Vigil-something."

"Vigilantism." Darcy sighed. "Yeah. Well, once I uncovered a possible lead on the van, I realized I had two problems. I knew I needed help. But maybe you remember what my colleagues said a few days ago: 'If you see them, call the real cops.' If I tell anybody about this, I'll get shoved aside, and if it turns up anything useful they'll forget I was ever involved." She practically vibrated with irritation. "The second problem is that this place we're approaching is, technically, outside of my precinct's jurisdiction. The right way to do this would be for me to notify Detective Black, but that would kill hours because he insists on doing everything by the book." Wally remembered the detective. He seemed pretty nice, all things considered. Darcy continued, "Franny would contact the other precinct, and explain the situation, and then they'd have to come to some agreement. And maybe the captains would have to talk. They'd have to do some handshake deal to let us come in and do a bust inside their precinct, or more likely they'd insist on having their own guys do it. But you can imagine how much enthusiasm this case receives outside of Jokertown. Missing jokers? Ha."

Wally said, "So you called me instead."

"I'm bending the rules a little, yes." She paused. Fidgeted again. "I've never done that before."

Wally smiled to himself. "How does that feel?"

"Like I want to write myself a ticket with a big fine."

Wally stopped smiling. "You, uh . . . I guess you must really want to catch these guys."

"Yes."

Darcy directed him to a junkyard situated partially beneath a section of the old elevated West Side Highway, right on the Hudson. *West Side Auto and Scrap,* according to the sign over the entrance to the yard. The sun had just set past the New Jersey refineries when Wally parked his car out-side the tall fence surrounding the property. The residual glow of sunset turned the underside of a low cloudbank pink and orange, casting enough ruddy light to turn Wally's iron skin the color of rust, and to show him that the junkyard was quiet.

A breeze whistled through the Slinky-curls of barbed wire atop the fence. Much of the yard inside was given over to stacks of smashed-up old cars, some of which were five or even six high in places. The ones at the bottom were a little older, and more pancaked than the ones on top. Few were car-shaped; many had been crushed into squares. Once in a while a stack creaked, or groaned, or rattled. Wally chalked that up to wind, or maybe rats. But aside from the wind, and the constant thrum of traffic along the highway, the yard was still. The dying firelight of sunset silhou-etted a tall crane deeper in the yard. The front offices of the junkyard appeared to be housed in an old double-wide mobile-home trailer. No-body came or went. And as the salmon-colored glow of sunset faded from the clouds, turning the sky a mottled violet gray, no lights came on in the trailer.

The shadows felt heavy. The weight of Darcy's focus gave everything a hard edge.

Wally wasn't sure how big the yard was. Maybe the secret club was deeper inside. Or maybe there was a secret entrance, like a trapdoor, and it was underground. The junkyard would be a swell place to hide some-thing like that. The entrance could even be in one of the cars, maybe the trunk. That's what he would do. He decided to keep an eye open for big cars that hadn't been squeezed into boxes.

They eased out of Wally's car. Wally threw the driver's-side door closed a half second before noticing Darcy had been careful not to make any noise with her door. She winced at the noise.

"Sorry," he whispered.

They tiptoed to the gate, which was chained and padlocked. Wally pinched a chain link in both hands and gently twisted it open. But the squeal of tortured metal wasn't much quieter than it might have been had he simply snapped the chain apart. Darcy winced again.

The gate creaked. Wally tiptoed into the deepening shadows of the junkyard with Darcy right behind him.

Within the warren of crushed cars and scrap metal, the sporadic breeze smelled like gasoline, mud, and the river. His feet clumped against the earth where the passage of heavy machinery had compacted bare soil. They kept to the shadows, slowly circling behind the trailer until he could approach it from the side with the fewest windows. Along the way, he did see a number of cars that hadn't yet been crushed into boxes, but they were so banged-up anyway that the doors and trunks didn't want to open unless he heaved on them or rusted out the hinges. He found no secret passages.

Darcy was light on her feet. He couldn't even hear her footsteps and she was right next to him. She whispered something about misguided chivalry, but he still insisted she stay behind him. Wally figured he made a pretty good shield for her.

They crept up to the trailer and crouched beneath a window. Darcy was too short to see over the sill. The pane was too grimy and the interior too dark for him to see anything when he peeked inside. But if there was any evidence connecting the junkyard to the joker kidnappings, surely it would be in the office. Wouldn't it?

Darcy whispered, "Wait!"

But the lock was flimsy, and Wally had already twisted the handle right off the door. Darcy crept back, pressed herself against the trailer. Wally eased inside.

It was even darker here than outside. A flashlight, he realized, would have been a very good idea. He was debating whether to go back for the one in the glove compartment of his car—did it have batteries?—when the *click* of a desk lamp replaced darkness with sterile white light. In the moment before Wally tumbled from the trailer, squeezing shut his dark-adapted eyes, he glimpsed a few cots.

Darcy had disappeared.

Wally tripped. There was a *thud* as somebody leapt on him and smeared Wally's face with goo.

The darkness that swallowed him smelled like cough medicine.

◆

He awoke outside. He knew he was outside, and not still in the trailer, because his face was coated with slime and dirt. His arms didn't work right when he tried to roll over; he flopped around like a walleye gasping for air on the bottom of a canoe. Everything tasted like an overdose of cough drops. He almost managed to sit up, but then the ground shook with the rumble and rattle of heavy machinery starting up, so he toppled over again, head spinning.

Spotlights, like big construction lamps, now flooded the junkyard with silvery light. More dirt, he noticed, was caked into greasy handprints on his lower legs and ankles.

"Can't believe he's already getting up," somebody said. "That dose would've put a rhino into a coma."

"Yeah, well, better luck next time," said a woman's voice. "Let's just get—" She was interrupted by the sound of sporadic gunfire. Wally knew that sound.

"Shit," she said. "The Iron Giant brought friends. Screw this noise."

Wally managed to lever himself up to his knees, swaying like a ship on high seas. He glimpsed a short woman with curly auburn hair sprinting toward a white van. But then a slippery foot on his back shoved him down again. A cloud of dust went down his throat. He coughed.

"Hey!" the other guy called after her. "You can't take off until I've taken care of this."

Somebody else was yelling now, too. It sounded like Darcy's voice. She had a pretty voice.

The rumble of machinery grew louder. Shadows slid across the ground, dark tendrils skimming across oil puddles and weedy slabs of broken concrete. Then there was a clink, and the rattle of chains. The crane, Wally realized.

A weird but somehow familiar tingly sensation took root in his belly, spreading through his chest to his arms, legs, and head. It differed from the medicinal wooziness; this felt like somebody had pressed a tuning fork to the roof of his mouth and it was vibrating his brain to pudding. He tried to roll over to see what was happening, but his arms and legs refused him. He couldn't think straight.

He'd felt this sensation before. Where?

For a moment he felt lighter . . . almost like he was floating. But then the ground fell away, all in a rush, and somehow he was falling *up* until his head and back and arms clanged against something large and flat. His body rang like a gong. Then he remembered.

Oh, yeah. When the kids stuck those magnets to my head. This felt the same, only times a million. Probably because they used this magnet to pick up cars. It made his brain feel cottony, like he had a bad fever.

The crane whined and whirred as the magnet retracted. Wally dangled high above the junkyard, splayed against the magnet like a fly on flypaper. His view of the yard bobbed back and forth, like the carnival rides he and his brother used to take on the midway at the Minnesota State Fair. Back before Wally's card turned.

It took most of his strength merely to bend his elbow, straining and contorting just enough to press his fingertips to the surface of the electromagnet. But he didn't touch metal. The working surface was laminated with a thin plastic coating. He couldn't make it rust. His arm slammed back against the magnet.

Oh, crud.

The crane arm lurched. Wally left his stomach behind. And then he was soaring across the yard: over Darcy, who crouched behind a car, reloading her gun; over a half-naked man with a towel around his waist, running away from her; past the trailer and the van parked behind it. He remembered there was something important about a van . . . But the magnet scrambled his brain and made everything feel gauzy and surreal, like dream logic.

The woman he'd glimpsed on the ground leaped into the driver's seat of the van. A cloud of exhaust coughed from the tailpipe. She must have floored it because the tires kicked up large clods of mud. The van spun around the trailer.

"You bastards!" screamed the little Gandhi guy.

Wally watched helplessly while somebody pulled him through the van's open side panel.

Wally became aware of a new sound, a thrum and a whine, like the groaning of a giant hydraulic press. Wally wondered where they were taking him. The crane swept him past more stacks of crushed cars.

Crushed cars.

Oh.

But he couldn't get smushed. Who would take care of Ghost?

The fright and worry hurt worse than any punch, any gunshot, any crocodile bite.

His struggles caused the magnet to swing like a pendulum. But each time he managed to wrench one arm or leg free of the magnet, it banged back when he went to work on another limb. He didn't have any leverage.

The crane pivoted. The maw of a giant press came into view. It was large enough to hold a big car, like Wally's Impala. The lid was a thick slab of steel on massive hinges, and the sides of the empty crusher comprised thick steel plates on massive hydraulic arms. That steel had been laminated, too. The whole thing stood on a pair of retractable legs, so that it could rock back like a dump truck to tip out the crushed cars. A generator rumbled off to the side. Wally caught a whiff of diesel fuel.

Another gunshot *crack* echoed through the junkyard. The crane jerked to a stop, which sent the magnet rocking wildly on its chain. Wally's head spun. Between the magnet, the spinning, and the diesel fumes, he felt like he might puke.

The van picked up speed. But it wasn't heading for the gate. Instead, it was barreling straight toward a wall of cubed cars. The magnet spun. Wally glimpsed Darcy again, now creeping to the other side of the crane. When his vantage spun around again, the van had almost reached the wall, but . . . Wally wasn't sure because the magnet made his brain all fizzy and he really wanted to puke and also he was dizzy. But he watched while something that sure looked like a tunnel or hole opened up to swallow the van. He expected a big crash, but instead the van just disappeared as though the wall of cars was fake, like a hologram in a movie. The magnet spun. He blinked. When he opened his eyes again, the van was gone.

Somebody shouted. The crane lurched back into motion, once again leaving Wally's stomach behind. The press drew closer. There was another *crack,* closer this time, followed by the *ping* of ricochet.

The crane stopped again. Somewhere, a distant voice said, "Wally!"

He thought about that. *Oh. That's me.*

"Uh, hello?" His voice sounded weird, like it was full of marbles. The magnet tugged on his jaw, making it hard to shout. "Up here."

The tingly sensation stopped as abruptly as somebody turning off a light switch. But before he had time to think about what that meant, the ground leaped up to hit him in the face. He belly flopped on the edge of the compactor. He bounced, crashed against a car cube, and skidded to a stop with one arm wrenched under his back.

"Ouch," he said.

It took a bit of work but eventually he managed to lever himself into a sitting position propped against one of the car cubes. The metal felt sticky, somehow, which was a little weird. The residual effects of the magnet and the goo crammed up his nose left him woozy. His eyelids made a weird clicking sound when he blinked. He was still sitting there, trying to clear his head, when Darcy walked up a few minutes later. She knelt beside him.

"Are you hurt?"

"I don't think so." His voice came out slurred. It felt like his teeth were trying to jostle each other out of the way.

Darcy sat with him while his head cleared. When he could think a little better, he asked her what happened.

"They got away," she said. "*Again*. And I'm probably going to be fired."

"Gaaagghhh—" It was hard to talk because his jaws kept repelling each other. He tried again. "Gosh, I don't know. I'd be in a real jam if not for you. I bet the Committee could help you out."

Darcy stood. She stared at the fence gate where they had entered the junkyard on their failed secret errand.

"You found the fight club," said Wally.

She frowned. "I'm not so sure. We found a few folks and a van. Big deal." She made a twirling motion with one finger in the air. "And anyway, they're all gone now. Where the hell did they go?"

"Oh, I saw the whole thing from up there. They drove away through the magic tunnel. Have you seen my hat?"

"I think that magnet scrambled your brain. You should probably see a doctor."

"Oh." Well, at least he wasn't getting smushed into a bloody cube.

She helped him to his feet. He tried not to lean on her, but she was stronger than she looked. "I think I should take you home."

Wally said, "But my car."

"No way. You are in no condition to operate heavy machinery. Not even yourself."

"Oh. Okay." They stumbled toward the outer gate. The door on the trailer hung wide open, and a pair of tire tracks had cut deep furrows in the dirt. They led straight to a wall of cars, which struck Wally as weird, though his head was too fuzzy to figure out why.

Darcy noticed the tracks, too. She stopped to study them. She stared, unblinking.

Then she said, "When you're feeling better, I want you to tell me exactly what you saw."

"Okay," he said. "Do you like kids?"

She shrugged, which made him wobble. "I guess. Why?"

"Good. I think you should meet Ghost," he said.

Galahad in Blue

Part Eight

TO MOST PEOPLE FORENSIC accounting sounded about as exciting and interesting as watching paint dry, but it was actually something
Franny enjoyed. Back at the precinct he began by drafting a request for a
warrant. He then called over to the courthouse to see who was signing
warrants that day.

Turned out it was Samuelson, which was great. He was a decent enough
judge, but when he wasn't hearing cases he got blow jobs from hookers in
his office. Which meant he liked to keep his office hours free of work. A
stupid man might have solved the problem by refusing everything, but
Samuelson wasn't stupid, and he knew that constant denial would lead to
challenges and questions, and have the opposite result of what he wanted.
The judge also knew that most warrants did result in lowlifes getting hauled
in, and lowlives and their overworked public defenders usually didn't challenge how a warrant got issued. Which meant he was a good bet to sign off
on this rather shaky house of cards that Franny had constructed.

As Franny walked down the hall of the courthouse, warrant tucked
into a folder briefcase, he hoped that the judge wasn't an aficionado of
American Hero, and had never heard of Michael Berman. The warrant
really was a fishing expedition, but like Jamal, he fully believed that Berman
was in this up to his neck.

Franny had timed it so he walked into the back of Samuelson's court-
room just as the lunch break was called. The judge's furry caterpillar-like

eyebrows drew together in a sharp frown when he saw Franny enter. Spectators, a bored city beat reporter, and the families of the victim and the accused shuffled for the big double doors. Only one person remained seated, a very tall, very leggy woman with hair a shade of red that was found nowhere in nature, black leather miniskirt, blouse with a plunging neckline, and stiletto heels. Yep, the judge was going to want to get Franny and his warrant out the door, and fast.

A sharp gesture, and Franny walked down the aisle and approached the bench. "What have you got, Detective?"

"Warrant for forensic accounting." Franny slid the paper across the bench.

"Come in my chambers."

Franny followed the judge through the doors behind the bench. It was a cliché of a judge's chambers—overstuffed armchairs, bookcases filled with weighty tomes that, judging from the dust, weren't getting touched. No reason to with every case online and available now. A sack lunch sat on the polished mahogany surface of the desk. The pungent smell of corned beef, kraut, and mustard hit his martini-abused gut, and Franny swallowed nausea.

Samuelson sat down behind his desk and flipped through the warrant. "Nice job," he said as he scrawled his signature.

"Thank you, Your Honor."

"Don't make a habit of this."

"No, sir."

Franny and the leggy redhead exchanged nods as they passed in the doorway.

Back at the precinct Franny put in calls to the IRS and faxed over the warrant. Once he had access to Berman's tax returns he would be able to bootstrap into Berman's bank accounts, and payments from those accounts would lead him to the credit cards. "And then we'll see what you're made of, Mr. Berman," Franny said to the fax machine as the final page of the warrant slid through.

"You know, it's never a good sign when you're talking to mechanical objects," Beastie Bester said as he lumbered in, heading for the copy machine.

"Yeah, well, when nobody, including my partner, will talk to me I'm all I'm left with." Franny hadn't meant it for it to emerge quite so plaintive.

"You could have turned it down," Beastie said gently.

"No, I couldn't have. I have my own traditions to live up to."

Eventually the material on Berman's finances landed in his e-mail inbox. Franny got himself a cup of bad precinct coffee. He began to dig into Berman's life as sketched by the producer's finances. First Franny looked over the W-2s and W-9s. Hollywood had been very good to Mr. Berman. Next he looked at bank statements for the past six months. Money flowed into the bank account and out just as quickly. There were a lot of overdraft charges.

He went back to the tax returns. The IRS had given him five years. What Franny found were gambling losses claimed as deductions against gambling winnings. That sent him digging into the credit card statements. There were a lot of charges at casinos in Las Vegas, Cannes, Atlantic City, Monaco, and *Kazakhstan*. Where the murdered Joe Frank, cameraman for Michael Berman, had also traveled. Franny went back to the bank statements and found ATM withdrawals at various gambling venues. Judging from the number of withdrawals, Berman had lost a lot more than he'd won.

Franny called Berman's bank and had the good fortune to end up with a representative who was a Badge Bunny. Once he'd scanned and e-mailed a copy of the warrant she was more than happy to help him, and was very disappointed when she discovered he was in New York City and she was in Houston. After an hour where his ear went numb she had given him online access to all Berman's checks for the past five years.

What he found had him jumping out of his chair, and pumping the air in triumph. Berman was a liar. He hadn't fired Joe Frank. As late as two weeks ago he had been writing checks to the cameraman. He was picking up the phone to call Jamal, when Deputy Inspector Maseryk walked up and dropped a file on his desk. "That big Committee ace Rustbelt and one of our meter maids have been playing detective, and they nearly got Gunderson killed."

"I told him not to," Franny said.

"Well, he didn't listen, and I'd like an actual detective to follow up. Maybe they'll have something useful. God knows we need something. I just hope it's not another of Darcy's fantasies."

"Yes, sir." Maseryk walked away and Franny slowly replaced the receiver. What he was doing with Jamal and Berman was strictly off the books. This was his actual job. And maybe the big ace did know something.

Wally Gunderson walked toward Franny's desk, the floor shuddering under his weight, and Franny watched in dismay as paper clips, sets of keys, staplers, and anything made of metal went sailing through the air to land like a flock of futuristic butterflies on the exposed metal skin of Rustbelt's face, neck, hands, and arms. Cops were yelling, and snatching at their suddenly airborne items. The big iron ace batted in alarm at the clinging objects and only succeeded in having them attach to each other in long strings that dripped from his fingertips. "Ah shoot," he said in his deep Minnesota accent.

Rikki, her over-developed chest heaving in alarm, rushed up waving her arms like a modern-day Chicken Little. "The computers," she yelled. "The computers."

Franny suddenly realized what she was ranting about. Rustbelt's magnetized skin was probably wreaking havoc on the hard drives. He reached up, placed his hands on Rusty's shoulders, turned him around, and propelled him back out of the precinct. The big head with its steam-shovel jaw drooped. "I'm sorry. I guess I got all magnetized by that magnet."

"Not your fault," Franny said as he plucked metal detritus off Rusty, and set it in a pile just inside the door. He spotted a coffee vendor's cart on the far side of the street down by the corner. "We can sit on the bench at the bus stop. I'll buy us some coffee."

"Sure," Rusty said, as he plucked off an overlooked paper clip.

"How do you take it?"

"Lotta cream and sugar."

Franny sprinted down the street and bought a couple of cups. Joining Wally on the bench Franny took a swig, and felt his gut rebel. He stared down into the black depths, and realized he had been subsisting on coffee for the past few weeks.

"What did you need from me, Officer?" asked Rustbelt. "Darcy wrote everything up, and I sure hope you fellas aren't gonna fire her. She works real hard to be a good policeman."

Franny set the cup on the sidewalk next to him. "Well, that's not my decision, but I'll certainly put in a word for her. I did read Darcy's report, but it's a little . . ." He considered the twenty-seven-page-long report filled with an exposition about the decay of cities, analysis of traffic patterns, traffic camera logs, parking violations, and a detailed sketch of a junk-yard, and finally settled on a neutral word. ". . . detailed. I just need to hear what happened when you reached that junkyard. Darcy's report was a little vague on exactly how the perps got away." Franny's pen was poised over his notebook.

"There was a tunnel, and this skinny guy wearing a towel. And he stuffed some stuff up my nose, and I got all woozy. Oh, and this red-haired woman. She was driving the car when it went into the tunnel."

"Was she a joker?"

"No, just a girl."

"Girl. So she was younger?"

"Yeah, I guess."

Franny asked a few more questions, but it seemed he had exhausted Gunderson's store of useful information. Vaporlock was old news. What was new was the woman, and the use of a clear ace power.

The bus pulled up, the doors opened, and the driver glared at Franny and Rustbelt. "Let me guess, you're just passing the time?"

"Sorry." Franny stood. Shook hands with Wally. "Thank you, Mr. Gunderson."

"Did anything I told you help?"

"I think so."

"May I tell Darcy? She's feeling real low right now."

"Sure," said Franny. He returned to his desk and his computer to search for aces who could open tunnels. It didn't take long to find one.

He called Stuntman. "Berman's got a gambling problem," Franny said. He paused for breath while Jamal gave a low whistle. "And Berman hadn't fired Joe Frank. He was still writing him checks as late as two weeks ago."

"Son of a bitch lied to me."

"Yep, but that's not the best part. I think I know how the jokers are being taken out of the city." Franny told Jamal about Rustbelt's testimony. "So, I went looking for an ace with a power like that. There is one. She was on *American Hero,* Tesseract. I looked up what 'tesseract' means. It's a four-dimensional analogy to a cube. I found some YouTube video of Tesseract doing her thing. She can make an opening in, say, Los Angeles, and reach through to Paris, or Beijing, or somewhere. She can make these openings big enough to walk through, probably even drive through."

"You have a real name?"

"Oh, yeah, sorry. Mollie Steunenberg." There was silence from the other end of the line. A silence that went on for so long that Franny thought they'd been disconnected. "Jamal? Hello?"

"I'm here. Mollie Steunenberg is Berman's assistant."

"Oh, holy fuck."

The Big Bleed

Part Nine

"**YOUR GUY JUST ARRIVED.** He's got the girl with him."

"Thank you," Jamal Norwood said. "We'll be there as soon as possible." Then he clicked off. He didn't want to be on the phone with Jack Metz any longer than necessary. Not that he had anything special against Upper East Side building managers, but this one was off-scale creepy.

He had proved to be useful, however. Metz's call meant that Michael Berman was back in the city with Mollie Steunenberg, aka Tesseract. Jamal knew it was unlikely to be for long.

It was early morning, mid-week, rainy, colder than it should be in New York this time of year. Jamal's physical and mental state matched the grim weather. He had been dozing, dreaming strange dreams about being chased down a street by the missing joker Wheels, feeling that he was late, ill-equipped, in danger.

On waking, he considered phoning Julia, something he had not done in over a week. But what would he tell her? *I'm feeling great!* Every conversation he could imagine ended in a lie, or a very uncomfortable revelation.

So he didn't. He distracted himself by watching TV with its news of the various campaigns, growing bored as the same stories repeated.

Eventually he turned to a movie channel and, to his amazement, caught the last half hour of *Moonfleet,* a cheap adventure feature he had worked on early in his career. In spite of its title, it had not been sci-fi, but rather a period piece about pirates and smugglers in the Caribbean (though the confusing title likely contributed to *Moonfleet*'s failure . . . that and an unappealing cast and incoherent script). Stuntman Jamal Norwood had one major gag in the piece, as a sailor who goes aloft during a storm only to have the yards break, plunging him to the deck of a ship.

Who was that young man? So eager, so fit, so certain he was making all the right decisions, making money, making himself into a star—

Right now Jamal merely wished he possessed that young man's health.

Franny picked him up a block from the Bleecker. "You're getting good at all this paranoid shit," the detective told him.

"A little too late."

"Don't be a pessimist."

"Don't be a cheerleader."

It was the middle of rush hour, a murderous time to be traveling from Jokertown to the Upper East Side. "I don't suppose you can use your siren," Jamal said.

"Sure, but it won't do us any good." They were completely gridlocked trying to reach the FDR. Eventually it did, and to Jamal's relief there were no unusual traffic problems.

As they turned into the building's parking lot, Jamal suddenly feared a Murphy's Law moment, that they would drive right past Michael Berman and Mollie Steunenberg heading out for a latte or breakfast—

Fortunately, no. Perhaps less fortunately, the attendant at the lot seemed all too aware of their business. "You know, my favorite TV series is *Baltimore Stakeout*," he said. "How do you get into that kind of work?"

"If you have to ask, you're not qualified," Jamal snapped.

They met up with Metz, who was as eager as a five-year-old on Christmas Day. "They're up there! You can hear voices."

"You actually saw them, though, right?" Jamal said.

Metz nodded.

Within minutes, Jamal and Franny were heading up the service elevator. Jamal carried a Watchman tuned to the cameras they had hidden in the apartment the night before, toggling from one view to the other. They were cheap Radio Shack–style equipment that couldn't be monitored remotely and of the two men one was too busy to man the cameras 24/7 and the other was too sick. No, the cameras were there because of Tesseract and her power. Both Jamal and Franny knew they needed to grab the girl first. Otherwise she'd be gone, and Berman with her. Jamal could see Berman and Mollie in motion in and out of the living room and hallway. They were out of view for minutes at a time, presumably in the kitchen, bathroom, bedrooms.

Jamal loathed stakeouts and had not prepared for this one. Thank God Franny seemed to be . . . the police detective had not only suggested hauling two folding chairs up the elevator, he produced water and an energy bar without asking. "I hope this doesn't take all day," Jamal said, knowing that he was now grumbling like a man twice his age.

They had deliberately chosen the back hallway as a site for the second camera because it gave them their best opportunity to surprise Tesseract and grab her.

"We should have miked the place."

"Well, we didn't," Jamal said. "So we wait."

Their planning for Operation Grab Michael Berman had been complicated because they were skirting the edge of legality. "I don't suppose you have any black bag team you could activate," Franny said. "To find this shit and install it."

Had Jamal still been on duty with SCARE, he could easily have given the task to just such a group—right after Carnifex signed off on the warrant and the budget. "Haven't you created a team of Jokertown irregulars?"

"Not yet," Franny said. "And if this goes tits up, not ever."

Then there had been the question of warrants. "I can get one," Franny had said. "Might take a day, or at least hours. What about you?"

Jamal shook his head. "Right," Franny said. "Hard to do that when your bosses have no idea—"

"—And you're on medical leave."

They could just have gone ahead, warrantless. But, eager as he was to put Berman, and by extension this whole gaggle of joker-nabbing criminals, out of business as swiftly as possible, Jamal was unwilling to allow those arrested under U.S. law to skate because he and Franny acted like movie cops. "Do what you can as quickly as you can."

While Franny worked the warrant issue, Jamal trolled through the audio and video shops on Eighth Avenue in search of surveillance gear—which turned out to be easy to acquire, though a bit hard on his credit card.

That night he left a message for Franny, then collapsed. When he awoke, yesterday morning, Franny's message was: "Warrant in hand; good to go."

Shortly after twelve-thirty P.M. Jamal and Franny heard raised voices from inside the apartment, Berman yelling something at Mollie and receiving a blistering answer in return. "All right," Franny said, "I withdraw my petty complaint about lack of audio surveillance . . ."

Wearing a T-shirt that displayed two of her more notable features and a pair of shorts that would, if worn in public, have gotten her arrested in certain communities, Mollie stormed into the hallway carrying a bag of garbage.

"Showtime!" Jamal whispered. Franny displayed a pair of handcuffs ("Double-locking Smith & Wesson," he had told Jamal earlier. "Bought them for twenty-five bucks!" He unlocked them—

—As Jamal pushed the door open, smiling and saying, "Hey, there!"

The girl was stunned into silence and immobility as Jamal wrapped her up—not the most unpleasant act he had performed in the past few weeks—allowing Franny to cuff himself to her, his left wrist to Mollie's right.

Now Mollie found her voice. "What the fuck?" she shouted, writhing and struggling and trying to slap Franny with her left hand.

Her voice brought Berman—in rumpled khakis and an *American Hero* T-shirt—into the hallway.

Jamal was ready for him—"Hi, Michael!"—diving at the producer and slamming him against the wall in a hammerlock, an action he had wanted to take for at least five years. He got a second pair of cuffs on Berman. "In case you're wondering, you're under arrest."

Berman had sufficient composure to say, "Do you have a warrant?"

Franny slapped the warrant on his chest. "Read, weep."

They hauled Berman into the living room. Jamal shoved him into an expensive-looking leather chair while Franny took Mollie to the couch. "Why are you doing this?" she asked the detective.

"So you don't pull your Tesseract trick."

"I don't need my hands."

"True. But if you go, you'll be taking me. And I'm guessing you don't want that."

"What if I need to pee?" Mollie said.

Hearing this, Jamal laughed out loud. "Then you'll still have Detective Black for company."

Suddenly the girl seemed less eager.

Berman had been complaining ever since being slammed against the wall. "This is brutality, plain and simple. I don't care what your warrant says."

"We don't care that you don't care," Jamal said.

"What's the charge?"

Jamal turned to Franny. "Detective?"

"Dealer's choice. Fraud, murder, accessory to both, terminal assholeism." Franny grinned at Jamal. "It was hard to narrow it down—"

Berman finally lowered his voice. He looked at Jamal, too. "Hey, Stuntman, who'd a thunk it?"

"You mean, who'd a thunk that you'd wind up in cuffs someday, Michael?" Jamal said. "Only every fucking person you ever met."

That actually seemed to sting Berman. He turned back to Franny. "Okay, what? You take us downtown? Is that the drill? When do I call my lawyer?"

"We could talk first," Franny said. "Isn't that right, Jamal?"

"I believe that Mr. Berman's cooperation at this time would be looked upon with some sympathy."

Berman seemed to think this over. Then, a dangerous smile—one that Jamal recognized—appeared on his face. "All right, then, yeah. A little conversation between friends." He cleared his voice and looked at Jamal. "Would you like to record this?"

Jamal set his phone on the table between them. "We'd love to."

"I am offering my full, voluntary cooperation here," Berman said. "Mollie, you're a witness."

"Wow," Mollie said, stretching a single syllable into a four-second snarl of sarcasm.

Berman held up his cuffed hands. "May we lose these?"

"What," Franny said, "you can't talk without using your hands?"

Jamal laughed. "He's telling the truth!"

So Jamal uncuffed Berman, who flexed his wrists and got slowly to his feet. "Time for the aria. You may recognize this."

"Jamal—" Franny said, a bit alarmed.

Jamal just waved a hand. "Watch and listen." He knew that for Berman, presentation and salesmanship truly over-rode all other concerns, even personal safety and dignity.

The producer faced them, hands clasped, eyes closed.

Then he opened them. "Okay, picture this. A talented, rich, ambitious, handsome young man with a flaw. A very human one . . . he wants money and power, not just for themselves. But for what they can give him. Which is love, right? What everyone wants. Picture Tom Cruise."

"Oh, you wish!" Mollie said.

Franny was still nervous. To Jamal he said, "Okay, what is this?"

"He's *pitching*!"

"He's *trying* to, Detective," Berman said. He actually seemed angry at the interruption.

"Continue," Jamal said.

"Thank you," Berman said. "Let's give our hero a name—Gene. Gene could never accept that he would be loved for who he was or what he wanted to be . . . so he went for the money. So, yeah, he's a bit of an unsympathetic character. But so was Rick in *Casablanca*. Or Charles Foster Kane. You don't have to like Gene, you just have to want to see how far he goes . . . the depths he will descend to." To Jamal he said, "He makes a lot of money."

"So I recall," Jamal said, knowing that Berman was playing him, but not especially concerned. He had always found the producer to be fascinating. How low *would* he go?

"But no amount of money is ever enough, right? Just like you never have enough love or—" And here he leered at Mollie. "—or sex—" Which made Mollie shudder.

"And earning it through work is ultimately unsatisfying. So Gene begins to gamble."

"Like every other rich asshole in Hollywood," Franny said. Jamal laughed: Mr. Police Detective was getting into this!

"It starts with sports, then gets into . . . more interesting sports. Cock-fighting, then the human equivalent. Fights to the death, especially with jokers. Insane visuals, tragic moments, and large amounts of money changing hands. Then, and here's where Gene's arrogance rises to the level of a Greek tragedy—which is pretty highfalutin for a Hollywood pitch, but you'll see why it works. He bets on his own television series, one of those survival game things in which spy cameras and crazy competitions are edited into episodes week by week, so audiences can vote on their favorites.

"This series becomes hugely popular, and there is betting everywhere, especially in Europe. Now, you can't just go to Vegas and make these kinds of bets, not for interesting amounts of money. You've got to find a place with a Wild West sensibility, or in Gene's case . . . Wild East. A casino in Kazakhstan." Berman glanced behind him. "If I'd had a few moments' notice, I could show you some visuals."

"If you'd had a few moments' notice, we wouldn't be here," Franny said.

"Gene goes big for a female winner whose name is probably not important—only to have her walk off the show! There's a little twist for you . . . she just changes her fucking mind, typical woman, something Gene can't control—making a far less-suitable male contestant the winner."

Jamal cleared his throat. "Less suitable?" He couldn't let Berman's comment pass without challenge.

Berman continued to play the game. "Let's just say, less suitable for our hero's purposes."

Jamal wanted to get to the point where Berman actually incriminated himself. "Michael, so far we're just taking our character down," Jamal said. "I like a good wallow as well as anyone, if the scenery is good and the dialogue is snappy."

"Oh, the scenery is fantastic. A bleak landscape in Kazakhstan, and set against it a city of mystery. Known as Talas when it was a major stop on the ancient Silk Road you'll now see it written as Taraz or Тараз, but it's the same place filled with history and secrets. And there are dangerous secrets in this casino palace in the middle of it. Beautiful Russian hookers for eye candy. Handsome Eurotrash men in tuxes. And wild bad guys like Dmitri, who is this huge fat guy, always wears a T-shirt, one of those sleeveless ones, even on the casino floor. Oh, and he chews gum. All the time. What makes him dangerous is his ability to crawl into your head. Fucks with you, makes you afraid. So afraid you freeze up."

"Noted," Jamal said. "But Dmitri isn't the star of your movie."

Berman smiled. "Nowhere near. He's just one of many threats. There is one far more dangerous, and the most unlikely villain you can imagine. Picture an elderly woman, call her Baba Yaga—"

"Michael," Mollie said, warning the producer. She had suddenly begun to pay attention.

He ignored her. "Obviously, given her business, she's not an ordinary old lady. Terrific casting possibility here, though. I'm thinking of one of those English actresses who were sex symbols a generation ago—"

"Wait!" Franny was laughing. "Your big villain is the world's scariest seventy-year-old woman? What does she do, whack you with her walker?"

Berman laughed. "Good one, Detective. Actually, no. Baba Yaga is an ace. She . . . changes people. And not in a good way. We're talking about furniture. So, at the same time Gene suffers a series of losses—huge amounts of money he can't pay—rather than transform him into a footstool, which she threatens to do, she comes up with a way he can pay her back: by using his skills and his team to, uh, recruit jokers for death matches at her casino. Next thing Gene knows, he's in business with a pretty young woman who possesses an amazing talent, one that allows her to move pretty much anywhere. There's a nice symmetry there too—this girl was also a contestant on our hero's show but in a later season. Ties everything together, you know? Anyway, this is the end of the first act.

"This team identifies interesting jokers and grabs them. Not by themselves, of course . . . Baba Yaga wants people she trusts at every step of the process. So Gene and his girl—"

"I was never your *girl*," Mollie snapped.

"I'm talking about the girl in this movie," Berman said, smoothly. "The jokers would be held in New Jersey until they had enough to fill a van for this talented girl to ship them to Kazakhstan."

Franny said, "Hey, is that where Father Squid is?"

"Who?"

"A very large joker who looks just the way the name suggests," Jamal said. "He's a priest."

Berman snorted. "He's not part of the pitch."

"He's an important figure in Jokertown," Franny snarled. "It's important for us to find him."

"I can . . . imagine a joker like that in Kazakhstan. So, sure, he's part of the cast, part of this new crew. Better fights, more money. Everybody's happy!" Then he lowered his voice. "Until one stupid cameraman sells footage of the fights."

Jamal had felt two different emotions as he listened to this presentation. First was amusement at seeing Berman in action—the producer's version of begging for his life and using the tools that have worked for him all his career.

Second was the satisfaction of having the dots connected for the missing jokers and dead cameraman Joe Frank. "Is there some point in the story where our hero fucks up?" Jamal said. "Where he is confronted by the police and possibly a handsome superstar of a federal agent, and he gives up the cameraman only to learn that he's been killed?"

Berman blinked. "The hero is stuck. He knows that the cameraman is in, shall we say, a tenuous situation, quite likely to be a victim of Baba Yaga's temper. But he has no choice, does he? He's trying to buy time—"

"What's act three?" Jamal said. "How does he get out of this?"

All during the pitch, Berman had been on his feet, moving between the couch and the television. Now, however, the producer was kneeling in front of the cabinet beneath his television, rummaging through various DVDs.

Until he came up with a gun, which he swiftly pointed at Franny. "This is how," he said, pulling the trigger.

Before he could react, there was a flash to Jamal's left—a change of light as, strangely, the couch seemed to open up and swallow Franny and Mollie. But only for a fraction of a second; the couch was in place again, spewing fabric as Berman's bullet blew through it.

Berman was training the weapon on him, but now Jamal was in motion, moving faster than he had in months. He slammed the producer into the entertainment unit, hurting himself in the process, but ensuring that Berman was unable to fire the pistol again.

He was ready to pummel the man . . . years of frustration made him want to smash the smug criminal bastard's face. But Berman was moaning, already defeated.

Franny appeared, dragging Mollie with one wrist, holding his weapon with the other. They had simply walked into the living room from the back hallway. "Do pitches usually end like this?" Franny said.

Jamal had no answer for that. After securing Berman's pistol, he pulled the producer to his feet. Berman groaned and stretched his back, which surely hurt like hell. "Michael, what did you think would happen?" Jamal said.

"Shoot the cop, then you. Then out of here."

"I'd bounce back."

"Sure. But not for a few minutes." *Possibly not ever*, Jamal thought.

"It's time we took Mr. Showbiz and his tape downtown," Franny said.

"What about me?" Mollie was blinking tears and now looked about fifteen—and frightened.

"What *about* her?" Franny said.

"We take her in, book her, she gets a lawyer. No way any lawyer is going to let her help us. And we need her to get the jokers. Or worst case, she gets bail and she's in the wind."

"So a little sin of omission," Franny said.

Which is how Stuntman wound up handcuffed to Tesseract.

Ties That Bind

Part Five

KAVITHA HAD SAID NO to his proposal.

"Why the hell not?" was what Michael had said in response, which in retrospect was perhaps not the most tactful way to persuade a woman to marry you. But he'd been genuinely shocked—he'd never actually thought she'd say no. And worse, Kavitha had refused to tell them why, even when Minal had started crying. And Michael had tried not to shout, but the discussion had gotten a little . . . heated, and they must have gotten pretty loud, because Isai woke up, and then Maya Aunty, and somehow it was two A.M. before they got everybody back to bed, and he'd just given up and collapsed. Minal wore his ring, but Kavitha didn't, and that was just wrong.

Maybe Michael couldn't find Sandip, but he could at least find out what was going on with his girlfriend. If he couldn't stalk his girlfriend, what good was it being a cop, anyway?

Michael called in sick to work the next day, *after* he'd left the condo.

She spent the morning at the studio, but at noon she left and didn't head for home. It was easy, following her. She might have ace powers, and jet set with the Committee on occasion, but Kavitha was still a civilian at heart. She didn't even look behind as she left the studio, walking a path that wasn't taking her home to the condo. And when she finally ended up in a frankly terrible part of town, she headed straight into one of the dingiest motels on the street. Michael waited a few beats, and then followed her in. She might see him, but at this point, he knew enough to confront her if he had to. He was going to get the truth out of her, one way or another.

He was in time to see the elevator doors closing, and to watch the indicator go up, up, up. Third floor. Michael took the stairs, as fast as he could, glad he'd kept up with the station's physical requirements, and emerged from the stairwell just in time to catch her disappearing into room 328. At that point, he abandoned all subtlety—because what the hell? Why in God's name would his girlfriend be meeting up with someone in a dingy motel? Was this why she'd refused to marry him?

There was just one likely explanation, but it made no sense. Michael found himself with one hand on the door, the other on his gun, fighting a sudden murderous rage. It was one thing to date more than one person— it was an entirely different thing to have one of them cheating on you. If she'd just told him that she wanted to see someone else—well, Michael still wouldn't like it, but he wouldn't feel the need to pound somebody's face in. He didn't think.

"Open up!" He shouted. "Police!"

The door suddenly swung open, with his fist still raised to pound again, and Michael almost fell inside before catching himself on the door frame. Kavitha stood just a step away, and there, legs and feet hanging off the end of the motel bed was . . . her brother. His torso swathed in bandages, looking like death warmed over, with terror in his dark brown eyes.

Michael took a quick, steadying breath. Carefully, deliberately, lowered his hand from the butt of his gun, suddenly ashamed of the urge that had put it there. And then he asked, in as calm a voice as he could manage, "Will one of you *please* explain what is going on?"

They didn't fall over themselves to explain. Not at first. The silence grew quite deafening, until Kavitha finally said, "Sandip. Tell him." She moved over to sit by her brother and took his hand in her own slim hand. She petted it gently, reassuring him, and finally, the kid opened his mouth to speak.

"They're killing jokers. Killing *people*." The words came stumbling out, and suddenly, shockingly, the kid was crying, big gasping sobs from deep in his belly, tears streaming down his face. Kavitha grabbed a towel by the side of the bed and started dabbing at his cheeks with practiced motions, as if she'd done this before. As if she'd been doing this for days.

"Tell me what happened," Michael said, in his calmest cop voice. On one level, he couldn't believe Kavitha had kept this from him—but he held the anger down, waiting for the facts.

And the story came spilling out. Sandip had been recruited a few weeks ago by the kidnapping squad; one of the disgruntled Tamils he'd tried to join up with had been a joker involved in the scheme. Sandip knew the basics of how to handle a gun, part of his revolutionary aspirations, though he'd never shot one outside the range. He didn't mind waving one around to scare people, though. Especially given how much money they'd paid him to do it.

"And not just money. Free drinks, as many as I wanted, and women too. Fucking gorgeous women just waiting for us. *Machan*, you should have seen the setup they had over there." The kid's eyes were wide and glassy.

"Over where?" Michael asked sharply.

Sandip huddled in on himself, and Kavitha put a protective hand on his arm. "I can't remember. They never really told us anything, but I heard some of them talking about it. Some tiny country, something stan?"

This was important. He had to tell the captain, as soon as he got the whole story. The kid was still babbling. "I don't know where it was, I'm sorry. I'm sorry!" He kept going on about how cool it had seemed, at first. Sandip had thought he was living the dream. And then they'd let him see the killings.

Now he was crying again as he talked, the words stuttering between jagged sobs. "I mean, they *told* me what was going on, but it's different when you see it. They said joker fight club, I figured it was gangsters, big guys, fighting it out to prove their manhood, y'know? Those were the kind of guys I was helping to grab. But the first real fight I saw, it was this little man, with glasses—he looked like a schoolteacher. Like the guy who taught my freshman history class. I kind of hated Mr. Matthews, but I didn't want to see him ripped apart into little pieces! The other guy started chomping on what was left of his stomach, and that's when I knew I couldn't keep doing this." Now Sandip was crying so hard that he couldn't talk anymore, and Kavitha took up the story.

"That's almost all of it," she said. "When they came back to New York on that trip, he took off. Got shot in the shoulder, but got away. He was too scared to go to the hospital, so he called me. It was the day your parents came for dinner. I snuck out that night, took some of our money, and rented him this place. Got medicine, bandages, dug the bullet out of his shoulder, patched him up and prayed that he'd survive it. You should have seen the shape he was in." Her voice was high, trembling.

Michael couldn't believe what he was hearing. "A week. You've kept this from us for a week?" No wonder she'd been wound up so tight; keeping secrets wasn't in Kavitha's nature. It must have been killing her to lie to them like this. That didn't make him any less angry. Rage was churning in his stomach.

"Michael." Kavitha stood up, came two steps closer, close enough that he could smell her fear. Although, perhaps wisely, she didn't touch him. "I knew you'd have to arrest him, send him to jail for a long, long time. But he's just a kid. That's what they do, you know." Her voice was shaky now, close to breaking. Kavitha took a deep breath, trying to steady herself. "To keep the brutality going—they take children, and make them part of their battles. We can't punish the children for what the adults have done."

Michael shook his head. His chest felt as if it were being stabbed with knives. He'd never thought heartbreak could feel so literal, so real. "Kavitha, you know better. He participated. Sandip is old enough to know what he was doing when he took those people to their deaths." She'd always been so committed to doing what was right. It was part of why he loved her. He'd known how she felt about family, but he'd thought she was better than this.

The boy was quieter now, doubled over and hugging his knees, swallowing his sobs.

She spread out her hands, helplessly. Despite everything, Michael was struck once again by how beautifully she moved. "He's my little brother," Kavitha said. "You should have seen him, bloody, with a bullet in him. He asked me to help him. I thought if I hid him for a little while, until it was all over . . ." She trailed off, clearly not sure what possible good ending there could have been.

If she had only come to him right away—he could have found some way to make it right. To protect the boy; as a juvenile, if Sandip had come in and told his story right away, maybe Michael could have saved him.

But now it was too late. "You lied to me for a week. You let these bastards continue their operation unimpeded. How many people did they grab, in the last week?" He could see the words hitting Kavitha, see her bracing against their assault.

How could they come back from this? Michael realized that she was never going to wear his ring, not now. He couldn't offer it to her after this, even if he understood on some level why she'd done it. He couldn't keep living with her; he could barely look at her. Oh, Isai. Sweetheart. This was going to tear their little girl apart. And Minal—would she still marry him? Or would he lose her too? If he made her choose between them, Michael didn't know who Minal would pick.

Kavitha stepped back, away from him. Let her hands fall to her sides. "What are you going to do, Michael?"

She knew the answer; she knew him too well. "What I have to."

Michael said the words, feeling the weight of them fall like a knife between them, cutting the ties that bound them together. "Sandip Kandiah, you're under arrest. You have the right to remain silent. Anything you say or do can and will be held against you in a court of law . . ."

Those About to Die . . .

Part Six

STANDING JUST OUTSIDE THE arena, hidden behind the doors that opened into it, Marcus told himself, *Just one more time.*

One more, and this is all over.

He knew he would hate himself for it later, when he was far from here and could look back. But that would be then. This was now. He had to get out of here. With Olena. He would do this for her, and then they would be free. They'd hide somewhere nobody knew him. It wouldn't matter where, because he'd have Olena.

Just one more death, and then never again.

The music died down and changed tempo. The announcer called for the crowd's attention. "Ladies and gentlemen, it's been an amazing night so far," he claimed, "but now it's time for the main event—a death match. Not since the time of the ancients, of Rome's mighty glory, have gladiators risked their very lives in the arena. But this bout goes even further back than that. Back to the very beginning. Back to the Garden of Good and Evil."

A different voice cut in, speaking a different language. Russian, Marcus guessed. And after that still another language, perhaps Chinese.

Marcus thought, *The world's watching,* but he hoped that wasn't true. Both for himself, and for what it meant about the world.

The English announcer picked up again, saying the first competitor, ladies and gentlemen, showed his murderous talent just days ago. He comes armed with the weapons the wild card virus gave him. Welcome him, ladies and gentlemen! *The Infamous Black Tongue!*

The doors in front of Marcus flew open. The rush of sound trapped in the small, claustrophobic space hit him like a physical force. He slithered into the bright lights of the arena. As soon as he was through, the doors shut behind him, trapping him inside. That was all right, though. He knew the way out. To kill. And he knew this arena. It was a friend. He passed through a rippling wave of tension in the air. Like heat but not. Like a scent but scentless. He sucked it in, feeding off it, filling himself with the rage he was going to need.

His eyes darted up to Baba Yaga's box. She was there, like always, with the twisted old man beside her. But this time someone sat on her other side, looking uncomfortable and nervous. And beautiful. Olena. She wore a tiny, tight red dress, and had her hair pulled up. She could've been a model, or a starlet on the arm of some Hollywood actor. He hated that she was so close to that evil woman and that horror of a man. Hated that the black-suited guards lined the back wall, a half dozen of them, staring at the arena from behind black sunglasses. They shouldn't be anywhere near Olena. He closed his eyes, reminding himself that once this was over she was going to be his. He would take her away from all this. That's what mattered.

When he opened his eyes again, Baba Yaga reached over and set a hand atop Olena's. She held it there, watching Marcus. The message was clear.

When the commotion died down the announcer continued. Facing the serpent would be a soldier of death disguised in godly robes. For years he pretended to be a man of the cloth, when he was really a man of the blade, a soldier of fortune with a past soaked in blood. They all knew the name he went by now. They'd all seen him in action.

As the translations rattled on, Marcus pulled his thoughts, and his eyes, away from Olena. *A man of the cloth?* he wondered. That didn't describe El Monstro. Or Nimble Dick. Or John the Pharaoh. Or any of the jokers he thought they'd match him with. They couldn't mean . . .

A door on the other side of the arena opened. A hooded figure lumbered through.

No! Marcus thought.

As if refuting him directly, the announcer shouted, "Bring in the Holy Redeemer!"

No, they can't do this!

The door slammed shut behind the priest. Father Squid reached up and pinched back his hood with his fingers. He stared at Marcus. He didn't look surprised. He didn't look horrified. But Marcus couldn't say what emotions did lie in the dark depths behind his large, round eyes.

"Ladies and gentlemen," the announcer intoned, "the serpent and the holy man! Only one of them can leave this Garden of Good and Evil alive. Who will it be? Which one should it be?" He reminded them that they could place bets electronically right up to the moment of first contact. That was the first thing that hushed the crowd, as many heads turned down to their mobile phones.

Father Squid approached him with his heavy steps.

"What are you doing here?" Marcus snapped. "You're messing up everything. You can't be here!"

The priest shook his head solemnly. "I'm the only one who should face you, Marcus."

"This a death match!"

"Who better than a priest to face death with?"

The man's calm annoyed Marcus. His fists turned to stones. Resentment surged through him. "Stop talking nonsense."

Shouts and jeers rained down on them, the audience urging them to fight.

"Marcus, God put us in this ring together. Nothing happens without his will. I understand it now."

Marcus wanted to grab him and shake him. He almost punched him. He wanted to. He was ready to. That's why he was here, to beat someone down. To kill. But . . . he couldn't make his fists do what they'd have to. He thought, *This is Father Squid.*

Father Squid looked away from him. He let his eyes range over the crowd. "We're not here for them. We're here so that you can become the man you are destined to be."

And then Marcus understood. The realization hit him with a physical force, stunning him, but also clearing the clutter from his mind at the same time. "You . . . you volunteered to fight me, didn't you?"

"I'm here to give you the last thing that I can. It's the only way you'll get out of here. Kill me, Marcus. Give in to the rage that you're holding back. Just this one last time."

The announcer piped up, saying something to the audience. Marcus concentrated through the announcer's voice and the crowd's taunts and the urge inside him to lash out. It was still there. He still breathed it in. It still egged him on. Just start it, his body seemed to be saying. Start it, and let death happen. He fought to get a word out. "Why?"

Father Squid closed the short space between them. He grasped Marcus by his forearms. Marcus tensed. His coils bunched, every inch of him screaming to unleash. The crowd roared, thinking something was finally going to happen.

The priest spoke slowly, clearly. "Because I led you into this hell. Because I've had my life, filled as it was with crimes—and with wonders. But for you, Marcus, the meaning of your life and work on this earth is before you. You can yet be a great man. I've always seen it in you, from the very first time I saw you—a frightened, angry fugitive, seeking help but not knowing how to ask."

"But you—"

Father Squid tugged on his arms, sharply. "Because there's no other way! And, as God sees and knows and plans all, this must be what he plans for us. No matter what you do, I absolve you. Now fight me!" The priest let go of Marcus's arms, pulled back, and slapped him.

The blow tossed Marcus to the side. Fury rushed through him. He swung back, fists cocked, poisonous saliva flooding his mouth. The crowd loved it. They rose to their feet.

"Kill me!" the priest bellowed. He slapped him again. "You have the rage. I see it in your eyes. Do what your body wants. Fight. Hate me, Marcus, for standing between you and your love. Kill me, and go with her and be free. Cut the bullshit and do it, Marcus!"

Marcus almost obeyed. He was so close. Father Squid was right there in front of him, offering the path to everything Marcus thought he wanted. Freedom. Olena. But hearing profanity come from the priest's mouth was another slap, one that brought with it a memory. Marcus saw the spinning of a teacup, thrown from his hand, chipped by his frustration. He heard that curse word, but to his shame it was his mouth that uttered it. A word said in anger. A teacup thrown. Chipped. He'd always regretted that. Always been ashamed of it. Always wished he could take it back.

"It's the only way out of here for you, and for me," Father Squid said, shoving him with one powerful arm. "I cannot take my own life, but I can give it. I give to you. It's okay, Marcus. Really. I'm not afraid. I will face my reckoning. If God allows it I'll see my Lizzie again, and that will be the greatest gift of all. What are you afraid of? Just do it. Poison me. And then do it. I'll feel nothing, if that's what you're worried about."

Marcus could poison him. He knew that. The father's aquatic skin, he figured, would absorb his venom in an instant. And then what? Break his neck? Choke him? It could be done, but knowing that he could just confirmed that he wouldn't. It was strange, how calming that realization was. He was going to lose everything. He would never have that life with Olena. He would likely die in the moments to come. He wouldn't have that future that Father Squid imagined for him, but he felt a resigned satisfaction at all of this. He could stay true to himself. He could go forward into his last moments without shame. He could make both Olena and Father Squid proud. That mattered more than anything else. The only thing he couldn't do was what the priest asked him.

Marcus glanced up at Olena. He saw in her face that she understood, looked more concerned than ever. Even from a distance, he could see her lower lip quivering. Slightly, ever so slightly, she shook her head. That was what Marcus needed. He slid forward and grasped Father Squid by the arms, just as the priest had done to him a moment before. "You really loved her, didn't you?"

"Lizzie?" the priest asked, coming in close to support him. "Yes, with all my heart. Loving her has kept me human. She was in every act of kindness I did."

"I'm sure she's waiting for you. You'll see her again, but not by my hand. That simply cannot happen. You mean too much to me."

As he spoke, the priest's facial tentacles went slack. He closed his eyes. When he opened them, they were again the ones Marcus had always known. Calm. Sad. Wise. A tear escaped one corner and trickled down into his tentacles.

Turning from him, Marcus projected his voice to cut through the crowd's commotion. "No, I won't do it. This man, he saved me. You understand that? When I was nobody, miserable, lost: he took me in and taught me I could be something. And you want me to kill him? No, I won't." He turned to Baba Yaga. His tongue quickened. "And fuck you, bitch, for starting all this. You got nothing on me. Not anymore. Not when you ask me to do this."

The old woman had risen from her seat. The crowd, looking from the players in the ring up to the standing woman, hushed.

Glaring down at Marcus, Baba Yaga's lips moved. She said, "Kill him if you want to live. If you want the girl." Her voice was just a whisper, but Marcus heard her clearly enough. Or did he see the words on her lips? Or just feel them, pressed from her mind to his? Whichever it was, there was power in that voice. Command. That voice could have told him to do a lot of things and he would've, especially for Olena. But this one thing he wouldn't do. Marcus shook his head.

Baba Yaga stared down. It was nearly impossible to hold her gaze. Marcus had seen hard men. He'd faced monstrous jokers. He'd killed men who wanted to kill him. But none of them had a face as deathly fierce as this old woman. The anger in her eyes pummeled him, seared him.

Watching must have unnerved the crowd. Whispers passed through the audience. Uncomfortable shifting. A few rose and then stood, unsure what was happening. One man, sounding drunk, said this wasn't what he paid for. The woman next to him shushed him.

"Marcus," Father Squid said, "you could still—"

"Never," Marcus said.

"I only wanted a future for you."

"A future with your blood on my hands? Never."

Baba Yaga's voice was small and cold, and yet reached them clearly. "You defy me? Foolish boy." She puckered her thin lips. She sucked in her cheeks, leaned forward, and spat.

The spittle fell through the wire mesh and down toward Marcus. Such a small action from such a small woman. *Pathetic,* he thought, *if that's the best she can do.*

Father Squid smashed into Marcus's side and shoved him away.

The small gob of spit landed where Marcus had been a moment before. It splattered on the side of Father Squid's cheek. The priest yanked his face away, but not quickly enough. He pressed his fingers to his tentacled cheek. He staggered. His body went rigid, fingers jerking spasmodically. His black eyes bulged, as if a great pain had bloomed inside him and he just then understood it.

Marcus slid toward him. He reached out, but Father Squid twisted away. He walked a few stiff steps before one of his legs buckled. In the complete hush of the arena, Marcus heard the snap of bone breaking. Not just once but again and again, a whole concussion of fractures. Father Squid went down. At first he grasped his leg, but he let go when it began to bend and twist. And then his other did the same. His head snapped back, banging against the floor. His torso bulged as if living things were moving beneath his skin. He rolled over and tried to push himself up. A wave rolled up his spine, audibly snapping vertebrae as it did. His arms and legs wouldn't support him. They were shattered, rubbery things, writhing.

And then he did rise, but not by his own power. The terror on his face made that clear. His body levered up from the floor, slowly, excruciatingly, supported on legs that were no longer legs. When he was upright, his eyes found Marcus. With great, trembling effort, he said one long, drawn-out word. "Lizzzzzzzzie . . ."

Before he was finished, the name rose into a scream. His torso snapped back from his middle and he became a molten form morphing out of all recognizing. His face went liquid. His eyes held their shape but they swam within the shifting chaos. His mouth was still a mouth and it screamed and screamed . . .

Until it stopped. Until all the horrible motion ceased. Marcus stared, recognizing what stood on the floor beside him, but not believing it. In the silence of the arena, Marcus—and everyone else—stared at the strange structure that was and wasn't Father Squid. The priest had been transformed into a prayer bench, complete with padded platform for the knees and an upper shelf for the faithful to lean against, heads bowed. Trapped in material that wasn't exactly flesh but wasn't wood or metal or plastic either, the father still breathed. His mouth stretched wide across the front portion of the bench. He saw still, through eyes that no longer had a face. Instead, they looked up from the shelf on which one of the faithful might tent their hands in prayer.

Galahad in Blue

Part Nine

FRANNY HAD FLASHED A badge at a cabbie, and shoved the hand-cuffed Berman into the back of the cab. He hadn't been gentle. They had wasted weeks, even shut down the investigation when all the while this man had held the key. And had kept silent while people died. Thinking about Father Squid and all the others trapped in a nightmare had Franny's hands clenching in impotent rage.

Wingman goggled at him as he blew in the door of the precinct, shoving the producer ahead of him. "Book this asshole."

"Okay. For what?"

"Attempted murder, assaulting a police officer, kidnapping, conspiracy . . . hell, being an asshole for that matter. Captain?"

"He's in," Homer said, still looking poleaxed.

Franny nodded. Homer called down to Sergeant Squinch and took control of Berman. Franny pushed through into the bullpen. Michael Stevens, seated at his desk, looked at him. Strain had etched lines around his eyes. He looked like a man who had lost everything. Franny ignored him, strode across the room to the office door, gave one pre-emptory knock and walked in. Maseryk looked up, a Jovian frown creasing his forehead. Surprisingly Mendelberg was also there, seated in a chair across the desk from the older man.

"Black, what the fuck?" the joker woman asked.

"I know where they're holding our missing jokers," Franny said. The two captains exchanged glances.

"Yeah, we do too," Mendelberg said.

Maseryk shot her a glance. "That might be a bit of an overstatement. We know they're someplace that ends in stan."

"How did you? Never mind . . . I've got more than that. They're in Kazakhstan, in a town called Talas," Franny said.

"Kazakhstan," Mendelberg repeated as if she were tasting the word.

Looking down into those bloodred eyes Frank remembered how Mendelberg had shut down the investigation, browbeaten him for arguing. He couldn't control it, he snapped, "Do you want me to spell it for you?"

That brought Maseryk out of his chair. "You better fucking climb down, Detective."

Mendelberg surprised him. She waved it off. "It's okay, Thomas." She turned back to Franny. "Where did you come by this?"

"Berman. He's being processed right now."

"You arrested him," Mendelberg said slowly.

"Yes."

"Why?"

Franny laid out what had occurred at the condo. For a moment the two captains just blinked at him, then Mendelberg reverted to form.

"Why is a SCARE agent involved in an NYPD investigation?"

"He had resources I . . . why are we talking about Norwood? Why aren't we—"

"Tell me everything," Maseryk ordered.

"That could take a while."

"Give me the *Reader's Digest* version."

So Franny walked them through it all. How the dead joker on a rural highway in New Jersey linked up with a SCARE investigation of smuggling. How the body led to the dog-training facility. How Jamal had run the names of the dead Russians that linked them to the KGB, how the DVDs had led to an *American Hero* cameraman, which had led to Berman, and how Berman had provided to the mysterious and very scary Baba Yaga the names of jokers who had auditioned for *American Hero*. "It sounds like there's a lot of former KGB goons so we better have SWAT—"

"Are you listening to yourself?" Maseryk interrupted. "This is Fort

Freak. NYPD Fifth Precinct. We don't have jurisdiction in Brooklyn, much less fucking Kazakhstan."

"And even if we could act how the hell would we get there? Flying carpet?" Mendelberg chimed in.

"We've got that handled."

Maseryk came out of his chair again. "You are not going to cause a diplomatic incident. And neither am I."

"So what? We're going to do nothing? These people are being killed." Franny clenched his teeth before even more intemperate words could emerge.

"Black, my first partner here, thirty years ago, taught me one hard lesson: when in doubt do nothing. Otherwise you're sure as fuck going to make things worse." The captain continued, forestalling the objections he saw rising to Franny's lips. "Now, nothing doesn't mean nothing. The first thing we're going to do is contact the State Department. Then I'll get on the horn to the UN, see if I can reach Lohengrin and the Committee. Your buddy can tell his people at SCARE. We rattle enough cages this Baba Yaga may shut down the operation."

"And bury the evidence. Literally." Franny spun and headed for the door.

"Black! Where are you going?" Mendelberg yelled after him.

"To do something."

"You walk out of here . . . it's your career," Maseryk warned.

"It's my soul if I don't."

Conversations in the bullpen were subdued. Franny realized the reality of a fight if not the details had penetrated to the assembled cops. Michael intercepted him before he reached the door. "I'll go with you," he said.

"How did you . . . ?"

Michael shrugged. "There's a place in the hall where every word from the captain's office comes through the vent. My dad showed me. I'm your partner, Franny. I haven't been a very good one up till now. Let me see if I can do something about that."

Franny read the shame and the sincerity in Michael's eyes. Jamal was sick, barely on his feet. Having another person . . . Franny shook his head. "You've got a kid. And I've heard you're getting married."

"Maybe not," Michael muttered.

Franny didn't have time to inquire. "Look, I appreciate it, but no. Now I've gotta go before the brass finds some way to arrest *me*."

Those About to Die . . .

Part Seven

MARCUS HAD TO DRAG his eyes away from Father Squid. They seemed heavy as stones. He lifted them and found Baba Yaga. She stood with her arms crossed, her lips pursed and her cheeks sucked in against the bones of her face.

You bitch, Marcus thought. At first it was a whisper. *You bitch.* But then, as he watched the smug satisfaction that lifted the corners of her lips, it became a scream. *Biittttcccchhhh!* All the rage and anger and confusion and determination to kill that he had overcome with Father Squid surged back into him with a vengeance. Poison-laden saliva flooded his mouth. He didn't think about what he did next. He just rose and did it.

He propelled himself upwards and crashed against the mesh that trapped the fighters in the ring. He pressed it up, his tail flexing beneath him. When the strained tension of the mesh pushed him back he fell with it. Gripping the mesh in his fists, he yanked down savagely, using the weight of his long body.

Dangling from it and looking through the lacework, he saw Baba Yaga turn to one of her guards. She jabbed her finger, indicating Olena. The burly, black-suited man stepped up behind her. He pinched Olena's shoulder in one hand. Using his other, he caressed her chin with the barrel of a handgun, lifting up on it to make her rise. She looked terrified.

Marcus shot upwards again, and then yanked down again. Up and down again, more frantic, failing with each attempt. The guard was leading

Olena away. The announcer was saying something. It sounded like he was ridiculing Marcus. The crowd, watching him thrash, began to relax again. A man decked out in African garb pointed at him, smiling. A red-haired woman in a tight black dress stood and thrashed in imitation of Marcus. Another man followed Marcus with his upheld cell phone, his freckled face tight in concentration as he tried to take a photo.

Hating them all, Marcus roared up into the mesh with renewed fury. He clenched it in his fists and wrenched his body around, his snake portion twisting him with all the force of his long, trembling muscles. He felt one section of the mesh give, just a single ringlet cord where it looped through one of the thick glass panels. He sensed it like a spider in its web. He let go and dove for the weak spot. He slammed his head and one arm through. Straining and cursing, he squeezed the other shoulder through, and then he wriggled like mad.

Marcus landed on the African man, driving his shoulder hard into the man's chest. The audience panicked. No laughter now. Shocked faces, people crawling backwards, shouting out, running for the exits. As much as he wanted to rage at them, Marcus had a different target. He squirmed toward Baba Yaga's box. He punched the man with the cell phone as he passed him and elbowed others out of the way.

Reaching up and grabbing the low railing of the box with both hands, he came up and over, face-to-face with a cadre of armed guards. Baba Yaga stood beside the wretched old man. Her face was wrinkled in concentration. Her lips puckered and her cheeks sucked in as if she were trying hard to gather enough saliva to spit.

For a terrible moment Marcus thought she was going to do to him what she'd done to Father Squid. The horror of it—even though he'd rushed to it—froze him in place. He watched her lips move.

She didn't spit, though. She was trying, and the guards were waiting for it. That was clear enough. Marcus realized she couldn't do it again! Her power had limits. There was exhaustion in her eyes. She clutched at a chair along the wall with one hand, needing its support just to stand. She gave up trying to summon her power and, said, flatly, disdainfully, "Shoot him, you idiots."

Marcus ducked under the box as the barrels of several Uzis fixed on him. He skimmed beneath it and shot up from the rear. Curling and coming up fast, he grabbed Baba Yaga by the shoulder. He spun her, and launched his tongue at her stunned face. It hit with a wet venom *thwack*.

The impact snapped her head back and flung her arms out. She fell into her guards, who scrambled awkwardly to support her, encumbered by their weapons.

Having poisoned her good, he didn't wait around for the spray of bullets he knew would be coming his way. He slipped back over the railing and dropped down into the stands. He landed hard. He glanced through the glass at the prayer bench that was the still-living Father Squid. He hated leaving him, but there was no choice. The father would want him to escape and live. So he was going to.

Gritting his teeth, he squirmed, whip fast, through the aisles and over seats. *Olena.* She was his last bit of business here. Get her, and get out. That's what mattered.

Many were heading, like him, for the exit doors. It was chaos. When bullets started to fly from Baba Yaga's box it only got worse. They tore up the seats and ricocheted off railings. Marcus weaved wildly, all curves, the point of his tail snapping behind him. He slithered over a row of cowering Japanese businessmen. He shoved a fat white man in a pinstriped suit out of his way, and bowled right through the blond, slinky, barely clad harem of women following an Arab-looking man in a long, shimmering robe. Someone behind him screamed, a high, piercing screech of agony that cut through all the other noises. Then the screamer died, battered down by the barrage of gunfire.

Marcus kept going, telling himself that nobody in here was innocent. They had come here to see people die. They may have gotten more than they bargained for, but who was to say they didn't deserve it?

When a man and woman, holding hands as they ran, went down right in front of him, Marcus realized the shots had come from the other side of them, from the mouth of the tunnel. The woman's long, auburn hair floated above her as she fell. Through the trailing screen of it, Marcus saw the shooter. The guard took aim with one hand, while his other clamped down on Olena's wrist. She twisted and yanked, making it hard for him to set his shot.

Marcus arched his body over the fallen couple. He reared high as he climbed the steps up to the guard. His tail cut a sinuous weave beneath him, a sidewinder motion that clearly unnerved the guard. He fired at Marcus's torso several times, only managing to graze his shoulder. And then, just before Marcus reached him, he lowered the gun and shot at his tail. Two bullets punched through his scales. The pain was instant, molten, as if red-hot iron prods had been slammed deep inside him. Roaring at the pain of it, the tip of his tail lashed at the shooter, catching his legs and flipping him. Marcus squirmed over him, pressing down as hard as he could. He bent and poison tagged him.

That done, he looked up at Olena. He stopped, unsure—now that he'd reached her—what to do. He stared at the perfection of features that was her face. She was too beautiful. Too beautiful for him, at least. He with venom on his tongue, blood on his fists, with the guilt of a murderer a searing brand on his flesh.

Suddenly, it felt impossible that someone like him had any claim on someone like her. He was speechless.

Olena stepped toward him, a hand held to her lips as her wide blue eyes took in the blood glistening on his scales. The concern on her face was exquisite, almost too generous to be believed. "Marcus, you are shot."

Marcus managed to say, "I'm okay." He wasn't sure it was true. His tail hurt with each pulse of blood through it. It took effort to keep the rhythmic surges of pain from showing on his face. "Olena, will you . . ." He hesitated. She watched him. "Can we get out of here? Will you come with me?"

The crowd had begun to squeeze around them, pressed against the wall, nervous but still frantic to escape down the tunnel. Olena scowled at them. "Yes. Get me away from these ones." She bent and retrieved the guard's handgun. With a few quick motions, she popped it open, checked something, and then slammed it closed again. Marcus didn't know what she'd just done, but clearly she knew a thing or two about handguns. Weapon raised in one hand, she beckoned him with her other. "Come. We go."

He didn't need to be told twice.

The Big Bleed

Part Ten

"THEY SAID NO."

Franny had returned from his delivery of Berman to Fort Freak with the bad news. He slumped on Berman's couch, accepting a glass of water delivered to him by Jamal and Mollie, who moved like participants in a three-legged race.

"What kind of 'no'?" Jamal said. " 'No' as in 'not now,' or 'not without SCARE'? Or 'no' as in 'never'?"

" 'No never nada.' They only thing Maseryk promised to do was tell SCARE so they could put the jokers on their to-do list."

"That's just what I didn't want."

"Well, will it make you happier to know he was going to add State, the Committee, the mayor's office, and I believe parks and rec?"

Jamal just closed his eyes. *Christ.*

"You two really know how to make a girl feel protected," Mollie said. "God." She tried to cross her arms, a gesture rendered impossible by her linkage to Jamal.

For the first half hour, Jamal had not found being handcuffed to Mollie Steunenberg to be a complete burden. She was pretty and bouncy and not wearing more clothing than necessary. Being free from Michael Berman improved her mood, too: she never reached flirty, but she had gone some distance from sullen.

But only for the first half hour. Four more half hours had passed, and now both of them were utterly sick of each other's company. "I don't like this any more than you do," Jamal told the girl. Her attitude had helped him make a decision. "Our only way out is forward."

"What the hell does that mean?"

Jamal turned to Franny. "We do this ourselves. Now."

He didn't have to spend much time or energy on the proposal, which was helpful, since he had diminishing amounts of both. For Franny, the pitch was simple: "Every hour that passes, some citizen of Jokertown dies."

For Mollie aka Tesseract, it was this: "The only way you're ever going to be free of Baba Yaga and the rest of her gang is if we take them out."

"Can we kill that old bitch?"

"It will probably come to that."

She was suddenly happier than Jamal had ever seen her.

The first sensation Jamal felt upon stepping through Tesseract's "door" from Berman's apartment into the gladiator compound inside Maxim's was dizzying vertigo.

Had Mollie bothered to consider the fact that the spatial orientation in New York, Eastern Time Zone, was radically different from that of Talas, Kazakhstan, Asian Crazy Time? Was it even possible? Or was this his illness at work, not only robbing him of his bounceback, but of *any* mental or physical resilience?

No matter. Jamal took in the huge digital television screen mounted above a wet bar, showing chaos in the arena itself. A camera operator was struggling to locate the action (*for whom?* Jamal wondered) as what looked like Snake Boy's torso slithered through a crowd of glitterati, knocking them sideways while zapping them with his poisoned tongue.

Nice.

Adding to Jamal's disorientation were the smell of the gladiator's quarters—heavy on cologne, perfume, and cigarette smoke—and the sound—hideous bass-heavy rap. Lounging on couches or bellied up to the bar were maybe a dozen jokers and twice that number of attractive "hostesses." And, holding a drink, his arm around a tall nat woman with un-nat breasts, Dmitri . . . fat, sleepy-eyed, sloppy, menacing.

Then Franny and Mollie walked in—looking as though they were holding hands like high school sweethearts, though most high school sweethearts weren't joined by handcuffs.

And, to quote Big Bill Norwood, a great deal of Hades came unmoored.

The jokers all sprang to their feet—those that had feet. Their eyes went wide—those that had eyes—with surprise or amusement. "What the hell is this?" growled an eight-foot-tall man-mountain joker Jamal knew as El Monstro.

Only Dmitri seemed to appreciate the situation. Shoving his goddess to one side, he smirked and turned his menacing attention to the intruders.

"Franny!" Jamal shouted and pointed. "Cap him!"

But Franny hesitated. And in that moment, Jamal felt as sad and sick and weak and afraid as he'd ever felt in his life. Worse than the day he'd broken his leg on the football field. He thought of Julia crushed, his parents dead, his own life ended. He wanted to crawl into a hole anywhere but here—*Dmitri at work.* Knowing what to expect in no way lessened the effect.

But that foreknowledge gave Jamal a few precious seconds of lucidity, and enough energy to raise the Glock. He snapped off three rounds that caught a surprised Dmitri in the back, shoulder, and, as he turned, in the face.

Down he went in a spray of blood and cranial matter.

"Oh my God!" Mollie was almost hysterical, and Jamal couldn't blame her. Franny stared. "Sorry, cop training." Blinking hard, he forced a smile. "I wanted to tell him to throw down his gun . . ."

Jamal stared at dead Dmitri. It seemed that someone else had pulled that trigger. There was no time to reflect, however. More goons with guns would be here soon. "Hey, people," he shouted. "We are here to take you back to New York!"

The unfortunately-but-appropriately-named Wartface was giddy about being rescued. "About fucking time! Can I hit anyone before we go? I've got a list!"

"Sorry." Jamal turned to Tesseract. "Do it!"

Without a word, Mollie opened a "door" to Fort Freak. They should be safe there, and it would allow the cops to remove them from the missing-persons list . . . once they calmed down. "There's the exit. Move!"

There was a mad rush. First the hookers, then the jokers flopping, crawling, hopping after them. They piled through the door, and Jamal imagined the chaos at the other end of the journey.

Two goons appeared from a side door, guns blazing in spite of the presence of at least two joker-gladiators. Jamal ducked: he knew these idiots were just spraying rounds. He squeezed off three rounds that were aimed no better, but served to force the goons to take cover.

As he reloaded, Jamal had a sudden surge of energy. Maybe he *was* some kind of adrenaline junkie, happy only when moving, chasing, shooting. It certainly fit the persona of Stuntman the ace from SCARE and Hollywood. Maybe he was seeing the endgame. All they had to do was grab the rest of the jokers—

Franny and Mollie were forced to duck as a lucky shot from one of the goons passed between them, shattering a mirror on the wall. Franny had finally lost his inhibitions, unleashing a spray of covering fire that silenced both goons.

Mollie was crying, whether out of fear or anger or the residual effects of the Dmitri mindfuck, Jamal couldn't know. He wondered what these Tesseract shifts did to the girl—God knew that bounceback drained him, even when he was healthy.

El Monstro had been lingering off to one side (his height made it impossible for him to truly take cover). Now the eight-foot-tall joker abruptly headed for the arena door. Jamal grabbed him. "Hey, big guy, where are you going?" He nodded toward the "door." "New York is that way."

"I'm not going. I like it here!" El Monstro insisted.

For a moment Jamal was furious—this was just the latest entry in a long litany of stupidity he had endured since learning about Wheels and the missing jokers. He was out of time, out of patience. He was not going to let this big goon stop him from completing this mission, no more than he had let Rustbelt stop him from winning *American Hero*! He trained his Glock at El Monstro's vast mid-section. "Look," Jamal said, "I don't know what they've done to your head here, but you're going through that door."

With no apparent windup, no warning, El Monstro simply swung one of his giant arms and metal fists toward him. It was slow, but still too fast for Jamal Norwood to dodge.

The massive fist slammed into the right side of his face.

It was worse than his first deliberate jump from a tall building, in *Halloween Night XIII*. He had time for the sickening realization that there was going to be no bounceback, that Stuntman was falling fading dying.

Galahad in Blue

Part Ten

EVERYTHING SEEMED TO SLOW down.

Franny's vision narrowed to a tunnel that showed him only Jamal's face, blood flying from his mouth, his right eye dangling loose, the deep indentation in the side of his skull. The agent seemed to collapse in stages, until he lay on the floor like a broken toy, casually discarded. Mollie was screaming in his ear, trying to hide behind him, yanking at the handcuffs that joined them.

Franny yelled. It wasn't even words, just an incoherent sound of rage and grief and denial. He brought up his gun.

And suddenly the dragging weight on his left arm was gone. He whirled in time to see Mollie, a paper clip clutched between her fingers, step backwards through an opening that afforded him a brief glimpse of the Eiffel Tower, flipping him the bird. Then the doorway snapped shut.

Of course the door to Fort Freak was also gone.

Trapped. Panic clogged his throat.

The whine of a bullet past his head brought him back to the precariousness of his situation. Franny dove behind a sofa. He heard El Monstro yelling to the remaining guards, "I'll get him."

Despite his ringing ears from all the gunfire Franny could hear and even feel El Monstro's footfalls as he closed on him. He leaped up and vaulted over the back of the sofa. He snapped off a few shots at the last remaining guard on the catwalk overhead, who ducked into cover.

El Monstro was closing. It wasn't that he was particularly fast, but he was so big that each stride covered a lot of ground. The buffet table was on Franny's left. Franny's eyes flicked across the offerings—deli meats, bread, cheese, a mound of caviar, a soup tureen set on a hot plate. The handle of a ladle invited someone to try a bowl.

Franny snatched out the ladle brimming with hot soup. The smell of paprika hit his nose. About half spilled as he whirled, but there was enough left in the big ladle for Franny to flick into El Monstro's face. The big joker howled, and clawed at his face and eyes. *Guess it was hot not sweet paprika,* Franny thought inanely. He closed with the big joker, screwed the barrel of his gun into El Monstro's ear, and pulled the trigger twice.

Until this day he had never actually fired his gun outside the range. Most cops went through their entire careers and never fired their piece much less killed someone. Now Franny had killed a man. A man he'd supposedly come to rescue.

It wasn't like in the movies. It wasn't even like watching Jamal shoot Dmitri. His knees suddenly felt like they'd been replaced with rubber bands, and he found himself sitting on the floor. A bullet creased the air where his head had been only seconds before.

There was no time for shock or regret. If he was getting out of here alive he needed to take care of that asshole on the catwalk, and find his way to the outside. After that—well, he'd think about after that once he got that far.

Access to the catwalk wasn't immediately obvious. There was another burst of gunfire from above that sent Franny scrambling for cover, but someone on the high ground always has the advantage, and Franny found himself knocked sideways from the force of the bullet that slammed into his left shoulder.

The shock wore off all too quickly, and the pain hit. It was worse then anything he'd ever experienced. When he broke an arm playing hockey, slashed his leg on a submerged tree while swimming in a lake that summer at camp nothing could match this searing agony. Franny screamed and fell to his knees.

Despite the torment some part of his brain kept working. *He needs to think you're dead.* Franny collapsed on the floor, the pistol hidden beneath him. With luck the goon would leave, or come down to make sure Franny was dead.

At which point Franny would kill him. Or try to kill him. Only, God, he didn't want to kill anybody else. Ever.

Blood was trickling from the wound. Franny could feel his shirt becoming wet and sticky. He listened to his heartbeats like a slow deep drum in his ears. The pain flared and ebbed also in time to that primal clock. Franny gazed into the staring eyes of El Monstro prone on the floor near him. He wanted to look away, but didn't dare move. He wanted to close his eyes, but didn't dare risk it.

Overhead Franny heard an agitated conversation in what he guessed was Russian. Two sets of footsteps. A door closing. Franny counted another thirty heartbeats and then cautiously climbed to his feet. Nothing. Pressing a hand to his shoulder he staggered to Jamal, knelt and, pressing his fingers against the SCARE agent's throat, felt for a pulse. There was none. He hadn't expected to find one. Not with the side of the agent's skull crushed in in that horrifying way.

"Eternal rest grant unto him, O Lord, and let perpetual light shine upon him. May the soul of this faithful departed, through the mercy of God, rest in peace, Amen." Franny lifted his head, crossed himself, pulled the cross from his collar, kissed it, and tucked it away. "I'll get you home to Big Bill and your mom and Julia. I promise," he said softly. It was stupid. It wasn't like Jamal could hear. But it did give him a purpose, and jolted him into motion.

Franny moved to the buffet table, shook out a napkin, folded another into a pad, and made a makeshift bandage. Got it tied using one hand and his teeth. Next task: Find a way out. He searched through bedrooms that smelled of sweat and jizz and perfume.

Eventually he found a door that looked like it might lead to stairs that would lead to the catwalk. It was locked. He went back and found the body of one of the goons either Jamal or he had shot. The man had taken a header off the catwalk, and his legs and neck were bent at odd angles. The Uzi was undamaged. Franny carried it back to the door. Bracing the gun against his hip, he held down the trigger. Bullets whanged and bounced, but eventually the lock gave up.

Up the stairs. There were a couple of doors off the catwalk. Franny picked one at random. It put him in a long hallway pieced by doors. At first he edged up to them, then took five-second looks inside, the Uzi at the ready. They were all empty and they all appeared to be offices. Computers that would have been old in 1990 sat on desks.

At the end of the hall was another closed door. Franny leaned against it. Partly to listen, partly because he needed to lean on something. Through the thick wood he faintly heard shouts, screams, and gunfire.

He really didn't want to face any more gunfire, but he couldn't wait for Baba Yaga and her goons to regain control. He had to add to the chaos and use it to escape. He sucked in several deep breaths, then pushed open the door.

He was in the casino proper. The usual dings and rings of gambling machines were muted. Many of the slots had been knocked over. Extremely well-dressed people were running in all directions. Women's discarded shoes littered the carpeted floor. Franny even spotted a forlorn toupee dangling off a chair like a dead squirrel. The room reeked of cordite and cigarette smoke.

Across the large, chandelier-hung room he spotted IBT writhing toward elaborate double doors. His tongue shot out like a lashing whip, leaving behind convulsing people. A young woman ran at his side, gripping his hand while with the other she held a pistol that she used with murderous skill.

"Marcus!" Franny yelled, but over the screams and gunshots and the crashes as people tore open cash boxes behind the cashier's stands he wasn't heard.

That looked like the way out so Franny followed in the snake-man's wake. He passed through a lobby with a coat check area, and a bench where a large man with a suspicious bulge under his shoulder was slumped. The mark of IBT's tongue was on his face. The doors were standing wide open.

Franny stepped out as a battalion of police cars swarmed up, lights blazing and sirens blaring. A loudspeaker blared out instructions in a language he didn't understand. But he was a cop. He could guess. He threw down the Uzi, and put his hands up, bit back a cry of pain as it hurt his wounded shoulder. "I'm a cop! *American*. **Police officer!!**" He reached slowly into his pocket to pull out his badge.

Somebody shot him.

The bullet ripped into his side. Franny fell. He heard people yelling. He vaguely felt hands rifling his pockets. The face of a young man holding aloft a saline bag, the swaying roof of an ambulance.

Darkness.

Galahad in Blue

Part Eleven

Epilogue

GETTING SHOT HURT.

Getting shot twice . . . well, that should have hurt twice as much, but it seemed like more. Ten times as much, at least.

The treatment after the fact hadn't been much better. The Kazakh police had handcuffed him roughly, despite the blood leaking from him. Since he had a bullet in his shoulder, and another in his side, he had lost all macho cred by screaming. That penetrated the language barrier and they had taken him to the hospital, where the personnel had seemed overwhelmed by the number of gunshot and poisoning victims as well as some old joker hunched in a wheelchair, a creature as hideous as he was pathetic.

Franny hadn't been sure what to expect from a Kazakh hospital, but it wasn't all that different from an American facility. He had been taken quickly into surgery, and awakened in a private room. He had a feeling this wasn't the norm, but the presence of two large, very unsympathetic Kazakh policemen at the door made his status crystal clear.

He kept demanding to see the American ambassador and kept being ignored. He'd then tried using the fraternity of law enforcement to generate some sympathy from his guards. That hadn't worked either. Maybe because none of them could understand a word he was saying.

He decided to get dressed even though his bloodstained shirt was gone; he didn't feel terribly effective clad in an open-back hospital gown. But when he opened the door, he found himself looking down the barrel of his guards' submachine guns. Franny had a brief moment of thinking the perps in New York would sure as fuck be impressed if he had one of those instead of his service pistol.

One guard snapped out something in what sounded like Russian. Or maybe Kazakh. He had no fucking clue. Franny indicated his bare if bandaged torso. "Hey, how about a shirt? T-shirt? Anything?"

The guards looked at him with disinterest and shut the door again.

Franny returned to the bed, sat down, tried to think. It was a hopeless effort. His thoughts kept returning over and over to those chaotic moments when Jamal had been killed. His throat felt tight, and he swallowed hard for a couple of seconds. He had liked the cynical SCARE agent. *I got Stuntman killed.*

He was now totally alone. When he failed to check in Maseryk would probably figure out where he'd gone. Maybe eventually someone from the NYPD or the State Department or SCARE or somebody would ride to the rescue.

"I got most of the jokers home," Franny said aloud to the room.

The room wasn't impressed.

The door opened, and his guards entered accompanied by a man with a secretive face and slicked-back brown hair that made Franny think of an otter. His suit was expensive. He wore a Rolex, and the wire from a radio earpiece ran down into his collar.

The guards grabbed Franny's arms, and frog-marched him out of the room. It hurt his shoulder and his side and he yelled. "Hey! What are you doing? Where are we going?" He was being hustled down the hall. "I demand to see the American ambassador! I'm a police officer, you can't—"

The man in the suit slapped him hard across the face. Franny chewed on the bright coppery taste of blood and shut up.

"Baba Yaga wishes to see you," the man said in a voice that had one of those unidentifiable but superior European accents.

A flock of moths seemed to have taken up residence in Franny's gut. He could feel a subtle trembling in his legs. Okay, he was going to die. He didn't have to face it whimpering like a girl. He stiffened his spine, glared at the otter, and said, "*I'm* under guard, but she gets to send fucking errand boys? She's a fucking criminal. Why aren't these guys—" He jerked a thumb at the two cops. "—on *her* door?"

"Because she is a respected member of the business community here in Talas, and you are American cowboy cop who is very much out of his jurisdiction."

The otter pushed open the door, and for the first time Franny faced the woman behind all of this madness.

She was a small, wizened figure, her dyed red hair shockingly bright against the stacked pillows. She seemed fragile until she lifted heavy eyelids, and gave Franny a piercing look out of the coldest, most calculating gray eyes he had ever seen.

He was pushed inexorably forward until he stood at the side of the bed. The two guards backed away. Baba Yaga's wrinkled lips worked.

Baba Yaga spoke. "So, this is the hero," she said, in English. Franny stared at her wondering what Berman had meant about furniture and footstools? "Stupid, stupid, boy," the old woman went on. "You have no idea what you have done. He is waking. And we are all dead now."

Franny swallowed. "We?" he said. "Who, we?"

Baba Yaga laughed and pointed at Franny. "You." She touched her breast. "Me. Them." Her gesture encompassed the otter and the cops and set the gem-encrusted rings to flashing. "Talas. Kazakhstan. Eventually . . . the world."

Somewhere far off, in a distant part of the hospital, people began screaming.

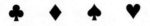

almost a woman

ALSO BY ESMERALDA SANTIAGO

When I Was Puerto Rican

América's Dream

almost a woman

Esmeralda Santiago

A Merloyd Lawrence Book

PERSEUS BOOKS

Reading, Massachusetts

Library of Congress Catalog Card Number: 98-86520

ISBN 0-7382-0043-3

Perseus Books is a member of the Perseus Books Group

Jacket design by Suzanne Heiser
Text design by Karen Savary Studio
Set in 11.5-point Electra by dix!

1 2 3 4 5 6 7 8 9-DOH-0201009998
First printing, September 1998

Find us on the World Wide Web at
http://www.aw.com/gb/

contents

"Martes, ni te cases, ni te embarques,
   ni de tu familia te apartes." 1

"Something could happen to you." 3

"I don't care what American girls do." 14

"Are you going to be famous?" 32

"But they're still illegitimate . . ." 43

"What's a Cleopatra dress?" 60

"Don't you want to sound Puerto Rican?" 75

"I don't care if the whole world is going." 90

"She's not exactly Method." 105

"Stop thinking and dance." 127

"It must be a sin to be so disrespectful to the Virgin." 138

"Who do you think you are?" 154

"Pearls bring tears." 170

"The music inside her . . ." 192

"What size bra do you wear?"   211

"It wouldn't look right."   238

"Your face is no longer innocent."   264

"Where were you last night?"   280

"For that slave-girl look . . ."   296

"It is the way it must be."   307

Acknowledgments   313

About the Author   315

"Martes, ni te cases, ni te embarques, ni de tu familia te apartes."

In the twenty-one years I lived with my mother, we moved at least twenty times. We stuffed our belongings into ragged suitcases, boxes with bold advertising on the sides, pillowcases, empty rice sacks, cracker tins that smelled of flour and yeast. Whatever we couldn't carry, we left behind: dressers with missing drawers, refrigerators, lumpy sofas, the fifteen canvases I painted one summer. We learned not to attach value to possessions because they were as temporary as the walls that held us for a few months, as the neighbors who lived down the street, as the sad-eyed boy who loved me when I was thirteen.

We moved from country to city to country to small town to big city to the biggest city of all. Once in New York, we moved from apartment to apartment, in search of heat, of fewer cockroaches, of more rooms, of quieter neighbors, of more privacy, of nearness to the subway or the relatives. We moved in loops around the neighborhoods we wanted to avoid, where there were no Puerto Ricans, where graffiti warned of gang turfs, where people dressed better than we did, where landlords didn't accept welfare, or didn't like Puerto Ricans, or looked at our family of three adults, eleven children and shook their heads.

We avoided the neighborhoods with too few stores, or too many stores, or the wrong kind of store, or no stores at all. We

circled around our first apartment the way animals circle the place where they will sleep, and after ten years of circling, Mami returned to where we began the journey, to Macún, the Puerto Rican barrio where everyone knew each other and each other's business, where what we left behind was put to good use by people who moved around less.

By the time she returned to Macún, I'd also moved. Four days after my twenty-first birthday, I left Mami's house, the rhyme I sang as a child forgotten: "*Martes, ni te cases, ni te embarques, ni de tu familia te apartes.*" On a misty Tuesday, I didn't marry, but I did travel, and I did leave my family. I stuffed in the mailbox a letter addressed to Mami in which I said goodbye, because I didn't have the courage to say goodbye in person.

I went to Florida, to begin my own journey from one city to another. Each time I packed my belongings, I left a little of myself in the rooms that sheltered me, never home, always just the places I lived. I congratulated myself on how easy it was to leave them, how well I packed everything I owned into a couple of boxes and a suitcase.

Years later, when I visited Macún, I went to the spot where my childhood began and ended. I stepped on what was left of our blue tiled floor and looked at the wild greenness around me, at what had been a yard for games, at the corner where an eggplant bush became a Christmas tree, at the spot where I cut my foot and blood seeped into the dust. It was no longer familiar, nor beautiful, nor did it give a clue of who I'd been there, or who I might become wherever I was going next. The *moriviví* weeds and the *culantro* choked the dirt yard, creepers had overgrown the cement floor, pinakoop climbed over what was left of the walls and turned them into soft green mounds that sheltered drab olive lizards and chameleons, *coquí* and hummingbirds. There was no sign we'd ever been there, except for the hillock of blue cement tile on which I stood. It gleamed in the afternoon sun, its color so intense that I wondered if I had stepped onto the wrong floor because I didn't remember our floor being that blue.

"Something could happen to you."

We came to Brooklyn in 1961, in search of medical care for my youngest brother, Raymond, whose toes were nearly severed by a bicycle chain when he was four. In Puerto Rico, doctors wanted to amputate the often red and swollen foot, because it wouldn't heal. In New York, Mami hoped, doctors could save it.

The day we arrived, a hot, humid afternoon had splintered into thunderstorms as the last rays of the sun dipped into the rest of the United States. I was thirteen and superstitious enough to believe thunder and lightning held significance beyond the meteorological. I stored the sights and sounds of that dreary night into memory as if their meaning would someday be revealed in a flash of insight to transform my life forever. When the insight came, nothing changed, for it wasn't the weather in Brooklyn that was important, but the fact that I was there to notice it.

One hand tightly grasped by Mami, the other by six-year-old Edna, we squeezed and pushed our way through the crowd of travelers. Five-year-old Raymond clung to Mami's other hand, his unbalanced gait drawing sympathetic smiles from people who moved aside to let us walk ahead of them.

At the end of the tunnel waited Tata, Mami's mother, in black lace and high heels, a pronged rhinestone pin on her left shoulder. When she hugged me, the pin pricked my cheek, pierced subtle flower-shaped indentations that I rubbed rhythmically as our taxi hurtled through drenched streets banked by high, angular buildings.

New York was darker than I expected, and, in spite of the cleansing rain, dirtier. Used to the sensual curves of rural Puerto Rico, my eyes had to adjust to the regular, aggressive two-dimensionality of Brooklyn. Raindrops pounded the hard streets, captured the dim silver glow of street lamps, bounced against sidewalks in glistening sparks, then disappeared, like tiny ephemeral jewels, into the darkness. Mami and Tata teased that I was disillusioned because the streets were not paved with gold. But I had no such vision of New York. I was disappointed by the darkness and fixed my hopes on the promise of light deep within the sparkling raindrops.

Two days later, I leaned against the wall of our apartment building on McKibbin Street wondering where New York ended and the rest of the world began. It was hard to tell. There was no horizon in Brooklyn. Everywhere I looked, my eyes met a vertical maze of gray and brown straight-edged buildings with sharp corners and deep shadows. Every few blocks there was a cement playground surrounded by chain-link fence. And in between, weedy lots mounded with garbage and rusting cars.

A girl came out of the building next door, a jump rope in her hand. She appraised me shyly; I pretended to ignore her. She stepped on the rope, stretched the ends overhead as if to measure their length, and then began to skip, slowly, grunting each time she came down on the sidewalk. Swish splat grunt swish, she turned her back to me; swish splat grunt swish, she faced me again and smiled. I smiled back, and she hopped over.

"¿*Tú eres hispana?*" she asked, as she whirled the rope in lazy arcs.

"No, I'm Puerto Rican."

"Same thing. Puerto Rican, Hispanic. That's what we are here." She skipped a tight circle, stopped abruptly, and shoved the rope in my direction. "Want a turn?"

"Sure." I hopped on one leg, then the other. "So, if you're Puerto Rican, they call you Hispanic?"

"Yeah. Anybody who speaks Spanish."

I jumped a circle, as she had done, but faster. "You mean, if you speak Spanish, you're Hispanic?"

"Well, yeah. No . . . I mean your parents have to be Puerto Rican or Cuban or something."

I whirled the rope to the right, then the left, like a boxer. "Okay, your parents are Cuban, let's say, and you're born here, but you don't speak Spanish. Are you Hispanic?"

She bit her lower lip. "I guess so," she finally said. "It has to do with being from a Spanish country. I mean, you or your parents, like, even if you don't speak Spanish, you're Hispanic, you know?" She looked at me uncertainly. I nodded and returned her rope.

But I didn't know. I'd always been Puerto Rican, and it hadn't occurred to me that in Brooklyn I'd be someone else.

Later, I asked. "Are we Hispanics, Mami?"

"Yes, because we speak Spanish."

"But a girl said you don't have to speak the language to be Hispanic."

She scrunched her eyes. "What girl? Where did you meet a girl?"

"Outside. She lives in the next building."

"Who said you could go out to the sidewalk? This isn't Puerto Rico. *Algo te puede suceder.*"

"Something could happen to you" was a variety of dangers outside the locked doors of our apartment. I could be mugged. I could be dragged into any of the dark, abandoned buildings on the way to or from school and be raped and murdered. I could be accosted by gang members into whose turf I strayed. I could be seduced by men who preyed on unchaperoned girls too willing to talk to strangers. I listened to Mami's lecture with downcast eyes and the necessary, respectful expression of humility. But inside, I quaked. Two days in New York, and I'd already become someone else. It wasn't hard to imagine that greater dangers lay ahead.

Our apartment on McKibbin Street was more substantial than any of our houses in Puerto Rico. Its marble staircase, plaster walls, and tiled floors were bound to the earth, unlike the wood and zinc rooms on stilts where I'd grown up. Chubby angels with bare buttocks danced around plaster wreaths on the ceiling. There was a bathtub in the kitchen with hot and cold running water, and a toilet inside a closet with a sink and a medicine chest.

An alley between our bedroom window and the wall of the next building was so narrow that I stretched over to touch the bricks and left my mark on the greasy soot that covered them. Above, a sliver of sky forced vague yellow light into the ground below, filled with empty detergent boxes, tattered clothes, un-paired shoes, bottles, broken glass.

Mami had to go look for work, so Edna, Raymond, and I went downstairs to stay with Tata in her apartment. When we knocked on her door, she was just waking up. I sat at the small table near the cooking counter to read the newspapers that Don Julio, Tata's boyfriend, had brought the night before. Edna and Raymond stood in the middle of the room and stared at the small television on a low table. Tata switched it on, fiddled with the knobs and the antenna until the horizontal lines disappeared and black-and-white cartoon characters chased each other across a flat landscape. The kids sank to the floor cross-legged, their eyes on the screen. Against the wall, under the window, Tata's brother, Tío Chico, slept with his back to us. Every so often, a snore woke him, but he chewed his drool, mumbled, slept again.

While Tata went to wash up in the hall bathroom, I tuned in to the television. A dot bounced over the words of a song being performed by a train dancing along tracks, with dogs, cats, cows, and horses dangling from its windows and caboose. I was hypno-tized by the dot skipping over words that looked nothing like they sounded. "Shilbee cominrun demuntin wenshecoms, toot-toot"

sang the locomotive, and the ball dipped and rose over "She'll be coming 'round the mountain when she comes," with no toots. The animals, dressed in cowboy hats, overalls, and bandannas, waved pickaxes and shovels in the air. The toot-toot was replaced by a bow-wow or a miaow-ow, or a moo-moo. It was joyous and silly, and made Edna and Raymond laugh. But it was hard for me to enjoy it as I focused on the words whizzing by, on the dot jumping rhythmically from one syllable to the next, with barely enough time to connect the letters to the sounds, with the added distraction of an occasional neigh, bark, or kid's giggle.

When Tata returned from the bathroom, she made coffee on the two-burner hot plate. Fragrant steam soon filled the small room, and as she strained the grounds through a well-worn flannel filter, Tío Chico rose as if the aroma were an alarm louder and more insistent than the singing animals on the television screen, the clanking of pots against the hot plate and counter, the screech of the chair legs as I positioned myself so that I could watch both Tata and the cartoons.

"Well, look who we have here," Tío Chico said, as he stretched until his long, bony fingers scraped the ceiling. He wore the same clothes as on the day before: a faded pair of dark pants and a short-sleeved undershirt, both wrinkled and giving off a pungent, sweaty smell. He stepped over Edna and Raymond, who barely moved to let him through. In two long-legged strides, he slipped out to the bathroom. As he shut the door, the walls closed in, as if his lanky body added dimension to the cramped room.

Tata hummed the cartoon music. Her big hands reached for a pan, poured milk, stirred briskly as it heated and frothed. I was mesmerized by her grace, by how she held her head, by the disheveled, ash-colored curls that framed her high cheekbones. She looked up with mischievous caramel eyes and grinned without breaking her rhythm.

Tío Chico returned showered and shaved, wearing a clean shirt and pants as wrinkled as the ones he'd taken off. He dropped the dirty clothes in a corner near Tata's bed and made up his cot.

Tata handed me a cup of sweetened *café con leche* and, with a head gesture, indicated that I should vacate the chair for Tío Chico.

"No, no, that's okay," he said, "I'll sit here."

He perched on the edge of the cot, elbows on knees, his fingers wrapped around the mug Tata gave him. Steam rose from inside his hands in a transparent spiral. Tata served Edna and Raymond, then sat with her coffee in one hand and a cigarette in the other, talking softly to Tío Chico, who also lit up. I brought my face to the steaming coffee to avoid the mentholated smoke that curled from their corner of the room to ours, settling like a soft, gray blanket that melted into our clothes and hair.

⌒

I couldn't speak English, so the school counselor put me in a class for students who'd scored low on intelligence tests, who were behavior problems, who were marking time until their sixteenth birthday, when they could drop out. The teacher, a pretty black woman only a few years older than her students, pointed to a seat in the middle of the room. I didn't dare look anyone in the eyes. Grunts and mutters followed me, and although I had no idea what they meant, they didn't sound friendly.

The desk surface was elaborately carved. There were many names, some followed by an apostrophe and a year. Several carefully rendered obscenities meant nothing to me, but I appreciated the workmanship of the shadowed letters, the fastidious edges around the *f* and *k*. I guessed a girl had written the cursive message whose *is* were dotted with hearts and daisies. Below it, several lines of timid, chicken-scratch writing alternated with an aggressive line of block letters.

I pressed my hands together under the desk to subdue their shaking, studied the straight lines and ragged curves chiseled into the desktop by those who had sat there before me. Eyes on the marred surface, I focused on the teacher's voice, on the unfamiliar

waves of sound that crested over my head. I wanted to float up and out of that classroom, away from the hostile air that filled every corner of it, every crevice. But the more I tried to disappear, the more present I felt, until, exhausted, I gave in, floated with the words, certain that if I didn't, I would drown in them.

⌒

On gym days, girls had to wear grass green, cotton, short-sleeved, bloomer-leg, one-piece outfits that buttoned down the front to an elastic waistband covered with a sash too short to tie into anything but a bulky knot. Grass green didn't look good on anyone, least of all adolescent girls whose faces broke out in red pimples. The gym suit had elastic around the bottom to prevent the sight of panties when we fell or sat. On those of us with skinny legs, the elastic wasn't snug enough, so the bloomers hung limply to our knees, where they flapped when we ran.

The uniform, being one piece, made it impossible to go to the bathroom in the three minutes between classes. Instead of wearing it all day, we could bring it to school and change before gym, but no one did, since boys periodically raided the locker room to see our underwear. With the gym suit on, proper hygiene during "the curse" was difficult, as we needed at least three hands, so most girls brought notes from their mothers. The problem was that if you didn't wear the uniform on gym days, everyone knew you were menstruating.

One girl bought two gym suits, chopped off the bottom of one, seamed around the selvage, and wore the top part under her blouse so that no one could tell if she had her period or not. I asked Mami to do that for me, but she said we didn't have money to waste on such foolishness.

Friday mornings we had Assembly. The first thing we did was to press our right hands to our breasts and sing "The Star-Spangled Banner." We were encouraged to sing as loudly as we could, and within a couple of weeks I had learned the entire song by heart.

Ojo sé. Can. Juice. ¿Y?
Bye de don surly lie.
Whassoprowow we hell
Add debt why lie lass gleam in.
Whosebrods tripe sand bye ¿Stars?
True de perro los ¡Ay!
Order am parts we wash,
Wha soga lang tree streem in.

I had no idea what the song said or meant, and no one bothered to teach me. It was one of the things I was supposed to know, and like the daily recitation of the pledge of allegiance, it had to be done with enthusiasm, or teachers gave out demerits. The pledge was printed in ornate letters on a poster under the flag in every classroom. "The Star-Spangled Banner," however, remained a mystery for years, its nonsense words the only song I could sing in English from beginning to end.

On a chill October afternoon, Mami, Don Julio, and I went to the airport to pick up the rest of my sisters and brothers, who'd stayed in Puerto Rico with our father until Mami could afford their plane fare. Delsa, Norma, Héctor, and Alicia were smaller than I remembered them, darker, more foreign. They huddled close to one another, holding hands. Their eyes darted from corner to corner of the enormous terminal, to the hundreds of people waving, hugging, kissing, to the luggage that banged into them. Birdlike, they lifted their heads, mouths open, toward the magnified, disembodied voices bleating orders from the ceilings. I wondered if I had looked that frightened and vulnerable only two months earlier.

We'd moved to a new, larger apartment on Varet Street. Tata and Tío Chico had been cooking all morning, and as we entered the apartment, the fragrance of roasting *achiote*, garlic, and oreg-

ano, the family milling around, laughing and talking, made it like Christmas.

We had many relatives in Brooklyn. Paco, Tío Chico's son, was short and muscular. His arms and face were always bruised, his eyes swollen and bloodshot, his nose bandaged, the result of his work as a wrestler. His professional name was El Santo. In the ring, he wore white tights and boots, a white leather belt, a white mask, a milky satin cape with a stand-up collar studded with rhinestones. He was one of the good guys, but although he usually won his fights, he always received a beating from the guys in black.

Paco's brother, Jalisco, worked in a factory. He was tall and lean like his father and groomed his mustache into a black, straight fuzz over his lips, like Jorge Negrete, the Mexican singer and movie star. Whenever Jalisco came over, I circled him like a febrile butterfly — offering drinks or food, or reminding him he'd promised to sing *"Cielito Lindo"* after supper. Mami never left me alone with him.

Tata's two sisters lived within a few blocks of our apartment. Tía Chía and her daughters — Margot, Gury, and La Muda — were close to my mother. They came dragging bags full of clothes and shoes they no longer wore. Gury, the youngest, was slender and soft-spoken. Her clothes fit me, although Mami said that the straight skirts, sheer blouses, and high heels Gury favored were not appropriate for a girl my age.

Her sister La Muda was deaf and mute. According to Mami, La Muda had been born with perfect hearing but as a toddler she got sick, and when she recovered, she was deaf.

"Then why don't they call her La Sorda . . ." I began, and Mami warned I was disrespectful.

La Muda read lips. If we spoke with our faces away from her, she shook our shoulders and made us repeat what we'd said while her eyes focused on our mouths. We quickly learned to interpret her language, a dance of gestures enhanced with hums, gurgles, and grunts that didn't seem to come from her throat but from a deeper source, inside her belly. Her hands were large, well mani-

cured, bedecked with numerous gold and stone rings that shimmered as her fingers flew here and there.

La Muda liked us to read the paper to her. That is, Mami or Don Julio read it aloud, while we kids acted out the news. La Muda's eyes darted from Mami's lips to our portrayals of that day's murders, car crashes, and results at the track, enacted race by race around the kitchen table. Her laugh, frequent and contagious, was deep but flat, as if, unable to hear herself laugh, she couldn't get the tone.

Her boyfriend was someone we'd known in Puerto Rico. He was a thin, laconic, dark-haired man who dressed in a beige suit. When we first met him, my six sisters and brothers and I were afraid of him, but he took a deck of cards from his pocket, performed some tricks, and after that we called him Luigi, which sounded like the perfect name for a magician.

Tata's other sister, Titi Ana, had two daughters who were closer to my age than La Muda, Margot, or Gury. Alma was a year older, and Corazón a year younger. They spoke English to each other, and when they talked to us or to their mother, their Spanish was halting and accented. Mami said they were Americanized. The way she pronounced the word *Americanized,* it sounded like a terrible thing, to be avoided at all costs, another *algo* to be added to the list of "somethings" outside our door.

When they walked into the apartment, my sisters and brother submitted to hugs and kisses from people who were strangers to them but who introduced themselves as Cousin this or Auntie that. Delsa was on the verge of tears. Norma held on to Alicia as if afraid they'd get lost in the confusion. Héctor circulated among the men, followed by Raymond, who chattered about Paco's exploits in the ring or about Don Julio's generosity with pocket change.

Luigi, his usually solemn face lit by the hint of a smile, performed new tricks, and the kids relaxed somewhat, as if this reminder of our life in Puerto Rico were enough to dissolve their fears. Margot had brought a portable record player and records,

which played full blast in the kitchen, while in the front room the television was tuned to the afternoon horror movie. The kids shuffled from room to room in a daze, overdosed on the Twinkies, Yodels, and potato chips Don Julio had brought for us.

The welcome party lasted into the night. Don Julio and Jalisco went to the *bodega* several times for more beer, and Tío Chico found a liquor store and came back with jugs of Gallo wine. Mami ran from the adults to the kids, reminding the men that there were children in the house, that they should stop drinking.

One by one the relatives left, and the kids once more surrendered to hugs and kisses. Our pockets jingled with pennies that the aunts, uncles, and cousins had handed out as if to pay for the party. Luigi escorted La Muda from the apartment. His pale fingers pressed against her waist, his too-big suit flapped around his scarecrow frame. As they walked out, the adults exchanged mysterious smiles.

Tío Chico and his sons were the last to leave. Tata and Don Julio went into her room and drew the curtain that separated their part of the apartment from ours. "It's time for bed," Mami reminded us. We got ready, Delsa and I on the top bunk, Norma and Alicia on the bottom, Héctor on the sofa, Raymond in the upholstered chairs pushed together, Edna and Mami in the double bed. She turned out the light, and the soft rustles of my sisters and brothers settling into their first night in Brooklyn filled me with a secret joy, which I never admitted but which soothed and reassured me in a way nothing had since we'd left Puerto Rico.

"I don't care what American girls do."

Like every other Puerto Rican mother I knew, Mami was strict. The reason she had brought me to New York with the younger kids was that I was *casi señorita*, and she didn't want to leave me in Puerto Rico during what she said was a critical stage in my life. Mami told her friend Minga that a girl my age should be watched by her mother and protected from men who were sure to take advantage of a child in a woman's body.

While my body wasn't exactly womanly, I knew what Mami meant. Years of eavesdropping on her conversations had taught me that men were not to be trusted. They deceived with *pocavergüenzas*, shameless acts that included drinking, gambling, and squandering money on women not their wives while their children went hungry. To cover up their *pocavergüenzas*, men lied. A man would call his wife *"mi amor,"* while looking over her shoulder at another woman passing by.

"A girl is smart to be suspicious of any man who talks sweet to her," Minga declared. "To her, his words are the most beautiful things she's heard. She has no idea he's said them a thousand times before . . . and will keep on saying them as long as there's some *pendeja* to listen."

According to Mami and her friends, women committed *pocavergüenzas* too. They flirted with men who were taken by more worthy women and lured those feckless men astray.

Having heard countless stories of deceitful men and wily

women, I decided never to become one of those calculating *putas*, but neither would I become a *pendeja*, who believed everything a man told her, or looked the other way while he betrayed her. There was a midpoint between a *puta* and a *pendeja* that I was trying to figure out, a safe space in which decent women lived and thrived and raised their families. Mami belonged there, as did her friends and female relatives. Her lectures, and the pointed conversations I was supposed to overhear, were meant to help me distinguish between a *puta* and a *pendeja*. But there was always a warning. One false move, and I ran the risk of becoming one or being perceived as the other.

I made a friend in school, Yolanda, a girl who spoke good English but spoke Spanish with me. Yolanda was the only Puerto Rican I'd met who was an only child. She was curious about what it was like to have six sisters and brothers, and I asked what she did all day with no one to play or fight with.

"Oh, you know, watch television, read, and I have my albums."

She collected pictures in three-ring binders, organized by type. "These are flowers," she said, pulling down a fat binder from a shelf over her bed. She opened it to a page cluttered with flowers from the Carnation milk can label. "And over here are lips." Pages and pages of lips, male and female, some with mustaches over them, others the disembodied smiles of movie stars. "This one is letters." Arranged alphabetically, hundreds of letters were pasted on the pages, uppercase letters sprinkled on the left side, lowercase on the right. Other albums contained product labels from cans, sanitary pad boxes, garment tags. Another held hair and beauty product advertisements cut out from newspapers and magazines. The fattest one held modes of transportation: cars, trains, cruise ships, ferries, bicycles built for two. Yolanda, I decided, spent too much time alone.

"Would you like to come to my house?" I offered. She had to ask her mother, but she was sure it was okay. The next day, she said her mother wouldn't let her. "I begged," Yolanda explained, her eyes misting, "but she's so strict with me." I was disappointed but understood, since Mami, too, was strict. But when I told Mami that Yolanda's mother wouldn't let her visit us, Mami was offended.

"What's wrong with that woman? Her place is good enough for you to visit, but ours is not good enough for her precious daughter?" After that, I wasn't allowed to go to Yolanda's apartment.

One day Yolanda asked me to accompany her to the library. I couldn't because Mami forbade unplanned stops on the way home from school. "Ask her and we'll go tomorrow. If you bring proof of where you live, you can get a library card," Yolanda suggested, "and you can borrow books. For free," she added when I hesitated.

I'd passed the Bushwick Public Library many times, had wondered about its heavy entrance doors framed by columns, the wide windows that looked down on the neighborhood. Set back from the street behind a patch of dry grass, the red brick structure seemed out of place in a street of rundown apartment buildings and the tall, forbidding projects. Inside, the ceilings were high, with dangling fixtures over long, brown tables in the center of the room and near the windows. The stacks around the perimeter were crammed with books covered in plastic. I picked up a book from a high shelf, riffled the pages, put it back. I wandered up one aisle, down another. All the books were in English. Frustrated, I found Yolanda, whispered goodbye, and found my way to the front door.

On the way out, I passed the Children's Room, where a librarian read to a group of kids. She read slowly and with expression, and after each page, she turned the book toward us so that

we could see the pictures. Each page had only a few words on it, and the illustrations made their meaning clear. If American children could learn English from these books, so could I.

After the reading, I searched the shelves for the illustrated books that contained the words for my new life in Brooklyn. I chose alphabet books, their colorful pages full of cars, dogs, houses, mailmen. I wouldn't admit to the librarian that these elementary books were for me. "For leetle seesters," I said, and she nodded, grinned, and stamped the date due in the back.

I stopped at the library every day after school and at home memorized the words that went with the pictures in the oversized pages. Some concepts were difficult. Snow was shown as huge, multifaceted flakes. Until I saw the real thing, I imagined snow as a curtain of fancy shapes, stiff and flat and possible to capture in my hand.

My sisters and brothers studied the books too, and we read the words aloud to one another, guessing at the pronunciation.

"Ehr-RAHS-ser," we said for *eraser*. "Keh-NEEF-eh," for *knife*. "Dees" for *this* and "dem" for *them* and "dunt" for *don't*.

In school, I listened for words that sounded like those I'd read the night before. But spoken English, unlike Spanish, wasn't pronounced as written. *Water* became "waddah," *work* was "woik," and wordsranintoeachother in a torrent of confusing sounds that bore no resemblance to the neatly organized letters on the pages of books. In class, I seldom raised my hand, because my accent sent snickers through the classroom the minute I opened my mouth.

Delsa, who had the same problem, suggested that we speak English at home. At first, we broke into giggles whenever we spoke English to each other. Our faces contorted into grimaces, our voices changed as our tongues flapped in our mouths trying to form the awkward sounds. But as the rest of the kids joined us and we practiced between ourselves, it became easier and we didn't laugh as hard. We invented words if we didn't know the translation for what we were trying to say, until we had our own language,

neither English nor Spanish, but both in the same sentence, some-times in the same word.

"Passing me esa sabanation," Héctor called to Edna, asking her to pass a blanket.

"Stop molestationing me," Edna snapped at Norma when she bothered her.

We watched television with the sound on, despite Tata's com-plaints that hearing so much English gave her a headache. Slowly, as our vocabularies grew, it became a bond between us, one that separated us from Tata and from Mami, who watched us per-plexed, her expression changing from pride to envy to worry.

One day Mami told me I couldn't go to school because I had to go somewhere with her. "Don't start with your questions," she warned, as I opened my mouth.

We took two buses, walked several blocks to a tired brick building with wire screens on the windows. Inside, the waiting area was crowded with women on orange plastic chairs, each holding a sheaf of papers. A counter divided the room, and behind it, three rows of gray metal desks were littered with stacks of folders, brochures, printed forms, and other papers.

APPLICATION FOR PUBLIC ASSISTANCE, the top of the forms declared, DEPARTMENT OF PUBLIC WELFARE: AID TO FAMILIES WITH DEPENDENT CHILDREN (AFDC). "Here," Mami handed me a pen, "fill them out in your best handwriting."

"But what's it for?"

"So we can get help until I find another job." She spoke in a whisper, looking right and left for eavesdroppers.

I filled out the forms as best I could, leaving the spaces blank when I didn't understand the question.

As the morning wore on, more women arrived, some drag-ging children, others alone. It was easy to pick out those who'd been to the welfare office before. They sauntered in, scanned the room to assess how many had arrived before them, went up to the

receptionist, took the forms, filled them out quickly — as if the questions and answers were memorized. The women new to welfare hesitated at the door, looked right and left until they spotted the reception desk, walked in as if prodded. They beseeched the receptionist with their eyes, tried to tell their story. She interrupted them with a wave of the hand; passed over forms; gave instructions to fill them out, have a seat, wait — always in the same words, as if she didn't want to bother thinking up new ways to say the same thing.

I hadn't brought a book, so I looked around. Mami elbowed me to stop staring. I immediately dropped my gaze to the floor. As I was about to complain that I was hungry, men and women straggled in through a back door and took seats at the desks behind the counter.

When it was our turn, the social worker led us to the far end of the office. He was a portly man with hair so black it must have been either dyed or a wig. He took the forms I'd filled out, scratched checks next to some of the squares, tapped the empty spaces. He spoke to Mami, who turned to me as if I knew what he'd said. He repeated his question in my direction, and I focused on the way his lips moved, his expression, the tone of voice, but had no idea what he was asking.

"I don't know," I said to Mami.

She clicked her tongue.

"Plis, no spik inglis," she smiled prettily at the social worker.

He asked his question again, pointed at the blank spaces.

"I think he wants the names and birth dates of the kids," I interpreted. Mami pulled our birth certificates from her purse, stretched each in front of him as he wrote down the information.

"Tell him," Mami said to me, "that I got *leyof*."

"My mother *leyof*," I translated.

"Tell him," she said, "that the factory closed. They moved to another state. I don't have any money for rent or food." She blushed, spoke quickly, softly. "I want to work, tell him that," she said in a louder voice. "*Cerraron la fábrica*." she repeated.

"Fabric no," I said. "She work wants."

The man's eyes crinkled, his jowls shook as he nodded encouragement. But I had no more words for him. He wrote on the papers, looked at Mami. She turned to me.

"Tell him I don't want my children to suffer. Tell him I need help until the factory opens again or until I can find another job. Did you tell him I want to work?"

I nodded, but I wasn't certain that the social worker understood me. "My mother, she work want. Fabric close," I explained to the social worker, my hands moving in front of me like La Muda's. "She no can work fabric no. Babies suffer. She little help she no lay off no more." I was exhausted, my palms were sweaty, my head ached as I probed for words, my jaw tightened with the effort to pronounce them. I searched frantically for the right combination of words, the ones that said what Mami meant, to convince this man that she was not asking for aid because she was lazy but because circumstances forced her. Mami was a proud woman, and I knew how difficult it was for her to seek help from anyone, especially a stranger. I wanted to let him know that she must have been desperate to have come to this place.

I struggled through the rest of the interview, my meager English vocabulary strained to the limit. When it was over, the social worker stood up, shook Mami's hand, shook mine, and said what I understood to mean he'd get back to us.

We walked out of the office in silence, Mami's back so straight and stiff she might have been wearing a corset. I, on the other hand, tensed into myself, panicked that I'd failed as a translator, that we wouldn't get help, that because of me, we wouldn't have a place to live or food to eat.

"You did a good job," Mami reassured me in front of Tata and Don Julio that night. "You know a lot of English."

"It's easier for kids," Don Julio mumbled between sips of beer. "They pick up the language like that." He snapped his fingers.

I was grateful for Mami's faith in me but couldn't relax until we heard from the welfare office. A few days later our application was approved. By then I'd decided that even when it seemed that

my head couldn't hold that many new words inside it, I had to learn English well enough never again to be caught between languages.

⁓

I woke in the middle of the night with something crawling toward my ear. I batted it away, but it caught in the strands of hair near the lobe. I stumbled in the dark, frantically searching for whatever was caught in my hair. By the time I reached the switch by the door, I'd pinched a crackly, dry, many-legged cockroach between my thumb and index finger before it could climb inside my ear canal.

"Turn off the light," Delsa hissed from her end of the bed. I threw the roach down, whacked it with a shoe before it scuttled away.

"What are you doing?" Mami sat up on her bed.

"A roach almost crawled into my brain." I felt dirty, and my fingers itched as if the roach were still between them.

"I'll fumigate tomorrow," she grimaced, then settled back to sleep.

I shook the sheets to make sure no more roaches lurked in the folds.

"Stop that," Delsa pulled on her end of the covers. In the bottom bunk, Norma and Alicia moaned and turned over.

Where there was one roach, I knew, there were hundreds. I imagined hordes of dark brown cockroaches poised at the cracks of the baseboard, waiting for me to switch off the light so that they could begin their march across the room. I'd seen them skitter for cover when I came into the kitchen for a drink late at night. Roaches roamed over the counter, inside the cups and glasses, around the edges of the paring knife, in the space between the sugar bowl and its cover. Mami bought ever more powerful poisons to spray the corners of our apartments. The roach poison made us cough and irritated our eyes. For days after she sprayed,

our clothes gave off the pungent chemical smell of Black Flag or Flit. But the roaches didn't die. They went away until the acrid poisonous gas dissipated, then returned, more brazen and in greater numbers.

Before we took a drink of water, we washed the already washed glass. Before cooking, we rinsed the scrubbed pots and utensils. Before serving, we ran every plate, bowl, cup, and spoon under water and dried it with a clean kitchen cloth. We kept food in tight-lidded containers, refrigerated what didn't fit in the cabinets, swept and mopped the kitchen floor every night before going to bed. But no matter how much we scrubbed and wiped and rinsed, the roaches always came back to parade across the floors, the counters, the dressers, the windowsills.

I lay in bed imagining an army of roaches crawling in orderly rows toward the bed I shared with Delsa. I pulled the sheets up and tried to cover my ears, but as I tugged my end, Delsa jerked hers down. I tried to cover my head with the pillow, but the bouncy foam balanced on my forehead, didn't conform to the shape I tried to impose on it, around the top of my skull, alongside my ears past the lobe. Images of roaches about to crawl inside me kept me awake. I was afraid to leave the bed. What if the legions of roaches I envisioned were marching around the floor? Before I could reach the light switch, I'd step on them in my bare feet. I squirmed, trying to wipe the images from my mind. I scraped the spot where I'd found the roach with a corner of the sheet, but no matter how much I rubbed, I still felt it. In fact, lots of crawly things crept over me, but as I reached to swat them, they moved to a different spot. I turned on my right side, then my left, because if I didn't stay in one spot for long, the roaches wouldn't have time to crawl inside the various orifices I imagined were their goal.

When the alarm rang, I slid out of bed, exhausted. I tiptoed, so that if there were roaches on the floor, I would step on as few of them as possible. The linoleum was bare, shiny clean, except for the yellowish ooze from the brown cockroach near the shoe I'd used in the middle of the night. There were no live cockroaches

to be seen. But that was no comfort. I knew they hid in the crevices of the baseboard, inside the cracks along the door jamb, under the bed.

~~~~~~~~

As fall became winter and the days cooled, we discovered that our apartment was unheated. Mami went to the *bodega* to call the landlord; sometimes the radiators clinked and clanged and got lukewarm, but not enough to reach the corners of the rooms. Tata lit the stove, and we spent most of our time at the formica table, in front of the open oven. Inevitably, one of us came down with a cold, and pretty soon, we were all up half the night wheezing and coughing.

Mami and Tata ran from one to the other with a bowl full of hot water into which they had melted a tablespoon of Vick's Vaporub. While Mami held the bowl under our noses, Tata tented a towel over our heads. Once each of us had inhaled as much steam as we could, Tata plastered leaves on our chests and backs with more Vick's Vaporub, then made us put on our warmest sweaters. The next day, Mami devised a concoction with Breacol cough syrup as a base, laced with her own formula of ingredients whose flavor didn't disappear despite the generous amounts of honey she poured into the bottle. The syrup was black, bitter, smelled like burnt cloves and camphor. She forced it on us, and within hours we no longer sniffled and our coughs were gone. From then on, as soon as one of us sneezed or showed a drippy nose, she brought out the sticky bottle, which was enough to cure us instantly. We called it *tutumá*, a mysterious name for that strange, powerful medicine that we didn't have to take to feel better.

Tata claimed that the first winter in New York was the hardest, because, coming from a warm climate, our blood was not thick enough. To thicken hers, she drank beer or wine daily, which also dulled the aches in her bones she swore didn't respond to

anything else. To thicken ours, she cooked soups and stews dense with *ñames*, *yautías*, and other Puerto Rican vegetables.

"But," I argued one day, "if we eat the same food we ate in Puerto Rico, it won't thicken our blood. It didn't while we lived there."

"She has a point," Don Julio chortled.

"We'll just keep getting the same thin blood we've always had," I pressed.

"What they need," Don Julio suggested, "is American food."

Tata was unpersuaded. "American food is not nutritious."

"But look how big and healthy American kids are," Mami allowed. "Their food must be doing something for them."

"They look like boiled potatoes," Tata asserted.

"But their blood is thick," Delsa argued, "and they never get sick."

In spite of Tata's mistrust of American food, Mami was willing to try anything to thicken our blood. At our urging, she bought a few cans of products we'd seen advertised on television: Franco-American spaghetti, Chef Boyardee ravioli, Campbell's chicken noodle soup.

"Yecch, it's slimy," Tata stared suspiciously at the potful of canned ravioli Mami heated for us. "I don't know how you can eat it," she grimaced, as we scooped every bit of sauce out of our bowls.

Mami gave us canned American food every day for a week, but our colds didn't disappear with anything but a spoonful of *tutumá*. So she lost faith in American food and only fed it to us as a special treat, never as a substitute for the hearty Puerto Rican meals she and Tata continued to prepare. When Tata asked why she let us eat it, Mami explained: "They should learn to eat like Americans—in case someday they're invited to an American home, they don't act like *jíbaros* in front of their food."

That silenced Tata and gave me an idea. "Mami, all American girls wear makeup to school."

"I don't care what American girls do. You're Puerto Rican and too young to wear makeup."

It was good to be healthy, big, and strong like Dick, Jane, and Sally. It was good to learn English and to know how to act among Americans, but it was not good to behave like them. Mami made it clear that although we lived in the United States, we were to remain 100 percent Puerto Rican. The problem was that it was hard to tell where Puerto Rican ended and Americanized began. Was I Americanized if I preferred pizza to *pastelillos*? Was I Puerto Rican if my skirts covered my knees? If I cut out a picture of Paul Anka from a magazine and tacked it to the wall, was I less Puerto Rican than when I cut out pictures of Gilberto Monroig? Who could tell me?

Mami's cousins Alma and Corazón were born in Puerto Rico, but their mother, Titi Ana, brought them to Brooklyn as toddlers. They lived on the corner of Varet Street and Bushwick Avenue, at the top of a six-story building with bow windows in the front. The hallways and landings were paved with black-and-white mosaic tiles. Huge windows let light into the staircase, whose wide steps and banisters were cool, cool marble, worn in the center from years of up, down, up. There were four apartments on each story, two facing Varet Street, two in the back. As I climbed to the sixth floor, I stopped at each landing to catch my breath, and to listen to the sounds behind every door or to smell the delicious aromas of dinner being prepared. Behind one door someone watched a soap opera, muted voices punctuated by organ music. I smelled brewed coffee across the hall, and further up, someone cooked salted codfish with eggplant. On the next level, *sofrito* sizzled into hot oil, and across the hall, the beans needed water, because they smelled scorched. A *merengue* played full blast behind another door, while across from it, the two apartments in the back were silent, and no fragrance seeped into the landing. By the time I arrived at the top and knocked on Titi Ana's door, I was hungry and my ears rang.

Corazón opened the three locks and chain on their door to

let me in. She held a bottle of Coke in her hand. "Help yourself," she said, nodding toward the refrigerator. "Alma's in there," she pointed to a door off the kitchen, and disappeared into her room. There was always a six-pack of Coca-Cola in Titi Ana's refrigerator, ice cream in her freezer, Hostess cakes in the cabinet over the sink. I grabbed a soda and knocked on Alma's door.

She sat on her bed, reading a heavy book about men with big mustaches. "I have a test tomorrow," she said, looking up. "History."

Alma's room was familiar, not only because I'd spent so much time in it since I'd arrived in Brooklyn but because it looked like the rooms of all the girls I'd met whose parents had money to spend on things other than the bare necessities. Her bed was white, covered with a ruffled, flowery spread that matched the curtains and the skirt of her dressing table. The linoleum floor was also a flower print, giving the impression that Alma moved and slept in a bright, flat, eternal spring. A window looked out over the roofs of two-and three-story buildings.

"There's a new *Archie*," she pointed to the shelf where she stacked her comic books, the most recent ones on top.

Archie, Veronica, Betty, Reggie, and Jughead were the only American teenagers I'd come to know. There were no Americans in our Puerto Rican neighborhood, and the few that went to the same school as I did kept to themselves in tight, impenetrable groups of chattering, cardigan-wearing, ponytailed girls and pimply, long-legged boys. Like Archie and his friends, they were not Italian or Jewish, Negro or Puerto Rican. They had short, easy-to-remember names like Sue, Matt, Fred, Lynn. They were the presidents of clubs, the organizers of dances, the editors of the school paper and yearbook. They looked like the actors on television: white-skinned, dressed in clothes that never were wrinkled or dirty, hair always in place, an air of superiority setting them apart.

My neighbors, mostly dark-skinned or identified by country of origin, lived in rundown, vertical apartment buildings. From *Archie* I learned about another United States — the trim, hori-

zontal suburbs of white Americans. Through him, I discovered that American teenagers' lives were very different from mine, their concerns as foreign to me as mine might be to them.

Archie and his friends lived in a world with no parents, made their own decisions about where to go and how to get there without consulting anyone but each other. My world was dominated by adults, their rules written in stone, in Spanish, in Puerto Rico. In my world, no allowance was made for the fact that we were now in the United States, that our language was becoming English, that we were foreigners awash in American culture.

Archie never ate at home. His meals, and those of his friends, were taken at Pop's soda shop, where their diet consisted of sandwiches, hamburgers, fries, ice cream sodas — food that could be eaten without utensils. In our apartment, Mami and Tata spent a lot of time in the kitchen, preparing thick *asopaos*, rice and beans, chicken fricassees, huge meals that required time to savor and a close connection to the cook, who lingered near us asking if it tasted good and checking that we ate enough.

Betty and Veronica talked and worried a lot about dating. At fourteen years of age, I was not allowed to go anywhere with a boy who wasn't my brother. We had no telephone, so unlike Betty and Veronica, I couldn't sit with shapely legs draped over the armrest of an upholstered chair chattering with invisible friends about boys. We had no upholstered chair. I had no friends.

Archie and his friends sometimes carried books, but they were never seen in class, or taking exams, or studying. Their existence revolved around their social life, while mine was defined by my obligations as a student and as the eldest sister. Neither Betty nor Veronica was called upon to be an example for younger siblings. They existed solely for themselves, their only responsibilities were to look beautiful and to keep their boyfriends happy.

From Titi Ana's kitchen, I plunged into Archie's bright, shadowless world, jealous of that simple life of fun and trivial problems so far removed from the realities of my own life. No one was ever born or died in Archie's world, no one shared a bed with a sister,

or bathed in the kitchen, or mourned an absent father. I wanted to live in those uncrowded, horizontal landscapes painted in primary colors where *algo* never happened, where teenagers like me lived in blissful ignorance of violence and grime, where no one had seven sisters and brothers, where grandmothers didn't drink beer late into the night and mothers didn't need you to translate for them at the welfare office.

⌐

Mami surprised me one day in front of my school. I trembled as she frowned at my skirt, which was midcalf when I left in the morning but now hovered above my knees. She scrutinized the smudged lines around my eyes, the faint traces of rouge on my cheeks. Every morning on the way to school, Yolanda and I ducked into the doorway of an apartment building on Bushwick Avenue and rolled up our skirts to the length other girls wore theirs. We drew lines around our lids with an eyebrow pencil stolen from Yolanda's mother. In school, the girls who took pity on those of us with old-fashioned mothers often shared their lipsticks and rouge and helped us tease our hair into beehives sprayed stiff. On the way home, we unrolled our skirts to their natural length; removed traces of makeup with spit; brushed our hair back into limp, decent ponytails.

As soon as she saw my mother, Yolanda dropped her head so that Mami wouldn't see her face. Mami grabbed my arm, dragged me across the street before I could shake off her strong grip. I avoided the eyes of boys who laughed, slapped each other five, gave Mami the thumbs up and called "Go Mamma" as we passed. She silenced them with a withering look that wiped the smirks from their faces. "*Títeres,*" she muttered, "so disrespectful to adults."

"Why did you have to spy on me," I screamed as we went up the stairs of our building. I expected a beating, the severity of which might be reduced if I showed the appropriate humility. But

I didn't care if Mami killed me once we got home. I'd been humiliated in front of the school, and I never wanted to go back there.

"I wasn't spying on you. I came to take you shopping," she said in a subdued voice, aware that the neighbors peeked under their chain stops to see what the yelling was about.

"You should have waited until I got home," I screeched, banging on the door, to which I had no key. Héctor opened it and held it as we stepped into the crowded room, and I slammed my books hard on the floor.

Mami grabbed my hair. "Who do you think you are?" she screamed, "talking back like that?" I raised my arms, tried to wrench loose, pulled my hair toward my scalp as she pulled in the opposite direction. "Don't think because we're here you can act like those fast American girls," Mami screamed, her face red, her eyes narrowed into slits, her lips taut. She pushed me away into the bottom bunk of the bed where Norma and Alicia sat, wide-eyed and scared. Tata appeared from the back of the apartment and stood between us. But Mami was done. I lay face down on the bed, stifled with rage, choked on the sobs that followed her beatings. I rubbed my burning scalp, wheezed without crying, beat the mattress with my forehead until Norma poked me with her toes. "Move," she said, "you're crushing our paper dolls." I raised my head to the bland stare of blonde, blue-eyed, red-lipped girls, their shapely bodies dressed in tight, short, revealing clothes. I swiped them off the bed, stepped on them as I stood up and climbed into the top bunk, Norma and Alicia's cries deafening mine.

That night, I lay next to Delsa and left myself and her, the apartment on Varet Street, Brooklyn, New York. I flew to the warm breeze of a Puerto Rican afternoon, the air scented with jasmine, the *coquí* singing in the grass. I placed myself at my father's side

as he poured cement, his shovel working quickly in the gray mud, scraping the edges, mixing them into the gooey center. As he worked, he sang a Bobby Capó *chachachá.*

The wheelbarrow full of cement squeaked as Papi pushed it closer to the wall he built. His brown arms corded from the strain, the muscles on his back bulged down to his waist. I fell asleep telling him about my day, about the walk to school along the broad sidewalks, about the crowded classrooms, about the gangs kids joined to protect themselves from other gangs, about how in the United States we were not Puerto Rican, we were Hispanic. I told him Mami was disappointed in me, accused me of being Americanized when all I wanted was to be like other girls my age. I talked to him the way I used to when we lived together and he and Mami made up after every argument. And I asked him to come get us out of Brooklyn the way he used to rescue us from the places Mami took us to when they fought. One of these days he would show up at the door, the way he used to in Puerto Rico, to convince Mami that he'd changed, that he still loved her. He'd write her long, flowery poems about happy homes and the love a man feels for the mother of his children. He'd soften her up with gifts — a flower in a paper cup, a half-melted coconut ice. These had worked before, and they would work again. Mami would give in and agree to return to him, and we would go back to Puerto Rico, where we would never be cold, where our lives would resume in our language, in our country, where we could be a family again.

<hr />

Papi wrote to say he'd married a woman none of us had ever heard of and had moved to a town none of us had ever visited.

I sat on the edge of Mami's bed reading the letter over and over, the tight, neat script, evenly spaced, wide-margined, so familiar and so painful.

I disliked his new wife instantly, swore never to visit them,

never to accept her. My letters to him, until then newsy and full of fears and confusion, became short salutations, lists of grades achieved in school and the progress of Raymond's medical treatments, which were successfully saving his foot.

Mornings, on my way to JHS 49, I yearned for my life in Macún. I missed the dew-softened air, the crunchy gravel of the dirt road, the rooster's crow, the buzz of bees, the bright yellow sun of a Puerto Rican dawn. I resisted the square regularity of Brooklyn's streets, the sharp-cornered buildings that towered over me, the sidewalks spotted with crusted phlegm and sticky chewing gum. Every day we spent in Brooklyn was like a curtain dropping between me and my other life, the one where I knew who I was, where I didn't know I was poor, didn't know my parents didn't love each other, didn't know what it was to lose a father.

With Papi married, our ties to Puerto Rico unraveled. He was the strongest link we had to the island, since most of Mami's family was in Brooklyn and Papi's sisters and brothers had never been an important presence in our house.

When I tried to find out if Mami was as disappointed as I was, she brushed me off, saying that Papi had a right to his own life and that we should never blame or disrespect him. But I couldn't shake the feeling of being cast adrift. By not including us in his decision to marry, Papi had excluded us from the rest of his life.

"Are you going to be famous?"

We knew Mami was in love, because she hummed and sang *boleros* as she cleaned or ironed. She was in love, because once she found another job, she bought a new outfit, which she hadn't done since we'd arrived in Brooklyn. She was definitely in love, we knew it, because her brown eyes shone and her lips were quick to smile, and she beamed when she looked at us as if we were the most perfect children any mother could have. We were sure she was in love, because Tata argued with her over every tiny thing and stood at the window when Mami left the house to see which direction she took. Three or four times a week Mami went across the street after work, stayed for an hour or so, then came back cheerful. She never stayed past nine o'clock, but Tata made it sound as if Mami was all over town until dawn.

When we finally met Francisco, who lived across the street with his parents, we knew Mami was in love because she was calm around him, and the hunted expression cleared from her face. She was thirty, Francisco twenty-eight, and the two-year difference in their ages didn't seem as big a deal to us as it was to Tata.

On a bright, late winter day moist with melting snow, we emerged one by one from our building, each carrying a box or a suitcase. Passersby stared with bemused expressions. We were afraid to provoke Tata, so we tiptoed in and out of the old apartment with our belongings until we'd moved everything but the

heaviest things to an apartment down the street. Paco and Jalisco came by at the end of the day to carry the furniture to our new place, and we settled into the two-room apartment before dark.

A few days after we moved, Francisco came for dinner. Afterwards, he and Mami talked in the kitchen while we watched *Candid Camera* in the front room. He left early but came back the next day, and every day for a week, staying later each time — until one morning he was still there.

"What do we call him?" I asked Mami, when it was clear Francisco had moved in. "We can't call him Papi . . ."

She squinted her eyes in my direction, as she did whenever I was disrespectful. "No, he's not your father," she finally said, as she paired socks.

"And he's too young to be Don Francisco."

"Yes, he is." She found a pair of panties and smoothed them. I could tell she was embarrassed, that I should stop asking questions and leave her in peace.

"Then what do we call him?"

"Franky, that's what his family calls him," she said curtly, handing me the panties and a couple of folded shirts. "Put these in Edna's drawer." Her eyebrows met over her eyes, which meant she was not about to answer any more questions.

I put the clothes away, but I couldn't stop thinking about it. Franky didn't sound official enough, since he was our stepfather. Well, not quite. Because he wasn't married to Mami, he wasn't technically her husband. But she hadn't been married to Papi either, and he had been her husband. Or had he? Not officially. Papi was our father, it said so on our birth certificates. But what was he to her? And now that Francisco was part of our household, what was he to us?

I couldn't ask Mami. It was disrespectful to pry into her personal life. But I knew that women who were married looked down on those who weren't. "Oh, she's just living with him," they said, with a wave of the hand and a disgusted expression.

I also knew that marriage in a white gown and veil — with a

walk down the aisle of a church, a priest, bridesmaids in colorful dresses, and groomsmen in tuxedos—was Mami's dream for me and my sisters.

"What happiness," she declared with a wistful expression, "to see a daughter walk down the aisle in a long white dress and veil!"

Mami hadn't married in a church, but we were supposed to. We never went to church, but someday we would each stand in front of a priest and receive the vows she never had.

"I sacrifice myself for you," she told us over and over. A fancy church wedding for each of us was one of the rewards she expected for that sacrifice.

Soon after Mami's belly started growing with his child, Francisco was rushed to the emergency room with a stomachache. When Mami returned from the hospital she told us he had cancer.

"But don't worry," she said, "he'll be well soon."

Her face was tight, her lips pressed together, her eyes scared, and we knew she was just saying that to make us feel better.

We moved to an apartment down the street so that Tata could live with us. Don Julio brought Tata's cot and small dresser, her radio and clothes, a few pictures of herself as a young woman, her altar. Now that Francisco was sick, she didn't gripe about him being too young or about Mami setting a bad example by living with him. Instead, she cooked and watched us so that Mami could go to the hospital right after work to spend time with Francisco.

A few weeks later, the landlord told us to leave because too many people lived in the three rooms he'd rented to a woman and two kids. We moved for the fifth time in a year. In the new apartment on Ellery Street, the bathtub was again in the kitchen, covered with an enameled metal sheet to make a counter during the day, removed at night so we could bathe. When the temperature dropped, the radiators stayed metal cold, and wind whistled through cracks in the casings.

We all had to transfer to new schools. Junior High School 33,

where I attended ninth grade, took up most of a city block. The cement playground and handball court were surrounded by hurricane fencing. Inside, the walls were the same amber-colored brick that covered the outside. The floors were shiny vinyl that squeaked when I wore sneakers, only allowed on gym days.

I scored well in a series of tests that Mr. Barone, the guidance counselor, gave me. I had no idea what the tests were for or why I had to take them, but Mr. Barone said they showed APTITUDE and POTENTIAL and that instead of going to the local vocational high school, I should apply to a school that would prepare me for college. While written English was getting easier for me to understand, spoken English still baffled me, so I agreed to an academic education not knowing what it meant and too embarrassed to ask. It was Mr. Barone's idea that I apply to Performing Arts High School in Manhattan.

"Why so far?" Mami asked. "Don't they have schools in Brooklyn?"

"It's a special school."

She frowned. "Special?"

"I have to apply . . ."

"A private school. We don't have the money . . ."

I explained that it was a public school for kids who wanted to be actors, dancers, or musicians.

She stared at me. "Do you want to be an actress?"

"I don't know. It's just a school."

"You'll do well there," Tata interrupted, "because you're so dramatic."

"There are no Puerto Rican actors on television," Delsa reminded everyone.

"What about Ricky Ricardo?" wondered Raymond.

"*Babalú!*" Edna beat an imaginary drum at her side and Alicia and Héctor joined her in a conga line, singing "*Babalú, Babalú Oyé!*"

"Stop that," Mami said, "the people downstairs will think we have savages up here."

"Ricky Ricardo is Cuban, and he's a singer, not an actor,"

Delsa continued once the kids settled. "And we know Negi can't sing."

"And if you could, Mami would never let you wear those skimpy costumes the vedettes wear," Norma warned. "Would you, Mami?"

"Stop this nonsense," Mami said, eyes back on her mending.

"You see!" Norma laughed.

Mami smiled but didn't say more.

I'd never considered acting as a profession, but once he suggested Performing Arts and I agreed to try out, Mr. Barone made a fuss over me, and that felt good. I didn't tell him that Mami might not let me go even if I were accepted. He helped me prepare for the required audition, chose a monologue, recruited Mr. Gatti, the English teacher, to coach me in the pronunciation of words that I memorized phonetically without knowing their meaning. Mrs. Johnson from Home Economics taught me how to enter a room like a lady and how to sit with my legs together.

I took every opportunity to show Mami I was preparing for my audition. I stood in front of her dresser mirror to practice my monologue, trying to overcome the lifelong habit of speaking with my hands, which Mrs. Johnson said was distracting. I felt like a paper doll, stiff and flat, a smile pasted on my face.

"You belong to a type that's very common in this country, Mrs. Phelps," I began. My sisters and brothers laughed at my attempts to be dramatic and repeated passages from my monologue, their faces twitching as they tried to be serious.

"Stop molestationing me," I yelled, and Mami or Tata shooed them into the next room, where I heard them laughing.

For weeks my sisters and brothers teased me about my lack of talent, while in school Mr. Barone, Mr. Gatti, and Mrs. Johnson helped me prepare. No one from JHS 33 had attended Performing Arts High School, and Mr. Barone made sure the whole school knew I was applying. Now, in addition to my family, everyone in ninth grade questioned my artistic ability.

"Hey, spick!" Lulu taunted as I walked into the girls' bath-

room one day. "You think you're better than us? Well, you're just a spick, and don't you forget it." She shoved me into the stall, and for a moment I thought she'd punch my face, but she was happy to spit on it, laugh, and leave me sitting on the toilet, so scared I might have peed in my pants.

I wiped my face with toilet tissue, pulled down my panties and did pee, holding back the tears. She wouldn't see me cry. Neither would she see me fight, because I'd never win. Lulu and her friends were tough, a gang of girls who sat in the back of classrooms passing notes to each other, smoked in the stairwells, picked fights with anyone they didn't like. They knew I was afraid of them, and they made sure I stayed scared. They tripped me in gym class, pushed me in the stairs, took food from my lunch tray. Because of Lulu and her friends, I only went to the bathroom in school if I couldn't hold it in anymore. Because of them, I walked home the long way, to avoid the corner where they stood mornings and afternoons, smoking, laughing, threatening passersby.

For months, Lulu and her gang ignored me. I was one of the kids they bumped into in the hall during period changes. But the minute they heard that I was applying to Performing Arts, Lulu and her friends began a campaign to put me back in my place.

"There goes the actress," LuzMari jeered, as I passed her in the hall.

"She thinks she's white," Violeta mumbled when I was excused from social studies to work on my monologue with Mr. Gatti.

"What?" Denise asked, as I waited to climb the rope in gym, "Eli Whitney not good enough for you?" Almost everyone from JHS 33 ended up at the nearest vocational school, which trained secretaries and nurses, auto mechanics and refrigeration technicians.

"It's just a school," I defended myself, but it didn't matter. Lulu and her gang, to whom I'd been invisible, considered me a traitor because I accepted the teachers' guidance.

"They're jealous," my friend Natalia suggested, as we walked

home from school one day. "They'll be pregnant and on welfare before we graduate from high school."

Natalia lived with her mother and sisters in a building down the block from ours. She was a native New Yorker, her English was perfect, and she spoke Spanish well enough so that I could speak a mixture of both without confusing her. Natalia's mother, like mine, worked in the garment factories of Manhattan, although mine sewed bras and girdles, while hers worked in sportswear.

On Saturdays we waved to each other as we helped our mothers lug shopping carts full of groceries up the steps. Weekday mornings, Natalia made breakfast for her two sisters and walked them to their school before she came to ours. Her mother picked the girls up in the afternoons, so Natalia and I went home together almost every day. When I first met her, I thought she was religious, because she never wore makeup, short skirts, or bright colors. Then I found out that she looked that way because her mother, like mine, was old-fashioned.

Because our mothers saw how strict they were with us, Natalia and I were allowed to be friends, as neither could be considered a bad influence on the other. We were both "good" girls who did as we were told, were expected to be an example to our siblings, and were supposed to take that responsibility seriously. Natalia was better at being a role model than I was, however. Goodness was in her nature, whereas I chafed at the idea that whatever I did was watched by six sisters and brothers who might then do the same. I worried that if I stumbled, Delsa, Norma, Héctor, Alicia, Edna, and Raymond were sure to fall behind me like a row of dominoes, never to rise again.

Natalia and I talked a lot about our future. She applied to the Bronx High School of Science, dreamed of becoming a doctor in one of the big hospitals, like Mount Sinai.

"I'll have an apartment on Park Avenue with a doorman and an elevator," she fantasized, hands pressed to her chest as if to contain the happiness it would bring her.

"When I become a famous actress, I'm going back to Puerto

Rico," I said, "to a farm in the country. And I'll have chickens and a rooster and maybe a dog."

"Why would you want to do that?"

"Because . . ." Could I tell her that I longed to return to Macún? That I missed the leisurely pace of rural Puerto Rico, the wild, green, gentle hills, the texture of the dirt road, from dust to gravel to sand to mud? I joked that the riches we hoped to make in our adult lives were meant to bring me back to where I'd started, while she dreamed of something completely different from what she'd known. She laughed politely, and I fretted that I had offended her by implying that my childhood was happier than hers.

"Are you going to be famous?" Raymond asked a few days before my audition.

"Leaf me a lone," I said, annoyed, and worried that maybe I was in over my head. I had memorized the monologue Mr. Barone had chosen and had practiced how to enter a room like a lady, how to sit without plopping on the chair, how to keep my hands still on my lap instead of using them to punctuate my speech. It already felt as if I were acting, and I hadn't even seen the school.

"Mami, the audition is next week, can you take me?" I showed her the paper on which Mr. Barone had written the school's address: 120 West 46th Street. She studied it as if there were more in it than the two numbers and two short words.

"When do you have to be there?" she asked after a long while, and I went limp with relief. I gave her the details, mentioned that Mrs. Johnson had suggested I didn't have to get dressed up, but that I should look nice. "I saw a dress that will look good on you," Mami offered, and I didn't argue that if she were to buy something new, I'd rather pick it out.

Several days later, she brought home a red plaid wool jumper

and new shoes. "This is a garter belt," she told me, unwrapping a white cotton and lace undergarment with straps ending in rubber buttons snapped onto a metal loop. "It's what we're working on at the factory. I made this one myself."

I'd watched Mami pull on her stockings, smooth them with her fingers, snap them on. I'd seen her stand with her back to the mirror to check that the seams were straight, then gently tug them into place. Until now, I'd not been allowed to wear stockings, and I knew the garter belt and the flat package that held a pair of "Nude" seamless stockings were a concession from Mami, an acknowledgment that I was no longer a child, although neither of us was ready to call me a woman.

"Thank you, Mami," I gushed, hugging her.

"For special occasions," she said, as she kissed the top of my head. "They'll look good with your new dress and shoes."

Over the next week, Tata ladled out larger portions of our meals, as if to fatten me up for what was to come. Aware of the attention I was getting, my sisters and brothers followed me with big, puzzled eyes, searching for what other people saw that they couldn't.

I felt the same way they must have. So many adults fussing over me on the one hand, while on the other, Lulu and her flock stepped up their threats and taunts, as if to keep me from getting too confident. I sensed that getting into Performing Arts was important not only for me but also for Mr. Barone, who strutted around the school telling anyone who listened that I was going there, even though the audition was still days away, and I might not impress the school with my dramatic talent. And it was important for Mami, who boasted to the relatives that I was going to be an *artista*, which brought the same images to my mind as it did to Norma's: curvaceous women in skimpy costumes with feathers in their hair.

The day of the audition, Mami took me to Manhattan, the first time I'd been out of Brooklyn since our arrival in New York. The elevated train ran level with the upper windows of warehouses and apartment buildings a few feet from the tracks. I tried to peek at what lay beyond them, inside the apartments that seemed an arm's length away. But the train moved too fast for me to see more than blurred images of shapes that might or might not be people inside shadowy rooms.

The school was one block from the bright lights and commotion of Broadway. It was a cold, blustery day, and Mami and I walked arched inside our coats, our eyes teary from the frigid winds. The few blocks from the Times Square station to the school were packed with people oblivious to the cold, who admired huge billboards on the sides of buildings or stared into storefronts, most of which featured posters of women with their private parts covered by a black stripe narrow enough to show they were naked.

On the corner of 46th and Broadway, there was a Howard Johnson's, and we went inside to warm up. The tables along the windows were occupied by people who looked as if they hadn't moved from that spot in years. Mami and I sat at the counter, where we were waited on by a woman with frothy platinum hair, turquoise eye shadow, false eyelashes, hot pink lipstick, and a face as wrinkled as a raisin. She called us "honey" or "darling," and once she had served our coffee and pastry, she came over several times to see if there was anything else we needed and to refill our cups.

I was nervous, but that didn't stop me from eating my pineapple danish and half of Mami's and drinking two cups of strong coffee with cream and lots of sugar.

"She eats, for such a skinny thing," the waitress said to Mami, and she nodded and smiled as if she understood.

We walked the half block to the school, and as soon as I was called into the audition room, I was sorry there was so much food in my stomach. My innards churned and churled, and if the interview wasn't over soon, I might vomit in front of the three

ladies in whose hands lay my future as an *artista*. But I managed to get through the monologue and a pantomime and to walk out of the heavy red doors of the school before throwing up between two parked cars as Mami held my hair back and fussed, "Are you all right now? Are you okay?"

On the way home she asked what had happened in the audition, and I said, "Nothing. I answered some questions and did my monologue."

I couldn't tell her that I'd been so nervous I'd forgotten everything learned from Mr. Barone, Mr. Gatti, and Mrs. Johnson. I raced through the monologue, toppled a chair, answered questions without understanding what I was asked. I wouldn't tell Mami how badly I'd done after she'd spent money we couldn't waste on a new outfit and shoes for me. I was ashamed to return to JHS 33 and tell Mr. Barone that I'd bungled the audition. Everyone would laugh at me for presuming I could get into Performing Arts, then fail to get in, in spite of all the help I'd been given. I imagined myself in school with Lulu and Violeta, LuzMari and Denise, who would never let me forget I thought I was too good for them. Mornings, while I took the bus to Eli Whitney, Natalia would be on the train to the Bronx High School of Science. I'd have nothing to talk to her about, because she'd be busy preparing for college, while I'd be sewing underwear in a factory alongside my mother.

As Mami and I rode back, the train charged out of the tunnels, clattered over the Williamsburg Bridge toward Brooklyn. The skyline of Manhattan receded like an enormous wall between us and the rest of the United States. My face away from Mami, I cried. At first my tears came from the humiliation of what I was sure was a terrible audition. But as we neared our stop in Brooklyn, I cried because the weeks of anxious preparation for the audition had left me longing for a life I was now certain I'd never get.

"But they're still illegitimate..."

As Mami's belly grew larger, she had trouble moving around because her legs and back hurt. She quit her job, and I again accompanied her to the welfare office.

"I need assistance until the baby is born and his father is out of the hospital," she had me translate.

"And how long have you and Mr. Cortez been married?" the social worker asked.

"We're not married," Mami said. "We've lived together for the past ten months."

The social worker pressed her lips together. "Does your first husband provide child support?"

"No."

"How long since you've been divorced?"

"Tell her," Mami said, "that your father and I weren't married."

The social worker gripped her pen, and her slanted, left-handed writing crawled across lined paper like rows of barbed wire.

"Then the seven older children are also illegitimate," she said, and Mami blushed, although I'd not yet translated.

"Their father has recognized them all," she had me interpret, pulling our birth certificates from her purse.

"But they're still illegitimate," the social worker insisted, ignoring the documents.

"What does that have to do with it?" Mami asked in Spanish, and I translated, burning with shame because her voice rose and I could tell she was about to make a scene.

The social worker didn't respond, kept on writing on her clipboard. "That's all," she finally said. "We'll let you know."

When we came home, I looked it up. *Illegitimate* meant born of parents who were not married. But the way the social worker's lips puckered, *illegitimate* sounded much worse. It had a synonym, *bastard*, which I'd heard used as an insult. Without my knowing it, the social worker had offended me and Mami. I wished I'd noticed, so that I could have said something. But what was there to say? She was right. We were illegitimate. I worried then that Mami wouldn't get the help we needed from welfare because she and Papi were never married, but a few days later, the help came through.

The word, however, stayed in my conscience a long time.

⁓

A couple of months after his son was born, Francisco died. Mami's usually lively and curious eyes dulled, looked inward, where we couldn't reach her with hugs and kisses. On her dresser, she lit candles that burned day and night, their heat like Francisco's spirit hovering in watchful anticipation of whether, and how, and for how long we would mourn him.

I couldn't cry my disappointment that our family had fallen apart again. Papi had refused to follow Mami to New York, unwilling to help us cope with a cold, inhospitable city. Francisco had left us as quickly as he had come, taking with him the commitment he had made to love Mami forever, to be the man in our house, to make us a complete family with a mother, a father, and children. Every time I passed the altar, I stopped to look at the orange flames floating over melted wax. I placed my hand over them and felt the heat, the solid warmth like an embrace, a promise.

I tried to imagine Papi's life. He'd moved, and I wondered

what his new house was like. Was it in the country or in a town? Was his wife prettier than Mami? Was she as good a cook? Did her daughters sit near him as he read a poem he'd written, as I used to do? I wrote him subdued letters and didn't dare ask about his life, afraid he'd write about how happy he was.

If Papi had come with us, Mami would never have fallen in love with Francisco, he wouldn't have died, and we wouldn't be on welfare again. Yes, Mami and Papi fought, but they always made up. Just like me when I fought with my sisters and brothers; eventually, we made up and went on as before. If we could do it, why couldn't they?

I resented the men who stood on street corners, or who sat on stoops with their elbows on their knees, their hands around a can of beer or curled around a cigarette smoldering between their legs. They might be somebody's father, but they had nothing better to do than to stare at young girls and women passing by and mumble promises under their breath.

<hr />

One morning, Mr. Barone bounded over as I entered the school. "Isn't it wonderful? Congratulations!"

My expression must have told him I had no idea what he was saying, so he stopped, caught his breath, and spoke slowly. "A letter came. You were accepted to Performing Arts."

"Oh my God!" I felt light enough to fly. Mr. Barone led me into the office, where the secretary, the other guidance counselors, and the principal shook my hand. "I can't believe it," I repeated over and over, "It can't be true."

"You worked hard," Mr. Barone said. "You deserve it."

On my way to homeroom, I ran into Natalia. "Guess what? I was accepted!"

She screeched, dropped her books, hugged me. "Oh, my God! I'm so proud of you!" She pulled away quickly, embarrassed at her enthusiasm. I bent down to help her collect her books.

"I can't wait to tell Mami," I said. "She needs good news."

"I wish I could see her face when she hears." Natalia stuffed some loose papers inside a notebook. She seemed about to hug me again but pulled her books into her chest. "I'm so happy for you," she said, and hurried down the hall.

I didn't realize I was smiling until Lulu passed me in front of the science labs, grabbed my arm, and asked, "What's so funny?"

"Nothing," I answered, suddenly serious, "nothing's funny." Lulu had lovely eyes — round, green, full-lashed. She blinked, seemed about to say something, but stopped when a teacher looked out.

"You girls better move on, the bell rang," she warned.

Lulu clicked her tongue at me, pushed me hard enough to let me know she could hurt me. "Wipe that shit-eating grin off your face," she growled, and went off in the opposite direction.

By the time I reached homeroom, Mr. Gatti was writing a question on the board for a pop quiz. He smiled and winked as I sat down. The telltale scratching of the speaker in front of the classroom let us know an announcement was coming. We dove for our books, intending to ignore the announcement for a few minutes of study.

"Ahem," the speaker started. "Girls and boys, ladies and gentlemen," Mr. Barone's crusty voice competed with the shrill feedback that accompanied the messages. "Ahem. I'm pleased to announce that one of our seniors, Esmeralda Santiago, has been accepted to Performing Arts High School."

I was embarrassed and pleased at the same time, didn't hear the rest of what he said. Mr. Gatti shook my hand. Andrea, the girl next to me, patted my shoulder. Someone applauded and the other students followed, except the too cool. I sat in awe for the rest of the period, aware that something good had at last happened to me, afraid that it was too good and that it would disappear before the day was over.

I ran home from school, burst in the door of our somber apartment, found Mami sorting papers on her bed.

"I got accepted, Mami. I got into Performing Arts." She looked puzzled. "The special school, remember? In Manhattan."

Her eyes widened. "*¡Ay, que bueno!*" she said, pulling me close for a hug. I held on to her. Mami's hugs were scarce these days, and I wanted to stay in her arms, to smell the flowery scent of her soap, so faint I buried my face into her neck to find it.

"What did Negi do?" Alicia appeared, and next to her, Edna and Raymond. As usual when one of us received Mami's attention, the others flocked to her, wondering how they could get some too.

Mami guided me to the other side of her papers. "Your sister was accepted into the school for *artistas* in Manhattan," she told them, and I was proud because I heard the pride in her voice.

"You're an artist?" Héctor asked from the other room.

"She's going to learn to be an artist, so that she can be rich and famous some day," Mami said with a smile.

I panicked. Is that what I was doing? "It's just a high school, Mami. So I can go to college."

"Didn't you say it was to study drama and dance?" she scowled.

"Well, yes . . ."

"Are you going to be on television with Ricky Ricardo?" Raymond asked.

"I don't know . . ."

"She's too ugly to be on TV," Héctor piped in from his corner.

Everyone laughed. Mami hugged me, kissed the top of my head. "I'm going to start dinner," she said. Performing Arts was never mentioned in that apartment again.

⌒⌒

A week later, Natalia wasn't in school. She was absent several days in a row, so I went to look for her. Though we lived a few doors apart, we'd never visited each other, and it was strange to stand in

an unfamiliar hallway knocking on a door I wasn't sure was hers. There was no answer. I knocked again, waited a while, pressed my ear to the door to listen for a radio or a television or a reason why no one heard my knock. All was silent, but the door across the hall opened a crack.

"Who's there?" asked a frail voice in Spanish, and when I turned, one eye and half a shrivelled old face peered under the chain stop.

"I'm looking for Natalia Pons. I think she lives here."

"They moved."

"But that's impossible. I just saw her, she didn't say anything."

"They're gone, that's all I know. Nobody has moved in yet, but someone will." She closed the door. Several bolts caught and the woman shuffled deep into her apartment.

I didn't believe her. Natalia hadn't told me she was moving. When I asked Mr. Barone why Natalia wasn't in school, he said the family had returned to Puerto Rico.

"But she never bean there," I said.

He shrugged his shoulders. "Her mother is sick."

Mami found out that Mrs. Pons had had an accident at work and that Natalia's uncle had come to take the girls back to Puerto Rico. It made no sense, but that's the way things happened in our neighborhood. People came and went with no warning, no farewells. My own family moved five times in one year, and there was never a goodbye or a backward glance. Each move was supposed to be for the better, and I wanted to believe that for Natalia, a move to Puerto Rico was good. But I also knew that Natalia's Spanish was really Spanglish, a mixture of English and Spanish that got the job done but was understood only by people who spoke both languages. What would happen to her in Puerto Rico? Would she still be able to study medicine? If she were accepted to the Bronx High School of Science, would she go?

I felt sorry for her, and for myself. The thing I wanted most, a return to Puerto Rico, came true for her. But her dream was the opposite of mine. She wanted to stay in New York, to be a success

American-style, surrounded by the things we thought would make us happy: the apartment on Park Avenue, the luxury car, the clothes and dinners out and nights at the theater. I curled into myself much the way Mami did, afraid to dream — no, afraid to speak my dreams aloud, because look at what had happened to Natalia's.

The candy store in front of JHS 33 was owned by an old couple. They lived behind the store, in a room on the other side of a door that was split in the middle, so that the owner's wife could talk to him as she sat at a round table before stacks of fabric scraps that she stitched into colorful quilts. The man's hands were mottled and swollen, his fingers round and unwrinkled, like hard sausages. Kids said that he was contagious, so we never touched him when he made change. He placed the coins inside a plastic bowl on the counter, and I picked mine up, threw them in my pocket, rubbed my hands against my skirt to get rid of his germs.

On the sidewalk in front of the candy store there was a metal bench for newspapers. The old man took the money for them through a small window in the storefront. Mornings, he sat by the window, watching the students go into school, vigilant of the rowdies who liked to run off with armloads of his newspapers.

If the gangs were acting up, I often ran into the store, browsed through a magazine, or took a long time to buy a candy bar — all the while peering over the counter to make sure the kids were gone. The man behind the counter knew that his store was a haven for those of us neither strong nor brave enough to stand up to the tough kids. If one of us came in and took a long time to choose a purchase, he leaned out the window over the newspaper bench and looked to the right and left along the sidewalk. With a gruff "What's taking so long?" he waved us over, growled the price of the item we held in hand, glowered if we put it back because we had no money. "Get out of here," he snarled, but we knew he was letting us know the coast was clear.

After Mr. Barone made his announcement about my acceptance to Performing Arts, Lulu's insults and threats became more frequent. Now that Natalia was gone and I walked alone, I left as soon as the bell rang, aware that Lulu and her gang were too cool to run out as if someone had chased them. But one afternoon after I crossed the street, relieved that once more I'd avoided her, Lulu stepped from the door of one of the abandoned buildings down the block from the candy store. Behind her were LuzMari and Denise. They surrounded me and pushed me into the cold, dark hallway, which smelled of urine and rotting wood. They punched and kicked me, their shrill voices a chorus of obscenities, their fists sharp and accurate, beating into my chest, my belly, my lower back. I fought back with kicks, scratches, and punches like the ones I used against my sisters and brothers whenever we tussled, only harder. The girls dug their nails into my arms and face, the back of my neck. I flailed against the six fists that pounded my ribs, the six legs that kicked my shins and crotch, the three toothy mouths that snarled and shrieked and spit, the six eyes that glinted in the musty darkness with fierce green hatred. I defended myself but, outnumbered, came out the loser, clothes torn and dirty, arms scratched, legs bruised, chest and back throbbing. As we fought, they screamed in English and I responded in Spanish, the obscenities I wasn't allowed to speak at home spewing from me like acid.

They left me sprawled against a pile of damp cardboard, screeched what must have been more threats, although I wasn't sure. I didn't know what they wanted from me, what I could do to make them ignore me as they used to. I didn't linger in the dark, smelly hallway. Creatures scurried in the depths of the abandoned building, I could hear them. I dusted myself off, found my belongings. When I stepped into the street, the candy store man stood on the sidewalk. He beckoned me in, handed me a frosty Yoo-hoo. From the back, his wife appeared with a damp rag and, mumbling

in a language that was neither English nor Spanish, wiped the grime and tears from my face, her rheumy eyes searching for open wounds on the inside of my arms and on my cheeks.

"Those girls," the old man said, and slapped his swollen hands against the counter. He didn't look at me as his wife wiped alcohol on my bruises, making the welts and scratches on my arms and legs sting and burn. He stared through the window at the street in front of the school, his shoulders slumped, a sad expression on his face.

"Go home, tell mama," his wife said, guiding me out of the store. I thanked them, tried to make eye contact with both, but they looked past me and waved me out, unwilling to accept my gratitude. I dragged myself home, each step like needles into my ribs and hips. Mami was in the bathroom when I came in, so I slouched into the front room, changed into clothes that hid the bruises on my arms and legs, spent the rest of the night bent over a book so that she wouldn't see the scratches on my cheeks, the swollen lip. After dinner I took a long, hot bath, covered my sobs by splashing water and belting out Mexican *corridos* about traitorous lovers and revolution. If Mami noticed, she didn't say a thing, and neither did my sisters and brothers, whose own struggles with bullies had similar outcomes.

For the rest of the year I avoided the candy store, ashamed but not knowing why, the nameless owners' kindness like a weight, unrelieved by the fact that Lulu never bothered me again.

⌒⌒〜⌒⌒

One day I came home from school and Mami's hair was in curlers. "Do you have much homework?" Mami asked as she set a cup of coffee in front of me.

"I have to study for final exams."

"We should buy you a graduation dress."

I'd given up on anyone noticing that in less than a month I'd be graduating from junior high school. My fifteenth birthday came

and went during the sad times, and it seemed that the same would be true for the last day of school.

"Can we come?" Edna asked.

"No. You stay here with Tata, we won't be long." Before Francisco's death, Edna and Raymond would have argued, cried, offered to be the best children in the universe if Mami took them along. But now they just looked disappointed.

"I'll change." I ran into the front room where two bunk beds, Franky's crib, and Tata's cot were lined up in rows. The windows that looked out on the street were open. Delsa, Norma, and Alicia were on the sidewalk jumping double dutch.

Tata lay on her bed, cuddling Franky, and when I came in, she looked up with a smile. I grabbed a dress from one of the hooks Mami had screwed into the wall because the apartment had no closets. With two towels pinched under the mattress of the top bunk I created a private space in which to change out of my school clothes and put on the cotton dress.

Mami was in her room, which served as a passage between the front room and the kitchen. Her bed was pressed against the corner under a window that opened to a dark air vent. Four mismatched dressers, with a drawer for each of us and a couple for Mami, lined the walls. She stood in front of the one with a mirror above it combing out her curls.

"We'll be back in a couple of hours," she told Tata as we went out. Edna and Raymond watched us wistfully.

"Bring us candy," Raymond begged as Mami shut the door.

Delsa, Norma, and Alicia stopped jumping rope when we came down the front stoop. Before they could ask where we were going, Mami scanned the street.

"Where's your brother?"

"He went to the corner," Alicia answered.

"What corner, who said he could wander off like that?"

"Héctor always does that, Mami. He goes off whenever he wants. . . ." Norma nudged Delsa before she could say more. "He'll be back soon," Delsa continued in a subdued voice.

"Don't stay out here too long," Mami warned, and walked toward Broadway.

"Where are you going?" Alicia called.

"To buy me a graduation dress," I called back, pleased to see my sisters' envious expressions. I hurried after Mami, whose decisive steps had already brought her to the corner.

It was the beginning of the month, when the welfare and social security checks came in the mail. Broadway was crowded with harried shoppers going in and out of stores, or standing at the bus stops with bulging bags at their sides. Overhead, the elevated train rattled by every few minutes, screeched to a stop at the station on Flushing Avenue. The beams holding up the train tracks divided the street into four lanes, the center two, where traffic moved in both directions, and the outside lanes for local traffic, always congested with double-parked cars, slow buses, and delivery trucks.

I followed Mami into the check-cashing office, a storefront with a huge sign above the door and a group of men loitering on the sidewalk. This time of the month, they were always there, waiting for their women to hand them money from the checks they'd cashed. One kissed and hugged the woman when she gave him money. Another took it without looking at her, stashed the bills in a pocket, and walked away without so much as a thank you. A third started arguing with the woman the minute she came out. She said she needed the money to feed the kids and to pay the rent and electricity. But he wrested it from her, counted it, and took off, leaving her in tears and cursing him while passersby walked a wide circle around her.

Inside, there were two long lines in front of two men behind thick glass. The cashiers wore white shirts, black pants with suspenders, and skullcaps. They had ringlets on either side of their face, like the vendors at the *marketa* and at the used furniture stores on Graham Avenue.

We stood on line behind a skinny woman struggling with a child. The little girl screamed and kicked, scratched at the hand

that held her tightly by the wrist. Those waiting stared at them, moved away without relinquishing their place on line. The woman yelled at the little girl to stop it, stop it, stop it, yanked her hand, smacked her, which made the child cry harder, fight more. The woman looked up at everyone staring, her eyes defying us to say something, and we shifted our gaze elsewhere. Inside their cages, the cashiers were the only ones who dared look back at her, their contempt directed at her, at the child, at all of us waiting on line.

When our turn came, Mami pulled a ballpoint pen from her purse and signed the welfare check in front of the cashier. She didn't look at the man insulated behind the plate glass, and he didn't look at her. Their transaction was silent, the air heavy with her shame and his disdain for people like us: female, dark-skinned, on welfare.

Before we stepped outside, Mami put her cash in her wallet, stashed it deep inside the purse she held tightly against her side, and led me out. The men glanced up expectantly and then turned from us, annoyed when neither of us was the woman they waited for.

"Which store are we going to?" I asked Mami as she led me past.

"That one." She glanced across the avenue, toward Dolores's Ladies Shoppé, where on the way home from school earlier that week, I had spotted the perfect thing in the window, a yellow sleeveless dress with a full skirt and a wide sash at the waist.

"Does my dress have to be black, or can I get a color?"

She looked at me quizzically as we crossed the street, didn't answer until we were on the other side. "You can wear any color you like."

My sigh of relief brought a smile to her lips, and she put her hand on my shoulder as we entered Dolores's Ladies Shoppé, where my dress waited, yellow as lemon peel, its bodice and skirt made of lace, the sash of nylon organza tied into a bow at the back.

"It makes you look jaundiced," Mami said when I tried it on.

I looked in the full-length mirror, at the golden glow on my brown arms and legs, at the light the dress reflected on my face. "I think it looks nice on me."

"Maybe she would like this baby blue one," Dolores rummaged through the clear plastic bags that encased every garment hanging along the walls of her cramped storefront.

"She doesn't like baby blue," Mami said, as she joined Dolores in her search through the plastic bags.

I narrowed my eyes to get a different view in the mirror, tried to see myself as a stranger might, and saw a young woman with dark brown hair teased into a flip, dark eyes with blue eye shadow on the lids and black liner all around ending in a tail at the corners. On my lips, pink frosted lipstick so pale that my lips looked white. On my feet, spiked heels with pointy toes. I looked like one of the Chiffons, the girl group that sang "He's So Fine." Opening my eyes fully, I saw the way I really looked, with shoulder-length hair in a loose ponytail, no makeup, brown loafers with knee socks.

"Here's one," Mami said. "It's more your color." She held up a navy blue dress with a square neckline, three-quarter sleeves, a dropped waist. It was like the dresses she always bought for me, simple and modest, not like the bold ones American girls wore.

I squinted into the mirror again. "I like this one." I sensed both of us brace for an argument. "It's my graduation, I should wear something dressy." I turned my back on her.

Mami stiffened, but she wouldn't make a scene before Dolores, who lingered near us holding two plastic bags with dresses as conservative and dull as the one Mami held. The yellow dress was luminous, made me feel special and pretty.

"You said I could wear any color," I reminded Mami, whose shapeless black dress hung from her shoulders unadorned, skimming her bust and hips without accentuating their fullness. Her black clothes, her belly still swollen from childbirth, her legs striped with varicose veins made her appear solid and heavy, earthbound.

The neckline of my yellow dress was cut above the gentle bumps of my growing breasts. The sash tied around a skinny waist, and the full skirt, made fuller by a built-in crinoline, appeared to lift me off my feet, off the dirty, scratchy rug in front of the narrow mirror in Dolores's Ladies Shoppé. Standing next to each other, Mami and I looked like darkest night next to brightest morning, each determined to get her way, knowing one would have to cede to the other, waiting until the last possible moment of uncertainty before she surrendered.

"Fine, take the yellow dress," she sighed, her voice brittle, exhausted, sad.

⁓

"I don't know what's with you," Mami muttered as we walked back to Ellery Street. "You've changed."

I hugged the plastic bag with my yellow dress. "I'm getting older, Mami." I chuckled, to make light of it, so she wouldn't accuse me of talking back.

"Older, yes," she continued, unappeased. "And stubborn, and disrespectful." She looked at me from the corner of her eye. "Don't think just because you're going to that school for *blanquitos* I'm going to put up with any *pocavergüenzas* from you." She turned the corner, and I dawdled after, trapped between thoughts.

When Mami and I went to the welfare or unemployment office, a box in the forms asked us to identify our race: White, Black, Other. Technically, Mami was white. Her skin was creamy beige, lacked the warm brown tones her children with Papi had inherited. My memory of my paternal grandparents was that they were white, but Papi and some of his sisters and brothers were dark brown, evoking a not-too-distant African ancestor. Franky, Mami's son with Francisco, was lighter-skinned than the seven older brothers and sisters. He had his father's pale complexion, dark eyes and hair.

When I had to indicate my race, I always marked "Other,"

because neither black nor white was appropriate. Pretending to be white when I was clearly not was wrong. If I could "pass," which I couldn't, there was always the question Puerto Ricans asked when someone became too arrogant about the value of their white skin: "*Y tu abuela, ¿donde está?*" Asking "Where is your grandmother?" implied that in Puerto Rico no one really knew the total racial picture and claims of racial purity were suspect.

I was not oblivious to race in Puerto Rico. I'd noticed that white skin was coveted by those who didn't have it and that those who did looked down on those who didn't. Light-skinned babies in a family were doted on more than dark ones. "Good" hair was straight, not kinky, and much more desirable than the tightly coiled strands of "bad" hair, which at its tightest was called *pasitas*, raisins. Blue or green eyes proclaimed whiteness, even when surrounded by dark skin.

I was neither black nor white; I was *trigueña*, wheat-colored. I had "good" hair, and my features were neither African nor European but a combination of both. In Puerto Rican schools I had not stood out because of the color of my skin or my features. I never had either the darkest or the lightest skin in a room. But when we lived in the city, I was teased for being a *jíbara* from the country. When in the country, my city experience made me suspicious to others.

At junior high schools 49 and 33 in Brooklyn, I was a recently arrived Puerto Rican in a school where most students were Puerto Rican, Italian, or black. I stood apart with the other recent arrivals because of my struggle to speak English. The few Americans in our schools, who were all white-skinned, lived and moved in their own neighborhoods and groups, closed to the rest of us.

When Mami accused me of wanting to go to a school for *blanquitos*, she guessed that most of the people at Performing Arts would be white and, therefore, richer than we were. In Puerto Rico, as in the United States, whiteness meant economic advantage, and when Mami talked about *los blanquitos*, she referred to people of superior social status more than to skin color.

The implication that I was reaching higher than I ought to by going to Performing Arts stung, but I wasn't about to defend myself to Mami. Any response to her assessment of me and what I wanted to do with my life would have confirmed her conclusions that I'd changed since we came to the United States. I had become too independent, she claimed, too bent on my own way, too demanding. All the attention around my application to Performing Arts High School had gone to my head. I had become ambitious and hard to please, always wanting more than I had or was entitled to.

She was right. I had changed. Some nights I lay in bed next to my sister wondering if she was changing too, if the Delsa in Brooklyn was different from the Delsa in Puerto Rico. Other than her growing ease with English, Delsa was the same high-strung, responsible, hardworking girl she'd always been. *She* wasn't applying to a high school in Manhattan. She was going to Eli Whitney to study nursing, a real profession that would bring her a good salary and steady employment. If I thought about it, none of my sisters or brothers seemed to feel the dissatisfaction with their lives that I felt.

I wanted a different life from the one I had. I wanted my own bed in my own room. I wanted to be able to take a bath without having to shoo the whole family out of the kitchen. I wanted books without a date due. I wanted pretty clothes that I chose for myself. I wanted to wear makeup and do my hair and teeter on high heels. I wanted my own radio so that I could listen to La Lupe on the Spanish station or Cousin Brucie's Top 40 countdown on the American one. I wanted to be able to buy a Pepsi or a Baby Ruth any time I craved one. In Puerto Rico I hadn't wanted any of those things. In Puerto Rico, I didn't know they were within my reach. But in Brooklyn every day was filled with want, even though Mami made sure we had everything we needed. Yes, I had changed. And it wasn't for the better. Every time Mami said I had changed, it was because I'd done something wrong. I defied her, or was disrespectful, or didn't like the same things as before. When she

said I had changed, she meant I was becoming Americanized, that I thought I deserved more and was better than everyone else, better than her. She looked at me resentfully, as if I had betrayed her, as if I could help who I was becoming, as if I knew.

"What's a Cleopatra dress?"

In the summer of 1963 we moved again, to an apartment above a drugstore on the third story of a building on busy Pitkin Avenue. Delsa and I shared a room that faced the street and, across the way, a Woolworth's and a Thom McAnn shoe store.

Unlike other places we'd lived in Brooklyn, no children played on Pitkin Avenue after school. It was a commercial block with stores crammed against each other, windows plastered with SALE signs and seasonal decorations displayed year after year by owners who watched their Puerto Rican and black customers with mistrust and resentment. Once the stores closed, the street fell asleep; traffic slowed; the buses that ran up and down Pitkin Avenue and Rockaway Boulevard chugged along, slow and easy, as if conserving energy for the frantic days.

Our welfare worker told Mami she was eligible for survivor benefits. Since Mami and Francisco hadn't been married, there was a lot of paperwork that I had to interpret and fill out. I was now better at telling Mami's story, at conveying her frustration at being *leyof* when she wanted to work, but it was a challenge to calm my nerves so that my English wouldn't flee the minute I had to speak. Many visits and interviews later, our claim was approved. Once confirmed, however, welfare reduced Mami's AFDC allotment, so the Social Security didn't help much.

After weeks of looking, Mami found a job in Manhattan. The sadness didn't leave her when she went to work. Her grief was like

a transparent box that allowed her to sew bras in the factory, to talk to us, to cook and shop, but held her in, untouchable. Mornings, her muffled movements about the apartment woke me as she got ready for work. She woke up early, showered and put on a simple black shift or a black blouse and skirt. She brushed her black hair into a tight bun, scrubbed her face, powdered her nose and forehead. She never ate breakfast, not so much as a cup of coffee. She tiptoed down the wooden stairs, which creaked in spite of her efforts.

I stuck my head out of the window. The sidewalks were empty, the darkness broken by rings of light under the street lamps. Mami looked left, then right, before stepping onto the street. She stiffened her back, raised her chin, pulled her purse closer to her side, and walked to the corner, where she turned right toward the train station. Her shadowy figure pushed through the darkness without a backward or sideways glance, gaze fixed on a point somewhere in front of her. She looked so sad and alone that I worried she'd disappear into the city and never come back. As she turned the corner, her steps faded into the sounds of Brooklyn. I tried to still the fear that made my head pound with a thousand frightening scenarios. She constantly warned us of all the some-things that could happen to us. But what if *algo* happened to her? Was she as afraid for herself as she was for us?

Over the jagged horizon, the sun punctured through thin, wispy clouds that turned pink, then melted into yellow. A soft roar accompanied the dawn, a low growl that grew louder as the city awoke. Within minutes, people hurried up and down the street, across the avenues, into and out of stores, their staccato steps muted by the first horns, distant sirens, muffled radios.

School wouldn't start for weeks. The days dragged long and humid, each like the other except for weekends, when Mami was home and we did errands or visited relatives.

The highlight of the week was *la compra*, the Saturday grocery shopping. When we were on welfare, *la compra* took under an hour and was dragged home in one shopping cart filled with

the staples of our diet: huge sacks of white rice, beans, cans of tomato sauce, onions, garlic, green peppers, fresh oregano, and *recao* for the *sofrito*. Mami also bought a couple of cans of Bustelo, the only Puerto Rican–style coffee we could find in New York, not as nutty-sweet as what we could get on the island; a five-pound bag of sugar; and evaporated or powdered milk for when there was no money to buy it fresh.

But when Mami worked, my sisters and brothers and I argued about who'd help her with *la compra*, because there would be cornflakes and fresh milk, Franco-American spaghetti, Chef Boy-ardee ravioli, and other canned American food. When Mami worked, there was Nestlé Quick, *queso del país* with guava paste, pork chops, hard salami on Ritz crackers, Cheez Whiz on Export sodas, beef stew with chunks of pumpkin and *yautías*, maybe a *pernil*. Mami was proud that even when things were bad, we never went hungry. "There's always bread and milk in the house," she said, "and there's always a cup of rice and a handful of beans."

But we didn't want rice and beans, milk and bread. We wanted Ring Dings and Yodels, pizza, Coca-Cola, Frosted Flakes, Jell-o, foods we never had in Puerto Rico and only got in Brooklyn when there was enough money or when the relatives gave us change for being well behaved during their visits. When we were on welfare, we talked about what we'd buy when we grew up and had jobs and could spend our money any way we liked.

"I'm going to buy the factory where they make Sno-Balls," Alicia said, and we tongued our lips, anticipating the sweet, coco-nutty, chocolatey, creamy-centered cakes sold in pairs that looked like flaky breasts under cellophane.

"I'll open a candy store so that I can eat Baby Ruths and Almond Joys any time I like," Raymond countered, and we agreed that a candy store with a variety of sweets was much better than a whole factory with only one kind.

When Mami worked and we helped her with *la compra*, we zigzagged up and down the market aisles looking for what new and tasty confection we might persuade her to buy. At home we

savored every morsel, licked our fingers to get the last taste of sweet from the tips, drained the bottle of soda until there was no more of the fizzy, tickly liquid, until the hard, smooth glass pressed firmly against our tongues.

Now that Tata lived with us again, Tío Chico found a room in the Bowery. We'd heard that's where bums lived, but Mami insisted Tío Chico wasn't a bum. "He drinks too much sometimes," she said, "but he works and takes care of himself."

No, Tío Chico didn't smell like the bums we passed on the side streets branching from Pitkin Avenue. He was clean, even if his clothes were rumpled, the collars of his shirts frayed, the soles of his shoes worn. He shaved at least every other day. When he didn't, black and white stubble grew around and inside the deep creases that ran from his nostrils to the corners of his lips. He had brown eyes like Tata's and a well-formed nose, long but not grotesque, well shaped. And he had beautiful, long-fingered, graceful hands.

Once he touched my left breast with those long fingers, gripped the nipple and pinched it. He'd been watching me comb my hair, and when Tata called him to the kitchen, I didn't move when he went past me, and he reached across and squeezed my breast. "Don't tell anyone," he muttered into my ear. On the way back, he dropped a dollar in front of me.

I could have told Mami what he'd done, could have used the dollar as evidence, but I didn't. I spent it on an ice cream sundae and told myself he was drunk. From then on, I avoided him whenever he came around, disappeared into another room, hid in the bathroom, or sat as far away from him as possible when he came to visit. His caramel, red-streaked eyes followed me when I walked around the apartment. I avoided his gaze, aware that we shared a shameful secret, weighing whether the blame should fall heavier on him who touched me, or on me who let him do it.

Now that Mami was working again, she had a telephone installed. "With you going to the city every day," she reasoned, "we need a phone so you can call if you get lost or *algo*."

Evenings we sat around the kitchen table discussing the "*algos*" that could happen. They appeared in daily newspaper reports of the crimes committed in the city, illustrated with grainy black-and-white photographs that electrified the imagination. We reenacted the more colorful events of the day, adding details not reported, but which we were sure existed. The day a suspected drug dealer was found hanged in his jail cell, Héctor unhooked his belt, tied it loosely around his neck, held it up, stuck his tongue out, crossed his eyes, and made hacking noises as his body shook in paroxysms that made us laugh until our eyes teared. When we enjoyed ourselves too much at the expense of the dead, maimed, or victimized, Mami stopped our parodies. "That poor man's mother," she'd sigh. Or, "How she must have suffered before he killed her." Her comments shamed us for a moment, but they didn't stop us from doing the same thing again the next day.

When crime threatened near, however, when Don Julio was mugged, or when our neighbor Minga was pushed into traffic and her handbag snatched, we didn't laugh. We huddled closer to Mami and to each other in speechless fear, visualizing the dangers outside our door, certain that the only safe place in the world was the four walls that enclosed us, small and vulnerable, in our mother's shadow.

Performing Arts High School was organized by departments: Dance, Drama, and Music. It was possible to tell students' majors by looking at them. The dancers had muscular calves and barely touched the floor when they walked, their feet turned out from

their hips like the hands of a clock at twenty past eight. The musicians carried black cases in a variety of shapes, drummed their fingers during academics, listened intently to the silliest prattle. The drama students were the worst listeners but the best talkers. I had the impression, when talking to other drama students, that during their brief silences they were just waiting their turn to hear themselves speak.

We were assigned homerooms, each divided roughly equally among music, dance, and drama students. Our day was split between our majors and academic classes. We had to maintain a high average in both, or we'd be asked to transfer elsewhere. Mrs. Schein, my homeroom teacher, congratulated us for our success in a process she said was highly competitive. "You demonstrate artistic as well as academic potential. By admitting you to Performing Arts High School, we're showing our faith in you as artists and as scholars."

I was flattered and inspired by her words, most of which I understood because she spoke in a deep, modulated voice, every word enunciated clearly.

"There is a dress code," she informed us. Boys were not allowed to wear jeans to school, and girls could not wear pants.

"What if it's a really cold day?" asked a girl with ratted hair and more makeup than the teacher.

"You may wear pants under your skirts, but in school you must take them off and wear a skirt or dress." Muted protests followed, but faded as Mrs. Schein continued. "You may not leave the school wearing theatrical makeup. It's unprofessional."

Professionalism was an important concept at Performing Arts. Most of the teachers were working actors, dancers, and musicians. They took themselves seriously as artists and expected us to do the same. "You have a gift," they each said at different times, "and it is our job to help you develop your talents, but it is also our responsibility to prepare you for the real world."

None of us, they stressed, should expect to become overnight successes. It would take an average of ten years after we graduated

from high school for our talents to be fully developed and recognized in "the business," and at least that long before we could make a living from our art.

The ten-year wait depressed me. How could I tell Mami that I faced three years of high school and ten years of struggle before I could support myself? I expected that, upon graduation from Performing Arts, I'd get a job as an actress and earn enough to help Mami. But according to the teachers, graduating from Performing Arts was only the beginning.

"The only people who make it," they never let us forget, "are those committed to their art, willing to sacrifice for the privilege of performing for an audience. You can expect to be 'starving artists' for a while before you're discovered."

When I told her what the teachers said, Mami was horrified. "I'm not working this hard to send you to a fancy school so you can starve," she warned. We both envisioned legions of actors, dancers, and musicians filling out forms at the welfare office as we'd done so often.

"I don't care what *monerías* they teach you at that school," Mami made clear. "As soon as you graduate, you better get a job."

We drama students were required to study dance so that we could develop a sense of how our bodies moved in space and prepare ourselves should we ever, in spite of our dramatic aspirations, get work in a musical. Although the school had high-ceilinged, wood-floored, well-lit, mirrored dance studios, they were reserved for dance majors. Actors danced in the lunchroom. The benches on the tables collapsed into the tops, and these were then pushed to one end of the room and stacked, leaving the tiled floor free. If we danced after the lunch period, we sometimes had to sweep crumbs off the floor.

It was a good thing that the lunchroom had no mirrors, for most of us weren't used to the outfits required for dance classes.

Girls wore black footless tights, a black scoop-necked leotard, and a dance skirt that had to cover us to midthigh. We danced barefoot, as did the boys, who wore black tights and a white T-shirt. The first day, we skulked into the lunchroom, the boys with hands crossed in front of the bulge enhanced by the required "dance belt," we girls hunched over our breasts, hugging ourselves.

Our dance teacher, Miss Lang, led us through what was for many our first formal dance class. Gawky and uncoordinated, we giggled as she demonstrated how to leap across the floor, toes pointed, head up, back straight. "Right foot out, left arm up," she sang, as she beat a rhythm on her hand drum that most of us defied with ungainly hops and turns. At the first class, it was clear that we needed to develop muscles we didn't know existed before we could execute graceful leaps or pirouettes that wouldn't land us sprawled on our behinds. The following week, and for many weeks thereafter, Miss Lang's dance class took place mostly on the floor, where she coached us through rigorous stretches that left us pained and sweaty. Students grumbled that we were actors, not dancers, and that we shouldn't have to take that stupid class, but I loved dance. I loved the open space before me in the lunchroom/ studio. I loved the weightless feeling as I leaped across the floor. I welcomed the dull aches after class, the stretched muscles that vibrated for hours, the rush of blood to my face, arms, and legs. It was the only time I was warm, the only time in the Brooklyn winters when my body moved the way I remembered it moving in Puerto Rico—free, open to possibilities, unafraid.

Most of my classmates were New Yorkers born and raised who spoke with the distinctive accent of the neighborhood where they'd grown up. Our teachers claimed they could tell what borough we came from simply by listening to us speak. In Brooklyn, for example, "I am" sounded like "Oyem," "here" sounded like "heah," "bathroom" was "batrum," and "in there" was "innair." I spoke

Brooklyn English with a Puerto Rican accent, a variation in a place where the goal was to get us to speak eastern standard speech.

Accent eradication was important, we were told, to widen the range of parts we could play. An actor must be versatile enough to change the way he or she spoke to fit the character being played. Standard speech laid the foundation for other accents, including, if necessary, the one we had when we first walked through the doors of Performing Arts High School.

My voice and diction teacher was King Wehrle from Kansas.

"You need a name that stands out," he told us when asked whether he was born King. "I changed mine when I came to New York."

He listed famous actors who had traded in their unimpressive names for the ones everyone remembered: Archibald Leish/Cary Grant; Eunice Quedens/Eve Arden; Betty Joan Perske/Lauren Bacall; Frances Gumm/Judy Garland.

"Do you believe a guy named Marion Morrison could get a part as a cowboy in the movies?" Mr. Wehrle asked. "No. He had to become John Wayne!"

When considering a change, Mr. Wehrle suggested we pick names with few letters, easy to fit on a marquee, easy to remember, and American, not foreign. "Anne Bancroft," he said, "not Anna Maria Italiano. Tony Curtis, not Bernard Schwartz. Kirk Douglas," he intoned in his most distinguished announcer's voice, "not Issur Danielovich."

So, in addition to having to wait ten years after graduation to make a living in my art, I also had to find a new name, since Esmeralda Santiago was clearly too long to fit on a marquee, hard to remember, and definitely foreign.

⌒⌒

If I looked at Performing Arts strictly along racial lines, Mami was right; it was a school where almost all the students and teachers

were white. In my tenth-grade class there were 126 students: fourteen black, three Puerto Rican, and two Asian. Two of the twenty-four teachers in the arts majors and two of the twenty-three academic subject teachers were black.

But as I walked the wide halls of Performing Arts High School, what I saw was not a school for *blanquitos*. Although it was true that those of us with dark skins were in the minority, the hierarchies set up along racial lines that I'd come to accept in junior high school weren't as marked. At Performing Arts, status was determined by talent. The elite of the school were the students who played the lead roles in scenes, or solo instruments in chamber concerts, or danced a solo or virtuoso pas de deux. The rest of us, whose talent had yet to develop, watched the stars of the school with a mixture of awe and envy. *They* wouldn't have to wait ten years to "make it" in "the business."

I recognized and accepted the hierarchy based on talent. It was fair, unlike those set up along racial lines. But there was another distinction among the students — more subtle, though not invisible. I was keenly aware of being a poor kid in a school where many were rich. In Brooklyn, most of my classmates came from my neighborhood and lived in similar circumstances, but Performing Arts drew from all over the city. As I talked to other students, the meagerness of my resources was made real. I knew my family was "disadvantaged"; it said so on the welfare applications. But it was at Performing Arts that I saw first hand what being "advantaged" meant.

It meant trips to Europe during vacations, extra classes on weekends with dance masters or voice coaches, plastic surgery to reduce large noses or refine broad ones. It meant tennis lessons and swim meets, choir practice, clubs, academic tutoring, dates. It meant money for lunch at the deli across the street or down the block. It meant taxis home.

Being disadvantaged meant I found my dance tights and leotard in a bin in the guidance office. It meant washing them and setting them to dry on the barely warm radiators of our apartment

and wearing them damp when there was no money to pay the heating bills. It meant a pass so that I could get a free bowl of soup and half a sandwich for lunch. It meant that, if invited to a party given by a classmate, I said no, because there was no money to buy presents for rich people. It meant never inviting anyone over, because I didn't want them to see the wet diapers hanging on ropes strung from one end of the apartment to the other. Or the profusion of beds that left no space for a proper living room.

Advantaged meant being able to complain about having too many things to do, all of them fun, being unable to decide whether to sleep over at Joanie's or to take an extra dance class at Madame's. It meant that papers handed in to the teacher were typed on crisp white pages, not handwritten with a cheap ballpoint pen on blue-lined notebook paper from Woolworth's. The advantage was not talent, nor skin color, it was money, and those of us who were disadvantaged had little or none.

I wasn't the only poor kid at Performing Arts — or in my class. There were many of us. We found each other and hovered on the fringes of the lucky few whose Monday reports of fun-filled weekends intensified our sense that our talent had to take us a long way, a very long way indeed, from where we were.

We learned to act by working on improvisations and scenes from well-known plays. For improvisations, the teacher set up situations, then let us work them in front of the whole class or in small groups. At any time, the dynamics could change; the teacher might send in another actor with different motivations or a conflicting situation right in the middle of our improvisation. Or a loud noise might intrude, or the situation might change naturally as the scene evolved. Besides developing our ability to think fast and concentrate, improvisations helped us work through the nuts and bolts of a scene by allowing us to discover a character's motivations and subtexts to the dialogue.

For scene work we were paired with partners. Teachers assigned plays and scenes appropriate to our talent and personalities, but they avoided typecasting, which was no challenge to the actor. For each scene we prepared "sides," half-page scripts with one side for our lines and cues written in block letters and the facing page for notes about meaningful subtext, stage directions, or motivation.

We didn't have sets. Wooden boxes with splintery corners created the illusion of a southern kitchen or a Roman Senate, depending on whether we were playing a scene from *Member of the Wedding* or *Julius Caesar*. The rehearsal space was the Basement, actually the ground floor of the school, with lockers at one end and entrance doors and stairways leading up on the other. We staked out areas of the Basement, hoarded boxes to create our set, and worked independently, while the teacher roamed from one group to another watching, questioning motivation, suggesting other ways to block the scene. At the end of class, we might be asked to perform our work-in-progress in front of the group. One-piece school desks/chairs were arranged in a semicircle so that everyone had a front row seat. Sometimes we were asked to perform in gibberish, to demonstrate that acting was more than parroting words from a page, that it conveyed a human experience independent of language.

My first scene was in act 1, scene 1 of George Bernard Shaw's *Caesar and Cleopatra*. I was paired with Roman-nosed Harvey, who was cast as Julius Caesar to my Cleopatra.

I was thrilled. That summer I'd read mostly biographies. Cleopatra was one of my favorite historical figures, and I'd acquired a lot of information about who she was, what her motivations might have been, what she looked like. As actors, we researched the characters we played, the fictional as well as the historical ones, on the theory that the more we knew about them, the better we could bring them to life on the stage.

I loved the preparation to act. I loved reading the entire play, even if I performed only a short scene from it. I loved figuring out

the character beyond what the playwright had written. I loved designing a costume and scrounging at home for materials from which to make it, since the school didn't provide wardrobe except for the performances at the end of the year.

I found a yellow tablecloth Mami had bought at the thrift shop. "Can I use this?"

"For what?"

"To make a Cleopatra dress."

"What's a Cleopatra dress?" She pursed her lips, a sign she thought I was asking for a fashion I wasn't allowed to wear.

"Cleopatra was an Egyptian queen," I explained. "She lived thousands of years ago, and she wore tight dresses."

"Why do you have to dress like her?" She took the tablecloth from my hand and examined it.

"It's homework. I have to dress like the people in the plays."

"In a tablecloth?"

"I told you, I'm making a dress out of it."

"It's got an *achiote* stain," she pointed out.

"That's why you might not want it anymore."

"I'll make it for you," she offered, still suspicious. I envisioned Mami's idea of a Cleopatra dress, nothing like what I imagined.

"We're supposed to make it ourselves," I lied.

"All right," she conceded, "but let me see it before you finish, in case you need any help." She wanted to make sure it wouldn't be too revealing.

I cut and sewed a tubelike dress so tight it required that I walk sideways, like an Egyptian hieroglyphic figure.

"Ay, *mi Dios*," Mami gasped when she saw it.

"You look like a banana," Edna volunteered.

"Shut up," I screamed.

"Shut up yourself."

"You're not wearing that in public," Mami said.

"It's only in school, Mami, for a scene in a play. I'll show you a picture." I minced to the bedroom, followed by my sisters' and brothers' giggles. To pick up the costume book I'd left on the floor,

I had to bend slowly from the knees. I took tiny steps back and opened the book. "Look, these people are Egyptian. See how they wear their clothes close to their bodies?"

Edna, Delsa, and Norma looked over Mami's shoulder at the picture, then at my dress.

"They didn't walk very far, did they?" laughed Norma. I sent her a hateful look, and she stuck out her tongue.

Mami studied the illustration, which showed the dresses to be transparent, which the damask wasn't. "I'm supposed to make it look like what they really wore." I tried not to sound desperate. "I'll only wear it in the classroom, in front of other students and the teacher."

"What are *they* wearing?"

I ignored her sarcasm. "My partner made a costume from a sheet, and another girl made hers from a drape." If I kept to the materials, maybe Mami wouldn't focus on the fit. "We'll be graded," I lied, "on how much our costumes look like the real thing."

"At least you can't see through it," Edna offered.

"Not that she has anything to show," Delsa snorted and slapped Norma five.

"You'll have to let it out," Mami said. "The seams are straining."

"Okay." I wouldn't do a thing to the dress. There wasn't enough fabric to let out, and Mami would never see me in it, as I'd wear it only in school, as Cleopatra. I looked in the small oval mirror over the dresser in the room I shared with Delsa. She was right, there wasn't much for me to show. Still, I didn't look like a banana. Bananas don't have breasts, and I did, even if my *nalgas* were flat and I had no hips. I raised my hands in a posture like the hieroglyph pictures I'd seen, and thought I looked pretty close to what Cleopatra might have looked like. At fifteen, Cleopatra was soon to be queen of Egypt, while I had to argue with my mother over every little thing. I wondered what it was like not to have a mother, and a chill raced up from my toes to my head. I had to

walk to the door and peek out to make sure Mami was still there before I could be warm again.

~~~~~~~~

The drama department taught the Method developed by Stanislavsky in his book *An Actor Prepares*. Method actors explored their deepest selves for the emotional truth that informed the moment lived on stage.

I refused to venture into my deepest self, to reveal my feelings, to examine my true emotions publicly. If I did, everyone would know I was illegitimate, that I shared a bed with my sister, that we were on welfare. The result was that I was accused by my peers of "indicating," the worst sin a Method actor can commit on stage. To "indicate" meant to pretend to be in the moment by going through the motions, rather than to actually live it.

It was humiliating not to be a good enough actress to fool my teachers and fellow students, but I simply couldn't abandon myself to the craft. I didn't have the skills to act while acting. Because the minute I left the dark, crowded apartment where I lived, I was in performance, pretending to be someone I wasn't. I resisted the Method's insistence on truth as I used it to create a simulated reality. One in which I spoke fluent English, felt at home in the harsh streets of New York, absorbed urban American culture without question as I silently grieved the dissolution of the other me, the Spanish-speaking, Puerto Rican girl most at home in a dusty, tropical dirt road. I created a character that evolved as the extended improvisation of my life unfolded, a protagonist as cheerful and carefree as my comic book friends Betty and Veronica, Archie, Reggie, and Jughead.

"Don't you want to sound Puerto Rican?"

One day I returned from the library to find a woman and a girl about my age surrounded by my sisters and brothers, sipping coffee and chewing cake around the kitchen table.

"Guess who this is?" Mami grinned.

The girl eyed me from under mascaraed lashes; and the woman, petite, corseted and skillfully made up, sized me up and found me deficient. I had no idea who they were and didn't care. "Friends from the factory?" I suggested, and Mami laughed.

"This is your sister Margie."

My mouth dropped in surprise, and I quickly closed it, because they laughed. Margie; her mother, Provi; my sisters and brothers, who were bunched on the side of the table closest to Margie, all seemed to think it was hilarious that I didn't recognize someone I didn't remember meeting.

"She's got the most expressive face," Provi giggled, and my cheeks burned. Mami crinkled her eyes at me and tipped her head toward Margie and Provi. I touched each one's shoulders with my fingertips, leaving lots of space between us, and kissed them lightly on the right cheek.

Provi had been my father's "wife" before he met my mother. I'd expected Margie to look like our father, with his high forehead, prominent cheekbones, broad nose, full lips. I'd expected his coloring, but she was lighter and looked more like my sister Norma, with the same tightly curled auburn hair, slanted brown eyes, regal bearing.

Mami served me coffee and cake. "Provi brought it from a bakery near her apartment in Manhattan." It sounded like a warning, but when I looked up, Mami's back was to me as she refilled her coffee cup.

Margie was uncomfortable at our table, her back to the wall, as my sisters and brothers jostled and pushed one another to stand the closest to her. Héctor brought out his entire bottle cap collection, and Edna drew flowers and birds and offered them for Margie's approval. Every once in a while, Margie smiled at me, and I wished we could go somewhere to talk. But there was no other place, no living room, no yard, no room that wasn't filled with beds or people. I was embarrassed and tried to read Mami's feelings. But she was serene, didn't seem to notice that Provi's eyes darted from the sink stacked with clean but battered pots and pans to the next room, where a rope was strung from the window to the door jamb. Under it, water dripped onto the dull linoleum from the diapers hung up to dry. Every once in a while, Delsa grabbed the mop, soaked up the puddles, then pushed her way back to Margie's side.

I was annoyed at Mami's composure. She should have been as ashamed as I felt. As soon as the thought surfaced, I banished it. Mami worked hard for us, and while I had less than I wanted, as the eldest I got more than my younger sisters and brothers. When they complained that Mami favored me, I argued that she didn't; but inside I knew she did, as did Tata. I settled back on my chair, seething, alternating shame with guilt, envious of Margie's fashionable clothes; her rolled, teased, sprayed hair; her meticulous makeup; the charm bracelet that tinkled on her right wrist, the Timex on her left. At the same time I longed to talk to her, to find out if she was in touch with Papi, if it hurt her when he remarried, if she remembered our grandmother, whom, Provi said, I resembled.

Mami spoke with pride about how much English we'd learned in a scant two years, about the school I attended, about how sweet-natured baby Franky was, about her job as a Merrow

sewing machine operator in a Maidenform factory. The two of them talked as if they were long-lost friends, when in fact for years Mami had referred to Provi as "that woman" and Provi must have had a few names for Mami when she wasn't sitting at our kitchen table drinking coffee and delicately chewing the too-sweet cake she'd brought.

Provi boasted about their apartment in Manhattan, where, she pointed out, Margie had her own room. About how Margie was one of the top students in her school, about how they'd lived in the United States so long, they were forgetting their Spanish while still learning English.

"And then what do we do?" she cackled. "We'll be mute, with nothing to say!" Mami and I exchanged a look, remembering our far-from-speechless La Muda.

I interpreted Provi's friendliness as an act. Used to the drama student's obsession with finding subtext in dialogue, I listened to Provi chatter but heard the unspoken "You weren't woman enough to hold on to Pablo," while Mami's unsaid "I had him for fourteen years, four times longer than you did" heated the air.

I imagined Provi was glad Mami was widowed, saw Francisco's death as a punishment for the wrong I guessed Mami had done her. Mami, younger and prettier, was, I suspected, the reason Papi had left Provi.

I sulked at my end of the table, listened to our mothers babble, aware they were still competing for my father, who wasn't there, who was married to another woman neither one of them had met. I heard nothing but criticism in Provi's remarks, only defenses in Mami's. I pitied Margie, whose shoulders slumped into the chair, as if she too was embarrassed by her mother's behavior. I resisted Provi's tight smiles and Margie's frequent attempts to make eye contact. Every second of their visit was a test we had to pass to rise to another level, but I wasn't sure what that level was, where it lay, if it existed. Margie had come too late, but I didn't know what she was late for, or whether and why I'd been waiting for her.

As Mami closed the door after them, she breathed a deep sigh. My sisters and brothers scattered to other parts of the apartment. Tata, who stayed in her room during the entire visit, stumbled into the kitchen and began chopping onions for that night's supper.

"Isn't Margie pretty?" Mami asked, not expecting an answer. Tata grumbled about "that woman." I was about to make a sarcastic remark but decided against it.

"She has nice hair," I allowed. "I like the way she lines her eyes, with the little tail at the corner," I added, to say something nice, and Mami fixed her gaze on me, as if seeing what wasn't obvious before.

"You have better hair," she said, running her fingers through it. "It's wavy, not so curly as hers. You can do more with it." She took my face in her hands, tipped it to the light. "As for her makeup, that line wouldn't look good on you. Your eyes are a completely different shape." She pushed my face to the left, to the right. "Maybe if the tail were shorter. . . . Why don't you try it?"

I dashed to the dresser where she kept the cosmetics she hadn't worn since Francisco's death. Breathless, I opened the zippered pouch. Inside, there was a mirrored plastic compact with a thin circle of pressed powder around the metal bottom, the once fluffy cotton pad flat and frayed around the edges. A smaller, round cardboard box held her powdered rouge, which leaked a fine red dust over two lipsticks and a stubby eyebrow pencil. I uncapped the point, whittled the wood with a Gem blade, and drew a curve on the back of my hand. When I tried it on my lid, the hard point slipped and left a faint ashen stripe, which I wiped with spit and toilet tissue. When I finally got it to sketch a dark line on my upper lid, I extended it to a jaunty angle, like a smile.

"What do you think?" I tried to still the thumps inside my chest that betrayed my excitement. Mami leaned against the counter, squinting as if evaluating an expensive purchase.

"It looks nice," she said. "But next time, make the tails shorter."

"Okay." Next time, she'd said. Next time! I ran back to the bathroom, erased the ends of the lines so that they didn't extend beyond the lids.

"Like this?"

"Perfect," she smiled. "That looks nice."

Tata watched from her post by the stove. "She's growing up," she said softly, and I pleaded for silence with my eyes. She turned with a grin. Mami smiled and went back to washing the rice.

In my room I stared at my reflection, fingered the thick dark lines around my eyes that made me look older, sophisticated. Delsa was in bed, wrapped in a blanket, her black curls peeking through the top.

"Quit it," she mumbled, though I hadn't made a sound. I left the room, curled up against the wall on Norma and Alicia's bed, and watched television. My eyes felt heavy, as if the black line added weight to them. During a commercial, Alicia stared hard at me, then trotted to the kitchen yelling. "Mami, Negi is wearing makeup."

"Shut up," I rushed after her and held her back.

"What's all the shouting?" Mami called.

"Negi's wearing makeup," Alicia repeated, fighting me.

"Leave your sister alone," Mami yelled, and I wasn't sure if she meant me or Alicia. "Next time I go to the drugstore," she said over her shoulder as she headed back, "I'll buy you your own pencil."

I let go of Alicia, who looked from me to Mami with a puzzled expression. She was nine, I was fifteen, and although Mami took my side in many arguments with my sisters and brothers, we both knew that something important had happened. I had stopped being a little girl because Mami wouldn't be outmothered by Provi.

⌒

It was always still dark when I left the apartment at five-thirty in the morning, my books and dance clothes in La Muda's old black

leather bag. The fifteen-minute walk to the elevated train station was a gauntlet of shadows under burned-out street lamps that lengthened the distance between abandoned buildings and parked cars. I walked in the middle of the sidewalk, eyes fixed straight ahead but alert, expecting danger from any direction at any moment. Once, a rat scurried in front of me. I didn't know what to do, afraid to walk, afraid to stand in the same spot. After a few seconds, I ran past the pile of garbage into which the rat had disappeared and added "bite from a rabid rat" to the list of "*algos*" that could happen away from home.

Even at six in the morning the trains were packed, and I often stood most of the way into Manhattan. That morning, I was lucky. When the train came, I spotted a space in the two-seater bench across from the conductor's booth. I took it, careful not to disturb the woman who slept on the seat closest to the door, her gloved hands pressed against a handbag on her lap. The passengers already on the train were black and Puerto Rican, but as we moved from East New York to Brownsville into Crown Heights, Prospect Heights, and Brooklyn Heights, the people waiting at the platforms were white and older than the passengers already on board. They pushed into the subway car as everyone squeezed together to make room.

A man elbowed his way toward the hang-strap above where I sat against the wall. He set his briefcase on the floor between his legs, grabbed the hang-strap with his left hand, unbuttoned and pulled open his coat, his right hand in the pocket. I kept my eyes on my book, only dimly aware of the movement in front of me, until I realized he was leaning in so close that he blocked the light. When I looked up to ask him to move, I saw that his zipper was open and his penis dangled outside his pants, not two feet from my face. I quickly looked down at my book, too embarrassed to say or do anything. His coat formed a curtain on one side, and the wall trapped me on the other. I pretended to read while I tried to figure out what to do. I could get up and move, but my bag was under my feet, and if I bent down to reach it, I'd be dangerously

Costco #241
1 Industrial Lane
New Rochelle, NY 10805

Member#	111369155000
Invoice#	9895
Date:	06/13/19
Time:	13:01
Auth#	00454C

VI Acct #
***********9206

Pump	Gallons	Price
9	6.497	$ 2.759

Product	Amount
Regular	$ 17.93

| Total Sale | $ 17.93 |

SALE- Card Swiped
Approved
TranID# 916409009895

Thank you
For your purchase of
Kirkland Signature
Fuel
Visit Costco.com
Search: Fuel

close to his wan, wrinkled penis. I considered but didn't have the nerve to look him in the eye and tell him to put it back where it belonged. As we reached a station and the train slowed, he dropped his arm from the hang-strap, covered himself, and waited until the train was moving, then raised his arm so that his penis was again in my face. I felt him stare while I struggled with what to do. I could grab the penis and pull hard. I could bite it. Without touching it, I could slam the pages of my biology text around it. But I sat stony-faced and silent, pretending to read, angry that I was being such a *pendeja*, wondering what I'd done to provoke him.

Theatrical makeup was taught in a room across from the auditorium's backstage entrance. The teacher, Mrs. Bank, a no-nonsense woman with a reputation for being exacting and difficult to please, was nevertheless beloved by those students who managed to impress her with their talent. I wasn't among her favorites. I had too little range as an actress to meet her high standards.

During the first class, she gave us a list of supplies, and I had to convince Mami the expense was necessary, that makeup was a real course in which I'd be graded. She frowned at the brushes and pencils, sponges, puffs, powders, and creams that cost more than what she put on her face. But she never said I couldn't have it.

Mrs. Bank moved us quickly through the rudiments of stage makeup. We began with techniques to enhance our natural features. Boys as well as girls were taught to apply foundation, lip liner, cheek color, and mascara. We were encouraged to study our faces, to learn their contours, to examine the shapes that made up our appearance, to look at ourselves not as who we were, but as who we could become.

To this end, we were taught to alter our features. Through skillful use of highlights and shadows, we learned to narrow a

broad nose and to flatten a pointy one. Eyes could be made larger, lips fuller, flat cheekbones rounded, high foreheads lowered.

I loved the class because I could apply as much makeup as I wanted and Mami couldn't complain, since I told her it was my homework to practice. I spent hours in front of the mirror making myself up to look innocent, sultry, elegant, Chinese. One of the assignments was to bring in a picture of an animal and to recreate the animal's features on our own face. At home, I made myself up as a tiger, a camel, an orangutan, then chased my sisters and brothers around the apartment, making the appropriate animal sounds, until Mami or Tata put an end to my grunts and their screams.

One of the last assignments of the semester was to make ourselves up as old people.

"Follow the natural contours of your face," Mrs. Bank instructed. "Darken the creases from your nostrils to your lips. Highlight along the edges to deepen them."

Most of us were fifteen or sixteen years old, and finding wrinkles on our faces was difficult, not because they weren't there but because we didn't want them to be.

"If you pucker your lips like this, then draw lines where the puckers are, you'll get some interesting wrinkles."

We followed her instructions, giggling as our faces aged under puffs and brushes.

"Most people have lines around their eyes," she pointed out. "Don't forget your neck and hands, they age too."

We drew liver spots on the backs of our hands. We powdered our hair to make it white. Jay applied a wart to his cheek. Elaine practiced a quiver in her voice to go with her frail, old-lady face.

At the end of the class, when Mrs. Bank asked us to evaluate the work we'd done, I looked closely at my wrinkled cheeks, at the curious eyes inside deep circles, and burst into tears.

"What's the matter?" Mrs. Bank, asked, alarmed.

"I'm an old lady," I whined in what I thought was a playful manner, to cover up my embarrassment.

Mrs. Bank smiled. "Not quite, not yet. Lucky for you, it disappears with Albolene cream."

"That's good," I giggled listlessly, "I'm too young to be old."

She moved on. I faced the mirror again and saw my grandmother, Abuela, whom I hadn't seen in three years. But if I turned to the left, there was Tata, the grandmother I lived with. It was frightening to see them both stare at me from my own face. Abuela's sad eyes, Tata's sensual mouth, Abuela's small nose, Tata's intelligent gaze. But I wouldn't admit that to Mrs. Bank or to the other students who laughed at my fear of growing old. Let them think what they will. They will never know, they can't ever understand, who I really am.

I had a secret life, one not shared with my sister, with whom I shared a bed. Or with my classmates, with whom I shared dreams of fame and fortune. Not with my mother, whose dreams were on hold since Francisco's death. My secret life was in my head, lived at night before I fell asleep, when I became someone else.

In my secret life I wasn't Esmeralda Santiago, not Negi, not a scared Puerto Rican girl, but a confident, powerful woman whose name changed as I tried to form the perfect me. Esme, I was once. Emmé, another time. Emeraude, my French class name. I tried Shirley, Sheila, Lenore, but names not based on my own didn't sound quite right. So I was Emma, Ralda, or just plain E.

In these dreams I had no family — no mother or father, no sisters or brothers, no grandmothers, no wrestling cousins, no drunk uncles, no deaf mutes. I was alone, sprung from an unnameable darkness, with no attachments, no loyalties, no responsibilities. I was educated, successful, professional. Whatever I did, I did well, with no false steps, no errors, no embarrassing mistakes that caused others to judge or to laugh at me.

I was the pilot of my own plane and flew around the world,

and everywhere I went people were happy to see me and no one asked where I was from. I was a movie star, and my character never died. I was a scientist, surrounded by test tubes and beakers, bunsen burners hissing blue flames as I received the Nobel Prize.

In my secret life I drove a convertible, and my house at the end of a long, sinuous driveway overlooked miles of green, rolling hills where it never snowed. I lived alone in my hilltop house, surrounded by books that I didn't have to return to the library. And every room was tidy, though I never cleaned.

In my secret life I wasn't Puerto Rican. I wasn't American. I wasn't anything. I spoke every language in the world, so I was never confused about what people said and could be understood by everyone. My skin was no particular color, so I didn't stand out as black, white, or brown.

I lived this secret life every night as I dozed into sleep, and every morning I resisted opening my eyes to the narrow bed in the narrow room I shared with Delsa, my chest tight with surprise and disappointment that it was all a dream.

⁓

"Eee, eee, eee, eee." I enunciated the vowels as Dr. Dycke, the head of the drama department, instructed. "Ay, ay, ay, ay. Eee, eee, eee, eee."

Raymond peeked around the door jamb. "What you doin'?"

"Practicing. Eee, ay, eee, ay, eee."

"Why?"

"So I can learn to speak English without an accent."

"Oh." He went away.

"Eee, eee, ay, ay, eee, eee, ay, ay."

A few minutes later Edna appeared at the door. "What you doin'?"

"Practicing. Eee. Eee. Eee."

"Practicing what?"

"Ask Raymond!" I closed the door on her face. "Ay. Ay. Ay.

Oo. Oo. Oo." The door opened. "Gettata here!" I screamed, then, "Oh, it's you."

"I have to find something," Delsa pointed at the dresser.

I backed up to let her through. "Eeu. Oo. Eeu. Oo. Ay."

"What *are* you doing?" She pulled a clean shirt from the drawer.

"That's it," I pushed her into the front room. "Everybody here!" I shouted. "Héctor! Norma! Mami! Tata!"

"What do you want?" Norma called from the back of the apartment.

Mami appeared from the kitchen. "What's all the yelling?"

"I want everyone here, so I can say this once."

"Say what?" Raymond asked.

"Norma! Héctor! Alicia! Get over here!"

"Quiet," Mami snapped. "Franky's sleeping."

"Hold on. I'm not as fast as I used to be." Tata shuffled toward the front room.

As everyone settled on the beds, the floor, the sofa, I began. "I have a class called voice and diction where I'm learning to talk without an accent."

"Why? Don't you want to sound Puerto Rican?" Héctor smirked.

"Let her speak," Tata said.

"It's part of my schoolwork," I pierced Héctor with a look.

"It sounded like you were imitating animals," Edna scoffed, and everyone laughed.

"Ha, ha, very funny." Unsmiling, I waited for them to settle. "I have to practice, and I can't have you interrupt me every five seconds to ask what I'm doing. So if you hear any weird sounds coming from the room, I'm doing my homework. Okay?"

"Is this what the yelling was about?" Mami asked.

"Yes. The kids were bothering me." I glared at Edna, Raymond, and Delsa. They looked at Mami, who stared at me hard. For a minute, she seemed about to scold me for making a big fuss out of nothing. But she turned to the kids.

"Let your sister be when she's doing her homework," she warned.

"It sounds like a zoo in there," Norma protested.

"Go to the other side of the apartment when she's practicing."

I backed into the bedroom, followed by Norma's "But it's not fair."

It wasn't. Since I'd started Performing Arts High School, Mami favored me. If I was reading and complained that the television was too loud, she made the kids turn it down. If I wanted to go to bed early, everyone was moved to the kitchen, where they could make a racket and I wouldn't hear. If I brought home a list of school supplies, Mami didn't say we had no money. She gave me enough to buy them or she'd get them for me without complaints about the cost. I knew how hard she worked to support us, so I didn't abuse her. But I felt guilty that so much of what little we had was spent on me. And I dreaded the price.

"I live for my children," Mami asserted. I was certain that no matter how hard I worked, I'd never be able to repay all she'd given up so that I could have what I needed.

Mami had dropped out of elementary school and didn't let us forget what a mistake she had made by not pursuing an education. While she never complained that we were a burden, her voice quivered when she told us it was hard to be both mother and father to eight children. Although she never talked about them, she must have had dreams once, but I was born, and every year after that, when one of my sisters or brothers was born, those dreams ebbed further and further as she focused on making sure we had dreams of our own.

"What do you want to be when you grow up?" she'd ask.

"A doctor," Delsa answered. She had high marks in school, better than mine, especially in math and science. And it was more likely that she'd be a doctor than that I'd ever be a good actress.

"A race car driver," Héctor announced, his eyes bright, his hands around an invisible steering wheel. At eleven years old, Héctor already worked at the pizzeria next door. Every few days

he brought home a couple of pizzas with plenty of sausages and pepperoni that Gino, the owner, gave him for us.

"Your son is a good worker," Gino told Mami, "You raised him right." Mami beamed at the compliment, and Héctor worked harder, and at the end of the week he gave Mami most of what he'd earned.

"And you, Raymond," Mami urged, "what do you want to be when you grow up?"

"A policeman," responded Raymond. "And I'll give you a ticket if you drive fast on my street," he warned Héctor. Raymond's foot, after three years of treatments, had healed, his limp gone. It was easy to imagine him in uniform, strutting down a street, looking for bad guys.

"I'll have my own beauty parlor," Alicia declared. At nine, Alicia already knew how to form her thick, black, wavy hair into many styles by skillful use of brush, comb, and bobby pins. "And I'll give you a permanent for free!"

Edna, who spent hours drawing curvaceous women in bizarre outfits added, "I'm going to have a dress store. And you can get all the clothes you want. For free!"

"Wow! I'm going to be a rich old woman," Mami laughed, and we giggled at the image of Mami being old. It was impossible to imagine she'd ever look any different than she looked then, her black hair tousled, the curls hugging her freckled cheeks.

When we talked like this, Don Julio and Tata watched with bemused expressions, as if they could see into the future and knew what our lives would really be like. They, unlike Mami, were old, and even through the haze of cigarettes that surrounded them and the slurred speech after too much beer or wine, they seemed wise in a way Mami didn't.

"Don't count your chickens . . ." Tata began, and she didn't have to finish to confirm what I'd already learned was true: that to announce what was to be was to jinx it.

Mami, Tata, and Don Julio often told me how smart I was, but I interpreted their compliments as wishful thinking. My grades

were average to low, and I'd failed geometry, which meant summer school and no job. I'd learned English quickly, but that was no surprise, since at Performing Arts we analyzed, memorized, and recited some of the best works written in the English language. My sisters and brothers hadn't the benefit of Performing Arts and could speak the language as well as I did, though with a Brooklyn accent.

Mami was proud that I went into the city every day by myself, returned when expected, was watchful that *"algo"* wouldn't happen. But I never admitted how scared I was early in the morning walking down our dark streets to the subway. I didn't mention that men exposed themselves, that sometimes they took advantage of a crowded subway to press themselves against me, or to let their hands wander to parts of my body no one should touch unless I asked them to. I didn't report the time I was chased from the subway station to the door of the school by a woman waving an umbrella who screamed "Dirty spick, dirty fucking spick, get off my street." I never told Mami that I was ashamed of where we lived, that in the *Daily News* and the *Herald American* government officials called our neighborhood "the ghetto," our apartment building "a tenement." I swallowed the humiliation when those same newspapers, if they carried a story with the term "Puerto Rican" in it, were usually describing a criminal. I didn't tell Mami that although she had high expectations for us, outside our door the expectations were lower, that the rest of New York viewed us as dirty spicks, potential muggers, drug dealers, prostitutes.

Mami was happy that I, at sixteen years of age, and now *"casi mujer,"* almost a woman, showed no interest in boys.

"She's too smart to get involved with those good-for-nothings around here," she asserted, when she knew I was listening.

And I didn't argue, although quality was not the issue. There were no boys my age in our neighborhood. And in school, some of the boys were homosexual, while those who weren't had no interest in girls like me. I was poor, talented enough not to embarrass myself on a stage, but only good enough to play Cleopatra

and other exotic characters. When the subject of dating came up in social studies class, I admitted that my mother didn't allow me to date unless chaperoned. That ensured no boy in the entire grade would ask. What was the point? If I asked Mami to let me date, I'd get a lecture about how boys only want one thing, and I wasn't willing to give it to anyone. All I had to do was look around me to know what happened to a girl who let a man take the place of an education.

In the cramped, noisy apartment where my mother struggled to keep us safe, where my grandmother tried to obliterate her pain with alcohol, where my sisters and brothers planned and invented their future, I improvised. When it hurt, I cried silent tears. And when good things came my way, I accepted them gratefully but quietly, afraid that enjoying them too much would make them vanish like a drop of water into a desert.

"I don't care if the whole world is going."

Mami emerged from mourning gradually. She curled her hair one day, or topped her black skirt with a gray blouse instead of a black one the next. Little by little, she abandoned drab clothes for dark blues and browns; then, a few at a time, she dug out the flower prints and bold patterns she favored. The high heels reappeared, along with bright lipsticks, jangly earrings, necklaces, nail polish. Her smiles returned. Small, shy smiles at first, then full ones, her whole face brightening, as if she were trying on her old self a little at a time, to see if it fit.

We adjusted our mourning to her reactions. We played the radio softly, and if she didn't say anything, we raised the volume. We danced around the apartment or sang in the shower, quiet *boleros,* and when she didn't object, *merengues* or Mexican *rancheras.* Visits from relatives became more frequent and lasted longer. La Muda came with Luigi, who looked sadder every day, even though he and La Muda now lived together in an apartment in her mother's building. Luigi said he didn't like New York. He couldn't find work and complained that the cold winters gave him arthritis. And it was true. His bony fingers, which once flipped through a deck of cards with lightning speed, were now clumsy, hindered by bumps and bulges around the knuckles. He no longer performed his magic but sat quietly when he came to visit, hands folded on his lap.

Tío Chico disappeared for weeks at a time, then showed up

in the middle of the day, sometimes sober, but most often drunk. Tata cleaned him up, cooked rich *asopaos* and strong coffee to help him get over his hangovers. He spent a few days with us, sleeping mostly, and then he fixed a meaty *sancocho* or rooster stew with red wine and lots of cilantro. He was a wonderful cook, and he, Tata and Mami each cooked a different dish for Sunday supper and then pretended to argue over whose food was better. Our downstairs neighbor, who was critical of the noise we made when we first moved in, now came up daily to sit with Mami or Tata and often stayed to dinner. Her eldest son, Jimmy, was a little younger than me. He had a long, pimply face, close-cropped hair, a wispy mustache, and big ears. My sisters and brothers teased that Jimmy liked me, and when he came over, I stayed in my room so that the kids would leave me alone. Whenever he heard steps coming down the stairs, Jimmy peeked to see if it was me and then said he was going out too and walked with me to the bus stop where I caught a ride to summer school. Almost every day when I came back, he was on the corner of Rockaway Avenue, waiting to walk me home.

"Mami, can I go to Alma and Corazón's after school?" I asked one day. She said yes, and after that I visited my cousins daily to avoid Jimmy's hopeful face at the bus stop after I'd spent the morning in summer school struggling with triangle congruent theorems.

Weekends, Mami took us to the beach at Coney Island. Carrying blankets; coolers packed with ice, drinks, and food; a stack of towels; a couple of plastic buckets and spades, we trooped into a subway already filled with people similarly burdened. Once, the picnic started there when a child complained she was hungry, and in no time, everyone was dipping into the fried chicken and the potato salad and passing it around to total strangers who were equally eager to share their coleslaw and sliced ham and cheese sandwiches.

The long street leading to the beach was lined with kiosks selling hot dogs and hamburgers, sodas, ice cream, newspapers

and magazines, sun tan lotion, stuffed animals. There was a wide boardwalk with games and more food stands, and, best of all, an amusement park with thrilling rides and a world-famous roller coaster.

But we weren't allowed to buy anything at the kiosks, because it was too expensive, nor could we go on the boardwalk, where "*algo*" could happen, or to the amusement park from which terrified screams came every few minutes as the roller coaster climbed and dipped on its rickety tracks. Holding hands, we fought the crowds toward the beach and, once there, pushed our way to a patch of sand big enough to settle our stuff and stretch a couple of blankets for one adult and seven children. Tata, who never came with us, kept Franky at home.

None of us could swim, so we looked for a spot near the lifeguard, although we wondered how he could tell anyone was drowning among the thousands of people screaming and jumping in and out of the water because it was fun to scream when you jump in and out of the water.

In order for the younger kids to play in the waves, someone watched them, while one of us sat on our blanket to make sure no one stole the cooler full of food, Mami's wallet, and our street clothes. I usually volunteered for this, as I found the beach, with its interminable, crashing waves, terrifying. The only time I'd been in that cold ocean, jumping waves with Delsa and Norma, a giant swell had thrust me under a ton of water and dragged me away. I was rescued not by the muscular lifeguard, who never saw me drowning, but by my mother and a bystander, who hauled me out sputtering and coughing, near death from humiliation.

One time after a day at the beach, we persuaded Mami to take us to the amusement park. We packed our stuff, took turns carrying the cooler and blankets, and wandered from one ride to the next, deciding which one we'd choose if we could only go on one, when Mami realized *algo had* happened: Edna was missing. We retraced our steps, called her name, searched in ever-tighter circles toward the spot where one of us always waited surrounded by our things. Mami was hysterical, calling for a police officer, but

there was none to be seen. Finally, one appeared, and in between sobs we explained that Edna was lost, described her, and waited for him to find her. He told us to stay where we were, disappeared for a few moments, then came back saying he had "called it in," an action that didn't satisfy Mami, who wailed that he was doing nothing while her child was in mortal danger. A few people gathered around. We explained what was wrong, told them what Edna was wearing, when she was last seen. Several men and boys went to search for her while their wives and girlfriends stayed with us, rubbing Mami's shoulder and telling her everything would be fine.

Then the crowd parted. An enormous chestnut horse, mounted by a burly policeman galloped toward us. Sitting in front of the policeman, her face ecstatic, was Edna. The officer handed her down to Mami, who hugged her, kissed her, thanked the police officers, the bystanders, God, and the Virgins for saving her little girl, while we pestered Edna about what it was like to ride a horse.

"It was fun," she said, "but his hair tickled my legs."

Back home, we joked and laughed about Edna's adventure, but for the next few nights, I fantasized about being rescued by a good-looking man in uniform atop a horse. I imagined the wind fanning my hair, his arm around my waist, and the way the horse's coat tickled my bare legs. I seized the image of the policeman and his horse as if it were a gift and ignored Mami's litany of the *algos* that could have happened if Edna hadn't been found on time.

~~~~~~

Mami was definitely out of mourning when she wanted to go dancing.

"A group from the factory is going," she told Tata.

"Hummph," Tata responded, an unspoken "I don't care if the whole world is going, you're not."

"Tito Puente is playing." Mami added casually. Tata dragged on her cigarette.

From where I sat reading, I watched Mami sorting socks

and underwear from the clean-laundry basket. Every so often, her eyelids flicked up to gauge Tata's mood. It was funny to see her behave the way I did when I wanted something: the not-so-subtle hints, the "all my friends are doing it" justification, the mention of a celebrity. Tata was as unimpressed with Mami's technique as Mami was with mine.

After a few minutes, she started again. "The girls need to be exposed to those situations, so they know how to behave in them."

Tata turned her head slowly toward Mami, fixed her with a withering stare. "You want to expose them to a nightclub so that they know how to behave in one?" Tata asked, each word enunciated with such clarity, she could have been one of Dr. Dycke's star voice and diction students, had Dr. Dycke spoken Spanish.

"Negi is studying to be an *artista*, she should meet other *artistas*," Mami said, inspecting a pair of socks.

"Those places aren't for decent women," Tata concluded after a while, and that seemed the end of it, because Mami got up, gathered the balled socks into the basket, and went to distribute them in the appropriate drawers.

She didn't give up. For days Mami badgered Tata until she agreed to watch the kids. Tata lived with us and rarely left the apartment, so it wasn't as if she had any plans on Saturday nights. But Mami didn't assume that Tata was our babysitter just because she was there, and she never left the building without telling Tata where she was going and when she'd be back.

Saturday night as we got ready, my sisters and brothers came in and out of the room as Mami and I dressed, giving unrequested opinions about what to do with our hair, makeup, and clothes. They were as excited as we were, as if seeing Mami so happy, dressed up for the first time in two years, were something to celebrate. When it was time to leave, Don Julio insisted on walking us to the station. He watched us go up the stairs to the train platform and waited until we were out of sight before heading back to Pitkin Avenue.

The club was on the Upper West Side. It looked like our neighborhood, with businesses on the street level and apartments

on the higher floors of four- and five-story buildings, only there were more people on the street. When we climbed up from the subway, we heard the music coming from blacked-out windows above a restaurant. Men loitered in front of the door leading to the club, their clean, pressed shirts tucked into belted pants with stiff seams. They eyed us, mumbled compliments. Mami grabbed my hand, pulled me close, practically dragged me inside, up steep stairs toward the deafening music. Our hands were stamped by a large woman in a tight, short, low-cut dress that displayed more flesh than I had in my entire body. When we entered the club, Mami craned her neck this way and that, a panicked expression on her face, as if, now that we'd come so far, she wasn't sure if this was such a great idea. She held my hand very tight, my fingers cramped, and towed me as she wove in and out of the crowd looking for her friends. When she spotted them, her grip eased, and I jiggled my fingers to get the feeling back.

I'd never been in such a large room with so many people, so many perfumes and after-shave colognes mingling with the pungent odor of cigarette smoke, hair spray, rum, and sweat. The women were dressed in glittery outfits, the men had slick and shiny hair, jewelry sparkled in the dark. The hot, steamy air of too many bodies too close together was dizzying.

The dance floor was in the middle of the room. It was packed with men and women whose hips seemed detached from their torsos, whose arms undulated in, out, around each other like serpents in a pit. Mami introduced me to her friends, but the music was so loud that I couldn't catch anyone's name. It appeared that the woman in the green sequined dress was with the man in the beige *guayabera*, and the woman in the pink taffeta was with the dark man wearing a baby blue suit.

The minute we sat, two men extended their hands in front of us. I looked at Mami to make sure it was okay to accept, and she nodded as she got up with her partner, a short, round man with a horseshoe of hair around a shiny pate. My partner was younger, skinny, smelled of cigarettes and sweet cologne.

I'd never seen Mami dance, had no idea where she learned

to do it, but she was good. Lips parted in a half-smile, eyes ablaze, cheeks flushed, she twirled and whirled as her partner guided her here, then there, pulled her in close and spun her in a tight circle. It was distracting to see her smile at unknown men who held her hand, pressed their fingers against her back, guided her by the elbow to our table.

If seeing Mami dance was new, experiencing strange men so close was newer. Even though I was already sixteen and *casi mujer*, I'd never had a boyfriend, had never been kissed by anyone not related. I didn't think I was ugly, but no one had called me pretty. At home, my sisters Delsa and Norma were frequently told they were lovely, while I was called "intelligent."

But on the dance floor, every woman who can dance is beautiful, and every man with loose hips and grace is dashing, regardless of facial features or body types. When my partner took me out and led me through the complex paces of a *salsa* number, I felt beautiful for the first time in my life. It was not what I wore, nor how much makeup I'd managed to get away with. The feeling came from the heat generated by the dance itself, had nothing to do with the way I looked but everything to do with the way I moved. I became the complex rhythms, aware only of the joy of moving freely, gracefully, in and out of the arms of a man I'd never seen, to music I'd never heard.

I danced with many men: short, tall, skinny, fat, old, young, dark, light. And so did Mami. Sometimes a man who took me out asked her to dance the next number. Or they danced with her, then asked me, and through hand gestures and exaggerated lip movements reminiscent of La Muda, complimented me on having such a pretty mother and her on having a daughter who danced so well.

The band played long, loud sets. I was surprised that it really was Tito Puente. I'd thought Mami had made that up to impress Tata, who was a fan. When Tito Puente's musicians took a break, another band came on and played slower numbers, as if to give the dancers a rest with a few *boleros* before the *salsa* started again.

The dance lasted into the small hours, and when we came out, I was practically deaf and so thirsty my tongue stuck to the roof of my mouth. Mami's friends invited us to an all-night diner down the street, and we took over two booths overlooking Broadway and ate fried eggs, pancakes with syrup, sausages, and many cups of coffee. From time to time Mami watched me to see if I showed any signs of exhaustion, but I was exhilarated, and only worried that we'd look like *jíbaras* on the subway at six in the morning in our party clothes.

We said goodbye to her friends, who informed us there was another dance the following week somewhere else. "We'll see," Mami said.

We arrived home as everyone was waking up with their questions about whether we'd had a good time and whether I'd found a boyfriend. We drank some coffee with the kids and with Tata, who glowered at our disheveled hair, streaked makeup, sweaty clothes.

"Yes, we had a good time," Mami allowed. "I think next time Delsa and Norma should come, don't you think?"

I agreed they'd enjoy it but hoped she would take me too, since I was the eldest. She smiled and dragged herself to sleep, while I sat up with Delsa and Norma, giving them minute descriptions of everything I'd seen and done the previous night. We agreed that if Mami was going to take us dancing, we should practice at home, and I promised to teach them the new steps I'd learned from my partners. When I finally got to bed, I lay awake a long time, revisiting every moment of the evening, while my body jerked in uncontrollable spasms of unreleased energy. I fell asleep lulled by the sounds of a remembered *bolero*, certain I'd never been happier than I was that night.

Now we went dancing almost every Saturday. Although Delsa and Norma were only fourteen and thirteen years old, it wasn't unusual

for there to be younger kids at the clubs. People brought their entire families: mothers, fathers, grandparents, children so young they toddled around, shook their diapered bottoms during the *merengues* while everyone clapped and encouraged them along.

Admission was half price for children under eighteen, free for those under twelve, which was how Mami was able to afford to bring us three oldest girls and, sometimes, Héctor. Drinks were sold à la carte, or one could buy a *servicio*, which consisted of a bottle of rum, two bottles of Coke, a bucket of ice, plastic cups, and sliced lemons. There were long tables arranged around the dance floor, eight folding chairs per table, a stack of cocktail napkins, and two aluminum ashtrays on each. Some places sold Puerto Rican fried food like *alcapurrías* and *pastelillos*, or bags of potato or corn chips. But most served only drinks. The only way to guarantee we could get a table was to order a *servicio*, so if we came alone, we always bought it, drank the Cokes, and brought the rum home for Tata and Don Julio.

We only went to clubs with live music, usually in the Upper West Side or El Barrio, but we never ventured into the Bronx or Queens, because Mami didn't know her way around those boroughs. At some dances we met people we'd seen at other clubs, and sometimes, if we had a particularly good partner, Delsa, Norma, or I told him where we'd be the next week. We didn't think of them as boyfriends. The only time we saw them was at the clubs, and the relationship was monitored by Mami, who, with a glance or a movement of her lips, made it clear we were getting too chummy with whomever we were dancing with and to ease up or she'd take us home.

Although Tío Chico had touched my breast once, and though I'd seen several penises dangling helplessly from the opened zippers of flashers, or triumphantly erect from a brazen truck driver's lap, I'd never come so close to men as I did on the dance floor. Some danced so close that they got an erection. When faced with this situation, we were to give them the benefit of the doubt. If they pulled away sheepishly, it was an accident.

If they pressed tighter, they were being fresh. We called them *rompemedias*, stocking rippers, because they danced so close, the friction made our nylons run. A man who got fresh risked being abandoned on the dance floor. A man on the dance floor alone was noticed by everyone and was sure to have trouble finding other partners. So most men were polite, maintaining a respectful distance while still managing to dance a *bolero* with enough heat to make a *puta* blush.

There were also the *pulpos*, octopuses, whose hands, instead of guiding us in intricate dance combinations, crawled over our backs, down to the buttocks, up under our arms, near our breasts, while their legs tried to insinuate themselves between ours. These men too were to be avoided.

Every once in a while, I didn't withdraw when a man got excited. We'd be dancing a slow number, and when I felt him growing, I pressed closer, to test his reaction. If he aggressively thrust himself toward me, or if, octopuslike, his hands and legs strayed where they shouldn't, I drew away, because it didn't feel as if I was giving him something, but as if he thought he was entitled to it. I liked the man who gasped in surprise, who tenderly pulled me closer, moved his hips in discreet slow circles around and against mine without missing a beat. I savored the power of being able to excite a man, to feel his hot breath against my ear, slow at first, then sharper, hotter, our bodies pressed into a sinuous whole that moved rhythmically across the crowded, steamy floor. I lost all sense of time, embraced and embracing, beautiful, graceful, trembling with sensations possible only this way, in this place.

When the *bolero* was over, my partner wanted to stay for the next dance. But I insisted he bring me back to my table. I didn't trust the feelings that made me dance that way, was embarrassed I let it go so far. I refused to look him in the eyes, afraid of what I'd see there. If he asked me to dance again, I refused, or told him I'd only dance fast numbers. I never acknowledged any part in what we'd done.

Later, shame was replaced with the thrill of his body against

mine, his face an anonymous blur, until all that was left was the tingle on my skin, the heat between my legs, the slow, billowing rhythm of the *bolero*.

Sometimes, in spite of Mami's efforts to keep us safe from a violent world, *algo* happened. We mourned President Kennedy's assassination with the rest of the country and bawled when John-John saluted the coffin as it went past. The radio and television brought us news of how at least thirty neighbors heard Kitty Genovese screaming as she was being stabbed to death and no one came to help. For weeks afterward, Mami was in a state if we so much as went downstairs to the pizza shop. But she wasn't the only one who worried. When she got off the train from work, Don Julio or Héctor was waiting at the bottom of the steps to walk her home.

The scariest thing to happen during that summer of 1964 was when whole neighborhoods like ours turned against themselves. We read about it in the papers, heard about it on the radio, saw the fuzzy, black-and-white images of people who looked like us running down streets that looked like ours, setting fires, beating each other, being chased by police — some of them on horses like the one that rescued Edna. The officers, all white men, dragged the dark-skinned rioters off the sidewalks littered with broken glass and garbage. They beat them with nightsticks, pushed them into police cars, then drove away followed by a crowd screaming and cursing, their faces twisted into grimaces.

Mami refused to go to work after news of a riot, and I didn't go to summer school. Our apartment was stifling, but we weren't allowed out. Don Julio, whose grown daughters lived in another part of Brooklyn, brought news of buildings set on fire, of crowds breaking store windows and taking whatever they could carry.

"I saw a man run off with a color television," he said. "And a woman and three kids dragged a sofa out of a furniture store and then went in and got a table and chairs."

We thought it was funny, but Mami didn't. *"Desordenados,"* she muttered. "If I catch one of you kids doing a thing like that . . ."

One hot night, we had just gone to bed when we heard screams, breaking glass, alarms going off.

"Get away from there! Turn out the lights!" Mami screeched when she saw us leaning out of the windows to see what was going on. A couple of blocks away a mob ran toward Rockaway Avenue, armed with bats and tire irons, banging everything in sight. She pushed us into the middle room, checked that the doors were locked, picked up the phone.

"Should we call the police?" I asked, ready to translate for her. "No," she whispered, "I just want to make sure it's working."

We huddled in the dark, listened for steps running up the stairs, or for the crack of splintering wood, or for an explosion, anything to indicate that the violence had reached our door. When we heard police sirens, Héctor crept over to the window, peeked out, crept back.

"They stopped them down the street. Nothing's going on out there."

After a while, Mami went to see. I followed, even though she whispered that we should stay where we were. The street was deserted. A block away, a couple of police cars were parked in the middle of the avenue, their lights flashing, their radios droning chatter. In the other direction there were more police cars, but no people. The sidewalks were littered with trash from upturned garbage cans and shimmering fragments of glass. Mami closed the windows, drew the curtains.

"Everyone back to bed," she ordered.

It was impossible to sleep. For hours the shrill store alarms kept us awake. Also the waiting. I was sure if I fell asleep I'd wake up in the middle of a fire or of a mob looting the drugstore on the street floor. But daylight came and nothing more had happened. The merchants whose windows were broken placed plywood over them, scrawled notes, or spray-painted "OPEN FOR BUSINESS" or "CLOSED UNTIL FURTHER NOTICE," depending on the damage.

When we shopped, they watched us with distrustful eyes, as if we'd been part of the violence, and we stared back, resentful that no one was immune from their suspicions and anger.

"As soon as I save enough for two months' rent and a security deposit," Mami sighed, "we're moving."

The night before the summer school geometry Regents exam, Ray Barretto was playing at a club in El Barrio.

"You stay home and study," Mami said.

"I don't need to. I have good marks in every exam I've taken."

"But if you fail this one, you have to repeat the course again."

"I won't fail. I know the stuff now."

"Fine, then, if you're sure."

"I'm sure."

I danced until my feet hurt. I danced until my throat was hoarse from yelling to be heard above the music. I danced until my eyes smarted from the smoke in the room, and from the melted makeup that dripped into them. I danced until my eardrums throbbed like Ray Barretto's congas. When the music stopped, we followed the crowd outside and found ourselves in the middle of a riot.

Exhausted and still dressed in our party clothes, high heels, and inexpensive but showy jewelry, we pressed together against the wall of a building and watched a crowd of men run past with bats, sticks, the covers of garbage cans. The entrance to the subway was half a block away in the opposite direction, and when the crowd thinned, we ran toward it and made it down the stairs as another angry group turned the corner. People who were at the dance were down in the subway station, and there was talk that the mob would come after us. The men in their *guayaberas* and pastel suits formed a line in front of the women and children, who converged at the far end of the platform, anxiously searching the dark tunnel for signs of a train. Above us, alarms shrieked, people screamed and cursed, cars screeched to a stop, glass shattered, and

heavy objects thudded to the ground. After a long time, sirens wailed. When the train finally came, we ran into it, pushed into the farthest corners, and didn't feel safe until the doors closed. As soon as the train moved, everyone relaxed, laughed at the foolishness of running from a crowd with no interest in us. But it was lame laughter; our fear was real; and although Mami, Delsa, Norma, and I made jokes and laughed along with everyone else, we didn't mention what had happened at home. It was too close an escape to joke about.

Three hours after we came home from our night of Ray Barretto and its aftermath, I chewed on a pencil trying to remember what postulates were and why x equaled z. But it was no use. The formulas, theorems, and hypotheses had fled. I failed the Regents exam for a second time, which meant I'd have to repeat geometry for the third time in two years.

Once school started, our dancing weekends came to an end. There was a lot of work and expense in getting seven children ready for school. We wore one another's clothes and received hand-me-downs from relatives, but Mami always bought each of us a new outfit and shoes for the first day of school. The girls got new book bags and new hairstyles. The boys got cropped haircuts, new pants, white shirts, and ties for Assembly. But clothes weren't the only expense. Pencils and pens had to be purchased, as did ruled pages, binders, construction paper, crayons, adhesive tape, glue. Teachers sent home lists of other supplies: gym suits and sneakers, maps, protractors, rulers, sketchbooks, dictionaries. Then there was carfare for me and Delsa, who had started high school, and a small allowance for us to buy a soda or a cup of coffee. As the weather cooled, we needed coats, gloves, boots, hats.

Sometimes, even with a full-time job and whatever overtime

she was able to put in, Mami wasn't able to cover all the back-to-school costs. Besides giving up our dancing weekends, we gave up the telephone, canned food, sweets. When we still fell behind, we went to welfare to request an emergency allowance for winter clothes, electricity, or to meet a couple of months' rent until things went back to normal. Mami had to take a day off work, lose that day's wages, then be told that welfare didn't help unless she had no job. Once, a welfare worker asked me why I didn't help my mother.

"I'm in high school," I responded, taken aback.

"You can work part-time."

"I don't have time. The school is an hour and a half from our apartment. . . ."

"What's going on?" Mami asked, when she noticed the welfare worker had lost interest in her to argue with me.

"He says I should get a job."

"She job school," Mami informed the welfare worker. Every once in a while she spoke a few phrases in English that were very effective. When she did, and if the person she was speaking to understood, she beamed with pride but didn't push her luck by trying any more.

On the way home, I told Mami that maybe I should get a job after school.

"I don't want you out on the street after dark."

"But Héctor has a job . . ."

"He's *casi un hombre*. It's different."

Héctor was twelve, long and scrawny and not "almost a man" from what I could see. But he was male and I was female, and that was the difference. As much as we could have used whatever money I might be able to bring in, it wasn't worth the risk of my being away from home after dark. *Algo* could happen.

"She's not exactly Method."

I wanted to play Scout in *To Kill a Mockingbird,* Eliza in *Pygmalion,* Laura in *The Glass Menagerie,* Sophocles' Antigone. But again I was cast as Cleopatra, this time with William as Julius Caesar.

Harvey, my first Caesar, played the character as a soldier, all macho bluster and strut. William played Caesar as an emperor used to being obeyed. I dug out the yellow tablecloth costume, tried to find a different approach to the same part. My first Cleopatra was kittenish and flirtatious; this one I decided to play as a cunning queen meeting an equally duplicitous opponent.

It was hard to get into character. The few times I tried to get away with what I wasn't supposed to, I was caught, so cunning didn't come easily.

"That's where acting comes in," Laura Figueroa affirmed when I explained my dilemma. She was one of the best actresses in the class, capable of any role, any accent, classic to contemporary. Her specialty, however, was old ladies. Not that she preferred playing them, but every time we were cast, I was Cleopatra and she was old. "Maybe you can model her character on someone you know." I shook my head. "Well, then, a combination of people."

"I wish I'd seen Elizabeth Taylor's Cleopatra."

"It might help, but she's not exactly Method."

At Performing Arts, we scorned movie actors. They "indi-

cated," and their acting relied on minute facial and eye gestures that were often no more than mannerisms. They seldom worked with their voices and seemed more worried about how they looked than creating a character.

It was crucial in our development as actors, we were told, to learn the difference between self-consciousness and self-awareness. A self-conscious actor was too earnest, too vigilant of his or her performance. Self-aware ones trusted that the weeks or months of preparation for a role helped them become the character, while maintaining a level of alertness that allowed them to react to the other actors and to the situation. A performance, we were told, was a living thing that changed and developed every time the actor stepped on stage.

I understood the concepts, observed and stored moments and situations in my "sense memory" for later, when I'd need to draw upon them. But I was convinced that my life didn't provide enough variety to make me a good actress. How could it, when every move I made was monitored by Mami? But whenever I so much as considered going against her wishes, a little voice went off in my head to remind me that between her and the rest of the world was nothing but hostile eyes and low expectations. Were I to fall, only my mother would be there to pick me up. Yes, there were seven sisters and brothers, but they were younger and more helpless. Yes, there was Tata, but she was often drunk. The other relatives were there, but they had children of their own, lives of their own, problems of their own. There was my father, far away in Puerto Rico, with his new wife and his new kids and his new life. If I didn't have Mami, I'd be alone. And at seventeen, I didn't want to be alone. Not yet.

My drama teacher, Mrs. Provet, called me to the office one day and asked if I'd be interested in a job on weekends, working as an usher in a theater.

"I can't work at night."

"It's on Sunday afternoons."

I accepted, happy that I'd finally make some money, eager for any exposure to the theater, even as an usher. I'd see actors at work, study their technique, and maybe get some pointers.

The job didn't require an interview. I was to report to the theater at noon on the following Sunday.

The address was in lower Manhattan. I came out of the subway station in front of a row of shabby two- and three-story buildings, not a theater marquee in sight. I looked at the directions and read the address again, walked up and down the block until I found a tattered awning over a dark doorway that led to a set of stairs. I was nervous, reluctant to go up, uncertain of where I was. The *algos* that could happen in dim halls of unfamiliar buildings repeated in my brain, but I silenced them, took a breath, and rose. At the top of the stairs were three doors and a ticket window. I knocked on the door marked "Office" and was greeted by a bearded gentleman dressed in black.

"I'm from Performing Arts," I introduced myself. "The usher."

"Oh, yes," he said, "Come with me." He led me down the hall. "I'm Mr. Rosenberg," he said, as he opened the middle set of doors. "I'll be selling tickets, and you'll be right here." He noticed me hesitate, looked in, and saw that the room was dark. "Uh, sorry," he said, flipping a switch, and we were in the back of a small theater.

"The numbers are on the armrests. See? You show people to their seats and make sure they get a program."

He rummaged behind a curtain against the back wall and pulled out a box full of printed pages in a script I couldn't read, but which I knew to be Hebrew. The stark black characters were similar to those in storefronts all over New York, and I'd learned that כָּשֵׁר meant that the establishment served kosher food, although I wasn't sure what kosher food was.

"Fold them in half like this," he demonstrated. "The play begins in an hour. You can watch from any seat that's free in the

back." He pulled out a flashlight from behind the curtain and handed it to me. "If people come late, wait until a change of scene to bring them to their seats. At the end, make sure they don't forget their belongings."

I sat on one of the hard wooden chairs that flipped up and folded the programs. When I was done, I walked down the stepped aisles to the foot of the stage. It wasn't raised high, only about knee height on me. The set was a kitchen in an apartment. A door stage right led to stairs going down offstage, and a window stage left led to a fire escape. A table covered in a checkered cloth, three chairs, a stove, curtains on the windows, and some dishes completed the set. A bare light bulb lit the stage, and I felt a sudden thrill. This was a real stage, in a real theater, and I was about to see a live performance by real actors.

In a few minutes, there was a shuffle of feet up the stairs. Mr. Rosenberg opened the doors, and I ran to my post at the back of the theater, took a bunch of programs in my hand, and handed them out as people showed me their tickets. They were mostly elderly, very orderly and polite, and seemed grateful to be shown to their seats, though it was clear that many of them were familiar with the layout and knew where they were going. Everyone was as dressed up as Mami and my sisters and I were when we went dancing. The women wore wigs, jewelry, furs. The men wore suits and hats, which they perched on their knees the minute they sat down. There was a strong scent of mothballs, cigars, and perfume.

When the lights went down, I stood in the back of the theater. The actors entered, dressed in the clothes I associated with the owners of secondhand stores and delis on Graham Avenue. They spoke Yiddish, a language that sounded familiar because I'd heard it in the *marketa*, at the check-cashing place, on the streets of Williamsburg.

Even though I didn't understand a word, I was caught up in the action on the stage. The drama revolved around a family whose son had strayed from the traditions they had brought from

their home country to the United States. He'd fallen in love with an American girl, and his family refused to meet her.

At the end of act 1, I applauded vigorously, along with the rest of the audience. A woman in front turned and smiled in my direction. When she passed me on the way out during the intermission, she asked if I understood any of it.

"I don't know the language, but I can follow the action. The actors are very good."

"Wonderful!" she said, and patted my hand.

When the second act began, a new character was introduced, and I was surprised to see Mr. Rosenberg on the stage. He played a grandfather or other older relative and made several impassioned speeches. At the end of act 2, he delivered a long monologue that brought the audience to its feet and had everyone, including me, in tears.

In act 3 the young man decided not to marry the American girl, and the play ended with the entire family on the stage around lighted candles singing a solemn, beautiful hymn. By this time I was sobbing, and the lady who had talked to me earlier came over with a Kleenex.

"Yiddish theater," she said, opening her arms in a dramatic gesture. "The best!" I thanked her, nodded agreement, and tried my best to clear the theater, but I was so distraught that I just sat in the back row crying and feeling stupid because I couldn't stop.

Mr. Rosenberg came out stage right, hopped down to the floor, made his way to me.

"I'm so sorry," I said, "I don't know what happened. It was so beautiful. Your performance. The song at the end. And the candles. I have no idea what you said. . . ." I blubbered on and on, wiped my face with the Kleenex, which by now was shreds in my fingers.

"It's all right," he said. "It's flattering," he added with a smile. He offered to introduce me to the actors and took me backstage to the cubicle dressing rooms. I shook each actor's hand, told them

how much I enjoyed the play. They looked at me curiously, and the woman who played Mamma touched my cheek. I was almost brought to tears again, but Mr. Rosenberg led me out.

"Come back in two hours," he said.

I ushered another show that day, and still the play moved me beyond words. For four Sundays in a row, I watched those actors perform the same play once in matinee and once in the early evening. No performance was the same twice. Their voices, their gestures, the level of concentration changed the dynamics each time they spoke their lines, making the play completely different and new.

Until then, a theatrical experience was a concept taught at Performing Arts, not one I'd had. But now I understood why my teachers at Performing Arts loved the theater so much, why they claimed the sacrifices were worth making.

After the sixth Sunday Mr. Rosenberg said he didn't need me anymore. "We're rehearsing for a couple of months," he said, "then we open another play." I was disappointed, told him to call the school when he needed me. A couple of months later, he did.

"Bring a handkerchief," he said, before he said goodbye. I did.

Mami was told about a dance in the Armory on Park Avenue. "It's been a while," she reasoned, "and it *is* almost Christmas."

I saved my ushering money for a dress and was allowed to shop alone.

"But don't come home with anything *estrámbolico*," Mami said.

"I don't want to look like a clown . . . maybe black."

"Ay, no! Don't get black." Mami had recently rid herself of mourning clothes. She was afraid that if she kept them, they'd bring bad luck. When I suggested she burn them, she flinched, and I understood that fire implied bad things for poor, dead,

Francisco. If she gave the clothes to someone not in mourning, they'd bring the recipient bad luck. So she stuffed them in a plastic bag, tied the bag with several knots so that the bad luck in them wouldn't escape, and put them out with the garbage.

"Red, then, since it's Christmas."

"Heaven forbid!" Tata said. Red clothes, she claimed, brought on heavy periods and, on a woman of childbearing age, miscarriages.

"I'm not planning to get pregnant any time soon," I reminded her.

"Still," she warned.

"Get something with all the colors in the rainbow," Edna suggested.

"Never mind, I'll figure it out," I replied. I used the excuse of looking for my dress to shop in Manhattan.

"Why can't you shop around here?" Mami asked, "or on Flatbush Avenue. They have lots of nice things."

But I didn't want to shop in Brooklyn. At Performing Arts, I'd learned that Brooklyn was not New York City. It was referred to as an "outer borough" by the mayor himself. Manhattan was the financial, theatrical, and artistic center of the United States. I wanted to be in it, to move from the margins into the center. I wanted to climb to the top of the Empire State Building, to gaze over the city and beyond it to the vast horizon that I knew existed but couldn't see from the ground in Brooklyn.

⁓

The dance at the Armory was the best we'd been to. Three bands played nonstop, and there were more Puerto Ricans than I'd ever seen in one enormous room. After the dance, Mami, Delsa, Norma, and I walked down Park Avenue looking for a place to eat, but there was none. The street, divided by an island of low bushes and scrawny trees, was mostly residential, and its businesses opened only during the day. Hungry as we were, we liked walking

on Park Avenue and, still giddy from the dance, laughed and joked and pretended to be rich ladies out for a stroll in the neighborhood. We left the Armory behind, but still we walked, our coats off our shoulders as if they were furs, our high heels clicking, our hands dangling limply from our wrists, toward an invisible *caballero.*

Lights flashed behind us. A police car pulled up ahead, and an officer climbed out and straddled the middle of the sidewalk like the sheriff in cowboy movies about to challenge the bank robber to a shoot-out.

"Good morning, ladies," he said. "May I direct you where you're going?" His fake-polite voice came out of a smirk, and his eyes, invisible under his cap, were like hands, roaming every inch of our bodies.

Mami placed herself between us and the cop, but she needed one of us to translate. Her face went from joy to panic in seconds, to the hard, serious expression she put on when she was afraid but had to be strong for the sake of the children. "Tell him we're just looking for a place to eat," she said to me, Delsa, or Norma, whoever spoke up. I jumped in front of her, smiled my most enchanting smile, and became Cleopatra, queen of the Nile.

"We were at a dance at the Armory, officer," I enunciated clearly. "It's such a nice evening, we decided to walk home."

"You live around here?" He tried to stare me down, but I held my noble bearing, though my knees shook.

"Yes, that way." I pointed with my whole arm, my whole body, to a faraway place, my palace, toward Brooklyn. Mami, Delsa, and Norma looked at me as if I had sprung horns and a tail. They pulled up and buttoned their coats, stood humbly before the police, hoping we hadn't done anything illegal and that I wasn't making it worse, while I prayed he wouldn't ask for an address.

"You were making a lot of noise," His voice lost its edge. "This is a residential neighborhood." Now he stated the obvious, somewhat sheepishly, I thought.

"What?" Mami yelled in English, as if to speak louder were to be better understood. "What the matter?" She sounded scared, definitely not like someone who lived on Park Avenue.

"We've been denounced for making too much noise," I said in Spanish, my voice low and even.

"What, you can't talk and laugh on Park Avenue?" Delsa snapped in Spanish, and I shot her a shut-up look. I turned to the officer.

"We'll keep it down." I, cunning Cleopatra, flapped my eyelids, smiled haughtily. "So sorry we disturbed the neighbors. Come on, girls." I waved them toward me and started to walk past him. "Thank you," I said, as the officer backed up to let us pass. Cleopatra, queen of the Nile, and her faithful retainers, who followed, puzzled, not certain we'd been dismissed by the law. I kept walking until I heard the patrol car door shut and saw it pull ahead and past us, down Park Avenue. The minute he was out of sight, we cracked up.

"How did you dare?" Mami laughed.

"I don't know. I didn't think . . . I just did it." We turned the corner away from Park Avenue, in case the police officer came around to see if we went into a building in the neighborhood.

"Wow, Negi, those acting classes are sure paying off," Norma said. "You made him believe we live on Park Avenue!"

I was elated. I'd just performed before the most critical and demanding audience I'd ever encounter — to rave reviews.

◦───◦

We went dancing again, not as often as in the summer, twice a month or so. At one of the clubs, Mami met, danced with, and fell in love with Don Carlos. He was gangly, with chocolate skin, a shy smile, a soft voice. He wore a dark suit with a white shirt and thin tie, and horn-rimmed rectangular glasses with green lenses. I thought he was blind. Why else would anyone wear dark glasses in an already dimly lit nightclub?

He danced with me, Delsa, and Norma, kept more than the required distance, stared over our heads the whole time, as if displaying any interest in us beyond the proper courtesy were forbidden. Afterwards, he took us to a diner, asked us about school, what we wanted to be when we grew up, the expected questions adults trying to ingratiate themselves with young people always asked. Delsa, Norma, and I asked him what he did (accounting), where he worked (Xerox), if he was married (divorced), how many children he had (three), and whether he was ever sick (rarely), while Mami kicked us under the table for our impertinence. But this was the only man Mami had shown any interest in since Francisco's death.

Mami must have told him which dances we'd be attending, because after the first meeting, every time we walked into a club, there he was. Delsa, Norma, and I soon figured out what was going on, especially since Mami didn't dance with anyone else. He sat at our table, and even though the music was deafening, he and Mami carried on animated conversations through the whole evening, even when they danced.

Delsa, Norma, and I teased Mami that she had a boyfriend, and she blushed, then asked us not to tell Tata. We liked sharing a secret with her, knowing something about her life that no one else knew. But we didn't like it when Don Carlos sat at our table. Men thought he was our father and didn't ask us to dance.

"He sits there with his dark glasses on, like a gangster or something, and scares the guys away," we complained to Mami.

The next time, he wore regular lenses on his glasses, thick as windowpane, through which he squinted as if they were the wrong prescription. It didn't help. Men now thought he was scrutinizing every move they made.

After weeks of courtship, Mami invited Don Carlos for Sunday dinner. When Mami told her a man was coming to visit, Tata's eyes narrowed, her lips puckered, and she walked away from Mami without a word.

"Good for you," Don Julio said. "You're still a young woman. You should have a husband."

"He's just a friend," Mami said, but her face turned red.

Sunday came and the house was spotless. The clothes-drying ropes strung across the rooms were down, the diapers folded and put away, the floors scrubbed, every bed made up with chenille bedspreads, the pillows discreet mounds at the heads. Mami was afraid Tata would be in a bad mood and embarrass her in front of Don Carlos, but Tata dressed early, took her place alongside Mami at the stove, and helped cook—at one point telling her she'd take over so that Mami could get ready.

Don Carlos showed up hours after we expected him, carrying a box of Italian cookies for us and a bottle of wine for Tata. He didn't bring anything for Mami, who was cold and polite to him, her face a hard mask. He wore his dark glasses again, didn't take them off the whole time he was with us. He never apologized for being late, made no excuses, sat at the kitchen table talking and drinking with Tata and Don Julio while my sisters and brothers paraded in and out checking him out, then running to the back rooms to compare notes. When he was about to leave, he asked Mami to walk with him to the front door, two floors below. He shook hands with everybody, even the kids, then followed Mami down the stairs. The minute he left, we started talking about him.

"He's an intelligent, well-educated person," was Don Julio's assessment.

"He makes a lot of money," Delsa informed every one. "When we go dancing, he pays, and then he takes us to breakfast and pays for that too."

"He treats Mami with respect," noted Norma.

"Oh, yeah? He showed up three hours late," Héctor recalled.

"Maybe he had to work," Alicia defended him.

"On Sunday?" I asked.

"He sure is tall," observed Raymond.

"But he's so skinny!" added Edna.

"All I can say," Tata finally spoke up, "is that I don't trust a man who won't look me in the eye."

Oh-oh, I said to myself.

As with Francisco, Tata and Mami argued over whether it was appropriate for Mami to bring a man into our family. Tata accused Mami of setting a bad example for us, and Mami insisted that at thirty-three she was still a young woman and deserved a life. If Tata didn't like it, she could move out. Don Julio took Mami's side, and Tata, outnumbered, accepted the inevitable. One evening Don Carlos came for dinner, and the next morning he was still there.

My junior year at Performing Arts turned out to be my best. My average was excellent, aided by near perfect grades in geometry, which, after three attempts, I'd mastered. My cunning Cleopatra was a success, and in spring semester, when we did character work, I was cast as one of the evil stepsisters in scenes from *Cinderella*. We were encouraged to use an animal as the physical model for the character, and I chose a camel, for its haughty look and ungainly walk.

I was a hall monitor, charged with checking that students wandering around during classes had a pass signed by a teacher. My favorite hall to monitor was on the dance department floor. I sat where I could watch a ballet class in session, could see the dancers hurl themselves through space, their controlled abandon making my own muscles ache for movement. I was envious of the training that made them so graceful and strong, the intricate steps they performed as the teacher called each movement in French.

The training for actors at Performing Arts was modern dance, its language English, its purpose to keep us from embarrassing ourselves if we had to perform musical theater. But I'd come to love dance class more than acting. While I knew I wasn't a great actress, I could see I was one of the better dancers in the drama

department. I practiced all the time. The semester we'd studied jazz and learned isolations, I'd begun to practice minute movements of my torso, hips, and back while waiting for the train, or while sitting in history class. At home, I couldn't sit still in front of the television while we watched *Candid Camera* or *The Jackie Gleason Show.* One eye on the screen, I stretched, did splits, counted out hundreds of pliés in first, second, third, fourth, and fifth positions while my sisters and brothers complained that my movements distracted them. To pick up something from the floor, I bent over from the hips, back straight, to stretch my thigh and calf muscles. I used the kitchen counter for a barre, leaped from one room to the other, held my leg up to my cheeks like the can-can dancers on *The Ed Sullivan Show.*

I knew I'd never be a ballerina; that wasn't my intention. At Performing Arts we learned that if actors had to wait ten years to make a living at their art, dancers were lucky if they could get that many years out of theirs. For me, dance was not to be shared but to bring me to a place nothing else did. I danced for myself, even when being led across a shiny floor by a skillful partner. It didn't matter if no one saw me dance. It only mattered that I could.

At the Yiddish theater, I ushered two shows every Sunday, for which I was paid at the end of the day in wrinkled bills. The company worked in repertory, alternating comedies with tragedies. When they were in rehearsals, I was laid off. When there was a performance, an actor staffed the ticket window, making me wonder if Mr. Rosenberg only chose plays in which one of the characters always made his first entrance in the second act.

I came to know the regular audience members by name. Mr. and Mrs. Karinsky took the same two seats in row C, center. Mrs. Shapiro and her sister Miss Levine liked front row, center, because Miss Levine was hard of hearing. Mrs. Mlynarski always brought a coffee cake for the actors, which she handed to me with cere-

mony, and which I was supposed to take backstage immediately while she stood at the door, a huge, immovable bulk, blocking anyone from entering until I returned and conveyed profuse thanks from the cast. Almost all the regulars knew where their seats were, and I wondered why Mr. Rosenberg paid me to usher, until the day Mr. Aronson had a fit of loud, hacking coughs. I came down the aisle with the flashlight to help him out of the theater and into the hallway, followed by a distraught and embarrassed Mrs. Aronson and another man who told me to get a glass of water.

"Don't worry," the man said as he bent over Mr. Aronson, who was turning blue, "I'm a doctor."

I couldn't find a glass anywhere, so I ran to the deli down the street and told the counterman that there was an emergency at the theater and could I please, please, please have a glass of water. When I returned, the play was in intermission and Mr. Aronson was sitting on the floor with the doctor on his knees at his side. He'd regained some color, and his coughs had subsided. He drank the water in little sips as the audience watched and hovered and commented on what was happening.

"You're looking better, Morey," Miss Levine said.

"It's his gallbladder," Mr. Klein diagnosed.

"Move away, he needs fresh air," Mrs. Mlynarski ordered everyone.

As the lights for the second act flashed, his wife and the doctor helped Mr. Aronson down the stairs and out of the building.

When everyone was seated and the play resumed, I broke into a sweat and shivers, imagining that one of the elderly people might some day have a heart attack or stroke during a performance, and there wouldn't be a doctor to help. Later, when Mr. Rosenberg was paying me and I expressed my fears, he reassured me.

"Don't worry," he said, waving his hand, "there's always a doctor in *this* house." He laughed, but I didn't get the joke.

Mami decided we needed an apartment that would allow everyone more privacy. She found one on the second floor of a two-story house, on a tree-lined street of identical houses, the stoop separated from the sidewalk by a cement yard behind a wrought-iron fence. She and Don Carlos took the bedroom in the back, Tata and we kids scattered our belongings in three rooms, one of which, the living room, faced the sunny street. The other rooms didn't offer much light, because their windows faced an air vent. When I was arranging my things in the middle room with Delsa and Norma, I noticed that a hallway off the kitchen was wide enough to hold a fold-out cot.

"Mami, can I take this room?"

"This isn't a room, it's a hall."

"If I close these doors," I shut the ones to the outside hall and to her room, "it still leaves me with a door to the kitchen, and I can put a cot in here, and a table, and have my own room."

Mami stepped into the room I'd created. "It's so dark."

"It's got a light. See?" I pulled the chain of an overhead bulb. "The room is useless. We don't need another entrance."

"Umm," Mami considered for a few minutes, then agreed. At the secondhand store we found a gold metal and glass vanity table with an oval mirror and matching chair covered in white vinyl. I dragged the folding cot into the hallway, where it hugged the walls tight enough so that the only way I could get into bed was by climbing over the foot toward the head against the door to Mami's room. The vanity table fit against the other entrance door. I screwed hooks into the wall for my clothes and stuffed my underwear into a basket that went under the bed. It was like living in a long box, but it was private, my own room, where I could keep my things and where I slept alone, even if every time I turned over I hit a wall with a leg or a foot.

"It sounds like you're fighting in there," Tata complained one

morning when I emerged from my room, elbows and knees bruised. "And you don't get any fresh air. You'll get sick."

"Maybe that room isn't such a good idea," Mami warned.

"I had a nightmare," I lied, "and there's plenty of air."

That night I began to train myself to sleep on my back, perfectly still: Cleopatra, surrounded by her belongings, in her sarcophagus.

As soon as school was out, I answered a classified ad for a summer job at a photographic developing company. I was interviewed by Mr. Murphy, a high-strung man who asked questions but never let me finish the answer.

He reviewed the job application. "You go to Performing Arts, right?"

"Yes, sir," I said, unable to hide the pride in my voice.

"What'd they teach you there?" He had an exquisite Brooklyn accent.

I turned on my standard speech. "I'm in the drama department, so we study acting, voice, and. . . ."

"What? You wanna be a movie star?"

"It's an academic school, too."

"Oh, yeah? Did you see *West Side Story?* You look like that girl there, what's her name, Mareer. You could play her."

"I can't sing. . . ."

"Not too many parts for Puerto Ricans," he broke in again.

"We're trained to play anything. . . ."

"What's this? Yiddish theater? D'you talk Yiddish?"

"I was an usher. . . ."

"What? They fire you 'cause you couldn't talk it?"

"No. They don't perform in the summer. . . ."

"That was some movie," he mused, and it took me a while to realize we were back to *West Side Story.* "What's her name won an academy award, didn't she?"

"Rita Moreno. She's Puerto Rican."

"Can you start on Monday?"

"Sure!"

"Eight in the morning. I'll have a card for you by the clock where you punch in." He stood up and led me to the door, "Yeah, Reeter, that's her name." He showed me out.

I was happy I had found a job but annoyed that it should have been because the boss loved *West Side Story*. I despised that movie, and it didn't help that every time I told someone I was a drama student, they expected me to lift my skirts and break into "I feel pretty, oh so pretty . . ."

Although I hadn't seen a stage performance of *West Side Story*, I'd read that the original Maria was played by an American actress, Carol Lawrence, while Anita was played by Chita Rivera. In the movie, Natalie Wood played Maria, and Rita Moreno was Anita. It was subtle, but it wasn't lost on me that the only virgin in the entire movie — sweet, innocent Maria — was always played by an American, while the sexy spitfire was Puerto Rican. And that wasn't all.

The Jets had a nice, clean, warm place to hang out, reminiscent of the malt shop where Archie hung out with Betty, Veronica, and Jughead. It was owned by a kindly old man who put up with all sorts of *pocavergüenzas*, including the near rape of Anita. The Sharks had a rooftop, and what did they do there? They argued over whether "America" was better than Puerto Rico.

"It's just a movie," Laura Figueroa reminded me once, when I was on a rant about *West Side Story*.

"It's not *just* a movie," I argued, "it's the *only* movie about Puerto Ricans anyone has seen. And what's the message? White Puerto Rican girls dangle from fire escapes singing sweet tunes to Italian guys, while dark-skinned Puerto Rican girls sleep with their boyfriends. Dark too, I might add."

"You're reading too much into it," she insisted.

When we read *Romeo and Juliet* in English class and Mrs. Simmons said *West Side Story* was based on the Shakespeare play,

I was disappointed. I thought the Bard could have done better. The death scene at the end of the play and the movie was the dumbest thing I'd seen. During the discussion, my classmates tried to help me see it differently.

"But don't you understand?" Brenda said. "They died for love."

"What kind of stupid reason is that?" I wondered.

"They couldn't live without each other," Ardyce explained.

"Oh, please! That's the most ridiculous reason over which to commit suicide."

"Obviously, you've never been in love," Myra sniffed.

"If I had, I'd still never kill myself over a guy."

"Even if he looked like Richard Beymer?" Roger asked.

"Especially if he looked like Richard Beymer."

"Cleopatra killed herself over Marc Antony," Jay reminded me.

"Not exactly. She thought Antony was dead and she'd lost her most important ally. With him gone, the Romans would strip her of her dignity." No one could invoke Cleopatra around me and hope I didn't have my facts straight.

Mrs. Simmons held up her hand to stop the discussion. "*Romeo and Juliet* is one of the great love stories of all time," she concluded, "but apparently, it's not for everybody." The bell rang. "Next week, we begin *Hamlet*." She smiled in my direction. "I think you'll like that one better," she said as I left the classroom.

My summer job consisted of stuffing negatives and pictures into envelopes, then mailing them to the people who'd sent in their film for processing. The film was developed next door, but fumes seeped through the wall into the room where I worked, which was dark and windowless. Two other women worked at desks doing the same thing I did, and one of them, Sheila, a black woman not much older than I was, was charged with teaching me how to do

the job. The other, an older Asian woman, mumbled to herself the whole time she worked and rarely looked up from her stacks of envelopes, negatives, and prints.

"That's what happens when you work here too long," Sheila said, tipping her head in Mimi's direction. "You go cuckoo. All those chemicals." She laughed, and I figured she must have been kidding.

"How long have you worked here?"

"Me? Oh, about seven months. I've got two kids to support, you know. I'm not like you, stayin' in school and all that." Sheila worked three days a week; the other two she was enrolled at a training program for nursing assistants. "I had to get my GED," she said, "then they made me take biology and chemistry and all that shit I slept through the first time. Do you have to study that in your school?"

"Yes."

"You like it, don't you?"

"I don't mind it."

"I wish I'd stayed in school. Now I got two kids to support. Don't you go thinking it's good to quit school."

"My mother wouldn't let me."

"I'm with her." She shuffled through some photographs. "Look at this fool in this picture here! What does he have on his head?"

"It looks like a bunch of bananas."

"You see the foolest people in this job. Check this one out . . . she thinks she looks good."

For hours, I stuffed people's memories into envelopes, to the sound of Sheila's chatter and Mimi's mumbles. Every evening as I stepped onto the sidewalk, I breathed the air of Brooklyn, fresh and clean compared to that in the building where I spent eight hours a day. I went home, changed, and closeted myself in my room to read, or to write rambling entries in a journal La Muda had given me for my seventeenth birthday.

I was paid every Friday. At home, I gave Mami a portion of

my salary and paid my sisters or brothers to do the chores assigned to me that I didn't want to do. The rest was spent on clothes for the coming school year, but my biggest expense was for books that I didn't have to return to the library.

My first purchase was Dr. Norman Vincent Peale's *The Power of Positive Thinking*. I liked his theory that negative thoughts result in negative actions. Mami, my sisters and brothers, friends in school had accused me more than once of having a morbid, negative streak. I hoped Dr. Peale's book would help me to think positively when life turned grim, which I was certain it would.

As Dr. Peale suggested, I made a list of the good things in my life:

1. I'd passed my third geometry Regents with a 96.
2. I had a job.
3. Mami had a job, was in love and happy again.
4. Delsa, Norma, and Héctor also had jobs.
5. With five people working at home, we now had more money than we'd ever had.
6. I had my own room.
7. Raymond's foot had completely healed, and the doctors said he didn't have to come for checkups any more.

Dr. Peale suggested ten things, but I could only come up with seven, which I interpreted to mean that I desperately needed the book.

To help me get into a positive mood, I memorized songs about the good life. At the library, I listened to scratchy recordings of Broadway musicals and learned to belt out "Everything's Coming Up Roses" like Ethel Merman. I sang "Luck Be a Lady Tonight" from *Guys and Dolls* as I showered every morning. But the song that I hummed in moments of doubt came from the despised *West Side Story*. I found it insulting that the only positive thing in Maria's life was Tony under her fire escape. But I loved his song, and promised myself that there would be something good every day, and that the minute it showed, I would know it. While in *West Side Story* good things were around the corner only for the

non–Puerto Ricans, I made myself believe that a miracle was due, that it would come true, and that it was coming to me. So I slowed when I turned the corner and imagined what a miracle might look like whistling down the river.

⁓

Since Don Carlos had come into our lives, we didn't go dancing as much, because the only time Mami saw him was on weekends.

"Isn't it strange?" Tata asked Mami, "that he doesn't live here?"

"It's because of his work," Mami explained. "It's too far for him from here to his job in the city."

"You and Negi go into the city every day," Tata pointed out.

"It's different. He has two jobs. One in the daytime and another one at night."

Whether Tata put doubts in her mind or not, by the middle of the summer, when Mami showed signs that she was pregnant, she began to question Don Carlos about his whereabouts during the week. From my room next to theirs I heard them argue. Or rather, I heard Mami. Don Carlos responded in a low voice, as if he didn't want anyone but Mami to hear his defenses. Sometimes, he didn't answer her at all, which infuriated her, so that she hurled accusations that he stubbornly refused to respond to. He just picked up his briefcase and left. When Mami cooled off, he returned, and things were fine for a while.

He told us he had three children. We pestered him about meeting them, but he always postponed the visit with one excuse or another. He said he worked as an accountant during the day and in the evening kept books and did taxes for private clients. During his courtship of Mami, he made a show of paying for our tickets and breakfasts after the clubs. But once he moved in, he had trouble opening his wallet. He didn't offer to help with *la compra*, didn't hand out spare change or offer to pay the phone bill when Mami couldn't keep up the payments and it was cut off.

"*Tacaño*," was Tata's assessment, as she tapped her elbow with

her fist. None of our relatives was rich, but neither were they stingy. They were generous with what they had, and Don Carlos's unwillingness to part with his money was interpreted as a weakness of character, a sure sign that there were other, more unpleasant traits in him that we had yet to discover.

"Stop thinking and dance."

~~~~~~~~

At Performing Arts, we read Shakespeare in English classes, but the drama department didn't cast us in scenes from his plays until we were ready. Now that we were seniors, with two full years of voice and diction and acting classes behind us, we'd finally get to perform some of the Bard's greatest scenes. I'd already expressed my dislike of *Romeo and Juliet,* so it was no surprise that I wasn't cast as a Capulet. I was to be—what else—Cleopatra, in iambic pentameter.

I was paired with Northern Calloway (no relation to Cab, he said), one of the stars of the drama department, equally at home in tragedy, comedy, or musical theater. I liked him, but his openness and subversive humor sometimes turned me off. When we were assigned act 1, scene 2 of Shakespeare's *Antony and Cleopatra,* I worried that we wouldn't work well together, but he was more disciplined than I'd expected. He helped me find aspects of Cleopatra's character that I'd underplayed or ignored. He advised that I give up the yellow tablecloth costume, because I'd developed mannerisms based on the limited range of motion the dress allowed.

I bought a pair of filmy nylon curtains, and made a transparent dress. After almost three years of seeing me concoct costumes out of sheets, drapes, and scraps of material, Mami no longer asked to inspect everything I made. But when she saw the sheer fabric, she warned me: "I hope you're planning to wear a slip under that."

I explained that the queen of the Nile didn't wear slips but agreed that, for the sake of decency, I'd wear the costume over tights and leotards.

~~~~~

I was in the hall reading the drama department bulletin board, where newspaper clippings of famous alumni were posted along with the year they'd graduated noted in a corner. At Performing Arts, one didn't just stand around. Every opportunity to exercise body or craft was to be taken advantage of, so as I read, I executed pliés in second position.

I felt someone standing behind me, and when I turned, I was face to face with a man with a large head topped by wild black hair, a big nose, piercing black eyes under shapely brows, and well-formed lips that didn't smile. I knew him to be one of the teachers in the dance department.

"You must be an Indian classical dancer," he declared in a deep voice with a hint of a foreign accent.

"No, sir. I'm a Puerto Rican actress."

He seemed annoyed at being corrected. "I didn't say you are, I said you must be. Come see me."

I was intrigued, imagining Indians in feathered headdresses and moccasins performing *en pointe* around a campfire. During a free period, I ran up to the dance office, but there was no one there. I tried a couple more times that week but never found him.

One day, Miss Cahan, a dance teacher in the drama department, stopped me in the hall and asked if I could try out for a play. "It's for a children's theater company."

She told me the audition was later that week, gave me the address. "Other students are auditioning," she added. "Don't be late."

The address was on Madison Avenue. A doorman had me wait as he called up my name and, after a few minutes, told me to go up to the fifth floor. The elevator operator, a short, swarthy man in a natty uniform that made him look like Napoleon stranded in

the wrong century, didn't look at me as we rose, pointed to the left when we reached a dim, carpeted hallway, waited until I pressed a button under the peephole of the apartment door. When the door opened, the elevator closed. Miss Cahan, dressed in tights, leotards, and a long dance skirt, greeted me and led me inside an enormous room with broad windows at the far end.

I was seventeen years old and had never been in an American home. Here I was, inside an apartment on the Upper East Side — thick carpets at my feet, dark brooding paintings on the walls, yards of fabric around the windows, two sofas, upholstered chairs, side tables with china and crystal figurines. I ached with envy.

Miss Cahan introduced me to Mrs. Kormendi, the writer and director of the play. Another Performing Arts student was in the room — Claire, whom I knew to be a superior actress. Her shoes were off, and she sat cross-legged on the floor at Mrs. Kormendi's left. The simple shirt and pants she wore, the casual "Hi" with which she acknowledged me, led me to believe that she lived in the apartment.

"Why don't you take your shoes off and put them under that bench." Miss Cahan pointed to a plush, upholstered piece of furniture I would have never called a bench, although I didn't know what else to call it. I wore a skirt, as always, because Mami didn't think decent girls wore pants unless they were on a horse.

"Maybe you should remove your stockings too," Miss Cahan said, "so you don't slip."

"Okay." I turned my back and discreetly unhooked the stockings from the garter belt and rolled them down, wondering why I needed to get undressed to audition for a children's play. Miss Cahan read my mind.

"I should have told you we were going to dance," she explained, "so you could come prepared."

"Oh!" I walked over, my toes digging into the plush carpet as I used to dig them into the soft, warm mud of Puerto Rico, then sat with legs folded under me on the floor, although there were about ten sumptuous chairs I longed to drop into.

Mrs. Kormendi explained that the play was based on an In-

dian legend. "India Indian," she specified, "not American." They were casting someone to play the goddess Lakshmi, who in the play was a statue that became a swan. I didn't ask how. There was quite a bit of dancing, the reason Miss Cahan was helping with the audition.

"All right, then," Miss Cahan said. "Let's try some things."

Mrs. Kormendi sat on the sofa with a clipboard on her lap and took notes while Miss Cahan led me and Claire through a series of steps unlike anything we'd ever done in dance class. They were stylized, dramatic postures that required we move in a wide, second-position plié, our torsos rigid, our arms and hands in gestures that demanded coordination and strength in muscles I had never used. I couldn't follow the choreography and stopped several times, embarrassed and frustrated, as Miss Cahan and Claire moved across the floor with ease.

Miss Cahan adjusted my stance. "Stop thinking," she said, "and dance. Don't worry about remembering the steps. Your muscles will remember."

That was a new concept. I worked hard in dance, pushed myself to leap higher, stretch farther. I never just let it happen. But I trusted Miss Cahan, who as a professional knew more about it than I did. I stopped thinking. Next thing I knew, the audition was over and Mrs. Kormendi promised to get back to us.

Claire and I rode the elevator down. While she and I were classmates, we didn't have much to say to one another. She was one of the smart, talented, popular girls who were cast in the best roles: Antigone or her sister Ismene, Juliet, Emily in *Our Town*, Frankie in *Member of the Wedding*. We parted in front of the building, but as I walked to the subway station on my way back to Brooklyn, I knew the part was mine. Claire might be an angelic ingenue, but I'd perfected exotic characters. Cleopatra, queen of the Nile, I was sure, was about to become Lakshmi, swan goddess.

A few days later, Miss Cahan asked me to stay after class and told me that Mrs. Kormendi wanted me in her play. I couldn't wait to get home and tell Mami that one full year before graduation, I already had a part in a play. Only nine more years of sacrifice, and I'd be a star.

～～～ɔ

The first rehearsal for Mrs. Kormendi's play was on a Saturday morning, at a studio on Madison Avenue not far from her apartment. A ballet class was in session when I arrived. I watched from the open door, but the teacher, a tight-faced woman with a sour expression, came over and slammed the door in my face. I was so embarrassed that tears came to my eyes, but I swallowed them when I heard steps down the hall. Mrs. Kormendi appeared as the ballet class ended and the hall filled with long-legged, haughty ballerinas.

Mrs. Kormendi kissed the sour-faced *madame* on both cheeks, and they talked as the room cleared. The dance teacher looked scornfully in my direction, and I heard Mrs. Kormendi say my name. I stripped to my tights and leotards but didn't dare warm up at the barre while *madame* was in the room. Her eyes followed me, and I expected her to apologize for her rudeness, but she didn't.

Within a few minutes the rest of the cast appeared, boys and girls no older than twelve years of age. They too stripped to their tights and leotards but weren't afraid to use the barre. By now the instructor had left, so I joined the kids, most of whom had obviously studied ballet before they could stand up. They went through exercises and stretches that I tried to copy, but I couldn't keep up with them.

When everyone arrived, Mrs. Kormendi handed out copies of the play, and we read through it. "Memorize your lines," Mrs. Kormendi instructed, "next week we begin blocking." Those of us who were dancing were to arrive at the next rehearsal two hours

before the rest of the cast, because the choreographer had to work with us.

The following Saturday, as I came up to the studio, I heard strange music, rhythmic stomping, bells jingling furiously from behind the open door. In spite of having the door slammed in my face once already, I couldn't contain my curiosity. In the room was the dance teacher who'd confused me for an Indian. He wore a sheet wrapped around his waist and legs and a long white shirt with embroidered designs down the front and on the sleeves. On his legs, he wore bells. His movements were fierce, low across the floor in a deep plié, his big toes curled up from the ground. He jumped, his arms and legs jabbed the air, his eyes rolled in his head, his mouth twisted into an evil grin, his head snapped back and forth on his neck, and then he landed in the same deep plié with toes pointed up. I'd never seen anything so savage or so beautiful. It couldn't be dance, but it couldn't be anything else. When he stopped, Mrs. Kormendi's voice called from inside, where she sat on the only chair in the studio, clipboard on lap. She waved me over to her side.

"You know Matteo, don't you?" she whispered.

"I've seen him around school." The other person in the room was Northern, my Antony, who smiled cheerily at my surprise to see him.

Mrs. Kormendi and I watched Matteo teach Northern the stylized gestures and facial expressions he'd just performed. When the rest of the actors arrived, Matteo taught us our first class in Indian classical dance, which had nothing to do with feathered headdresses and moccasins. It was an ancient dance form, actually six ancient dance forms, each associated with a different part of India, and each having distinctive music, choreography, postures, costumes. The dance he was teaching Northern was based on Kathakali, the dance theater of Kerala, while the rest of us were to learn Bharata Natyam, associated with southern India. Matteo demonstrated some of the ways the two dance types differed in style and in the kind of stories the dancers told with their bodies.

He explained that historically, Kathakali was performed by men, Bharata Natyam by women. He spoke with reverence of choreography passed down generation to generation by dancers who were often ostracized for their dedication to their art. He showed pictures of sculptures based on the movements he was about to teach us.

He put us through a class more demanding than any I'd ever taken. It wasn't just the physicality of the dance that was so challenging. It was that what we were learning was more than theater and more than dance. It was a complete art form that combined theater, dance, music, and spectacle. It had its own unique language; every gesture had a name, every emotion a gesture. When I looked in the wall-size mirror of the studio, I saw what Matteo must have seen the day I was doing pliés in front of the Performing Arts bulletin board. I didn't look like a Puerto Rican actress from Brooklyn. I looked like an Indian classical dancer.

~~~~~~~

Matteo taught at a studio on the Upper West Side. He charged more money per class than I made from ushering. I called Mr. Murphy at the photographic developing company, and he offered me work on weekends and whenever I could come in. The problem was that between school, rehearsals, and the work it took to pay for classes, I didn't have time to go to Matteo's studio. And he didn't appreciate dancers who weren't committed to the art. I took classes with him a few times, but mostly I paid attention to what he taught during rehearsals, came even when my character wasn't involved, and soon learned the dances in the play, including the attendant's story dance and Northern's ferocious devil dance.

As rehearsals evolved, I abandoned my fantasy of being whisked on wires above the stage like Mary Martin in *Peter Pan.* Lakshmi spent the entire first scene standing on one leg inside a temple while the princess cried and prayed, in despair from being

in love with the prince but betrothed to a rajah who was really a devil. At the beginning of scene 2, a sitar thrummed, my cue to begin the transformation from stone to swan. My fingers trembled, my eyes flicked from side to side, my arms softened and fluttered. Flying was simulated by *mudras*, hand gestures that were slow and tentative at the beginning, then fully realized into the sinuous movements of a creature discovering she's no longer hard stone but a soft, graceful bird. In performance, when my fingers came to life, the audience gasped, and by the end of the dance, they were on their feet, clapping.

La Muda came to the last show. My dance, so much like her wordless language, was the best I'd ever achieved. As I transmuted from silent stone to effusive goddess, I *was* La Muda, trapped in silence but avid to communicate, speaking with my body because voice failed me. When I danced, I had no tongue, but I was capable of anything. I was a swan, I was a goddess, I vanquished devils.

When Mami was five months pregnant, she found out why Don Carlos didn't have money to spare and didn't come home every night. He'd told us he was divorced, but the truth was that when he wasn't with us he was with his wife in the Bronx. Mami found out when the wife called and cursed her, her ancestors, and every future generation into eternity. When Mami confronted Don Carlos, he admitted that he wasn't technically divorced but insisted that it was only because the paperwork hadn't come through. Neither Mami, Tata, Don Julio, nor any of us believed him. In my eyes, the courteous and soft-spoken Don Carlos became just another *sinvergüenza* who promised more than he had any intention of delivering.

Respectful attention gave way to a mouthy, aggressive insolence that Mami punished. Her threats, slaps, and insistence that we owed Don Carlos proper courtesy and deference because he

was an adult and the father of our soon-to-be sister or brother didn't change our behavior. Instead, a bitter grudge sprouted where there had once been affection, and although eventually Don Carlos did divorce, did introduce his children to us, and did loosen his wallet, for me at least the damage was done. I'd never forgive him for reopening the still tender wounds caused by Papi's surrender of us to an American fate and Francisco's death.

But what scared me most about Don Carlos's betrayal was that Mami was not immune to the seductive power of a man with a sweet tongue and a soft touch. "Men only want one thing," she'd said so many times that I couldn't look at a man without hearing it. If *she* could fall under the spell, how could I, younger and less experienced, hope to avoid the same destiny?

⌒⌒

Mami worked until a few months before she was due, and then we humbled ourselves at the welfare office. After we explained the situation, the social worker came to the apartment unannounced to make sure Don Carlos wasn't hiding behind the shower curtain or in the closets.

Because we hadn't been warned, the apartment was the familiar chaotic mess I found comfortable but embarrassing, because I knew people shouldn't live like that. The beds were not neat, because they served as seats when we watched television or did our homework. The dishes hadn't been washed, because it was my turn and I always waited until the last minute if I couldn't bribe one of my siblings to do them. Mami hadn't been to the laundromat, so there was a pile of soiled clothes spilling out of the hamper. The bathroom was adorned with drying bras, panties, and stockings, as well as with a few hand-washed shirts and blouses on hangers. Franky's nose was snotty, and no one had helped him clean it. Mami's back ached and she'd been in bed all day, one of the reasons the apartment was such a mess. Tata's bones hurt, so she'd begun to drink early and now sat in the kitchen smoking,

her caramel eyes on the doughy social worker who went from room to room opening cabinets and drawers.

While the social worker was there, we were subdued, afraid to look at her, as if we'd done *algo* and she'd caught us. Mami trailed her, with me and Delsa to interpret. The kids sat on their beds pretending to read because, while I translated for Mami in the kitchen, Delsa ran back to warn them to behave. Don Julio was due any minute, and we worried that the social worker would think he lived with us, which he didn't. Even so, it felt as if he shouldn't visit, as if we shouldn't know any men.

The social worker was thorough. She wrote cryptic shorthand symbols in a pad, pushed her glasses up, opened the refrigerator, made a note, checked inside the oven. When she asked questions, we weren't sure if she was making conversation or if she was trying to trap us into admitting there was a man under the bed or behind a door, even though we knew there wasn't one.

Once the social worker left, the apartment looked smaller and meaner than before she came. There was a dead roach in the corner. The trash barrel was full. Grease congealed on the dirty dishes. The walls had peeling paint, dark wood showed under the torn linoleum. The ill-fitting secondhand curtains were too heavy for the rods. Everything looked worse, which, I supposed, made us look as if we really needed the help.

The noncommittal social worker was the first American to see the way we lived, her visit an invasion of what little privacy we had. It stressed just how dependent we were on the opinion of a total stranger, who didn't speak our language, whose life was clearly better than ours. Otherwise, how could she pass judgment on it? I seethed, but I had no outlet for my rage, for the feeling that so long as I lived protected by Mami, my destiny lay in the hands of others whose power was absolute. If not hers, then the welfare department's. I closed myself off in my room and cried into my pillow, while my family joked and laughed and imitated the social worker's nasal voice, the way she peeked inside the cabinet under the sink, as if a man could fit there. It was not funny

anymore to laugh at ourselves or at people who held our fate in their hands. It was pathetic.

I fell asleep bathed in tears and didn't hear the screams when the world went black, didn't hear Mami shuffle from her room to the front of the apartment, bumping into furniture as she counted heads to make sure we were together in the utter darkness of Brooklyn. I didn't hear her call my name as she and Tata ordered the kids to huddle close until they could figure out what had happened. When I woke up, I was blind, and opening my eyes made no difference. I thought I'd died, but I could feel. I screamed Mami's name and heard her "We're in the front!" I groped my way out of my room, through the kitchen to the open living room windows, where my whole family was crammed against each other. People were on the street, talking in subdued, intimate voices. The warm yellow light of candles flickered in our neighbors' windows.

"What happened?" I asked.

Delsa shushed me. Through the static of her battery-operated radio, we heard the news. New York and the entire Northeast were blacked out. I went back to the window. Above the scrawny trees, over the ragged flat lines of buildings, tiny bright lights beckoned and danced, the first stars I'd seen since we'd come to Brooklyn.

"It must be a sin to be so disrespectful to the Virgin."

In the depths of winter we moved to a single-family house on Stanhope Street. I no longer had a room to myself but shared with Delsa, Norma, Alicia, and Edna while the boys—Héctor Raymond, and Franky—slept in another room. Mami put the soon-to-be-born baby's crib, her double bed, and the dressers in the middle bedroom, the only one with a door. The downstairs had a small living room and dining area and a good-size kitchen. Tata's cot went into the pantry, across from the rice, flour, dry beans, cans of tomato sauce.

Having a whole house to ourselves made us feel rich. No downstairs neighbors to bang on the ceilings because we made too much noise. No one upstairs walking heavily overhead, shaking the light fixtures. But it also meant no super if the toilet broke, and when there wasn't enough heat, it was because we hadn't paid the bill, not because the landlord was stingy.

We lived close to the relatives again, and I could visit Alma and Corazón on the way home from school. They too had moved, to a roomy but dark apartment on Flushing Avenue, half a block from the elevated train. Alma had graduated from high school and worked as a secretary for a sock wholesaler. Her office was a few blocks from Performing Arts, and every week we met for dinner in the city. We got along so well that we soon came up with a plan

to share an apartment as soon as I graduated from high school and could find a job.

"It'll have to be a two-bedroom," Alma said, "I need privacy."

"Yes, and I hope you know I can't cook."

"Neither can I. We'll eat out," she suggested.

We combed the classifieds for a sense of what we'd have to pay in the Upper East Side, our first choice. Alma had read somewhere that we shouldn't spend more than the equivalent of one week's salary, and it was soon clear that a two-bedroom apartment anywhere in Manhattan was out of the question.

"We might have to look in Queens," she suggested, to which I objected. "I don't want to live in the outer boroughs."

"We'll keep looking, then." The next week we went over the listings again. We figured out how much to put aside for a security deposit, the first month's rent, furniture, towels, sheets, curtains, and rugs. If we were thrifty, if Alma got a raise, if I found a good job, we'd be able to afford an apartment six months after I graduated.

"We'll move in for Christmas," I said, "and throw a housewarming party." I imagined an apartment not unlike Mrs. Kormendi's, filled with people whose faces were a blur because I didn't know them yet.

It was so much fun to plan our lives as single girls in Manhattan that we didn't think of asking our mothers.

"The only way you're leaving my house," Mami vowed when I broached the subject, "is as a married woman."

"But I don't want to get married."

"Decent girls don't live alone in the city."

"We won't be living alone. Alma and I will be together, in the same apartment."

"Still," she spat out, and when I was about to make another point, she held up her finger in my direction, "just because you're in that school for *blanquitos*," at which point I tuned out.

Alma had the same argument with Titi Ana, and we had to accept that, according to our mothers, two young women living

together were still alone if there was no man to keep an eye on them.

⁓

Charlie was born in February, and Don Carlos used the birth of his son to insinuate himself back into our lives. He showed up with a scarf for Mami one day, a birthday present for Franky, an outfit for Charlie. He played gin rummy with us, or sat with Tata and Don Julio until late at night, then climbed the stairs to Mami's bedroom when he thought we were asleep. As soon as he left for work, Tata ragged on Mami for taking Don Carlos back. When he returned at night, she served him supper, muttering insults under her breath. "*Sinvergüenza*," she said as she set down his rice and beans, "*desgraciado*," as she poured his coffee.

Mami was embarrassed by Tata's candor, but Don Carlos didn't seem to care. He ignored Tata, his eyes trapped behind his tinted glasses, a half-smile on his lips as if what she said were amusing but not offensive. He tried to win her over with presents: a jug of Gallo wine, a carton of cigarettes, a velvet painting of John F. Kennedy and Martin Luther King facing each other across the bleeding heart of Jesus. Tata took his offerings but didn't let up, until I wondered if Don Carlos enjoyed the abuse Tata heaped on him, if part of the reason he wanted to live with us was to hear an honest accounting of what kind of person he was. I figured he must love Mami to put up with her eight children and bristly mother. And she loved him, because pretty soon, Don Carlos's dark suits hung in her closet like giant bats, and her fingers caressed the cuffs and collars of his white cotton shirts as she ironed them every morning.

⁓

Luigi and La Muda couldn't live together, but neither could they live apart. They separated, reunited, separated again, came to-

gether in teary reunions when he'd just happen to drop in during a family gathering. La Muda, Mami, and Tata had long conversations that we were not allowed to watch. I managed to need something from the kitchen whenever La Muda visited, and since I was *casi mujer*, Mami didn't shoo me off as she did my younger sisters. During one of her visits, La Muda swatted the side of her face, which seemed to mean that Luigi hit her. It was hard to believe that such a quiet, gentle man would hit anyone, least of all the woman he loved. But it was even harder to believe that La Muda would lie about something like that.

A few days later, he came to see us, his sad figure stooped inside his suit as if he'd shrunk and his clothes had grown around him. He had decided to return to Puerto Rico. We begged him not to go, but he said he couldn't stand the cold any more.

"Look at my hands," he moaned. The bumps on his knuckles were huge, the fingers curled over one another into loose fists. I looked away.

He walked back to the train station, his steps a painful shuffle down the street. He'd aged so much in five years that it was hard to imagine he'd been young, had performed card tricks, had been vibrant La Muda's lover. I sensed we'd never see him again, and less than a month later, we learned he was dead. It wasn't clear what killed him. Arthritis, someone said. He died in excruciating pain under the warm Puerto Rican sun. Someone else whispered that Luigi was so in love with La Muda that, unable to live without her, he had committed suicide. He had drunk himself to death, went a third theory, less believable because we'd never seen him drunk. We never knew. He simply disappeared from our lives, consumed by pain, grief, or liquor, a memory of pale graceful fingers scattering magic into the air.

⌒‿⌒

The spring of my senior year of high school brought daily updates from my classmates on acceptances to colleges they had applied

to and I hadn't. Mrs. Provet, Dr. Dycke, and the school guidance counselor encouraged me to continue my education.

"I can't afford to go to college," I said to them. "I need a job so I can help my mother."

"Maybe you can work part-time," Dr. Dycke suggested.

"Most colleges have work-study programs," Mrs. Provet added.

But I wasn't interested in college just yet. I wanted to be out in the world, to earn my own living, to help Mami, yes, but also to stop depending on her for my every need.

Mr. Murphy offered me full-time work in his lab in Brooklyn, but I'd already decided to seek work in Manhattan, in one of the gleaming new office towers that sprouted from the ground like defiant, austere fortresses. The only problem was that I had no skills to bring to a business.

Performing Arts offered a typing course, designed to teach us a practical skill should our talents not be recognized the minute we graduated. I sat in the front row of the classroom, feet flat on the floor, back straight, head up, eyes focused ahead, fingers poised over the keyboard, as Mrs. Barnes called out the letters we were to press without looking.

"Capital *T*, lowercase *r*, capital *J*, lowercase *m*, Shift Lock, H P S V, semicolon."

Each keystroke was a nail that hammered my future onto a rubber platen. If not an actress, a secretary. If not a dancer, a secretary. If not a secretary, what?

Senior Showcase was the last time my class performed in front of the whole school. I had expected to portray another Cleopatra in an obscure play by an unknown playwright, since I'd already interpreted all the famous Cleopatras. But I was surprised to be cast as the Virgin Mary to Laura Rama's Bernadette of Lourdes.

When I told Mami I was to play the Virgin Mary, she was

ecstatic. Unlike Cleopatra, queen of the Nile, Mami knew the Virgin to be a respectable character who didn't wear outlandish clothes or heavy makeup. She offered to make the costume, but the school provided it.

The first day of rehearsals I learned that my part didn't require acting in the traditional sense. I was to be a dancing Mary, with no dialogue. While my classmates blocked their scenes, Miss Cahan and I worked on a dance of apparition in a corner of the Basement.

Mine was not a religious family, so my idea of the Virgin Mary was based on what I'd picked up from devoutly Catholic Abuela, my father's mother, who went to church every morning and prayed the rosary every evening. "*Santa Maria, madre de Dios,*" she'd taught me, and in my dance improvisations, I tried to come up with decorous, evocative movements, befitting Holy Mary, Mother of God.

Miss Cahan, however, offered a less pious interpretation. Her vision of Mary was according to the Martha Graham school of movement: geometric, hard-edged, abstract. I made my entrance in one deep lunge, firmly planted my right leg, straightened it as the left rose parallel to the floor. Eyes focused on the ground, arms outstretched, back flat, I balanced on the right leg, while the rest of my body formed the cross-stroke of a *T*. I held this position until Bernadette of Lourdes noticed me and went into a trance. Then, still on one leg, I straightened my body, while my left leg swung up, up, up into a standing split, which I held with my right hand. Not very modest, this Virgin Mary with her privates exposed.

Laura Rama knelt at the foot of the stage, while I circled the back like a hungry tigress, my long robes hissing, Bernadette's terrible vision. Not once in the entire dance did my hands come together in the traditional prayer pose, nor did my arms gently open to encompass humanity. I was a warrior Virgin, mourning my Son. Torso contracted, I sought Him in my empty womb. Arms stretched back, I arched my heart toward Heaven, daring God to take me instead of Him, who suffered on a cross. When I

made my exit, in the same powerful lunge that brought me on stage, there was a pause, followed by scattered claps and, finally, real applause. I ran down the stage steps, through the back door into the makeup room, where I collapsed into a nervous heap. Northern ran over from the wings.

"That was great!" he said with a grin. "Great costume too!"

I laughed and thanked him, under the impression that he was joking about how I had finally left behind the yellow tablecloth of my Cleopatra days. As the next group of actors ran out for their scene, I bent over from the hips to stretch my back, my legs apart in second position, and noticed that, with the lights of the makeup mirror behind me, my virginal robes were transparent. I rose in a panic. During my dance, I'd been lit from behind to enhance the dramatic effect of the Grahamesque choreography.

I dropped to my knees, covered my face with my hands. Around me, my classmates ran back and forth, preparing for their moment on the stage, while I tried to make myself disappear.

After the performances, everyone gathered for a reception in the Basement. When I came down, Mami, my sisters and brothers, and Don Carlos circled me.

"Ay, *Santo Dios*," Mami was breathless, "it must be a sin to be so disrespectful to the Virgin." She was flushed, scanned the crowd as if God Himself were walking toward us to punish me on the spot.

"We saw right through the dress," Delsa announced, and people clustered around another student turned toward us and chuckled.

Miss Cahan came over. "It was wonderful." She kissed me. "Lovely."

"My costume . . ." I burbled on the edge of tears, "the robes . . ."

"Don't worry," she assured me. "You were great."

The Basement hummed with the chatter of proud teachers and excited students. For three years we'd been one another's critics, but this night everyone loved everybody's work. As we

hugged, kissed cheeks, and applauded ourselves, my family backed away. The distance was not much, a few feet at most, but it was a continent. I felt their pull from where they bunched in a corner of the room, talking and laughing, isolated in the noisy crowd of voluble actors and jovial teachers. I couldn't walk away from them, but neither did I want to be with them and miss the camaraderie of actors after a show. I was pulled by Mami, Don Carlos, and my siblings in one direction, while my peers and teachers towed me in another. Immobile, I stood halfway between both, unable to choose, hoping the party wouldn't move one inch away from me and that my family would stay solidly where they were. In the end, I stood alone between both, and when it was clear no one missed me in the spirited gathering of actors and teachers, I ambled back to Mami, and in a few minutes we were on the train to Brooklyn.

Back home, I suffered through a depiction of my dance by my sisters for the benefit of Tata, Don Julio, and the kids who hadn't come. Seeing them recreate my Virgin Mary was so funny that I laughed until tears sprouted. Later, when we'd all gone to bed and the house was still, I cried for real. I didn't know why, didn't want to know. I just let the tears fall and hoped that in the morning my swollen eyes wouldn't give me away.

I asked Papi to come to my graduation. He wrote back that he'd see. "We'll see" usually meant no, so I didn't insist, but I was disappointed. In the five years I hadn't seen Papi, I'd grown at least five inches, had learned to use makeup, had acquired another language, had become independent enough to travel around Brooklyn and Manhattan on my own, had worked at two jobs, had become a dancer, had managed to avoid the *algos* that could happen to a girl in the city. And he hadn't been there.

I wondered if he had any idea what our lives were like in New York. My letters seldom described the conditions under which we lived. Even when things were at their worst, I didn't ask for help.

It was his responsibility to determine his children's needs, not ours to beg him to take care of us.

Sometimes I was so angry with him, I wished there were a way to tell him, but I couldn't bring myself to be disrespectful, to risk his anger. My letters responded to his newsy chatter, but I expected more from him. I longed for the small, tender acts that marked our life in Puerto Rico. The time he took to explain things. The hours we spent side by side hammering nails into walls. His patience when he taught me to mix cement, to place a cinder block over squishy concrete, to scrape the mud oozing from the bottom of the block with a triangular spade. I missed the poems he wrote, the silly jokes he told, the melodies he hummed as he worked. Now that I was almost a woman, I missed my father more than ever. But I couldn't tell him, afraid that my need resembled a demand, or looked like a criticism of Mami's ability to take care of us. Instead, I stifled the hunger for a father who had become more and more of an abstraction, as illusory as the green flash of a tropical sunset.

Just before final exams, men in fitted suits appeared at Performing Arts. Within minutes a rumor spread that they were Hollywood producers casting a movie. They visited a few classes but were more interested in the architecture of the school than in the students or teachers. A few days later, however, some of us were told that we'd been chosen to audition for the film version of Bel Kaufman's *Up the Down Staircase*.

"Mami, I've been discovered!" I crowed as soon as I came home.

"Discovered doing what?" she asked.

I explained what little I knew. They were making a movie of a famous book about a school. The writer had once been a teacher at Performing Arts. The producers had come to look around, because they might film there and might choose kids to play students in the movie.

"¡Ay que bueno!"

"You'd better be careful," Tata broke in. "Sometimes those movie people just want to meet young girls."

Tata had never met any movie people. As far as I knew, she'd never been to the movies, so her warning went in one ear and out the other. Still, it was a relief when I went up to Warner Brothers for my interview and there were no couches in the casting director's office.

Mr. Jeffers was a square-jawed, ageless man whose practiced smile nevertheless elicited a toothy response. He sat behind a huge desk piled with black-and-white photographs of every aspiring actor in New York City. I didn't have a head shot, but he said that wasn't necessary.

"We're looking for real people," he said, "not necessarily professional actors."

He didn't give me a script to read from but instead asked questions designed to get me to talk. I figured he wanted to make sure I didn't have an accent, so I enunciated every word in standard speech, modulating my voice as I'd been taught. Satisfied, Mr. Jeffers stood to show me out, and I was surprised by how short he was. He took a business card from a wallet in his pocket and handed it to me. When I reached to take it, he took my hand in his, curled my fingers around the card.

"This is my direct line," he said. I nodded but didn't dare look him in the eye. Was he flirting, or was he being nice? He led me through a maze of halls and offices toward the reception lobby.

"Call me tomorrow," he said and flashed his perfect smile.

That night I met Alma for dinner and we talked about the interview.

"It's weird. He didn't do anything, other than hold my hand a little too long."

"You think he was coming on to you?"

"I think so, but I'm not sure."

"We can't be suspicious of every man we meet," Alma suggested.

"Maybe I was reading too much into it. But I keep hearing,

'Men only want one thing,'" I mimicked Mami's voice, but Alma didn't notice.

"It's the same with me." She thought for a few moments. "Maybe our mothers just haven't met any nice men."

"They're nice at the beginning," I reminded Alma. "Then, when they get what they want . . ."

"Now you sound just like your mother!" Alma laughed, and I was embarrassed but had to agree.

Since Mami and Titi Ana had shot down our plan to move in together, men had replaced apartments as the main topic of conversations during our dinners out. In my household, there were Don Julio and Don Carlos, and we had frequent visits from Mami's male uncles and cousins, who came alone as often as they showed up with wives or girlfriends. But Titi Ana didn't encourage male relatives to come around, especially if Alma and Corazón were alone while she was at work. When it came to men, I had firsthand knowledge and long experience compared with Alma, whose main contact with men was her boss, the sock wholesaler. Sometimes we talked about what kind of man we'd like to marry.

"Rich," I said when she asked.

"But how about other qualities? A sense of humor, kindness?"

"No," I insisted, "just rich." She laughed because she thought I was kidding. "Let's say our mothers are right and men only want one thing," I continued, "what's the point of giving it to just anybody? It's the only thing we have to offer."

"No, I don't agree with you," Alma's dark eyes grew larger. "You can't think that way."

"Why, not? Men think that way about us."

"No, Negi, that's wrong." She shook her head back and forth as if trying to dislodge my words from her brain.

"I'm not kidding. When I'm ready to give up my virginity, it's going to the highest bidder."

"Oh, my God, that's terrible! Don't joke about it. It's not funny."

I loved seeing her flustered. With Alma I could be outrageous

and say things I wouldn't dare say in front of anyone else. What made it fun was that she believed me. I tried out the craziest ideas on her and she took them seriously. I spoke without thinking, for the sheer joy of seeing her reaction, of arguing a point with her, of hearing myself express opinions I didn't know I had until they spilled out of my mouth.

"Just wait," I said. "The first man I do it with will be a millionaire."

"Just make sure you love him," she warned.

"Of course," I said. "Once I know he's rich, I'll fall in love with him." And then we laughed.

When I called Mr. Jeffers, he said he'd like me to try out for Carole Blanca, a featured role, the most prominent part for a Puerto Rican actress in the movie.

"Come prepared to perform a short monologue," he said. "And call me afterwards."

"But won't you be there?"

"No, that's not my department," he chuckled. "Good luck."

The audition was in a rehearsal studio on West 49th Street. Several chairs were set up against the wall of a hallway that led to a closed door. As I reached the top, a woman flew out from inside, asked my name, checked me off a list attached to a clipboard, pointed to the last unoccupied chair, and then disappeared behind the door.

Three actors were ahead of me. They dismissed me as soon as they realized I wasn't competition. They were called into the audition room one at a time, and I moved up the line. When my turn came, the woman who had first greeted me led me into a small, dark theater with a tiny stage that wasn't even raised off the audience level.

Several people huddled in the back. Miss Silver introduced me to an elegant man, Mr. Pakula, who was the producer, and to

a rumpled man with a thick mustache, Mr. Mulligan, the director. We talked for a few minutes as they asked the usual questions; then Mr. Pakula pointed to the stage and said they were ready for me.

"You can use any props that you find down there," Mr. Mulligan suggested, which meant he wanted to see me handle a prop. I'd chosen the scene from *Member of the Wedding* in which Frankie tells John Henry she wants to leave their small town. I hadn't practiced the scene with props, but I found a bench against a wall and incorporated it into the monologue. When I sat down in the middle of it, the bench shuddered on its hinges, and I jumped up but stayed in character and played it as if the whole thing had been planned. It was the best audition I'd ever given. Mr. Pakula and Mr. Mulligan shook my hand, told me I'd done well, and said Mr. Jeffers would let me know in a couple of days, as soon as they met everyone being considered for the part.

I was proud of myself. I'd reacted appropriately to every situation, and I hoped to get the role. Even though it was after five, I called Mr. Jeffers, who sounded friendly and excited.

"You did great this morning," he said.

"You mean this afternoon," I corrected him.

"If they were making a decision right now, you'd be it," he assured me, and I could almost see his brilliant smile over the phone. "Come in tomorrow afternoon. I'll probably have good news for you."

That night I couldn't sleep. I had images of myself as Carole Blanca, my first major role in a movie, made by Warner Brothers, a famous Hollywood company. It wasn't legitimate theater, but my training at Performing Arts would ensure that I rose above the indicated performances of movie actors. I'd be brilliant. It would be the first time in my short acting career that I would play a Puerto Rican. Not Maria or Anita or any of the Sharks' girlfriends. I was to be a character with a name, a smart girl, someone my age.

The next day, when I went to Mr. Jeffers's office, he seemed surprised to see me.

"You said I should come today," I reminded him.

"Yes, of course," he was flustered, appeared confused, as if I were the last person he expected. "You're Esmeralda Santiago?"

"Yes."

"Right. Give me a second." He shuffled through some papers. It took him a while, and I had the impression that he was stalling. Finally he asked if I'd brought a head shot.

"You said I didn't need one."

"Right, I did." He shuffled his stacks some more.

"If this is not a good time," I offered, "I could come back."

"Yes. No. It's fine. That's fine." He took a couple of deep breaths, held them in, placed his hands in a prayer pose in front of his nose, stared at me for a few seconds until I looked away. "The truth is," he exhaled, "I had you confused with another girl."

"Oh."

"The other girl . . ." He leaned in, as if about to whisper, but his voice was the same as before. "The truth is," he repeated, "you're not right for the part."

"But you said . . ."

"The other girl, she looks more, how do I say this? Well, the truth is," he said for the third time, and I wished he'd lie because the strain in his voice told me that, whatever he was about to say, I didn't want to hear.

"The other girl looks more Puerto Rican."

"What?"

"You just don't have the look. You're a pretty girl. This is the movies. It's about the look."

"I'm too pretty to be Puerto Rican? Is that what you're saying?"

"You don't look Puerto Rican enough. But you'll be in the movie, don't worry about that. There are many other parts . . . a whole classroom of kids . . ."

I felt myself leave my body and rise to a corner of the room. There was Mr. Jeffers, looking somewhat hapless and small, and I, across from him my hands gripping the armrests of the chair as if

loosening them would make me hurtle through space. He was blubbering, or so it seemed, his brilliant smile fading more and more every time he flashed it. He wrote something on notepaper, handed it over the desk, and the me sitting on the chair took it, read it, folded it, put it inside the small pocketbook on my lap. He stood up, stretched his hand out, and I was no longer above my head. I was shaking his hand as if he'd done me a favor. I walked out of the building in a daze; went straight to the library; found a picture of Rita Moreno, another of Chita Rivera, a third of José Ferrer. They were not ugly people. They were beautiful Puerto Ricans. But did they, I asked myself, "look" Puerto Rican? Had I not known that they were, would I have said, there goes a *compatriota*? Knowing who they were, I could not know what I would have done if I hadn't known. I only knew that according to Mr. Jeffers, my one connection with the entire motion picture industry, Puerto Ricans were not pretty people.

When I came home, I didn't mention the humiliation. I announced in chirpy tones that I'd been hired to act in the movie, that I'd be paid, that the ten-year rule obviously didn't apply to me. One week before graduation, and I already had a job as an actress. I convinced myself that it was more than I could have hoped. As we'd been told over and over again, rejection was part of the business. You couldn't take it personally.

⌒⌒⌒

The auditorium at Performing Arts was filled to capacity. When we marched in, dressed in our caps and gowns, the audience stood up to applaud. It was our final performance, the last day we'd appear in the auditorium as students. Papi wasn't there. From the corner of my eye I caught Mami's proud smiles. Next to her Don Carlos, in his suit and dark glasses, stood tall and dignified, proud too, even though I wasn't his child. I'd been allowed two guests. I'd pleaded that I was the first of nine children to graduate from high school, that my mother wanted to make an example of me

and bring all the kids to watch. But the auditorium at Performing Arts was small. Only two guests per student.

During the program, many of my classmates were called up to receive special honors or prizes. My name wasn't called, but it didn't matter. I knew what I'd accomplished. Neither my mother nor my father had studied beyond elementary school. And here I was, in a foreign country, in a foreign language, graduating from a school for dreamers.

Had I stopped to think about my future, I would have been afraid. But what I felt on that bright June day was the thrill of achievement. I'd managed to get through high school without getting pregnant, without dropping out, without *algo* happening to me. I had a job as an actress in a movie, not a starring role, but at least I'd be paid, and who knew, I might be discovered.

But first I had to go home to Brooklyn with my mother and stepfather to celebrate with my sister the clerk at Woolworth's; my brother the pizza cook; my other six sisters and brothers; my grandmother and her boyfriend; my cousins the deaf mute, the wrestler, and the Americanized sisters; with my alcoholic uncle. That world in Brooklyn from which I derived both comfort and anxiety was home, as was the other world, across the ocean, where my father still wrote poems. As was the other world, the one across the river, where I intended to make my life. I'd have to learn to straddle all of them, a rider on three horses, each headed in a different direction.

"Who do you think you are?"

A week after graduating from Performing Arts, I stood in the middle of an elementary school playground in El Barrio, surrounded by other hopefuls on the first day of filming for *Up the Down Staircase*. Mr. Mulligan's assistant told us that we could expect work every day for a couple of weeks. The playground was to be our base while the crew filmed exteriors in front of the school and across the street.

Most of the other teenagers in the movie were from local schools, but a few were professionals with commercial and film credits. They'd been around sets and came prepared with books, knitting, cards, and board games to pass the time between takes.

The story line for *Up the Down Staircase* followed a young teacher, Miss Barrett, at her first job in a New York City school filled with underachievers. There was the class clown (Jewish), the ugly fat girl (white), her best friend (the part I didn't get because I didn't look Puerto Rican enough), the future young Republican (also white, also fat), the sensitive, doomed boy (Puerto Rican Negro), the Italian rebel with no cause, the slut. Sandy Dennis played the idealistic teacher. A supporting cast portrayed an assortment of other types: "Committed Teacher," "Frustrated Spinster," "Fascist Principal," "Alcoholic Poet."

Every time I learned the name of someone associated with the movie, I went to the library to look the person up. The director, Robert Mulligan, had won an Academy Award for *To Kill a Mock-*

ingbird, produced by Alan Pakula. Tad Mosel, a respected playwright, wrote the screenplay. And the character actors—Roy Poole, Eileen Heckart, Maureen Stapleton, Ruth White, and Vinnette Carroll (who was a teacher at Performing Arts)—were legitimate theater actors, as was the star, Sandy Dennis, who'd just costarred with Elizabeth Taylor and Richard Burton in *Who's Afraid of Virginia Woolf?* I was proud to be in the midst of so much talent.

Most of the exteriors were filmed in El Barrio, outside the elementary school and the streets around it. We were called to the location early in the morning and were often there until late afternoon. We did a scene several times and then waited for the lights, camera, and sound to be ready for another take from a different direction. It was tedious work, but it did give me a lot of time to read, to learn to play Monopoly and Scrabble, to chat with the other extras. Like me, they hoped to make such an impression in the movie that they'd be discovered, go to Hollywood and become stars. We did everything we could to gain the attention of the director, producer, and crew. We massaged sore shoulders, carried coffee, flirted, listened attentively to dumb jokes. It paid off. After the exteriors were shot, some of us were chosen to be featured in the classroom, which meant more work and higher pay.

The production moved to a high school near Lincoln Center, where the hall, stairway, and some of the classroom and office scenes were filmed. Then we were called to a sound stage in the West 20s, where the classroom was recreated complete with a giant transparency of the view outside the windows of the school we'd just left. The walls moved out of the way for the cameras, lights, and technicians who ran around between takes to adjust lights or microphones or to powder Sandy Dennis's face or spray her hair.

When she wasn't needed on the set, Miss Dennis went to her dressing room or sat in a director's chair, where she was approached for autographs by kids brave enough to risk being shooed

away. She was friendly, seemed to enjoy it when one of us talked to her as if she were a normal person and not a movie star. Sometimes she did things that we didn't know how to interpret. Once, we came back from lunch to film a scene that required deep emotion and concentration on everyone's part. We rehearsed the scene numerous times, having been warned before the break that the scene was difficult to shoot, that we should listen, concentrate, follow directions carefully to make it easier for the featured actors. We were nervous, and when Miss Dennis came in, we focused and prepared for the moment. Mr. Mulligan called "Action!" in a soft voice. Sandy Dennis's face twitched, she opened her mouth, and out came a long, ripe, thunderous burp. Everyone froze in place, Mr. Mulligan called "Cut!"

Miss Dennis giggled. "I shouldn't have beer at lunch." We cracked up. It took us a while to settle down because the minute Mr. Mulligan called action, someone laughed, and pretty soon the entire cast and crew were giggling.

Usually, a stand-in Sandy Dennis's height and coloring took her place while lights and cameras were adjusted. But sometimes Miss Dennis did it. One day she sat at her desk while technicians worked around her. My desk was directly in front of hers, and every once in a while she looked up and smiled. Then, out of nowhere, she asked if I had any sisters or brothers.

"Yes, I'm the oldest of nine children," I said.

"Nine!"

"Five girls and four boys."

"Hasn't your mother heard about birth control?"

Someone behind me snickered. "She doesn't believe in it," I mumbled, because I didn't know what else to say. Miss Dennis nodded, no longer interested, and began a conversation with Liz, who sat next to me.

Birth control was in the news because of the recently developed pill to prevent pregnancy. Whenever we discussed it at home, it was agreed by the adults around the kitchen table that "the Pill" was nothing more than a license for young women to have sex

without getting married. The fact that my mother, grandmother, and almost every other female relative of ours had sex without marriage was not mentioned. If I pointed that out to them, I was scolded for being disrespectful. In any case, I would never suggest that Mami avoid having babies. While being in a large family was hard for all of us, there was not a single sister or brother I'd rather not have.

For myself, however, I'd decided that I'd changed enough diapers for a lifetime and planned to sign up for the pill as soon as there was any possibility I'd need it.

Sometimes, when we were dismissed from the set of *Up the Down Staircase* early, I window-shopped on Fifth Avenue or spent hours at the Lincoln Center Library listening to Broadway musicals. From time to time, men approached me.

"Excuse me, is this seat taken?" They pointed to the empty chair next to me, and I felt like saying, "Yes, my invisible cousin is there," but never dared. Next thing I knew, I was carrying on a conversation with Dan or Fred or Matt or Kevin. Sometimes they invited me for a cup of coffee. We sat across from each other discussing theater, since most of the men I met in the middle of the day on weekdays in Manhattan were unemployed actors. As I listened to them expound on whether the Method was passé, or whether legitimate theater actors were selling out if they did commercials, I tried to determine if this qualified as a date. I didn't know what the rules were for dating, never having done it. And I felt pretty stupid asking people who did know about it, like the girl who played the slut in *Up the Down Staircase*, or Liz, my seat mate on the set. I read *Sex and the Single Girl*, Mary McCarthy's *The Group*, some Harold Robbins, trying to figure out what one did on dates, should I ever have one. But my encounters at the library never went further than coffee, and there were no other candidates.

Delsa had a boyfriend, Norma had a boyfriend, Héctor had a girlfriend. But none of them dated. My sisters' boyfriends came to our house on Sunday, had dinner with us, sat in front of the television with the younger kids, then left at a respectable hour. Héctor's girlfriend came with her mother, or Héctor went to her house and did what Delsa's and Norma's boyfriends did at ours. They were not permitted to go anywhere as couples without a chaperone, most frequently one of the younger kids because they had to be looked after, couldn't be ditched, and snitched if anything untoward took place.

Because I had the most freedom, I could get away with a solo clandestine date in the city. I hadn't tested it, since no one asked, but I began to plan for the day when I'd have to do it. Every day toward the end of summer, as *Up the Down Staircase* wound down, I stayed out later, giving one excuse or another for coming home long after expected. Most of the time Mami scrunched her brow, narrowed her eyes, pursed her lips, any of the familiar grimaces I understood meant she had misgivings but was not about to give into them yet. In the interest of not raising suspicions for what I wasn't doing, I didn't take advantage. I slowly raised the threshold of her permissiveness, and when she complained I was late too many days in a row, I didn't go out if there was no filming the next day. I played with my sisters and brothers or went shopping with Mami or hung around the house reading, my hair in curlers in an attempt at a new hairdo, and tried to act as if I had nothing to hide, which I didn't, certain that someday I would.

⁓

Although I'd worked hard to be discovered on the set of *Up the Down Staircase*, when the movie wrapped there were no offers from Hollywood, so I had to figure out what to do next. I gave myself a month to be cast in another movie, a play, or as a dancer with a company. I bought *Backstage* and *Variety* every week, made a list of the auditions for which I might qualify, called casting

agents, appeared at rehearsal studios where try-outs were announced. But there were no parts for a Puerto Rican ingenue/ Cleopatra/Indian classical dancer.

Late summer and early fall was a rough time for Mami because of the enormous expense of getting the kids ready for school and another winter. I'd made a lot of money over the summer but had spent most of it on dance classes and a wardrobe appropriate for an actress/dancer who needed to make a good impression at auditions. I gave Mami a portion of each paycheck, and Don Carlos also helped, especially now that Mami was pregnant again. But it wasn't enough, so we moved from our house to a smaller, third-floor apartment where the rent included utilities.

The owner of the house, Doña Lila, lived on the second floor with her two sons, one of whom was a couple of years older than me. Neftalí was slender, with a dark *café con leche* complexion and startling green eyes. He was the handsomest man I'd ever seen, and his deferential manner, soft voice, and tender smile made me flutter and tingle whenever he looked my way.

My sisters and brothers noticed I liked Neftalí.

"How come you don't sit around the house with your hair in curlers any more?" Héctor asked.

"Yeah, and you go up and down the stairs twenty times a day," added Alicia.

"You used to pay us to take the garbage out when it was your turn," Raymond complained.

"Come on, Negi," Norma begged. "I'm not making any money from you."

Neftalí came upstairs frequently, joined the domino and gin rummy games around the kitchen table that competed with laughter from the television set in the other room. He was a terrible player, which made him fun to play with, since we wagered on every game. He came on Sundays, like Delsa's and Norma's boyfriends. He liked to read, which I appreciated, but his favorite books were serial science fiction novels, which I didn't understand. He was a high school graduate and talked about going to college. In the meantime, he worked in the garment center, pushing carts

loaded with newly made clothes from the factory where they were made to the warehouse from where they were shipped. He said it was like lifting weights and let my younger brothers dangle from his bent arm to show off his biceps.

"You're in love! I knew you didn't mean it when you said . . . you know," Alma blushed, "about your virginity going to the highest bidder."

"I'm not going to have sex with him or anything," I protested, but I blushed too, though for a different reason. For days I'd fantasized about kisses from Neftalí's *café con leche* lips. And more than once I'd let my hands skitter across my body, imagining they were his. "Anyway," I continued, "we haven't even been alone yet. Mami doesn't take her eyes off me whenever he's around."

Which was true. But it was also true that Neftalí didn't show any interest in being alone with me. There were plenty of opportunities. He could have walked with me when I went on one of the many errands I volunteered to do for Mami. He could have waited for me at the train station when I came back from work. He could have come up while Mami was at work and the kids and Tata watched television. But he did none of that. He seemed content to join my family, to gaze at me from time to time with his unnerving green eyes, to gamble lavishly against the hand dealt me in gin rummy.

"He'll act when the time is right," Alma guessed. "He knows your mother expects things to be done a certain way."

"I wish I knew if he liked me, at least."

"He wouldn't visit so much if he didn't like you."

But I wasn't so sure. If he liked me, he should show it. He should send flowers, hire mariachis to serenade me, bring me chocolates, write poems. He should do something romantic that proved he cared about me in a way he didn't care about anyone else. When he did nothing, I followed the advice in *Sex and the Single Girl* and played hard to get. If I heard his step up the stairs, I disappeared into my room. I paid my sisters and brothers to do my errands again, so that I no longer went past his door four or five times a day. I stopped announcing when I'd be home.

One day I came back to find Doña Lila at our kitchen table. "He's not violent," she murmured between tears. "He never hurt a fly." Mami and Tata huddled by her, rubbed her shoulders, made humming sounds meant to soothe. I thought one of her sons had been accused of killing somebody and silently prayed that it hadn't been Neftalí.

"*A Neftalí lo llamaron del servicio*," Mami answered my silent question, but I had no idea what she meant by "Neftalí was called by the service."

"He's been drafted," Delsa interpreted.

Mami and Tata rubbed Doña Lila's shoulders, tried to convince her that just because Neftalí was drafted didn't mean he'd go to Vietnam. But none of us believed that. More than once Mami thanked *Dios* and the *Vírgenes* that Héctor was only fourteen. She and Tata prayed out loud that the war would end before he was old enough to be drafted and sent to what we feared was certain death.

It was hard to make sense of what was going on in Vietnam. The images were so incongruous. We watched news reports of soldiers having a great time, soldiers who laughed and made rabbit ears behind one another's heads as sober newsmen talked about casualties. We saw the landscape, lush and tropical, the long beaches lined with palm trees that reminded us of Luquillo, on Puerto Rico's northern coast. Cheerful soldiers, picturesque rice paddies, reporters who leaned manfully against army trucks, spoke into the camera while behind them young men in fatigues cavorted or carried one another in stretchers. It didn't seem real.

But here it was, my first potential boyfriend, about to go to war. It was too much like the radio *novelas* I'd listened to as a child, where the handsome hero went to war, while the beautiful heroine stayed home, wrote soulful letters, and fended off suitors not nearly as worthy as her beloved. I was torn between feeling sorry for Doña Lila and the romance of a boyfriend in a faraway country fighting for democracy.

That night Neftalí came upstairs, and I didn't hide. Don Julio and Don Carlos, both of whom had fought in Korea, told him

what he could expect in basic training. "They'll make a man out of you," Don Julio joked, and Neftalí smiled shyly and looked my way.

The next day I made sure to take the garbage out, and there was Neftalí at the bottom of the stairs, with his family's trash.

"Will you wait for me?" he said, so softly that I heard "Will you weigh it for me?"

I looked at him with what must have been a stupid expression because he came closer and repeated his question.

"I'll write to you," I responded.

"I'll speak to your mother," he said, "to make it official."

I'd been waiting eagerly for pledges of love from Neftalí and the tingles and flutters that accompanied thoughts of him were now tremors and shivers. "What do you mean, official?"

"*Tú sabes*," he murmured with a shy smile, and leaned over for a kiss.

I backed away. "No, I don't know." This was not the way I'd imagined it. He was supposed to get down on one knee, to say he loved me, to offer a diamond ring, at least to use the word "marriage" in a complete sentence. It wasn't right that he expected me to propose to myself as we stood in a dim hallway holding bags heavy with trash.

"What's the matter with you?" he said, an edge to his voice so familiar, it could have been Mami's.

I slid past him out the door to the barrels. "What's the matter with *you*?" I wanted to ask but didn't. I was sure he didn't know any more than I did. I felt like crying. He came up behind me.

"I thought you liked me," he whined, and the sound grated.

"I don't." I couldn't stop myself from being mean. A few minutes earlier he'd been a dream, and now I was telling him I didn't like him. What *was* the matter with me? I ran into the building, up the stairs, into my room, buried my face in the pillow. I sobbed as if Neftalí had done something terrible, when all he did was love me. Or did he? Why didn't he say it? I was confused, unable to understand why I'd responded as I had. I was ashamed.

He'd stood on the sidewalk holding the garbage, looking at me as if I'd lost my mind. Which is what it felt like. I was crazy, nuts, *loca*. Who'd want to come anywhere near me?

"Neftalí hasn't been up to see us in a while," Mami said a few days later, her eyes searching for a reaction. I shrugged my shoulders.

I stepped past Neftalí's door on my way to work and back on tiptoe. A part of me hoped we'd cross in the hall, and we'd talk and I'd apologize, but I didn't know what to say after that. So it was a relief when, after a week, Doña Lila came to say that Neftalí had gone to visit relatives in Puerto Rico before reporting to basic training. She watched me as she made the announcement, and there was resentment in her eyes. But she never said anything, and neither did Mami, and neither did I. There was nothing to say. I played out the scene with the trash bags in my head hundreds of times, trying to find a reason for my behavior. But it was no use. I'd behaved badly and couldn't forgive myself.

My month deadline to get an acting or dancing job came and went, and it was clear that I'd have to find another line of work. I answered a classified ad, and the week before Labor Day I was met at the door of the personnel office of Fisher Scientific by Mr. Kean, who had the characteristic turned-out, shoulders-back, lifted-from-the-hips posture of a former ballet dancer. He asked me to fill out an application, then took me into a small room with a typewriter on a small table. From a shelf by the door, he picked up a kitchen timer, a spiral-bound book, and a sheaf of paper, which he set next to the typewriter.

"We have openings in typing," he said, "so let's see how fast you do it." Mr. Kean watched as I put the paper in the typewriter and lined it up so that the edges were even. He opened the spiral-bound book to a random page, placed it next to the typewriter, set the timer, and said, "Start."

I typed as fast as I could, but I'd had no practice since the course at Performing Arts and made so many mistakes that when the bell rang, I was ashamed to show Mr. Kean the page.

"I see," he marked the mistakes in red. "Don't feel bad," he assured me, "not everyone was born to type." He laughed, and that made me feel better. "Let's see what else we can find for you." He led me to his desk in a corner of a room full of desks that reminded me of the welfare office. He riffled through a box of three-by-five cards, pulled out a couple, read the notes scribbled on them, then dialed a number. "Don't worry," he said. "There's a job in the mail room."

We took a rickety elevator to a room the width and depth of the building. Rectangles of fluorescent light fixtures cast bluish light over everything and everyone. The room was a labyrinth of gray metal desks in rows. Wide aisles divided the purchasing department from international sales from the noisy corner where typists sat, clickety-clacking for eight hours a day broken by two fifteen-minute coffee breaks and a half-hour lunch. At the far corner, in front of a row of dusty windows with a view of rooftops, was the mail room. It wasn't a room at all, but a section divided by a long table flanked by file cabinets in a horseshoe, with just enough room between them to make a passageway into the work area. Under the windows there were two more tables, and at the end a wooden desk with an armchair. Mr. Kean knocked on the table as if it were a door. A stately blonde woman stood up from behind one of the cabinets where she'd been putting folders away.

"Come in, dear," she smiled. She had an aristocratic air perfectly appropriate in spite of the setting. Mr. Kean introduced us, and Ilsa Gold interviewed me standing up, even though there were chairs under the tables by the window. Mr. Kean led me back to his office, where his phone rang, on cue, the minute we reached his desk. "You're hired," he announced in such cheery tones that I was certain he was as happy for me as I was for myself.

Ilsa explained my duties. I was to open the mail in the morning, sort it, distribute it, pick up outgoing mail in the afternoon, run it through the postage meter, and get it ready for the mailman, who came by at the end of the day. In between, I was to retrieve and file documents in any of the fifteen cabinets that formed the horseshoe of our office. By the end of the first day my fingers were shredded with paper cuts. The next morning, I showed up with Band-Aids on every finger. Ilsa looked at me curiously but didn't say a thing.

There was more work than two people could handle. Ilsa said she'd hire another person to help us, but that the right candidate hadn't come along.

"I'm very particular about who works for me," she assured me. She spoke with an accent that became heavier when she was nervous or had to talk on the telephone. I asked her where she was from.

"Far away," she said with a mysterious smile. I felt bad for prying.

The best part of my job was when I collected or delivered the mail. It gave me a chance to visit the departments, to chat with the secretaries or typists, the purchasing clerks, the salesmen. One of them, Sidney, was always at his desk when I came around.

"He's a good boy," Ilsa said, which made me giggle. "What's so funny?"

"He doesn't look like he's ever been a boy, he's so serious."

"As he should be," she said, but didn't elaborate and I didn't ask because she was frequently enigmatic, and when I asked her to explain, she clammed up or found something to do that minute.

Fisher Scientific had an employee cafeteria, but because someone had to be available should a file be needed, Ilsa and I didn't take our breaks together. In any case there was a hierarchy that determined who took breaks with whom. After a few awkward attempts to join people who were friendly when I came to drop off or pick up their mail, I learned that my place was with the clerks and other low-level employees. The supervisors, managers, and

executive secretaries sat in their own groups, like high school cliques on an adult level.

There was a lot of gossip during the breaks. Gus drank too much. Phil's marriage was on the rocks. Loretta was pregnant with no husband in sight. People's problems kept us in suspense from morning coffee break to lunch to afternoon coffee break, as details emerged over the course of the eight-hour workday. When nothing juicy happened, there was the question of how women dressed for work. Brenda was too conservative and wasn't it a pity, because she had a nice figure. Lucille, however, was not nearly shapely enough for the revealing outfits she insisted on wearing. Penny's frequent hair color changes made her bald, and that was why she wore wigs. Jean's legs were too thick for miniskirts. Roberta wore too much perfume.

I worried that if I wasn't there, my coworkers would talk about me, so I rushed to the cafeteria the minute my break was due and stayed until they all headed back to their desks. At home, I repeated the gossip for the amusement of my family, who followed the stories as if they'd met the people involved. For dramatic impact, I exaggerated or added details not present in the first telling. Pretty soon I believed my version was the real thing and was surprised when facts veered from what ought to have happened, given the scenario I'd invented.

One day, as I came down the stairs of the elevated train on my way home, I was surprised to find Neftalí waiting for me. In the few weeks since he left for Puerto Rico, I'd sent him off to war, where he distinguished himself. I had received his love letters, responded with cool but interested reserve, obtained vows of enduring love, married in a cathedral with my sisters and brothers in attendance, gone on a honeymoon to Tahiti, and was about to bear twins—all in the fifteen minutes it took me to walk to and from the train station. Faced with him, I realized that the Neftalí

of my imagination was taller and better dressed than the Neftalí in real life. He was also more poised. The flesh-and-blood Neftalí hung his head and mumbled hello while I asked myself what I could have seen in him a mere three weeks ago.

We walked side by side down the crowded sidewalk. It was a mild September afternoon, and the stores were open. Each door was an entrance into a cave rich with treasures: tropical fruits and vegetables; newspapers and magazines; colorful candies in shiny wrappers; racks of plastic-covered dresses, blouses, and skirts. People ducked in and out, their shopping carts squeaking behind them. Crumpled brown bags bulged with musty-smelling coats from the secondhand store. Women sat on their stoops while their children skipped rope, roller-skated, pitched bottle caps against a wall.

Neftalí and I dodged in and out of the crowd, enough space between us to fit a small child. I wished he'd try to touch me, to steal a kiss, something to indicate we were more than just neighbors. But all he did was tell me about his trip to Puerto Rico, which made me jealous.

"I hadn't been since I was kid," he said. "Those *quenepas*, man. You can't get them here."

I ignored that he'd called me "man" because I tasted the round, crackly skinned, slippery, sweet, solid-centered *quenepa* of my childhood.

He touched my shoulder and I jumped back. "You were in a trance," he explained.

"I'm sorry."

"Anyway, I was wondering if you'd like to live in Puerto Rico."

"Someday."

"Then we can settle there. In Ponce, so you can eat all the *quenepas* you like. I picked out a *solar* for a house."

"Are you planning to marry me?" I asked, incredulous.

"You like me, don't you?" Then, in an accusatory tone, "You act like you do."

"Is this a proposal?"

"You want me down on my knees?" He kneeled on the sidewalk, like in church, clutched my hand. "Is this what you want?"

People steered around us on the sidewalk. "Say yes!" somebody called, and there was laughter.

"Let go!" I pulled my hand back and ran up the street.

"Who do you think you are?" he yelled after me. "You're a big movie actress now. Is that it? I'm not good enough for you, is that it? Is that it?"

His voice faded into the clatter and thrum of the street. I ran as fast as my high heels allowed, my purse banging my side as if someone followed me with a stick. Who did I think I was? I wasn't sure, but I knew for certain I wasn't about to be Neftalí's wife.

There were times when I left our apartment, caught a train, rode for an hour, rose from the subway station to the crooked streets of the Village, walked six blocks to Fisher Scientific, rode in the elevator, and realized where I was only when the doors opened to the fluorescent glow and clatter of typewriters in the huge room where I worked. It was an enormous stage lit on all sides, with an audience that could see every action from any angle. A daily theater in the round.

Ilsa professed that she had hired me because of my attitude. "You're positive and enthusiastic," she asserted. "You'll go far if you keep that up."

Sometimes my face hurt from smiling, from maintaining the alert demeanor of someone excited about what she did. But the truth was that my job was boring. Hours of filing papers that I couldn't read because Ilsa made a face if the stack in front of me hadn't decreased every time she looked in my direction. I looked forward to the half hour I spent delivering and picking up the mail, which at least allowed me to chat with the other employees. But it took enormous energy to talk without saying much about myself. People were shocked when they learned I was the oldest

of nine children with a tenth on the way. Their reaction embarrassed me, as if it were my fault Mami was fertile.

When my coworkers asked for details, I made light of our living situation. "Nine children, three adults in a four-room apartment," I grinned. "It sounds worse than it feels," I insisted.

If pressed, I admitted that Mami wasn't married to the man whose baby she carried, had, in fact, not married the father of any of her children. My coworkers' eyes crinkled, their lips tightened as they judged what kind of woman Mami was and, by extension, what kind of girl I was.

"But I'm not allowed to date," I joked, to let them know I understood the irony but that my family had values that ought to command respect.

More than once I was told I didn't "sound" Puerto Rican. "You don't have an accent," Mr. Merton, one of the supervisors, remarked, and I explained about Performing Arts and standard speech. When he implied that I didn't "act" Puerto Rican, I swallowed the insult. "Maybe you haven't met enough of us," I suggested, hurt that he was surprised Puerto Ricans could be competent, chaste girls who spoke good English.

I smiled, did my job, gossiped. At the end of the day, I retraced my steps to Brooklyn, sometimes in the same haze in which I left, but exhausted, the performance having gone on too long.

"How was your day?" Mami asked each evening as I walked into our apartment.

"Good," I smiled brightly, and ducked into my room to change. Delsa, used to the routine by now, climbed down from the top bunk of our bed and left me alone.

I wiped off my makeup, then stripped. Esmeralda Santiago remained in the folds of each garment I took off and put away. Naked, nameless, I lay on my bed and slept. Half an hour later, Negi emerged, dressed in the comfortable clothes I wore at home. Another performance was about to begin, this one in Spanish.

"Pearls bring tears."

After weeks of interviewing people, Ilsa hired another clerk, Regina.

"She's beautiful, isn't she?" remarked Ilsa one day, as Regina walked away from us.

"She's giving them whiplash," I laughed.

Every man in the office craned his neck when Regina strolled by. Their eyes followed her as she moved from desk to desk, her hips and buttocks undulating in a most un-American fashion. Some of our male coworkers actually broke into a sweat when Regina came near. When she spoke, in a throaty voice with a Brazilian accent, her shushes and hums sent visible ripples through men's bodies.

Regina seemed unaware of her beauty. She dressed in long skirts, sleeved blouses with prim collars, squat-heeled shoes. She favored drab colors, wrapped her shoulder-length hair into a loose bun at the nape of her neck, wore little makeup, just a dab of lipstick and mascara.

Ilsa assigned me to train her. Regina followed me around long after she learned the simple tasks involved in our work as mail/file clerks. At first, I was annoyed that whenever I turned around, there she was, beautiful and dazed. Then one day, as we walked down for our coffee break, she thanked me.

"What did I do?"

"I am, how you say, culture shock," she confided. "In Brasil was not so." She opened her arms as if to embrace the world.

"In Puerto Rico," I said, "it was not so either."

Neither of us needed to say more to understand what the other meant, but I still didn't know why she thanked me.

"I have not friends here," she said. "Only you."

I was so touched, I hugged her.

During our breaks, we didn't sit with the other clerks but took a table by ourselves and talked about our lives. She was an only child who had nursed her mother through a three-year battle with breast cancer. When her mother died, Regina's father sent her to New York.

"I cry every day in three months," she said. "Is horrible see your mother die a little bit, a little bit." She lived with her paternal aunt, who had an important job at the Fisher Scientific offices in New Jersey. "She say me three month enough tears. I must get job. And soon I have get marry."

"Who are you going to marry?"

"I don't know."

I imagined her aunt to be the evil stepmother in fairy tales, and soon Regina's predicament was added to the stories I embellished for my family's benefit. Mami and Tata were ready to adopt her.

"Poor thing," Mami said, "motherless and alone in this city."

"And that woman," Tata added "*no tiene corazón.*"

Mami nodded that Regina's aunt did sound heartless. "*Pobrecita,*" she repeated, as she shook her head for poor Regina.

Because Regina's English wasn't very good, and because Ilsa was nervous on the phone, I was in charge of answering the calls to our office. Most of the time people called to request a file, or to warn us that they had a large mailing and we should allow extra time for pickups. One day, just as Ilsa left for her break, the phone rang. It was Sidney, who was always so pleasant to me. His office was twenty feet from ours, and he usually just walked over to ask for whatever he needed.

I turned around to make sure he was at his desk, and he waved. "How can I help you?" I waved back.

"Go out with me Friday night." He smiled.

"On a date?" I turned away because I didn't want him to see my excitement.

"Yes. Dinner, a movie, whatever you like."

"Dinner sounds good," I said into the phone, softly, because Regina had noticed what was going on and looked from me to Sidney with amusement. "Thank you," I hung up, then felt stupid for thanking him. I was afraid to look toward his desk, in case he could see me blush.

"He's very nice," Regina volunteered.

"How do I ask my mother?" I wondered aloud, and Regina laughed.

Mami wanted to know who Sidney was, what he did, where we were going, how long we'd be gone. "Bring him home so we can meet him."

"I'm just going out to dinner with him Mami. I'm not going to marry him."

"It shows respect," she said. She was right, but I couldn't imagine Sidney in our apartment filled with people and furnishings. What would he think if Tata happened to be drunk when he came by? Or if Mami wore a housecoat and rollers in her hair, as she often did when we were home? Or if Don Carlos were there, in his suit and dark glasses, sitting silently at the kitchen table, a bemused smile on his lips? Or if Don Julio, his face battered like a boxer's that had taken too many hits to the head, lounged with the kids in front of *The Lawrence Welk Show?* What if my sisters and brothers giggled about the way Sidney looked? He was short, wore thick rectangular glasses that slid down his nose and left deep red grooves along his nostrils. He spoke in a soft, whiny voice that sounded as if he were complaining, even when he wasn't. His hands stuck from the sleeves of his suit small and childlike, and never rested anywhere for more than a few seconds. I found them graceful, but Mami would surely imagine them deftly undoing my bra.

Ilsa was shocked that I was going out with Sidney.

"He asked you?" she asked, incredulous.

"Of course," I answered, annoyed she thought I had asked him.

She looked toward his desk, a somber expression on her face. "Interesting," she mused.

"Is there anything I should know about him?"

"No, dear," Ilsa said, "it's just . . . I'm surprised, that's all. He's a good boy. You have a good time."

The day before the date, Regina accompanied me to Gimbel's. I liked to shop alone, but I was worried about making a good impression and needed help in choosing something appropriate. Regina was the perfect person to restrain my impulses for theatrical, colorful, or dramatic clothing. When I came home with a new navy blue suit, low-heeled shoes, a demure handbag, Mami couldn't hide her smile.

"What's wrong with it?" I asked.

"Nothing," she said. "It's okay." She turned away to stifle a giggle.

"It's an old lady outfit," was Tata's opinion.

"I got it in the junior section," I explained, but as I looked at it, the suit seemed more Regina's style. "It's elegant," I added, repeating Regina's words. "It looks better on." I couldn't persuade anyone.

As I dressed the next morning, I told myself that it was better for me to seem conservative and old-ladyish than like a hot *tamale* right out of *West Side Story*. When I walked into the office, people stared, and some commented on how cute I looked, which made me feel better.

Sidney wasn't in his office all morning, and I worried that he'd changed his mind and wouldn't show up. During lunch, Regina pulled a small pouch from her handbag.

"Wear these," she said. Inside the pouch was a string of pearls. "They were my mother's," she explained. "They will be nice for your special night."

The pearls hung heavy in my hands, languid like a tropical

afternoon. I coveted them. My desire embarrassed me. "Regina, I can't wear these." I handed them back reluctantly. "What if I lose them?"

"You will take good care, I know," she said. "Please accept to wear them."

I hugged the pearls around my neck and she fixed the clasp. When she sat back to admire them, Regina gently straightened the collar of my blouse. She smiled sweetly, her eyes misted. "You remind me of my mother," she said. I had to swallow hard to keep from crying.

Sidney walked into the office five minutes before five. "I'm sorry. There was a lot of traffic from New Jersey in the tunnel."

I assured him it was all right, relieved that he'd shown up.

"Go," Ilsa said, "put on some lipstick. We'll finish here." I ran to the rest room and fixed my face and hair, straigthened the pearls around my neck. They shimmered pale against my cinnamon skin.

"I thought we'd eat near where I'm parked," Sidney suggested, as we walked down the street in a direction I'd never taken. The air was moist, and a cold wind blew from the Hudson, cut through my cloth coat until I shivered. We walked down a cobblestone street, around huge delivery trucks backed up to loading docks.

"Are we going far?" I asked after a few blocks.

"Just around the corner," Sidney said.

The restaurant was in a basement. An awning flapped over the door with a name written in such dark characters that it couldn't be made out. Inside, two brick walls were lined with booths, each lit with a single flickering candle inside a red glass. The cloths and napkins on the tables glowed a fluorescent white, floated in the darkness, each with its red circle of light. It reminded me of my grandmother's altar in Puerto Rico, the mystery of the rosary she recited every evening.

We were the only patrons. The bartender looked up when we walked in, nodded us to a booth. In the dim room, Sidney's fea-

tures softened. His eyes, enormous behind his glasses, were kind, and there was a sadness in them that made me want to be nice to him.

A waitress appeared from the back pushing bobby pins into a frothy beehive. "I'll take your drink order," she informed us.

I'd never had an alcoholic beverage anywhere but with my family, at Christmas, when Mami made several bottles of *coquito* with fresh coconut milk and Puerto Rican rum. When I asked for a Coke, both Sidney and the waitress were disappointed. He ordered a whiskey sour.

"Don't you drink alcohol?" he asked.

"Only at home," I answered, and he laughed. It took me a while to understand why. "I didn't mean it that way. I mean . . ."

"I know what you mean, don't worry about it."

We chatted for a few minutes about life at Fisher Scientific, where he worked as a microscope salesman. He liked the work, because he visited clients in several states, instead of being stuck in the office all day. He'd recently moved out of his widowed mother's house into his own apartment.

"It's not much," he confided. "I hate living alone, but I liked it less when I lived with my mother."

We ordered dinner from the specials board, discussed movies we'd seen, places we'd like to visit, books we'd read. We talked about our coworkers, and he told me something I didn't know. Ilsa, my supervisor, was Hungarian and had survived Nazi concentration camps.

"She doesn't like to talk about that part of her life," Sidney confided.

"I don't blame her." It explained a lot. Her accent, for starters. The faraway look that came over her, as if she heard voices.

"Look at her left arm sometime," Sidney suggested. "She has numbers tattooed right here." He touched me near the inside of my elbow.

He was easy to talk to, a generous listener. We sat at our table long after we'd eaten, sipping coffee, talking about dance and

music. He played the violin, and I admitted I knew nothing about classical music except what I'd heard at Performing Arts assemblies.

"MOTE-zart," he corrected my attempt to name composers. I dug a piece of paper from my handbag, wrote down more names. "How do you pronounce them?" I asked. "BATE-hoven." I repeated after him. "Rack-MANNY-nov. Pooch-EE-nee."

It was drizzling when we left the restaurant.

"How about a walk? I have an umbrella in the car."

At first, he held the umbrella so that I was protected and he wasn't. When I pointed out that he was getting wet, he drew closer, took my hand, kissed my cheek. I quivered with pleasure, with the romance of a stroll down a cobblestoned street in the rain with a sweet man who played the violin.

"If my mother knew I was out with a *shiksa*, she'd kill me," Sidney blurted out.

"A what?" I stopped so suddenly that he walked a few steps before he realized I wasn't with him.

"A *shiksa*. A girl who's not Jewish."

I didn't know if he was insulting me or if I should feel flattered that he'd gone against his mother's wishes to be with me. I understood why Ilsa was surprised that Sidney had asked me out. He wasn't supposed to. "Is it against your religion?"

"Sort of," he said, but I heard "Yes."

"Then you'd better not bring me home to meet her." He gaped at me as if the thought scared him. "It's a joke," I reassured him, and he smiled, unconvinced. "It's getting late," I decided.

We ran to where he'd parked, as if to get away from whatever had come between us. The rain picked up the minute we entered the quiet, protective hull of his car. I directed him to Brooklyn. Squinting against the glare of other cars, Sidney paid close attention to the street signs, the turns he'd have to take on his way out. I tried to make conversation, but he stopped me. "Just a second, I have to concentrate. At the pizzeria," he continued talking to himself, "I go right, then left. Got it." He turned to me. "This is your street," he grinned, "which one is your building?"

Our Venetian blinds were drawn, but, through a slit, Mami peered out of our third-floor window at the street below. I waited for Sidney to get out of the car, come around, open the door, hold the umbrella so that I wouldn't get wet. We went up the stairs — slowly, because I heard running, things shoved, doors slam. At the top landing, I fumbled for a key I didn't have, since there was always someone home, then pretended I'd forgotten it and knocked. Mami opened the door. She wore a maternity top and slacks, had combed her hair into playful curls, had dabbed her lips with color. I wondered if she had been dressed like this for hours, or if the running around I'd heard was due to the family getting ready for Sidney. My sisters and brothers sat on the couch and chairs, stiff as starch, their faces scrubbed, hair slicked. A flowered bed sheet divided the kitchen and living area from the front room, where I could hear Tata shushing Charlie. The kitchen smelled of freshly brewed coffee.

I introduced Sidney to Mami, then to each kid. The younger ones giggled shyly and hid behind the older ones.

"Would he like some coffee and cake?" Mami asked. On the table was a supermarket coffee cake still in its box.

"No," I answered, "he has to go." Sidney looked from me to her, expecting me to translate the exchange. "I told her you have a long drive to New Jersey."

"Oh, right, yeah." He seemed startled to be reminded of his home state. I led him to the door.

"See you Monday," I promised, letting him out. Nine pairs of eyes followed our every move. It was a relief when Sidney waved goodbye from the threshold, made his way down the stairs. Tata shuffled out from the other room, Charlie in her arms. "Is he gone?" she cackled. I closed the door and turned to face my family, who expressed their opinion.

"He's so short!"

"He has a big nose."

"His coat smelled bad."

"His glasses are so thick."

"That's how come he took Negi out. He's blind and couldn't see her."

I made a feeble attempt to defend Sidney, "He's a sweet man," but it was useless. I gave up and added to their mirth by revealing that his hobby was the violin. They thought that was really funny.

Mami looked at the clock on the kitchen wall. "At least he behaved like a gentleman and brought you home early. It's not even ten o'clock," she noted.

"Maybe Negi couldn't stand to be with him anymore," Delsa snorted.

"Where did you get those pearls?" Tata asked, suddenly serious.

"Regina lent them to me. They were her mother's."

"Take them off," she shrieked. She lurched toward me, about to remove them from my neck. I covered them with my hand. "Pearls bring tears," she warned.

"Ay, Tata, stop with your superstitions." The pearls felt warm against my neck.

"They bring tears," she repeated, "especially if they're someone else's. And a dead woman's!" She came at me again. I ducked into my room and closed the door. The pearls felt lovely. There was no way I'd believe they brought tears. All I had to do was listen to the laughter on the other side of the door.

⌒⌒⌒

I thought it might be awkward to see Sidney the following week, but he was away for the first three days, and by the time he returned, I was in love with Otto.

Otto was a big man, with golden skin and hair, a deep voice that rumbled out of a barrel chest. We locked eyes when I went to deliver the mail in the International Department. For the rest of the morning, we exchanged glances across the blue-gray fluorescence of the office. He disappeared at lunch but was there when I came to pick up the outgoing mail from his desk.

"You are Esmeralda, yes?" he asked. The way he pronounced my name, the yes at the end of the sentence, was like a song that repeated in my brain for hours. "I am Otto," he said. I stretched my hand to shake, and he held on to it, squeezed it gently before releasing it. I almost melted on the spot. He handed me a stack of letters addressed to Germany. I thanked him and continued my rounds, aware that he watched me. Although I'd always resented it when men brazenly scanned my body, I welcomed it from Otto, made sure to stay within his sight the whole time I picked up the mail. That night I fantasized about what it would feel like to be in Otto's arms and continued to dream about him over the days that he didn't return to the office.

Christmas blinked red and green in the neighborhoods of New York City. At home, we folded notebook paper into triangles, then cut out fanciful shapes to create snowflakes. Héctor carried Raymond on his shoulders as he taped the snowflakes to a corner of the ceiling. Don Carlos lifted Franky up to impale a blonde angel atop the Christmas tree. Tinsel tears dripped over the plastic branches laden with fragile balls in brilliant colors.

It was an abundant Christmas. Everyone in our household old enough to work had a job. Sundays vibrated with the thump-thump-thump of relatives climbing the three flights of stairs to our apartment. Most of them carried wrapped boxes to be placed under the tree, near which the younger kids kept watch as if the bounty might disappear if left unguarded for a few minutes.

La Muda and Gury came up one day with a bag of clothes, which Delsa, Norma, and I divided among ourselves, since Mami was pregnant and couldn't fit into any of them. From the bottom I pulled out a pale pink chiffon and taffeta party dress, the cuffs of its long sleeves and modestly scooped collar dotted with pearly beads.

"Is it bad luck," I grinned toward Tata, "to wear these pearls?"

"Not the fake ones," she chuckled, and La Muda gestured snipping off the collar and sleeves of the dress to indicate that if the pearls were real, I'd have a sleeveless dress with a very low neckline.

"You can wear it to the dance at the Armory," Mami suggested, and my sisters and I cheered, because we hadn't been dancing in months.

Sometimes I met Alma, and we spent hours on Fifth Avenue, among tourists who shoved and pushed each other before the elaborate displays the stores put on to lure us inside. When it came to spending our money, however, Alma and I went to Herald Square, where our salaries stretched further. One day, as we browsed the shoe bin in Ohrbach's basement, I looked up to a familiar face. I froze, struck by the sight of Greta Garbo bent over a stack of flat gillies at 30 percent off. She wore a black turtleneck and coat, her pale, angular face luminous under the brim of a soft black hat. When she felt me stare, she turned and disappeared in the crowd. By the time I signaled to Alma, Garbo was a memory.

That week I went to a hairdresser and had my shoulder-length hair cut blunt to chin level and parted in the middle, like Garbo's. I bought a black felt cloche, which I pulled over my ears, trying to duplicate the effect of Garbo's soft hat. It was useless, I looked nothing like her, and all the hat did was squish my hair. When I took it off, it looked as if I'd been wearing a bowl over my head.

The presents I bought were stored at Alma's, so that my family wouldn't discover what Santa Claus-Negi was to bring them. In Titi Ana's apartment, Christmas was observed quietly, with a few strands of colored lights around the windows, a small tree by the television set, a modest pile of gifts wrapped in bright paper. I spent the night in the small room off the kitchen thirty yards from the elevated train tracks. After Titi Ana, Alma, and Corazón went to bed, I stood at the window and watched trains rattle past. The people inside were ghosts, gray specters framed in darkness. Their anonymity made me homesick for the warmth of our noisy apartment. I crawled into bed, lonesome and invisible behind the lace curtain of Titi Ana's window.

The dance at the Armory was on a Sunday night. We stayed until the band played its last note, then had an early morning breakfast at a diner. Back home, I had just enough time to shower, change into daytime clothes, and head back into the city and my job at Fisher Scientific. Only half awake, I stumbled through the morning until Ilsa suggested I go home and get some rest. It was already dark as I walked to the subway station, strangely quiet for midafternoon. The cold air revived me just enough to keep me upright. My feet, sore from hours of *salsa* and *merengue* in high heels, throbbed with every step.

I was about to cross Hudson Street when someone grabbed me from behind and pulled me back to the sidewalk. I struck back with my elbow, hitting my attacker in the face, and started in the opposite direction, but stopped as a truck barreled past. Then I realized the man behind me was trying to keep me from being run over. When I turned around, there was Otto, his fingers pressed to his lips.

"Oh, my God, I'm so sorry!"

"I thought I was a hero." He tried to smile but the cut on his lip hurt.

"There's a little blood on the side." I offered a tissue, but he bent his face in my direction. I was too embarrassed to look him in the eye as I wiped the blood off the rapidly swelling lip. "You need ice."

"There's a coffee shop," he said, guiding me in its direction.

As we walked, his hand at my elbow, I wished the previous night hadn't been so much fun. My eyes were swollen from lack of sleep, my hair, in its Garbo cut, stuck out in frizzy curls because I hadn't had time to wash and straighten it. I'd worn no makeup, had grabbed the first thing I reached in my closet—the suit I'd worn on my date with Sidney—which made me look, I now realized, like a nun in street clothes.

But Otto didn't care. We sat across from each other at a window booth. "Charming," he kept saying, and I had no idea how to respond except to stammer "Thank you," which he found even more endearing.

Unlike Sidney, Otto wasn't easy to talk to, because his accent was heavy, his grammar confusing, and the pack of ice at his lips caused him to mumble. He liked restaurants or restoring, cooking or küchen, Audubon or autobahn. After many attempts, I understood he wanted me to go to a Christmas party with him at his sister's house in Long Island.

"I have to ask my mother," I said, embarrassed that at eighteen I needed permission to go to a party.

"Charming," he repeated.

He walked me to the train, and on the way to Brooklyn, I remembered his strong hands on my shoulders. He'd saved me from being run over by a truck. It was the most romantic thing that had ever happened to me.

"Not alone!" Mami said, when I asked her if I could go to Long Island with Otto.

"It's to his sister's house."

"I don't care if you're going to see the pope. You can take one of your brothers with you, or one of your sisters. But you're not going that far alone with a man I've never met." No argument could persuade her that I was old enough to take care of myself.

Regina sympathized with my problem and came up with the perfect solution. "I will come," she suggested. Although Mami had never met Regina, she agreed that a young woman who had been so recently orphaned and had picked the unflattering navy blue suit as appropriate wear for a date was the perfect chaperone. Otto thought it was a wonderful idea that Regina come with us. His cousin Gilbert needed a date for the party.

"He will like your friend," Otto assured me, and the date was fixed.

He offered to pick me up in Brooklyn, which I knew would impress Mami. The evening of the party, Don Carlos and Don Julio decided to stay home, doubtless at Mami's suggestion. Dressed in his black suit, Don Carlos sat across the kitchen table from Don Julio, also dressed up in a pressed shirt and new pants. They were joined by Héctor and Raymond, the two oldest boys in

the family, their faces scrubbed, hair newly washed and combed back. I dreaded the moment Otto would walk into this pitiful attempt to protect my virtue.

I was ready twenty minutes before Otto was to arrive. My intention was to introduce him to everyone and then get out of there as fast as possible.

When Otto and Gilbert appeared at our door, however, it was clear that it would take longer to leave than I had planned. They dominated the room—two large, Teutonic men who spoke little English. They wore suits, which, rather than make them look respectable, added to their bulk, their maleness. Mami frowned and exchanged a look with Tata, who smiled vaguely and left the room to attend to a screaming Charlie.

Otto handed me an orchid in a plastic box. I pinned it on myself because there was no way I was going to let him get that close in front of Mami. The concern on her face was worrisome. I wished Otto and Gilbert had picked up Regina on the way so that Mami wouldn't envision me alone in a car with two men for so long as a second. But it was too late. Don Carlos, who spoke good English, managed to get a phone number and address for where we'd be. He handed Otto his business card, made him take down our phone number—as if I didn't know it—while Mami made sure I had identification on me.

"*Por favor*, Mami," I pleaded, "you're embarrassing me."

"What do you mean embarrassing you?" she asked, her voice rising enough for Otto and Gilbert to take their eyes off Don Carlo's green lenses and look in our direction. Mami smiled at them, then turned to frown on me.

"We better go," I suggested, avoiding her gaze, "or Regina will think we're lost." I hoped that mention of Regina would remind Mami I had a chaperone and that she'd relax a bit.

"Call when you get there," Mami said, as she watched us trudge down the stairs in silence.

Otto and Gilbert spoke German to one another, laughed. I waited for a translation, but none came. Before climbing into

Gilbert's car, I looked up. My entire family was at the window, surrounded by blinking Christmas lights.

Maybe this was a mistake. These two men I barely knew could drive me somewhere, rape me, throw me off a bridge. I couldn't relax the entire drive to Lefrak City, where we were to pick up Regina. It didn't register when Otto mentioned that Gilbert and Regina had already been out on a date until we parked in front of her building and she ran out. She looked spectacular, dressed in a form-fitting dress under a fur, spike heels, her mother's pearls gleaming at her throat. Her perfume invaded the car, a flowery scent that lingered in the air.

"Wow," I commented, and she laughed.

"Is not every day I go to party," she said, and even the men were delighted with the happiness in her voice.

Otto's sister lived in a street of identical houses behind broad lawns. Santa Claus, reindeer, elves, and miniature carolers vied for attention with thousands of tiny lights on the roofs, eaves, and window shutters of almost every house. Something about the neighborhood was familiar. Then I remembered that Archie and Veronica, Betty, Reggie, and Jughead strolled along an identical street, without the decorations, in the comic books I'd devoured during my first year in Brooklyn.

It was easy to tell the house where the party was, because many cars were parked in front of it and the window shades were up. We came up a walk lit by strings of Christmas lights on the ground. Inside, the house was warm, smelled of cinnamon, cloves, and burning wood in a fireplace. A blonde, big-boned woman met us at the door, and Otto kissed her on both cheeks. She was Minna, his older sister. They looked alike, but Minna spoke much better English.

"I'm so happy you're here," she said, pressing my hand, "Otto has told me so much about you." Regina and I exchanged a look, wondering what he could have said, as we barely knew each other.

Minna treated us like honored guests, introduced us to everyone there, offered us drinks and miniature sausages from a tray.

Her husband, Jim, was American, but as blond, blue-eyed, and German-looking as everyone else in the room. He wore *lederhosen*, and I wasn't sure if it was really a national costume or a joke. His principal job was to keep everyone's glass full, which he did with gusto. From time to time he broke into song, and the company joined in what I took to be German Christmas carols.

We'd arrived as dinner was being served. The dining room table was heaped with food arranged by type. A turkey, a ham, a platter of meatballs, and cold cuts were set next to a variety of cheeses, whipped cream, butter. Beside them were colorful bowls of vegetables: chunks of yellow squash, milky mashed potatoes, green string beans dotted with tiny white onions, blood-red beets. Several trays held crusty breads, rolls, seeded buns. A sideboard was devoted to cakes, puddings, cookies, chocolate-covered nuts, and fruits. It was the most bountiful spread I'd ever seen, each food group set off from the other with ribbons and pine boughs.

Otto and Gilbert led us through the buffet, encouraged us to taste everything. They laughed at how diligently I kept the different flavors from contaminating one another, and at Regina's face when she tasted the whipped cream and it turned out to be not sweet, but spiced with horseradish.

After dinner, we went down to a finished basement with chairs along the walls, a bar, a Hi-fi with a stack of records that dropped one by one onto a lazy turntable. Nancy Sinatra insisted that her boots were made for walking, the Monkees were daydream believers, and the Young Rascals promised good lovin'. Otto and Gilbert flailed their arms and legs in a style I'd come to associate with American dancing, which now appeared to be an international technique. Used to the graceful, seductive movements of *salsa, merengue,* and *chachacha,* I was frustrated by the distance between our bodies, the sense that we weren't dancing together, but near each other. That changed when Percy Sledge wailed about when a man loves a woman. Someone turned the lights down. Otto took off his jacket, pulled me close, and I was finally in his arms, my head resting on his broad chest. Each time

Percy Sledge's voice rose, Otto drew me closer, and I didn't resist. As the song ended, Otto took me by the hand and led me up the stairs. Regina watched us, smiled, buried her head in Gilbert's shoulder.

"Where are we going?" I asked, but Otto didn't answer. We went down a hall. He opened a door into a dark room, but I refused to go inside. "Let's go back," I suggested. He pressed me against the wall and kissed me.

It was wonderful, his kiss. Soft, warm lips. The heat between our bodies. The slow insinuation of his tongue into my mouth. Irresistible. Each time we came up for air, he guided me closer to the door. A couple went past us into another room, and I caught a whiff of Regina's perfume. Otto mumbled some words into my ear, which I didn't get. "Please," he begged and I understood that I'd better get out from between him and the wall. His kisses were insistent, his hands strayed. I was overwhelmed, certain that if I waited a moment longer, I wouldn't be able to resist his curious fingers, his hot tongue, the desire to rip my clothes off and present myself naked before him. He was a big man, but I was a muscled dancer. With effort, I pushed him away and ran back to the crowded basement, where the Troggs sang about their wild thing.

I sat on one of the chairs against the wall, tried to calm my breathing. Otto had not followed. I was grateful not to have to face him just then.

Minna came over and sat next to me. "Are you having a good time?" she asked.

"Very nice," I responded, my voice tight. She didn't notice.

"My brother really likes you," she confided. "He's never brought a girl for us to meet before."

"I like him too," I admitted, hoping that if she conveyed that message, he might forgive me for what I'd just done.

Two small windows high on the wall faced out to the walkway in front of the house. Huge snowflakes twinkled among the Christmas lights. Minna followed my gaze. "How lovely!" she exclaimed. "Look, everyone," she called, "it's snowing."

Several couples stopped dancing to ooh at the sight. Otto came down the steps. I expected him to be angry, but he wore a sheepish expression, smiled sweetly, sat on my other side, squeezed my hand. He turned to the window where everyone was staring, and I turned in its direction. To my horror, there were my mother and Don Carlos marching toward the front door, fat snowflakes pelting their resolute faces.

⌒⌒

"Oh my God," I stood up so fast, I slipped and fell to my knees. Otto helped me up, and I ran up the stairs. I opened the door before they could knock. "What are you doing here?" I shrieked. Mami's lips were pressed together. She looked behind me at the festive house, the leftovers of the meal still on the holiday table, the curious faces that followed us to the door.

"You didn't call," Don Carlos responded. "We were worried about you."

A giant hot wave of humiliation, relief, and shame, rolled over me. Ten minutes earlier I'd almost given myself to Otto. What if Mami had found me naked in bed with him?

Minna appeared at my side, put her arm around my shoulder, invited them in, offered them a drink. But Mami declined with a strained smile, pointed to the taxi at the bottom of the walkway.

"And your friend?" she asked.

"She's in the bathroom," Minna said, too quickly.

"Where's my coat?" I croaked. Jim retrieved it from a closet by the front door. Mami stared at him—a grown man in green leather shorts with suspenders, red knee socks with dangly felt balls on the side. Otto helped me into my coat, tipped his head sympathetically when I pulled it closed and crushed what was left of the corsage he'd given me. "Thank you," I said to no one in particular.

I wanted to die, wished that on the way home, the taxi would crash and kill us, so that I never had to face Otto again. But the

driver was careful, drove slowly, which gave me plenty of time to scream at Mami and Don Carlos.

"How could you do this? I'm old enough to take care of myself!"

"Lower your voice or I'll shut your mouth for you."

The source of Mami's anger was an enigma. I argued that I'd asked her permission, had brought Otto home for her to meet, had found a chaperone. She knew where I'd be, who I'd be with, when I'd be back. Don Carlos repeated that I'd forgotten to call when I got there, but I reminded him they had Otto's sister's number. Why hadn't they called to see if I'd arrived safely? They'd gone to great trouble and expense to come get me, to humiliate me in front of my friends, to teach me a lesson I didn't need. I was hysterical all the way back to Brooklyn. As soon as we got home, I tore the pink dress with the fake pearls off me and ripped it to shreds. The tiny pearls dislodged from the fabric, plinked onto the linoleum floor, rolled into the crevices along the baseboard where roaches lurked.

～～ ◡ ⌐

Regina didn't come to work on Monday, but Otto was there. Ilsa and I were scrambling to open and sort piles of mail by ourselves when he approached the long table that divided our department from Purchasing. He was the same person as two days before, but now I saw him through Mami's eyes. Unlike Neftalí and Sidney, Otto was a man, not a boy. That didn't make him less attractive. As he stood in front of me, I couldn't stop blushing. Shame and desire alternated, fused until they were the same.

"We can have coffee, yes?" he asked. Ilsa frowned from her desk.

"My break is at 10:30." I was happy that he'd talk to me after Saturday night's fiasco. Ilsa coughed discreetly to let me know I should go back to work. Before he left, Otto bowed in her direction, which I found gallant but she found infuriating. She muttered a few words in her language that sounded hostile.

"Why don't you go out with Sidney anymore?" she asked later.

"I'm a *shiksa*." The defensive tone in my voice surprised me as much as it did Ilsa, whose eyes flickered wildly for a few seconds, then looked away.

Everyone in the cafeteria stared at Otto and me sitting by ourselves in a far table. He held my hand through the fifteen minutes I was allowed for coffee. In his halting English, he apologized for getting "fresh," which astounded me, since I had had as much to do with it as he had.

"Your mother and father is very good," he assured me, "they take good care."

"They treat me like a child."

"It is good," he consoled me. "You are not American girl. They are very free."

"I want to be free," I hinted, but he didn't get it.

"You are perfect," he smiled. "My girlfriend," he murmured, and, had I been standing, my knees would have buckled under me.

Later, we had lunch in the coffee shop where he had once nursed the wound I caused him. He had to go to Switzerland next, he informed me.

"We write each other," he offered.

I was late getting back, and Ilsa put on a face. She glared at the piles on the tables. My apology didn't affect her mood. Later, as we filed a stack of documents in side-by-side cabinets, I apologized again.

"It wasn't right," she relented, "for me to be so cross. It's not you I'm mad at, it's him." She tipped her head in the direction of the International Department. "And it's not him," she amended. "It's them." I had no idea what she was talking about. She fixed me with her blue eyes. "I had a very bad experience with Germans," she explained. Then I understood.

"But Ilsa," I argued, "they can't all be bad."

"To me they're all the same."

"But it's not fair."

"Fair? Was the murder of six million Jews fair?" Her voice rose, but not so loud that anyone else heard. I stammered that no, it wasn't, but that it was equally wrong to judge a whole nation by the actions of a few.

"A few!" She was appalled. "The whole country stood by as Jews were murdered. My mother, my father, my sisters and brother." The passion in her voice was hypnotic, and I remained silent, hoping she'd continue, but she bit her lips and said no more.

"I'm so sorry, Ilsa." I touched her arm, and she pressed my fingers and smiled sadly.

"I hope you never have to hate," she murmured.

Regina came back two days later, still weak from a bad cold. She'd heard about Mami and Don Carlos coming to rescue me in Long Island.

"How horrible for you! Minna said you were so shamed. Everybody felt bad."

"It's all right. Otto was impressed," I laughed.

"Gilbert and me, we see each other more." Regina blushed.

"Don't tell Ilsa," I warned.

Unable to convince Mami to let me stay out after I was due home, I could see Otto only at work. Over the next few days, we took lunch or coffee breaks together. Ilsa scowled every time she saw me leave without Regina, but I didn't care. Whatever feelings she had about Germans were hers, not mine. Used to being judged because some Puerto Ricans did bad things, I wasn't about to do the same to Otto.

I expected Otto to want something to remember me by. I snipped a few strands of my hair, tied them in a thin red ribbon. But he didn't ask, and I was too embarrassed to admit such a silly thing had occurred to me. He left right after the New Year. Other than holding my hand and giving me an occasional peck on the

cheek, he never touched me as he had the night of the Christmas party. His gentlemanly behavior proved that Mami was right: "A man who really cares about you respects you." I appreciated it but couldn't erase the sensations of his tongue in my mouth, his hands on my breast, his probing fingers. He was a man, and his kiss had made me feel like a woman.

"The music inside her..."

Fisher Scientific was to move its offices to New Jersey after the first of the year. Regina, Ilsa, and I were offered promotions if we transferred to the new location. With the promise of a job in New Jersey, I made a case for moving closer to work, as Regina's roommate. Mami vetoed the plan. "There's plenty of work in New York," she claimed.

Before the company moved, I took advantage of a benefit they offered. They paid part of the tuition for employees who wished to continue their education. Don Carlos, who studied accounting in night school, encouraged me to look into a community college. They were less expensive than the famous New York universities, he said. They also offered evening and weekend classes, which meant I could work and study.

I applied to Manhattan Community College because it was on 51st Street, off Sixth Avenue, close to the theater district and dance studios where I still took lessons. Courses focused on business, advertising, and marketing. I signed up for those that allowed me to be out of classes by one o'clock in the afternoon. After school, I picked up temporary jobs as a receptionist in nearby offices.

Soon after classes started, I went to the college bookstore to buy supplies. On line ahead of me stood a young woman about my age whose presence overpowered the hallway leading into the bookstore. She wore knee-high brown boots, a leather miniskirt, a

brown chiffon blouse through which her black bra showed. Her hair was ratted into a mass of golden curls held back with a leopard print chiffon scarf whose ends draped over her shoulder. Her makeup was elaborate, complete with false eyelashes.

Tired with the long line ahead of them, the two people in front of me left in disgust. The young woman turned around, smiled radiantly, and introduced herself as Shoshana. "We're in the same English Composition class," she informed me.

We chatted while we waited our turn, continued over lunch at the Horn & Hardart. She lived in Queens with her parents, who were as old-fashioned as Mami.

"It's stupid. I spend half my time arguing with them," she complained. Her mother was particularly critical of the way Shoshana dressed, which didn't surprise me. If I were to wear anything half as flashy as Shoshana's most conservative outfits, Mami would lock me up.

Shoshana was born in Israel, came to the United States the same year I did. Her parents were Holocaust survivors, so it took me a while to tell her about my German boyfriend.

"It's true then," she mused, "that Puerto Rican girls prefer blond, blue-eyed men."

"Where did you hear that?"

"In school. A classmate told me."

"Maybe she was speaking for herself."

"You have a blond, blue-eyed boyfriend," she pointed out.

"Yeah, but it just worked out that way. The first guy I dated was Jewish," I added. "But he couldn't bring me home to his mother."

"What, and give her a heart attack?"

When I was with Shoshana, I felt happy, even if she sometimes made assumptions, like Puerto Rican girls wanting blond boyfriends. If she offended me and I set her straight, she nodded as if she understood and moved on to other things. I did the same with her.

Shoshana could date, if she dated Jewish men.

"I'm being loyal to Otto," I gave as my reason for not going out with anyone.

"Do you think," she asked, "that he just sits at home on weekends thinking of you?"

Otto's letters weren't as frequent as I would have liked, but they brought news of evenings at the opera, the symphony, museums. He described hikes in the woods in such detail that it felt as though I were there. My news was less interesting, mostly reports on my courses, the New York weather, and the people I met as a part-time receptionist. Occasionally, I fabricated this or that highly accomplished man who took an interest in me. Otto never responded to my attempts to make him jealous. I also invented friends happily married to foreign men, stories about marriage by proxy, in which the bride and groom were in different cities (the Corín Tellado romances I still read had lots of those), and marriages in which everything was arranged by the bride while the groom lived in Europe. He never responded to those hints either.

Shoshana insisted that as far as she could tell, Otto and I were pen pals, in which case, I should go out with whomever I chose.

"My mother doesn't want me alone with men until after I get married," I admitted.

"My mom's the same," Shoshana chuckled. "It's because they're from the old country."

Shoshana said the reason our mothers said no so much was that we asked them too many questions. "Does she have to know everything you do?" Shoshana asked. She suggested we get part-time night jobs, but that we should tell our mothers we worked every night. That way, the nights we didn't work, we could go out.

We answered an ad for telephone operators, evenings only, and were interviewed by Mr. Vince, a perfumed, coiffed, man who wore a pinkie ring, tight-fitting pants, and a shirt unbuttoned to display his hairy chest. He hired us on the spot and put us to work that same night.

Our job was to return phone calls from people who'd in-

quired about how to win a fabulous vacation. The company advertised destinations on television. Viewers called a special number, actually an answering service, and were asked their names, phone numbers, the best time to call, and which commercial they'd seen.

Mr. Vince said that we couldn't use our real names when returning the calls. We should each pick one that was short and easy to remember. Shoshana became Miss Green and I Miss Brown. He gave us a script. "You're an actress, you shouldn't have any trouble with this," he grinned.

We read aloud before Mr. Vince let us make the first call.

"Good evening Mr. (or Mrs.) _____. This is _____, returning your call. How are you tonight?" (Give them a chance to respond. If they ask how you are, thank them.) "You inquired about a chance to win a vacation in _____. Have you ever been to _____?" (Yes: "It's a fabulous place, isn't it?" No: "Oh, you'll love it.")

To qualify for the prize, the prospect had to agree to a sales visit. If they accepted, we transferred them to Mr. Vince, who set the date and time. We were paid by the hour, but if Mr. Vince sold a certain number of vacations to prospects we'd contacted, we received a commission and the chance to go on the fabulous vacation ourselves.

"How many do you have to sell?" Shoshana asked.

"I'll let you know when I sell them," Mr. Vince laughed.

We worked in cubicles, each with a phone, a stack of pink message slips, a few #2 pencils, and notepads. At first Mr. Vince monitored our end of the conversation by standing behind us when we talked to prospects or by listening on an extension. But once he was sure we were talking to his clients and not our friends ("You do that, you're fired," he threatened), he wasn't as strict. Sometimes he left us in the office alone, since he was not kept very busy. In spite of our best efforts, most prospects refused a sales call to make them eligible, if they purchased another trip from Mr. Vince, to win the fabulous vacation. As soon as he left the

office, Shoshana called her boyfriends. I didn't have anyone to call, so I talked to her boyfriends, too.

"Are you as beautiful as Shoshana?" they asked, and I answered that no one was as beautiful as Shoshana, which she loved.

Many of the calls we returned were from people with no intention of ever going on vacation. "You can't let them waste your time," Mr. Vince scolded. "I'm not paying you to be their friend."

But I liked listening. Given interested silence, people talked. They complained about inattentive spouses, ungrateful children, undeserving nieces and nephews, greedy neighbors. The dead were recalled with regrets.

"*I didn't know how much I depended on him until he was gone.*"

"*She was an angel, and I didn't appreciate her.*"

"*He never knew how much I loved him.*"

More than once I was brought to tears by the voices that floated out of the darkness into my ear. No one was happy. I let them talk, asked questions, pointed out the snares they'd stumbled into that left them sad and lonely. If I listened carefully, I might hear myself speak twenty years from now, or thirty, or even fifty. Would my life be summed up in a series of regrets and resentments? Would I wish to turn back time, to relive this or that moment, as so many of my callers did, to change the outcome? How could I tell if a decision I made today would haunt me for years to come?

"I hope you never have to go through what I went through," a woman began her tale, and I paid close attention. Each life was a message I had to decode, clues for what lay ahead. Not a blueprint, but a road map from which to choose a path.

When we weren't in classes or working, Shoshana and I went to tapings of television shows. Manhattan Community College was only a few blocks from the CBS and ABC studios and two blocks

from NBC. In the daytime, we sat in the audience of game shows, hoping we'd be picked as contestants. We never were. After a while, the NBC pages recognized us and moved us to the front of the ticket line or saved places for us in the studios. They were pleasant, clean-cut young men in neat blue uniforms. We each had a favorite. Mine was Andy, a pudgy redhead with freckles on every visible part of his body, including his earlobes and knuckles. He worked the evening shift most of the time and always made sure I got in to watch tapings of *The Johnny Carson Show*. Andy reminded me of comic-book Archie. He had the same goofy grin and dreamed of writing the jokes Johnny Carson read off cue cards during his monologue.

"You mean those are not his jokes?"

"There's a whole army of writers who make Johnny funny," he confided.

"But the ad libs . . ."

"Oh, those are his," Andy said. "The man is funny. But the writers make him funnier."

Because he worked nights like me, Andy and I could only go out days, if I didn't have a class. We visited museums and art galleries, ate lunch from hot dog vendors on Fifth Avenue, sat in coffee shops for hours, each engrossed in a different book.

"That's what you do on dates?" Shoshana asked. "You read next to each other?"

I explained that with Andy, what I had was a friendship, not a romance.

"Oy!" she slapped her forehead. "You're hopeless."

"He's all I've got," I laughed.

"I know some guys," she offered.

Sammy and Josh were Israeli premed students. Shoshana had dated Josh a couple of times, and he had asked her to introduce his best friend to a girl. That's how, on a damp Sunday morning in June, I sat stiff and fearful atop a horse in Van Cortland Park.

"You have to show the horse who is boss," Sammy asserted, his speech garbled by the cigarette in his mouth.

"He's the boss," I said.

"No, no, no, no." Sammy shook his head, and ashes flew in every direction. "You are the boss. You!"

It was hard for me to believe I could dominate the quivering creature between my legs. His malevolent eyes rolled back wetly to focus on me, petrified on his sagging back. He stomped his hooves into the gravel the way Trigger did when Roy Rogers asked him to count, only this horse wasn't counting. He was, I was certain, anticipating the moment Sammy handed me the reins to take off, with me helplessly bouncing atop him, or dragged alongside, still attached to the stirrups. I suggested to Sammy, Shoshana, and Josh that I'd be happy to sit on a bench and wait for them to come back from their ride. But Shoshana insisted that this was a fun date. The horses in Van Cortland Park, Josh claimed, were old, docile, one false step from the glue factory. Sammy swore he was an expert horseman and would ride alongside, in case I needed him.

The horse knew where he was going. No matter what I did with the reins, he trudged forward, followed Josh and Shoshana's horses as if he were attached to them. I loosened my grip and looked around. Beside me, Sammy chatted in a low murmur about his experiences on kibbutz, where he worked as an electrician. He was very thin, with abundant black hair and eyes that probed from beneath luxurious eyebrows. He sucked unfiltered cigarettes one after the other. His fingertips and teeth were stained an opaque mustard color, and from time to time he doubled over with rumbling coughs that turned his face red.

The path was wooded near the stables, but as we came around a curve, it opened into a long stretch alongside a busy avenue. Cars and trucks rumbled past, but the horses were used to the congestion and paid no attention to it. They ambled along placidly, the clop of their hooves an incongruous contrast to the whir and horns of traffic. Josh and Sammy spoke to each other in Hebrew, and Shoshana and Sammy changed places, so that she rode next to me.

"The guys want to canter," she explained.

"What's that?"

"When the horses go fast."

I gripped the reins again. I expected a "Hi-yo, Silver," or some other exclamation to make the horses go, but Josh and Sammy simply dug their heels into the animals' sides, and they took off. Shoshana's horse and mine pursued them, even though I, at least, did nothing to encourage mine. I pulled the reins with all the power in my arms, but the horse ignored me. Shoshana's horse was even faster and soon whizzed past me. Then, way ahead, I saw Shoshana fly through the air and land on her side, inches from the avenue. In a move to make Annie Oakley proud, I slid off my horse while he was still moving and rushed to her side. She was unconscious. Within seconds, traffic stopped on the avenue, Josh and Sammy appeared, and the horses could be seen cantering (if that's what they did when they ran fast) toward the stables, their reins flapping uselessly along the ground.

"I'm a doctor, I'm a doctor," Sammy and Josh yelled, to keep people away from Shoshana.

"You're not supposed to move someone . . ." I started when Sammy turned her over, but he gave me a look to wither poison ivy, and I backed away.

She moaned, opened her eyes, and it was a relief to see she was alive. Josh and Sammy hovered over her until an ambulance wailed its way to us, then I rode with her while the guys followed in Sammy's car. She was pale but conscious. I held her hand all the way to the hospital, and when they took her away to be examined, I called Mami.

"Has someone told her mother?" Mami asked. I hadn't, and probably Sammy and Josh hadn't either. Mami said it was Shoshana's mother I should be calling and not mine.

Josh and Sammy ran in, and while Josh went into the room where they'd taken Shoshana ("I'm a doctor, I'm a doctor!"), Sammy called her mother. Josh was escorted to the waiting room, and we sat in silence until a doctor came out and led us back to

Shoshana. She lay on a high bed, her golden curls framing her face like a halo. The white sheets added to the angelic effect. She looked both vulnerable and sexy, and the three men were jelly. The guys spoke to her in Hebrew, and then she asked if she could be alone with me. Once they left, she smiled mischievously.

"He's cute, isn't he?"

"Which one?"

"The doctor."

"Which one?"

"The real one, silly. We're going out next week."

Shoshana was in the hospital a few days. She was released in time for her date with Dr. Diamond, who testified when she sued the people who rented the horses. They settled for enough money to allow Shoshana to spend the rest of the summer in Israel. "But you should go out with Sammy while I'm gone," she suggested.

Dashing as Sammy was, I preferred my quiet afternoons with Andy. Shoshana rolled her eyes. "You'll die an old maid!" We laughed. We were both nineteen, and although we were desperate for love, we knew there was still time. After all, this was America, not the old country.

———◦———

I hadn't seen Neftalí since the day he had tried to propose on the street. His mother, Doña Lila, still came up to visit, but I rarely saw her. Then, shortly after Cibi was born, Mami decided the apartment above Doña Lila's was too small. We moved to a single-family house with a huge yard and large, bright rooms with high ceilings. At the rear of the house was a small room off the kitchen, which I claimed. It was big enough for a single bed, a desk, my mirrored vanity table and matching chair. I spent the "summer of love" in that room, loveless, writing term papers about the history of public relations and the use of humor in outdoor advertising.

One day I came home and Mami and Tata were at the dining room table, their faces so somber I knew someone had died.

"Who?" I asked.

"Neftalí." Mami said.

I dropped onto a chair, overwhelmed with images of Neftalí riddled with bullets in a foxhole in faraway Vietnam. But that's not how it happened. Neftalí, Mami informed me, had been rejected by the army because he was a heroin addict.

"He was arrested," she said, "and he jumped out the window of the police station."

"There were spikes on the fence . . ." Tata added.

I raised my hands and motioned for them to stop. It was too much, too fast. My brain was still working on Neftalí being rejected by the service. Mami and Tata waited for me to signal I was ready for more, and then they repeated the information, as if it hadn't been clear enough, and filled in the details.

Doña Lila had such an attack of *los nervios* when she was called by the police that she was hospitalized. Neftalí hadn't told anyone the army didn't want him. When he was arrested, he jumped, according to Doña Lila, because he was ashamed everyone would find out he was on heroin.

"That's why he always wore long-sleeved shirts," Tata mused, and I stared at her.

"I never noticed that," I cried, and went into my room, followed by Mami and Tata's concerned gaze.

I threw myself on the bed and closed my eyes. Images of Neftalí popped into my head in confused sequences. Neftalí hoisting my brothers on his arms to show off his muscles. Did he wince because it hurt the needle tracks? Neftalí's flat nails against Tata's Spanish playing cards. Did he always lose because he couldn't concentrate? Neftalí's green eyes that made me shudder. Was the look I interpreted as mysterious actually blank? It was hard to reconcile the romantic hero I had wanted him to be with who he had been: an addict who'd rather jump out a window than confront his problem.

One Sunday afternoon, my half sister, Margie, came to visit. In the two years since she had first come to our apartment on Pitkin Avenue accompanied by her mother, we had moved four times, and Margie at least once. She had recently married Nestor, a warm, sociable man several years older. He stood behind her, his left hand lightly touching her waist, as Margie introduced him and tried to remember our names. When we had last seen her, there were only eight of us, and she was surprised that the family had grown so fast in two years.

Mami and Tata immediately began preparing *arroz con pollo* and stewed pinto beans. Nestor and Margie sat at the kitchen table talking about their new apartment in Yonkers.

"Why so far?" Mami asked.

"It's just over the border with the Bronx," Nestor said. But anything outside the confines of Brooklyn or north of the garment district in Manhattan was foreign territory to Mami. To her they might as well be living in another country.

Margie and Nestor were interested in every bit of news we could give them. They asked what schools we attended, what jobs we held, how tall we were. She apologized several times. "I don't mean to be nosy," she said. "But it's been so long since we were together." I was touched by her need to connect with us, to feel a part of our family. Nestor played with the boys as if he'd known them forever, and Margie talked to the sisters, helped Mami and Tata in the kitchen, jiggled Charlie and Cibi on her knees. She was comfortable, as if this were her house, her mother and grandmother, her siblings. I was enchanted by how open she was, how sweet and unpretentious. Before they left, Margie asked Mami if we could visit her now that she had her own place.

"Of course!" Mami said, and hugged her.

A few weeks later, Margie met me at the Yonkers train station. We walked the few blocks to the yellow brick building on a hill where she and Nestor lived in a sunny, cheerful apartment decorated with the optimism of newlyweds.

"This is where you'll sleep." She opened a door to a small

room near the kitchen. A single bed was covered by a fluffy comforter and matching pillows. A lamp topped a wicker side table with drawers. At the foot of the bed lay a set of towels, a basket with tiny soaps, a shower cap. She reached under the bed and pulled out a small basket. "If you get your period, here are the tampons." A box of Tampax was propped into a well of pink tissue paper like an offering to the goddess of menstruation.

I'd never touched a tampon, since Mami warned I could lose my virginity if I used them. Just having Margie think that I wore them made me feel grown-up, privy to the secrets of a married woman. She no longer needed to worry about her virginity, and I wondered if offering me the tampon was a test to see if I worried about mine.

Nestor was due from work, so Margie asked me to set the table. At home, setting the table meant putting platters of food in the center so that everyone could come and get their share. Margie used place mats, knives, forks, a dinner plate, a salad plate, a water glass, a coffee cup and saucer. She had to remind me to put each on the table. A pitcher had to be filled with ice water. Paper napkins had to be folded into a triangle, placed to the left of the plate. Matching salt and pepper shakers had to be retrieved from the cabinet and lined up with the bottle of ketchup, the sugar bowl. It took me as long to set the table for three people as it took her to cook the entire meal, because I kept getting things wrong. I closed my eyes and tried to remember restaurant settings, but that was no help. Most of my dining-out experience was in coffee shops and the Automat, where one was lucky to get utensils.

"No, the water glass goes to the right of the plate," Margie corrected me. "The salad plate on the left, like this." She was kind, but I took her criticism personally, which made me sullen and uncomfortable during the meal. I offered to clean up, to make up for my ineptitude in other areas. She stayed in the kitchen with me, which under other circumstances I would have welcomed. But I was so self-conscious that I was bound to break something. She cleaned up the glass from the floor and sent me to watch Red

Skelton with Nestor. I was glad they went to bed early and curled up under the plush bedcovers, neither comforted nor consoled.

The next morning I woke to the smell of fried eggs and coffee. Margie bustled in the kitchen while Nestor read the paper and sipped his *café con leche*. I ducked into the bathroom to wash up. On the counter top a Water Pik gleamed white and clinical on the shelf next to the sink. I was afraid to touch it, because I didn't know what part of Margie or Nestor's body the tiny hose went into. It looked marital, as intimate as the cottony tampons wrapped in white paper. When I came out, Nestor was finishing his breakfast.

"I better get ready for work," he said, moving toward the bathroom. Margie set a plate in front of me neatly arranged with two fried eggs, a slice of ham, toast cut into triangles. Then she sat at the table and nibbled on a piece of bread, chatting about what we would do later. It was hard to concentrate on what she said because of the sounds coming from behind the bathroom door. The hum of electrical appliances, gargles, running water were a counterpoint to Margie's plans to walk to the park, have lunch at a local diner, shop. When Nestor came out, a fresh, clean scent of peppermint and orange saturated the room. Margie accompanied him to the door, where they kissed and muttered endearments. Once he was gone, Margie went into the bathroom, and the buzzing and gurgling resumed.

"Don't you wash up after every meal?" she asked when she came out, and I mumbled yes, which wasn't true, but I knew I should. "You can use the Water Pik if you like," she said. Still afraid to touch the hose, I pushed a button; water squirted out of it in a stream like a baby pissing. "Do you know how to use it?" she called from the kitchen, and I was thrilled that my older sister was about to impart adult knowledge. She came into the room, unhooked the hose, squirted water inside her mouth, the way the dentist did when he fixed my cavities. I was disappointed beyond words, which must have shown because, halfway through her demonstration of the proper technique, she crossed her eyes, curled

her lips into a weird grimace, and let water dribble down her chin. Our eyes met in the mirror, and we set each other off in a fit of giggles that lasted the better part of the morning because, every time I looked at her, she put a finger in her mouth, hummed and gurgled, crossed her eyes, and pretended to brush her teeth.

We talked a lot about our father, whom she hadn't seen in years, but with whom she corresponded. I had lived with him many more years than she had, and she was surprised to learn that he sang well, and that he wrote poems and *décimas*.

"His handwriting is so tiny," she laughed, and showed me a sheet in his slanted script, each letter neatly drawn, the accents over the *is* nearly horizontal. It was Papi who gave her our address. "He loves your letters," she told me, which made me feel good and guilty at the same time, because I never wrote as much as I should have.

Over the next few weeks, my sisters and I took turns spending time with Margie and Nestor. They came to visit, and we went home with them. Or she met one of us at the train station, and in a couple of days they'd both return with us to Brooklyn and have some of Mami's good cooking. She once wrapped her arms around Mami and muttered that she wished she were her mother. Mami repeated the comment every time one of us was especially annoying or disrespectful, to let us know other people appreciated her when it seemed that we didn't.

One Sunday afternoon, Nestor informed us that they were moving to Miami. "Of course, you're welcome to come see us there," Margie offered. That was unlikely. If we had any money for travel, our goal was always Puerto Rico, where none of us had been in seven years. When we hugged goodbye, I knew it would be a long time before I'd see Margie again.

⌣⌒⌒◞

In mid-August, I received an invitation to the premiere of *Up the Down Staircase* at Radio City Music Hall, to be followed by a

party at the Warwick Hotel. Almost all the actors who had played students in the classroom were there, dressed up. We were asked to come early so that we could be photographed on the grand staircase. Like me, many of the other students had never been inside Radio City, and we tried our best not to appear too amazed. But once in the upholstered seats of the theater, I couldn't help myself. I gawked at the high ceiling, the gilded decorations, the hundreds of seats sloped toward the enormous stage. For the first time I saw the Rockettes' precise kick line, the long legs that moved as one, the tappety-tap that seemed to come from every corner of the room.

Once the movie was shown, it was difficult to concentrate on it, because my fellow actors and I cheered or giggled every time we saw ourselves or one another. At the party, we exchanged stories about what we'd been up to since the movie wrapped. Sandy Dennis had won an Oscar for *Who's Afraid of Virginia Woolf?*, and the rest of us did our best to make our paltry accomplishments sound equally splendid.

My performance would not earn any awards, would more than likely not be noticed. But seeing myself on the screen renewed the desire to stand before an audience. After more than a year of office jobs and uninspiring college courses, I longed for the nervous excitement before the curtain rose, the hums and rustle of an expectant audience, the applause.

Once more I scoured audition notices in *Backstage* and *Show Business*, and on the bulletin boards of the International School of Dance, where I took classes. I had visions of dancing with an established group like Matteo's, but I was soon discouraged. While I'd come a long way as a dancer in four years, my competition began as children. They could take classes every day, could devote their lives to dance. Many of the traditional beginner dances, like Allarippu, had become second nature to them, and they'd moved on to more complex choreography that required a wider range of expression and technical expertise.

I went to dance class whenever I could afford the time or

expense, practiced at home even when my family complained that the jangling ankle bells and atonal Indian music drove them crazy. Every time I considered dropping out of college and using my money from temporary jobs to support my art, I rebuked myself for being self-indulgent and unrealistic. An artist should sacrifice for her art, I knew that. A part of me loved the romance of being a starving artist. But the voice that spoke loudest asked what chance an undertrained Puerto Rican Indian classical dancer had of supporting herself.

Our house on Glenmore had a finished basement as well as a second floor, where Mami set up the kids' beds. We had room to spare, Mami said. Maybe that's why one day her cousin Lólin appeared at our door on the arm of the man she had eloped with.

Lólin was thin, with dark soulful eyes and a quiet manner. She was delicate and graceful, wore her long hair down, a wide black ribbon between narrow shoulders. She spoke in a hushed, kittenish voice, made frequent use of the Spanish diminutive, as if she could make herself smaller through speech. It didn't surprise me that she introduced her "husband" as Toñito rather than Antonio.

He was as slight and quiet as she was, with nutmeg skin, dark hair, Taíno features. They came with few belongings and no money, but they were obviously in love. Every time he looked at her, she blushed and dropped her lids. When she did look at him, her gaze was like a caress, soft and slow and full of meaning.

Mami wasn't thrilled to have them at our house. She liked Lólin, but she wasn't comfortable with a handsome, lusty young man—not our brother—in his undershirt near me and my sisters. I was nineteen, Delsa seventeen, Norma sixteen, Alicia fourteen, Edna thirteen. We knew what Lólin and Toñito did at night in the room in the basement that Mami assigned to them. And although they did their best to be discreet, it was difficult to ignore the soft

moans and whispers coming from their room, the way her hand stroked his thigh when they sat together, the way his arm kept her close when they watched television.

Mami's aunts and uncles, cousins—Gury, La Muda, and Margot—and other relatives who rarely showed up at our house all came to see Lólin and Toñito as if they were the main attraction at a circus. In Puerto Rico, Tío Pedro was not happy with his eldest daughter's choice of husband. The many telephone conversations I overheard were pleas for him to be flexible, to accept Toñito, to respect Lólin enough to allow her the consequences of her decision. But Tío Pedro was stubborn. The aunts and uncles, the cousins, Mami and Tata sat at our kitchen table for hours, discussing what to do. From time to time, the romantic chords of a guitar were heard from the basement, where Toñito strummed love songs while Lólin reclined on her side.

The relatives complained that Toñito was irresponsible, because he showed up with nothing to his name but that blasted guitar. They predicted the relationship couldn't last. Lólin was used to comfort, they noted, since Tío Pedro was a merchant who provided well for his family. She was temporarily blind to Toñito's charm, they suggested, and as soon as she realized what a laggard he was, she'd crawl back to Puerto Rico to ask her father's forgiveness. Of course, it was assumed Tío Pedro would never forgive her or accept Toñito, so the gossip was tinged with compassion for poor, misguided Lólin.

My sisters and I watched the drama. For years Lólin and her sister Tati had been held up as examples of "good" girls, and here was Lólin, having eloped with a good-looking guy who, by all accounts, had no skills with which to support her. And in Puerto Rico, Tati, who was younger, had already married, borne a son, and been abandoned. Tati, who was so pretty, lively, and always carefree, was now a tragic figure. Lólin's disobedience didn't conform to her mild, serene nature. The female aunts and cousins still used Tati and Lólin as examples—only this time they were negative models.

About Tati they said, "See what happens when a girl is too eager to get out from under her parents' care and protection?" Lólin's defiance they blamed on her docile ways. "All this time she was the perfect daughter," they mused. *"Pero llevava la música por dentro."* When they said that Lólin carried "the music inside her," they looked at us hard, to let us know that if we were too well behaved, they suspected we were up to no good.

When Tío Pedro relented and Lólin and Toñito returned to Puerto Rico, the relatives shook their heads and suggested it was Tío Pedro and Titi Sara's overprotectiveness that had caused so much trouble for their daughters. Had they been more permissive, Tati might have waited to get married, thereby avoiding abandonment at a young age. Lólin would have met many men and not fallen for the first *manganzón* to make eyes at her.

My sisters and I were advised to learn from their mistakes, to place ourselves between Tati's impatience and Lólin's audacity. It was a path with no precedent in our family. Each aunt and uncle, each adult cousin was a model of impulsiveness and contradiction. Not to mention Mami and Tata, who both spouted rules they didn't live by and were prime examples of the aphorism, "Do as I say and not as I do." Tata warned us not to smoke or drink as she sat at the kitchen table with a cigarette in one hand and a beer in the other. Mami talked about church weddings for us, then used herself as an example of how tenuous nonsanctified unions were.

"But Don Carlos was married to that woman, and he divorced her to be with you," I started, and she shushed me.

"That marriage was over long before he met me," she said, which was true, but that wasn't my point.

"Get an education so that you can get jobs in offices, not factories," Mami frequently advised us. The next day she showed us a beautifully stitched bra. Her face flushed with pride, she went over every seam, pointed out how tricky it was to get the double needles to turn just so, how delicate the fabric was to work with, how unusual the new closures. She made useful and lovely things

with her own hands. When she was laid off, she lamented that her skills were not enough to support her children.

"Don't be like me," she insisted, "learn a profession, don't depend on factories for your livelihood."

The more time I spent at home, the more confused I became. We never went to church, but I should marry in a cathedral. A good girl, I should not be too good or my goodness was suspect. If I was too anxious to leave home, my life could turn to tragedy. If I lingered under Mami's protection, I was sure to be deceived by those more knowledgeable in the ways of the world.

There were times I left the house for school or work with the intention of never coming back, but I didn't have the courage to run away. Sometimes I stared at the shiny subway tracks, at how easy it would be to throw myself upon them, but the thought of being mangled by tons of moving metal made me step back when the train rumbled near.

The home that had been a refuge from the city's danger was now a prison I longed to escape. I was exhausted by the intensity of my family life, by the drama that never ceased, the crises that rose out of nowhere, subsided, made way for others that in their turn were mere preludes. I was tired of the constant tug between the life I wanted and the life I had. I dreaded the loneliness that attached itself to me in the middle of my raucous family. I didn't blame them for my unhappiness, but neither did I want to contaminate them with it. I wanted to be, like Garbo, alone. I wanted to become La Sorda, deaf to my family's voices, their contradictory messages, their expectations. I longed to cup my hand to my mouth, the way singers did, and listen to myself. To hear one voice, my own, even if it was filled with fear and uncertainty. Even if it were to lead me where I ought not to go.

"What size bra do you wear?"

The second semester at Manhattan Community College, Shoshana and I signed up for Fundamentals of Mathematics. The course was not required of business majors, but in the fall of 1967, it was taught by gorgeous Mr. Grunwald. Shoshana was thrilled, because he was not only the handsomest man she'd ever seen but also Jewish. She reasoned that since the class met three times a week and Mr. Grunwald had office hours for extra help, there would be many opportunities for him to fall in love with one of us.

"But what if he falls in love with you and I get jealous?"

Shoshana considered this a moment. "Let's not do that. Let's say that what's good for you is good for me and vice versa. That way there's no jealousy."

Shoshana had no sisters, and I did. Her proposal was noble but unrealistic, and I told her so.

"All right then. If he chooses me over you, then you have to promise to back off. I'll do the same."

"That sounds better," I agreed.

The first day of classes, Shoshana and I took seats side by side in the front row of the room, which was filled with females dressed, like us, in our best outfits. When Mr. Grunwald walked in, we sighed as one. Not too tall, not too short, perfectly proportioned from head to toe, Mr. Grunwald was as gorgeous as Shoshana had promised. His dark blue, nearly violet eyes were

intelligent and gentle. His sandy hair curled around his ears and below the collar of his shirt. He was clean shaven, with a wide, chiseled jaw, sensuous lips, a perfect nose. He wore a light brown corduroy jacket with suede elbow patches, tight jeans, a button-down indigo shirt with a subtly patterned tie. When he wrote his inscrutable formulas on the chalkboard, his handwriting was crisp, the numbers perfectly formed, the x forceful and mysterious. He claimed he wasn't teaching us math, that he taught logic; but it looked like math to me.

"He's good-looking and everything," I said to Shoshana, "but the course looks too hard. I'm dropping it."

Shoshana would have none of that. "All you need is a C − to pass," she said. "I'll help you."

After class, Shoshana consulted her careful notes and re-peated almost everything Mr. Grunwald had just said. Twice a week, I went to his office, and he corrected my dismal quizzes and tests in front of me. He wore cologne, a fruity scent that filled my nostrils as he leaned in to show me how the sine and cosine related to the tangent. He spoke with a drawl, the vowels long, soothing as a siesta. I wanted to live in his diphthongs, engulfed by his *os* and *us*, caressed by his *is*. But Mr. Grunwald's passion was in convex regions and the vertex of a parabola. Just as it didn't occur to Shoshana that Mr. Grunwald wouldn't fall in love with any of us, it didn't seem to occur to Mr. Grunwald that I, and every other girl in his class, was in love with him.

One day, as he tried to help me understand what would never make sense, Mr. Grunwald leaned back in his chair. "Let's not work on this anymore," he suggested.

Humiliated that he should give up on me, I apologized. "Math has never been my subject."

He rubbed his face with both hands. "What is it that you hope to do with your college education?" he asked from inside his fingers.

"Get a good job," I answered.

He dropped his hands, glared at me. "Doing what, exactly?"

"Advertising, I guess." Sweat collected on my forehead, my upper lip. "Or marketing . . ."

"You have no idea, do you?" The tone of his voice, its low register, the soft look that accompanied his words, made tears come to my eyes. I shook my head. "What would you like to do?" he asked, and I wanted to say kiss you all over, which was what I was thinking, but I shrugged my shoulders instead. "Shoshana mentioned you're a dancer," he added. "Are you any good?"

No one had asked me that, and it took a few seconds to decide to answer honestly, without false modesty. "I'm very good," I said. "Considering how late I started."

He smiled. "Modern dance? Ballet?"

I smiled back. "I'm probably the only Puerto Rican Indian classical dancer you've ever met."

The rest of the extra help period was spent describing to Mr. Grunwald the subtleties of Bharata Natyam. He was attentive, made comments that let me know he was listening.

"Indian music progresses mathematically," he interjected once, and I stopped talking to consider it. He watched me think, as if it were a new experience.

"I . . . I guess so," I finally said. Mr. Grunwald chuckled, which made me feel stupid for coming up with such a dumb response.

When I told Shoshana that I had spent my extra help session talking to Mr. Grunwald about dance, she was ecstatic. "He likes you! Now he'll probably ask you to a musical."

"That's not the kind of dancing I do," I protested.

Shoshana was over her infatuation with Mr. Grunwald now that she was dazzled by the Principles of Advertising teacher. Mr. Delmar was older than most of the professors at Manhattan Community College. He had salt-and-pepper hair, gray eyes, features embellished with wrinkles deliberately placed to enhance his handsome face. He wore expensive, fitted suits that accentuated an elegant physique, slim and long legged. Mr. Delmar strolled the halls of the college as if he owned the place and drew admiring

glances from males and females alike, young or old. I disliked him instantly, found his finished air too self-conscious and calculated. But Shoshana said that was because I'd never been anywhere. "He's so sophisticated, so European," she sighed.

With each of us mooning over a different teacher, there was no jealousy. Our conversations focused on how far we'd go if one of them asked us out. We were both willing to give up our virginity if Mr. Grunwald or Mr. Delmar gave us the slightest hint that they wanted it. After repeated attempts to gain his attention, Shoshana decided Mr. Delmar wouldn't date her while she was still his student. She gave up on him for the fall semester and set her hopes on the spring. As for me, the only way to impress Mr. Grunwald was to become immersed in reflection symmetric figures. I wasn't about to do that, even with the promise of a night of passion as its outcome. I continued my long, rambling letters to Otto, whose responses were shorter and less frequent.

"You should break up with him before he breaks up with you," Shoshana suggested. I stopped writing, and I could almost hear the relief all the way from Switzerland.

Just down the hall from our lockers at Manhattan Community College was a student lounge. Shoshana and I never went in there to study, because loud music came from behind its heavy, closed doors. We liked music, but we also liked to hear ourselves talk. Between classes, we preferred to walk to a nearby coffee shop or to the Automat, or we'd meet our page boys at the NBC commissary. But one day I needed coffee in a hurry and made my way to the lounge. The room was big, with a few battered chairs, a sagging couch, a row of vending machines that offered candy, soda, pastries wrapped in plastic. Under the lone window was a small table with a coffee maker, packets of sugar, a stack of paper cups, a jar of Cremora.

As I entered, it felt as if I had strayed into another country. To my left, the room vibrated with Motown music from a portable

record player. Black students sat or stood in small groups arguing politics as the Supremes sang about "The Happening." To my left, at an equally loud volume, Eddie Palmieri's rhythms punctuated the sounds of Spanglish. The center of the room was nearly empty, except for a few white students adrift between the two lively continents. Most of the people in the room were familiar to me because we saw one another in classes or in the halls. One of them, Gloria, waved me over to the mambo side of the room.

"Are you Puerto Rican?" she asked. When I said yes, she turned to the group. "You see!" She turned to me again. "These guys here didn't believe me." One of the boys, Felix, was in a class with me.

"You knew I was Puerto Rican," I chided him.

"I told them," he chuckled, then turned his hand palm up toward another guy, who slapped it.

"You were in that movie about the school, right?" another girl asked.

I flushed with pleasure at being recognized. "*Up the Down Staircase*, yes I was."

"Told you!" another round of palm slapping. The bell to signal the start of a period rang, and all of them scrambled to gather their belongings.

"See you later," I said. No one responded. I left, surprised that there was talk about me but that the minute they met me, no one cared. I wondered if I had left a poor impression and replayed the scene several times. Was I friendly and open enough? Did I appear too proud of having been in a movie? Was there anything I could have done to make them like me? They had stood close together in a semicircle as we talked, as if I were being interviewed. But then they dispersed, dismissed me.

Perhaps I was oversensitive, Shoshana suggested later, because most of the students at Manhattan Community College were black or Puerto Rican and my best friend was Jewish.

"Maybe deep down inside you feel you should be friends with them and not me," she pouted.

"Remind me to skip Psychology next semester," I responded.

Since she had started that course, everything anyone said or did was open to interpretation. But it did bother me that Shoshana felt that way and that a part of me — a tiny, hidden part — agreed.

A few weeks after school started, I lost my night job because Mr. Vince went out of business. In spite of months of advertising and thousands of calls to prospective clients, he hadn't sold enough vacations to keep me and the other telephone solicitors employed. Shoshana had quit the job months earlier, before she went to Israel for the summer. Several men and women came and left, but I worked with Mr. Vince until the end, and he was close to tears the day he let me go.

"Soon as I get on my feet again," he promised, "I'll give you a call." He paid me an extra week's wages as a bonus.

I went to the student employment office at the college, which had a program through which I could get credit for work related to my major. The counselor sent me to the Advertising Checking Bureau. My supervisor, Mrs. Davis, promised me a flexible schedule. "Your education is more important than a job," she assured me.

Mrs. Davis was a petite, gray-haired lady who dressed in A-line skirts and frilly blouses with tightly secured cuffs and collars. Her desk was close to the entrance door, turned toward the room lined with glass-paneled offices for managers and higher-ranked supervisors. The three employees in her department faced Mrs. Davis along the only row of windows. Each desk and shelf over the radiators under the windows was covered with mounds of newspapers, magazines, folded posters, radio and television copy.

My job was to check that the ads for accounts assigned to me ran according to the arrangement between the manufacturer of the product and the retailer. The manufacturer paid for part of the advertisement. My job was to ensure that if Amana paid 30 percent of the cost, the Amana product took up at least 30 percent of the

column inches for the newspapers or magazines, or 30 percent of the radio and television copy. Each "checker" kept track of several accounts in a geographic area. I handled large and small appliances in the Upper Midwest. Every day I came into the office, there was a stack of clippings on my desk and a list of which accounts had which arrangements with which retailers. Often, instead of a clipping, there was an entire newspaper, which I skimmed until I found the advertisement for my client. I came to know the vagaries of weather in Ypsilanti, Michigan, the price of wheat in Kankakee, Illinois, the results of local elections in Onalaska, Wisconsin. For the third year in a row, Tracey Dobbins of Rock Rapids, Iowa, won top prize for her calf at the 4-H exposition. Mrs. Sada Ulton's pickled rhubarb was the best-selling food item at the county fair. Danny Finley scored the winning touchdown at the Emmetsburg High School Homecoming game. It was a world so far from Brooklyn that I was lost in it, awash in church suppers, agricultural fairs, births, deaths, local theatricals. From time to time, Mrs. Davis stopped by our desks to ask how things were going, or to wonder if the RCA logo was prominent in the ad for Sam's Appliance Mart. But like her three employees, she was a reader, and she often chuckled at the antics of Blondie and Dagwood, or snipped recipes from the pages of the *Philadelphia Inquirer*.

Without the excuse of a night job, I came home every evening. I had supper, then closed myself in my room to do my homework, most of which involved preimage objects to which Mr. Grunwald had us apply identity transformations.

The more time I spent away from home, the more it felt as if I were a visitor in my family. Our house, with its noise and bustle, was like a pause between parts of my real life in Manhattan, in dance studios, in adventures with Shoshana, in college, in the social calendar of Mishawaka, Indiana. Weekends when I didn't have school or work, I caught up with my siblings' lives. Delsa had a boyfriend named George. Héctor excelled at gymnastics in high school. Alicia sang in the school choir.

Mami, thirty-six years old and pregnant with her eleventh child, looked worn. Her step was slow, her skin had lost its luster, her hair, cut short to frame her face, was brittle and broken at the ends. After being unable to afford dental care for years, she went to the dentist during the summer, and he pulled out her teeth. Her face collapsed into her mouth, her youthful look vanished. The dentures didn't fit well, and she was in pain for months before the dentist agreed to fix them.

Tata moved out for a few weeks to live with Don Julio, came back, moved out on her own again. I went to see her at the boarding house where she lived in one room crammed with a bed, an easy chair with torn upholstery, a hot plate, some chipped dishes and glasses. By the window she had set up her altar of family relics and saints, who were supposed to bring her luck when she played *bolita*. She won enough times to keep her faith in them. The bathroom was in the downstairs hallway, and she kept a chamber pot under her bed so that she wouldn't have to make the trip up and down the stairs more often than necessary. After a few weeks there, she returned to the basement once occupied by Lólin and Toñito. She grumbled and complained about the activity in the house. Now that we were older, she didn't find us as charming as when we were little. The only one she still doted on was Franky, who at four years old was still cute and didn't talk back when she scolded him.

I floated in and out of family activities, took note of major changes. Don Carlos lived with us. Norma dyed her hair red. Don Carlos moved out. Cousin Paco gave up wrestling. Don Carlos came back. Delsa achieved straight As in math. Héctor helped Raymond get a job at a pizza shop. Crises rose, subsided, rose again, kept Sunday afternoons lively as aunts, uncles, cousins, and their families appeared unannounced to share in the good food and gossip that kept everyone entertained from week to week. I made excuses, disappeared into my room, or left the house as soon as I could get away, sometimes with one of my sisters or brothers but more often alone. I took in a double feature, lost in Holly-

wood's version of life, with its elegant women, manly men, nonexistent children, predicaments resolved by guns or marriage, and sometimes both. Sometimes I went to visit Alma and Corazón, sat in their quiet apartment talking about books and listening to American rock and roll.

Corazón loved the Doors and the Bee Gees. "Listen to this," she said, as she put on an LP. She sat back on the couch, I plopped next to her, and we closed our eyes and listened. She understood the lyrics of the songs, I didn't. "What does the chorus say?" she asked.

"Come and maybe like my buyer?" I guessed, and she roared with laughter.

Alma wrote poetry. One of her poems was published in an anthology. She placed a sliver of paper as a bookmark on the page where her name in italics looked authoritative and precise. The poem was titled "They," a sonnet about impotence and powerlessness. The last line, "They will not let me," was such a surprise that I looked up at her to ask whom she meant, but her face was so proud and pleased with herself that I didn't dare.

On the bulletin board of the International School of Dance, someone posted a "Models Wanted" flyer, no experience necessary. I called the number and was told that the models were for a photography school. In exchange for posing, models received an eight-by-ten glossy from each student who took a picture. There was no nudity involved. Models brought a couple of changes of clothes and their own makeup. I told Shoshana, who immediately agreed we should do it.

The school was in a loft in the West Forties. There was a small dressing room with a lighted mirror and a closet for the models to hang their clothes. We were asked to put on "natural" makeup and wait to be called. There were two other girls, Sharon and Beverly, who planned to use their pictures in modeling portfo-

lios. They were taller, with better cheekbones, so they ignored me. Shoshana they eyed with envy. She was as tall as they were but more shapely, and her features, well proportioned and very pretty, were designed to be photographed.

We sat in a row of chairs outside the dressing room. Within a few minutes the instructor appeared, trailed by a group of young men.

"Ladies," he began. "The way this works is, for the first hour or so everyone gets to pose, and everyone gets to take a picture. But if one of the students and one of the models develop a special affinity, then you may work together individually over there in the seamless." He pointed to a huge roll of white paper dangling from the ceiling onto the floor, "Or on the set." His hands fluttered in the direction of a dark gray backdrop with cloudlike blotches painted on it. "Is everyone ready?" We nodded, and he led us to another lit seamless area, where we posed in assorted groupings while the students clicked furiously, moved around for different angles, and tried to stay out of one another's way.

I felt silly striking "Mod" girl poses, but Sharon and Beverly were expert at it. When the instructor asked me and Shoshana to step out so that they could be photographed first together, then individually, I saw what a difference aptitude for modeling made. Sharon butterflied her elbows, placed her hands on her hips, and somehow made herself look two-dimensional. Beverly's specialty was motion. She jumped, and she managed to float in the air long enough for the photographers to take many more pictures than they could take of me standing still. It was impressive to see how effortlessly Sharon and Beverly went from pose to pose, each one different, each one striking. Shoshana and I looked at each other in dismay. No way could we do that.

We were surprised when, at the end of the first session, Sharon and Beverly were told to go, but three young men asked to photograph me and Shoshana together. We were posed in profile, first facing each other, then both looking in the same direction. The three young men worked as a team, set up lights for one another, took turns at a portrait camera set up on a tripod, while

the instructor stood in the background and offered suggestions for how to pose or light us. We were also photographed individually, in different clothes and with changes in our makeup and hair, which Shoshana and I did for each other. The session took the entire morning. At the end, we were exhausted, but the instructor asked us to come back on a different day for another group of students, and we agreed on the spot.

"Can you believe it?" Shoshana exulted. "They sent the professionals away and liked us better!" A career we'd never considered was now possible. "If we get good pictures," Shoshana suggested, "we can put together a portfolio and go to the agencies." We imagined that Eileen Ford herself would sign us and put us on the cover of *Vogue*.

"Competition for Twiggy!" I crowed.

"Although I think you're more *Seventeen*," Shoshana mused.

"I've never seen a model with my complexion on that cover," I sulked.

We did several more sessions at the photography school. The eight by tens the students gave us were high-contrast, black-and-white glossies, different from what we had imagined as we posed.

"Do you think we can really use these for a modeling portfolio?" I asked Shoshana one day as we went over our photographs. Deep shadows distorted our features, dramatic juxtapositions made us turn the pictures on their side to see if we could recognize ourselves.

"They're arty." She was as unconvinced as I was. Nevertheless, we each bought a black portfolio and arranged our pictures with the "arty" ones in the back. It was Shoshana's idea that once we got our portfolios together, we should consult our advertising teachers. "After all, they have agencies and see thousands of models," she reasoned.

Her professor was the dashing Mr. Delmar. Mine was Dr. Henning, long as a basketball player, with huge feet and hands, a massive head topped by curls of gray hair. He wore suits that hung in folds and drapes around his body like tweed togas.

When I asked him if he could look at my portfolio, he sug-

gested I come to his office, which was over a Tad's Steaks on Seventh Avenue. It was a small dark room at the end of an equally dim hallway that smelled of grilled meat. Mr. Henning sat behind a massive oak desk in front of a window. Smoky gray light fell on him from behind, highlighted the dust that floated in the air. He pointed to a leather chair across his desk, and I sank into its musty rasps and squeaks.

"These are very nice," he said, poring over the pictures. He turned the portfolio over, as Shoshana and I did, to figure out the more artistic photographs. He looked up. "How tall are you?"

"Five feet, four inches."

"Fashion models are taller," he said. "At least five-eight. But you might be able to do catalogue work. What size bra do you wear?"

"I beg your pardon?"

"I'm not being fresh," he reassured me. "There's a market for models who do women's intimate apparel, bras and girdles, that sort of thing." I was aghast, and it must have shown, because Dr. Henning raised his palms toward me, as if to protect himself from something I might throw. "This is for respectable catalogues like Sears and J. C. Penney's." He unfurled himself from his chair to reach for a thick book behind him. "Let me show you."

I waited until I could speak without breaking into tears. "Thank you, but . . ."

He leafed through until he reached the back pages. "They don't usually photograph the face, so no one will recognize you." He tipped the catalogue toward me. Black and white images of female torsos wearing cotton bras were printed along the left and right margins. Blocks of print gave particulars for styles, price, sizes available. "There's quite a bit of money in it," he promised.

"It's not the kind of modeling I had in mind," I said, trying to stay composed. I shook with anger and humiliation, but I didn't want to say or do anything stupid. After all, he was my teacher and would grade me at the end of the semester. "Thank you, anyway."

"Don't decide right now. I know it's not the sort of thing a girl jumps into." He returned the catalogue to its place.

"I'm sure it's not my thing." I took my portfolio. He walked me to the door. "I appreciate the time you took."

The long hall felt longer with him staring after me from the threshold. I tried to walk so that my hips didn't swing from side to side, my breasts didn't jiggle. No part of my body should appear suggestive in any way to someone who had just recommended a career for me as a bra model. Had the thought just occurred to him as he looked at my pictures? Or had he checked me out from every angle while I sat in class jotting down famous advertising slogans? How could I face him again? Never in tight clothes, that was for sure.

Shoshana didn't think I should have been offended. "Someone has to model bras," she reasoned. "Why not you?"

"I'm not even allowed to wear a bikini. How can I tell my mother I model bras?"

"You tell her too much," she said.

"That's not the point, Shoshana!"

She ignored my irritation. "Doesn't she make bras?"

"Yes she does. But that doesn't mean she wants me to wear them without a shirt."

Shoshana's appointment with Mr. Delmar went much better. He thought she could be a model, but she needed more pictures. "Get some that are straightforward, less of this artsy-fartsy stuff," was his assessment.

Since I was about four inches too short to be a model, I didn't want to be photographed any more.

"You can use them when you go on auditions," Shoshana suggested. "Didn't you say they always ask for a head shot?"

I'd long felt at a disadvantage during auditions because I didn't have a composite or a head shot, which cost more than I was willing to invest in my career as an actress. But these photographs were nothing like the head shots other people brought to auditions. We made another appointment to be photographed,

and this time, we brought simple clothes, wore little makeup. Again we were snapped together, but at the end of the session, different students asked us to pose for them individually.

The young man who asked me was Indian. He was bony, slightly taller than I, stoop-shouldered. He spoke in a soft, deferential voice, a musical English that at first sounded too fast for me to understand. Once I became used to it, I liked his forceful explosives and snappy vowels, the way every syllable was differentiated from the other.

"My name is Shanti," he said, as he set up lights for a portrait.

We worked well together. He was gentle and considerate, gave me breaks between setups, made little gestures with his lips, or his head, or his bony fingers to get me to move, or to hold a pose. It was as if we'd known each other a long time, and at the end of the session, he asked if it might be possible to do some exteriors.

"Is that okay with the school?" I asked.

"Yes, sure," he said. "We're supposed to learn that too."

We met that Sunday afternoon in Central Park. We walked around, and when he saw a nice background, he had me pose before it. After a couple of hours, he had enough pictures, and we went home, but not before he had asked me to meet him again the following weekend, this time in the Village.

The next Sunday we wandered around, and he snapped me next to a group of hippies in outlandish clothes and unkempt hair. I was uncomfortable around them, which showed in the photographs. The hippies made faces at the camera while I stood primly in front of them, my purse clasped to my bosom. He then photographed me in the midst of a group of old men observing a chess game. I had no idea how chess was played and watched the game intently to see if I could get a sense of it. But there was such little action, it was impossible to figure out, and when I looked up to see if Shanti was done photographing me, I gazed into the eyes of my math teacher, Mr. Grunwald. Behind him, Shanti snapped a picture of me looking shocked.

"Hi!" Mr. Grunwald seemed happy to see me, strangely, since in class he ignored me so that he could focus on people who understood scalar multiplication. He grinned. "Do you always travel with a photographer?" he asked. I introduced him to Shanti, and the three of us walked down the rows of chess tables crowded with spectators, as if the game held real excitement. Mr. Grunwald said he lived nearby and often walked to the park to see the players. He laughed when I suggested there was nothing to watch. Beside us, Shanti neither spoke nor took pictures, and I felt his sullenness grow like a balloon being pumped with air. Mr. Grunwald felt it too, because after a couple of blocks, he excused himself and went in the opposite direction.

"Is he your boyfriend?" Shanti asked, the minute Mr. Grunwald was out of hearing.

"No. He's my math teacher," I blushed.

"I see." He sounded annoyed, which made me mad. What business was it of his whether Mr. Grunwald was my boyfriend or my math teacher? "Maybe we're done for the day," he said.

"All right." I looked in the direction Mr. Grunwald had taken, wondering if I might catch up with him.

"Fine, then," Shanti said, and stalked off. He quickly disappeared in the crowd, while I stood in place, surprised at his reaction. In the two weeks we'd worked together, it hadn't occurred to me that Shanti's interest might be more than professional. It was hard to imagine that when he looked at me through the lens, he saw more than a model. I walked around the Village for a while asking myself whether I wanted to be the object of Shanti's affection as well as his art. When I realized that my wanderings were meant to run into Mr. Grunwald again, I knew the answer.

The following week Mr. Grunwald asked me to stay after class. As everyone filed out, he handed me a copy of *Backstage* with an audition notice circled in red.

"I saw this," he said, "and it sounded perfect for you."

"Are you an actor?" I should have known that such a handsome man was in the theater.

"No," he said, "but my roommate is."

Shoshana waited outside, and I shared the news that Mr. Grunwald had a roommate. Her face fell. When I asked her why she looked so disappointed, she gave me her opinion.

"He's homosexual."

"Oh, please!"

"Think about it. He's single, lives in the Village, has a roommate."

It was the most ridiculous reasoning I'd ever heard. If anyone should know about homosexuals, it was me, I argued, since I was surrounded by them in dance classes. But Shoshana could not be dissuaded. She said some homosexuals didn't look it. "I bet his roommate," she curled her tongue around the word, "is swishy."

There was only one way to tell. We must see the roommate. If we followed Mr. Grunwald from school, we'd see where he lived. We might be able to catch a glimpse of the roommate through the window. Or, if we waited outside Mr. Grunwald's door, we might see them come out together.

In the excitement of planning how to follow Mr. Grunwald without being seen, I almost forgot why he asked me to stay after class. The audition notice in *Backstage* called for an ingenue for a children's theater company casting a Broadway-bound production of an Indian fable. It was a dream come true—a part I was qualified to play that took advantage of my looks and training. I called to set up a time and was told I didn't need to prepare anything because I'd read from the script.

If Shanti would talk to me again, I could learn an Indian accent and throw in a few Hindi words if necessary. We met for lunch, and as he showed me the pictures he had taken the previous week, I listened to his inflections, tried to capture the rhythm of his speech. He laughed at my attempts to mimic his accent.

"You can't learn it in one day," he chuckled. "It takes a lifetime."

The audition was at Michaels Rehearsal Studio on Eighth Avenue. Several other actresses waited ahead of me, but a couple

were too old to be ingenues, and none looked as Indian as I did. I'd made myself up to appear as Indian as possible without wearing a sari, my hair parted in the middle and braided, eyes done up with kohl, a dot of red nail polish in the middle of my forehead.

When I was called in, Bill, the director, and Vera, the producer, exchanged a look. They asked some questions about my prior experience, then said they were ready to hear me read from the script. In the scene, a character named Soni explained to a character named Babu that she was a prisoner in a tower because her uncle planned to marry her to a rajah. Soni was allowed to leave the tower to pray at a temple, but she had a chain around her waist, which her uncle pulled when it was time for her to return.

As soon as he heard my poorly executed Indian accent, Bill interrupted and asked if I could read it straight. Vera then asked me to improvise a scene in which a monkey entered through a window and offered to help Soni escape from the tower. I did my best to appear surprised, scared, curious, grateful. At the end, Vera took my phone number and said she'd get back to me.

Bill and Vera were professional and noncommittal, didn't give me a clear sense of whether or not they liked my audition. I wanted to play Soni more than anything in the world, and as I left the studio, I reviewed everything I'd done and said, tried to figure out if there was more I could have done to assure me the part. It was a Saturday, almost time for matinee performances. I walked on Broadway, past the marquees with the names of famous plays and actors, the tourists who gawked at tawdry posters in front of the pornography shops vying with legitimate theaters. I turned the corner and stood in front of Performing Arts's chocolate facade with its heavy red doors. I pressed my forehead against the glass. The familiar wooden boxes were stacked near the lockers in the Basement, the desks arranged in a semicircle, as if a scene were about to be performed for students and teachers. I shook with anxiety and had to lean against the front pillars of the shuttered

school until I no longer felt lightheaded and the trembling had stopped.

⁓

I hung up the phone and slumped against the wall of our kitchen. Mami panicked. "What's the matter?"

"I got the part," I spoke to myself, unbelieving. "I'm going to be in a play." I looked up at her. "On Broadway."

"Is that good?" she wondered. She knew it was when I pulled Cibi from the playpen in the middle of the kitchen and danced her around the house. "I'm going to be on Broadway. I'm going to be a star," I sang. Cibi chortled, drooled on me. I put her back.

Tata dragged herself from her room in the basement, Delsa and Norma left the television on in the living room and ran into the kitchen. Raymond and Franky appeared from the yard. The rest of my sisters and brothers came down from the bedrooms. The house was full of people I loved eager to hear good news. Without knowing what the fuss was about, my sisters and brothers, my mother and grandmother, could tell it was a wonderful thing because I was so happy. I repeated what Vera told me. The play was for young audiences. It was one of a repertory of other plays performed in schools and theaters around the Northeast. The company, Children's Theater International, had won several honors and awards.

My family was impressed. They didn't ask if I'd wear any of the bizarre costumes they'd seen on me, the bells strapped to my ankles, the nail polish dots in the middle of my forehead that had to be removed with acetone. They didn't joke about the strange sounds that came from my room when I practiced my Indian dances, which would increase now that I was to perform regularly. They were as glad as I was, which made my joy greater because it was wonderful to do something that not only made me feel good but made everyone else smile.

I called Shoshana, Shanti, Alma and Corazón, everyone I knew. I would have told total strangers if I had had the courage.

Rehearsals began that week, in a loft on Christopher Street in the Village. Some of the cast had performed in other Children's Theater International productions, *Petey and the Pogo Stick* and *Hans Brinker.* The play I'd be in, *Babu,* had been in repertory the year before.

"You might know the girl who played Soni," Vera said. "She went to your school. Priscilla López."

"Yes, she graduated a year before me." I was thrilled to be playing a part originated by Priscilla, one of the most talented actors at Performing Arts when I was a student there. Vera also told me that, while they liked the fact that I was an Indian classical dancer, my role didn't require dancing.

"There is one scene where a dancer performs," she said, "but we already have someone to do that." I was disappointed, but got over it after I had read the entire script, which made it clear that my character, Soni, had a bigger role to play in the story than the dancer who attended the rajah.

The title role of Babu was played by Allan, an actor and singer whose openness and warmth won me over instantly. In the play, he rescued Soni from her prison tower, and it didn't take much acting for me to fall in love with him at each performance, and to remain besotted between shows.

Allan and Bill had known each other for years, had worked together, and were good friends. Both had marvelous, trained voices, and I often asked one or the other a question just to hear them speak.

The other member of the cast I came to know well was Tom. In the first scene of the play, when Soni and Babu met, Tom, in his role as the monkey god, sat in the lotus position in a niche on the set. After Soni was dragged offstage by her evil uncle, Babu prayed for a way to help her escape. The audience screeched when Tom opened his eyes and spoke, because they didn't expect a statue to come to life.

After rehearsals I often joined Bill, Allan, or Tom for a cup of coffee or a late dinner. They'd been in the theater much longer than I and told funny, poignant stories about mishaps and humiliations onstage and off.

Vera lived in Westchester County and commuted to rehearsals. She was like an anxious mother one moment, all business the next. If one of us coughed, she handed out lozenges retrieved from her ample bag, but if we were late, she made sure to let us know that next time we should try harder. She frequently reminded us about our responsibilities as actors. "Just because this is children's theater," she often said, "doesn't mean we patronize or talk down to our audience."

We rehearsed evenings and weekends, and each time I left the studio I felt lucky to be among such gifted, committed people. It was fun to improvise with Allan and Tom, then to work from the script with Bill, who worked us hard but made us feel as if we were the most brilliant people he'd ever directed. Over the weeks of rehearsal, the character of Soni evolved as I better understood what Bill expected from my performance.

"Not so stylized," he scolded, when I tried to introduce Indian dance movements into Soni's actions.

With college in the morning, the Advertising Checking Bureau in the afternoons, and Children's Theater International evenings and weekends, I again spent most of my time away from home. I met Shoshana in classes, and we often had lunch together before I went to work.

We didn't forget Mr. Grunwald. One day we followed him in the subway to his stop at Waverly Place. He was easy to stalk. He was oblivious to his environment, seemed lost in deep mathematical thoughts, and kept his eyes focused on the obstacles in front of him but no further. Once he entered the subway, he immersed himself in a thick book with a parabola and formulas on the cover. From the next car, Shoshana and I watched until he got up from his seat and stood by the doors. As soon as they opened, he got off. We waited, then followed at a distance, trying not to draw attention

to ourselves in spite of the nervous giggles that attacked us every time we realized what we were doing. Mr. Grunwald climbed the station steps, and we lost him in the throng on the street. But soon Shoshana spotted him buying a paper at a newsstand. He dropped some coins in the vendor's hand, turned a corner, and vanished.

"Now that's weird," said Shoshana, as we peeked around a building to a street of brownstones with neat stoops and flowerpots in the windows. "He must have gone into one of the houses."

"It must have been the first one," I pointed out, "he didn't have time to walk too far." No sooner had I spoken than Mr. Grunwald emerged from the first door on the street, led by a fluffy white dog in a hurry to get to a hydrant.

"What did I tell you?" Shoshana said, triumphant. Whether Mr. Grunwald was homosexual or not, his choice of dog certainly balanced the equation, as he would have said, in the direction of Shoshana's suspicions. "A swishy dog," she proclaimed, as if I hadn't noticed. "Oh, I'm so sorry," she pouted, when she noticed my expression.

"He doesn't look like the kind of man to have that type of dog," was all I could say.

Shoshana walked me to a nearby restaurant, where she ordered a cup of soup and a sandwich to make up for my disappointment. When I was fortified, we talked about how hard it was to find the right man.

"Maybe we're too choosy," she mused. "We'll end up old maids."

"He could at least have had a German shepherd," I said, fixed on the image of the magnificent Mr. Grunwald attached to the fussy dog.

The restaurant window faced a busy intersection near the subway entrance. A mishmash of hippies, businesspeople, ancient men and women, beggars, and street musicians paraded up and down for our entertainment. In the middle of Shoshana's description of her ideal man, she yelped as if pricked and pointed behind me. On the sidewalk, walking in our direction from the train

station, was Mr. Grunwald, still led by the fluffy dog, his arm tight around the waist of a leggy, redheaded woman. Every few steps they stopped and kissed, to the annoyance of people behind, who were forced to circle around them, their faces crimped in displeasure. They passed no more than three feet from us, oblivious to the rest of humanity.

"The dog is hers," I guessed.

When I told Bill and Allan the story, they laughed.

"Do you like German shepherds?" Allan asked.

"At least they're real dogs, not walking mops." Bill and Allan looked at each other, then laughed some more. It was weeks before I realized what was so funny. One day Allan had to rush back to his apartment on the Upper West Side. He lived on the second floor at the rear of a brownstone, and as we came up, the deep-throated barking of what could only be a huge dog filled the hallway. "Wait here," Allan said, as he clicked open the three locks on his door. He slid into the apartment while I waited in the hall. In a few seconds, he opened the door, his left hand on the collar of the biggest German shepherd I had ever seen. "This is Tristan," he said. The dog's nose dove into my crotch, and Allan had to restrain it to keep it from pushing me further against the wall. "He likes girls," Allan grinned. He clipped on the dog's leash, and we walked half a block to Central Park, where Allan played with Tristan while I leaned against a tree. It was touching to see the warmth between them, the way the dog followed Allan's every move, stopped if Allan stopped, moved when Allan did. Watching them, I knew that this was the first man outside my family I had felt affection for. I'd fallen in love with several — Neftalí, Otto, Mr. Grunwald — but what I felt for Allan was unlike the romantic fantasies I had created around other men. I didn't daydream about marrying Allan, or even kissing him. I wanted to be with him, to talk and be silly and hear his stories. I loved his laugh, the way his eyes sparkled when he was pleased or proud. Between us, there were no sexual games. Had there been, I would have been disillusioned.

Shoshana didn't understand my relationship with Allan. She and I often discussed whether it was possible for a man and a woman to be friends without being sexual. She didn't think so; I did. Or rather, I hoped it was possible. I couldn't imagine that for the rest of my life, every encounter with a man was to be appraised against a possible sexual tryst. As an example of my ability to have male friends who were not boyfriends, I pointed to my frequent meetings with Shanti.

"He's in love with you," Shoshana insisted. "You just refuse to admit it."

Shanti's devotion was flattering. We worked well together and continued our collaboration, in spite of the fact that we were often testy around each other. He constantly criticized my diet, which consisted primarily of street-vendor hot dogs smothered with sauerkraut, washed down with a Yoo-Hoo, or pizza and grape ade, or creamy eclairs and coffee.

"You're a dancer," Shanti reminded me, "you should eat better."

"At least," I retorted with a disdainful look at his cigarette, "I don't smoke."

On a warm and sunny winter day, we sat on the steps of the Main Library on Fifth Avenue after he took a series of pictures of me atop the lions that guarded the entrance. "You're not the most beautiful girl I've photographed," he admitted. "But when I look at you through the lens, I see myself."

"Don't scare me that way," I snapped.

Whenever Shanti went metaphysical on me, I turned nasty. He once said our souls were connected, and I stared at him as if he were crazy. "I have no soul," I finally spit out.

He was silent for a long time, then spoke in a near whisper. "I see your soul even if you don't."

It was my turn to be speechless. His faith in something within me that he could see and I couldn't made me feel inadequate and immature. I had to defend myself. "You see what you want to see, not what's there."

Another time he insisted on reading my hand. "Over here is the life line," he stroked a curve from between my thumb and index finger to the crease on the inside of my wrist. "It will be a long life," he assured me. "But these," he pointed to a series of ragged lines, "indicate illness."

I pulled my hand away. "That's nonsense," I said. "I don't believe any of it." The truth was that it scared me to think he could know anything about me from my hands. If so, were there other signs, in the shape of my lips or eyebrows, the way my hair curled? If there were, I didn't want to know what they meant. What difference did it make if I had ten, twenty, fifty years to live? Or if the next day I'd be run over by a car? Why would I want to know what lay ahead?

"I can't predict what will happen," he protested, "I can only interpret what has happened already."

"I can do that," I retorted.

No matter how mean I was to him, or how much he criticized me, we always found time to be together. We knew that the pictures he took were not commercial, would never end up in a magazine, or be printed by the hundreds as head shots for auditions. Weekends, we still met in Central Park, or Lincoln Center, or the Empire State Building, where he took pictures of me looking as remote and inaccessible as I was to him. Every week, he handed me a few eight-by-ten glossies, which I studied as if they were a puzzle, each feature, shadow, line a piece of a larger, undefined whole. I felt protected by their formality, their solemn stillness. But it unnerved me when he captured another me, whose eyes beseeched the onlooker for something I couldn't define.

⁓

As the day neared for my Broadway debut, I settled into my role as Soni. We performed at local schools, which gave me a chance to become familiar with the set and comfortable in my two costumes. Bill and Vera planned several more shows after the New

York run, and a tour out of town. I prepared Mami for the possibility that I'd go away for two weeks or more with the cast of *Babu*. Other than occasional overnight stays with my cousins Alma and Corazón and the visits to Margie in Yonkers, I'd never slept away from home. I expected Mami to make a fuss, but she just asked a few questions about where we'd be going and seemed at ease with the possibility.

Even though Mr. Grunwald gave me a C as my final grade in his class, I invited him to the opening. After all, he was responsible for the audition that had won me the part. We both knew a C was generous, considering my negative progress in mathematics or, as he called it, analytical thinking. For the final paper, we were supposed to state a theory and, using logical progression, prove it. I set out to prove that civilization began in Puerto Rico.

"But you said the theory didn't have to be true," I argued when we discussed my paper. "You just wanted us to make a logical case for it."

"You didn't do that," he maintained.

The play was to open for a limited run at the Longacre Theater during the Christmas holidays. Just a few months before, Sandy Dennis had starred in *Daphne in Cottage D* on the same stage. At the first dress rehearsal, I was assigned her dressing room, which featured a star on the door. Every time I pushed the door open, the star right before my eyes filled me with pride, which I had to contain so as not to appear conceited. I wanted to share my happiness with someone without seeming vain or boastful, so I wrote to Papi in Puerto Rico. I sent him a copy of the program, which featured Allan and me in our "crown jewels," the elaborately sequined and embroidered costumes Robert De Mora had designed for the finale. I described the hours of work it took to put a show together, the people involved, the fanciful plot. I told him about the dressing room, the wall-size mirror surrounded by lights, the private bathroom, the rug, the rundown but comfortable couch in which I took naps between performances. Because he wasn't there to see it with his own eyes, Papi saw it through mine,

and for the first time I was glad he didn't live with us, because now there was someone whose vision of my world depended on my version of it.

The stage of the Longacre was huge. A few hours before the opening, I stood in the center, peered at the rows of empty seats, and saw not a deserted theater, but a challenge. My task was to transform a roomful of adults worn out from Christmas shopping and children fidgety with expectation into an audience. If I believed that I, a Puerto Rican girl from Brooklyn, was an Indian princess captive in a tower, rescued by a monkey, married to a prince, my audience would believe. If I could do that, I could do anything.

Mami and my sisters and brothers came to the first show. I was so nervous that I raced through it and was dazed and exhausted for the curtain calls. When I returned to the dressing room to change, I was greeted by a huge bouquet of flowers from Bill and Vera, another from Mr. Grunwald, a third from Shanti. Within minutes, the room filled with people. When she came backstage, Mami carried more flowers, somewhat wilted from having to share her arms with Franky. Mr. Grunwald stopped by, waved at the confusion from the door, disappeared.

Bill and Vera made a point of being nice to Mami, and she later told me she could see they were respectable, sober people.

"You take good care my daughter," Mami told Vera, when she mentioned the tour.

"I'm a mother, too," Vera responded. "Don't worry." Mami hugged her.

Don Carlos brought his kids. La Muda showed up. Shoshana came with Josh and Sammy. Shanti took pictures of me putting on makeup, as well as in the captive-in-a-tower costume.

"This looks nothing like what Indian girls wear," he complained. "It's for a harem."

"The designer took creative liberties," I said, "but the costume works on stage, which is what matters." He shrugged his shoulders.

Every day before a show, I got off the subway from Brooklyn,

walked slowly along Broadway, listened to the commotion as if it were a marvelous song. Taxi horns blared. Tourists chattered in a plethora of dialects, all of them incomprehensible but familiar. The Hare Krishnas clinked their finger cymbals, pounded their drums, chanted their joyful tune. Peddlers offered legal and illegal bargains. I turned the corner and smiled at the bold *Babu* on the marquee of the Longacre. In front, there were huge posters of Allan and me, of Tom as the monkey god, of the rajah and his dancer. I entered the theater through the stage door, floated as if in a dream into my leading-lady dressing room, and caught an image of myself in the enormous mirror. I was not the most beautiful girl Shanti had ever photographed, nor the most talented actress graduated from Performing Arts. Alone with my reflection, I wondered what had brought me here. I was grateful, but I didn't know whom to thank.

"It wouldn't look right."

Because Vera lived in Westchester County and ran a children's theater series there, she organized several performances of *Babu* at schools in her area. The cast met at the rehearsal studio, and Bill drove a brown-and-beige Volkswagen van along the Hudson River north toward Scarsdale or Bronxville, Tarrytown or Elmsford, Mamaroneck or White Plains. We didn't spend much time in the communities where we performed, because the cast couldn't wait to get back to the city. Some claimed pollen allergies, exacerbated by the mere sight of trees. Others remembered childhoods in similar communities and were morose and pensive the whole way there and back.

The polite, mostly white audiences of Westchester County were a contrast to the outspoken children of New York City schools. When the curtain parted to reveal me praying before a stone god on the stage of an auditorium in a suburban school, there was appreciative applause and intense attention. At the Brooklyn Academy of Music, Town Hall, or schools in New York City, the applause of third, fourth, and fifth graders was accompanied by whistles and commentary. It took great concentration to wait while teachers tried to control students who called out "Hot mamma!", "Baby!", or "Hey, sweet thing!" Once the audience was relatively quiet, Allan made his entrance, discovered the captive Soni, a chain tied around her waist. As we discussed my predicament, a yank startled me and the audience, who couldn't see Bill

or the stage manager dragging me off while I pleaded with Babu to help me. In the suburbs, this was a moment of high drama. In the city, the kids screeched. "Follow her, man!" they yelled — obvious, though not dramatically efficient, advice.

The schedule of performances intensified as spring neared and the promised tour developed. I took time off from college and from the Advertising Checking Bureau to go to Maine, New Hampshire, Massachusetts. The plan was to drive north to Bangor, then perform our way down the coast toward New York. Bill, Vera, and the cast traveled in the VW bus, while the stage manager followed in a truck that carried the set and costumes.

Early on a Sunday morning, we met on the corner of 55th Street and Sixth Avenue. The familiar VW bus was parked on the curb, a rental truck behind it.

"Nanook of the North!" Allan joked when he saw me, bundled up as if our destination were the North Pole and not New England. It was mid-March, and although New York was beginning to bloom, I had consulted regional newspapers at the Advertising Checking Bureau and knew to prepare for foul weather, from snow to sleet to implacable rain.

The cast negotiated where to sit, a process Vera likened to her four children bickering about who'd be in front and who needed frequent bathroom stops and who must sit by a window or they'd throw up. The city peeled away as we drove north on Interstate 95. Every time a familiar exit appeared, someone told a story about a summer stock playhouse, or about being stranded in New Haven in a blizzard, or about out-of-town tryouts that never made it into town. Lee, who played Soni's nurse, began a round of camp songs, none of which I knew. While everyone sang, I clapped my hands or whistled.

We stopped for meals at diners sometimes five or ten miles from the highway. Millie's Coffee Haus, Aunt Polly's Place, the Towne Line Diner, the Harbor View (with no water in sight) — all offered delicious, inexpensive food on enormous platters. We were a coffee-drinking group and usually entered diners in the throes of

caffeine withdrawal, which made us irritable and impatient until the fragrant black liquid hit our systems. Veteran waitresses recognized our dazed looks the minute we walked in, desperately sniffing the air. They didn't ask if we wanted coffee. They poured full cups as we sat down, then handed us chatty menus with a long list of offerings. Along the back of the counter, refrigerated cases held golden-crust apple pies, lemon meringues, crunchy cobblers, puddings, creamy tapioca. Except for Lee, who was a strict vegetarian, we were indiscriminate eaters, eager to taste local specialties, like Rhode Island's coffee milk, Massachusetts's clam chowder, New Hampshire quahogs, Maine steamers.

We spent our first night in Lewiston, Maine. Bill and Vera were nervous about the accommodations in local bed and breakfasts. They relaxed when we pulled up to a pretty Victorian house on a hill.

"It looks like a storybook house," I exclaimed, charmed by the lace curtains in the windows, the gingerbread eaves, the etched glass door. The owner of the house, a rosy woman named Mrs. Hoch, had a fire going and muffins in the oven. Lee, Allan, and I stayed with Mrs. Hoch; the rest of the cast and crew went to other houses nearby.

We went to dinner at a local restaurant. The minute we walked in, I sensed how much we—ten New York types in urban wear—stood out from the rest of the patrons. I was the darkest person in the room, and the stares I drew felt like darts. The waitresses joined a couple of tables as we huddled at the door. I was embarrassed by the commotion we caused, conscious that we were out-of-towners in a small community. Every action was noticed by the locals, who blinked us away whenever one of us looked in their direction. I made a point of sitting between Allan and Bill.

"I feel so dark," I muttered. Bill smiled and put his arm around me.

The color of my skin was something I noticed every day when I stripped naked for a shower or bath. When I tried on new clothes,

the color of my skin determined whether I could wear certain greens or yellows. Black, I noticed, made me look paler, white had the opposite effect. Hot pink gave me a healthy glow, whereas certain blues created ashen shadows around my eyes and lips. It was important for me to know these things when choosing costumes, because at Performing Arts we were taught that a character's choice of color said a great deal about her. The principles I learned there seeped into my choice of everyday clothes. I favored bright, tropical hues but avoided distracting patterns. Other than the color of my clothes, there was nothing about the style to make me stand out. My skirts were never too short, nor my pants too tight, nor my blouses too low-cut. So it was the shade of my skin, I thought, that caused people to stare in Lewiston, Bangor, and Portland, in New Hampshire, Massachusetts, Rhode Island, and Connecticut. Wherever we stopped to perform our Indian fable, I was the darkest person in the room, the diner, the school, the store, the entire town.

"I must be the only Puerto Rican ever to have visited Woonsocket," I joked once, after a particularly tense visit to a diner. The others chuckled, but no one said more. The color of my skin, my Puerto Rican background, were not topics in the garrulous discussions in the VW bus or at meals. Just as the others took their whiteness for granted, I was to do the same for my darkness. Only they didn't draw stares as I did.

At first I was intimidated by the attention. As the tour progressed, I grew defiant, interpreted the stares as a challenge, made sure that at restaurants I sat where everyone could see me, a dark face among light ones. When that didn't change the way I felt, I decided to educate people about Puerto Rico. A blustery morning in Salem, Massachusetts, recalled the warm, soft dawns of the Puerto Rican countryside. As I walked the shore in Newport, Rhode Island, with my fellow actors, I felt compelled to describe San Juan harbor. A side of pilaf next to my meat loaf elicited memories of my mother's tender rice. I took every opportunity to mention Puerto Rico and Puerto Ricans, even when the subject

of conversation had nothing to do with ethnicity or culture. Waiters, school custodians, the doorman at one of the hotels where we stayed, the clerk at a pharmacy where I went to buy sanitary pads, a cashier at L. L. Bean—all learned that I was Puerto Rican, that Puerto Rico was in the Caribbean, that Puerto Ricans were American citizens at birth, that we spoke Spanish as our first language, that English was a required subject in our schools. Yes, there were a lot of Puerto Ricans in New York, but there were also many in other cities, such as Chicago and Miami. If I relieved their ignorance about me, maybe they would look at the next Puerto Rican who came through with respect rather than suspicion.

When the tour was over and we returned to New York, I felt worldly. I'd traveled into the vast horizon of the United States that I couldn't see from the ground, but the trip made me wary of venturing farther into the continent. What would it be like if, as Vera and Bill planned, we toured the South? Could I be forbidden from restaurants? I knew the laws didn't allow that, thanks in part to Martin Luther King, Jr., whose portrait hung in our living room. But I also knew laws meant nothing to people who hated. I wasn't black, I wasn't white. The racial middle in which I existed meant that people evaluated me on the spot. Their eyes flickered, their brains calibrated the level of pigmentation they'd find acceptable. Is she light enough to be white? Is she so dark as to be black? In New York I was Puerto Rican, an identity that carried with it a whole set of negative stereotypes I continually struggled to overcome. But in other places, where Puerto Ricans were in lower numbers, where I was from didn't matter. I was simply too dark to be white, too white to be black.

⌒

The weeks following the tour were a flurry of catching up. I had been absent from college for fifteen days and returned to assignments missed and hundreds of pages to be read in order to get to where my classmates were. At the Advertising Checking

Bureau, a daunting stack of clippings on my desk had to be examined and approved. Mrs. Davis smiled as I scanned the pages without catching up on the latest news from Grand Rapids, Michigan, or Baraboo, Wisconsin.

Shanti called to arrange more sessions, but I couldn't do it. He'd quit the school of photography to take a job in a lab, enlarging other people's pictures. "I can develop color now," he said proudly.

We performed *Babu* a few more times, and then everyone bade a teary goodbye for the summer and dispersed to other repertory or stock companies away from New York. Bill and Vera promised us work in the fall, a tour in the Washington, D.C., area. A new production was to be added to the program, a Japanese fable this time, with a part for an ingenue.

I planned a summer devoted to work and college, so that I could take the fall semester off to perform in *Babu* and, hopefully, in the new production. One of the courses I signed up for, Survey of Art History, required weekly visits to museums. Sometimes I dragged one of my sisters with me, usually Edna, and we spent Saturday or Sunday afternoons staring at paintings neither of us understood. At home, I wrote a paper about the art work assigned that week. My weekends became stressful, because although I appreciated the art, I couldn't explain it. From time to time, Tata or Mami knocked on the door of my room because they heard moans. I was frustrated by the challenge of paintings to which I had an emotional reaction but about which I could find nothing to say.

"If the artist wanted to say other than what's in the picture," I argued with my teacher, "he should have been a writer, not a painter." She insisted that painting was filled with vital clues and subtleties that rendered meaning but that each detail had to be studied individually.

"If you stand in front of a painting long enough," Miss Prince assured me, "its meaning will become clear."

One Sunday afternoon, as I stared at Seurat's dots, a woman

approached me. "I'm sorry to disturb you," she smiled sweetly, "but do you have any idea how to get to the restaurant from here?" She had blonde hair teased into a bouffant made famous by Jacqueline Kennedy eight years earlier.

I dug out the brochure with a map of the museum galleries out of my purse and traced the route she should take to the first floor. As we were bent over the map, a man approached. "Hi," he grinned. He was obviously related to her, with the same alert eyes, sandy hair, cheery smile, and mellifluous southern accent. She introduced him as her brother Avery Lee, herself as Patsy. "You've been so kahhnd," she said, stretching the word until it seemed endless. "Would you join us for coffee?"

We walked downstairs, and she told me she lived in El Paso. "But I just love coming to New York," she said, "the museums, the wonderful restaurants . . . Do you live here?"

By the time we arrived on the first floor, Patsy had extracted from me that I lived in Brooklyn, was single, a college student, a dancer and actress. "Oh, my goodness," she gushed, "you sure do have an interesting life." As we joined the cafeteria line, she remembered she had to call her husband. I directed her to the telephones and was alone with Avery Lee, who'd followed us in attentive silence the whole time Patsy elicited my history.

"Shouldn't we get something for her?" I offered, but Avery Lee said he didn't know what she liked. The next few minutes were awkward as I waited for Patsy to return.

"I have to be honest with you," Avery Lee confided. "She's not coming back."

"Why not?"

"Because we planned it this way."

Had we not been in as public a place as the Met's cafeteria, I would have panicked. "What do you mean?"

"You were by that painting a long time," he said. "I stood next to you, but you just stared and stared."

"I was doing my homework," I admitted.

"I didn't want to scare you, so I asked Patsy to see what she could do."

"*Are* you related to each other?" I asked.

"Of course. She's my sister." Despite his ploy, there was about Avery Lee an openness that I liked, and his accent, so slow and easy, was reminiscent of the adorable Mr. Grunwald. Avery Lee looked nothing like the math teacher, however. Physically, he was more like Otto — big and muscular, with thin, determined lips and a square jaw.

"You probably know the shows to see in New York," he guessed, "because you're an actress." He was also under the impression that I could recommend the best restaurants. I had to admit that the cultural life of the city was something I read about but didn't participate in because of its cost.

"Then you can be our guide," he suggested. "You know where to go, and we're here to have a good time." When I hesitated, he insisted. "Come on. Patsy has her husband, and I'm here by myself. You can be my date," he grinned.

I told Mami that I had a job as a guide to Texan tourists. The next morning, I appeared at the apartment building where Avery Lee and Patsy were staying with friends. The doorman called up my name, and in a while Avery Lee came down alone. When I asked after Patsy, he said she had a migraine.

We hopped in and out of taxis, visited the Empire State Building, the Museum of Modern Art, Lincoln Center. We had lunch at the Waldorf Astoria. He wanted to have dinner at the Plaza, but I wasn't dressed up enough. So we went to Bloomingdale's.

"Avery Lee, I'm not comfortable with you buying me clothes," I protested. "I'll go home and change." But he wouldn't hear of it.

I chose a simple dress on sale, but then we had to get shoes and a purse to match. I was torn between the pleasure of buying what I could never afford with my own money and worry about its real cost.

"I know what you're thinking," he read my mind, "but believe me, I love doing this for you. I love to see you smile."

So I smiled my way through the junior department, where

Avery Lee bought me an outfit for the next day too, when we'd see *Man of La Mancha*, and a bikini and coverup I was to wear to the beach the day after.

It felt strange to check two shopping bags at a fancy restaurant, but that's what we did. The candlelight, the wine he ordered for dinner, the slow drawl of his speech were all intoxicating. I had to excuse myself several times and go to the ladies' room, where I leaned my face against the cool wall until my head didn't spin any more and I could speak without slurring my words. After dinner, we walked hand in hand around the fountain in front of the hotel. The last man I'd kissed had been Otto, a year and a half earlier. Avery Lee was an equally passionate kisser whose hands strayed, the way Otto's had.

"I'll get us a room," Avery Lee offered, and headed toward the Plaza.

I sobered up right quick. "No. I better go home."

He squinted, as if the colored lights of the fountain weren't bright enough to see me. He turned his back, stuck his hands in his pockets, took a few steps away from me, and I fully expected him to kick the ground, hang his head, and say "Aw, shucks."

"Home?" he asked instead, as if the word were newly minted.

I sputtered that the subways were dangerous if I waited much longer. My shopping bags were still at the hotel, but I was reluctant to go back there with him, afraid to weaken and agree to follow him upstairs. I waited outside while he retrieved them. In the back of my mind I heard Shoshana's voice, "You idiot! He's a Texas millionaire!" Losing my virginity at the Plaza would have been the perfect end to the perfect day, but I couldn't bring myself to do it. As Avery Lee walked me to the train station, gloomy and silent, I felt the need to explain.

"You should know that I haven't come this close to giving in with anyone before," I confessed.

He grinned, kissed my forehead, handed me my shopping bags. "See you tomorrow," he said.

For the next three days we met, ate, saw plays, walked in Central Park, kissed at every opportunity. It rained the day we were

supposed to go to Jones Beach, so we went to the movies instead. "This is what they call petting, right?" I whispered, after a particularly breathtaking session of kisses and caresses.

"Yeah," he huffed.

"What's the difference between necking and petting?" I asked, and he demonstrated. Each evening he tried to get me to come to a hotel with him, and each time I resisted. One night he accompanied me all the way to Brooklyn. We kissed, we talked, kissed some more.

"Come with me to Texas," he offered, as the subway rumbled near my station. "I'll get you an apartment, a car, whatever you need."

"Are you asking me to be your mistress?" I asked coyly, because I thought he was kidding.

"Yeah!" He grinned, but this time I wasn't charmed.

"If you're going to all that trouble, why not marry me?"

"Because it wouldn't look right," he confessed, "for me to have a Spanish wife."

I was so stunned I almost missed my stop. The doors rattled open, were about to clang shut when I jumped out, too fast for Avery Lee to lumber after me. The train pulled away and left him still sitting on the plastic bench, astonished at my agility.

I must have misunderstood. He couldn't have meant what he said. Not once in the past few days had I sensed Avery Lee's impression of me to be tainted by the stereotype of the hot-tomato Latina. I was the virginal Maria of *West Side Story*, but he envisioned me as the promiscuous Anita.

I walked home through the dark Brooklyn streets to our house, let myself in the door, changed into my pajamas, and lay face up, staring into the dark. It was wrong to have accepted the clothes he bought me, the dinners, the theater, the romantic ride in the horse-drawn carriage through Central Park. Necking and petting, I learned from Shoshana, were okay so long as I wasn't just teasing him. But I was ashamed of how close I had come to tangling with him on a bed.

Early the next morning, he called, begged me to meet him.

"I have to explain," he said, and I agreed to meet him at a coffee shop near my job.

"It didn't sound right," he stammered as soon as we sat down, "the way I said what I did."

"Can you make it sound better?" I was determined to make him squirm, as I had all night long, remembering his kisses, feeling dirty and used.

"Hell!" he exclaimed, blushing when patrons at the coffee shop turned to look at us. He leaned toward me. "My daddy has had a Mexican for twenty years," he confided. "He loves her more than life," he added.

"A Mexican what?" I bit out.

"I'm being honest with you," Avery Lee sulked.

My eyes itched, and I was having trouble breathing. Under the table, my hands shook with the desire to strangle him. But he was impervious to my emotions. He gently turned my face toward his. In a murmur, he told me that he had political ambitions, that he had to marry a "good ole Texas gal" from a prominent family. Someone who could help him get elected. "Hell," he sat back and exclaimed again, "LBJ himself did it that way. The marriage means nothing."

I stood up, gathered my things. "I don't want to be your mistress," I hissed. "Right now, I don't even want to be in the same room with you."

"Sit down," Avery Lee ordered. "Everyone's starin'."

I sat down, defeated. It was too late to make a dramatic exit, to act self-righteous. Avery Lee wrote a phone number on his business card. "This is mah private lahhn." Oh, those long vowels! "Call me when you change your mahhnd." I stared at the paper, at his hopeful, foolish face. I wanted to spit into it. He stood up, helped me out of my chair, walked me to the Advertising Checking Bureau half a block away. At the elevator, he tried to kiss me, but I backed away. When the doors opened, I gulped some air, pushed my shoulders back, swallowed the hurt that tightened my throat, tickled my eyes. As the elevator rose, I absorbed Avery Lee's

insult as thoroughly as newsprint absorbs ink. Maybe I *was* too proud and ambitious. Maybe the years at Performing Arts, the exotic dance training, the movie work, the Broadway show had caused me to develop a higher opinion of myself than I deserved. Maybe Avery Lee saw the real me, a "Spanish" girl, good enough to sleep with but not good enough to marry.

That night I pulled out Shanti's photographs and studied them. In one, I sat on the grass, my body toward the camera, my face in haughty profile, gaze on a distant horizon. A scarf was tied around my forehead — Cleopatra's diadem. When Shanti took the picture, he made me hold the pose a long time. "Be still," he murmured over and over, until I had to stop breathing to satisfy him.

In another photograph, I leaned against the granite wall at the top of the Empire State Building. Behind me, Brooklyn floated in a soupy gray cloud like the suggestion of a city, nothing but pale rectangles and bruised smudges. Between me and Brooklyn, the East River was a flat, icy sheet. That photograph was taken on a cold, blustery morning just as the sun cut through the clouds, so that half of me was overexposed, the other half obscure. My expression was desolate, as if I'd just heard bad news.

As I leafed through the portfolio of my stillborn modeling career, I didn't see myself. I saw Avery Lee's Spanish girl, earnest but sad, eyes wary, and in each picture, alone, the edges of the photographs a box encasing loneliness.

⌒⌒

Days later, as I leaned toward an approaching bus on Fifth Avenue, a man tapped my shoulder and asked for directions to Rockefeller Center. I turned and met the sea-green eyes of Jurgen, who was clearly not lost, but captivated by my own dark brown pupils.

"I know where it is," he admitted. "There's a restaurant there. Will you join me for tea?"

I followed Jurgen to the restaurant on the lower level of

Rockefeller Center, which in winter looked out to a skating rink but in summer offered tables shaded by bright umbrellas.

Jurgen spoke excellent English with a charming accent. Whenever he made a mistake in grammar or pronunciation, he struck his lips with his index and middle fingers, as if the fault were in the mouth and not the brain. He was born in Hamburg but didn't live there. "Where, then?" I asked.

"All over," he chuckled.

His skin was translucent, its planes smooth and even. His lips frequently curled into a roguish smile that showed small teeth, flat, as if filed along the bottom.

Like many people in New York, Jurgen was just passing through. He'd buy me tea at Rockefeller Center, then return to Germany, or wherever his next stop was.

"Los Angeles," he said. "Then Egypt."

"How wonderful," I sighed, and he laughed.

As we talked, I slipped into the familiar, vague responses to the typical questions. But Jurgen was a careful listener, who asked for details no one else bothered to gather. Before the waiter refilled my glass of iced tea, I'd told Jurgen everything there was to know about me, including that I was a virgin, was not allowed to date until after I got married, and had recently been offered a position as the mistress of a Texan too ambitious to marry a "Spanish girl." He listened, chuckled, softened his eyes with concern. When tears dribbled from my eyes, he fished out a handkerchief from his pocket and pressed it to my cheeks. As he wiped away my tears, I was ashamed to have said so much and excused myself, intending to slip out another door and into the subways. But first I had to go to the bathroom, wash my face, comb my hair, apply lip gloss. When I came out, Jurgen was in the hall leading to the rest rooms. "I thought you were lost," he said.

He led me to the street, and we walked up Fifth Avenue toward Central Park. On 54th Street, he took my hand, and by the time we arrived in front of the Plaza at 59th and Fifth, his arm was around my shoulders and mine was around his waist. As we

strolled through Central Park, I told him that the last German to hold my hand had saved me from being run over by a truck. He joked that Germans had great timing.

I asked where he'd been born and he told me about his childhood in Hamburg. His mother and father still lived there, he said, but he hadn't seen them in a couple of years. He asked if I missed my father, and I nearly broke down again.

"You must think I'm a crybaby," I apologized.

"No," he stroked my hair, "it's sweet."

It was easy to be with Jurgen, to talk to him about things I had never shared with anyone but Shoshana. Every once in a while I remembered we'd just met and wondered what it was about him that made me feel as if we'd known each other for ages.

We walked to a restaurant across the street from Lincoln Center. Jurgen introduced me to the bartender, Donny, at whose apartment he was staying.

"Where are you from?" I asked, upon hearing his accent.

"Ireland," Donny chuckled. He had black hair and blue eyes, was shorter than Jurgen, stocky, somewhat older, although he claimed to be the same age, twenty-nine. He and Jurgen exchanged a few words in German. I could tell Donny said something about me because of the warm, proud look Jurgen gave me.

"Where did you learn to speak German?" I asked Donny, and the men exchanged a look.

"He speaks terrible German," Jurgen laughed. "Like schoolboy." Donny blushed. We chatted for a while, and then Donny invited us to come with him and his girlfriend to Jones Beach the next day. When I hesitated, Jurgen offered to call my mother and ask permission.

"No, that's okay," I told him, certain he was laughing at me.

Jurgen said he had a meeting and asked me to come with him to Donny's apartment so that he could change.

"I can't," I said, "I should go home."

"It won't take long," Jurgen insisted. "It's very close."

Donny encouraged me from his post behind the bar. "Don't

worry, he's an honorable man. He won't bother you. You have my word."

"I'll walk with you to the corner," I offered. When we arrived there, Jurgen took my hand and led me down the street. "It's really time for me to go," I protested. "My mother will worry."

"It will only take a minute," Jurgen said, "for me to put on my suit."

The apartment was two blocks away, in a yellow brick building with no doorman but with two secure doors. Inside, the wide hall was dim and cool, the walls and floors covered with a mustard-colored tile that echoed the shash and click of our footsteps as we walked toward the elevator. We stood side by side as we rose to the fifth floor. My heart raced as I mentally reviewed every kick and strike my wrestling cousin Paco had taught me and my sisters in case we needed to defend ourselves.

The apartment was at the end of a long hall with a window that looked toward the Hudson. Inside there were two tidy, sparsely furnished rooms and a galley kitchen with no dishes, pots, or food anywhere in sight.

The minute we entered, Jurgen tried to kiss me. I resisted but then figured that if I gave in to the kiss, he'd relax, and I could make my getaway. He was gentle, didn't press himself against me, or place his hands where he shouldn't. He stepped back, took my hand, kissed it reverentially. "We are meant for each other," he said.

"Huh?"

He looked into my eyes. "Marry me."

"I beg your pardon?"

"Marry *me*," He struck his hand against his chest, as if he were saying, "Me Tarzan, you Jane."

"You must be kidding!"

"I am very serious."

I couldn't control the giggles. He stood before me, my hand in his, the roguish smile on his lips. It occurred to me then that he was a psycho and laughing at him wasn't smart.

"Yes?" he prompted.

"We met three hours ago," I reminded him.

"Yes?"

I wanted to get out of there alive. "All right, let's get married."

"Wonderful!" He hugged me, kissed my eyes, my forehead. "My wife." Now, I thought, as he tries to get me to the bedroom, I'll kick him and run. Jurgen released me, stepped back. "I go dress now," he said. "Wait one moment, please." He dragged a straight chair from its place against the wall, held it for me as I sat. Not too smart, I thought. He's going to tie me to it. "Pardon me," Jurgen said, and went into the bedroom. I sat on the edge of the chair, not ten feet from the half-open door, calculating the best moment to escape. He moved in and out of my vision as he changed his shirt, put on a tie, a jacket. Each time I was about to jump up and run, he turned toward me with a smile. He combed his hair, stepped to the hall door. "Let's go tell Donny," he said.

I jumped from the chair into the hallway, confused but glad we'd soon be outside so that I could run. On the way down, Jurgen talked about how long he'd waited for the right girl and how lucky he was to have found me. He claimed to have fallen in love with me as I stood on the curb on Fifth near 48th. "I am not impulsive man," he claimed, "but I follow my, how you say, instinct?"

We'd be married in the United States, Jurgen suggested, fly to Germany to meet his family, then settle in Egypt. It was the most surreal conversation I had ever had with anyone who didn't live inside my head. Every fantasy of princely men I'd ever dreamed up was coming true. As if there were such a thing as love at first sight, romance, intelligent, charming men with money willing to spend it on me — to marry me, even. "Can you dance?" I asked, certain there was a flaw in this too perfect plot. To prove he could, Jurgen tangoed me in the door of the restaurant where Donny still stood behind the bar serving tired businessmen.

"Married!" Donny's eyebrows rose so high they disappeared into his black hair. When he recovered, he congratulated Jurgen. "I told you he was an honorable man," he winked. "Now I'll have to propose to Laryssa," he grimaced, and we laughed.

Jurgen had to go to his meeting, but he asked me to wait with

Donny until his return, when we'd celebrate our engagement with dinner and champagne.

"Jurgen," I began, about to tell him that the game had gone on long enough, that I didn't want to marry him — or anyone — I'd only known for, let's see, four hours? What came out was, "I have to call my mother."

"Should I speak with her?" Jurgen offered, his eyes earnest. It was then I knew his proposal was no game.

Jurgen stood in front of me, waiting for an answer. He had Neftalí's green eyes and hushed voice, Otto's height, coloring, and accent, Mr. Grunwald's perfect physique. There was even a little of Avery Lee in him — the same roguish smile and confident air. In the second it took to transform Jurgen into the personification of all the men I'd ever loved, I surrendered.

We stood by the phone at the back of the restaurant getting our story together. We'd known each other a year, were introduced on the set of *Up the Down Staircase* by Sandy Dennis herself, had dinner a few times, recently met again, and decided we couldn't live without each other. "She'll want to meet you," I warned, and he offered to pick me up on Sunday when we went to the beach with Donny and Laryssa.

When I called Mami and told her I was engaged, she was suspicious, asked all the expected questions, and listened carefully to my answers. Jurgen got on the phone and told her, "I *mucho* love your daughter. Very *mucho*." When he returned the phone to me, she allowed that he sounded nice.

"Are you bringing him home now?"

"No, Mami, tomorrow. We're going to the beach. He'll come get me, and then you can meet him."

The minute I hung up, I was sorry I'd called. Before I had called Mami, I could have changed my mind, could have said goodbye to Jurgen, could have given him the wrong phone number and avoided midtown for a few days until he'd flown away. Jurgen noticed my mood.

"Come with me," he said. It seemed strange that he'd bring

me to a business meeting, but by now it was all so unreal that nothing surprised me.

We took a taxi to a luxury car dealership on Tenth Avenue. Sport cars and sedans glimmered behind the huge plate-glass windows, some with their doors open to show the interior. As we walked in, a florid man approached us. He towered over Jurgen, and I had trouble envisioning him behind the wheel of the Porsche toward which he led us. From their exchange it was clear that Jurgen was interested in a Porsche just like the blue one in the window. He was there for a test drive, and after introducing me as his "fiancé," Jurgen took a Porsche out for a spin in the crowded streets of Manhattan, where it could go no faster than a Ford. The florid man waited at the door of the dealership when we returned, fawned over Jurgen, who talked about horsepower and torque while I wondered how it was that nine hours earlier I had left Brooklyn still mourning Avery Lee's rejection and was now sitting in a Porsche dealership with my future husband.

We had an early dinner, and then Jurgen took me to see the all-black production of *Hello Dolly*, with Pearl Bailey. After the theater, he wanted to take me home, but I convinced him that wasn't necessary. He walked me to the train station, gave me Donny's phone number, and insisted I call as soon as I got home so that he'd know I'd arrived safely.

On the train home I marveled at what a strange day it had been. According to the papers, half my generation was supposedly high on LSD or other hallucinogenics. I had had nothing stronger than coffee and a couple of glasses of wine at dinner, but it felt as if I were "tripping." Any moment, I'd wake up in my bed in the back room of our house on Glenmore Street in the East New York section of Brooklyn, and the whole day would have been a dream. Or maybe I'd died, and this was Paradise. Or maybe it was hell, and my punishment for not being religious was to spend eternity having a good time in the afternoon as the fiancé of a rich, good-looking man who could afford to buy Porsches and then having to go home to Brooklyn.

As soon as I walked in the door, I called Jurgen, to make sure that he existed and that the entire afternoon had not been an extended fantasy. He sounded relieved that I had called, told me he loved me, asked for directions to my house the next day. I fabricated a history about me and Jurgen for Mami, Tata, Don Carlos, Don Julio, and those siblings who had waited up. When I finally crawled into bed, I believed every word of every lie I'd told them. Jurgen and I were in love, would marry, travel to Germany and then Egypt, where we'd live happily ever after in the shadow of the pyramids.

At the exact time when Jurgen promised to pick me up, the roar of a sports car drew my brothers to the cement yard that divided our house from the sidewalk. The family had been up for hours, cleaning and straightening up for the imminent arrival of my fiancé. He pulled up in a black Porsche, not the same one that had been on the sales floor, nor the one he had test-driven. I fretted that I might not recognize him when next I saw him, but there was no mistaking the clear complexion and rakish grin. Donny was in the passenger seat. They both kissed me on each cheek, and I introduced them to the family. I hadn't brought any men home since Otto, and I watched Mami's face for her reaction. She was taken by Jurgen's gallantry, his easy charm, the bunch of flowers he handed me, the box of chocolate-covered cherries he gave her, which endeared him to my sisters and brothers. The only one with a scowl on her face was Tata, who had been forced to change from her comfortable cotton housedress into the black lace dress she had worn to pick us up at the airport seven years earlier.

When we entered the house, every surface gleamed and smelled of Pine Sol, Pledge, or Windex. Jurgen and Donny sat on the edge of the recently purchased plastic-covered sofa in front of the new console television set. With help from those of us old enough to work, Mami had managed to decorate the house to her taste, with new furniture, pretty curtains, a lace tablecloth for the largest dining room table she could find, the seats of its high-backed chairs sealed in plastic.

Jurgen and Mami talked through me or my sisters and brothers. She asked him the same questions she'd asked me the day before over the phone, and a few more based on the information I'd made up the previous night. Jurgen was cool and relaxed, pretending that his English was worse than it actually was when he didn't know what I'd told Mami. She was both puzzled and charmed by him, but when he formally asked for my hand, she conceded it with a smile.

Jurgen informed us that because of his travel schedule, the wedding must be in less than a month. I nearly slid off the armchair, but Mami wasn't fazed by the challenge. "We'll have to order your dress tomorrow," she said.

Even though Mami and Tata had prepared a meal, I wanted to get away before Mami discovered the truth. I reminded Jurgen and Donny that we still had to pick up Laryssa. The Porsche had drawn curious neighbors to the windows and sidewalk. We came out of our house, trailed by my mother and siblings, and I couldn't hide the pride I felt. If I had been one of the neighbors, I'd have been jealous of me as I climbed into the bucket seat next to my good-looking fiancé. Donny squeezed his pudgy frame in the tiny back seat, and within seconds, Jurgen revved the many horses in his chariot and we peeled off, scattering dust and litter into the sidewalks of East New York.

It was impossible to hold a conversation in the Porsche. It was a noisy car, especially with the top down. Jurgen turned up the radio. Diana Ross wailed that a love child was never meant to be as Jurgen raced from Brooklyn to Long Island. The wind pelted my hair against my cheeks, into my eyes. I sank further into the seat, but that didn't help. Every time I moved, I received a mouthful of my own hair.

Laryssa's house sat in the middle of a pine grove in a community of homes that were copies of one another except for the landscaping and color. As we walked into the house, a cat slithered under a LA-Z-BOY in front of a console television set much larger than ours. Laryssa greeted us dressed in a yellow top and turquoise shorts, her blonde hair tied into a long ponytail. She offered us

iced tea and a tuna sandwich in the sunny kitchen with a glass door that overlooked a yard with a swimming pool. Two people lounged by the pool, didn't come to greet us, and Laryssa didn't take us out there to meet them. She left us in the kitchen and went to change. A young woman came out of one of the bedrooms, her hair in curlers, her slender, well-tanned body clothed in a sheer baby doll with frilly panties. Donny and Jurgen exchanged a look.

"Hi," she purred, "I'm Jen. Laryssa's sister." The men stood up to shake her hand and, as an afterthought, introduced me. Jen poured herself a glass of tea, excused herself, went back down the hall into the door through which Laryssa disappeared. Within seconds, there was yelling, to the effect that Laryssa should have told Jen that she had guests. Laryssa countered that Jen shouldn't walk around half naked. "In the middle of the day, too!" Laryssa screeched. The men and I quietly munched our sandwiches and sipped our iced teas, our eyes on the shut door. The two sisters continued their argument, which ended when Laryssa stormed out of the room, a packed beach bag over her shoulder. "Let's go," she said. Before she led us out, she called through the door. "See you later Mom, Dad!" The two figures by the pool waved without turning around.

Laryssa and Donny went in her VW Beetle. Jurgen and I followed, and, over the roar of the Porsche's motor and the wind, Jurgen said, "That's what I don't like about American girls." He didn't elaborate, which left me to wonder if he meant Jen's near nakedness, the argument between the two sisters, or the parents who didn't care who their daughters went out with as long as they weren't disturbed.

At the beach, we drove around the parking lot a couple of times, bypassed several likely spots until Jurgen pulled up next to a copper-colored Jaguar convertible, inside which a young man was slumped fast asleep in the driver's seat. Jurgen hurdled out of the Porsche, banged the nose of the Jaguar with his fists, and the young man awoke with a start, his black eyes round with panic.

When he saw Jurgen, he jumped out, hugged Jurgen warmly, and the two chattered in German until Jurgen remembered I was there.

His friend's name was Felipe, but everyone called him Flip. "Are you Spanish?" I asked.

"Mexican," he said. He had straight black hair and slanted eyes; skin browner than mine; a muscled, slightly bowlegged body. He wore rubber flip-flops, walked with a side-to-side roll, on the outside edge of his feet. From what I could gather, Jurgen, Donny, and Flip had arranged to meet at Jones Beach. Flip had driven the Jaguar from California, which explained why he passed out on a beach blanket under Laryssa's umbrella and slept the rest of the day. Jurgen went over the car with the same attention he had invested in the Porsche the previous day. He lifted the hood, looked at the motor, opened and closed the doors, examined the body, popped the trunk and inspected it.

"It's a good car," he finally said, and shook Flip's hand.

I had on the bikini Avery Lee had bought me, yellow with white squares, not nearly as small as Laryssa's. The men also wore tiny bikinis, which made me feel overdressed, even though it was the first time I'd revealed my abdomen in public. Because I couldn't swim, I sat in the sand while Donny, Laryssa, and Jurgen cut long, elegant strokes into the waves and then floated back. In or out of the water, Laryssa and Donny were all over each other. Jurgen kissed me a few times, but I was so uneasy making out half naked in public that he gave up.

At the end of the day, Laryssa went home in her car. We pulled up in front of our house, Jurgen and I in the Porsche, Donny and Flip in the Jaguar. Mami came to the front steps, and Flip called out to Jurgen, "Watch out man. They say the daughters end up looking like their mothers." The three men laughed. Mami, who understood, scrunched her face into her most unattractive expression. I sent a killer look toward Flip, who shrugged and gave me a sheepish smile.

"He always make jokes," Jurgen said. He walked me to the

260 ~ Almost a Woman

stoop. We planned to meet the next day in the city, which I confirmed in front of Mami. He backed toward the car, waved from the driver's seat, then left, followed by Flip and Donny, who laughed uproariously at something one of them said in German so that I didn't understand.

"Why didn't you ask him in?" Mami asked, looking after them.

"I'm sandy and itchy and tired," I complained. "I need a bath."

It bothered me that Flip had said something so hurtful in front of Jurgen, who indulged it. Who was Flip, anyway? He claimed to be Mexican, spoke fluent German, but other than his name, didn't say a word of Spanish to me. He drove across the country in a Jaguar, arrived that same morning at Jones Beach, of all places, and when Jurgen opened the trunk, there was nothing in it. Where was his luggage? He didn't even have a change of clothes in there.

And where did Jurgen get a Porsche? He didn't have it the day before. Why was he buying one if he already owned one? Why did he have a car in New York when he didn't live in the city? The Porsche could have been Donny's. Did bartenders make enough money to own late-model sports cars? I was confused and wary, certain that something strange was going on, not sure what it could be.

The next day, Jurgen and I walked through Central Park on our way to the Lake. He planned to rent a rowboat and take me for a ride. I reminded him that I couldn't swim, was afraid of water, dreaded the thought of being further than a few inches from firm ground. But he was adamant. We had to do this, he said, because rowing was one of his favorite sports. He was on a team, he claimed. Since we were to be husband and wife, I should learn to love the things he loved.

"Can I wear a life vest?" I asked.

"You don't need one," he laughed. "I'm an excellent swimmer."

"But I'm not!"

He said it worried him that I didn't trust him with my life. "I will save you, I promise."

The boat looked bigger once we were inside it. Jurgen placed his jacket across my lap, rolled up his sleeves, pushed off the dock. "Relax," he chuckled. "Let go of the sides."

He rowed to the center of the lake, secured the oars, leaned back with a contented sigh. He looked perfectly at home surrounded by water; his hair gleamed gold in the sunlight; his eyes deepened to a blue-gray color, a bottomless ocean. I gripped the sides of the boat. "Can we go back now?"

"Not yet," he said. The graveness in his voice, the way his body tensed made me shudder. "You have been open with me," he murmured. "You have introduced me to your family. They are honest people. Your mother is a good woman. But you have not asked about me."

"Don't say any more," I covered my face with my hands. The fairy tale was about to end. Now, I thought, he'll confess he's really a waiter at that restaurant where Donny works and has a wife and five kids in Hamburg. "I don't need to know." We floated in silence for a while, I with my hands still pressed to my face. I felt his eyes on me, and when I looked up, there was a troubled expression in them. So many questions crowded my thoughts that I didn't know where to begin. "Are you married?" I finally asked. He laughed so hard the boat shook. Then he noticed I was serious.

"No, *liebchen*, I'm not married," he said softly.

I mimed picking up a notebook, a pen, adjusting invisible glasses. I tightened my lips, put on a reedy voice. "Very well, sir, do you have any children?"

He played along. "No, madame."

"Are you really from Hamburg?"

"Yes, I am, madame."

"What is your date of birth, sir?"

We were silly for a while, and then Jurgen took up the oars and brought me back to dry land. As we walked along a shaded

path, I asked another question. "What is it that you do? For work, I mean."

He stopped, turned, searched my eyes. "You really want to know?"

The way he asked made me wish I didn't. I nodded.

"I fly planes," he said, then started walking again.

I guessed he was an airline pilot, but he shook his head. Did he fly for a cargo company? No. For the air force? Not that either. I gave up.

"I steal planes," he declared.

I guffawed. He smiled absently. "What do you do with the stolen airplanes?" I giggled. "Hide them in your garage?"

"I sell them."

According to Jurgen, it was easy to steal a plane. "Small ones, not jumbo jets," he stipulated. He put on a pilot's uniform, walked into a hangar, chose a plane, flew it to Mexico, sold it.

"So you steal planes and sell them in Mexico," I snickered.

"Or other places. Depends who orders one."

"You have seen too many 007 movies," I concluded.

Jurgen smiled. I was sure he was pulling my leg. "Are Flip and Donny in on this?" I joined his game.

"No. They prefer cars." Jurgen went on to tell me that he'd dreamed of flying since he was a child and had learned to do it as a young man. When he took planes, he flew very low, to avoid radar, he said. Sometimes, over the ocean, he saw enormous schools of fish, whales, dolphins. He'd flown all over the world and described dangerous air currents around mountains, sudden pockets of air, thunder-and-lightning storms he'd flown into that he feared would ground him forever. It sounded as if he were narrating a dream, but as he spoke, my skepticism ebbed until it hit me that I was about to marry a man who stole planes for a living.

"I can't believe this," I moaned. I walked over to a nearby bench and sat down because my knees couldn't hold me up. Jurgen put his arm around my shoulder.

"Don't worry," he whispered into my hair.

"Don't worry? Jurgen, now that I know this, I'm a criminal too. I'm supposed to go to the police or something. . . ."

He stroked my cheek, swore that he must be truthful with me, that it wouldn't be fair if he weren't. In any case, once we were married, I couldn't be made to testify against him should it come to that. I wanted to ask why he didn't wait to tell me until after the wedding but reminded myself that wasn't the issue.

"I'm leaving for Los Angeles," Jurgen said. "When I come back, I will marry you, if you still want me." He was sincere. I could hear it in his voice. In some twisted way, his confession was responsible. Still, a part of me wondered if he had fabricated the story to scare me away because the whole marriage thing had gone too far and he didn't want to hurt my feelings.

He escorted me to the subway station. He'd been teaching me a few words of German, and he drilled me as we walked. We pretended that our plans to get married had not changed with his disclosure. On the train back to Brooklyn, I decided that Jurgen wanted to test me. It didn't seem right that if he really did steal planes, he'd tell someone he barely knew. But then, this was the same man who had proposed after three hours. "I am not impulsive man," he'd told me a couple of days earlier. I made a mental note to look up the word, to see if there was a meaning I'd missed the first time.

Should I call the police? The story was unbelievable. I had no proof. I imagined the scene: a Puerto Rican girl walks into a police station, claims a German she met on the street and agreed to marry after three hours confessed that he steals planes and that his friends steal luxury cars. I could hear the laughter.

Jurgen left for Los Angeles. He didn't give me a phone number where I could reach him but promised to call daily. I didn't believe him, so it was a surprise when a bouquet of roses arrived, and that evening, when the phone rang, it was Jurgen. "Hello, *liebchen*," he whispered. "Do you still want to marry me?"

"Your face is no longer innocent."

I spent the next week shopping for my wedding dress with Mami. Jurgen's daily phone calls wore away my reluctance, convinced me that we belonged together. He swore that he would no longer steal planes. He'd been considering a job offer in Egypt, piloting the private jet of an Arab prince, which he'd decided to accept. His life had been transformed, Jurgen claimed, by me. Mine was about to be transformed by him. It was a fair exchange. I'd save him from life in prison; he'd save me from life in Brooklyn.

Mami and I picked out a champagne-colored silk moiré dress and coat ensemble for me to wear when I met Jurgen's parents. As she had planned for so long, my sisters would be my bridesmaids, my brothers groomsmen. Franky, who was five, was to be the ring bearer; Donny, Jurgen's friend, the best man. I picked La Muda as the maid of honor. Papi would come from Puerto Rico to give me away. Mami found a priest to marry us even though I'd never been to his church. Jurgen kept abreast of the plans through daily phone calls. I worried about the cost of the wedding, especially when we advanced money that wouldn't be refunded. But according to the etiquette books I consulted, the bride's family bore the expense.

When not shopping for my trousseau, I echoed the phrases in the Berlitz "Teach Yourself German" long-playing records I found at the library. On my wall was a map of Egypt with a big red circle around Alexandria, where Jurgen said we would live —

not Cairo, as I had imagined. I didn't believe in karma, astrology, palm reading, handwriting analysis, reincarnation, extrasensory perception, astral projection, transcendental meditation, Nostradamus, "Chariots of the Gods," or any of the other mumbo jumbo every young person in the United States was supposed to be obsessed with in 1968. But what was I to make of the fact that I, who had spent three years perfecting the role of Cleopatra, was about to move to the city of her birth and untimely death?

Even though it seemed preordained that I should marry Jurgen, doubt niggled at me. He didn't appear to be a violent man, but by his own admission he was a criminal. What if he'd done worse things and hadn't told me about them because I didn't ask the right questions? It frightened me to think that he'd take me to Egypt and then I'd be stuck there with no one to help me if he turned out to be a drunkard or a wife beater.

There was another thing that bothered me: I couldn't convince myself that I loved Jurgen. Was I crazy to expect to love a man I'd met only a few times? It troubled me that although I looked forward to his calls, I had forgotten what he looked like. What shape were his eyes? What shade his hair? If I loved him, his features should be embedded in my memory. How tall was he? Did he write with his left hand or his right? I didn't know whether he had birthmarks, or whether he parted his hair. As the day approached for Jurgen's return, I grew nervous and wished to stretch the time so that it wouldn't happen in two weeks, ten days, five days, three.

"I can't do it," I cried on the phone two days before his arrival.

"What do you mean?" He knew exactly what I meant.

"It's happening too fast. I'm not ready. . . ."

"Don't you love me?"

I dreaded that question from him. In the two weeks we'd been engaged, no one had asked it, not even Jurgen. It was the silence that confirmed it, the fact that I didn't interrupt him and say, "No, that's not it, that's not it at all."

"I see," he said after a while.

"Maybe if we had more time to get to know each other," I hedged halfheartedly.

Jurgen heard the uncertainty in my voice, didn't attempt to change my mind. Had he tried, I might have wavered, at least for a while. "All the plans we had," he said sadly, which were Mami's exact words when I told her the wedding was off, though she was angry rather than melancholy.

We lost several hundred dollars in deposits for a wedding dress, the hall, bridesmaids' dresses. I told Mrs. Davis at the Advertising Checking Bureau not to give my job away because I wasn't moving to Egypt. At first, it was embarrassing to explain to people that I'd changed my mind, but after a while, I was proud of it. I saved myself, I thought. I've done something most women don't do until it's too late.

Shoshana had been in Israel all summer. "Are you still a virgin?" she asked the minute we saw each other again, and I had to admit I was, and so did she. "Not that I didn't have plenty of chances," she amended, which led to my telling her of my adventures with Avery Lee and Jurgen.

"What is it with you and Germans?" she wanted to know.

"I don't pick them," I defended myself, "they pick me."

She signed up for courses at Manhattan Community College, but I didn't, because I wanted my days free for Children's Theater International. To supplement my part-time salary at the Advertising Checking Bureau, I found a job distributing flyers in front of a bank on Park Avenue. One day a woman with a neatly trimmed Afro and an African print dress stopped to talk to me. She had an agency for "exotic" models and wondered if I had any interest. We made an appointment for the next day, and I showed up at her office on Sixth Avenue and 40th Street with my portfolio of photographs by Shanti. The door was locked. Every once in a while a phone rang inside, but no one answered. I waited in the hall for half an hour and then gave up, annoyed to have missed an afternoon of work for nothing.

I walked to Woolworth's on Fifth Avenue, where the public

phones were in mahogany cubicles with doors that shut tight for privacy. As I settled into the first booth, a man peered inside, and when I looked up, he moved on. He'll just have to wait, I thought. I called the temporary jobs agency to let them know I was available for the next few days. Then I called Mami to tell her I'd be home early to pack my room, since we were moving again, to a house on Fulton Street in the Brownsville section of Brooklyn. Mami was excited, because Titi Ana had agreed to rent an apartment in the house, which meant Mami could afford to buy the building. Our cousins Alma and Corazón would live with us. I came out of the phone booth in a much better mood than I entered it.

"Excuse me," a voice startled me, and when I turned around, there was the man who'd peeked into the phone booth. I was sure he was about to complain that I had talked for too long, but he smiled and pointed to the portfolio. "Are you model?"

"Trying," I grinned.

"I am film director," he said. "I am looking for leading actress for my movie." He had a heavy accent, hesitated between words as if to make sure of the pronunciation.

"Where are the auditions?" I asked, excited but trying to be businesslike.

"I write down for you." He tore an edge of paper from a note in his pocket, wrote a name and phone number, handed it to me.

"Ulvi Doğan," I read.

"Dawn," he corrected me. "Like the morning."

"Where are you from?" I asked.

"Turkey. And you?"

"Puerto Rico." I introduced myself and promised to call the next day.

"Very good," he nodded. "In the afternoon, I will be there."

That evening, I called Shoshana to tell her that a Turkish film director wanted to audition me. "Come with me," I asked.

"What if there's no part in the movie for me?"

"Just come and keep me company."

The appointment was on East 58th Street, nowhere near the

theater district or the rehearsal studios used for auditions. "This feels a little weird," I said to Shoshana as we stood in front of the white brick residential building. She suggested that maybe the film company had rented an apartment for the interviews.

The doorman called up my name, directed us upstairs. We rang the bell directly across the hall from the elevator, as he instructed. It was opened by the man from Woolworth's, whose broad smile dimmed when he saw Shoshana. He asked us in.

"I hope you don't mind," I apologized, "but my friend is an actress too. In case you need extras . . ." He nodded.

The room we walked into was in black and white. Two black leather armchairs, a matching couch, what looked like a black leather-topped table were arranged around a shag rug with black-and-white squares. On the stark white walls were four enormous posters, grainy black-and-white closeups of the same woman in the throes of sexual ecstasy. Shoshana and I looked at each other.

"Mr. Doğan," I began to excuse us and get out of there.

"Call me Ulvi, please. Have a seat, please." He ushered us to the armchairs. "May I offer you Coca-Cola?"

Shoshana said yes, and I glared at her. As Ulvi opened the refrigerator, spilled ice cubes from a tray, opened and poured the Coke, Shoshana and I whispered to each other. She thought the apartment was tasteful, the pictures as arty as the ones in our portfolios. "She's fondling herself," I hissed.

Ulvi returned with our Cokes. He sat on the couch, leaned back, crossed his legs. He wore brown leather loafers with no socks. Shoshana noticed too. While we sipped our drinks, he told us that his film was to be shot on Long Island. I asked to see the script, and he placed his hand on a neat pile of papers on the coffee table. "It is not ready yet," he said. He asked us about our acting experience. Shoshana had been in a couple of high school plays. I listed my credits, which impressed him. Shoshana wondered what he had directed, and Ulvi said his film had won top prize at the Berlin Film Festival. The posters on the wall began to look more artistic.

Ulvi leaned toward me, touched my hand. "I am sure I can use you in my movie," he said. "But we must do screen test. Yes?"

"Yes, of course," I said.

He leaned back, his hands fingertip to fingertip, and said he had a part for Shoshana too, but smaller. She beamed with gratitude. I asked when the screen test would be, and he said he had to arrange it but needed my phone number to let me know. He didn't ask for Shoshana's. He led us to the door, stood in the hall until the elevator came.

"You're going to be a star!" Shoshana shrieked, as we walked down the street.

"The screen test might be awful. . . ."

"Did you see how he looked at you? Every movement you made . . . he watched so carefully!"

"I didn't notice."

"I can say I knew you when . . ." she giggled.

I dared not hope. Ulvi talked like a director, and Shoshana pointed out it was easy to check if he really won in Berlin. We walked to the library, and sure enough, there it was on page 42 of the July 8, 1964, *New York Times*. The audiences were surprised, the paper said, that the award went to *Dry Summer*, a Turkish film. They described Ulvi as its "youthful producer," and Shoshana and I agreed that he did seem youthful, if not young.

We parted at the subway station, Shoshana still certain that Ulvi represented my big break.

He called to say that the screen test would be that Sunday, so I put on my best outfit and appeared at his door. There were no cameras in the apartment, no lights, no film crew. I wondered if I was too early, but Ulvi said no, the cameraman was late. I asked, "Should I come back?" But he suggested we talk until the crew arrived.

Was the script ready yet? I wanted to know. "My writer is very slow," he said with an indulgent smile and a shrug of the shoulders.

After five minutes of chitchat about who I was, what I did,

where I lived, the phone rang. He spoke in Turkish, a language I'd never heard. Its sound was soothing, at least, the way he spoke it, in a hushed, intimate voice, a raspy whisper. From time to time, as he listened to the caller, he lifted his hand in a "just one moment" gesture.

He had huge, very dark brown pupils; straight, fine, black hair; a high forehead. Deep lines ran from his nostrils to his lips, which seemed drawn on his face, their shape precise, flat. His nose made a straight line with his forehead, flared to a wide base. In profile, he looked like a museum fresco of an Etruscan horseman or a Mesopotamian king. The majestic air was enhanced by his movements, which were slow, studied, as if he had to be careful or he'd knock something over.

Once he hung up, he asked me about Puerto Rico. He'd never been there but had attended film festivals in Cartagena, Colombia, and in Venezuela, Costa Rica, and Mexico. Along the way, he had picked up a few words of Spanish. "*Señorita,*" he said, "*¿Cómo está?*" I congratulated him on his excellent accent. "It's English I have trouble with," he grinned.

I assured him he spoke well, that I understood everything he said. He thanked me with another self-effacing shrug. The phone rang again, and this time he spoke German. Although I couldn't understand the words, there was no hesitation in his voice, as there was in English.

When he finished his call, we discussed the film that had won the Golden Bear in Berlin. He said it was a love story, which he had produced and directed. He had also played the romantic lead. The lead actress was now a big star in Turkey. "But I discovered her," he stressed.

He said he had spotted her sitting on the steps in front of his office building. She was waiting for her mother, the cleaning woman. She'd never acted in films, but as soon as he saw her, Ulvi could tell she had star potential. When he saw me at Woolworth's, he recognized the same qualities he saw in her.

I was flattered, but aware that we were alone in his apartment

decorated with posters of women masturbating. Arty or not, it was impossible to look anywhere in the apartment without my eyes landing on a nipple, an inverted navel, pubic hair. After a half hour with no film crew in sight, I stood up. "I should go."

Ulvi suggested we take a walk. "They will be here by the time we get back," he promised.

As we strolled down 58th Street toward Fifth Avenue, I asked him where he had learned German.

His eyes widened. "Do you speak too?"

"No," I laughed. "Some of my friends . . ." I waved them away.

He nodded. He had lived in Germany for years and spoke the language fluently. "Better than Turkish, sometimes," he chuckled. We lamented how hard it was to retain one's first language when there were few opportunities to practice. We agreed that the longing to go back to the home country, even after years of being away, never disappeared.

"But when you return," he said, "they don't appreciate." He became a celebrity in Turkey after his film won the awards. But the press attacked him. He held his hands palms up, seesawed them up and down, "They criticize me for this, for that, for nothing." I appreciated his thoughtful answers, enjoyed our conversation, which meandered from one subject to the next. His soft voice and relaxed manner were comforting. As Shoshana had noticed, he watched me intently. At first, I was uncomfortable with his earnest attention. But then I realized he had to do that because he read lips. Not because he was hard of hearing, but because it was another clue to interpreting what I said. I did the same. Even after seven years of intensive English, I focused on the speaker for clues other than language to help me understand. When I spoke, I still translated simultaneously from Spanish, and I was certain Ulvi had to do the same from Turkish via German. No wonder he talked so slowly.

There was a parade on Fifth Avenue. Marching bands led acrobatic cheerleaders with colorful pompons. Slow-moving floats

trimmed with crepe paper streamers carried young women dressed in evening gowns. Their white-gloved hands wiped the air in perfect arcs, as they waved to the right, the left, the right again.

Later, I wondered at which point during the parade he took my hand. Or why, as a float went by filled with polka dancers, he put his arm around me. Or how it happened that, when the Middletown Police Athletic League Band marched by playing their version of "Winchester Cathedral," my face was against his chest, and I smelled his skin, clean, a nonscent really, captivating.

We returned to his apartment. While I'd been kissed, touched, had known the contours of a man through his clothes, it was different when we were naked. His skin was the color of toasted walnuts. No tan lines marred the even tones from hairline to soles. His chest was furred with a heart of straight black hair which ended in a point under his ribs. His abdomen was flat but soft, undefined by muscles, a long, smooth, flesh table on which I laid my head to listen to his life. When I moved higher, his heart thuthumped against my ear, soothed me to sleep upon his chest. Or, if I snuggled down to his navel, the sounds of a noisy brook gurgled intermittently. I traced my fingers from the top of his head, down his broad forehead across the frown line etched from temple to temple, to his nose, a wide-based pyramid above soft, cool lips. At rest, he appeared sad and solemn, but I made him smile. His chin was dimpled in the center, a shallow depression where I stuck my tongue to feel fine, prickly stubble. His neck was long, with two deep furrows webbed from ear to ear, like scars. I caressed his chest, the fuzzy valentine of straight, black hair, a heart over his heart. And the flat expanse of his unblemished belly.

After we made love he made phone calls. Naked, I wrapped myself around him, his left arm under my head, mine across his chest. I pressed close until our brown skins were one. I could not think of what I'd just done, refused to answer the voice that asked, "Why him?" Why not Otto or Avery Lee or Jurgen? Why had I not resisted, had in fact joyfully thrown off my clothes on the black leather chair?

He spoke his foreign language and I listened to the muffled words, chuckles, whispers. Once he held the phone to my lips and said, "Say hello," and I said "hi" into the speaker, not knowing who I greeted. After a while I grew jealous. I writhed this way and that, generated warmth, straddled him, rolled back onto my side until he engulfed me, until I felt his weight, until I sank under his long, dark body, until I couldn't breathe. It was when I pushed him off, gently, with a whimper, that he moved aside, stroked my face, and called me "Chiquita."

"Who?" I pushed up on one elbow, searched his face.

"You are Chiquita," he smiled, "my little one. That is what it means, the Spanish word *chiquita?*"

"Yes," I said, appeased. "Little one. Little girl," I amended and lay back.

Sated, I returned to Brooklyn, tingling with secrets. Late at night, the A train was filled with workers returning from the evening shifts. Most of them dozed or read the papers with wary intensity, seeking confirmation for their worst fears. A man in overalls slept on the seat against the conductor's booth. A woman in a nurse's uniform pulled her purse close when I sat across the aisle. Another woman, thin and nervous, tugged at the tired curls around her shoulders, the window behind me a grimy mirror into which she peered desperately. From time to time both women stared at me, then averted their eyes. Can they tell what I've been doing? I wondered. Are there telltale signs?

No, he was careful not to mark me. My skin left hotter than it arrived, but there were no marks, no signs that we'd been naked for hours. I sought his smell on me, but that too was gone. He had insisted we shower after sex. We went in together, my hair wrapped inside a thirsty towel, and on his knees, he soaped and rinsed. His hands sometimes a caress, sometimes a probe, he erased all traces of our lovemaking, all evidence that he'd been with me, inside me. Hot water pounding my back, I closed my eyes and let his fingers, slippery with soap, explore, between my toes, behind my knees, across my buttocks. I dripped with desire, but he whispered,

"Not now, no more. Enough for today." He wrapped me in his huge black towels, rubbed the corners against my skin until every drop was soaked away. I returned to Mami's house hungry, thirsty, impatient for the next day, when I'd return to his black-and-white apartment and strip down to nothing and let him touch me again where no one ever had.

⁓

"You did what?" Shoshana's long lashes fluttered. "When? How?"

It was hard to explain *how* it had happened. Not the mechanics of sex, but how I went from fledgling movie actress to the director's . . . what? I couldn't name what I'd become.

"Why him?" Shoshana wanted to know.

There was no way to answer that question either. No, he wasn't as handsome as Neftalí, Otto, Avery Lee, or Jurgen. In the week we'd been together he hadn't taken me to any restaurants, the theater, not even the movies. He'd spent no money on me. He hadn't asked me to be his girlfriend, his mistress, his wife. He'd made no promises whatsoever. He seemed to have no expectations except that I show up at his apartment at the agreed time. When I suggested I should get birth control, he told me not to worry. "I take care," he said, and he did.

"So," Shoshana smiled wickedly, "did you get the part?"

Ulvi admitted that he had never had any intention of putting me in a movie. "I want you for me," he said, "nobody else."

"Wow!" Shoshana was impressed.

In order to spend more time with Ulvi, I changed my schedule at work. I checked ads mornings, then spent the afternoon with Ulvi. I was usually home for dinner, then hid out in the room I shared with Delsa in our new house on Fulton Street. I didn't want to give Mami a chance to study me, afraid that she suspected, that my secret life with Ulvi showed in the way I moved or behaved.

One day I ran into Shanti on Fifth Avenue. He'd been mean-

ing to call me, he said, because he wanted to take color photographs of me. His fingertips on my chin, he moved my face from side to side to capture the light. "Your face is no longer innocent," he concluded.

"Neither am I," I snapped back. He winced. "I have to go." I left him on the corner of Fifth and 44th, my throat tight. I ran into the Algonquin Hotel, through the bar, downstairs to the cramped ladies' room. I stared into the mirror for a long time but couldn't see what he saw. Was it only visible to others?

Vera called to discuss the Children's Theater International season. They wanted me back as Soni in *Babu* and as a Japanese princess in a play inspired by kabuki theater. After the read-through at the rehearsal studio on Christopher Street, Bill gave a couple of us a ride uptown. I was on my way to Ulvi.

"How was your summer?" Bill asked, and the others shared stories of summer stock and dinner theaters. I was the last to leave the VW van. "You've been quiet," Bill remarked as he pulled up to the corner of 58th Street and Third Avenue. I was about to tell him where I was going but was unable to speak his name.

"I can't even begin," I stammered.

He squeezed my hand, "It's amazing how one summer can change your life." I leaned over and kissed him on the cheek. I loved him, I loved Allan, I loved so many people. Did I love Ulvi? I must have, to give myself so willingly to him. Yet what I felt for him was nothing like what I felt for Bill and Allan, for my family, for Shoshana. I could easily say I loved them. About him the best that I could say was, "I make love with him."

What did that make me? After years of fantasizing about romantic love, I had landed on the black-and-white sheets of a man who was not romantic in the traditional sense. No flowers, no candlelit dinners, no talk of the future beyond the next day, when we'd be together again. Being with Ulvi was like being suspended in time. After the first long conversation we had, there were no more discussions about our lives.

"I don't care about your family, your friends," he said when I

tried to tell him. "I only want you." It was freeing not to have a past with him. But it bothered me that if he weren't interested in my life away from him, how could I justify asking about his life away from me?

One Monday afternoon, I met Shoshana at the Automat. We put our coins into the slot and the square glass doors unlocked so we could pull out bowls of macaroni and cheese.

"I have to tell you something," Shoshana said, excited. Soon as I sat across from her, she spilled her news. "I did it!"

It wasn't hard to guess what "it" was. "When? Who?"

She went to a party that weekend, met a Turkish man. "Younger than your guy," she added. "Now we've both lost our virginity to Turks," she giggled.

When I told Ulvi the story, imagining he'd enjoy the coincidence, his eyebrows crept together, his lips tightened. "She is a very dumb girl," he said.

"What do you mean? Should she worry about Ali? Do you know him?"

"There are a thousand Alis," Ulvi yelled. I'd never heard him raise his voice above a murmur, and the change scared me. "How can you have such a friend?" he continued. I didn't understand what he meant. When I pointed out that she wasn't doing anything worse than what we did, Ulvi looked at me sternly. "It is not the same. She is cheap girl."

I was stunned. His assessment of Shoshana was so unfair, I argued. He'd only met her once. She was a wonderful person, warm, funny, intelligent. How could he say such a thing?

"I know million girls like that," Ulvi muttered, and the contempt in his voice made me shiver. He took me in his arms, stroked my hair, kissed me. "You are such naive girl," he said. "There are so many things I must teach you, Chiquita." He was tender, gentle. The circle within his arms was a world in which I felt protected, a place where I could admit my ignorance. Yes, I was naive, but in his arms my innocence was treasured. In his arms, I didn't have to think, didn't have to plan, didn't have to do

anything but respond to his caresses. When he held me, I didn't question or challenge him, because I knew nothing. Not even the true nature of my best friend.

~

Late at night, Fulton Street was quiet, the shadows solid as walls. I walked on the side of the street closest to the playground, where the hurricane fence stretched tall and forbidding between me and the swings, slides, monkey bars. To my left, cars were snugly parked and locked for the night, but in some, people-shapes moved in wary anticipation. As I passed them, my heart beat faster than my feet could walk. I pressed close to the fence, eyes straight ahead but alert to unexpected movements. A low voice mumbled, "Hi, sweetheart," another "Hey, baby," and danger propelled me, almost lifted me off the sidewalk, but I wouldn't run, not unless chased. If I ran without provocation, they'd know how scared I was, so I walked—fast, but confident that I'd reach the door to our house, that I would have time to insert the key in the lock, turn it, push open the heavy door, and be inside before anyone could reach me.

Once safe, I leaned against the door and breathed until my backbone didn't tingle and my heart beat its normal rhythm, until my insides felt as composed as my face, wiped of its frightened expression, until my hands no longer trembled and my knees were stable. I unlocked the inside door and opened it to the dim hallway, where I listened for Mami's footsteps, for her disapproval at the end of the hall, for her dark, sad eyes heavy with disappointment and reproaches. But it was too late. She was asleep on the edge of her bed, feet still slippered, knees curled up, nylon nightgown bunched around her thighs. Her right arm was bent over her face to block out nightmares, while her left gripped the bar of Ciro's crib, where the baby slept in a tight lump.

I tiptoed past her door into the room with the bunk beds against one wall and the bed that Delsa and I shared against the

other. In the airless darkness I again felt the thrill of danger, only this time it wasn't fear of an unseen attacker. The memory of Ulvi's hands was like traces on my body, charged my skin with an energy I was certain anyone could see, could feel. When I crawled into bed next to my sister, she stirred, and it was natural that I should roll over and spoon into her the way I did with him. But she was my sister, and had I wakened her for a hug, she would have flailed and cursed and pushed me off the bed. I lay face up, arms alongside my body, took up as little space on the narrow bed as possible. The deep, even breath of my sisters and brothers was as soothing a sound as I ever heard, but it didn't lull me to sleep as it once had. I was too conscious of that other breath, miles away in the sparsely furnished apartment of my lover. My lover! Again I wanted to turn over and embrace the body next to me, but it was Delsa's. I hugged myself instead, closed my eyes, imagined my arms were his, that I was in the enormous pull-out bed with the black sheets, where reaching out for warmth was greeted with a moan of pleasure, not annoyance.

In the morning, Mami pointedly kept her eyes on me as I went to and from the bathroom, but she didn't ask where I'd been. When I set up the ironing board, she moved aside without a word. Her serenity was unnerving amid the chaos of making breakfast for my sisters and brothers and helping them get ready for school. "Watch the babies," she pointed at Charlie and Cibi, who were trapped in the playpen. She walked Raymond and Franky to the door, waited there until they turned the corner, then returned to rescue Ciro from his crib, where he'd been whimpering for some time. I pressed my clothes and watched her out of the corner of my eyes, aware that her silence could explode into an argument at the slightest provocation. Her walk was a heavy shuffle across the linoleum. Three babies in two years had left her soft and fleshy, eyes permanently swollen from lack of sleep, features slack, as if her muscles didn't have the energy to animate her face. I averted my eyes from her exhausted figure, ashamed that I was adding to her burden.

I played with the babies, kept as far from Mami as the crowded kitchen permitted, then disappeared into the bedroom to change. When I came out, she was at the table with her morning cup of black coffee in front of her and Ciro on her lap.

"I'm going to work and then I have a rehearsal," I said.

She looked up, pursed her lips, nodded. I was grateful for her silent censure, for another day in which she didn't confront me with her suspicions, and left the apartment with a sense of triumph, hollow, because she refused to fight.

"Where were you last night?"

Ulvi's opinion of Shoshana didn't keep me from seeing her whenever possible. There was no one, including him, with whom I felt more comfortable or had more fun. We met for lunch, visited museums, took long walks along Fifth Avenue, chatting about our love lives. Shoshana's relationship with Ali didn't last, but it wasn't mourned. No longer his student, she began an affair with Mr. Arthur Delmar, the Principles of Advertising professor.

"Why didn't you tell me," Shoshana asked, "that sex with an older man is so much better?"

"I have no basis for comparison," I reminded her.

"I wonder how old he is," Shoshana mused. "Not as old as my father, I hope."

Papi was older than Mami, who was thirty-seven. I hadn't seen Papi in seven years and had a hard time conjuring an image of him. Was he old and wrinkled? Did he have a pot belly? Did he wear glasses? Ulvi looked younger than Mami, but he wouldn't tell me his age. Arthur had gray hair, and we figured he was Ulvi's senior, but Shoshana wasn't about to ask him directly. "I don't want to know," she said, with a flick of the wrist.

We had no illusions about a life with either Ulvi or Arthur. Even if Arthur proposed, Shoshana would never marry him, because he wasn't Jewish. "I have to think of the future of Israel," she said seriously.

I didn't have a whole nation depending on my choice of

husband, but neither did I expect Ulvi to marry me. He was blunt when he said he didn't want to involve me in his life. "Why not?"

"It is complicated," he responded, then kissed away my anxious frown. "Don't worry," he said, "it is nothing for you to concern." If I asked more questions, he silenced me with caresses. "I will never hurt you," he assured me, and so far, he hadn't.

Ulvi insisted that our lives away from his bed be private, which led me to suspect secrets much worse than Jurgen's. One afternoon when he had to go to a meeting, he asked me to wait for him in his apartment. It was the first time I'd been in his place alone, and I decided to take advantage of it. If I found anything illegal or incriminating, I swore to leave and never come back. He was so fastidious that it took a long time to search the apartment, because I had to leave everything exactly as I found it. His belongings were put away in a precise order imposed on every shelf, drawer, cabinet. The black towels were folded in thirds lengthwise, then in thirds again, stacked so that no edges overlapped. There was nothing in between, behind, or under them. He wore no undershorts, but in spite of my first impression, did wear socks, which were paired and doubled into rows at the bottom of the dresser drawer. There wasn't a gun there, nor bags of marijuana, nor love letters. His shirts, pants, and jackets hung by color, each in their own section of the closet. There was no false wall or safe behind them. His shoes lined up on the floor, each with a cedar shoe tree inside. Nothing fell out when I tipped one after the other. He wore no jewelry, used an electric razor, didn't slap on aftershave. There were no drugs in the medicine chest, not so much as an aspirin. The kitchen cabinets held a set of china for four, white dishes with a black border. There were sixteen glasses, four each in descending sizes, adorned with playing cards showing the jack, queen, king, and ace. In the refrigerator were a few vegetables, a container of orange juice, butter, a few eggs. Other than the woman masturbating on the walls, there were no pictures anywhere, no prizes for his film, no clippings, no press releases. I found no credit card receipts, no savings passbooks, no checkbook.

Everything in the apartment was brand new, carefully selected so that it all matched. Expensive too. The towels were thick and fluffy. His clothes had designer labels, were made from fine materials like wool, silk, cashmere. His shoes were thin-soled, leather-lined, soft. On the top shelf of his closet was a set of suitcases, thick black leather with brass fittings closed with a combination lock embedded in the center. There was something in the largest suitcase, but I didn't open it, because it was too heavy for me to lift down.

Used to the chaos of my home in Brooklyn, Ulvi's apartment seemed sterile, its order sinister. It was so clean, so tidy; even the corners bore no traces of dust, crumbs, or stray pieces of thread. After I examined everything and found nothing to make me suspicious, I opened the leather couch into a bed and lay in it, thinking about what it meant. He was a man with no history, ageless, rich enough to live in a luxury apartment building two blocks from Bloomingdale's but not so wealthy as to spend lavishly. There were so many questions I wanted to ask, but whenever I tried, he deflected my doubts with kisses. The only way to get him to talk, I decided, was to get out in public, where he couldn't distract me with his touch.

When he returned from his meeting, the first thing he did was to search inside the closet where the towels were kept. I wondered if I had missed something, but it was too late now. He didn't ask if I had riffled his things, but I had the feeling that he knew, although he didn't say a word. He never left me alone in the apartment again.

⌒

My cousin Alma lived with her mother and sister in an apartment on the second floor of Mami's house on Fulton Street. When they'd lived farther away, I spent more time with Alma, because we made it a point to get together for dinner every so often. Since I'd met Ulvi, however, my friendship with Shoshana had grown

stronger, while my relationship with Alma had cooled. There was more to talk about with Shoshana, without the danger that my secret life would get back to Mami.

Alma and I had spent hours talking about getting an apartment together. Our mothers made sure that wouldn't happen. My goal now was to have a place of my own, where I could come and go as I pleased. At twenty years of age, I argued, I was old enough to take care of myself. Mami insisted that the only way she'd let me go was on the arm of a man, preferably a legal husband. Alma, who was a year older, still lived at home, Mami pointed out. With Titi Ana and Mami backing each other up, neither Alma nor I had any chance of getting our way.

Shoshana argued that I was too considerate of Mami's wishes. To become a woman, she asserted, I must rebel against my mother. What she said made sense, and I went so far as to discuss it with Alma, who agreed with Shoshana. Still, I couldn't bring myself to defy Mami, just as Alma didn't oppose Titi Ana, and Shoshana didn't confront her own parents. Alma devoted herself to her work; to her sister, Corazón; to her books. Shoshana and I schemed, planned, dreamed, nurtured secrets. But none of us stood up to our mothers and said, "I'm leaving you. I can stand on my own. It's time for me to claim my life."

We spent as little time at home as possible. Shoshana had Manhattan Community College, a job at a shoe store on 34th Street, and Arthur to keep her busy. I had Children's Theater International, the Advertising Checking Bureau, and Ulvi. Together, Shoshana and I had our dates.

Whether on the street or in a restaurant, Shoshana and I were often approached by men eager to take us out. Most of the time we accepted but followed strict rules for these unexpected dates. We only went to dinner at nice restaurants, never for drinks at a bar. We refused alcohol. We agreed on a curfew, and even if the men were fascinating, left when the time was up. We arrived together and left together. We never left the other one alone with a date. Most of the men were content to talk, but a few offered us

money for sex. In that event, Shoshana and I executed a dramatic exit. After the agreed-upon signal, we rose from the table as one and stalked out. Ninety percent of the time, the men were so stunned that they sat with their mouths open while other diners stared after us. Once, a man yelled obscenities as we walked out, which only confirmed our decision to get out of there fast as we could.

We didn't think what we were doing was wrong or that we were cheating on Arthur or Ulvi. They never took us anywhere, as if afraid to be seen with us. The strangers who escorted us to dinner were thrilled to have us by their side, brought us to elegant restaurants, urged us to order the most expensive entrees. We were, we knew, decoration, a line on their expense reports. But we didn't mind. Their conversation, which to their wives or girlfriends might have been stupefying, was fascinating to us, who'd never met an accountant from Peoria or a personnel director from Albuquerque.

The first thing we established about a date was where he lived. We preferred men from out of town, because there was no chance we'd see them again. Then we asked whether he was married, if there were children. If he lied, he only fooled himself. If he shared pictures of his wife and kids, stories about Little League games and school plays, we did his family a service by easing his loneliness and keeping him from actions he might later regret. We had nothing to lose, enjoyed a nice dinner with interesting conversation, and felt virtuous because we were saving a family while still being loyal to our boyfriends.

We learned to spot the boasters and posturers, whose lies and exaggerations added to our mirth the next day, when we traded impressions of the previous evening. As with my sisters and the men we danced with at clubs, the "stocking rippers" and "the octopuses," Shoshana and I had code names for our dates.

First there were the "Groovies," who tried to impress us with their hipness by using adolescent expressions as often as possible. Shoshana and I, both native speakers of other languages, were not as in tune with American slang as native English speakers. Most

of the time, a Groovy's use of slang was like another language to us, and we listened in awe of how idioms that sprang from our generation set us apart from them. Because we had learned English as a second language, Shoshana and I were obsessed with its proper usage. We spoke in schoolroom grammar, looked down on the second type, the "YKs," who couldn't put a sentence together without adding "you know" between phrases. A Groovy patronized us, a YK was never specific, let sentences disintegrate into generalities. If we were feeling wicked that day, we prodded YKs to say more, until it was clear to him that no, we didn't know. Shoshana maintained that YKs were threatened by real ignorance, because by saying "you know," they avoided a display of their own.

The third group, Daddies, were older men who, sometime during dinner, compared us to their daughters. "You remind me so much of Lindy," one said to Shoshana, and she prompted him to describe Lindy. Before we knew it, we'd heard the story of his life, with details about in-laws, best friends, alimony payments, visitation rights. Daddies were the most likely to want to see us again, but another of our rules was no repeat dates. Groovies assumed we could find them a drug connection. YKs were the most likely to offer us money for sex.

Shoshana sometimes discussed our dates with Arthur. I kept them from Ulvi, who wasn't interested in my life. Our relationship was a bubble isolated from the rest of our existence, confined to the white walls of his tidy, one-room apartment.

Rehearsals for the new Japanese-inspired production for Children's Theater International were on evenings and weekends, while performances of *Babu* took two or three mornings a week. With the exception of Tom and me, most of the actors from the previous season of *Babu* had to be replaced due to other commitments. Allan had joined the Broadway cast of *Fiddler on the Roof*, so a new actor, Jaime, took his place in the repertory.

Like me, Jaime was Puerto Rican, but born in New York. We recognized the irony of two Puerto Ricans playing Indian royalty.

"There's something wrong with this," Jaime complained. "We should be out there fighting for the rights of our people."

Jaime was proud of his heritage, determined to do what he could to preserve Puerto Rican culture in New York. In El Barrio and the Bronx, in parts of Brooklyn, other young Puerto Ricans, some of them members of the Young Lords, campaigned to improve the lives of their *compatriotas*. My cousin Corazón was involved with a group in the Lower East Side that offered art and photography lessons to Puerto Rican high school students. My brother Héctor and my sister Delsa were involved in youth organizations in our neighborhood.

My own social conscience was pathetically underdeveloped. I felt no obligation to "our people" in the abstract, felt, in fact, weighed down by duty to my people in the concrete: Mami, Tata, my ten sisters and brothers.

"That's a cop-out." Jaime charged that I used my family as an excuse to avoid involvement in the Puerto Rican struggle. "And what's with the Indian dance?" he scolded. "We need to champion *our* art and theater. Let the Hindus worry about their own."

My devotion to Indian dance, I argued, wasn't part of a conspiracy to promote their civilization over Puerto Rico's. My love of Indian classical dance and its music didn't extend to any other part of the subcontinent's culture. I didn't like curry or spicy foods, didn't dress in saris, didn't pray to Krishna, Shiva, or Ganesh, sneezed whenever incense burned near me.

"You don't get it," Jaime argued, "if we lose Puerto Ricans to other cultures, we lose Puerto Rican culture."

"What do you think happens to us here?" I contended. "Do you think we're as Puerto Rican in the U.S. as on the island?"

"More," he argued. "We have to work at it here."

I saw his point, but that didn't make me want to rush down to the nearest community center to dance the *plena*. Why should I be less Puerto Rican if I danced Bharata Natyam? Were ballet dancers on the island less Puerto Rican because their art origi-

nated in France? What about pianists who performed Beethoven? Or people who read Nietzsche? It was useless to argue with him. Even if I won, Jaime's judgment of me, unsparing and consistent, made me question my loyalty to my people.

In spite of Jaime's accusations that they were a cop-out, I still defined "my" people as Tata, Mami, Delsa, Norma, Héctor, Alicia, Edna, Raymond, Franky, Charlie, Cibi, Ciro. On the periphery there were also Papi, Don Carlos, Don Julio, La Muda, Tía Ana, Alma, Corazón, and the many aunts, uncles, and cousins in New York and back on the island.

For as long as I could remember, I'd been told that I was to set an example for my siblings. It was a tremendous burden, especially as the family grew, but I took the charge seriously, determined to show my sisters and brothers that we need not surrender to low expectations. To avoid the hot-tomato label, I dressed neatly but conservatively. I didn't smoke or drink. If I was in a situation where drugs were being shared, I walked away, so as not to confirm the stereotype of Puerto Ricans as drug abusers. There were enough alcoholics in my family for me to know that it wasn't fun, or pretty, and that whatever a drunk sought to abolish with liquor never went away.

The first Puerto Rican drug addict I met was Neftalí, who paid for it with his life. Maybe he felt good after he injected poison into his veins, just as Tata felt good when she drank beer. From where I stood, sober and straitlaced, the high wasn't worth the low, which for Tata, at least, came earlier every day.

The only people I knew who used drugs were American college students. They held smoky court in a corner of Manhattan Community College or hovered in disheveled groups in the streets of the Village near NYU and the rehearsal studio. They offered to "share" with me, but I refused. I had no desire to alter my consciousness, nor to escape reality. If I took even one "trip," I'd never return. Stubbornly, I observed every second of my ungroovy life, felt every pang of pain, shouldered humiliation, succumbed to joy, leaped into passion.

Mami drilled into me that I had only one asset. I wasn't the

prettiest of her six daughters, or the strongest of her children, but I was, she often said, intelligent. It was the power of that intelligence that I trusted. If my one asset was to work for me, my brain needed to remain unfogged and focused. My clear-headed self-absorption kept me sober. It also convinced me that in spite of Jaime's censure, I could be of no help to "my" people until I helped myself.

Jaime and I were too professional to let the prickly relationship we had offstage affect our performance in the happily-ever-after world of children's theater. But we were never as close as I'd been to Allan, who had demanded less and accepted me as I was. With Allan gone from the cast, and to avoid Jaime's frequent rebukes, I drew closer to Tom, the only other actor left from the Broadway production. He was easy to be with, funny, a good actor, a lithe dancer. He made it clear from the beginning that his friendship with me was not as disinterested as Allan's and Bill's. When I told him I was involved with someone, however, he confessed that he was in love with a dancer. "But I had to try," he said, with an impish grin.

For the new play, A *Box of Tears*, Robert De Mora, who'd also worked on *Babu*, designed a spectacular set and elaborate, clever costumes. I played a mermaid who disguised herself as a turtle and was caught in a net by a peasant fisherman. After a series of adventures, he became a prince and I a princess and we lived happily ever after. My mermaid costume was heavily sequined in emerald green and drew applause from the audience when I made my entrance. I wore a wig of long, green hair, made of a material so fine that it floated around me as I moved and gave the impression that we were under water. When I became a princess, my kimonos were traditional in design, my wig elaborately combed and decorated.

A consultant was brought in to show us how to move like Japanese people, including the proper way to bow. She also demonstrated how to put on the three layers of kimonos and gave me some tips on how to walk in the sebutan shoes without falling

over (very small steps). During performance, we wore Kabuki-style makeup. I arrived at the theater two hours before curtain to transform myself from Puerto Rican Indian classical dancer to Japanese mermaid. First I applied a thick white paste to my face, which obliterated my features. I then drew in the slanted eyes, straight eyebrows, bow lips in the photograph Kyoko gave me as a guide.

In one of the scenes, I was required to perform for the ocean king in my mermaid costume. Kyoko taught me how to sing "Sakura" in Japanese and choreographed a dance using fans to tell the story of how the fisherman caught the turtle/mermaid. After hearing me sing, Bill and Vera decided that I should just move my lips while Kyoko sang and played the koto.

I loved the play, the extravagant liberties De Mora took with costumes and set, the jokes we played on stage to break each other's concentration. My first words were spoken into a microphone offstage, while I was still a turtle in the hands of Tom as the fisherman. Rather than say my lines as Tom expected, I gurgled watery noises that were magnified through the whole theater. The first time I did that, Tom was disoriented, looked around as if the voice had come from heaven. In a later scene, as I performed my fan dance, Tom had his back to the audience. He often made goofy faces at me, while I struggled to maintain the dignity of a buddha.

My sisters and brothers couldn't come to my performances, because they took place during school hours, but I was enjoying myself so much that I wanted to share it with someone. Well aware that he preferred to keep our private lives private, I still urged Ulvi to come see me perform at the 92nd Street Y. The huge auditorium hummed with children bussed in from schools all over the city. It wasn't until I was putting on my makeup that I envisioned Ulvi in the audience surrounded by fidgety, chatty, precocious New York City schoolchildren. Naturally fastidious, he'd probably notice the pungent smell a roomful of children discharged. He'd frown at their shrill voices, at the way they ran down the aisle to claim a seat next to their best friends. With Ulvi in the audience,

it was difficult to concentrate, because I worried that the context for the performance would affect his enjoyment of it.

We'd agreed to meet at his apartment afterward, and when I entered the black-and-white room, he didn't even greet me. He took me in his arms and loved me, and I knew that he knew the performance was for him. That every pore was focused not on the children who were the primary audience, but on the dark scowling face at the back of the theater who now covered my breasts with kisses.

Mrs. Davis at the Advertising Checking Bureau called me into a manager's office because she needed to speak to me in private. She'd been informed, she said in her best supervisor's voice, that I was no longer a student at Manhattan Community College. My job was designated as "cooperative education," which meant I received credit for working, but only if I was enrolled in school. Since I wasn't, Mrs. Davis suggested that I take a full-time position elsewhere in the company, so that another student could be hired. Because of my performing schedule, I couldn't work forty hours a week, so I quit the Advertising Checking Bureau. As the holidays approached, however, it was clear that my income from children's theater couldn't keep up with my expenses, even after I dropped dance classes and workshops. Bill and Vera promised there would be more shows in the spring, as well as a tour, but they couldn't say how many dates, nor when the tour might be. Just as the year began, I was forced to leave Children's Theater International and look for a real job. I sobbed my goodbyes to Bill, who was also leaving for San Francisco, to Vera, to Tom and Jaime. It was difficult to imagine that I would no longer wear De Mora's outrageous mermaid costume, that there would be no chain dragging me offstage. In the year and a half I worked in children's theater, I came to love the enthusiastic responses of our audiences, the tension when the hero or heroine was in danger, the giggles at the

pranks of the monkey god, the cheers at the end when the prince and princess appeared in their full regalia, their future a cheerful certainty.

My own future didn't look so great. January wasn't the best month to look for work. Everywhere I went I was told business was winding down from the Christmas "rush." The best the employment agencies could do was to send me to do inventory at department stores, whose stock had to be counted before the discount sales began. It was tedious work, and I resented the prospect of counting thousands of shoes, dresses, coats that I couldn't afford to buy, even at a discount.

Shoshana came to my rescue. She had dropped out of college and was about to start a job as a sample model for a manufacturer of junior dresses and skirts. She talked to the owner of the shoe store where she worked and convinced him that he should replace her with me. But I was not good at selling shoes. When a woman asked how white go-go boots looked on her, I tended to be honest —a virtue in life but not in retail. Mr. Zuckerman suggested I find another line of work. After a number of interviews in offices that demanded more skills than I could offer, I was hired at Lady Manhattan. When I told Mami, she was upset. "All this education so that you can work in a factory?" she wailed, and I assured her I'd be in an office, not at machines.

Now that I was employed nine to five, Ulvi and I changed our trysts from afternoons to evenings and weekends. When I wasn't with him, I saw Shoshana or went to the movies or met Alma for dinner. Alma had just started a job as a secretary at NBC, where most of the pages I knew had graduated to better-paying work as assistant producers and writers. She admired her boss, who was said to be headed for great things in the company. I met him once at her office. He looked like a younger version of Mr. Rosenberg, the producer of the Yiddish theater where I was an usher, only more high-strung.

My boss at Lady Manhattan was Iris, a woman in her thirties with kind hazel eyes, cropped auburn hair, and a body type Sho-

shana described as *zaftig* — not fat, but not quite skinny either. As her assistant, I merited my own office outside hers, where my job was to maintain her files, answer her phone, keep track of her appointments, order her lunch, get her coffee, handle her correspondence. When she interviewed me, Iris didn't give me a typing test, and it wasn't until a week into my job that she realized she should have. It took me an entire morning to type a simple one-paragraph letter with duplicate. Every time I made a mistake, I took out the original and the carbon copy behind it and started over so that both would be perfect. Iris took one look at the pile of Lady Manhattan letterhead and carbon paper crumpled in the wastebasket and shrugged her shoulders.

"Never mind," she said. "I'll type it myself."

In her office, Iris had a wall-size bulletin board on which she pinned swatches of color for the previous, current, and two upcoming fashion seasons. Her job was to purchase the fabrics that the designers used for the blouses Lady Manhattan manufactured. She was good at her job, Iris told me without prompting, and if I was smart and paid attention, I could learn a lot from her. She had me sit in on meetings, ostensibly to take notes, but she admitted it was so that I could "learn the ropes." Together we came up with the names of the next season's colors. I suggested "Teal" — she called it "Mediterranean Blue." Never having seen that sea, I couldn't argue with her. When I offered "Dark Orange" she countered with "Pumpkin Spice." If I saw navy blue, she envisioned midnight. It was clear to everyone else at Lady Manhattan, but not to generous Iris, that I didn't have the poetic or hyperbolic instincts necessary for success in the garment industry.

The office building where I worked was seven blocks from the Broadway theater where Allan was in *Fiddler on the Roof*, starring Harry Goz. Allan was in the chorus and also understudied the role of the idealistic student who married one of the daughters, at that time played by Adrienne Barbeau. One day he called my office to let me know he was taking over the role that evening and that he could get me a ticket to see him. I called Ulvi to cancel our time together. He didn't ask why, and I didn't go into details.

I'd seen *Fiddler on the Roof* when Allan was first cast. It was wonderful to see how he had grown in the role. He lent a boyish charm to the romantic part, an innocence that endeared him to the audience. Afterwards, I met him backstage, and he introduced me to Adrienne and to Harry Goz; to Florence Stanley, whom I'd met in *Up the Down Staircase* and who played Yenta in *Fiddler*; to Bette Midler, who portrayed the oldest daughter. After they signed autographs at the stage door, we walked across the street to eat at a long, tunnel-like restaurant whose walls were decorated with signed photographs of Broadway actors. The bar was smoky, crowded with garrulous actors still high from a performance. In the juke box, Diana Ross proclaimed someday we'll be together, its chorus repeated over and over again by a mushy group in a corner bidding goodbye to one of its members.

It was very late when I arrived home. Mami raised her head from her pillow, waved me in, went back to sleep. The next day, I was exhausted at work, and while Iris went to a meeting in New Jersey, I asked the switchboard operator to handle calls, locked myself in Iris's office, and slept for two hours on the floor. When I checked, there were several messages from Ulvi. He was home, and, even though it wasn't one of our nights, he insisted that I come to his apartment because he needed to talk to me. He was furious, I could hear it in his voice.

"What's the matter?" I wondered, but he refused to talk about it over the phone. "Come after work," he said.

He prepared dinner for me, as he often did. His concoctions were simple — sautéed vegetables sprinkled with feta cheese, salad, steamed spinach with a soft-boiled egg in the center, roasted eggplant. I came to appreciate the subtle, delicate flavors of fresh vegetables — seldom served at home, staples in Ulvi's diet. This time he cooked steamed cauliflower with generous helpings of store-bought Hollandaise sauce, my contribution to his diet. He wasn't as fond of the dish as I was, and it made an impression that he bothered to make it for me. We ate in silence on the leather-topped coffee table. I could tell something was wrong, felt the tension in the room as solid as the four walls. As soon as we

cleared the dishes, he led me to the pull-out sofa bed, sat on one corner, pointed to the other, where I sat, one leg folded under me.

"Chiquita," he began. "Where were you last night?"

I told him about the play, Allan, the rest of the cast, the smoky, noisy restaurant. He listened attentively, asked about Allan. When did I meet him? Where? Was Allan my boyfriend before he met me?

"Oh, no," I laughed, "it's not like that with me and Allan. I love him very much, but not that way. We're friends."

Ulvi nodded, a finger curled to his lips. "Tell me, Chiquita, do you have many men friends?"

"Yes," I answered truthfully.

He stood up and in three strides was at the door. "Get out!" He was so angry he glowed red.

I was stunned, unable to move, speechless. He opened the door and repeated his words with such venom that I had no choice but to push myself off the couch, pick up my purse, and leave the apartment. He slammed the door after me. In the elevator, in the lobby, outside his building, down to Third Avenue, I was carried by the force of his rage. What had I done? What could I possibly have said? I walked to the train station, waited behind a column, my thoughts focused on every word I had uttered in his presence. In channeling my English through Spanish, had something been lost? Did he misunderstand what I'd said as he translated English through German to Turkish? Or had I broken some Turkish taboo by spending an evening out with friends? Turkey was a Muslim country. Followers of Islam didn't drink. Was he offended that I went to a bar? No, he was angry that I had male friends. Was that forbidden to women in Turkey? Is that why he reacted so violently? I held my sobs until I reached home — earlier than usual, Mami noted with raised eyebrows. I locked myself in the bathroom, filled the tub with scalding water, soaked and sobbed for an hour, while outside a sister or brother periodically banged on the door because they had to pee.

It was over, just like that. The most words Ulvi and I had

exchanged since the day of the parade led to our first and only fight. Was it even a fight? Didn't a fight require at least two people? It was so one-sided. I didn't get a chance to defend myself. From what? Had I done anything to deserve the way he'd treated me? His fury was so unexpected, swift as a scorpion's sting, as painful. "Get out," he said. With two simple words he kicked me out of his life. As I tossed in bed next to Delsa that night, I moaned and wailed so loud that Mami came to see what was the matter.

"Something I ate," I said, "made me sick to my stomach." Five minutes later she brought me a cup of chamomile tea with honey. I sipped it in front of her, and from time to time, bent over with sobs, pushed my arms against my stomach to still the hurt that pulsed not there, but a little higher up and to the left.

"For that slave-girl look . . ."

Iris noticed that I looked drawn and exhausted the next morning. She called me into her office and asked what was the matter. It was impossible to contain the tears that lurked so near the surface; they flowed against my will.

"Oh, you poor thing," Iris said. "A man did this." I nodded, my face in my hands. She came around her desk to where I sat and put her arms around me. She rubbed my back, offered me tissues, pushed back the hair matted on my cheeks. But she had no words of womanly wisdom that could help me get over the pain. "He's a dog," she finally said, although she'd never met him. Again I nodded. She gave me the rest of the day off.

I called Shoshana at work, and we agreed to meet for dinner. I left the office and walked briskly up Seventh Avenue to Central Park. It was a cold, drizzly winter day, and my red eyes, swollen face, and occasional sobs went unnoticed by passersby. As I reached the spot where Jurgen had confessed his occupation, my heartache turned to anger. How dare Ulvi throw me out of his apartment with no explanation? What kind of a stupid fool was I to do as he asked? What would have happened if I'd refused to leave, if I'd argued with him? A couple of times I turned toward Ulvi's apartment. But as I played possible scenarios in my mind, they seemed melodramatic, too much like a *telenovela*, too close to what was expected of a passionate Puerto Rican who'd been wronged. I squelched the desire to kill him and walked on, letting

the drizzle soak me through until I reached the Metropolitan Museum of Art. I stood in front of the Seurat painting where I had first met Avery Lee and was sorry I'd said no to him. Had I said yes, I'd be living in luxury in El Paso, where it never rained. Avery Lee didn't expect more from me than what I gave Ulvi. And he could speak English. I stared at the painting for a long time but still could find no more meaning in it than the first time I saw it.

At dinner, Shoshana urged another bowl of chicken soup to chase away the sniffles that were no longer caused by tears for Ulvi but by the cold I caught after walking in the rain. By the time I told her the story, it no longer hurt to speak of him.

"I can tell you'll be over him soon," Shoshana predicted. "It's not like you to suffer for long." My head was so heavy I couldn't think fast enough to agree or disagree. On the subway to Brooklyn, I jotted down her words on a scrap of paper and folded them inside my wallet. No, it wasn't like me to hold on to pain for long. Why bother? A new setback was bound to come soon enough.

I missed three days of work. Tata and Mami nursed me with broths and the dreaded *tutumá*, which tasted no better now that I was twenty than when Mami had first invented it in my thirteenth year. I slept, lulled by the whirr of sewing machines. Mami had a business at home now. She brought in cut garments from a factory; then she, Titi Ana, and a couple of other women finished sewing them on the machines set up in the living room. Tata watched Charlie, Cibi, and Ciro, who sometimes wandered into the makeshift *fábrica* to be admired, cuddled, and cooed over by the women.

By Saturday morning I felt better but stayed in bed reading. Shoshana called to see how I was doing. At the end of the conversation she told me the real reason she called.

"I didn't want to say anything the other day, when you felt so bad. . . ." She was returning to Israel to fulfill her military service, which she'd put off for some time. She'd be gone for months. "If the Arabs don't do something crazy, I might make it back," she

joked, but I didn't laugh. She didn't have much time, but we arranged to meet for one last dinner. Losing my best friend at the same time as my lover sent me back to bed for another day, but on Monday I dragged myself to work. There was a stack of messages on my desk, most of them for Iris but a few for me. "Ulvi called," the receptionist who handled the calls had written on at least five pink slips. On the most recent one she had scribbled "Urgent!" and in parentheses, "He told me to write that," with an arrow pointing to the word. I didn't call him. Every time I looked at the slips, I remembered his fury, the cruel turn of his lips when he told me to get out of his apartment.

I met Shoshana for dinner, and afterwards we walked on Fifth Avenue as we had done so often, toward the Plaza, intending to retrace our steps to Grand Central and the subways. But in front of the fountain, a man approached us. He was a producer, he said. His film was being screened at the Paris Cinema across the street. Would we like to see it?

It was an inscrutable black-and-white film in a Slavic language neither of us could identify. The subtitles didn't help. Shoshana and I giggled through the whole thing, as serious moviegoers hushed us and the hapless producer walked nervously up and down the aisles peering into the faces of his audience, trying to determine who dared laugh at his masterpiece. We ran out of there as soon as the final credits rolled, no longer able to stifle our laughter. As we walked to Grand Central arm in arm, we knew that our free-spirited adventures ended that night. It would be months before Shoshana could return to the States, and by then who knew where I'd be? We hugged, and Shoshana promised to write as soon as she arrived in Haifa. I didn't remind her that every time she left for Israel, she swore to write but never did. Within minutes of our parting, I felt the loss of the best friend I'd ever had, the only person, I thought, who really knew me.

I hadn't forgotten Ulvi, but in the five days since he had slammed the door behind me, he'd become like the pain left after a cut. Most of the time I didn't feel it until I banged up against it. The day after my dinner with Shoshana, I answered Iris's phone.

"Chiquita?" His soft, tentative voice made me lightheaded, and my first instinct was to hang up. First he apologized for his behavior of the previous week. Then he wanted to see me because he had to explain. "Maybe you don't understand," he guessed, "why I am upset."

The use of the present tense didn't throw me off, because Ulvi frequently confused the present for the past. I insisted we meet in a restaurant, not his apartment. "If you want to talk," I said, "it will be better." When I saw him in front of the Magic Pan on East 57th Street, I almost flew into his arms, restrained myself, let him kiss my cheek, pulled away for fear of losing my resolve.

He thought about what happened last week. "You are a child," he said. "I forget sometimes."

I reminded him that I was twenty and a half years old, not ten. He showed his indulgent smile. "To me, you are my *chiquita*," he said. "Always."

He was angry that night, he continued, because we had a date and I broke it at the last minute to be with another man. I explained that Allan was not "another man" in the sense I understood Ulvi to mean, but my dear friend. The reason for the short notice was that Allan, as an understudy, didn't always know ahead of time when he'd perform.

"Why don't you tell me this?" Ulvi asked.

"Because you didn't ask. You never do. You don't want to know about my private life, remember?" It was impossible to keep the resentment from my voice, the sarcasm that crept into the final three syllables. Ulvi winced. We sat in silence for a few minutes. I felt him struggle with a response. There was no possibility of kissing my emotions away here, in a busy restaurant with fake French food. I couldn't be appeased with promises that he'd never hurt me. He already had.

It took him a long time to formulate what he wanted to say. He thought he was the only man in my life. It disturbed him that I felt free to see other men.

I answered that we'd never talked about our "relationship" in a way that made me feel I couldn't date others. If it made him feel better, I assured him, I hadn't had sex with any other man but him. The relief that swept over his face startled me. What did he expect?

We left the restaurant, circled the block, ended up on his street. He grinned, pulled me close, kissed me, and I dissolved through my thick winter coat. His arms felt familiar, his lips like mine. He was the perfect height, no need for me to stretch or scoot down to place my head on his shoulders, for him to wrap his arm around my waist. We walked with the same purposeful stride, our feet hit the pavement at the same time, synchronized through an internal mechanism neither of us controlled. Our lovemaking was a dance, each part of our bodies attuned to its complement in the other, as if we were not two but one. Afterwards, as I lay content in his arms, he said he wanted me always by his side. It wasn't a promise, a proposal, a declaration of love. But I understood it as all those things.

Over the next few days and nights we drew closer. Reluctantly, Ulvi opened up, talked about himself and his obsession with his film, *Dry Summer*. Its success had surprised him, because the favorite for the top prize at Berlin had been *The Pawnbroker*, with Rod Steiger. "No one expect me to win," he laughed. "Not even me." He became famous overnight, traveled around the world for festivals and competitions, made money. He bought a white Rolls Royce, which he drove from New York to Hollywood. There, he met Kim Novak and Angie Dickinson. The Hollywood producer Sid Solow let Ulvi spend a few weeks in his guest house while Ulvi tried to get a film deal. In spite of his efforts, however, *Dry Summer* couldn't pick up a distributor in North America. Wherever Ulvi went, he was told that the film was lovely but that if he wanted to show it in the United States, it needed more sex and better music. He sold the Rolls Royce, invested the money in

the film. He hired the Greek composer Manos Hadjidakis, who'd scored *Never on Sunday*, to create new music for *Dry Summer*. Ulvi found a girl who looked like Hulya Kocigit, the love interest opposite him in the film. They drove out with a cinematographer to Long Island and shot new scenes. He was now reediting the film to incorporate the sex.

"Did Hulya agree to that?" I wondered.

"She's a big star in Turkey now. She doesn't have time."

The editing suite was on the second floor of a rundown office building half a block from Woolworth's, where Ulvi had first seen me. His editor was a long-legged older man with white hair, sad eyes, a deeply lined face that seldom smiled. Hans reminded me of Bela Lugosi, both in the way he looked and in his speech, which was heavily accented. He worked at an upright Movieola, his fingers flying from the editing machine to the ashtray at his side. In a back room was another Movieola rented to another filmmaker.

Every day after work I met Ulvi at the editing room, a few blocks from my office. Once he was done, we went to his place, ate, took long, frigid walks down Fifth Avenue or through Central Park, and talked — or rather, he did. I cherished his every word, his intonation, the pauses and hesitations of his speech. He prefaced many of his confidences with "I don't tell anyone this, Chiquita," which made me feel included in his life, privy to secrets.

Ulvi hired a writer to create new subtitles for the film. He worried that the money he had left was dribbling away into making the movie attractive to American audiences. Evenings, after he walked me to the train station, he went to Manos's apartment above the Acropolis restaurant on West 57th Street to work on the score. Manos didn't like to compose during the day, Ulvi said, so their sessions began after eleven at night and ended in the early hours. It was an exhausting schedule, but Manos claimed his creativity was at its peak late at night. Since Manos had won an Academy Award for *Never on Sunday*, Ulvi felt he must indulge him. He hoped that Manos's score would increase interest in his film.

When I worried about his health because he worked so hard, Ulvi thanked me but said he had no choice. "This is my only chance, Chiquita," he confided.

Over the next few weeks my days, evenings, and weekends were consumed by Ulvi. I didn't spend time with anyone else—not my family, not my friends, not my cousin Alma. Able to afford dance classes again, I stopped going to them after Ulvi and I went to a Satyajit Ray movie.

"That's the kind of dance I do," I told him, referring to the Bharata Natyam sequence at the beginning of the film.

"Is ridiculous dance," was Ulvi's opinion. "Not for you."

The next time I went to a workshop, I watched myself in the studio mirror, self-conscious about the stylized movements, the affected expressions, the atonal music. I looked ridiculous in my sari and ankle bells, the dot in the middle of my forehead.

From then on, every free moment was devoted to him. While Ulvi worked on his film, I read in a corner of the editing room. Sometimes I was sent out for coffee or lunch, or to pick up or deliver a package. Johan, who rented the other Movieola in the suite, asked me to translate his film. He and his brother Fritz had documented an archaeological expedition into the Colombian jungle. Many of the scenes were in Spanish, a language neither Johan nor Fritz understood. I translated the Spanish scenes into English, then translated the whole film into Spanish so that he could have a movie in each language.

While he and Hans edited, I saw scenes with a younger, ardent Ulvi but never viewed the entire movie from beginning to end. The nude scenes were skillfully shot, one in a cornfield, another in front of a loom on which was stretched a half-finished carpet. The actress looked enough like Hulya that, through clever lighting and positioning of her face, the transitions were smooth, if not perfect.

Days in the garment center, I failed to come up with evocative names for primary colors. I couldn't type a letter without wasting ten sheets of stationery. Iris's busy schedule meant that I

was often alone in the office, overcome with boredom, willing the phone to ring so that I could take a message. It felt wrong to collect a salary when I had nothing to do, so I decided to improve my secretarial skills. I bought the book *Teach Yourself the Gregg Shorthand Method*, but between Spanish, English, Spanglish, high school French, the Turkish that came backwards and forwards from the Movieola, and the German that Ulvi, Hans, and Johan spoke among themselves, there was no more room in my brain for another language.

Mami no longer asked where I'd been, who I'd been with, what I'd been doing. It was as if, with ten other children to look after, my activities held no interest for her as long as I was home every night. I seldom saw my sisters and brothers, because I made it a point to leave the house as early as possible and returned way past everyone's bedtime. One Sunday, Ulvi couldn't see me because he had to visit friends in Long Island. I planned to stay home that day, but two hours after I woke up, I left the house, suffocated by the clutter and disarray, the confusion, the people running in and out of rooms, up and down the stairs. I longed for Ulvi's quiet, austere room, its systematic order no longer sinister but soothing. Without him there, however, I couldn't go to his apartment. I spent the day at the movies, watched the double feature twice, and came home at the same time as always.

Ulvi surprised me one day. He took me to dinner at an expensive restaurant because he wanted to celebrate meeting some people interested in his film. They had shot a couple of low-budget films in Italy and were interested in Ulvi as a director for another film they wanted to produce. Ulvi said they were impressed by his reputation as an art film director, an image they sought to promote for themselves.

"It is a good possibility," Ulvi said, and as he downplayed it, I knew he was relieved. The burden of financing every aspect of *Dry Summer* was lifted just when he ran out of money. "I only have enough for one month," he told me, and I wondered what might have happened if the partners hadn't come along.

When we returned to his apartment, Ulvi took my hand, kissed it. He asked me to close my eyes and clicked a cuff bracelet on my wrist. It was heavy gold mesh, about one and a half inches wide, with gold braid along the edges. I was speechless, embarrassed by the extravagance of such a gift.

"What's this for?" I stammered

"You have been good girl," he murmured.

"But you can't afford it."

"Don't worry," he said.

Later, naked save for the bracelet, I turned my wrist this way and that to catch the shimmer of the gold against my skin. I wondered what the bracelet was worth, whether hundreds or thousands of dollars.

"I feel funny taking this when I know you need money," I offered.

"I said don't worry," he snapped.

On the way home that night, I pulled the sleeve of my coat over the bracelet so that no one on the train could see it and mug me. Because I knew Mami would notice it, I concocted a story about a friend who wanted to sell it. Was the bracelet worth the $25 she asked? Mami thought the price was more than fair.

I wore the bracelet everywhere, with casual or dressy clothes, because it pleased Ulvi to see it on me. When I showed it to Iris at work, she said it reminded her of shackles. "For that slave-girl look," she added.

Over the next few weeks, Ulvi gave me other expensive gifts. An Hermés leather agenda book, a sterling silver key ring from Tiffany's in the shape of a heart. He also took an interest in how I dressed. He insisted that when we were together, I not wear makeup. "I don't like painted woman," he said. He accompanied me shopping for clothes. Before making films, he had worked as a textile engineer in Germany and was particular about what went next to his skin. When I chose a garment, he rubbed it between his fingers, weighed it on the palm of his hand, turned it inside out to see if the pattern was stamped or woven in, and to check the finish on the seams. He eliminated most of my choices. "This

is for cheap girl," he sneered, then picked something else. "This one better for you."

"Cheap girl" was his biggest insult, the exact opposite of "elegant girl," who dressed well and behaved appropriately according to a complicated system of etiquette and demeanor that Ulvi swore I needed to master. "If you are going to be with me, you must learn."

I wanted to be with him, so I attended to his lessons. When we were out, I was to mirror his movements, so as not to embarrass myself. I was to eat if he ate, with the utensil he used, to speak less and listen more, to withhold my opinions. He made me aware of my limitations, promised to help me overcome them. "You are poor girl with small mind," he said once and repeated often. When he noticed I was offended, he explained that he meant not that I was stupid but that I was unsophisticated, because I'd been too well protected.

"It is what I love about you, Chiquita," he told me. "I can teach you everything." He wanted to be Pygmalion, and I became the stone upon which he sculpted Galatea. Whenever it felt as if he controlled too much of my life, I complained, but he shushed me with caresses and a promise. "You will be by my side, but you must do as I tell you." To be with him, I had to discard who I was and evolve into the woman he wanted to be with. "I have thousand girlfriends," he boasted, "but only you I care." It was the closest he could come to saying he loved me, but for me it was close enough.

Gradually, he introduced me to people in his life. Each encounter was a test I had to pass to move on to the next level. First I met Hans, Johan, and Fritz and comported myself well in the stuffy editing room. Then he introduced me to Bruce, the writer who helped him with the subtitles, and to his delicate wife, Diana. Peter, the Iranian cameraman who filmed the sex scenes, and his wife, Barbara, were next. When he introduced me to the man he called his best friend, Tarik, I knew he trusted me. Each little piece of his life I was allowed to share felt like a victory, because I'd earned the right to be with him, by his side.

Manos finished most of the score and planned to record it

with a Juilliard-trained group of musicians who performed under the name *The New York Rock and Roll Ensemble*. I came to the recording studio and met Manos for the first time. He was enormous, with an engaging grin; small hands with short, fat fingers; merry ebony eyes.

After the first couple of sessions in the recording studio, Ulvi told me not to come anymore. The musicians and their girlfriends smoked pot constantly, and Ulvi worried that they were into other drugs. "I don't want you around that," he said, and I was grateful for his concern.

The day he admitted how old he was, I understood why he had kept it a secret for so long. He was thirty-seven, the same age as Mami, seventeen years older than me. I'd studied psychology at Manhattan Community College, was aware that Ulvi was the classic father substitute, but it didn't matter. He took care of me in a way no one else did. In his arms I felt safe and protected. Wrapped in his embrace, I had no responsibilities except to do as he said. "Don't worry," he assured me, "I take care everything." He was clear about what he expected from me. Unlike the other adults in my life, he didn't say one thing and do another. If he didn't want me to drink alcohol, it was because he didn't drink. If he frowned on smoking, he didn't smoke. He didn't want children, so he took care I didn't get pregnant.

He needed a disciple; I needed to be led. I felt myself submerge into his need like a pebble into a pond, with no resistance, no trace I'd ever been anywhere or anyone without him. With Ulvi I wasn't Negi, daughter of an absent father, oldest of eleven children, role model for ten siblings, translator for my mother. I was not Esmeralda, failed actress/dancer/secretary. My head against Ulvi's chest, my arms around his neck, I was what I stopped being the day I climbed into a propeller plane in Isla Verde, to emerge into the rainy night of Brooklyn. After seven years in the United States, I had become what I stopped being the day I left Puerto Rico. I had become Chiquita — small, little one. Little girl.

"It is the way it must be."

⤳

In April Ulvi and I took long walks in Central Park along paths that he seemed to know intimately. "I jog here," he said, which surprised me because he'd never told me he was a runner. From time to time he liked to leave the paths and walk on the grass, his eyes scanning the green for four-leaf clovers. It impressed me that he always found one, plucked it, pressed it between the folds of a dollar bill. Later, in his apartment, he taped it flat, carefully cut around it. He sent them to friends, he said, and once gave one to me. "It will bring you good luck," he claimed. I kept it in my wallet as he instructed but noticed no difference in my fortunes.

"Maybe I'm immune to good luck," I joked, but he didn't get it.

Our walks in the park usually ended at the zoo, where we visited the sad, caged creatures who paced back and forth with the same tenacity they'd display if they were going somewhere. We stopped to watch the seals slither in and out of murky water, their coats a-shimmer. A crowd gathered around the pond when they were fed, but I found their silly antics for a dead fish pitiful.

Shanti had taken numerous pictures of me in the zoo, by the monkey cages or on a bench surrounded by pigeons, which an old lady fed from a plastic bucket at her side. Every time I passed those spots, I remembered Shanti's Crayola brown eyes, the way he tilted his head to let me know how I should place mine.

When Ulvi and I walked around the Lake, I remembered

Jurgen's content look as he lifted the oars, dipped them in the water, pulled them toward his chest to propel us across. Ulvi liked to sit in the lobbies of fancy hotels like the Plaza, the St. Regis, the Waldorf. I didn't tell him about the dinners Shoshana and I had had in the restaurants of those hotels, about the lonesome men eager to spend their money and their time on a couple of girls hungry for male attention.

The restaurant in Rockefeller Center where Jurgen and I had first talked still served expensive meals under bright umbrellas, but I didn't tell Ulvi I had once sat in their shade to cry on the shoulder of a stranger because Avery Lee had asked me to be his mistress. Ulvi, who talked as if I'd never remember a word he said, didn't ask about me. The less interest he had in my life, the more ashamed of it I became, ashamed of a life before him, without him.

A few weeks short of my twenty-first birthday, we were walking in the park when Ulvi doubled over. I helped him to a nearby bench, and he sat for a while, refusing my offer to accompany him to an emergency room. "It's nothing, Chiquita. I get this before," he said, and I didn't press him but insisted we take a cab back to his apartment. He lay down for a few minutes, which he said made him feel better. Before I left, he promised to see a doctor.

"I need operation," he told me a few days later.

The only people close to me to have needed operations were Raymond, whose injured foot and subsequent surgeries were the reason for our one-way trip to Brooklyn, and Francisco, Mami's love, my brother Franky's father. Raymond's operations had saved his foot. Francisco had suffered through numerous procedures that couldn't save him. Instinctively, I ignored the successes and focused on the failures of medicine. Like Francisco, Ulvi would go for surgery, and I wouldn't see him again. I wasn't strong like Mami, couldn't survive the months of black despair.

"Don't be so scare, Chiquita," Ulvi took me in his arms, pressed me close while I sobbed into his chest. "It is only hernia operation. Nothing to worry."

But he couldn't convince me. My head filled with images of Ulvi, dead. Ulvi, a ghost to haunt me forever, as Francisco had haunted Mami. It took me a long time to calm down, and then Ulvi told me the rest. It was minor surgery, he wouldn't be in the hospital more than a couple of days; but he didn't have insurance, and his savings had run out. The distributors who wanted to release *Dry Summer* arranged for a hospital and a doctor to perform the surgery at no charge, in Fort Lauderdale.

"Why so far?" I whined.

"It is the way it must be." He waited for me to argue, and when I didn't, he continued. Even though he was in pain, he wanted to finish the film before he left New York. The new subtitles had to go in, the film had to be remixed to incorporate Manos's music and new sound effects. He needed a couple of weeks, and then he'd fly to Fort Lauderdale to have his surgery. He didn't know when, or if, he'd come back to New York. He spoke matter-of-factly in his simple, declarative English, each word carefully chosen. I sat with legs folded under me, my hands pressed between my thighs. For some time, I'd dreaded a conversation like this, had known that one day Ulvi would leave my life as swiftly as he had entered it. I was glad he wasn't going to die; he was just going to Florida. As he spoke, I made myself withdraw, until we were not at opposite ends of his black leather sofa but in different continents.

Once he laid out the plans, Ulvi leaned further into his corner of the couch, pressed his hands together, his fingers to his lips, and spoke so softly I had to strain to hear him. "You can come with me."

I'd waited, hoped for those words, certain I'd never hear them, relieved when he said them. I surprised myself, then, when my response was that my mother would never let me go.

"You must leave her, then," Ulvi declared.

There was no way to explain to Ulvi, who didn't know Mami, why the thought of leaving my mother so that I could go to Fort Lauderdale with my lover terrified me. He hadn't been there when

she showed up on Long Island in the middle of a snowstorm to rescue me from sex with Otto. He hadn't heard the pain in her voice when she mourned her unfinished education, young, unmarried motherhood, men who betrayed her. He hadn't been with her at the welfare office, had not stood solemn and scared as she humbled herself before people who would conquer her pride because they couldn't vanquish her spirit. He'd never placed his head on her lap, had never listened as she revealed her dreams for her children, who would, she hoped, be smarter about life than she had been. He hadn't seen Mami's face light up at the thought of me, her eldest daughter, dressed in a white wedding gown en route to a cathedral.

"Maybe if we get married," I suggested, pathetic even to myself.

Ulvi shook his head. "No, we cannot get married."

No explanation followed his refusal, and I didn't seek one. He was somber, patient. His eyes watched me with the same intensity as they had, months ago, when Shoshana and I sat in this room trying to impress him so that he would put us in his movie. This, I knew, was a test of my loyalty. If I refused to follow him to Florida, I would fail.

Over the seven months we'd known each other I'd relinquished my will to his. I'd stopped seeing my friends, stopped dancing, ran from work straight into his arms. But I still went home at night to sleep under Mami's roof. Without saying the words, Ulvi was asking me to give her up too, to choose between them.

In all the time we'd been lovers, it had never once occurred to me that I'd ever have to make such a choice. One day, Ulvi would return to Turkey; or to Germany; or to who knew, who cared where. It would be Ulvi who would leave my life, not Mami. Over the years of watching Mami, La Muda, my aunts and cousins as they loved, lost, loved again, I'd learned that love was something you get over. If Ulvi left, there would be another man, but there would never, ever be another Mami.

"You think about," Ulvi advised when I didn't respond right away. For the first time since the first time, I left his apartment without taking my clothes off once. I rode the train to Brooklyn. The heavy, dusty air of the subways was suffocating, made it impossible to breathe, muddled my thoughts so that I didn't know where I was, where I was going, or why. The express hurtled between Nostrand Avenue, Utica Avenue, Broadway-East New York. I got off the train and switched to the local for one stop, to Liberty Avenue, a block from Mami's house. It was dark, but earlier than I usually came home. Mami and Tata had cooked a vat of *arroz con pollo* and stewed pinto beans.

"Ay, Negi, you're early, that's good," Mami said. "Let me serve you some dinner."

She was cheerful because it was Saturday and she was paid on Friday, which meant there was a big, generous *compra* in the pantry. The sewing machines in the living room were quiet, covered with sheets so that the younger kids knew not to touch them. Héctor, Raymond, and Franky were in the cement backyard, throwing a ball around. A little dog snapped at my ankles. Where had it come from? Did we own it? How long had we had it? I changed into my stay-at-home clothes and sat with Mami and Tata in the kitchen, and the three of us ate their good cooking, while in the next room, the television blared a variety show.

My sisters and brothers sprawled on the floor or on the plastic-covered furniture and laughed and pointed at the outlandish costumes and performers. Somewhere one of the babies cried, another screeched, the dog yipped. Tata lit up a cigarette, opened a beer. Mami screamed at Edna to pick up Ciro so he'd stop crying. I stood up, put my dishes in the sink, and burrowed into the room I shared with Delsa, into the bed I shared with Delsa. Covers pulled over my head to block out the noise, the confusion, the drama of my family's life, I knew, just as Ulvi knew when he asked, that I'd already made my choice.

acknowledgments

This is what I remember, as I remember it. Memorable statements, compelling confessions, and intriguing questions have contributed to the recreated conversations in some scenes.

The names of members of my immediate family are real, but circumstances have forced me to change others. For example, so far, there have been twelve Franks and five Normas in my life. While I can tell one from the other, it was harder to do that on the page. To avoid confusion, I've nicknamed or renamed some people.

Then there are those people whose names I can't recall. Some might be minor characters in a novel, but in real life, if they're remembered, they're not minor at all. I beg forgiveness from those who recognize themselves but whose names are different in these pages. Please understand that, while I may have forgotten your name, I still remember you.

Several individuals have helped shape this book. I am particularly indebted to my editor Merloyd Lawrence, whose confidence and encouragement are the greatest motivators any writer could ever hope for. Whenever I was overwhelmed by the emotions the writing of this memoir evoked, I called my friend and agent Molly Friedrich, whose reassurances kept me on course. My writing buddies Terry Bazes, Ben Cheever, Joie Davidow, Audrey Glassman, Marilyn Johnson, and Mary Breasted generously put aside their own work to read this manuscript at various stages. *Mil gracias,* dear friends.

The Santiago/Cortéz/Martínez clan has been gracious and supportive, even if they sometimes disagree with my version of events. Individually and collectively, my mother, father, sisters, and brothers manifest what respect and *dignidad* mean to a Puerto Rican.

And finally, my husband, Frank Cantor, and our children, Lucas and Ila, have figured out when I need to be alone and when I need a hug. You make me sing. (But don't worry, I won't do it in public.)

about the author

Esmeralda Santiago is the author of *When I Was Puerto Rican,* a memoir, and of *América's Dream,* a novel.

GERARD S. SLOYAN

CHRIST THE LORD

HERDER AND HERDER

1962
HERDER AND HERDER NEW YORK
232 Madison Avenue, New York 16, NY

Illustrations by Sister Mary Irenita Ciarlo, O.S.F.

First Edition 1962
Second Impression 1963

Grateful acknowledgment is made to Hi-Time Publishers, Inc., for permission to reproduce the copyrighted material contained in this book, both text and illustrations; to Atheneum Publishers, for the quotation from Ignazio Silone's *Fontamara*; to Duckworth Ltd., for Hilaire Belloc's *Sonnets and Verse*; to The Macmillan Co., for Eileen Duggan's *Poems*; to The Bruce Publishing Co., for *The New Testament* translated by James Kleist and Joseph Lilly; and to the St. Anthony Guild Press for *The Holy Bible* in the translation made for the episcopal committee on The Confraternity of Christian Doctrine by members of The Catholic Biblical Association of America. The poem on page 96ff is from *The Eagle's Word* © 1961 by Gerald Vann, O.P., and reprinted by permission of Harcourt, Brace & World, Inc.

Nihil Obstat: John T. McGinn, C.S.P., Censor Deputatus
Imprimatur: Patrick A. O'Boyle, Archbishop of Washington
June 19, 1962

The *nihil obstat* and *imprimatur* are official declarations that a book or pamphlet is free from doctrinal or moral error. No implication is contained therein that those who have granted the *nihil obstat* and the *imprimatur* agree with the content, opinions or statements expressed.

Library of Congress Catalog Card Number: 62–17231
© 1962 Herder and Herder, Inc.
Printed in the United States of America

BT
301
.2
.S57
(1)

Introduction

It takes a certain foolhardiness bordering on insensibility to attempt again what the four evangelists have done so well. To bring alive on the printed page the Jesus of Nazareth whom Christians venerate as the world's Savior and whom countless others consider one of the wisest and holiest of men is to court failure. Yet it is common to those who believe in any person or cause to give testimony to their faith. Friends everywhere speak enthusiastically of friends. When the faith concerned has a more than natural quality, when the partner in friendship is someone believed in as true God and true man, the likelihood of written testimony to this faith and love does not diminish but rather increases. It is, in other words, entirely to be expected that Christians should write about Christ.

The chapters that follow are in that long-standing tradition. They do not comprise a "life of Christ" in the classic sense, the kind of thing that began with the 14th century Carthusian Ludolf of Coblenz and has culminated in modern works such as those of Lagrange and Prat. The chapters are much more like the gospels themselves from which they derive, being a series of thematic considerations based solidly on the existing faith of the Church in Jesus Christ. Many important pieces of gospel witness are absent from these pages: the narrative of Zachary's vision in the Temple, with which redemptive history proper begins; the story of the man born blind; the Transfiguration. If any principle of selection is at work here it is an attempt to feature aspects of the Lord's saving ministry that are less familiar to many. These outlines for consideration are supple-

mentary, above all. The faith of Catholics and of many other Christians in the full divinity of Jesus Christ is clear and strong; their supernatural belief in his full human status is often not so firm. There is a general understanding that "Jesus was a Jew"; the actual implications of his relation to his people Israel have never been brought home to large numbers. That the eucharist is the food of Christians, and that the Church is Christ's mystical body, all know; how, exactly, they stand in relation to Christ in glory, who will return to raise them up at the Last Day in virtue of the eucharists they have received in the Church, many have not pondered on. It is to provide the opportunity to learn or to recall such truths that this modest volume exists.

The speech employed is the language of every day. The examples, one hopes, are commonplaces of modern life. Occasional resort to levity, however painful to the discriminating reader, is an attempt to levitate the spirit and not to debase the message. St. Augustine, after all, demands *hilaritas* as the condition of instructing in Christ. The word had a slightly different meaning in the Fifth century but it connoted "cheerfulness," at the very least.

The deep-seated wish of the writer is that he will create in the reader a threefold sense of dissatisfaction: at his own imperfect familiarity with the New Testament, at the writer's bumbling attempts to direct him to the riches that are there, and with life generally—which is to describe that hunger and thirst for holiness which will have its fill only when Christ the Lord returns and "is all, in all."

The Author

Contents

INTRODUCTION 5

1. THE JESUS WHOM THE FIRST BELIEVERS PREACHED . 7
2. THE BAPTIST'S CRY: JESUS TESTED IN THE DESERT . 12
3. JESUS CALLS HIS DISCIPLES 18
4. THE FIRST OF JESUS' SIGNS 24
5. JESUS CASTS OUT DEMONS 31
6. JESUS RETURNS TO NAZARETH 38
7. THE ENEMIES OF JESUS 44
8. THE FRIENDS OF JESUS 52
9. THE MOTHER OF JESUS 58
10. THE STORIES JESUS TOLD 65
11. JESUS THE LAWGIVER 72
12. THE IRONY OF JESUS 81
13. JESUS, THE BREAD OF LIFE 88
14. JESUS THE GOOD SHEPHERD 96
15. THE AUTHORITY OF JESUS 104
16. THE SINLESSNESS OF JESUS 110
17. THE PRAYERFULNESS OF JESUS 118
18. JOY IN FOLLOWING JESUS 126
19. JESUS AND HIS OWN PEOPLE 132
20. JESUS, THE SUFFERING SERVANT OF THE LORD . . 140
21. ARE YOU HE WHO IS TO COME? 149
22. THE RAISING OF LAZARUS 156
23. THE MEALS JESUS TOOK 162
24. JESUS ENTERS JERUSALEM 169
25. JESUS TEACHES ABOUT THE LAST DAYS . . . 176
26. THE MASTER TAKES LEAVE OF HIS FRIENDS . . 183
27. THE LAST SUPPER: VOW AND REMEMBRANCE RITE . 191
28. AGONY AND TRIAL. "I AM HE" 200
29. JESUS DIES BECAUSE HIS WORK IS FINISHED . . 208
30. DEATH THE LOSER IN A DUEL WITH LIFE . . . 215
31. THE FORTY DAYS AND THE PASCHAL FAITH . . 224
32. JESUS SENDS ANOTHER TO SUSTAIN US . . 232

1

The Jesus Whom the
First Believers Preached

There's a great deal to be said for knowing Jesus Christ if you hope to spend a lifetime calling yourself a *Christ*ian. *Really* knowing him, that is. Knowing who he is and what he stands for. Believing in him—throwing in your lot with him for good.

DO WE *REALLY* BELIEVE?

On the day of our baptism, every one of us declared that we accepted our Lord Jesus Christ as God and Savior. Most of us said this through our godparents. This is the faith that made Christians of us—that made us members of Christ in his one, holy, catholic and apostolic Church.

The big question is this: do we really believe it *now?*

Do we mean it with all our strength? We'd like to believe it, yes, but perhaps we don't know enough about our Lord to "go all out" for him. That is why really getting to know him is something that should make a tremendous difference in our lives.

ARE WE CHRISTIANS, OR FRAUDS?

Most of us have no time for fakes or frauds, people who sail under false colors. The most obvious types are the professional "con men." At the amateur level you have the athlete who shaves points in a basketball game for a gambling syndicate's cash.

Most of us, however, get caught up in the more ordinary kinds of fakery. We copy homework like crazy, or fill out padded expense accounts.

Do you remember the knife-like words our Lord threw at the phonies he met? You will find them in chapter 23 of Saint Matthew's Gospel.

There is still another way of playing the fraud. Most of us were born into a community of people who believe in Christ— our family, our parish, our neighborhood. We said we were *Catholic* because everyone else said we were. It did not take much thought or effort.

Once in awhile we thought about it a little, about what it meant to be a Christian—when we made our first communion or came to love someone who was not a Catholic and didn't bother about church. Perhaps then we thought a little harder about the big difference between *saying* we were a Catholic and *being* one.

DO WE KNOW CHRIST?

Sometimes it seems that the more we learn about Jesus Christ, the less we know him. What sort of person was he? If he was truly the Son of God in human flesh, how could anyone stand having him for a daily acquaintance? or having him as an enemy—that's even harder to understand. So *getting to know him* may be the trouble.

It could be that we are bothered by the idea of what Christ is supposed to mean to us *now*, granted all that the Bible and the Church say about him is true. To some of us, Christ may seem too "far away and long ago." In church we are told that he is the *central figure* in our lives and in history. But when we walk downtown on Saturday night, in the parks, past the cheap movie theaters and the "gin mills" we think, "Who's kidding who?"

DID JESUS EVER MEAN
EVERYTHING TO ANYONE?

The best way to get facts is to go back to sources. What did our Lord's first followers think about him? To find that, we go to a book in the Bible called "The Acts of the Apostles." Saint Luke wrote it some time after the year 65 A.D. Its first part tells the way the disciples preached about Jesus around the year 30, when he arose from the dead and went back to his Father. When we read Acts we learn what Christ meant to those men and women who were willing to suffer for him. We need to have him mean that much to us now!

Those first disciples felt terribly close to Christ—and to one another. Why? Because the Holy Spirit had let them know exactly who their great teacher was. During his lifetime they never did get the point entirely—but later they did. And then, instead of wanting high places in Jesus' kingdom, their only

boast was that they were disciples of Jesus of Nazareth. Why were they his followers, his friends? Because of what they *knew* about him. He was not merely their friend; he was the *Lord!* (For the Israelites—or *Jews,* as they were later called—only God was "the Lord").

How could these strict Jews say that about a *man?* Because the Holy Spirit had assured them that Jesus, whom wicked men had killed, and who rose again from the tomb, was "Lord." Men had no other savior but him. To believe in him was to have life. (Jesus said that, himself. See John 6:47). So nothing that the mobs or rulers did could shake them or weaken their faith in him.

What about us? Can we take it—the jibes, the sneers sometimes—and remain loyal and unshaken?

HOW MANY OF US WOULD
GO ALL OUT FOR CHRIST?

Most of the ideas we need to grasp about Jesus are in that story of the strong, courageous faith of the early Church in Jerusalem that we find in Acts. In the first place, without faith we cannot be sure who Jesus is. Saint Paul tells us we can't even say his name, except in the Spirit. (I Corinthians 12:3) That means if we want to understand Jesus we have to ask God the Holy Spirit, the third person of the blessed Trinity, to make our personal Pentecost—our confirmation—mean something to us.

Then we have to *know* Christ as his disciples did. They had their warm memories of him. We can "read all about it" in the New Testament. They knew him in the breaking of the bread—we can know him in the eucharist.

WHAT DOES 'GOING ALL OUT
FOR CHRIST' MEAN?

Going all out for Jesus means loyalty. And *loyalty to Christ means the cross!* It is strange, but the cross won't bring only misery. It will bring a sense of security in life, and purpose—yes, it will bring *real* joy—not just a wandering about aimlessly, looking for random kicks, but a sense of deep-down, lasting happiness. For the worst that *can* happen, *has* happened. CHRIST WAS CRUCIFIED! And Christ won the victory! He is in the glory of the Father. If we stay faithful to him, the glory that is his will be ours too.

WHAT TO DO?

There is *one condition* that cannot escape our notice when we read the Book of Acts: *If we don't spread the good news about Christ's victory over death and sin, it soon stops meaning much to us.*

No wonder we feel a little rocky about the whole business of who, exactly, Jesus is. We don't pray enough—to the Holy Spirit for light and guidance. We don't read enough—of God's love for us in the Bible. We twentieth century disciples don't fulfill our duty of confirmation enough—by telling the good news to others.

Lots of communions received, did somebody say? Good, wonderful—but *that is not enough.* Look at Acts 2:42 and you'll see that that's only part of it.

2

The Baptist's Cry:
Jesus Tested in the Desert

Have you ever heard about whole towns putting on "Pioneer Days" pageants? Usually the men have to grow beards and carry flintlock muskets. The women make their own pinafores and dustcaps. Why all this? Because we have a romantic idea that our people were braver and more resourceful in the old days. When the wagon trains went west, everything was different—we like to think.

It is much the same with religious groups. Most of the small Christian churches that are called "sects" have this mark in common: they want to capture the simplicity of the early days of the Church. They read the Bible with great care, especially the *Acts of the Apostles* and the letters of Saint Paul. Then they try to copy the smallest details they read

about. They want to live *exactly* as the New Testament says the first Christians lived. No changes; no developments; everything just as it was centuries ago.

LONGED FOR THE OLD DAYS

Well, the people of God in the Old Testament, his beloved people who called themselves "Israel" (at that time they weren't known as "the Jews"—that came much later), thought in pretty much the same pattern. They made a romantic ideal out of their own early history. For them, nothing had ever been quite the same since their wanderings in the desert, back in Moses' time.

In those days, according to the writing of Ezechiel, one of their great teachers, God had come upon Israel. She was like an abandoned, newborn child. First, God raised her. Then he showered all kinds of gifts upon her. Then he took her as his own bride! This is a poetic way of speaking, of course, but it helps us to understand. If we think of Israel as the bride of God, it is easier for us to learn what Jesus meant in many of the things he said. The love between God and Israel was so strong in the early desert days that Israel, like a bride, endured hardships that she had never been able to put up with since. At least, that is the way people liked to remember it.

ISRAEL'S FAITH FAILED

The place where all these memories centered was the desert. This *desert* does not mean the broad sands to the east of Israel's homeland, stretching out toward the River Euphrates, in what is today called Iraq. It was not the kind of Foreign Legion desert that makes us think of palm trees and camels. No, it was a narrow little neck of land to the south and west

13

of them, which joined Asia to Africa. Today there is a canal on the part that is closer to Africa, the Suez Canal, near Egypt. "East of Suez"—you may be familiar with that phrase. Well, the land *immediately* east of Suez is a rocky peninsula called *Sinai*, where it's impossible to live. It was grim —it *is* grim. Something like Alcatraz, only miles and miles of it.

When Israel (the people of God, the bride) was in this rocky desert, the people grumbled terribly. They wanted to be back in pagan Egypt, where at least the water was fit to drink and they could eat meat regularly. Then God put their faith to the test at the rock where Moses struck his rod. Israel failed the test miserably!

GOD'S LOVE DID NOT FAIL THEM

Even then, God's love for his people would not let them down. Food fell from heaven—manna. There were quail. The people's worn clothes and battered footwear became like new. And for all of God's goodness to Israel, what did she do in return? The Israelites turned against the Lord, their strong lover; they turned against his servant, Moses, and made idols to worship. In general, the Israelites couldn't get off that rocky Sinai peninsula fast enough!

It's funny what changes the years will bring! The boy who used to whine about the cold water in the tub grows up to be the man who is forever praising its good influence on his character. In the same way, Israel centered all her loving memories on that desert stay of "forty years." The only way she could ever be "saved," that is, rebuilt as a people of God, was by acting out again her whole history as a people. She would be tested again as once she had been in the desert, but this time she would pass the test. She would cross over the Jordan River—as she did years ago

under Joshua—and come up out of the water of this same stream into the "promised land"—the "kingdom of God."

JOHN THE BAPTIST HAD A MESSAGE

Do you have the picture? Can you see now why John the Baptist had gone into the desert? John had everyone talking. For he went into the wasteland, dressed like the prophets of old, eating the same wild food. Why? Because the Lord would begin the work of saving his people *in the desert*. (The men of Judea who have left us the "Dead Sea scrolls" fled from the cities and towns of their time to live in the desert—for the same reason as John's).

Then a call came from God to John the Baptist, a call that came to no one else. John was to preach to all the people sorrow for sin and a complete change of heart—and he did. He gave them an *outward* sign, too, which showed that they meant to change *inwardly*. He led them into the Jordan where they were covered by the waters—and they came up out of the river, ready to hear about a new life in the "kingdom of God."

That is what John prophesied was coming upon them. He taught that the eighteen centuries of longing—since Abraham's time—were shortly to come to an end. And thousands of people believed him. It is more correct to say that the people believed God, and were convinced that John was a true prophet speaking in his name. (Mark 1:1-8)

THEN CAME THE NAZARENE

And then came Jesus: at first only an onlooker at the edge of the crowd. He had come to begin the work his Father sent him to do. Jesus came up to John, who recognized him and did *not* want to give him the sign of sorrow for sin—

15

the waters of the Jordan. But Jesus insisted. "And the heavens were torn apart" at the moment Jesus came up out of the water. The dove, a sign of God's Holy Spirit, hovered low over the waters, just as had happened at the creation of the world. The voice of God the Father was heard: "This is my Son, my beloved. My favor rests on him." (Mark 1:9-12)

Then Jesus was sent into the desert by the Spirit, where he put man's enemy, Satan, to flight by succeeding in the three tests where his people, Israel, had failed. He won a smashing victory in all three encounters because his trust was wholly in his Father.

You can look all of this up for yourself. First, read Saint Matthew's Gospel, starting with chapter 4. Then turn back to the Old Testament, to Deuteronomy 8:3 for Jesus' first answer; to 6:16 for his second; his third answer is found in 6:13.

THE END OF THE LINE,
THE GREATEST GIFT!

It is sometimes difficult to understand fully what our Savior said and did. Often it takes study, chiefly study of the Old Testament. One may even say that Jesus cannot be known— let alone loved and followed—unless we picture him as someone at the very end of a long story of God's love for men: the climax, the greatest gift.

One wonderful thing about the Bible is that you can find your own life story in it. It is the story of every man's life in miniature. The Old Testament is a story of growing up from infancy with never-ending favors done by a loving parent—and endless acts of ingratitude by a fickle and ungrateful people who take the parent for granted. The New Testament is an image of what we ought to be—ourselves at our potential best—just as Christ and the Church he founded is the people of God at its best.

16

BAPTISM 'CHRISTS' US

We are called *to be Christ,* in fact. That is the whole meaning of our baptism.

Our Jordan was the font in which we were baptized. The "land of promise" we are walking about in now is the Church, for God does not plan to give men any higher or better life on earth than life in the Church. For you, the question is: Has Satan challenged *you* in the desert yet? Not by little, everyday temptations that we can charge to weak nature, but by big ones—the kind that Israel and our Lord both endured. The temptation to pride, the temptation to satisfy every desire you experience. The temptation to trust in yourself, and not in God.

YOU ARE GOD'S BELOVED!
WHERE ARE YOU GOING?

You, since your baptism and confirmation, are God's beloved on whom his Spirit has descended. Are you well into your public life? What are you doing, for your part, to help save the world?

3

Jesus Calls His Disciples

Leadership is a funny thing. It's like charm in a woman, as Sir James M. Barrie says in one of his plays, *What Every Woman Knows:* you either have it, or you don't.

Some leaders show no air of self-importance—others are full of vanity. There are bullies among the leader class—and gentlemen. There are strong men—and cowards. Some attract all men equally—others make their point with a small "in-group" and through them influence others. Many of this second type are despised by the non-leaders, *but they follow them, all the same.*

JESUS THE LEADER

Jesus was in that select group of persons who could have a few intimate friends—say fifteen or so—yet never lose his personal appeal to thousands. Even now, you don't feel that *you* cannot be close to Jesus because John was such a good friend of his. The special relation of Jesus with Peter does not seem to interfere in the least with his relation to *me*.

Do you see what we're getting at? It's hard to define, but you meet a few persons in life who have this same gift. They seem to be able to *give themselves completely* to a *limitless number* of individuals—and not only while they are talking to them!

JESUS THE FRIEND

What we have just said seems to describe *friendship* as well as it does *leadership*. That's because a leader is a friend at his best. The fine feature about it is, there are certain areas —the things you are interested in, for example—where *he* follows *you*.

When we read the gospels with care, we immediately see something of the magnetic quality of Jesus' personality. It's true that he acquired a good number of close friends who had been ready-formed in piety by John the Baptist. These friends took religion seriously, eight or ten of them at least. They really cared! When John turned them over to Jesus they went to him direct. This gives us a good clue to the character of Jesus! Although at the moment he was an unknown, these new-found friends followed him immediately.

WHAT PEOPLE LOOKED FOR
IN JESUS

Remember, Jesus wasn't even from Judea, and it's hard to imagine the contempt the sophisticated people from the south (Judea) had for the bashful bumpkins (the "hicks") of the north
(Galilee). We have grown used to the idea that Jesus is of the
tribe of Juda and the house of David. We are also likely to think
that all pious Jews at the time of Christ were clear as to where
the Messia was to come from. Not at all! There were all sorts
of conflicting theories. The most commonly held was the "house
of David" theory, for the people thought he had to be a king.
Down along the Dead Sea, however, the monks of Qumrân
were expecting a "Messia of Israel and Aaron" (two!).

Some of the priests thought he had to be the son of a priest
(which Jesus wasn't). And to imagine that a descendant of David would successfully re-establish the throne—well, that was
as much expected from Galilee as that the next president of the
United States will be a Mississippi Negro. "Study the Scriptures and you will find that prophets do not come from Galilee."
(John 7:52) That was a well-known gibe, a bit of contempt,
which the Jerusalem leaders hurled at the Galileans. Most of the
twelve men Jesus chose as his apostles were from Galilee. Yet,
that did not keep Nathanael from wise-cracking, "Can any good
come from Nazareth?"

WHAT PEOPLE FOUND IN JESUS

New friends of the Nazarene left their families and their careers
to follow him! The only adequate explanation of this fact is the
personal pull which Jesus exerted on them. They were really
drawn to this man!

In the first place, he was mysterious. There was so much you
couldn't know about him. What could be known was admirable,

but there was so much more *to* this teacher! And no one could see it all on one visit, the way it had been with the Baptist. John dressed like a prophet, he ate like one, and his message was very close to that of an Isaia or a Jeremia. To hear him was to recognize his type immediately.

Jesus was different. He was a quiet type; not mousy, just quiet. An ordinary town-dweller, he wore the clothes of his time. He had no special badges of discipleship, no "campaign buttons" to give out, such as long fasts or assigned daily prayers. All Jesus did was look a man in the eye. If he thought he had the goods, he said, "Follow me." That didn't mean, "Walk this way." It meant, "Be of my company—ten, twenty years, a lifetime!" Jesus let them know that the reign of God they all awaited had arrived—and was somehow centered on him.

WHY PEOPLE FOLLOWED JESUS

When these people quit their work to follow Jesus, they weren't thinking of God's glory entirely. They meant to be right there when the major plums were given out. After all, he did choose twelve—and Israel had twelve tribes. They put two and two together and got *twelve:* jeweled thrones (they thought) on which they hoped to sit and judge their own people. Nice, high-minded motives!

You know what they got. Nights out under the stars without even a *foxhole.* (Funny that the bloody business of war should steal a term from the gospel of peace!) They walked forever, and they policed huge crowds, and they went hungry. He promised them even more when he asked, "Can you be drenched in the bath of suffering that I will be drenched in?" They said yes—and when they said it they probably meant it. (See Mark 10:38; Matthew 20:20-23).

HOW JESUS CALLED THE DISCIPLES

John, in the fourth gospel, is interesting when he tells how Jesus first called his disciples. It's at the end of the first chapter —but he skips all around Jesus' public career to make his point. First, the Baptist calls him "the lamb of God"—a title for the Messia in popular religious writing of that time. (See what wonderful use the Apocalypse makes of it, from 5:7 to the end of chapter 7). Andrew then calls him "Messia." Philip adds "the one spoken of by Moses in the Law and by the prophets." (Dt. 18; Is. 53) Nathanael reaches the climax: "Son of God," he says, "King of Israel." (Read John 1:36, 41, 45, 49).

Then Jesus answers this great litany of faith in him by naming the title he liked best of all, the one he gave so much meaning to: "Son of Man." (John 1:51)

You ask, what can this possibly mean to *me?* If you've been baptized—and confirmed—you might as well know the box you're in. "Can you be drenched in the bath of suffering that I will be drenched in?" he asks you! The trouble is, some of you have begun to realize all that he expects of you. You may not like it. Cheer up. You can run. (Three of his bravest did, in the garden). You can sell out. (No need to name the poor fool who did that "because he was a thief," John 12:6).

OR YOU CAN STAY AND FIGHT!

The plan to stick with Jesus has a good deal in its favor. "No man ever spoke as this man speaks," the crowds said. And they were right. Listen to him—just once! If all that he did were to be set down in detail, it's doubtful the whole world could hold the books that would need to be written—this is the thought that concludes the four gospels.

There is an even better reason for staying with him. You may not see heaven wide open, and angels going up and coming

down upon the Son of Man. But you'll gain a friend in him, at a time when you may need one desperately. Then a funny thing happens. You gain a whole lot more friends. People begin to look more and more like him.

It's no use to push this. You have to find out for yourself if it's true, or just something the four evangelists made up.

4

The First of Jesus' Signs

Why did Almighty God send his Son to us? God's reason for sending Jesus to us was that he wanted to speak to us.

God had spoken to his beloved people Israel many times before: through the forefathers of the nation—Abraham, Isaac and Jacob; through the great prophets, starting with Moses. After the prophets, he sent men of wisdom to speak a word of love to his people. These men wrote great religious songs like the psalms, and many wise sayings by which God hoped to make Israel a holy nation.

But the last and greatest Word he spoke to his people was his own Son—a Word clothed in the fullness of manhood—as the last gospel of the Mass says: "The Word was made flesh."

MANY WAYS OF 'SPEAKING'

We men have any number of ways in which we can get ideas across to one another. Spoken words are surely the commonest way. Written language comes high on the list. But even before writing, there is the gesture, the *sign*. A shrug, a rolling of the eyes, a finger drawn across the throat, can speak volumes. If there is some circumstance where we can't speak (like being behind the wings during a play), we act the whole thing out so as to get our meaning across. Have you ever seen someone go through a set of gestures which say, "Run upstairs and get the dishes for the second act"?

There is a game played with signs where you act something out in brief sketches to get your meaning across. You know it—it's called *charades*. Perhaps you've seen it played on television where, unfortunately, it isn't played very well. There, it's pretty much a case of making syllables with one's hands, the way deaf people do in sign language.

In a really clever game of charades, someone who is a good actor and has a quick mind does an entire short play, without words, to get across a book title or a witty saying. In this, husbands and wives should not be on opposite sides because they know each other's thoughts too well. Their minds work together and so it's a giveaway.

ISRAEL USED SIGNS,
ALMOST RIDDLES

In Old Testament times, the prophets used to act things out that way in order to teach the people. Sometimes they would use an object, like an almond tree or a frying pan or a clay pot. That seems strange to us. If we had something to say to thousands of people, we'd print it in the newspapers or go on television. We would say it directly, so that no one would miss our mean-

ing. The Israelites were different. They liked to speak with their hands and with their whole bodies. Above all, they liked to speak in *signs*, almost in riddles, to get their most important messages across.

JESUS, TOO, USED SIGNS

Are you getting the picture? And do you suppose that Jesus our Lord, who was the greatest of the prophets ("Nay, and more than a prophet," he once said of himself), would speak to God's people in a way entirely different than they were used to? Of course he wouldn't. Jesus worked signs to convey his meaning—just as did all those men before him whom God had sent with messages to the people.

Jesus spoke to his fellow Jews in a language of gesture which they understood as well as they did their own Aramaic speech. They knew very well what his signs *stood for*—oh, maybe not always right away, but after they had thought about them. They understood because they had nearly two thousand years of memories to draw on.

CHRIST'S REASONS FOR HIS FIRST SIGN

There is really little need to review the details of the first *sign* Christ worked at Cana, near his home town of Nazareth. You have been hearing of the miracle of the water-made-wine ever since you started going to Mass. Why did Jesus do it, besides wanting to show his power as the Son of God? He had several reasons: one, to do a kindness for the family that was embarrassed; then, to teach us something about the power of his mother's influence with him—that he finds it difficult or impossible to refuse a request from her; also, he wanted to teach his mother that she had to give him up now, to do his great

work. But the real reason he worked the sign at Cana is more important that all of these!

THE REAL MEANING OF THIS SIGN

Remember, Jesus worked this first sign at a wedding, or rather at the great feast of celebration that followed a wedding. The water Jesus changed was not just any water. It was found in *six* water jars (not *seven*, Israel's sacred number like the *Sabbath*—the seventh day—meaning the holiness of God). No, there were *six* jars—one short of perfection.

The water was there for the guests to wash their grimy hands, and their feet, dusty from the roads, before they dared to eat. This was part of strict religious custom, according to the Pharisees. So you see, the water jars were a *sign* of Israel's religion. They stood for the Law of Moses, as it was interpreted by the rabbis of Jesus' time.

When Christ changed the water into wine, therefore, he didn't only work a great miracle. He performed a *sign* that could have had a great deal of meaning for the onlookers, especially if they were looking for the "kingdom of God"—as we know his newly made fishermen friends were. Right before their eyes they saw the Law (the water) give way to the new teaching that he would give them (the fiery red wine). It was like saying outright that Christ considered himself superior to Moses, the great lawgiver.

Then remember, it took place at a wedding feast! Every pious Israelite knew that the wedding feast was the sign of a final union in love between God and his people. Israel was like his virgin bride. (Remember, we talked about the "bride" before, in an earlier chapter?) And when *this* great marriage banquet was celebrated, that would be the last age of the world.

'MY HOUR HAS NOT YET COME'

Long after the miracle had taken place, Jesus' disciples turned over in their minds every word of his, every glance. Was this, they wanted to know, the coming of God's kingdom in glory? It was—and at the same time it was not. "My hour has not yet come," he said quietly. Later, he would suffer for men's sins and be glorified. That would be his "hour."

But this day at Cana was indeed the beginning of the "last times." He was, after all, Israel's Messia, the only Son of his Father, come to save all men. He let his mother and his new friends know this by working a sign—a sign that meant that the long-expected "kingdom of God" had arrived.

NOT READING TOO MUCH,
ONLY SEEING WHAT'S THERE

Can we be sure of all this? It may seem like reading an awful lot into the story. Not really. It's only seeing in the story all that's there. Saint John gives us the clue by his solemn and mysterious ending: "This first of his signs Jesus did in Cana of Galilee. By it he revealed his glory and led his disciples to believe in him."

Those disciples didn't believe that Christ could work miracles —for they *saw* the miracle, and you don't believe what you *see*. No, what they began to *believe* in was his *glory*—and this, for the reporter John, meant his being glorified by his Father as the chief figure of the Last Days on the earth.

Israel's long awaited wedding feast (the sign of God's union in love with his people) had really begun in the person of this Jesus of Nazareth.

WHERE DO YOU COME IN?

Some of you who read these lines are married, and many will be. We could of course speak of that in connection with Cana. But this first of Jesus' signs was not worked for *some* of his followers, but for *all* of his followers.

What one meaning does it have for all of us? Chiefly this: *to believe in Christ is to let yourself be changed totally by God.*

Read that prayer in the offertory of the Mass, the one the priest says over the water as he pours a few drops into the wine. It's all about changing us into God, just as the Son of God was changed into one of us. What it means is that the eucharist can make an entirely new person out of us!

Have you ever thought of that? That at the Mass it is not only the bread and wine that is changed—but, most of all, *you yourself?* That means that every Mass is Cana—a happy feast between God and his people as bridegroom and bride.

All this the gospel is trying to say to us—if only we will let it.

5

Jesus Casts Out Demons

You might be surprised to learn how much Jesus had to do with the devils of hell! You might, that is, if you're not in the habit of reading the four gospels.

Open your New Testament to the Gospel according to Saint Mark—the second of the four gospels and the shortest one. The first half of it might almost be called a book about "casting out devils." Mark sometimes calls them "demons"—but more often his term for them is "unclean spirits."

MODERNS CALL HIM 'EMOTIONAL DISORDER'

It is important for us to know what place these terribly unhappy creatures hold in our belief as Christians. Nowadays very

few moderns except Christians—and not all Christians, at that—believe that there are any such thing as devils.

You will learn, if you haven't already heard it, that most modern people are satisfied that what used to be called "possession by demons" was really epilepsy or some serious mental illness. People were just ignorant in ancient times, the moderns say. The people in biblical times did not know how to explain all the strange behavior of sick people. Because they could not account for it otherwise, they blamed it on "devils"—that's what the moderns charge.

TOO MUCH, TOO LITTLE, BOTH DANGEROUS

That is one way to be wrong about demons: to disbelieve in them entirely. The other way—and this is just as much opposed to the faith of the Church—is to believe too much in devils. This usually takes the form of telling stories about "possession" which are like glorified ghost stories. In a way—though the teller usually doesn't know this—multiplying these tales takes for granted that Christ hasn't really broken the power of Satan by his death and resurrection.

You remember the task we set ourselves at the beginning of this book, don't you? We said we would look into those events in Jesus' life that were especially important to him, and to the disciples who wrote about him. These are the things that have to be important to us—even though we haven't heard of them before, even though they sound a bit queer the first time we do hear of them.

IMPORTANT TO UNDERSTAND
THE DEVIL

That portion of the gospels about demons is extremely important. We *must* understand it if we are to get the full message of the Master about the work he came to do.

Jesus, you see, is holiness itself. In the gospels, that is the clearest fact about him. He is holy with the holiness of God!

Now, ever since the people we call Israel had known their God (and the "Lord"—which was their special name for him—was a holy God from the very first), they'd had some idea of the opposite to holiness: a terrifying, dark someone whom the Bible calls "the adversary." The Hebrew word is "Satan"—a creature who is "set against" God.

EVIL IS A PERSON, NOT A THING

The first parts of the Bible to be written are not clear on him at all. All sorts of vague and uncertain statements are made in the earliest portions of Scripture about the force of evil. What *does* become clearer and clearer, as the Bible period continues, is that evil isn't only a *thing*, it is a *person*. Rather, it is persons without number, who once were with God, but who now are against him.

All this supposedly happened long before there were any men on the earth. The first one to make clear what happened between God and the angels was the Christian author of the Book of the Apocalypse (the last book in the Bible). He tells, in his chapter 12, about a mighty struggle in heaven between the archangel Michael, and the proud angel "Satan or the devil" and his disobedient followers. "This is the hour of victory for our God, of his power and royal rule, when his Christ wins the mastery, for the accuser of our brothers has been hurled down,

33

he who accused them before our God day and night." (Apocalypse 12:10)

JESUS BROUGHT FREEDOM
FROM FEAR

In our Lord's time, even though the Bible hadn't much to say about devils, the common people lived in deadly fear of them. When Jesus came, he made it his business to set them free from many fears and superstitions. Every word he spoke removed another burden that their religion teachers had put on their backs.

Jesus would say, "This is what the Scriptures say . . . but this is what I say." What *he* said was what the Scriptures really meant. The Scriptures had always meant love and obedience, never a set of back-breaking rules and regulations. It is strange, but that is what the rabbis of Jesus' time had made of the Law which was given to their fathers out of love on Mount Sinai.

For all these reasons you might expect Jesus to say, if it were true: "The Scriptures seem to be describing certain evil spirits who hate God and hate men. Actually, though, this is just a manner of speaking. Like so many of the 'traditions' of the Pharisees, this idea of devils is only a human invention that has grown beyond all bounds. There aren't any devils: that's just a way of describing ignorance and fear and superstition."

CHRIST RECOGNIZED THE DEVIL;
DEVILS WERE FALLEN ANGELS

Did Jesus say that? He said nothing of the sort. He dealt with some of the sick whom he cured as if they were precisely that: sick men. With others, he acted quite differently. He did not speak directly to the sick person, but to other individuals, to

wicked spirits who were dwelling inside the sick. Jesus never stopped to argue with these unclean spirits. He simply commanded them to go, and to leave the sick person in peace.

When Jesus spoke to the demons, Israel had its first absolute certainty that evil was real in the person of fallen angels.

That may sound strange to us, but it is quite true. Remember, the people of God were uncertain about a great number of things until God's own Son came to earth. If you read about the sin of Adam and Eve in the garden (chapters 2 and 3 in Genesis), you will see that evil is described there under the form of a snake—the great sign, for ancient Israel, of heathen religion, that is, all that is opposed to God.

This uncertainty about who or what evil, or the evil one, was, continues all through the holy books. You find "Satan" mentioned—in the book of Job and in the prophet Zacharia, *but only Jesus settles the problem finally*. He is the first one to give us complete certainty about the devil.

DEVILS CAN'T TOLERATE HOLINESS

God has an ancient enemy, Jesus teaches us, who is also man's enemy. The "Son of Man," as our Lord loved to call himself, comes from heaven to break the power of this evil one. The very first service he does is to *identify* him. The devil really *is*. Let there be no mistake about that!

Secondly, the devil's hold over men is broken because he cannot accept the fact, he cannot stand it, that one of these men, one of these creatures whom he despises, is holiness itself! "What have we to do with you!" they shriek. They call him "the holy one of God"—a truth that not even people of good will were yet able to say about him. Jesus' tone is firm—and final. "Go out of him!"

JESUS CALLED SATAN
LIAR, MURDERER

Really, it's great to see what Jesus thinks of Satan. He calls him a liar (remember the lie the serpent told Eve?) and a murderer (recall the story of Cain?) from the beginning. Jesus has no fear of the devil, nor respect for him. He despises him. Once when dozens of his disciples returned to him in high spirits, after casting out demons in his name, Jesus said, "Yes, I was watching Satan fall, like lightning out of the sky." (Luke 10:18)

When we pray the great prayer of Christ's saving death on Good Friday, we say a wonderful thing. We rejoice: "He has broken the serpent's tooth of hell!"

HAVE YOU MET HATRED FOR GOD?

How about you? What does it all mean to you? Perhaps you recall your first experience of evil, and it made you sick. We don't mean by committing evil—that's too awful to think of; but the shocking mystery of deep hatred or disregard for God!

Have you run into that yet? It can take any number of forms, like the dirty-picture industry: those people who make millions by trying to destroy the image of God that exists in man. They turn man into not just an animal but into something that is a mockery of human or animal existence.

Something else you may have known at first hand is slow, burning jealousy: the kind that destroys everything it touches. Another face of evil is hatred between two persons who would rid the earth of each other if they thought they could. They're too superstitious, or too afraid of punishment, to kill—so they just hate.

Maybe what's bothering you is a bad habit that *looks* like evil. It has an ugly face, and it's all around you. You've tried everything you could to be rid of it, but it keeps cropping up

again no matter what you do. You may be tempted at times to lose hope. You say, "I don't need any explanation about the devil. He seems to be everywhere I turn."

That is why it is important to know what the gospels tell us about Jesus and the demons. *He has defeated them, smashed their offensive—right, left and center!*

JESUS LIVES IN US!
CHRIST CONQUERS!

What's important to keep in mind is that, ever since our baptism, Satan has been put to flight before us. Jesus lives in us. Every time we take holy water we recall that we have been made new in Jesus Christ. "If God is with us, who can be against us?" Saint Paul asks.

Be fearful about the power of evil to destroy us, yes, but most of all, have an utter contempt for it, because the great gift Jesus brought us was the forgiveness of sin. Satan is finished— *kaput*—all washed up! Christ conquers! Christ rules! Christ is in command!

6

Jesus Returns to Nazareth

One of the hardest things about growing up is that not everybody does it at the same time. (If they did, that would make matters even worse!) As it is, young people don't seem to know how their parents think. And this is every bit as true in reverse: parents would take a rocket trip to the moon if they thought they could find out there how their children think.

When you get right down to it, the big gap in life is not so much between youth and middle age, as between two quite different ways of looking at things. Just glance around you and see if that isn't so.

A quick glance at the "laws of the heart," and you see how true it is that age doesn't really make the big division in life. It isn't money, either, or brains. The real difference is a matter

of "outlook," for lack of a better word: our way of thinking about God, and other people, and the world in general.

Doesn't it seem to you that people who think exactly as you do are fairly few? You *seem* to be on the same wave length as dozens of others. But deep down inside you, if you'll admit the truth, you know that there are only about half a dozen persons in the world who seem to understand you.

JESUS HAD THE SAME PROBLEM

Because this business of understanding one another is so vital, it's a comfort to know that, when God's Son became man, he had the same problem as everybody else. Jesus had it much more, in fact, because his idea of what the savior of the world should be (the only right idea on this subject) and everyone else's idea were a world apart. You may say that the reason Jesus came to earth was to make his idea of "salvation" everyone else's.

At the start, very few people knew what Christ meant when he said that God's kingdom had already come. In particular, his own family members did not understand him; and that is a hard fact for *us* to understand.

The gospels give the names of four of Christ's kinsmen ("brothers" is the ancient name for close relatives). They are called James and Joses, Simon and Jude. There are women cousins in the family, too, but we don't have their names.

JESUS WAS THE 'ODD' COUSIN

We don't suppose it's true of all of them, but some at least had no sympathy whatever for this "odd" cousin of theirs. Even poor Mary, his mother, who loved and trusted him perfectly, is dragged along with them. Women in those days didn't assert their rights the way they do now. Mary was probably

just glad to get a look at this good son of hers—whom she wasn't seeing much of any more.

When Jesus came home to his own town of Nazareth things reached the worst pass of all. His own townsmen tried to take his life! He managed to escape them, though. Unbelievable, did you say? No, not really. You see, Jesus had a bad habit of telling the whole truth to people at the time they were worst prepared to take it in. It was always the right time, of course. Jesus was no fool, and he was never merely argumentative. When he argued, his arguments were always based on his thoughts, never on his temper or his prejudices. And he sailed right in! Good grief (as Charlie Brown would say), but he had nerve!

JESUS PAID THE PRICE!

He paid the price, of course. Everybody who has both brains and guts pays the price. What we mean to say is, "they get you in the end." That isn't just being cynical but factual. They do—the *they* being people who have neither brains *nor* guts, or one but not the other. If, besides these two qualities of intelligence and nerve, you have goodness as well (when you're good all the time and on principle we call it "virtue")—the opposition is just *sure* to get you somehow.

Jesus had the keenest human intelligence God ever gave a man. He had a nerve like steel, and holiness higher than that of all the saints and angels together. Notice how we keep speaking of his human qualities. That is most important.

CHRIST SAVED US THROUGH HIS MANHOOD

Even though Christ is God's only Son and in every sense equal to the Father, it is through his holy manhood that he saves us. Don't ever lose sight of that great Catholic truth. It is all too easy to do just that. He wouldn't have all those human gifts

40

unless he were the Son of God. But because he has them, we call him brother, and savior, and Lord.

That's what makes everything easier. When your own older brother has been through every suffering before you—suffering which you are enduring now; when you know how much more he had to take than you, because he was so much holier and brighter than the people who couldn't understand him—then you can put up with a lot!

This is especially true when your own family doesn't understand you. We're not talking, for the moment, about all those thousands of selfish people who want to have everything in life their own way. We're talking about those cases where a person wants to be a perfect disciple of Christ, wants to *go all out* for him—but the people he lives with daily don't seem to have any idea of what he is getting at. The cases that are sadder still are those where family or friends *do* know, *are* aware—and oppose this kind of life bitterly.

DOES YOUR FAMILY UNDERSTAND?

Making fun of the other fellow is the big weapon of hurt pride. "Who does she think she is, running off to Mass all the time!" That's known as the gentle-sneer approach. Another is the deep-dig-direct: "I may not be much on religion because I'm earning food and clothes for the lot of you. But believe me, my religion is as good as yours, and if you ask me a damn' sight better." Fact is you hadn't asked him. He's very dear to you. You had just hoped with all your strength that he would understand the ideals you're trying to live by.

'I AM THAT MAN'

"So he came to Nazareth, where he had been brought up," Saint Luke writes. (4:16) First, he went to the synagogue on

41

the Sabbath, as he regularly did. Nothing new about that. Then he asked the man in charge of the service to hand him the scroll. Again, nothing new. He read from the prophet Isaia, chapter 61, at the beginning of the chapter.

It was all about someone whom the Lord would anoint with oil, so that he could spread the good news to the poor—those depressed and deprived people who had no earthly hope in this world. This "someone" on whom the Spirit of the Lord rested was going to let the prisoners out of jails, give sight back to the blind, and let the broken victims of tyrants go free.

"I am that man," said Jesus. "This text has come true in your hearing this day."

GOD BELONGS TO EVERYBODY!

Well, they all hoped that "someone" would make Isaia's prophecy come true. Jesus was a local boy: "the carpenter's son," they called him. Their first feeling was one of surprise—not anger. *What, then, turned them against him?* As we've said before, he sailed right into them. He reminded them that being a Nazarene was nothing; indeed, being an Israelite was nothing. *What really mattered was the free choice of a holy God.*

Jesus told them a couple of stories to make his point— stories about the days of the prophets Elia and Elisha. In both stories, God worked wonders not for Israelites but for Gentiles: people from Phoenicia (the widow of Sarepta, whose son the Lord restored to life) and from Syria (the general of the king's army, Naaman). Our Lord's point is that God helps *whom* he wants to *when* he wants to. No one can say, "That isn't fair," because *he* is the Lord.

In the same way, Jesus said, Nazareth shouldn't expect to see him work the miracles he had done in the neighboring towns, on some sort of "native-son" principle. God is not committed to geography, nor to home ties, nor to Jewish blood. He is ab-

solutely supreme over everyone and everything, and he is a holy Lord.

IS IT A SIN TO BE DIFFERENT?

And there, it seems, is where most of the trouble lies when you try to follow Christ very closely. The first thing you know, you're not doing what everyone else on the block is doing. You become different! And being different is the one "sin" people can't stand: not being a carbon copy of themselves.

The next step after that is, you're supposed to consider yourself *better* than everyone else. You never said that for a minute. You never thought it, in fact. They say it.

What can you do about it? Probably nothing. Like Jesus himself, you have to follow your clear call from God—and take your lumps.

It would be pleasant to report that, after a while, everyone will begin to understand you, and to love you. Some will. Not all, though. In fact, not many.

WISECRACKS DID NOT FAZE JESUS —DO YOU TAKE THEM IN STRIDE?

But Jesus didn't let rebuffs from his neighbors and townsmen bother him too much. He didn't let wisecracks or the opinions of men stand in the way of his carrying out the great mission God had sent him to earth to accomplish. He kept right on doing his Father's will. So should you, so should we all!

7

The Enemies of Jesus

The four gospels are filled with mysteries. In the last chapter we were speaking about Jesus' being rejected by his own family and townspeople. Before that we dwelt on the dark mystery of evil, especially as it is reflected in the evil wills of the "unclean spirits"—the devils of hell.

MOST MYSTERIOUS OF ALL!

But perhaps the most mysterious thing of all about the earthly life of Jesus is the way it ended, and why it ended as it did. Not even his closest friends were prepared for that. If we were to read the gospels for the first time, without knowing their ending, it is very unlikely that we would be prepared for the climax.

It was God's will, of course, that Jesus should die for the sins of men. Now, no human mind can fathom the depths of God's love for us and all that he means to do out of that love. It will always remain a mystery why Christ died—it's as mysterious as God himself. But at still another level, the level of human motives and the like, the violent end of Jesus is almost an equally great mystery.

WHY DID THEY TURN ON CHRIST?
WAS IT HIS POPULARITY?

Consider this: Jesus was an extremely popular person. Despite the fickleness of all crowds everywhere, he could not have lost his hold on the people completely in a matter of weeks or days. The common people listened to him willingly, the gospel says. (See John 7:31) They marveled at him at every turn. "No one ever spoke the way this man speaks." (John 7:46) He was not accepted at home by his own people, it is true (Mark 6:5-6), but strangers thought he was great!

The reason for this popularity? Christ represented for them a hope they had never had before. He told them they were worth something. These poor, "marginal" farmers who could scarcely raise enough food to eat, these day-laborers with crooked backs who hadn't a single decent day in prospect this side of the grave, began to think that maybe life had some meaning for them after all.

It wasn't that he promised them riches, or even freedom, the way a modern leader of downtrodden peoples might do. He didn't seem to care a fig for economics or politics as solutions to their problems. All he cared about was these people *as persons:* the poor. And they cared for him in return *so much* that the four gospel writers could scarcely express it in words. Some of the popular demonstration of affection was selfish and self-seeking, but much of it was genuine.

45

HIS ENEMIES WERE NOT
THE CROWDS

Another thing that kept happening—in a way it *had* to happen
—was that Jesus told the crowds they hadn't much to hope for
from their religious leaders. You see, he was terribly interested
in religion as something of the *head* and *heart*, but the religious
leaders of that time were strong for it as a thing of *prestige* and
pocketbook. They were not only doing *good* at religion; they
were doing *well*. The leader class was riding high. Jesus represented a popular threat to them on two fronts: that of *power*,
and that of *income*.

HIS ENEMIES WERE THE 'DICTATORS'

Those are the two threats no dictator can stand. That is why
Castro in Cuba, or Kadar in Hungary, or name-your-strongman
always tries to put religion out of business. First he tries to
make it work for *him*. (The Chinese "People's Republic" is
playing it that way; so is the Communist régime in Poland).
When this doesn't work, the dictator moves in. He shuts the
churches, closes the schools, seizes the properties. *The one thing
he can't stand is opposition*. When he can't *buy* the opposition,
he *crushes* it.

'OFFICIAL RELIGION'
WAS DICTATING

It isn't always the case that religion is the *victim*, however. Sometimes religion itself is the *dictator*, and ordinary people are the victims.

In our Lord's time it was *official* religion that couldn't stand the opposition of real religion which Jesus represented. It tried to silence the voice of the greatest of God's spokesmen, his Son. Because the leader class in official religious circles couldn't silence him, it turned murderer like Cain.

BETTER THAT ONE MAN
SHOULD DIE?

But the blood of Jesus cried out from the ground, like innocent Abel's. Cain's question had been, "Am I my brother's keeper?" (Genesis 4:9) The high priests and the scholarly "doctors of the Law" decided that their answer to this question should be "No." Or rather, after keeping a good eye out for

themselves, they chose to be the keeper of every Jewish brother they had—except Jesus of Nazareth. They said, "It is better that one man should die [that a little blood should flow, in other words] than that the Romans should come and take away our holy place and our nation." They made it a clear choice between the temple area in Jerusalem and the power they wielded within it, and a just man. Justice lost!

IT WAS MONEY—BUT NOT ONLY MONEY

Oh, they might have carried on at the temple with Jesus the victor over them, but they had the grim prospect of seeing their revenues shrinking to almost nothing. After all, hadn't he said once that the time would come when people wouldn't worship in Jerusalem any more, but "in spirit and in truth?" (John 4:24) What's the "percentage" in a religion like that? the leaders figured.

The other thing that infuriated them was that Jesus, in his talks to the crowds, spoke of the leaders' evil lives, and they knew it. He made fun of their spirit of unbearable self-importance. He described them as a pit of snakes; as the filthy, buggy underside of a stinking tomb. (See Matthew 23: 33, 27).

HOW TO LOSE FRIENDS AND ALIENATE PEOPLE

There's a lesson for you in how to lose friends and alienate people! Jesus didn't care a bit. He had come to bear witness to the truth and he couldn't rest until the job was done. His enemies—the rich and powerful elements in organized religion—were ready to murder him after his first few public talks, but they knew they had to go slowly, slowly, for fear of the crowds. The crowds had a sort of natural instinct for the truth, and

when they came face to face with truth in the form of a Man, many of them threw in their lot with him for good. (John 7:40) "I will follow you wherever you go" (Luke 9:57), one man said.

DICTATORS KNEW INSECURITY THEN; WE HEAR MUCH OF IT TODAY!

The priests and the lawyers didn't dare finish him off early and so they watched—and waited. The man of passion will kill in a blind rage. The cool, crafty hater takes his time. He can wait. When the enemies of Jesus thought they had waited long enough, they sprang. (Matthew 26:3-5) Being natural cowards, of course, they used the services of one of his friends as an informer. (Vv. 14-16)

Nowadays we talk about "insecurity" quite a bit. The court psychiatrist will prove how this man steals cars and that one molests girls because neither was brought up properly. The offender had parents who neglected him or helped warp his character. They never made him feel sure of himself in a normal human way, and so he took steps on his own. He went to great lengths of crime or violence to prove that as an individual in his own right he could *do* things, like anyone else.

There seems to be quite a lot to this theory. You've known some pretty warped characters in your day, haven't you? What their trouble frequently seems to come down to is *insecurity*. It is fairly clear that the Jerusalem gang of bully-boys had a bad case of it. They were not on God's side because their prayer lives had dried up long ago. Their temple-sacrifices had become empty ritual, strictly a matter of profit and loss.

THERE'S NO SECURITY
WITHOUT GOD!

The Old Testament prayers called the psalms say that a good man's strength is the Lord. All his security should be in him. But that was far from the case with the priests and the scribes and their different hangers-on. They trusted chiefly in the coin of the realm. Another thing that gave them a feeling of security was pride of ancestry: descent from Abraham, Isaac and Jacob, from Moses and all the prophets (whom their forefathers had murdered, as Jesus somewhat tactlessly reminded them). In a word, they were insecure because they didn't possess the living God—only toys and trinkets, like money and the blood of Abraham. (See John 8:33).

'I COME TO MAKE ALL THINGS NEW'

When Jesus came along he threatened it all, and they panicked. He not only made them quake at the thought of losing their own spot in the local universe, he let them know that *true religion was about to be shared with the Gentiles.* For eighteen centuries, God had performed his mighty acts in the midst of his own people—tiny Israel, his chosen. The Lord God began to say through Jesus his beloved Son that her uniqueness of privilege was at an end.

The prophet Isaia had promised it, and now it was coming true: the *new temple* was to be a house of God *for all peoples.* (Isaia 56:7) A *new sacrifice* would be offered from this time forward, not just in Jerusalem, but from sunrise to sunset throughout the world. (Malachia 1:11) *A new creation*, a royal race of priests from every nation under heaven, would do in spirit (that means, taken at its fullest, in the Holy Spirit) what the sons of Levi did in the blood of goats and heifers.

In a word, the true religion was branching out. It was

going to have a place *for all men of good will* everywhere. It was going to have no place whatever for the greedy power élite, into whose hands it had fallen as almost a private possession. As Jesus put it in one of his stories, the owner of the vineyard was going to come and take the property away and put it in other, worthier hands. (Matthew 21:41)

CHRISTIANITY KNOWS NO BARRIERS

That is the way things are from now until the end, when Jesus returns in the glory. Christianity means bigness, broadness; no frontiers of the mind or of the human spirit. To be the enemy of Christ means to have a heart full of barriers. Really, the correct spelling is "barrier$," for that's the highest one of all.

51

8

The Friends of Jesus

The proverb says, "You can choose your friends, but you can't choose your relations."

Choosing our friends is an important part of growing up. If we are truly mature, no matter what our age, we tend to select as friends people who will bring out the best in us. When young people tag along with a fast crowd (they like to think they're *with* them because they're wanted, but it's really "tagging along"), parents begin to get nervous. It isn't only that they panic at the thought of drag-strips, or cruising around all night whistling at girls. (Dressing to be whistled at?) That *does* give parents something to think about, but those bits of foolish behavior are only symptoms of a deeper-lying condition known as "immaturity."

IT'S A STATE OF MIND

There should be no misunderstanding here. Losing one's life in a highway crash or forefeiting one's chastity isn't to be dismissed airily as "only a symptom." Each has something pretty final about it. But *the state of mind that leads up to these tragedies,* or any other you may care to name, *is the underlying cause of them.* If the Christian can be rid of that state of mind (or avoid ever acquiring it), then *life will be a simpler, happier business all around.*

IT WORKS BOTH WAYS

Getting to be mature is the remedy for immaturity. The pattern of our friendships is both the sign that maturity is taking place and the best guarantee that it will take place. If that sounds like a roundabout sentence, it's because the whole thing is a roundabout process. Our friends help us to grow up; yet we pick good friends only if we're already in the process of growing up.

Sometimes we pick friends who don't look like such a good bet to help anybody—themselves or us—but they turn out to be good friends and good for all concerned. Why so?

CONFIDENCE IN FRIENDS HELPS

Well, because we figured things out right; because we could see good qualities in them that others couldn't pick out, qualities that perhaps hadn't begun to develop much yet. We made an act of faith in them as possible good friends, and by the very confidence we showed, we helped bring about a change in them. It also proved to be a good thing for us, this business of working to bring about a change.

53

THE 'MASTER' WAS MATURITY ITSELF;
CHRIST RESPECTED EVERYONE HE MET

Let's give a look at the pattern of friendships in Jesus' life. We have to start by recognizing how mature he was from the beginning. It isn't just that Christ was a man of thirty-odd years when we first meet him. He was fully mature in ways that a great many people of that age are not. Self-composed, thoughtful, prayerful; "outgoing," extremely interested in the well-being of others—all these things Jesus of Nazareth was. They add up to being mentally and emotionally mature.

Notice in the gospels how much respect he shows for everyone he meets. There is one great exception: he is blistering with phonies and frauds! With everyone else he is fairly stern —or serious, if *stern* is too strong a word. *But he meets them on a man-to-man basis that is calculated to bring out the best that is in them.*

THEY WEREN'T 'THE PIOUS TYPE'

Take, for example, the fishermen whom he recruits as his disciples early. They aren't pious types by Pharisee standards or the standards of the scribes—those members of the Pharisee party who knew the Scriptures inside out. Look at Simon and his brother Andrew, and the other brother-combination, James and John: none of the four could be called "learned in the Law." But they were pious in another way, in that they "looked for the kingdom of God."

There was a good bit of self-seeking in it. They hoped that Israel would triumph over all her enemies, and that they would be there for the final "kill," so to say. Still, they had left much behind them to follow the preaching of John the Baptist. He was down along the Jordan's banks in Judea, to

the south, whereas their home place was to the north by almost a hundred mountainy miles.

That switch couldn't have been easy, especially when what awaited them at the end of their journey was a good, stiff going-over by John, a man who preached a hard life and a total change of outlook. Jesus picked them as his friends because they were already men of action and men of decision who had a basically religious view of life.

They were a pretty immature crowd, though. Petty, that is to say. You remember Nathanael's famous sneer, "Can anything good come from Nazareth?" He himself was probably from Cana, just a few miles away. *Big* deal! It was all Squaresville, Galilee, no matter how you looked at it, but Jesus paid no attention to this provincialism of the mind. He was fishing for men who would really mature and amount to something, and he knew he had come across a few good types.

FAULTS EVEN IN YOUR BEST FRIENDS?

Sometimes they nearly drove Christ crazy with their bickering and their self-interest. He came down from the mountain where his face and his whole body had shone for a brief moment with heavenly glory, and he ran into a lack of faith in his own friends that prevented the Father from working a cure. (Mark 9:14-29) Even on the home stretch—on their way to Jerusalem to see him suffer and die—two of them began a silly, schoolboy quarrel over who would sit on his right hand and who on his left in "the kingdom." (Mark 10:35-40)

This underlines the fact that we all encounter curious weak spots in the character of even the best of our friends. We then have to decide whether they are worthy of our continuing friendship. If they are, why we keep on working at helping them to mature. Quite unlike Jesus, we are helped to become

55

more complete human beings by helping them. It is a mutual self-help process.

FRIENDSHIP NEEDS TO BE WORKED AT

This doesn't mean that we have "snobism" as a goal. It just points out the fact that friendship is a very special thing that needs to be worked at hard. Having everyone as a brother in Christ is a goal for all of us. To make friends of a special few, though, is a life work for everyone.

The unique thing about our Lord is that he can make a special, close friend out of millions and millions of people who have been baptized into him. No one else can do that. That is because no one has a heart with the capacity his has.

JESUS HAD 'BAD-RISK' FRIENDS

The other type of person that "the carpenter, the son of Mary" (Mark 6:3) attracted to himself was the rag, tag and bobtail sort that didn't make the social register. The Samaritan woman at Jacob's well embarrassed the disciples into silence when they came back from buying food in Sichar. (John 4:27) They got her number fast. There were tight-fisted tax collectors ("gougers," actually, not professional men who did a professional job; see Luke 5:29-32). There were people who hadn't been to synagogue service or to the temple for a pilgrimage feast for years. (John 7:49) Then there were the people of thoroughly mixed up lives who had got themselves in the mess of making a living from the mystery of sex. (Luke 7:36-39)

The men of Jesus' day who were officially "good"—who swung morality about like a club, rather than held it in awe for the gift of God that it was—couldn't understand how Jesus could make friends from people such as these. Their

trouble was, they didn't know what holiness meant. Therefore, they couldn't see how he, who was all-holy, could purify those he came close to *just by being near them*, if only they would let it happen.

BEING CLOSE TO HIM CHANGES US

Perhaps that is the one thing we need to know most about the friendship of Jesus: it can burn away our sins and our shortcomings completely, it can change us into different persons —if we'll let it.

DO YOU EVER FEEL JUST 'NO GOOD'?

The things that discourage most of us aren't the sins of the "sinners" in the gospel. They may not even be the sins that every normal person is supposed to know all about and be troubled by. All right, so much the better for us. But every single one of us does want to throw in the sponge at some time or other because of sheer discouragement at being weak, or unimportant, or just "no good."

That's the time to remember that *our real importance lies outside ourselves.* We are holy because Someone who is holy loves us, and the love he bears us makes a change in us. In other words, because we have a friend in Jesus, nothing need ever be quite the same again. We can even come to experience a strength and holiness in ourselves by which we are able to be of help to others who are weak.

They badly need the friendship of Jesus Christ. *Will you bring it to them?*

9

The Mother of Jesus

It is part of Catholic faith to honor Mary as the mother
of God. It is part of Catholic piety to hail her as the holiest
of the saints of the Most High. She is our chief friend and
helper in that heavenly company. As Queen of Heaven, she
is high above the angels, too.

OUR LADY IS NOT INDEPENDENT,
HER MEANING IS THROUGH CHRIST

There is no belief about the Virgin Mother that is not very
much a part of our belief about her Son. The "mystery of
Christ" includes the mystery of Mary. That means that, in
God's plan to save us, Mary has no independent place. She

is forever someone who has meaning only in light of the work of her Son, Jesus, as our high priest. He is the one and only person who acts as a link between God and the human race. His mother is never far from him as he fulfills his unique role.

Jesus Christ is the great offerer of himself, whole and entire, to God. Mary, however, is the one who provided him with his human frame and form. Therefore, it is right to say that much of what he gives to God as our priest he got from God through her.

TO BE INTIMATE WITH CHRIST,
THE 'MARY PATTERN' IS A MUST

Mary also is a "giver," along with Jesus, in the sense that his self-giving (or "sacrifice") is the model for hers and our complete giving over of self to God. No one—absolutely no one —can be in the intimate personal relation with Jesus that each of us is called to, without patterning himself on Mary, the first believer. He alone is the way, but she directs us in following along this way. If we do follow, then what is offered to God is not Jesus only but "the whole Christ," he and we together.

MARY IS SO OFTEN MISREPRESENTED;
SHE IS A PART OF OUR REDEMPTION

A little instruction on the mother of Jesus seems necessary because we daily come across such soupy—and downright questionable—teaching about her in Catholic writing. There come to mind immediately several devotional journals on our Lady that enter Catholic homes, only because the publishers managed to get the householders' names and won't "let up." The difficulty is that, while Mary is always presented in

them in a mother-and-son relationship, she seldom appears in the context of the whole mystery of our redemption.

MARY IS NOT BY NATURE ONE WITH GOD; SHE IS BY NATURE ONE WITH US

It is God the Father who saves us through his Son, in unity of the Holy Spirit. In this work of God, the three are inseparably one. They are the great God who saves. They cannot have a human creature allied with them, so to say, in this work of saving men—except the one human creature that stands in a unique and special relation to the second person, or Son, whom we call the Word. *That creature is the human body and soul of Jesus.*

Now, the body and soul of Mary, despite the closeness in words and deeds and mannerisms to her Son, is not something that can be identified by nature with the work of God to save us. No, our Lady is forever aligned with us, because she is forever a creature of God who needs saving like everybody else.

Another way to put this is to say that God is joined to no human creature so closely as he is to the body and soul of Christ in the mystery we call the "incarnation." (That word means simply, "taking human nature").

BAPTISM RELATES US CLOSELY TO GOD, BUT MARY'S RELATIONSHIP IS UNIQUE

But—and this is a big and important *but*—of all the cases where God has come especially close to creatures by showing his choice and affection for them, he has never come closer to anyone than to Mary. Sometimes, because of her part in the mystery of the incarnation, we call her the daughter of

the Father, the mother of the Son and the bride of the Holy Spirit. That is surely a correct way to speak of Mary.

The same cannot be said of any other Christian. Yet, of each one of us, it can and must be said that, at our baptism, we came into a distinct relation of love with each of the three persons in God. In the case of no two human beings is that relationship identical. Just as you and your brother or sister mean something different to each of your parents (and they to you)—though there's love in all directions—so you stand in a relation to Father, Son and Spirit that is *like* our Lady's, but *by no means the same* as hers.

WHAT MAKES THE BIG DIFFERENCE? GOD'S CHOICE—MARY'S ANSWER

What makes the difference? Two things: God's choice of her, and her response. First, he did not pick you out for the same role as Mary in the work of our salvation. She was given the more important task, you the lesser one. Yet if either you or Mary were to fail, it could be said that God's plan to save us had failed, in greater or lesser degree.

Second, given the fact of the difference in "vocations" (i.e., different work to do, different call from God), there is another major unlikeness between the mother of God and you. When we say "you," we mean everyone who ever lived, since no one has ever given so generous a "yes" to God as Mary since he began issuing calls to man to make man holy.

TWO KINDS OF VOCATIONS: A *GENERAL,* AND A *SPECIAL* VOCATION

A vocation is a very common thing in life. Everyone has one. The call is not issued to each one of us to be a priest, the father of five, a day-laborer and an insurance salesman, all at the

same time. The rule is, of course: different roles in the work of our salvation, different calls.

The four listed above are special vocations. The general vocation issued to all Christians—indeed to all men, if we carry out Christ's missionary command—is a call to holiness *in Christ*. The Father issues it. The Holy Spirit makes its acceptance possible. Every man is free not to answer it, but such a man is properly termed a fool if he understands it and turns his back on it.

MOTHERHOOD AND VIRGINITY!
SUFFERING AND HUMILIATION

How did Mary receive her vocation? You know the steps, surely. First, she was born into a holy nation, a priestly people. Then came the vocation to marry Joseph. After that, the angel's message, and with it, a call to two roles that seemed to cancel each other out—motherhood, and virginity. Mary couldn't understand this. No one can. But because it was God who issued the call, she said, "Let it be done." (Read Saint Luke's gospel, 1:26-38).

Her next call was to suffer deeply over the loss of her young Son. (Luke 2:41-52) When he grew up and left his home, going off to preach about his Father, he once told a crowd of people who had reported to him that his mother and his brothers were waiting outside, that doing his Father's will was a greater and more important thing than being related to Jesus. (Matthew 12:46-50)

SCRIPTURAL REFERENCES TO OUR LADY PUZZLE US; 'A SWORD SHALL PIERCE . . .'

On another occasion, Jesus had a perfect opportunity to join a woman in praise of his mother. Instead, he turned it into praise of anyone who heard the word of God and kept it. (Luke 11:27-28)

These references to Mary in the gospel are very puzzling to us. They certainly do fulfill, however, what the old man Simeon said would happen to her: "A sword shall pierce your own soul, so that the thoughts of many hearts may be revealed." (Luke 2:35)

IS DISCOURAGEMENT THE SWORD THAT 'PIERCES' YOUR HEART?

If the normal human individual were asked what his biggest hardship in life was, he'd probably say, "Discouragement." That's the sword that pierces his heart. Friends and family don't seem to understand; one's work is hard; most boys don't make the teams they try out for; most girls can't manage to interest the one boy in the school they really want to like them. Result: *discouragement*. What is life all about? Almost everyone will tell you: "One big defeat, one setback after another!"

WHAT ABOUT SETBACKS? ASK MARY! SHE KNOWS—AND SHE'LL HELP YOU

Ask Mary what life is about. She *really* knows. She'll tell you that it's one great mysterious plan of God to bring us to himself. Most of the time, she will say, he doesn't provide us with many clues. He is good at reminding us (as he re-

minded her) that sentiment doesn't come first, or even family ties.

Obedience is what matters: doing his will—which, incidentally, is by no means an easy thing to discover. He teaches us through setbacks much more than through easy victories. The goal is great, so the price is high. It was so with Mary, greatest of the saints. It is so with us.

"Behold your mother," Jesus said from the cross to his disciple. (John 19:27) Ask Mary, he is saying, the meaning of life. It is chiefly a plan, God's plan, framed out of love. If you do not come to believe that, life is almost unendurable.

10

The Stories Jesus Told

Abraham Lincoln was our great storytelling president. He'd had lots of experience as a backwoods boy, grocer's clerk, flatboat operator, lawyer, judge and Illinois politician. By the time he got to the White House, he seemed to have at his disposal ten thousand witty tales from his younger days, ready-made to suit the occasion.

LINCOLN'S HUMOR WAS EVER READY

It didn't matter if the point in question was the appointment of a federal judge, McClellan's skill as a general, or the financing of the Union Army. Lincoln always seemed to know some "character" from his Sangamon County days who once

had an adventure that paralleled perfectly the issue under discussion.

"That reminds me of old Sim Cooley," the President would say, if the conversation got around to cheerful coincidences that were totally unplanned. "He said that the happiest man he ever knew in all southern Illinois was the fellow who managed to cut a bee tree down on his wife."

ABE'S YARN SUGGEST THE PARABLES—
BUT CHRIST'S STORIES ARE BETTER

It is almost impossible to read about President Lincoln's yarns without being reminded of the parables of Jesus. Our Lord was just such a storyteller as that. His stories have passed the test of time much better, however. The chief reason for this, of course, is that he is the eternal Son of God, while Lincoln was a good man trying to serve God. Even so, Jesus wins out if you apply only the rules of good oral prose. His stories were better, even as stories.

Our Lord did not invent the form of storytelling that he used. He became the perfect master of a style that the rabbis (i.e., the teachers) of his own day employed all the time. They in turn got it from centuries of usage.

The Old Testament has a number of wonderful parables, such as the story of the trees that chose a king, in the Book of Judges (9:7-21), or Nathan's tale about the rich man who, when he had a guest, robbed his own poor neighbor of his little ewe lamb. (II Kings 12:1-4) Look these stories up. You'll enjoy them. And if you have your Bible out, look up the ones in Ezechiel 17:22-24 and II Samuel (i.e. II Kings) 14:1-20, as well.

PARABLES POINT UP
HUMAN BEHAVIOR

You will notice immediately that a parable is a story which makes some point about human behavior; in it, certain things are made to stand for other things. *Any tale, however brief, in which figures of speech are used, and one major comparison is identifiable throughout the telling, is a parable.*

Mashal is the way Jesus would have said the word for this kind of speech, in the Hebrew language. But, of course, the gospels were written in Greek, and our word *parable* is like the Greek word that was used for any *mashal* or comparison. The same Greek word was used by the gospel writers to describe a riddle, even though Hebrew has a different word for *that*.

CHRIST NEVER USED THE FABLE
NOR POINTED TO PEOPLE BY NAME

We shouldn't say "any comparison" because there were certain types that our Lord never used. For example, he never employed a fable, the kind of story in which animals or trees are given the power of speech.

He never told a story about real people by name, a thing that Lincoln did *all the time.* There is only one proper name in all of Jesus' parables, that of the poor beggar Lazarus. But that was like calling him "Joe." It didn't mean a particular person at all.

CHRIST RARELY USED ALLEGORY:
VINEYARD OWNER'S SON IS BEST

Lastly—and this is very important—only very rarely did Jesus tell an allegory. *An allegory is that type of parallelism*

67

in which one person or thing represents another all through the story. The best known of his allegory-parables is the one about the sower and his seed. Jesus goes on to explain it by saying that the seed is the word of God, and the path and the thorns and the birds are all the different states of the human heart as the word comes to it. (Read Matthew 13:4-9; 18-23)

That sower story is surely the best *known* allegory of Jesus. Yet the most important one is the story about the wicked men who killed all the collectors of rents for the vineyard, and finally the vineyard owner's son. Undoubtedly, Jesus meant to describe the stoning of all the prophets and lastly, his own destruction at the hands of the leaders of the people. He got his point across, all right, because this tale so infuriated his listeners that, after hearing it, they began their final plotting against his life. (Read Matthew 21:33-46).

BEING FARMERS OR FISHERMEN HELPS, BUT PARABLES OF LOVE AND MERCY NEVER CHANGE

It's pretty hard to get the full impact of our Lord's stories if we don't happen to be farmers (Mark 4:24-32) or fishermen. (Matthew 13:47f.) Probably an even worse handicap is not knowing how business transactions were carried on in his day (Luke 16:1-13; Matthew 20:1-16), or how cruelly desert chieftains—the gospel always calls them "kings"—dealt with their enemies and with their friends. (Luke 19:27) A few simple clues can help us, though.

Despite all the differences between his day and now, the rules for the human heart do not change. His parables of love and mercy are as easy to understand today as the day they were spoken.

CHRIST MAKES A SINGLE POINT

The chief thing to remember is that most of the parables of Jesus have a single point. Look for *it*. Everything else in the way of detail is added just to make the story interesting.

THE KING NOT ALWAYS GOD

Secondly, the king or the wealthy man must not be taken to stand for God the Father every time. Or, better, when he does stand for him, he does so in this way: that just as kings and grasping men can always be expected to act the way they do—cruelly, skin-flinty, taking revenge—so God can always be expected to be in fact the way he is—supremely just, forgetting nothing, kind.

BEING AN ISRAELITE
ISN'T A TITLE TO GLORY

A final important clue is that, when Jesus is talking about the "kingdom" that his people expected, he has the important task of correcting their many wrong notions about it. His big job is to make clear to them that being a son of Abraham or Israelite, or even being an observer of Moses' Law in full Pharisee style, will not do. God the Father has another set of qualifications, which Jesus has been sent to remind them of. These are *mercy* and *justice* (holiness)—and *sorrow for sin*.

CHRIST EMBRACES *ALL* MEN

That is why so many of our Lord's stories—all his "kingdom parables"—are Israelite-versus-Gentile stories. The laborers-in-the-vineyard is the best known of these. (Matthew

20:1-16) Who are the eleventh-hour crowd but Greeks and Samaritans and "sinners" of every kind, namely all others but the pious observants of the Law who think they have been out in the heat of the sun since Abraham's time.

The story of the wasteful son and the good boy who stayed at home is in exactly the same vein—Luke 15:11-32: "My son, you are always with me, and all that is mine is yours." So is the briefer story called "the parable of the two sons": "Son, go and work today in my vineyard." He answered, "I will not," but afterward he regretted it and went. The other answered, "I go, sir," but he did not go. Which of the two did the Father's will? (Read Matthew 21:28-32).

THEY'RE COLORFUL READING—
CAN YOU FIND *YOU* IN THEM?

Earlier, we put the question of what the parables can mean to us. Well, we must get to know them, first of all. There are a good many more in the first three gospels than turn up in the various Sunday gospel readings. So comb your Matthew, Mark and Luke to discover the great variety of colorful tales that Jesus left behind him. Look especially in Matthew 13, then 18 to 25; Mark 4, and Luke 7 to 19.

Then see where it is possible that the story is being addressed to you. You may not know all the customs of those times, but you can see whether there is anything of the priest or levite on the Jericho road in you. (Luke 10:25-37)

Have you got as far as the wedding feast—the eucharistic table—without a wedding garment—a real spirit of faith, in eating the body of the Lord? (Read Matthew 22:12).

How does the Father "run out to meet you when you are as yet afar off"? (Luke 15:20) Have you ever really decided, with respect to life in Christ—the "kingdom of heaven"— that it is such a treasure that everything you own must be

exchanged in order to come in possession of it? (Matthew 13:44-46)

DON'T DISMISS STORY-TELLERS
THE WORLD LIVES ON STORIES!

There's one thing to remember about a teller of stories. He can always be dismissed by serious-minded types as a clown. Lincoln's enemies dismissed him that way. With Jesus' enemies, it was the same. "A spinner of yarns. Entertainment for the children. Who can be expected to listen to him?" they might have said.

Remember this: the world lives, not by its statesmen or treaties or battles, but by its stories. A simple tale can bear the weight of the profoundest truth man is able to bear.

Don't dismiss these parables by making the terrible mistake of thinking that you know them. All right, maybe you can finish five or six of them when someone starts one, just because you've heard it read so many times at Mass. Can you tell the one about the house built on sand? The rich man who was a fool? The king planning a war?

These stories won Jesus his best followers. They saved his life more than once. They earned him his fiercest opposition, and finally death. In twenty centuries, they have never faded from human memory.

What have you let them do for you lately?

71

11

Jesus the Lawgiver

The Italian novelist Ignazio Silone writes about the poorest of the poor in the mountain towns of his own country. In one of his books entitled *Fontamara* he is describing the importance of lawsuits and the law in his area, which is not at all unlike the country in which Jesus Christ spent his earthly years.

WITH NOTHING ELSE TO SHARE
THE POOR SHARE THEIR MISERY

"All the families," he writes, "even the poorest ones, have interests to divide among themselves, and if there are no goods to share, they share their misery. Therefore at Fontamara there is no family without some suit pending.

"As is known, the suits die down in the lean years, but they become bitter as soon as there is money with which to pay the lawyer. And there are always the same suits, unending lawsuits that are passed on from generation to generation in interminable hearings, eternal expenses, in blind inextinguishable bitterness—to establish the ownership of some thornbush grove. The grove may burn down, but the suit continues even more bitterly." (Dell Laurel edition, p. 17)

This fighting over an absolutely worthless piece of property gives us some idea of the misery of the very poor. But of course suing other people in court for no good reason is not confined to the poor. The rich do it too. In their case, it is a sign of something quite different: the unhappiness born of greed and of owning too much.

LAWSUITS COMMON IN JESUS' DAY

When you read the gospels you get some idea of this constant wrangling in the law courts we are speaking about. One day a man called to Jesus out of the crowd, "Master, tell my brother to divide the inheritance with me." (Luke 12:13) Jesus wouldn't have anything to do with the case. He told the man that no one had appointed him a judge over his claim—even though, later, he was to say that he would be the judge of all men at the end of the world. (Matthew 25:31ff.)

Instead of giving an answer, he told a story about a grasping rich man who "couldn't take it with him." Read it in the twelfth chapter of Saint Luke's gospel. It's a great lesson on the folly of piling up too much cash.

COURTS WERE PART OF ISRAEL'S
RELIGION; CHRIST KNEW THEM

In the middle of the Sermon on the Mount, Jesus refers to going to law over one article of clothing. (Matthew 5:40) Mind you, a shirt! And when he wants to tell people about the wrongness of most human anger—not just murder—the best way he can do it is to name two courts of law—the one in the local town, and the "supreme court" at Jerusalem—and finally the flames of Gehenna, the holy city's refuse dump, which signified punishment, by its fire.

All of the law courts the gospel speaks of were part of the religion of Israel. There was no such thing as what we would call a civil court. Religion governed the lives of the people in every aspect.

Whenever "lawyers" come up in the gospels, they are not very pleasant people. Almost always they are enemies of Jesus because he is a threat to their pretensions as "doctors of the Law" and "rabbis" (teachers). He blasts them once for a whole chapter's length. (Matthew 23) They are sometimes called "scribes"—like our word scribblers—because, in those days, to be skilled in reading and writing was to be concerned about the one great writing: Moses' Law.

DID CHRIST OPPOSE
THE LAW OF MOSES?

Actually the Law was God's Law and Moses was only his scribe. Why, then, should Jesus, who always referred to God as "my Father," set himself against the writings that had come from heaven to men through the great lawgiver, Moses?

You can guess the answer to that one. He didn't. Never for a moment did our Lord take a position contrary to the writings of the Old Testament.

CHRIST OPPOSED ABUSE OF THE LAW

He was opposed only to the people who were making a fat source of income out of the Torah. Torah is the Hebrew word for Law. A better translation, perhaps, would be The Instruction. Another abuse of the Law in those days was to employ it just to parade your knowledge.

Probably the worst abuse, though, was to think that your own human opinion of what it meant was more important than the words of the Law itself. Or going against its clear and direct meaning, and saying that some other complicated meaning—worked up by rabbis who were dead no more than one or two hundred years—was to be preferred.

ABUSED RELIGION SERVES MEN
TRUE RELIGION SERVES GOD

All of these abuses were just ways of making religion serve men! And religion, of course, *true religion,* is the way man serves God.

JESUS LOVED THE LAW—
THE REAL HEART OF IT!

The best statement we can make about Jesus and the Law is to say that he loved it and he kept it. Not a brush stroke, not the tiniest Hebrew letter—"i"—would go unfulfilled, Jesus said. The end of the world might be expected to come sooner. Read the verses near Matthew 5:18.

But the more we read the gospels, the clearer it becomes that Jesus means something quite different by "fullfilling the Law" than did the men of his time who were lawyers or scribes. The phrase, for them, meant keeping to some unimaginative, wooden sort of interpretation of a precept that

had sprung up by human pedantry or genius. By "fulfillment," Jesus meant going to the heart of the meaning of a precept as it came from God.

A GOOD LAWYER IS NOBLE—
A GOOD JUDGE, NOBLER STILL

For a young person to want to become a lawyer is a fine ambition. It is a higher ambition still to aspire to becoming a judge. A lawyer tries to get justice for his client but a judge, or court of judges, has the heavy task of deciding where justice lies in a particular case.

Only God knows the answer to that question in *every* case, but only the judge who fears God and loves his will can come close to being perfectly just all the time.

Everybody knows the jokes they tell about crooked lawyers. Sometimes they're not so funny, especially if your father or your brother is trying hard to be a good lawyer. These gags are especially unfunny to the family that has received an important, fair decision with the help of a lawyer, a man who has worked maybe years on the case. Ask a Negro American who is familiar with the NAACP how much justice his race has achieved through the law courts. Quite a lot, he'll tell you.

THE CONSCIENTIOUS LAWYER
WAS A FRIEND OF CHRIST

In the same way, we would make a terrible mistake if we thought that Jesus was against lawyers who interpreted the Scriptures, as a class, any more than he was against the Law itself. On the contrary, the pious interpreter of the Law was his ready-made friend. Such a one was very close to all the ideals Jesus stood for.

Once he said that the whole body of laws in the Bible,

those that we know as the ten commandments and all the lesser ones about worship and human life and property, could be summed up in two: love of God and neighbor.

At this a lawyer praised him for having got the meaning of the Scriptures straight. Jesus saw that the man had spoken wisely and he said to him, "You are not far from the kingdom of God." (Mark 12:34) The reason why Saint Joseph and our Lady and Saint John the Baptist were such *just* persons—another word for holy—is that they let the Law of God, given by Moses, make saints of them.

TEN ARE TOO MANY?

The story is told of a French actress—alas, the poor French actress, basically a sodality type—that her sole comment on the ten commandments was: "Il y en a de trop"—"There are too many of them."

Don't laugh too soon. There's a little streak of that mentality in all of us. The speed limits are set too low, we think. The parking meters don't give you enough time for your nickel. The feud with a friend—heh! friend—seems the only reasonable way to keep in touch with a stinker or a catty type like that. The once-married man has all the charm. The nicest girl at work has a husband she ought to get rid of.

REMEMBER THE DIFFERENCE:
GOD'S COMMAND—AND HUMAN LAW

The list could go on all night. It would name all the cutting of corners we'd like to do to suit ourselves when it comes to laws and commandments. There's one big difference between a human law and a command of God, however, and we need to get it straight.

78

Laws are passed by governments—federal, state and local —to make it easier to be a good citizen. It is possible to argue them: "Our taxes are too high in this town."—"Why don't they put drinking drivers in jail instead of just revoking their licenses?" But in the main, good laws are made by good lawmakers. Keeping them is surely a key to considerable happiness as a member of the human family.

GOD NEEDS NO RULE BOOK
HE LOOKS IN OUR HEARTS

When God draws up his commands he doesn't need to consult a heavenly rule book on how to make life hard for his creatures. He looks in the human heart, and he makes his laws accordingly. That is why Christianity is such a simple religion. It is not something that can be captured in lists of ten or six or even 2,414. It is simplicity itself, as it came from the lips of the Master: "Thou shalt love."

GOD'S LAWS WILL FREE US,
NOT MAKE US MISERABLE

We hope that by this time in your reading of these pages you're dipping deeper and deeper into the gospels and the Acts of the Apostles. The right way to follow up on the present chapter is to dig into Saint Matthew's gospel hard. Matthew is called "a Christian rabbi." His great concern is to show how Jesus is the new Moses, seated not on Sinai but on the mount from which he teaches. (See Chapters 5, 6, 7).

"Of old it was said to you," says Jesus . . . "but I say . . ." He doesn't deny or twist the former meaning. He tells what Moses meant, at its highest and deepest.

God isn't out to make us miserable with rules. He sent

his Son to set us free not from rules but from the bondage of rules. The great law of love of God and fellowman sets us gloriously free. Everything that holy Church requires us to do is just a way to make sure we'll enjoy our liberty best.

12

The Irony of Jesus

There probably has never been a time in our national history when there was more attempt at comedy, and less genuine humor, than nowadays. Millions of dollars are being spent for well worked up "routines" and gags. What do we get for it? (Besides ulcers for last season's comic, when the Trendex ratings can't buy him a thirteen-week contract).

NOT FUNNY, JUST VULGAR!

We get twenty million Americans, sitting stony-faced as they listen to something genuinely funny, and howling with laughter a few minutes later at the crudest kind of exchange of insults.

This pattern is having a real and a serious effect on our

81

national character. We are becoming a nation of loud-mouthed bullies. The worst of it is, we confuse this diseased condition of soul with *fun!*

WARPED MINDS CAN BE CRUEL

One autumn day last year, two Los Angeles teenagers drove up behind a man of eighty-seven and a woman of seventy who were proceeding at four miles per hour in a three-wheeled electric cart. The kids were in a 1951 sedan. You've guessed it! They pushed them off the road from behind—just for kicks.

"It's not against the law to push a cart, is it?" one of them asked. "The old people weren't hurt, were they?"

As a matter of fact, the man and woman had broken a few bones and suffered numerous cuts; but to be "hurt," in the language of these baboons, you need to have a fractured skull. A police captain in Los Angeles said afterwards, "We're up against a complete disregard for everything. You can't give a reason for it. The standards seem to have disappeared, and we have kids without standards."

WARPED HUMOR, WARPED MIND!

What we do have are kids with a warped sense of what's funny who have been helped to become that way by a billion-dollar industry. Not all comedy is cruel. Some of it—a fairly small percentage, it would seem—is good humored and uproariously funny.

THE JEWISH COMIC A FAMILIAR FIGURE

Many Jewish people are in the field of comedy for a livelihood. Some of them are not especially amusing. They trade

in jokes—buy them and memorize them and spiel them off—
as they might trade in dry goods or real estate.

However, some of our most genuinely funny Americans are
Jewish. Their gifts have enriched the national life greatly.
One thinks immediately of Jack Benny, Sid Caesar or Danny
Kaye. One of the funniest of American writers—you don't
see him much, but you do see other people spouting his stuff
—is a man named Goodman Ace. Look for his name some
time on the television credits. When it says "additional dialogue by . . ." that usually includes anything really comical
that was said by the funny man himself.

JEWISH HUMOR A LITTLE SAD

One important thing about Jewish humor is that it is always
a little sad. Even at its highest peak it is touched by pathos.
The reason is fairly easy to see. The Jewish character has been
molded by suffering.

For centuries upon centuries, the Jew has felt the flick
of the whip: Assyrian, Egyptian, Roman; then Polish, Russian,
German. Persecution is like hanging. You never quite get used
to it. But you do develop a few little ways to survive, and one
of them is laughter. Often it's deadpan laughter, the kind you
manage when your throat has just been cut.

Another mark of Jewish humor is that it makes its cleverest
thrusts by saying the most outrageous things with a straight
face, when the exact opposite is meant. There is a place in
Herman Wouk's novel, *Marjorie Morningstar* (born "Morgen-
stern") where Marjorie, who has been loafing around the
house for months, starts taking a shorthand course so she
can get a job with a theatrical producer. Her mother has every
good reason to suspect this burst of energy, and she says to
her: "Shorthand! My God, watch out, you might end up useful."

'IRONY' MARKS JEWISH HUMOR

We call that kind of speech "irony." It isn't exactly sarcasm. Sarcasm is usually out to hurt: to wound and leave a scar. Irony is different in that it includes a built-in antiseptic. It provides the opportunity for a person to look within and laugh at himself, which is nature's best remedy. Marjorie's mother was dead serious. If the girl had any sense at all she could see that her mother wanted to see her "end up useful" more than anything else in the world. *Irony is the last-resort language of an injured love.*

DID JESUS ENJOY A JOKE? WAS HE WITTY?

There have been oceans of ink spilled over the question: Did Jesus ever laugh? You can't prove from the gospels that he did or didn't. Of course the gospels are incomplete records. The men who wrote them had a very serious purpose: to print a word picture of the Savior of the world. Maybe they just left out all of his lighter touches.

One thing that is perfectly clear from the gospels is that Jesus and his friends lived a life of joy. Now, some joyous people are completely serious at all times. They may not be humorous, but they are always in good humor.

Jesus was the "man of sorrows" of the great poem in the Book of Isaia. (52:13 to 53:12) It is very clear that he was convinced of this. (Look up Mark 8:31; 9:30, 10:32ff; Luke 24:25ff.).

Christ never made himself out to be a victim of fate, or a man so taken up with his own sorrows that he couldn't feel for another's. Yet, he *is* pretty serious in the gospels. No matter how you view him, our Lord can't be described as a comical sort.

CHRIST'S HUMOR SUBTLE;
IT NEVER HAD BARBS

Several traits about him are worth remarking:

—he never ridiculed or made fun of anyone except men of obvious bad will, genuine hypocrites. When he called Herod a fox, he wasn't tearing him down, just looking into his heart.

—he always dealt with ordinary people so decently that they came to trust him completely.

—he seemed so bent on the work he came to do that you feel he hadn't time for small talk.

Yet, he did exhibit a wry sort of humor from time to time. For example, when the man in the parable of the great supper gave as his excuse:

"I have married a wife and therefore I cannot come." (Luke 14:20)

"It is easier for a camel to pass through a needle's eye, than for a man to enter the kingdom of God when he is rich." (Luke 18:25)

"The scribes swallow up the property of widows under cover of their long prayers." (Luke 20:47)

That is pretty subtle, as humor goes. It wouldn't make you throw your head back and roar, but you might say to yourself inwardly: "Clever! What a grasp of the situation he has!" Our Lord wields a scalpel when he speaks, not a length of lead pipe.

IRONY IS THE LANGUAGE
OF REJECTED LOVE!

Jesus is at his best—in that he is most a son of his people— when he says, along with the prophet Isaia: "The heart of this people has grown dull. Their ears have grown hard of hearing. They keep their eyes shut so that they will never

see with those eyes—or hear with their ears or understand with their heart and turn back to me. Then I would have to heal them." (Matthew 13:15)

In other words, the Jewish mother's words, "Watch out, you might end up useful!" have the same flavor as Christ's caution to Israel: "Careful, Israel. You might end up sorry for your sins. Then I'd have to take you back, and I'm not sure I have time for that!"

This same Jesus, when he was too heartsick and tired for irony, said to his people, "Jerusalem, Jerusalem, murderer of the prophets . . . how often have I been ready to gather your children together, the way a hen gathers her chickens under her wings; but you would have none of it." (Matthew 23:37)

Irony, we repeat, is the last-ditch language of rejected love.

THE JOKER: HEALER OR HEEL?

"When he threw that ax at me I thought I'd split."

Are you the funny man in your crowd, the poor man's Jerry Lewis?

The question is, even though you always leave 'em laughing, are your gags as much fun for the people they are *on* as the people they are *for?* Here's the acid test: *how much acid?*

There is a huge difference between the wit of Jesus Christ and the laughter of the devils in hell. When he gives a swift answer, he does it to make the hearer think. Jesus wants him to reflect, to become more of a person than before. When Satan plays the comedian, he wants to destroy a person utterly—strip him down to nothingness and howl after him with the hollow laughter that rings in hell. Sara in the Old Testament laughed at the promise she would be a mother, laughed it to scorn. The boy Chanaan laughed at his father Noah's nakedness. The passers-by laughed at the man on the cross. That is all so

different from what Dante calls "the eternal light which loves and laughs."

"How can I describe this generation? They are like children sitting in the market-place and shouting at each other: 'We piped for you and you would not dance [Jesus, who went to parties]. We wept and wailed and you would not mourn.'" [John the Baptist, who went to none] Matthew 11:16ff.

What is your idea of fun?

When you joke, which are you more like—healer or heel?

13

Jesus, the Bread of Life

God sent his Son to earth to show us the way to heaven. It's as simple as that.

Heaven is not some far-off place that happens to you when you die if you stay out of the messier kinds of mischief. It is by no means as simple as that.

NO PARADISE IN ORBIT

Last summer Mr. Khrushchev, full of good lemon juice and bad catechism, said this to a United States correspondent:

"As to paradise, we have heard a lot about it from the priests. So we decided to find out about it for ourselves. First we sent up Gagarin, but he found nothing in outer space.

It's pitch dark up there, he said; no Garden of Eden, nothing like heaven. So we decided to send another. We sent Titov and told him to fly for a whole day. After all, Gagarin was only up there an hour and a half. He might have missed paradise. Well, he came back and confirmed Gagarin's conclusion. He reported there was nothing out there."

Little Nikita was probably taught the difference between heaven and helium as a small boy. He just seems to have forgotten. If that's the kind of moonshine the priests were peddling in the Ukraine sixty years ago (and we doubt it), Marxism begins to look good.

For ourselves, we rather think that Khrushchev *minor* missed lots of C.C.D. classes.

'I AM THE WAY . . . ' TO HEAVEN

God's Son came to earth because man had lost the way to heaven. Jesus said: "I am the way . . . he who follows me walks not in darkness but has the light of life." (John 8:12) The man who follows Jesus does not inhabit a murky outer space, but has the light of life.

God is light, he is all light. In the Gloria of the Mass we call Jesus "Light of Light" because his whole being, as true God, comes from God the Father. Our Lord has another, further glory: not what he had with the Father from the beginning, but what God gave him to crown his manhood when he had finished the work he came to do. In explaining how he got this glory, Saint Paul says: "That is why God has raised him to such a height, given him that name which is above every other name . . . He dwells in the glory of God the Father." (Read Philippians 2:6-11).

IS HEAVEN A 'PLACE'?

Jesus sits at the Father's right hand, enthroned as Lord and Christ. This is heaven, the place where the glory dwells. Is it a "place"? It scarcely matters. We have to use words.

"Up" is scarcely a direction here. It means "where God is." The important thing is, *the glory of God is already shared.* It is meant to be shared further still: with you, and me, and every man who comes into the world. We are called to life, the same life Jesus Christ lives in the body *now*.

You might say that this is the whole of Christianity: a call to share in the glory Christ has at this very moment.

IT ISN'T 'BEING GOOD'
IT'S 'BEING DIFFERENT'

Christianity is not simply "being good." Many people who are not Christians are good. They keep the commandments, even though they may never have heard of them as such. They may not recognize the commandments as given to *them*, but they do live by them.

No, Christianity is not so much "being good" as it is "being different," totally different. It means being "graced," changed in body and soul, in thoughts and speech and ambitions. Nothing is quite the same again in our games, or work, or marriage, or citizenship—because Christ has come and we have received him. He leaves no one the same. Rather, he hopes to leave no one the same. His great prayer to his Father is that no one will remain alone, but that all may become one in him. (See John 17:20-21).

Now this is something unheard of and new in the world's history.

90

THE SPIRIT, THE SANCTIFIER
IS THE CHANGER-INTO-CHRIST

How does Christ bring about accomplishing the change? We scarcely need to review this, it should be so well known to all. First of all, he leaves to the Holy Spirit the actual work of changing. The Spirit is the sanctifier, the changer-into-Christ. This change comes about as a result of *a personal relation with Jesus Christ now, in his glory*.

SAINT, OR CONDEMNED!
NO ONE IS UNCHANGED

Nobody can live through this contact with the Holy Spirit unaltered. Either he becomes a saint or he condemns himself.

When we say "this contact makes a saint of him," those are not just empty words. They have a meaning. They describe *the living contact between a person in this life and the person of Jesus Christ in glory*. Today—not centuries ago, on dusty roads in Galilee.

CHRIST EXISTS NOW
IN BODY AND SOUL

As of this morning there is no Jesus of the dusty roads—nor of the cross nor of the resurrection. But this morning there is a Lord Jesus *existing in glory*. He is not a soul or a spirit. He is a man like us who has a body and soul. His body is different from ours in that *it is deathless now*. Disease and pain cannot destroy it; food and drink no longer nourish it. It is completely changed. It exists *in glory*. More accurately, Christ himself exists in glory, and not just his body. He is the eternal Word, and he is glorified, perfect man.

WHAT DOES 'GLORY' MEAN?

The big question is, what is this glory we have been speaking about? Unless we know, we can't say, "I'm for that." Without understanding, we can only guess what the glory of Christ means. No one really has a passion to stand like a light and *shine* for all eternity. Glistening and gleaming is all right for a sunbeam but if you're a lively human being it has limited appeal—especially forever!

Of course anyone who thinks of Christ's glory in terms like that is running several catechism lessons behind Khrushchev. Christ *in glory* means Christ *fulfilled*. All that man could ever hope to be, *he* has become. The desires, the dreams of poor, striving mankind, Jesus realizes in himself.

Most important, in glory he has the power to be present to each one of us. In glory, he holds out to us the same sort of fulfillment that he has. That is the gift of glory: reaching our full perfection as sons of the Father.

JESUS' GLORIFIED BODY HAS NO LIMITATIONS!

If you and I are in Wyandotte, Michigan, we may dream of life in Ouray, Colorado, but our immediate influence in Ouray is pretty slim. To be "in the body" is to suffer this limitation of not being able to get around. But to be Jesus Christ in glory is to be in contact—direct, full and instantaneous contact—with this man in Wyandotte, that woman in Ouray, and millions of others all over the world.

THE EUCHARIST, CHRIST'S
PLAN TO STAY CLOSE TO US

What is Jesus' formula for remaining close to all those legions of human beings who have heard of him and believe in him? Is it that, being the Son of God, he can think himself anywhere he wishes? That's no answer. You and I can do almost as much.

Look at the title of this chapter. The answer lies there, of course. The bread of life is God's gift of the eucharist to us. *It is that sign by which the glorified body of Christ becomes present to us. If we eat of this bread, the glory that is his in the body is "sown" in us.* Like makes like, says the proverb. Saint Paul calls us "one body in Christ" because all of us who eat the sacrament-body of Jesus are being prepared to have a glorious body like his.

EVERY MASS A TASTE OF HEAVEN
'I AM THE BREAD OF LIFE . . . '

The eucharist, in other words, is *the great point of contact between Christ and us.* When we eat this supper of the Lord, we are getting ready to sit down at the heavenly feast. "Here I am, standing at the door and knocking," says Jesus. "If anyone listens to my call and opens the door, I will come in to him and have supper with him and he with me." (Apocalypse 3:20)

That is a description of every Mass, because in it we offer and receive the richest food that God has given to men: the body and blood of his Son. It prepares us for that great and unending meal of the Father's house, the heavenly eucharist, the blessing-in-praise that has no end.

THE 'LIVING BREAD' DIED?

"I am the bread of life," Jesus said. "Your fathers ate the manna in the desert and they died. The bread which I speak of, which comes down from heaven, is such that no one who eats of it will ever die. I am the living bread which has come down from heaven . . . He who eats this bread will live forever." (John 6:48-51, 58)

Hasn't the Master a forceful way of saying things? Yet, here is a puzzle. The same Jesus who said that eating his body and drinking his blood would bring life and not death, himself *died*. "Every time you eat this bread and drink the chalice of the Lord, you proclaim the Lord's death until he comes," was the way Saint Paul explained this to the Christians at Corinth. (1 Corinthians 11:26)

Do we keep remembering the death, then, of one who conquered death? That's precisely the point. "Christ has been truly raised to life. He is the first fruits of those that have fallen asleep in death. For since man is the cause of death, a man also is the cause of resurrection from the dead." (I Corinthians 15:20-21)

CHRIST, CONQUEROR OF DEATH, GIVES US GLORIFIED BODIES

Now we have all the pieces we need in this mystery—not *puzzle*, but *mystery*—of the life-giving food that is the Lord's body. First, we eat the food which is both a sign, and actually *is*, the body of the risen Jesus. It is the human body of one who has overcome death: he dies no more. It gives the possibility of deathlessness to those who eat it. It is like a seed which causes a tree, but at this moment cannot be recognized as a tree.

Second, it is a food which all of us who believe in Jesus

Christ eat in common. It has the same effects on all of us, individually (an increase in the ability to love, a capacity for glory), and as a people of God. We are one Church, one body of Christ, because his one body is our common food.

LIFE'S ALL-IMPORTANT TRUTH: THE EUCHARIST COMPLETES US

Lastly, and most important of all, this food of the eucharist gradually fulfills us—makes us to be complete individuals who find happiness in union with others: Jesus the Lord and a whole host of brothers. The hardest cross in life, the deepest cause of unhappiness, is unfulfillment or a sense of incompleteness. You must experience it.

Are you taking the proper remedy for it—regularly?

14

Jesus, the Good Shepherd

Thus Jesus spoke to them in symbol; but they could not grasp
his meaning. So he went on:[*]

> *I AM the door of the sheepfold.*
> *Those who climb in elsewhere*
> *are robbers and plunderers:*
> *to them the sheep will not listen.*

> *I AM the door.*
> *He who enters in through me*
> *will be safe and sound:*

[*] John 10: 6-16, Tr. by Gerald Vann, O.P. *The Eagle's Word*, Harcourt,
Brace and World, 1961.

he can come and go as he will, freely,
and will find pasture for his sheep.
The robber comes only to steal,
    to kill, to destroy;
I am come that the sheep may
    have life, rich and full
    and abounding.

I AM the good shepherd.
    The good shepherd
        lays down his life for his sheep.
    The hired man,
        who works for a wage
        but is no true shepherd,
        has no real care for the sheep
        since they are not his own;
    so when he sees the wolf coming,
        he abandons the sheep and runs
        off, and the wolf harries
        the sheep and scatters them.

I AM the good shepherd.
    I know my sheep, lovingly,
        each of them by name,
        and they know me,
    just as the Father knows me
        and I know the Father
    And I lay down my life
        for my sheep.
    Other sheep I have,
        not of this fold:
    I must lead them to pasture, too,
        (and they will listen to my
        voice):

so there will be but one flock
and one shepherd.

In the last chapter we were talking about the nourishment we get when Jesus is our food. The idea comes from him, of course, not from us. He keeps saying the same simple truths in a hundred different ways—always hoping that he'll get through to us. This time he talks about sheep and shepherds.

Now the chief task a shepherd has is to see that his sheep get good nourishment, and are safe. As animals go, sheep are a little dumb: timid, eyes down to the earth while they nibble away, ready to follow the crowd in any direction in case of panic. The threat of wolves or mountain lions causes the worst panic. But starvation and thirst are other possibilities if they aren't led to good grazing lands and water holes.

MOST PEOPLE ARE TIMID

In a word, sheep remind us of us human beings generally. Men like to think they are independent, tough-minded, and all that. Actually, most people are fairly timid. They stay busy all through life holding down jobs, paying for a home, bringing up their children. They nibble away, eyes down, and are pretty frightened when great threats come along, such as war, or lesser troubles, such as losing their jobs. There are many other fears that grip people: for example, the thought that their children won't turn out right (fall prey to "wild beasts," one way or another); or will marry unhappily; or won't remember them when they, the parents, grow older (the constant fear of not having good streams and hillsides).

ISRAEL KNEW HER SHEEP

It would be a mistake to think that the hearers of Jesus didn't grasp his meaning in John's tenth chapter because they didn't know about sheep and shepherds. They knew *all* about them. Maybe some of you readers live on sheep ranches or near them. Most of you, though, have to rely on books or on a movie to know how sheep behave.

Not so the people of Galilee or Judea! They recognized immediately how a well-fitted sheepgate, usually bolted and barred, but swinging freely when opened, could mean life and death to the animals. The gate (or "door") was the best assurance the sheep had against their enemies, whether men or beasts.

Israel knew grazing as a way of life better than she knew city-dwelling or farming. The very name "Hebrew" once meant *wanderer or nomad:* not the sandy-desert kind, but the fringes-of-civilization kind. The nomad has no house, no farm, no bulky store of possessions. Unless he is to steal from other men, he has to transport his source of livelihood with him wherever he goes.

Flocks and herds are the best way to do this. When you read about Israel's great ancestor, Abraham, you see that his wealth is measured in "flocks, herds . . . asses and camels." (Gen. 12:16) His son-in-law, Lot, was rich in the same way: "flocks, herds and tents." (Gen. 13:5)

NOBODY LIKED A SHEEPMAN

Often neighbors in biblical times had arguments when there were more cattle, sheep and goats among them than there was land to support them. (Even Abraham and Lot, who really liked each other, had to separate because of this). And *nobody* liked a sheepman in those days, any more than today. Why? Well, chiefly because the sheep used up too much of the water that

100

people needed. Also they nibbled so close to the ground that they first ruined the land for farming and then caused soil erosion in the heavy spring rains.

Most important of all, the sheepmen would get the best out of everyone's land and then move on. They packed up their sense of responsibility with their goatskin tents and traveled off to the next valley. For this, all the farmers and the town-dwellers despised them.

'THE LORD IS MY SHEPHERD'

Yet this was Israel's earliest way of life, and so she looked upon her great God as a shepherd set over her. "The Lord is my shepherd," this people prayed, "I shall not want . . . You are at my side with your rod and your staff." (Ps. 22:1, 4) And in another psalm she sang: "O Shepherd of Israel, hearken, O Guide of the flock of Joseph!" Their forefather, Joseph, had fed them during days of famine, from his position of influence in the Egyptian court. Now it is the Lord himself who is being called on to care for Joseph's offspring: "Rouse your power, and come to save us." (Ps. 79:2-3)

THEY KNEW ALL TOO WELL!

You can see now, can't you, why, when Jesus spoke, "they could not grasp his meaning"? It should be pretty clear. Using figures of speech such as "I am the door," didn't confuse the listeners in the least. They were used to speaking in symbol language all the time. The heart of Hebrew poetry is figurative speech of this very sort.

JESUS' 'I AM' TROUBLED THEM

No, they were troubled by two things: Jesus' repeated use of the phrase I AM, which was identical with the way the Lord had described Himself to Moses at the bush, and our Lord's claim to be *the good shepherd* who *gives life.*

That was enough to give pause to any Jew of Palestine. It seemed clear that Jesus was identifying himself with the limitless God, who had made the heavens and the earth. If there was any truth in Jesus' words, it was frightening to the hearer; if there was none, it was not a good way for a pious Israelite to speak. What Jesus' words amounted to was: "In all the praise you give to Israel's Lord, you speak to me."

'OTHER SHEEP . . .' A THREAT

Something else was involved, "the other sheep not of this fold." In Jerusalem, crowds didn't *want* to understand that one, because they knew all too clearly what was meant. It was a threat —not veiled, but clear—that this teacher would go to the Gentiles, there to preach one great kingdom of God made up of Jews and non-Jews alike.

"And they will listen to my voice." That phrase has a thousand overtones. It is exactly what the prophets had said of old. If God's own people, so dearly beloved—ached for, longed for by him—do not hearken to his voice, he knows to whom he can go.

Nowadays we take a battery of psychological or IQ tests to prove whether the wheels are turning upstairs—or whether there are any wheels to turn. In the old days it was simpler: they asked whether a person knew enough to come in out of the rain? Could he blow hot soup? tell a hawk from a handsaw?

The Bible has a wonderful test of good sense in the things that matter most. Isaia says, in the Lord's name:

The ox knows its owner,
And the ass its master's manger;
But Israel does not know me,
My people have not understood.

Isaia 1:3

ARE YOU SMARTER THAN SHEEP?

Even the poor dumb beasts are smarter than people who don't put all their trust in God.

What do you put your trust in? Doing things "the smart way"? Lots of horsepower under the hood, or cash in the bank? Whatever it is, it won't do if it isn't the Son of Man who is a good shepherd to his sheep. That's really what our holy religion is all about: not about requirements and things to learn, but a lover who cares for us when we haven't the sense to care for ourselves.

We're all a little bit like sheep, even the keenest of us. Yet thinking for ourselves is absolutely essential. Getting all the facts isn't easy, mind you—never was, never will be. Do you tend to think of Catholicity as a great joint venture with Christ the leader, who thinks along with us and sometimes for us?

That is what it is, of course. He knows all that can happen to us, good and bad. He will be door and shepherd and all to us, if we do but one thing. We have to unstop the ears of our pride and listen to his voice.

15

The Authority of Jesus

You've probably seen the television show "Youth Wants to Know." The kids who appear on it are quite brainy. They are representative, if not of all modern youth, at least of those most likely to "want to know."

SOMEONE ALWAYS IN CHARGE

Youth wants to know many things, but "Who's in charge here?" isn't one of them. Someone, however, is always in charge. That's authority. There's nothing wrong with this—but it can be aggravating, because it's a system that works all the time.

Psychologists say that human beings have all sorts of needs, wants and drives. It doesn't seem that the "will to be bossed" is one of them.

Is this the case? Is authority a "pain in the neck"? Before we give a snap answer, we need to consider three separate yet related terms. One is *anarchy*, another is *authority* and the third is *discipline*.

ANARCHY MEANS NO BOSS

Anarchy is the state of things when there's no one in charge. That's exactly what the word means in Greek: "no boss." Mutiny at sea, rebellion on land, bedlam in the school bus: all have the one thing in common—total lack of authority. Nobody thinking, nobody calling the plays; everybody shouting. Are they happy? Yes, probably—the way small children and the insane are happy when they're let loose. There's a sick joke that has a mother saying to her children with a sweet smile: "Go out and play in traffic, dears." That's the spirit of anarchy: no bosses, no rules—and no protection. Why? Because no one *cares*.

AUTHORITY HAS THE SAY

Authority is a different matter. You know what it is without needing a definition: *Authority is the voice of someone who knows or who has the say in things.* When the people who have the say also happen to know, it makes things much easier. Serving under authority is hard for all of us. But when authority is both intelligent and kind, obeying it is less of a chore.

DISCIPLINE MAKES DISCIPLES

Discipline is perhaps the hardest of the three to define. It doesn't mean repression of liberties. It isn't a term for bossing a tough gang like the Capone mob, or having the strictest teacher of the school for homeroom. Discipline is the fine art of being able to

learn—of being a disciple. The man who can be taught has disciplined himself. The loudmouthed idjit hasn't. Discipline is something that comes from inside a person, not from outside. Unfortunately when we speak of it we usually mean "enforced discipline," and that's the degradation of a very fine word.

From the gospels we learn that one thing that drew the crowds to Jesus was that *he spoke with authority*. More than that, *he acted with authority*. That doesn't mean that he bossed people around! That was the last thing the poor peasants of Palestine needed. The Romans told them what to do. Rich landowners told them what to do. The religious leaders told them what to do. All three classes spoke in firm, hard tones, demanding enforced discipline.

"AUTHORITY" WAS GOD'S POWER

Consequently, any teacher who came along and said, "This is *really* it," wasn't going to attract a crowd very readily. But we miss the force of the gospel word "authority" entirely if we think that all it meant was a firm tone in Jesus' voice, a piercing eye, and a conviction that he was a true teacher sent from God.

No, "authority" was a word with a special religious connotation for the Jews. It didn't mean any *human* way of acting, but the power of *God himself*. That is exactly what the crowds thought they saw in Jesus of Nazareth—divine power. And oh, how they longed for it!

They had been without a true prophet for more than four hundred years, until the Baptist came along. They thought the heavens were closed against them. The Lord had visited his people in Moses' time, when he led them out of Egypt by his mighty outstretched arm. Centuries later he set them free from a second captivity, this time in Babylon. But that was now more than five hundred years ago. Persians, Greeks, Romans—everyone had trampled on them since. Had they any hope? What

106

could be the meaning of God's promise made to Abraham, re
newed in the Law given to Moses, repeated sternly but lovingly
through the mouths of all the prophets? Oh, how they wished
they knew!

Then there came this strange man from upcountry, Galilee,
who had never been trained as a rabbi, but *who spoke and
acted with the very tone of God.* That is what is meant by the
authority of Jesus. *He was a man who acted with the full power
of God.*

GOD "AUTHORS" OUR FAITH

The word *authority* has *author* in it, and that word means someone who gives growth or increase. Not only the people who turn
out three-hundred page books are authors, but all those who
start something and see that it continues. President Kennedy is
the author of the Peace Corps, a plan for aiding underdeveloped
nations by helping them to help themselves. General George
Marshall was the author of the Marshall Plan for feeding Europe after World War II.

But the great author of all that is is the God who is the
Father of our Lord Jesus Christ. The most wonderful thing that
he begins in us is our faith in him. This spirit of perfect confidence he means to bring to fulfillment in us. He would never
get such a wonderful work started if he didn't intend to end it
fully, in the glory of union with Himself.

Jesus' authority was not just meant for the Jews. He saw to it
that it would reach all of us—through his Church. When someone says to you, "The Roman Catholic Church is a religion of
authority," what does that mean to you? Do you automatically
say to yourself: "It certainly is a religion of authority. Not only
does it have a set of rules for what to do and what not to do,
but it even has a whole hierarchy of people telling other people
what to do." This sounds as though you are missing the whole

107

point of the teaching of Jesus. If God is a God of *love*, he doesn't stand around barking orders all day. If Christianity is a religion of *love*, there must be more to it than rules and commands.

MORE THAN PRECEPTS HERE

There is—a great deal more. Try to think of it this way. You have been given the Spririt of Christ in your hearts. That gives you the power to cry out to God, "Father!" as only a son can do. You are sons in the only Son. When your Father speaks to you through his Son, in the gospel proclaimed in the living Church, he does so with *authority*. What he is the author of is a whole way of life that is love.

We listen to him attentively, in the spirit of disciples. We are well-disciplined, in other words, so that we may learn. We love God's authority, and that of his Church, because it never means anything but good to us. It is a *voice of love*, and it demands an answer on our part *in terms of love*.

JESUS CAME TO FREE US

Right now you're a Catholic, a member of his Church. Do you think you will always be one? If Christ came back in glory, would he find faith on the earth?

Many people who were born Catholics aren't Catholics any more. They have thrown off the authority of Christ, or else they've said that his authority hasn't any connection with the Catholic Church. Do you know why they've done this? Generally, it's because they never understood what his authority meant. They thought it was a set of rules: rules about marriage, about birth control, about obeying the bishop. How little they knew about the inner nature of faith in Christ. It is true, Jesus said, "If you love me, keep my commandments," but the opera-

tive word in that sentence is love. If all Christianity consisted in was keeping rules, there'd be very good reason to drop out. The Pharisees had rules, plenty of them. That is why Jesus came to set men free. His whole task was to set men's feet on a path of love and obedience leading toward a kind Father. Does your Catholic faith mean *that* to you?

BREATHE HIS LOVE

If it doesn't, you've got a worry on your hands because you're mixed up in something really big that you haven't got a grip on. Do you think that the Catholic religion is nothing more than a list of rules and regulations for people who can't think for themselves? You must begin to realize that you are committed to a religion that is a willing response of love to a love that surrounds you like the air you breathe. Start "breathing" this love —and you'll find a lifetime of happiness in store for you.

16

The Sinlessness of Jesus

If you have ever served Mass or taken part in a recited Mass you will remember having said in the Confiteor, "quia peccavi nimis," which means, "because I have sinned exceedingly . . ." Have you really sinned exceedingly in thought, word and deed? That's a question everyone must answer for himself. It's a question that has to be faced, because the great work of Jesus was to save us from our sins. If we don't understand something of sin, we will never understand him. The best description of Jesus Christ we can give is: "He is the one who is everything that sin is not."

JESUS WAS NEVER REPENTANT
BECAUSE HE NEVER SINNED

One thing that is very clear from the gospels is Jesus' complete lack of sorrow or regret for his own actions. He associated with sinners, and they were strongly attracted to Him. But he never indicated that what he had in common with them was sin. He could forgive them—and he did—only because he himself was sinless.

NOT EVERY SIN
IS MORTAL SIN

In Chapter 5, when we were speaking of Jesus and the demons, we tried to point out the difference between what are sometimes called our sins and *sin;* between the human weaknesses that are part of everyday life, and that unspeakable revolt against a holy God which we call evil. It is, of course, the difference between venial sin and mortal sin, the latter being the tragedy of bringing death of spirit to ourselves.

To be death-dealing, sin needs to be something that is a seriously wrong, of its nature; but it must be more than that. It must be carefully and hatefully thought out. If it is a question of passion, it must be willingly allowed to grow. Then, and then only, does it qualify to keep us from possessing the holy God forever.

That information may come as a relief to some readers who have gone through agonies of worry thinking that all "sins" are serious sins. Generally speaking, the more you worry the less likely they are to be mortal offenses against the love God has for us.

DON'T UNDERESTIMATE SIN;
THAT'S THE OTHER EXTREME

There are some Christians, however, who have another danger to contend with. That is the notion that practically nothing they do is seriously sinful. People with this outlook tend to think that sin is some kind of thing or stuff that you "catch," the way one has sinus trouble or scarlet fever. And just as most people think they're never going to die, or can't pick up a disease, so they have a tendency to think that no matter how they behave on dates, deal with their parents or their marriage partners, lie and cheat, they can never qualify as serious sinners.

FREE WILL IS FRIGHTENING!
YOU CAN LOSE GOD FOREVER

But of course they can. That is the frightening mystery of freedom of choice. You *can* choose against the love of God that enfolds you, and you *can make it final.*

VENIAL SINS, MULTIPLIED,
BREED INDIFFERENCE TO GOD

The thing to fear in life is gradually coming to lose the idea of the holiness of God. Venial sins, when they are multiplied, bring this about. Venial sins are small acts of unfaithfulness, of broken honor, of disloyalty to a lover who has a claim on our perfect loyalty. These little choices against a great love bring a person to a point where he doesn't care, one way or the other, any more.

ONE WHO LOVES INTENSELY
CAN ALSO HATE INTENSELY

Now a person who no longer cares, but who had a friend once whom he loved, can turn on that friend in hate. *He can hate no one else as he can hate someone he once loved.* This turning-in-hate we call sin, when the friend is God. "Sin" in this sense has no adjective to go with it. It needs none. It is just sin, simply sin—the mystery of a free human being turning on his loving Father in rebellion. We could call it "mortal," perhaps, but no qualifier is necessary to establish that it means an end to God's life in the soul.

JESUS DESIRES HOLINESS;
HE IS HOLINESS HIMSELF

We call Jesus of Nazareth sinless because rebellious thoughts such as these never had a moment's place in his mind. What the Father wanted, Jesus in his turn wanted and wanted with all his human strength. He desired it immediately and fully. This longing for God's will to be done, this adoration of his will once it is known, we call in a creature *holiness*. In God, his very will which is he himself, *is* holiness.

Jesus was holy in two ways, the way of God and the way of man.

You mustn't think of his human holiness as an endurance contest: Jesus constantly biting the bullet, bent on obeying the Father's will regardless of how painful he found it. It wasn't that way at all. He recognized God's will immediately. His human will fell right in with it, even though later this would cost him something in physical pain, or in his emotions, or wherever else men pay a price.

WILL HOLINESS EVER BE EASY?
HOW LONG CAN I HOLD OUT?

We must insist on this because some followers of Jesus have
their major problem not with "sins" nor with *sin*, but with advancing in holiness. They get as far as knowing that this is
mostly a change that the Holy Spirit brings about in them, not
one that they work in themselves. At first they trust in his action as fully as they know they should.

Then they begin to wonder, "How long can I hold out? Do
things get easier? Will I ever get to recognize God's will fairly
readily? The way it is now, I go through torments of indecision,
and when I act I am never quite sure if what I choose is the
right thing to do."

The problem may be different in your life. It may take this
form: "Knowing God's will is not so hard for me. It's *doing* it
that causes the grief. Will I ever leap to do it, as Jesus did in his
earthly life? I want to be a saint, but the very *attempt* is so
great a hardship that it makes me want to chuck the whole business."

IF SINNERS, WE'RE SLAVES!
JESUS CHANGED US TO SONS

A furious crowd shouted at Jesus once, "We are the descendants
of Abraham, we have never been slaves to any man. What do
you mean by saying 'You shall be free?' "

"In very truth I say to you," said Jesus, "everyone who commits sin is a slave. The slave has no status in the household, but
the son is at home there forever. If then the Son sets you free,
you will be free indeed." (John 8:34-36)

What a sense of relief those words of Jesus bring! He gives
security—not gilt-edged, locked-in-the-vault security. Neither
is it the rustproof, mothproof kind. He does provides relief from

life's greatest captivity, fear. You are sons, he says, along with the only Son, because the Father has made you so. You have the run of the house—his house, my house. Be holy, as I am holy. If the Son sets you free, you will indeed be free.

THE SECRET OF CATHOLICITY:
AS SONS, WE ABANDON FEAR!

The secret of Catholic life, Christian life, is that in it you throw off your fears. The big fear is that there is a hard set of laws to keep that you won't be able to keep. But this is getting things all in reverse. *Christian life is freedom from this fear and from every other fear; it is power to live as a family member lives.*

A son is perfectly at ease in his own house. He doesn't tiptoe around in the kitchen. This is his home! All his actions come naturally to him there, from turning on the TV to sitting down at table with the rest of the family. If it is a happy home, his actions are not only natural, but a pleasure to him. He knows exactly how to behave himself and he gets a certain delight out of behaving the way he does.

WE CHOOSE RIGHT; EACH TIME
IT'S EASIER, AND WE'RE HAPPIER

It wouldn't do to pretend that there's no challenge in Christian life. Being a red-blooded citizen of the United States or Canada these days, and staying faithful to God, can make a pretty stiff combination. The points worth stressing, however, are these:
1. growth in holiness is something God brings about in us more than we do ourselves (though we must accept freely his gift of holiness) ;
2. Jesus wants to share his own holiness with us;
3. gradually it *does* work out that way—in other words, each time we choose to make our will agree with God's will, the

115

choice becomes easier. And, each time we do so we make the choice faster and with more happiness. Why? Because we come to resemble Christ. The family likeness between the only Son of the Father and his many sons, becomes evident to all; it even becomes plain to us.

JESUS BECAME ANGERED
WHEN ACCUSED OF SIN

Our Lord, when he was provoked at his enemies in Jerusalem, once said, "Which of you can prove me guilty of sin?" (John 8:46) He wasn't just hurt or insulted by them, as you or I would be. No, Jesus knew he was being accused of selling out to his Father's great enemy, Satan. Jesus, who was *total holiness*, was being called *unholy*. That was the one thing his honor and his love for his Father could not stand.

YOU CAN LIVE WITHOUT SIN!
WHY DON'T YOU?

You've got a perfect right—yes, *you*—to holler "foul" when anyone links your name with serious sin. Serious sin is not a necessary part of life. Christ is acting through his sacraments all the time to destroy the possibility of sin in us. The chief "effect of sin"—of Adam's sin—is the individual mortal offense against God's love; but *by God's grace it need never take place.* St. John goes as far as to say: "We know that no child of God commits sin." (I John 5:18)

We repeat: *a serious fall doesn't ever need to happen,* no, not once in life. You can go from early childhood through to the grave as someone perfectly charitable, perfectly chaste, perfectly honest and perfectly truthful.

Did you know you could? Had anyone told you that the sinlessness of Jesus is something that you can possess if you let

116

the Holy Spirit have his way in you. Read the whole first epistle of St. John, which makes this very explicit.

Your cue is there.

Why don't you take at face value the Christian teaching on the total victory Jesus can win over sin *in you*.

17

The Prayerfulness of Jesus

"Beads and prayerbooks are the toys of age," wrote the cynical poet Alexander Pope. Everyone knows what he is referring to: the special religious fervor of those advanced in years.

Maybe he's right. Many elderly people attend weekday Mass. ("Cramming for their finals," one wiseacre has put it.) Afternoons and evenings, too, one often sees older people in the subdued light of the church. Their movements are stiff and slow; they're in no hurry now. They have no obligations. No one waits for them. With gnarled fists, they clutch their rosaries or leaf through their missals.

OLD FOLKS AREN'T EMBARRASSED
THEY LOVE GOD TOO MUCH

The bitter poet seems to have accused these senior citizens falsely. How could he have known that they had been prayerful most of their busy lives; that they'd never had enough leisure to pray as much as they wanted to. Now, with time to spare, they are making up—and they care little what others may think. There is no embarrassment about them. They kneel or stand as they please, following the Way of the Cross at the pace that best suits them. They love God much and they speak to him freely. They have known pain at his hands, but they have also known great joy. They pour out their hearts to tell him so.

How wonderful it is, though, when the young are prayerful. They are not "benched" by arthritis or age. They have perfect freedom of movement. There are a thousand interesting things they could be doing. Yet, they choose to pray . . . to pray much!

THERE'S MORE TO PRAYING
THAN MUMBLING PRAYERS

Praying, however, isn't the same as *saying prayers*. Not at all. Sometimes, in fact, *saying prayers* just gets in the way of real praying.

What, then, is prayer? Prayer is an experience of closeness to that Holy One who is our God. At times we will be moved to speak to him with words. This is not always the case, however. It is enough that we have a sense of his presence, that we are aware he is near, that we know our lives are touched at all points by him who alone is sacred.

FROM DUST, TO GOD,
THERE IS A BRIDGE

He *is*, and we *are not*. He is the All-Holy; we are but dust and ashes. We bow our heads at the thought of him. We are ashamed. We shrink before the mystery of his great majesty. Our own nothingness humiliates us. Yet, there is a bridge by means of which we may reach him. That bridge is his Son. Jesus is God and man. Therefore, we and God have Jesus in common. Moreover, the love that the God-Man bears us casts out any fear we might have. *Awe* and *dread* before the almighty God remain, but *fear* is no more! The blood of the cross is a tide that has washed all fear away.

SOME DON'T SAY MUCH
THEY "DRINK HIM IN"

Occasionally you meet a young man or woman who gives much time to prayer. It may be a college football player who is in the chapel whenever he isn't out on the field or at the books. Or, perhaps it's a young mother who comes to the church at 1:45, though she doesn't have to pick up her first-grader until 3:00. When these people pray, they don't *say* much. They simply experience the majesty of God, and words become unnecessary— sometimes impossible. They just kneel or sit there and "drink him in."

The prayer of Jesus was prayer such as that. He could kneel in perfect silence for hours, drinking in the glory of God. God was the very condition of his being, so to say. As the sun is to plants, or temperature is to bodily health, so the great God and Father was to Jesus of Nazareth.

OUR GREATEST CHRISTIAN
PRAYER: AN *ACT* OF CHRIST

It would be wrong to give the impression that prayers made up of words or actions are not important. Our *greatest Christian prayer* is an action (more properly an act) of Christ: the Mass. Here his work of saving us is done in the sign language of bread and wine, of gestures and of prayers. And in the very heart of the Mass we find the prayer that he himself taught us, the Lord's prayer. It has always had a place of honor in the Mass, to prepare our hearts for the body of the Lord.

JESUS PRAYED FOR FRIENDS,
FOR ENEMIES, FOR HIMSELF

The Church has many prayers with words—our Mass book is filled with them. They are simple and direct prayers which speak all the thoughts and desires of men.

Indeed, the gospels give us ample evidence that Christ prayed with words. He prayed for his friends: "O Father! I will that those whom you have entrusted to me shall be at my side where I am. I want them to behold my glory, the glory you bestowed on me because you loved me before the world was founded." (John 17:24)

He prayed for his enemies: "Father, forgive them; they do not know what they are doing." (Luke 23:34)

Jesus prayed the night of his arrest, while his whole being shuddered in dread at this evil which was taking place: "My Father, if it is possible let this cup (i.e. this bitter dose of pain) be spared me! And yet, not as I will but as you will." (Matthew 26:39)

THANK GOD IN JOYFUL PRAISE

Most of all, however, he prayed during his lifetime in joy and praise to his heavenly Father. "He looked up to heaven and after uttering a blessing in thanks broke the loaves into portions." (Mark 6:41) "Father, I bless you thankfully for giving ear to me . . . I know that you will always hear me." (John 11:41ff.) "I praise you with a blessing, Father, Lord of heaven and earth, for hiding these things from wise and learned men and revealing them to simple ones." (Matthew 11:25) Here Jesus referred to God's great work. Through the life and death of Christ, God worked out his plan to save men, a plan which, until that time, was hidden in the depths of his being. In his prayers, Jesus acknowledges that marvel.

THANK GOD FOR REDEEMING US! THAT'S REAL PRAYER!

This acknowledgment of man's salvation is the core of the whole business. If you think that prayer means "delight in saying prayers," you're quite wrong. Nor does it describe a feeling of inner satisfaction that God is there as a partner in conversation. Actually, you may have no awareness of him in the sense of being joined to a conversation partner, and yet engage in some fine prayer.

But of course you must have *some* awareness of him, for as we have said this is the meaning of prayer. To be present before God, in some way, with any part of your mind or heart, and to wish to acknowledge the marvel of his goodness in saving us—*that* is prayer.

GO TO GOD THE FATHER
THROUGH HIS OWN SON

If you get discouraged, therefore, about trying to pray, it may be that you are on the wrong trail. Take, for example, this business of *feeling* that your prayers are being heard. Whatever God is like, the one thing about him we can be sure of is that *he is completely different from us.*

It's true, we describe him in words very similar to the words we use for people: spirit, person, father, goodness. But these words all add up to a description of human beings. They can never capture the reality which is God. This is something no human tongue can describe.

That is why people who tell you that they have nice, cozy conversations with God (who answers them, moreover!) probably have a very limited idea of God. They're really talking to themselves.

WE FIND PRAYER HARD
JESUS FINDS IT EASY!

This problem of prayer to the divine majesty would be reason for real discouragement if it were not for one thing. That thing is the *prayer of Jesus.* You see, there is a close union between what is man and what is God in Jesus. His manhood unites him with us, making him our brother. Because he is also God, however, Jesus is much better able than we are to think human thoughts of what God is like.

We find prayer hard. Jesus finds it easy. It is his element, just as water is the element of a fish. He thrives on prayer. It is conversation with *men* that is strange to him, for men are not holy as his Father is holy.

Yet, he longs to talk to men so that he can put them in touch with his Father. When we want to speak to God, therefore, we

should do it through Jesus. He is man as we are men. We can picture him in our imaginations, read his very words in the gospel. He comes *alive* to us. He leads us to that God whom we could never come to know on our own.

JESUS LEADS US IN PRAYER; HOLY SPIRIT PROVIDES POWER

When we pray to God through Christ, the words we choose are not our own. They are supplied by the Holy Spirit, whom Jesus sent us for this very purpose. The Son *leads* us in prayer, but the Holy Spirit *provides the power* to pray. "He will guide you into all the truth," our Lord said, just before he left us. The one great truth we need guidance in is how to speak words of trust and love to our Father who is so high above us. On our own, we might make a botch of the job. Jesus, therefore, leads the whole Church in a chorus of praise. To be of the Church is to pray gloriously under the skilled direction of Jesus Christ our head.

The correct term for the Church's prayer under the headship of Christ is *Liturgy*, that is, a work of the people of God.

18

Joy in Following Jesus

A Mr. Joyboy is one of the main characters in Evelyn Waugh's novel, *The Loved One,* in which he pokes fun at American burial customs. Mr. Joyboy is the chief mortician at "Whispering Glades," and he has charge of the Slumber Room, the Orchid Room and all the other plush accommodations for "viewing." He takes extreme pleasure in his work, deriving great satisfaction from making a big fuss over preparing the corpses (whoops! "loved ones").

IT CAN BE A GIRL—OR A SOAP
OR EVEN 'JOY TO THE WORLD'!

Every crowd has its joyboys; anything for a gag. They don't get enjoyment from fussing over the dead. They're all wrapped up in *life*. Everything is a big joke. A laugh a minute.

Joy can mean lots of things. For instance, it is a girl's name. *Joy* is supposed to make dishwashing a . . . pleasure. *Joie de vivre* is "zest for life" in French, with all sorts of overtones of wacky gaiety. *Filles de joie*—they're not such happy types at all, but in a grim and gritty business.

There was a time when "Joy to the World" meant that Christ the Savior had come—now it means four weeks of unbearable TV assault on the ears.

HOW DO YOU DEFINE 'JOY'?

What is the definition of true joy? *Joy is what comes to him who heeds the commands of Christ and dwells in his love.* "I have spoken thus to you, so that my joy may be in you," Jesus said, "and your joy may be complete." (John 15:11)

That definition of joy isn't at all like the other examples. If it is the correct meaning of joy, then serious people who seldom smile can be filled with joy, and those with the noisiest laughs may never know it. In such case, sorrow is not necessarily the opposite of joy, for the keeper of Christ's commands may lose mother or husband in death, may be bitterly disappointed in love, may never succeed materially in his life's work, and yet continue on in the love of God without interruption. *All through his time of trial and sorrow, he never loses joy.*

NOTHING GLOOMY ABOUT 'JOY'
LOVE OF CHRIST IS THE KEY

A joyful person doesn't mean a fixed grin suspended in mid-air like the Cheshire cat's. He needn't like early rising, algebra, or broccoli, homely girls or overtime at no extra pay. If he delights in *doing God's will in a spirit of love,* however, he will know joy.

JOYBOYS ARE SAD CASES!

Contrariwise, some of the youthful joyboys of our time who get a thrill from cruising around town in a car with a case of beer don't know much joy. They are sad cases and sad soaks, in the strict sense. Nothing has ever given them deep-down satisfaction. Their young lives are terribly unfulfilled.

Depression and gloom are their companions—daily, not just "the morning after." They know little of the joy of Christ, and so in the deepest sense they do not know joy.

JOY HAS A LONG HISTORY—
THE ISRAELITES KNEW JOY

The idea of joy has a long history among the people of God. If you examine the Old Testament carefully, you'll see that religion is always a *sacred* and a *serious* business for Israel, but it is never a *glum* business. Long-faced religion—the Puritanical type—is simply unheard of there.

One thing you do find in the early days of Israel is a wild, frenzied sort of dancing and song—religious "exaltation," it is called. It is much like the revival meetings you read about at which people get "carried away in the Spirit." All this happened back in the early biblical period when the religious prac-

tices of Israel were quite different from what they came to be later.

The notion of joy is the thread we are following, though. Like cheerfulness, it keeps breaking in. For the Israelites, joy was all tied up with music and song. It was the state of heart of anyone who gave praise to the Lord. The Lord, in turn, rejoiced over the love his people bore him, just as a newly married man rejoices in his bride. (See Isaia 62:5). The people bowed their knees to God in adoration and sang the joyous songs of David and the court musician, Asaph.

After their bitter exile in Babylon, they came back singing. When they set up the worship of the Lord in the temple, again they did it with joyous song. "They sacrificed great sacrifices that day . . . God had made them joyful . . . and the joy of Jerusalem was heard afar off." (II Ezra or Nehemia 12:42)

'YOU CAN'T HAVE ONE WITHOUT THE OTHER'

The meaning of all this can't be missed. What the Bible is saying is that music, song, religion, and joy are all mixed in together. You can't have one of them, in the truest sense, without the others. Does this make sense to you? It should, because aside from the fact that it's as clear as crystal in God's holy Book, it seems to be written everywhere in the book of the human heart.

MUSIC IS MEANINGLESS— WITHOUT LOVE OF CHRIST

Yet, it would be foolish for us to suppose we could experience real joy in the Lord by merely delighting in music and song. A lot of impressive singing and organ music (if your parish is fortunate enough to have these) is meaningless without

129

everyone's joining in much of the time. In turn, the popular participation which the Church is stressing in our day can be empty formalism without that necessary consent of each one to follow Christ in one's heart.

IT'S MORE THAN EMOTION—BUT
RELIGION NEEDS JOYOUS SONG

In other words, *religion is not chiefly an experience of emotion.* But, conversely, *there is no true religion without emotion.* Whoever seeks the joy Christ promised, and does so without joyous celebration in song, has exchanged Christianity for some other religion.

For a while—perhaps for a century or more—a persecuted people can hold on to its Catholic faith without the religious ceremonies, without its song. After that (and usually well before it) *joy in believing* steadily dies among this people, almost by a law of nature—a law of grace, we should say. Unless whole congregations can full-throatedly sing out their *Kyrie* and their *Sanctus*, their *Hospody Pomilui* and their hymns full of great music and great words about the mystery of faith, they will gradually lose first their enthusiasm and later their balanced Christian faith.

THIS JOY BUSINESS IS NOT SO
EASY; IT LACKS OPPORTUNITY

See if this isn't true with you. When was the last time you were carried away with joy at the experience of having brothers in Christ? Was it, for example, at Sunday Mass in your parish church when the *entire* congregation prayed and sang together? Or was it, perhaps, in the municipal auditorium last October, or a city park a year ago, when you and your fellow Christians, in full-throated chorus, sang together the praise of God through

Christ the high priest. Whenever it happened last, we'll wager it was too long ago.

You may have wished to experience this spirit of joyfulness more often, but you have not had the opportunity. You discover that this Christian joy business is not so easy, when so few in the Church seem committed to working at it. How about happiness through silence—can this be more readily experienced? Think it over carefully. Is it not true that happiness and peace are hard to come by unless we regularly experience Christian exultation and joy?

CHRIST'S FRIENDS
SHARE HIS JOY

"Then I heard a voice like that of a great crowd, like the noise of rushing water and of mighty thunders, and it cried, 'Alleluia! Now the Lord our God Almighty reigns! Exult and shout for joy and give him glory, for the marriage of the Lamb has come.'" (Apocalypse 19:6ff.)

This is a word picture given us by one of the inspired writers of the early Church. It explains the kind of joy there will be in the last age of the world, the time we are in now. It refers to Jesus Christ, the Lamb of God, and his love for a holy people—a people as close to him as a woman is to a man in marriage. Christ spoke of how his friends should share in his joy, when he prayed, "I speak these words so that they may have my joy within them in full measure." (John 17:13) "Be always joyful," says Saint Paul. (I Thessalonians 5:16) "Count it all joy . . . when you meet . . . trials." (James 1:2) "All joy is yours . . . The Lord is near." (Philippians 4:4-5)

We want him near. We need that joy. In the eucharistic celebration he comes nearest of all. Then, let's sing out the praises of the Lamb as if to burst our throats.

131

19

Jesus and His Own People

Whether you happen to come from the State of New Mexico or the Province of Ontario, chances are you have a lively attachment to your home place. If you go off to the armed services, to college, or traveling where your work takes you, no one will mind it too much if you push the glories of your native state or province. People will rather expect it, in fact.

It's the same thing with being an American, a Canadian or a Puerto Rican. There are few men so attached to the whole human family in general that they can't work up a little special enthusiasm for people of their own country or nationality. We praise this outlook. We call it the virtue of *patriotism* or love for one's homeland.

RAMPANT NATIONAL PRIDE
HAS LED TO WORLD WAR

When these natural sympathies get out of hand, however, a diseased state of mind sets in. This is termed *nationalism* or, sometimes, *racism*. Premier Mussolini of Italy and Germany's *Führer*, Adolf Hitler, in recent history, were *nationalists*. Both were trying to restore to their people a pride in their achievements as a nation, but they went too far. They carried their nationalism so far, in fact, that the rest of the world was forced to defend itself against these two dictators, even to the point of war.

Perhaps you've heard something about Hitler's racist theories. He believed that the branch of the Aryan peoples known as *Nordics* was the "master race" (in German, the *Herrenvolk*). As a scientific theory it isn't worth much, but if you happened to be tall, blond and handsome and lived in Germany thirty years ago, it could be very appealing. Hitler himself didn't fit his own description of a Nordic, but it could have cost you your life to say so in public.

ISRAEL A PROUD NATION
GOD HAD CHOSEN IT

Jesus of Nazareth was born into a people which held some views much like the ones just described. In the case of the Israelites, however, the situation is rather complicated. You see, the undeniable fact was that God had done special favors for the people Israel. Israel was his son, his beloved. Israel was his chosen people. The entire Old Testament is a record of God's agreement (covenant) with this priestly nation, an agreement to make it great above all the peoples of the earth. This was an agreement which he swore he would never go

back on. (Read Genesis 17:4-8; 28:13-15; Exodus 6:7; Leviticus 26:45; Deuteronomy 7:7-11; 30:15-20).

But, this did not mean that the Lord God wasn't interested in the other peoples on the globe. In the first book of the Bible (Genesis chapter 10), you find a list of tribes from all parts of the Near East. Israel was only one out of this group, and the Israelites knew it. They were certain that *God was Lord of the whole world,* even though he did have a special interest in them. After all, they said in their holy books that man, not just Israelite man, was made in God's image and likeness. (Genesis 1:26ff.)

JEWISH NATIONALISTS
EXCLUDED NON-JEWS

When those religious reformers whom we call the *prophets* came along, part of their message was to remind the people that the Lord willed to save *all men* and not only them. Many people didn't like to hear this, for they had become very *nationalistic.*

By Jesus' day, the idea of the unity of the human race and the importance of every individual was losing ground even among the rabbis. After they returned from the Babylonian exile in 538 B.C. their nationalism reached such a fever pitch that some were teaching that only a circumcised Jew could know happiness in "Abraham's bosom," an expression they used for a blessed after-life.

You pick up a hint of that in Saint John's gospel, where he says very briefly: "Now Jews do not associate with Samaritans." (John 4:9) The point of Saint John's story was precisely that Jesus, although a Jew, did not consider himself too good to associate with Samaritans. He did that very thing, as a matter of fact, when he spoke with the Samaritan woman at the well of Israel's great forefather, Jacob. Our Lord had

134

made a friend from among these people who were traditionally the enemies of the people Israel.

JESUS SCOLDED ISRAEL
PRAISED THE GENTILES

At every chance he got, Jesus scolded his own Jewish people. ("This wicked generation" was his favorite description of them!) On many occasions, he compared the heathen nations favorably with his fellow Jews. He spoke of the Queen of Sheba (Matthew 12:41ff.), the widow in Sidon back in the days of the prophet Elia, and the general in the Syrian army, Naaman (Luke 4:24-27), in more favorable terms than he did the Jews.

Jesus seemed to take special delight in multiplying examples of good religious conduct among foreigners, and of his own people's ingratitude to God. "Nowhere in Israel have I found such faith," he said once, after a Roman soldier expressed certainty that Jesus would cure his servant. (Matthew 8:10) *Nowhere* in Israel, mind you. Though Israel was still the favored son—the people God meant to have for his own—Jesus found more faith in a Gentile. On one occasion a crowd of his own people were quoted by Jesus as saying to him: "We sat at table with you and you taught in our streets."

What will his reply be when it comes time to judge them? "I do not know where you come from. Out of my sight, all of you." (Luke 13:26ff.)

LOVE FOR HIS PEOPLE
CAUSED CHRIST'S ANGER

Instances could be multiplied of the anger Jesus showed at the sins of his own people, the annoyance he exhibited toward their pettiness. Yet he loved them deeply. It would remind

135

you of the way parents put their children in their place when they get fresh. Whammo! They lose their tempers and sail right in because they love them so much. Mothers are forever praising the local talent: "Why can't you be more like Imogene McNasty? You never see *her* doing a thing like that!" Yet, these are the reproaches that are born of love.

The thing to look for in the gospels is not the flare-ups of Jesus, but his overall approach to "the Jewish question." Read carefully and you'll see that, in a word, he was mad for Israel. He had to be; after all, didn't he do always the things that pleased his Father? And wasn't the Lord God partner to a romance with Israel that went all the way back to Moses' time in the Sinai desert? "I passed you by and saw that you were now old enough for love . . . I swore an oath to you and entered into a covenant with you; you became mine, says the Lord God." (Ezechiel 16:8) Here, the prophet was referring to God's special love for Israel. The love that Jesus bore it could never be less than that.

And what a marvelous love he had for the holy city! He wept at its faithlessness: "O Jerusalem, Jerusalem, the city that murders the prophets and stones the messengers sent to her! How often have I longed to gather your children as a hen gathers her brood under her wings, but you would have none of it." (Matthew 23:37)

JESUS' FIRST CONCERN: THE LOST SHEEP OF ISRAEL

Jesus' extreme concern for Israel is evident in his policy on preaching and teaching. "I was not sent except to the lost sheep of the house of Israel," he said. (Matthew 15:24) In other words, the gathering of the scattered flock, which had been the work of all the prophets, was equally his task. When Jesus first sent his twelve friends out to preach his instructions

were, "Do not go in the direction of the Gentiles, nor enter the towns of the Samaritans; but go rather to the lost sheep of the house of Israel." (Matthew 10:5-6)

Does that sound strange to you? You knew Christianity was a world-wide religion, of course, and have always heard that Jesus came to save *all* men. Well, he did, but his first and biggest concern was "his own sheep." (John 10:3)

ISRAEL IS THE FAVORED SON
GENTILES ARE THE "PRODIGAL"

We can understand why Israel will always be the favored offspring from the parable of the prodigal son. Upon the wasteful boy's return home, there is great celebration. The father says to the older son, who is angry and refuses to join in the festivities, "My son, you are always with me, and everything I have is yours. We *had* to celebrate this happy day, for your brother has returned." (Luke 15:31-32) The people Israel is the elder brother. Everything God has belongs to him. Israel's position was never safer. Yet, when the Gentiles came to believe in the true God, after centuries of false religion and sinful conduct, it was necessary to rejoice. The Jewish people were asked to join in, in celebrating the wanderer's return.

We have it from the lips of Jesus himself that, "Salvation comes from the Jews." (John 4:22)

HIS PROMISE MADE ISRAEL
GOD'S PEOPLE FOREVER

Eileen Duggan, an Australian poet, wrote a piece some years ago called "Nationality." Toward the middle of the poem, these lines occur:

137

> Discountried and diskinged
> And watched from pole to pole,
> A Jew at heart remains a Jew—
> His nation is his soul.

It has to be that way, don't you see? The promise made by God was to his own, special people—forever. Though the land God gave the Israelites for their own was taken from them by the Greeks and the Romans, God never changed his promise.

Some of the Jewish people have a homeland once again, the state of Israel. Praise God for that! But they are not there on the same terms as we find in the biblical promise.

Nevertheless, God is found faithful to his promise even apart from that holy land. Because he isn't tied down to one little portion of earth, we must look to see what relation he continues to have with his chosen people if we are to discover whether he is faithful or not. God passes the test. He proves his faithfulness by the love he bears his beloved Son Jesus, the perfection of the chosen people. Though Jesus became "a light of revelation to the Gentiles" (Luke 2:32), he never stops being "a glory to the people Israel." God is in a continuing relation of love to all Jews, forever, because of his promise, and its wonderful fulfillment in becoming incarnate in Jewish flesh and blood.

ELDER BROTHER ISRAEL IS FOREVER FIRST HEIR

But, are we not all sons of the one Father? And is not Jesus himself our peace? "Gentiles and Jews, he has made the two one, and in his own body of flesh and blood, has broken down the enmity which stood as a dividing wall between them." (Ephesians 2:14ff.)

138

However, *the Jewish people will forever be the first heir to God's promise.* We must never forget that. God "has them with him always." All that he has is theirs. For he has never said, "I gave my promise to Israel once, but when I sent my Son I called the whole thing off." That would be nonsense. God cannot act in such a way. He is the Lord, and he changes not.

We who are Gentiles must hold our elder brother Israel in awe—this rightful son of the household. If we do not, we make a mockery of an ever-faithful God. Read chapter 9 of St. Paul's letter to the Romans. Then read chapter 11. Then adore the inscrutable will of God for the mysterious love for his people Israel that will forever be his.

St. Paul wrote: "By their (Israel's) false step, salvation has come to the Gentiles." (Romans 11:11) In other words, God permitted Israel's defection in order that all men might have an opportunity for salvation. If the Jews had accepted Jesus immediately, Christianity could scarcely have become universal. Undoubtedly, they would have kept this faith as narrowly national as they had kept Judaism.

Is their rejection final? Paul, who continued to love his people despite the folly of some, and who proudly wrote of himself, "I also am an Israelite, of the posterity of Abraham, of the tribe of Benjamin," made it very clear that *their rejection is not final.* He wrote, "A partial blindness only has befallen Israel, until the full number of the Gentiles should enter." (Romans 11:25) After the nations have had their full opportunity to enter the Church, Israel will have its second chance and not fail. Why? "Because," said Saint Paul, "God does not revoke his gifts and his call." (v. 29) God loved his son Israel in ancient times, even when he was faithless. He loves him still. He always will. He shall yet bring him home to himself, the loving Father!

20

Jesus, the Suffering Servant of the Lord

Some families still have servants. Not many, but some. Nowadays, most people who have someone working for them have an employee rather than a servant. You see the difference, don't you? *Servant* is a word that is passing out of use in this part of the world, because the social order it describes is disappearing. A more correct way of expressing it would be to say that, generally in the Western world, the relation of master and servant is giving way to that of boss and worker or employer and employee.

'AT YOUR SERVICE!' IS
NO SIGN OF LOWLINESS

It is no disgrace to be a servant or, in modern terms, an employee. The only time this arrangement becomes disgraceful is when one man treats another *as his servant*. To order a person around and to forget his dignity completely is the greatest injustice one human being can do to another. It doesn't matter whether this involves an army general and a private or a corporation's president and vice-president. No one is ever free to disregard the basic worth of another individual.

Many times the "servant" may really be the master. For example, the filling-station employee who gives you a bright smile and says, "At your service!" is far from being at the bottom of the social ladder. By his courtesy and willingness to help, he qualifies as master of the situation. On the other hand, a man who seems to be the master, if he is governed by pride and the desire to domineer those who are close to him, is actually the slave.

JESUS WAS PROUD
TO BE A SERVANT

This should all be very clear to you. It is well to recall it, though, because the notion of "servant" (which was close to that of "slave" in ancient times) plays a big part in the gospels. We cannot understand Jesus Christ in glory, King and Lord over angels and men, unless we know that in the days of his flesh, one of the proudest titles he claimed was servant.

His mother, too, was a servant. You remember how she agreed to God's plan as soon as the Angel Gabriel had explained it to her. "Regard me as the humble *servant* of

141

the Lord," were her words. "May all that you have said be fulfilled in me." (Luke 1:38) And when she praised God's goodness in song for choosing her to have a part in man's salvation, she called herself "his lowly maid." (Luke 1:48)

ISRAEL WAS *SERVANT* BUT NEVER *SLAVE*

In this, both she and her Son were like their people, "his servant Israel," whom God had kept faith with ever since Abraham's day. (Luke 1:54) Although the people Israel were servants, they were not "slaves to any man," as the crowd angrily told Jesus once during an argument (John 8:33); they were trusted servants of a loving Master. "You whom I have called my servant, whom I have chosen and will not cast off—fear not, I am with you; be not dismayed; I am your God." (Isaia 41:9ff.)

When their prophet Isaia wrote that way, putting speech on the lips of the Lord himself, Israel did not feel humiliated at being called a servant. This was a high title. So much confidence had been placed in them as the Lord's servant that the word conveyed to them only the holiness and splendor of their Ruler in heaven. "I will strengthen you and help you, and uphold you with my right hand of justice" (Isaia 41:10), he promised this servant of his.

THE BIBLE SPEAKS OF INDIVIDUAL SERVANTS

There are many other Bible passages where "servant" is a term of highest praise for the people of God. Often, too, it will stand for a pious individual Israelite, such as the author of one of the psalms, or the inspired writer of the Book of Wisdom: "Give me wisdom, the attendant at your throne,

142

and reject me not from among your children; for I am your *servant,* the son of your handmaid." (Wisdom 9:4-5) When God gave this gift of wisdom to the servant who asked for it, he became a magistrate, a king, or a temple builder —all of which roles were fulfilled holily in the Lord's service.

THE MASTER WILL NOT
FORGET HIS SERVANTS

The relation between the Lord and his servant, the people Israel, is a tender one of love and affection. "Servant" in the Bible means trusted son rather than laborer or slave. How could anyone hope for a stronger bond between God and a holy nation than is expressed in the following lines:

> "Remember this, O Jacob,
>> you, O Israel who are my servant!
> I formed you to be a servant to me;
>> O Israel, by me you shall never be
>> forgotten:
> I have brushed away your offenses
>> like a cloud, your sins like a mist;
>> return to me, for I have redeemed
>> you."
>
> (Isaia 44:21ff.)

OUR LORD PRACTICED
WHAT HE PREACHED

Since serving the Lord had placed Israel at the very top among the nations, it is no wonder Jesus taught that "he who would be a prince among you must be your servant, and he who would be a leader . . . must be your slave." (Matthew 21:26ff.) He wasn't the type to hand out empty advice, either.

143

He practiced what he preached. Because he was a true son of Israel, he, too, was a servant. Remember his words: "Why even the Son of Man did not come into the world to be served but *to serve* and to give His life as a ransom for many." (Mark 10:45)

TO BE A SERVANT, ONE
MUST PAY THE PRICE

The statement that he gave "his life as a ransom for many" is the clue to the whole idea of service as the Scriptures use it. You don't just *serve* the Lord. You pay the price for the honor of being his servant. This price is the offering of your life—your *total* being—to God.

It may seem harsh to put it as directly as that, but there's no other way to express the great truth that Jesus taught. He was a good and faithful Servant and entered into the joy of the Lord, but not before he had paid the price of his own life.

'BY HIS STRIPES
WE WERE HEALED'

To understand why it had to be so, we need to know four wonderful songs or poems in the Old Testament. These are called the Servant Songs. They all come from the same prophet's pen, that inspired author who wrote the second part of the Book of Isaia. The theme of the four poems is the same: that the Lord has a servant who will suffer much at the hands of Israel's enemies. The sufferings of this servant will end in death, but this will be no tragedy, for his guilty brothers will be judged innocent as a result of the death of this innocent sufferer. (Read these songs in Isaia 42:1-8; 49:1-6; 50:4-9; 52:13—53:12).

144

The Servant Songs are sad, all right. Reading them reminds us of the sufferings of Christ as the gospel describes them:

> He was pierced for our offenses,
>   crushed for our sins
> Upon him was the chastisement that
>   makes us whole,
>   by his stripes we were healed.
> We had all gone astray like sheep,
>   each following his own way;
> But the Lord laid on him
>   the guilt of us all.
>
> (Isaia 53:5-6)

THE REAL MEANING WAS LOST

The interesting thing about these beautiful prophecies is that, in our Lord's day, their real meaning was lost. The students of the Scriptures read them in such a way that they made the prophecies refer to the sufferings of the Lord's enemies! But the clearest thing about the Servant Songs is that the servant is God's great friend, not his, nor Israel's, enemy. In a general sense, this servant is the people Israel who must suffer for being faithful to the Lord. Upon more careful examination, you will see that a specific individual is being spoken of—a single member of this holy, suffering people.

> If he gives his life as an offering for sin,
>   he shall see his descendants enjoy a long life.
>
> (Isaia 53:10)

JESUS, THE MESSIA, IS
THE SUFFERING SERVANT

What Jesus, the Messia, did was to take these sad poems that seemed to describe defeat, and attach them to the figure of the glorious leader whom the people were waiting for. None of the rabbis of his time wished to do this. Nevertheless, Jesus said that Israel's Messia and the Suffering Servant were one and the same person. He said, more shocking still, that *he* was that person. "The Son of Man will be betrayed into the hands of men and . . . put to death . . . They will mock him and scourge him and spit upon him . . . (he will) suffer much, be rejected by the elders, the high priests, and the Scribes, be put to death, and after three days rise again." (Mark 9:31; 10:34; 8:31)

To make sure that His followers had understood him in his lifetime, Jesus said during his risen life: "This is the gist of the Scriptures: the Messia must suffer and on the third day rise from the dead." (Luke 24:46) He described it as necessary for the Messia to suffer so that He could enter into his glory.

YOU, TOO, WILL BE
CALLED TO SERVE

It is easy to say that everyone baptized into Christ must suffer and die with him if he hopes to enter into his glory. It is difficult, though, to understand exactly what this will mean to *you*. Until he sends you suffering, almost nobody in the world can get across to you what to expect.

Don't worry about it now; but when the blows begin to fall, or the taunting begins, or the attacks from without and within threaten, think of your model, Jesus, the suffering

147

servant, and say to yourself: "Well, here we are! Right on schedule. The servant is no better than his master. My master is the Lord of all because he served his brothers in suffering. Why can't I give it a try?"

21

Are You He Who Is to Come or Look We for Another?

The poet Belloc has a verse that runs,

> *Kings live in Palaces, and Pigs in sties,*
> *And youth in Expectation. Youth is wise.*

The name of that piece of solemn nonsense is "Habitations." "Home is where the heart is," says the proverb. We dwell in what we wish for, in other words. So it isn't such a nonsense verse after all. The dwelling place of youth *is* expectation.

KNOWLEDGE OF GOD'S WILL
FILLS US WITH HOLY HOPE

Now *expectation* and *hope* are first cousins. In one sense there isn't too much difference between them. Perhaps *expectation* has a ring of "I-think-it-will-happen" about it; *hope* has more the idea of "I-want-it-to-happen-but-don't-know-how-it-will-come-about." If that distinction is a correct one, then *hope* is the weaker word.

Yet, when *hope* is used in a Hebrew or a Christian sense, it has always been, and still is, a strong word. It describes a state of mind that is rooted in the known reality of God's love. He wills only good for us. The knowledge that we have of his will and his plan for us fills us with holy hope.

He will do everything, in other words, that is necessary to help us be with him in his glory. The utter certainty that this is so, we call HOPE.

IS HOPE ACTIVE NOW, OR
IS IT FOR A DISTANT FUTURE?

That seems to put things off quite a bit, doesn't it? No matter what age you are you tend to think that you won't be with him in his glory for a good number of years. Must we say, then, that hope has to do with a distant day in that it looks ahead twenty or fifty years? That would make a kind of useless virtue out of it—one that is almost bound to dry up for lack of exercise.

But of course that would be to think of hope much too narrowly. Hope is something that is ever-present, since God's care and his plan to save us are ever-present. Confidence, or trust based on certainty, is a thing of every moment. So hope is as actual to us now as our needs are. We hope at all times because our progress toward the Father, in Christ, continues

at all times. The continued need of God's help, plus the continued certainty of receiving it, add up to a hope which is always active.

MOST JEWS EXPECTED
A POLITICAL SAVIOR

In Jesus' day, the people of Galilee (his home territory in northern Palestine) and Judea (the south, where Jerusalem was located) were full of expectation. It would be good to report that they were also full of hope. But since *hope* is the stronger, truer, religious word, it is impossible to make such a report. In those times, great crowds of people had a trust in God's power to save them that was like a counterfeit bill: the eyes weren't quite straight, the lines were wobbly. They trusted more in their being sons of Abraham than they did in Abraham's God. The majority of the Israelites were more interested in being free politically than in being free from the slavery of sin.

We shouldn't, of course, neglect mentioning that there were many who had a solid hope that the Lord would be faithful to his promises. Among these were Mary, the mother of Jesus: "He has given help to Israel, his servant," she sang, "mindful of his mercy to Abraham and his children's children, forever" (Luke 1:54); old Zachary, father of John the Baptist: "He promised by the lips of his holy prophets that he would save us from our enemies and from the hands of all who hate us" (Luke 1:70-71); and Simeon: "Now Your promise is fulfilled; for my eyes have seen the deliverance which You have prepared before the face of all the nations." (Luke 2:29-31) These three saints under the Old Law represent a large class known as the "pious poor" in Israel— those whom Jesus praised in his first two beatitudes. (Matthew 5:3-4)

151

These are three cases in which those who possessed hope in the Lord, in its truest sense, lived to see their hope fulfilled.

JESUS' MIRACLES
FULFILL PROPHECY

All through the gospels we pick up hints of a popular belief in a mysterious personage referred to as "He who is to come." You get a reference to it in the question which the disciples of John the Baptist put to Jesus, having been sent by John for this purpose: "Are you he who is to come, or shall we look for another?" (Matthew 11:3) Jesus answered by naming some of his miracles which were roughly the same as those listed in the book of the prophet Isaia. (26:19; 35:5f.) These miracles were given by Isaia as necessary signs of the "last days": the blind see, the deaf hear, the lame walk. Jesus reported these things and the greatest marvel of all: "The poor have the good tidings proclaimed to them." (Matthew 11:5)

Jesus used the same words about "the expected one" to describe himself when he quoted a psalm that says, "Blessed is he who comes in the name of the Lord" (Matthew 23:39); and after feeding the five thousand with five loaves and two fishes, the people marvel and say, "This is indeed the prophet who is to come into the world." (John 6:14; see Deuteronomy 18:15)

ISRAELITES CONFUSED
ABOUT THEIR SALVATION

The people of our Lord's day had all sorts of titles for the person God would send to deliver them. They also had a variety of notions about what "deliverance" or "salvation" meant. As we've hinted above, the really good people knew that being set free from the weight of sin was the big thing. Still, all

152

of them—even Mary and Zachary and Simeon—quoted passages out of the Scriptures that spoke of their deliverer as scoring a smashing victory over Israel's enemies, who were also supposedly God's enemies.

At times, "the expected one" is called "the Holy One of God," whether by a demon (Mark 1:24), or by the fisherman friend of Jesus, Simon Peter. (John 6:69) The angels at Bethlehem call him a "Savior" (Luke 2:11); so do the Samaritans, those neighboring people sandwiched between Galilee and Judea who had the same beliefs as the Jews, by and large. (John 4:42)

It is to a Samaritan woman at Jacob's well that Jesus says, when she tells how she expects "the Messia who will tell us everything," "I am he who am speaking to you now." (John 4:26) That was a remarkable thing to say to a foreigner! He almost never told a fellow Jew he was the Messia. No doubt this was because the word *Messia* had come to mean all sorts of wrong things in his day.

'CHRIST' IS A TITLE—
NOT A PROPER NAME

Messia is the Hebrew word for an anointed servant of God. In Greek, the way to say it is *Christos*. It is a title, therefore, not a proper name. "Jesus is the Christ," we who believe in him say, as we might say, "John F. Kennedy is the president," or "Elizabeth is England's queen."

The word *Messia* was on everyone's lips during Jesus' lifetime. That, in a way, was what was wrong with it. Jesus warned His friends, "If anyone says to you, 'Look, here is the Christ; see, there he is,' do not believe it." (Matthew 24:23) So there must have been plenty of candidates for this honor in his day.

"Can it be that the rulers have really come to know that this is the Christ?" the crowds in Jerusalem asked about

153

Jesus. "Yet . . . when the Christ comes, no one will know where he is from," some objected. (John 7:26ff.) Evidently there was some mystery associated with his appearance on the earth. More than that, on the basis of their own Scriptures the devout had come to believe that the Christ would continue forever. (John 12:34)

Great was the faith of the common people in the coming Messia, and they asked, seeing Jesus "When the Christ comes will He work more signs than this man works?" (John 7:31) Obviously, Jesus was doing as many and as great wonders as these men of good will were ready for in their wildest dreams. Yet not all of his miracles together satisfied the Scribes and Pharisees, who kept asking for a "sign" in proof of his claims. (Matthew 12:38)

ISRAEL BELIEVED THE CHRIST
WOULD BE AN EARTHLY RULER

Let us put the pieces in this puzzle together now, to discover just what Israel hoped for in the Messia. First, the Jewish crowds thought their God would do great things for them, and they were right. He had promised it. They thought that when he sent his anointed king to save them it would be the last age of the earth, and in this they were right, too. They likewise thought that Israel would defeat all her enemies in battle, and that the Messia would rule under God over all the peoples of the earth.

Here they were very wrong. You might say that Jesus was put to death because he told them how wrong they were.

For what our Lord did was change the popular idea about a lightninglike "coming of the kingdom." He let them know that the Messia and the Suffering Servant were one and the same, *and he was that one*. The people were terribly slow to get the idea; some of them never got it. Even after he rose

from the dead, his best friends asked an old, old question that was by then clearly the wrong question: "Lord, will you restore the rule to Israel at this time?" (Acts 1:6) He tells them that they'll never know God's secret answer to that one, so will they please get on with spreading the news of salvation to the ends of the earth. *And, this advice to get busy with the spread of the kingdom is just what you and I need.*

MESSIA OF ISRAEL'S HOPE
IS OUR HOPE OF GLORY, TOO

When Jesus came, he was the Messia of Israel's hope. In the hearts of believers, those with true hope, his coming was glorious, triumphant, although many others did not see this.

When he returns, when he comes back to us, his glory will be made plain to all, believer and unbeliever alike. Meanwhile it is hidden. Like God's love in the soul, it can only be seen by the eye of faith.

Let us sum up in black and white what we Christians hold about the Lord's Anointed who has come in human flesh:

Jesus Christ, our hope of glory. The Son of Man who will come back to us on the clouds of heaven. The Lord, the just judge, who will say, "Come, you blessed of my Father."

All this we can be certain of. This is the substance of our hope.

22

The Raising of Lazarus

Can you remember clearly your first personal experience of death? High school is the time when many have their first taste of "fell sergeant death," so swift in his arrest. Seeing a member of one's own family, or a school friend, lying still in a satin-lined casket can be a bitter experience for youth. Do you recall your first encounter with this intruder?

It seemed so unfair at the time. No one had ever warned you that death could be so cold, so motionless, so final as this. When the dead person's body went into the earth—if he was the first person close to you to die—life seemed strange and unreal for days!

EVERYONE FINDS DEATH
DIFFICULT TO ACCEPT

When someone alive and active yesterday lies dead today you wonder how people can go about their business, especially if that person was very close to you. You are puzzled that some who suffer a loss can be so calm about sending telegrams to all the relatives and calling on the phone to make the "arrangements."

An empty feeling, hard to describe, comes over the young person who experiences his first death. That emptiness is real, palpable. It crowds out completely what seemed impossible to displace—life! Everything appears somewhat false and useless for weeks after death—if it's a boy or girl's first death.

DEATH ISN'T SO BAD WHEN YOU
DON'T THINK ABOUT IT

As people grow older they get used to death—death *for others*. That's the deceptive thing about it; when you think about death or talk about it it's always someone else's. Paradoxically, the less you think about death, the more easily you grow accustomed to it.

JESUS IS VICTOR OVER DEATH

Victory over death was accomplished in the life of Jesus of Nazareth. It is his great achievement. When Peter delivered the first Christian sermon, he said that the Master had not been left in the grave; his flesh did not see decay. "God has raised up this Jesus—of that fact we are all witnesses." (Acts 2:32) Though Jesus has a tomb, his is very different from all other tombs. It is empty. He sits at the right hand of God. The proof that God had made Jesus Lord and Christ, said Peter, was

157

that no tomb could hold him. His proper element was not death, but life.

THERE IS A MESSAGE ABOUT CHRIST'S DEATH IN THE STORY OF LAZARUS

Are you familiar with the mention of Lazarus in the song sung at a funeral, as the body is carried down the aisle of the church to the door? It is called *In Paradisum*. The words go like this:

> *May the angels lead you into*
> *paradise,*
> *The martyrs receive you at your*
> *coming*
> *And guide you into Jerusalem the*
> *holy city.*
> *May the angel choirs bid you*
> *welcome—*
> *Give you rest eternal in the company*
> *of Lazarus,*
> *Once a wretched beggar.*

This was the Lazarus of Christ's parable. (Luke 16:19-31)

There is another Lazarus in the gospels. You will remember that he is the man whom Jesus brought back to life after he had been dead four days and his body had begun to stink with decay. The true story of this Lazarus has an important message in connection with your death, and with Christ's death. Let us examine it.

JESUS DID NOT HURRY TO CURE LAZARUS; HE HAD HIS REASONS

Jesus had been a good friend of a certain two sisters and their brother, whom he used to visit at their home in Bethany.

158

Lazarus lay dying, and his two sisters sent word of this to Jesus. The Lord did not run off in haste to visit him, however, least of all to cure him on the spot. He very calmly said when he got the news: "This illness will not result in death. No, it is to promote the glory of God. Through it, the Son of God is to be glorified." (John 11:4) Then for two days Jesus didn't make a move. Rather strange conduct, wouldn't you say?

JESUS USED LAZARUS' DEATH
TO PROMOTE GOD'S GLORY

Jesus then went back to Judea (where both Bethany and Jerusalem were located). He knew that his enemies were out to destroy him; he also knew that he would accomplish the work he came to do in the time the Father had given him, neither more nor less.

First, Jesus told his friends that Lazarus was asleep, meaning to say in hidden language that he was dead. They missed his point, so he came out with the direct statement: "Lazarus is dead. For your sakes I am glad I was not there, so that you may believe. Come now, let us go to him." (John 11:15)

Do you see how Jesus thinks? It is always in terms of the unveiling of the mystery of God. This unveiling God accomplishes slowly, through His Son. Jesus came for the very purpose of helping make this *revelation* (unveiling). He does not wish to uncover completely the mystery of God's love for us—that would be impossible—but to share it, to enlighten us on the unspeakable riches of his tender care.

MARTHA BELIEVED THAT
LAZARUS WOULD LIVE

The funeral had already taken place when Jesus arrived at the outskirts of the town. Martha ran to tell him the sorrowful news.

Jesus and Martha had a profound conversation right there on the spot. It is given in the gospel of the Mass on the Day of Death or Burial. (See John 11:21-27). Jesus promised Martha that her brother would live. She was a pious Jew, and had the same convictions about the raising up of the dead from their graves as Jesus did. She already believed in what Jesus reminded her of and said so. It is as if a priest were to comfort someone at a funeral, and the person were to agree with what was said because he had the same faith as the priest. Jesus and Martha held to the belief of the Pharisee party that the dead would rise again.

MARTHA HAD GREAT FAITH IN JESUS, SON OF GOD!

Then Jesus said to her: "I am the resurrection and the life. He who believes in me will live, even if he dies; no one that lives and believes in me shall be dead forever. Do you believe this?" "Yes, Lord," she replied, "I firmly believe that you are the Messia, the Son of God who was to come into the world." (John 11:25-27) Do you see the point? She goes from a general faith in the resurrection to a particular faith in Jesus as the Christ.

JESUS CALLED LAZARUS BACK FROM THE TOMB

Once Martha had said that, Jesus had accomplished all that he had hoped for in Lazarus' death—with her at least. Then he went off to the rock-hewn tomb of Lazarus to try to move other hearts to have faith in him, and in the Father who had sent him. Making his way through the noisy, wailing crowds, he disregarded the stench of a body four days dead, went into the little cave and cried out strongly, "Lazarus, come forth." (John 11:43) When Lazarus emerged, bound hand and foot with linen

in the custom of those times, Jesus said, "Unwrap him and let him go."

YOU ARE EITHER JESUS' FRIEND OR HIS ENEMY

Many believed in Jesus that day. Some did not. Those who did not reported to his enemies this latest sign of power, and the supreme council in Jerusalem (the Sanhedrin) began to plot against his life.

That's the way it is with the Son of Man. You're either with him or against him. There is no middle road. The more power he shows from on high, the more you trust him, or hate him.

If you believe in him, you do not fear death—your own or anyone else's. You know that it is chiefly a way God has to show forth his glory—the glory of the resurrection that he will share with men who have the faith in Christ that Martha had

23

The Meals Jesus Took

Jesus did nothing without a reason. The more you read the gospel, the more you see the truth of this statement. He never acted on the spur of the moment, nor gave answers thoughtlessly. At the same time, there is no evidence that Jesus lived under any strain. He moved from one action to the next with a calm certainty which said, "I do always what pleases the Father who sent me."

(Read John 8:27-30 for Jesus' policy on the conduct of his life; also John 4:34, where he considers doing the Father's will his meat and drink).

JESUS ALWAYS HAD A REASON—
EVEN WHEN HE ATE HIS MEALS

This attitude of deliberateness is seen in the least of his actions —even in the meals he took. There is no record of his taking meals in the normal routine fashion. It is true, he was hungry after his long fast in the desert, as anyone would be. (Matthew 4:2) Later, when vast crowds pressed around him, in his adopted town of Capharnaum, he and his disciples "could not even take a meal." (Mark 3:20) Yet the impression is clearly given by the gospel that every time he ate or drank, he did so to promote the kingdom of God.

This can be seen in his visits at the homes of "sinners." In the gospel this word does not usually mean evil men. Like a modern definition from Moscow, it meant what the religious leaders decided it should mean, namely people who did not keep the Law of Moses as those in power interpreted it. That is why when we read that Jesus "reclined at table (stretched out to eat a banquet meal, a Greek custom) with sinners," we know that the company wasn't half bad. (See Mark 2:15-17).

Eating with tax collectors was another thing our Lord did fairly often. That was a slightly different matter. Tax collectors were almost certainly crooked, in an official sort of way.

RICH ZACCHEUS WAS IN NEED
SO JESUS ATE WITH HIM

When we read in the gospel, for example, about Zaccheus, "a high official among tax collectors and rich as well," (Luke 19:2), we know both what his bank balance was and how it got that way. Surely he was a dishonest man. Yet Jesus ate with Zaccheus because he was rich and therefore greatly in need.

Jesus said, "Zaccheus . . . today I must be your guest."

Down Zaccheus scrambled from the tree he had climbed to

get a better look at Jesus. He welcomed the famous teacher joyfully. Jesus said of him, presumably during the meal he took, "Today salvation has visited this household, because he, too, is a son of Abraham. After all, it is the mission of the Son of Man to seek and save what is lost." (Luke 19:9-10)

TO THE ISRAELITES, A FORMAL
MEAL MEANT SOMETHING SACRED

One thing we need to know about Jesus and meals, especially the formal meals he took as an invited guest, is that the Old Testament period looked upon the banquet meal as a sign of something holy. A father and his family would celebrate sacred meals at a common table laden with rich foods. An example of this is the great supper held at harvest time which is called *Sukkoth* (Feast of Booths, or Arbors). A rich man would also invite guests in great numbers when his son was being married, in those days. When he did this he was celebrating the marriage of the Lord to Israel, as well as that of his son to his bride.

MOST SACRED OF ALL MEALS WAS
BANQUET TAKEN AFTER SACRIFICE

Most sacred of all, however, was the banquet meal taken after a sacrifice had been offered. In this practice, whatever was offered to God—say a ram, a lamb, or some grain—was given by God back to the Israelite who offered it. It was "consecrated," changed into God-like food, by being offered to God. When God returned it to the people, they ate as their food something that properly was his. In doing so, they came very close to God. After all, they were being nourished by sacred food—food that had been made God's special possession.

Now Jesus was a faithful son of his people. He took part in all of Israel's customs, the religious ones above all. He attended

the usual banquets on the three great feasts of pilgrimage to Jerusalem each year (Passover, Weeks, and Booths). He also attended many a wedding banquet and family celebration.

THE JEWS WERE CERTAIN OF GREAT BANQUET ON ARRIVAL OF MESSIA— THE LAST AGE OF EARTH

The special celebration that the Jews of Jesus' time hoped for was the banquet of the End Time or the last age of the earth. They would eat it when the Messia came, they thought. It would be then that the close friendship with God that had dawned in the garden of Eden would be renewed.

In the meantime, every meal in celebration—the Passover and all the other feasts—provided a way to speed the coming of the Messia. This would bring God's deliverance. Under his anointed king, the holy people would sit down at God's table and eat and drink in his kingdom. The Jews were sure of this, just as sure as you are that the sun will come up tomorrow.

'YOU SHALL EAT AND DRINK AT MY TABLE,' JESUS VOWED

Jesus put a stop in his lifetime to a lot of foolish guessing about the future. But one idea that he never discouraged was that the last age would be like a great meal of celebration. "You have stood by me in my trials," he said to his friends toward the end of his lifetime. "Therefore, just as my Father has willed that I should inherit kingly power, so I in turn vest in you the rights of kingship; you shall eat and drink at my table in my kingdom . . ." (Luke 22:28-30)

PARABLE OF THE GREAT SUPPER—
DO YOU KNOW ITS MEANING?

Our Lord once told a parable about a great supper. In it, it was made very clear that the master's house had to be filled to capacity. (Luke 14:22) Even if the host needed to force the guests to come in, he meant to have a full house. Surely this was a reference to the way Jesus felt about his kingdom, the Church. It would be filled first with Jews, then with Gentiles; and there would always be room for more.

NOT EVERYONE WILL SIT
AT HIS FATHER'S TABLE

Jesus did say, however, that not everyone will sit at his Father's table. He put it this way: "Many will come from the east and west and in the company of Abraham, Isaac and Jacob, will recline at table in the kingdom of heaven." (Matthew 8:11) At the same time, born citizens of that realm will be thrust out into the night because they do not have the faith that a heathen Roman soldier had. They will complain, our Lord predicted; they will cry out bitterly: "We ate and drank under your eyes, and you taught in our streets." (Luke 13:26)

Jesus will say to such people: "I tell you, I do not know who you are. Get out of my sight, you pack of evildoers." (Luke 13:27)

YOU, TOO, MAY BOAST
YOU ATE WITH JESUS

Other people, who do have faith, will be able to say the same thing of Jesus as Saint Peter did: "We . . . ate and drank with him after he rose from dead." (Acts 10:41) This will be perfectly acceptable to the Father. In Peter's case, he is naming

166

the special reason why he and the other disciples had been given the task of preaching the good news. They had already taken a meal with Jesus, Lord and Christ, in the kingdom of God.

'THIS IS MY BODY: TAKE YOU AND EAT'

This meal was the Last Supper, that final sacred meal that Jesus ate with his twelve friends. All the food and drink he ever took led up to this meal. When, on another occasion, he had multiplied the bread by miracle at the lakeshore, he acted just as his Father had done through Moses when he sent manna from the sky to feed the Israelites in the desert. Jesus' miracle recalled the miracle in the desert and it looked forward to the great banquet of the Last Supper.

The chief sign of discipleship that Jesus left behind him was given at the final meal eaten before the coming of God's kingdom in glory. Jesus said as much. In fact, he took a vow not to drink wine again until the kingdom of God was set up. (Luke 22:16) Days later, when it was established at a new level by his resurrection in glory, he was free to drink "the fruit of the vine" again.

Jesus is the *true* bread from heaven—we have his word on this—as opposed to the manna which was only a sign. He said that if men eat his body and blood they will have life to sustain them until the Last Day. He gave them his body and blood at the Last Supper. He gives this same body and blood to us, in the eucharistic celebration. (Read chapter 6 in St. John's gospel; it is the closest John comes to discussing the institution of the eucharist).

WILL YOUR MEALS LEAD YOU
TO HEAVEN'S HIGH FEAST?

Mealtime is happy time, charity and love time. Have you found it so? Would you be ready to have Jesus come to your dining room table, your plant or school cafeteria, and offer you his body and blood there? Do you treat your family meals as sacred banquets, serving God in all that you say and do while you're eating?

If your meals mean all this to you, each one of them is tied in with your next eucharist. Both your meals and your eucharists will then look forward to the table of the Lord at heaven's high feast.

24

Jesus Enters Jerusalem

There is excitement in store for anyone who gets the chance to travel. One thrill that travel may bring you is the sight of the cathedral dedicated to our Lady in Chartres, France, as you approach it from Paris. The outline of the huge church pierces the skyline, rising from the flat meadows and farms like a ship sailing on a sea of wheat.

Another such thrill is the one that comes with first spying the cathedral at Pisa in Italy, with its famous leaning tower, as you approach it through the hill country from Florence.

WHAT SIGHTS STIR YOU MOST?
DO THEY TELL OF GOD, OF MAN?

Most people experience a clutching at their hearts when they see the Capitol at Washington. Or when leaving the United States aboard a ship, they watch the Statue of Liberty fade in the waters of New York harbor. Greater still is their elation when, on their return, the Great Lady, the symbol of freedom and security, welcomes them home.

People sometimes feel cheated because no one has ever told them how much it would move them to gaze suddenly upon these sights. All these buildings tell something about God, something about man.

Since our chief concern in these pages is Jesus of Nazareth, we will want to know what sights moved him most deeply. Great natural beauties? Man-made wonders?

THE CITY OF JERUSALEM
TOPPED HIS LIST

Surely the most moving sight that Jesus ever gazed on was the holy city of Jerusalem. Its chief feature for him was the temple being built by Herod the Great. Psalm 121 sang (and Jesus must have prayed it often): "I rejoiced because they said to me, 'We will go up to the house of the Lord!' And now we have set foot within your gates."

Psalm 83 took up the same theme: "How lovely is your dwelling place, O Lord of hosts! My soul yearns and pines for the courts of the Lord."

ALL JERUSALEM SHARED
THE TEMPLE'S HOLINESS

These snatches from the psalms underline the point we wish to make. There was no major distinction between sacred buildings

and other buildings for Jesus and his people. Their whole outlook was sacred. The capital city, Jerusalem, was not just a fine city; it was the stronghold of their God. His shrine or sanctuary was the central place in it. A holier or more splendid setting anywhere in the world they could not imagine. Everything in Jerusalem shared, in some way, in the holiness of the central shrine.

Jesus loved Jerusalem because it was the city of King David, his ancestor of a thousand years before; but also, and above all, it was his Father's city. The temple was there with its holy of holies (that dark, empty chamber where only the high priest, a descendant of Aaron, went once each autumn to sprinkle blood for the people's sins). This room had long ago housed the stone tablets of the Law, before they were lost in battle. In front of this room, the holy of holies, was the "holy place," where reminders of God's special protection of the Jews were located: the seven-branched candlesticks, Aaron's rod, and the twelve round, flat loaves of bread reminding the people of the manna from heaven which had fed the twelve tribes in the desert.

JESUS LOVED THE TEMPLE, HIS OWN 'FATHER'S HOUSE'

Jesus would never have been inside that part, of course. He did not belong to a priestly family, being a member of the tribe of Jacob and not of Levi. The whole nation of Jews, however, was priestly. Everyone was terribly interested in the morning and evening sacrifices offered to the Lord by the priests of Aaron's line. The holier an individual Jew was, the more he cared about what went on in the temple. And Jesus was the holiest of Jews!

On the day he made such a commotion in the temple area about the changing of money for profit, he called the buildings "my Father's house." (John 2:16) He loved the temple dearly, yet he knew it would not remain standing very long. During his

171

public career it had already been under construction for forty-six years. Another forty-one or two and down it would come—ruined by the Romans in 70 A.D.

CHRIST RISEN IS OUR TEMPLE
AND OUR HIGH PRIEST FOREVER

Although Jesus could foresee this destruction, it was not that which he meant to prophesy the day he said, "Destroy this temple, and in three days I will raise it up." (John 2:19) No, he was speaking of the temple of his body. The risen body of Jesus would be the new sanctuary for all to worship before. When it would be taken up in the glory of his ascension, it would become the focal point of all human prayer.

Jesus became not only our temple, but our high priest as well. By his ascension, he went behind the veil of the heavens (as Israel's high priest went behind the temple veil), not once a year, but once only. His prayer to the Father upon his arrival in heaven was a perfect one, because he had completed the work he came on earth to do. Jerusalem's temple found its fulfillment in the temple of the Lord's body.

JESUS WEPT OVER JERUSALEM
BECAUSE HEARTS WERE HARD

All these things we must know if we are going to understand Jesus' feelings toward Jerusalem. At the end of his young life, this strong, self-controlled man who had lived in the outdoors for a couple of years cried—actually cried—over the city he loved so much. "Jerusalem, Jerusalem!" he said, "The city that murders the prophets and stones the messengers sent to her. How often would I have gathered your children as a hen gathers her young under her wings; but you would not have

it. Behold your house [did he mean your temple?] you will find abandoned, a prey to desolation." (Matthew 23:37ff.)

It seems fairly clear from these words that Jesus is foretelling the destruction of the city he loved so much. He says, "I've tried—tried with all my strength. But I just can't reach your hearts."

CUSTOM WAS TO MEET
VISITORS AT CITY GATES

We are getting ahead of our story, though. It is not right to quote Jesus' lament over Jerusalem before he has entered Jerusalem. He has been making his way solemnly southward to Judea to suffer and to die. There are stops along the way: at Jericho to see Zaccheus, at Bethany to visit the Lazarus household, and at the Mount of Olives just east of the city. Then Jesus instructs two of his friends to unhitch an ass's colt in a nearby village, explaining to the owner, "The Master needs it."

Off the little procession goes, once ready, in the fashion of pilgrims from out of the area entering the holy city. Nowadays when we have important visitors, we meet them at the airport, the dock or the depot. In those times, the Jerusalem residents would go out to the edges of the city to escort the pious travelers in on foot. "Open to me the gates of holiness," they would all sing, "I will enter them and give thanks to the Lord . . . This is the day the Lord has made; let us be glad and rejoice in it." (Psalm 117:19, 24)

'BLESSED IS HE WHO COMES'
GREETED JESUS' ENTRANCE

These verses are taken from the psalm most commonly used to welcome pilgrims at Passover time. A couple of lines in it

173

are very important to the story of Jesus. The crowds sang out: "Blessed is he who comes in the name of the Lord. We bless you from the house of the Lord." (Psalm 117:26)

That sounds harmless enough. Did not any good Israelite come to Jerusalem "in the name of the Lord"? Why shouldn't this shout go up from the temple court to greet Jesus? But his enemies didn't see things that way. They thought that Jesus was accepting honors that should have been reserved to the Messia alone—certainly not to him. They tried to stop the demonstration, the branches of olive and palm strewn out before Jesus, as the sleepy little long-eared beast moved along bearing its holy burden, the Savior of the world.

"Hosanna (meaning 'Save us!') to the Son of David," the people cried. (Matthew 21:15)

JESUS ENTERED IN TRIUMPH
BUT ENEMIES WERE THERE

Do you hear what they are saying? Jesus' enemies said angrily. "Rabbi, rebuke your disciples," they ordered. (Luke 19:39) But Jesus said to them, "I tell you that if these people keep silence, the very stones will cry out."

In, in he went to the heart of the city he loved more than any place on earth—knowing that it would destroy him.

THE CHURCH AS JERUSALEM—
THE MASS AS THE TEMPLE

Think, for a minute, of the Church in our day with all its people, as if it were a splendid city—Jerusalem, in fact. Now think of the temple in that city as if it were the sacrifice of the Mass, the holiest of human actions that goes on day and night within the Church. Now think of Jesus as he comes back to earth in

triumph—not on an ass's back this time, but riding on the clouds of heaven.

Often asked by his friends—simple fisherfolk who didn't know a great deal of theology—what the signs of the last times would be, and how they might expect his coming at the end of the world, Jesus gave a long and detailed answer in the special language of a part of the Bible called *apocalyptic*. His chief answer to them was: Whenever the Son of Man returns it will be sudden and swift. No one can quite prepare for it. But try. If you are ready at heart, then the great suffering that surrounds all men will not be so great for you.

We shall have more to say about this answer of his in the next chapter.

YOU MUST ANSWER THIS ONE

"When the Son of Man comes, will he find faith on earth?" (Luke 18:8) *You* must answer this question. Is your faith a thing of habit? A thing of school or Sunday Mass-time? Are the dark things that go on in the side streets of the city of God —the pious hypocrisies, the cheap little bargains that go masked as acts of religion—the only things Christ will find when he comes back?

There was a destruction of Jerusalem, once, by Romans who did not understand the holiness of religion. Could there ever be a destruction by the holy God, who knows all about the holiness of religion?

Jesus keeps weeping for us. We in the holy city of the Church still have time to change.

25

Jesus Teaches About the Last Days

Every once in a while you read in the newspaper about someone who says the end of the world is coming soon—say in 1985, or this July, or next Thursday. In these days of nuclear stockpiles it would take only one madman at the head of a government to bring about the end—of the planet earth at least; but that is not the kind of thing we mean.

The people who issue statements on the date the world will go up in flames are always "religious" types. They do not issue forecasts or predictions. They utter *prophecies*. Now why on earth should religion be interested in the date when the earth is going to end, whimper or bang? Do these prophets really have a clue, or are they just trying to get their names into the newspapers?

PROPHETS SPEAK FOR GOD,
TEACHING MEN GOD'S TRUTH

The best way to attack this problem is first to see what a prophet is. A prophet is a man who speaks for God. He addresses men in the name of God. Moses was a prophet. Isaia, that Old Testament writer we quote so often, was another. For us Christians, the last and greatest of the prophets was Jesus of Nazareth.

A true prophet, says the Bible, is a man on whom the Spirit of God rests. Now God is all-holy, so a prophet will be holy. But the real test of a prophet is this: what he teaches in the Lord's name either *is* true, or *will come* true, because God is truth itself. (Deuteronomy 18:15-22)

In applying this test to men who claim to have special, inside information about the end of the world, we ask whether they qualify as prophets. First, are they really holy? Are they well-balanced mentally, not fanatics? Do they love and honor the Scriptures, or do they have the Bible as a sort of disease? Part of sainthood, you know, is being mentally sound. Someone has put it this way: "Holiness is wholeness."

HOLY SPIRIT SPEAKS
THROUGH THE CHURCH

Test number two for your modern prophet is this: is he part of the Church, the "pillar and bulwark of truth" (1 Timothy 3:15), as Saint Paul calls it? No one can tell the Holy Spirit what he can do and can't do, of course. That goes without saying. (See Mark 9:37-40). It is absurd to think that he can move only Catholic hearts and speak only through Catholic tongues. He will never speak through other churches, though, if they take positions on Christian matters that go against the Church's teaching. We have Jesus' word that the Spirit of truth will

177

never do this. (See John 16:13). Prophecy is a gift of the Church. The Church has always had prophets. She is very careful to listen when a holy person claims to have a vision or to hear heavenly voices. Her real prophets in every age are, of course, her bishops—by virtue of their teaching office.

But notice this. Even though Jesus is Israel's and the Church's greatest prophet, his disciples could never get him to make a prophecy on the date the world would end! He did give us this important warning: "No pupil is above his teacher." (Matthew 10:24) In other words, watch out for the man who foretells what Jesus would not foretell: "But about that day and hour no one knows, not even the angels in heaven, nor even the Son, but only the Father." (Matthew 24:36)

JESUS *IS* COMING —
SWIFTLY UNEXPECTEDLY

That is the one important thing we ought to underline in this discussion: although we know that the end of the world is coming, we do not know *when*. Sometimes we see signs along the highway which say, "Prepare to meet thy God," or "Jesus is coming soon." These are good signs, bearing important reminders. They speak the language of the New Testament. They come from a time when the first Christians thought that Jesus would quickly return to them, after only a brief stay with his Father. The trouble is he has been gone for more than nineteen centuries now. He may be gone for thousands more. The right word to describe his coming back to us, therefore, is not "soon" but "swiftly" or "unexpectedly." Whenever it happens, it will take us by surprise.

There is only one thing to fear about the end of the world—or our own death, the end of *our* world. That is, will we have our hearts ready when it comes? Nothing else about it should frighten us.

178

IN THE EUCHARIST, GOD
COMES TO JUDGE US LOVINGLY

Every time we receive the body of the Lord, it is God coming to judge us through his Son. He judges us lovingly when he does come. Only if he were to find us in sin would the eucharist be a judgment of "guilty" against us. But God has no desire to find us in sin. He wants to judge us favorably again and again throughout our lives, so that the final judgment will be like all the others: "Enter into the joy of the Lord." (Matthew 25:23) In other words, "Share to the full your master's happiness."

How did we get started on all this talk about the end of the world? Actually it is Jesus himself who launched the topic. The idea comes up in the gospel many times in one form or other. The Master always dodges it, or answers his questioner shortly. Finally, Jesus meets the issue head on. Read the two long passages in the gospel, one in chapter 13 of Saint Mark and the other in chapters 24 and 25 of Saint Matthew, in which our Lord gives a long description of the Last Days.

JEWS OF JESUS' TIME HAD
MANY IDEAS OF LAST DAYS

To understand the gospel on this point we need to know how much the Jews of Jesus' day were influenced by thoughts of the final age of the world. Nowadays, people can hardly be made to think about death. They shudder and say: "It's too gruesome." It is almost impossible in the 1960's to get a conversation started about eternal life. But in those times, anyone who happened to ask in a crowd of pious Jews, "I wonder what the Last Days will be like?" could settle down and listen to a good four-hour discussion.

The trouble with all this talk was that it was a threat to true religion. Instead of dwelling on the *message* of the prophets, the

179

people spent all their time on the *language* of the prophets. Some rabbis taught there would be a thousand years of peace and plenty, for example. Others said ten thousand times ten thousand. The heavens would cave in. The moon would turn to blood. The earth would be consumed by a raging fire, so as to be cleansed by it. The one central and certain fact, however, was that the Lord would win out over all his enemies. Through God's anointed king, this victory would be achieved. All nations of the earth would bow down before the Messia of God. This would all come soon, soon, soon!

DID GOD'S PROPHETS
DECEIVE THE JEWS?

You may very well ask how this wild talk got started. Israel had been truly taught by God through Moses and the prophets, had she not? Did God work some of this teaching into Scripture? If so, it seems he was deceiving his chosen people. But that is unthinkable. God cannot deceive. What was the story on all these "prophecies"?

Here are the facts in the case: the Hebrew language is filled with rich figures of speech. That means you have one word doing the work of another, time and again, like "lion" for courage, or "a broken reed" for someone you can't depend on. When some men taught others in writing, as did those Israelites whom the Holy Spirit helped to write down the teachings of the prophets, they did it in the most beautiful poetry imaginable. When they described how the Lord would destroy Jerusalem unless she changed her ways, you could not help knowing she was doomed.

Gradually, as the centuries passed, the people laid more and more stress on the language of the prophets, and less and less on what the prophets were getting at. What was the result? A disease—a real disease in the religious spirit of the people.

They began to outdo one another in the tall tales they manu-factured about the marvels of the End Time. They substituted apocalyptic writing (all sorts of "revelations") for prophetic.

WILD GUESSES CONFUSED
WITH THE TRUE RELIGION

By the time Jesus came to earth, this business had become a national pastime, like gambling on a lottery or boasting about fishing trips. The dangerous thing about this "prophesying" (guessing, really), was that it was terribly mixed up with the true religion taught by the prophets. It was so mixed up that Jesus spent most of his public life trying to untangle the two ideas. The people never completely succeeded in understanding what the prophets were trying to say because this apocalyptic type of writing got in the way.

Time and again the crowds, and even Jesus' close friends, the Twelve, asked him if the kingdom would come soon. Once in a while, Jesus would use a phrase from a book of prophecy in the Bible. In the main, though, he would not go along with the wild-eyed, popular religious beliefs we have been speaking about. To make sure of this, he wouldn't even use the poetic terms of those biblical books. When people tried to steer him in that direction, he firmly went in another.

TRUE RELIGION WAS THE
PEACE OF GOD—TO JESUS

True religion for our Lord was something calm and peaceful. It was a thing of the head and the heart—not a bundle of emotions tied up with politics and visions and explosions in the heavens. Jesus did keep saying (or hinting) that the king-dom would be set up soon—indeed, had been set up already. (See Luke 10:9; 17:21). His kingdom, while visible, was simple

181

and silent, and to accept it would require faith. (See Mark 4: 26-29). Toward the close of his life, our Lord was again approached on this topic by his friends. He met it squarely. These simple fishermen, who had heard what the rabbis were teaching, asked him what the signs of the Last Times would be, and how they might expect his coming at the end of the world. (Matthew 24:3) Slowly, patiently, he answered. On this occasion *only*, he used the language the Jews had at their command to speak about these things. It was the *language* of the prophets. Using it, he spoke the *message* of the prophets. The return of the Son of Man, he said, will be sudden and swift. No one can be fully ready, but everyone must try to be. If your hearts are ready, said Jesus, then the sufferings that men will experience when God comes to judge will not be so great for you. (You must read Matthew 24 and 25, Mark 13, and Luke 17:26-37 to get the Master's full message).

WE MUST BE PREPARED
FOR HIS SECOND COMING

Are we clear on this matter of the Last Days? Jesus *will* come back. He will come in spendor. His coming will be unexpected and we must prepare for it, for Jesus will judge us.

The terrible destruction of Jerusalem by the Roman armies, which happened some forty years after Jesus' time, like the sack of that same city by the Babylonians in 587 B.C., gives us some inkling of what God will permit in the way of judgment. What God wants us to think about, though, when we receive his Son in the eucharist, or think about our own death, is how he wants to judge us *in his love*. The joyous sentence of Jesus to be spoken at the judgment is the classic place in Scripture for that: "Come, the elect of my Father! Take possession of the kingdom prepared for you at the beginning of the world." (Matthew 25:34)

26

The Master Takes Leave of His Friends

Do you know a poem of Shelley's called *Ozymandias of Egypt?*
You find it frequently in textbooks of English literature. It's
about a man who is trudging across the desert and comes
upon a statue that has been standing for centuries. He removes
from the base some of the sand that has been covering it, and
slowly reads the inscription: "My name is Ozymandias, king
of kings: Look on my words, ye Mighty, and despair!"

You see immediately what the poet is getting at. Poor old
Ozymandias and his opinion of his own importance. Is *he* ever
dead! So are all the kings and emperors and popes who ordered
great tombs built over them so that no one would ever forget
them. The only ones who live on in human memory, it seems
(aside from dictators) are those who serve other people. States-

men, artists and musicians, for example, leave something behind them—gifts, for all to enjoy.

FORGET YOURSELF—IF YOU WANT TO BE REMEMBERED

Actually, the best remembered men are the saints—those heroes of unselfishness who forget their way into the remembance of everyone who comes after them.

The moral seems to be, "If you want to be forgotten, remember yourself; and if you want to remembered, forget yourself."

Throughout these pages, we find ourselves discussing Jesus of Nazareth. He is Israel's Messia. He has a higher title still. He is the Lord. The earliest act of faith made in him by Christians describes him as "both Lord and Christ." (Saint Peter said that in Acts 2:36). An important question to ask about him is this: in what sense does he still live on in the world? Some people who do not believe Jesus is the Son of God say that we Christians have just decided to keep on saying forever how wonderful it was that he died for our sins. The fact is, however (these people say), that Jesus was only a man. He lives on only in our memories, not in glory at the right hand of God the Father.

The honest believer needs to ask himself, "Does Jesus still live or is he like Ozymandias, except that men have buried him under a different pile of sand? Have they just decided to honor him as God?"

WHO *IS* JESUS TODAY? WHO IS HE IN MY LIFE?

Some Christians experience this difficulty on their own. Every Christian needs to face it. It would be plain foolishness to raise every question about Jesus except the really big one. That ques-

tion is not, "Who *was* he?" but "Who *is* he?" Who is he to me? Today. In my life. Is he a character in history whose words and deeds we remember admiringly, or is he someone living and acting *now* in the world right outside the door? Does he still have all the power of God he showed when he lived in the land of Israel and among its people, or is he a great teacher from the past?

Jesus is the King of time. Jesus is the Lord of history. All the ages lie open before him as if they were a single moment. The weaver's apprentice of fourteenth century France and the businessman of Stockholm in the twenty-second century are present to him just as truly as his mother Mary was present to him in their home at Nazareth, although in a different way. Ever since his return to heaven from which he came, he has been alive and active to save us. He is ever-present to his Father and ever-present to us. He rules over us from his place of honor at the Father's right hand; the way he does it is by being the Servant of us all. He is ever-living, to make intercession for us. (Hebrews 7:25) He has entered into heaven itself, "where he now presents himself in the presence of God on our behalf." (Hebrews 9:24)

IN THE CHURCH, JESUS
COMES AS OUR FRIEND

The worst mistake we could make about Jesus would be to think of him as someone out of the past. The gospel was written because the early Christians who hadn't known him in life wanted a record of his words and deeds. But the first way they came to know him was to meet him every day in his brothers in the community of love they called "the Church." They met him in the sacraments they received, especially the meal of celebration that contained him, the eucharist. The chief

185

thing the eucharist did for them is what it does for us, namely form a community of charity.

Christ was active in each one of these holy signs—in baptism, in confirmation, in the eucharist—by uniting himself to all those who received them in a spirit of faith. During his earthly days, he approached people as individuals, not just in a crowd. He always came to them as a friend. He was never high-and-mighty, never looking for reasons to scold or blame, always open in his manner and deeply interested in people on a man-to-man basis.

When he comes to us in the Church through the holy sacraments, he always comes in that same spirit.

JESUS EXISTS FOREVER
AS THE IMAGE OF GOD

The one thing that sets Jesus apart from the heroes and saints of all the ages is that he is not the prisoner of time. He is not someone (like poor Ozymandias) who once had influence but has it no more. He has won out over the centuries and over distances and over death. In a word, he *is*, because the Father has raised him up in glory. Because he exists forever as the "image of God" (II Corinthians 4:4), Jesus is a special person, an individual, to a multitude of men.

That is the faith in him that you and I have through the Church. That is the faith in him that the gospel is a reminder of. He does not simply speak to us out of a book of writings. He speaks to us in a living community of people (the Church) who reflect his love in their lives, who "belong to Christ, and Christ to God." (I Corinthians 3:23)

We are constantly quoting in these pages the words of Holy Scripture. The Bible is God's message from heaven to men. All of the books that go to make it up are the written record of a spoken Word, the Word God speaks to us through his Son. In

fact, his Son *is* that Word. God's message to us and his only Son whom he sends to save us are one and the same. After Jesus, the eternal Word of God, went back to his Father, he continues to speak to us through his Church.

CHRIST IS THE WORD
GOD SPEAKS TO US

There you have the simple truth of how God speaks to his sons. It is a very important matter to grasp. We need to treasure it for a lifetime. There is a single Word of God, you see, and that is Christ. God speaks to us through this Word each time the Church celebrates a sacrament. The men who have faith in Christ hear God speak every time they receive a sacrament, but in the eucharist most of all.

God speaks to us through the Bible, too, particularly the New Testament. When the two go together, for example when a long and beautiful part of the Bible is read at Mass, or when a couple gets married, or a sick person is anointed, and the Bible is read as part of the ceremony, you have God speaking to his people. He does it in two ways: in a sign that you see, or taste, or touch—the sacraments—(for example, the living body of the Lord), and a sign you hear—the Scriptures. Jesus is the whole content of this twofold message. God "says" Christ to us; that is the Word he utters. He wants us to answer by saying "Amen," that is, "I believe," once we have heard this Word spoken.

Is it safe to assume that you're going to let God speak to you for the rest of your life? Let's hope so. The chief occasion to hear him is when you offer Christ to the Father in the eucharist and receive him back again as your food. Penance is another time when God will speak to you through Christ—then at your marriage, or your priestly ordination, or when you are anointed in illness.

READ SCRIPTURES TO HEAR
GOD SPEAK IN SACRAMENTS

But God can better "get through" to you in these sacraments if you are constantly reading the Scriptures as well, to learn what Jesus intends the sacraments to do for you. That New Testament of yours—the gospel especially—should be so well thumbed by the time you die that everyone will be able to say: "He let God try to speak to him through the holy sacraments." That is what happens any time we open the gospel, even at random. God speaks to our hearts. Then we hear his words proclaimed in the Mass. Finally, we walk forward to the holy table and let God speak his perfect Word, his Son, to us in the eucharistic gifts.

A most important section of the gospel of Christ is that series of four chapters according to Saint John numbered 14 through 17. There the Lord Jesus speaks at length to his friends at the Last Supper. You should read it often. It is a very good way to be put in touch with the spirit of the Master. The whole fourth gospel—Saint John's—is written in such a way that anywhere you open it you meet the whole person of Jesus in his ideas and his words. It's like sawing the trunk of a tree at any point: a good clear cut gives you its whole life history in the rings. In the same way, any part of the gospel—but these four chapters in particular—gives you the whole Jesus, Son of God and Son of Man.

YOUR LOVE WILL MARK
YOU AS JESUS' DISCIPLE

"A new commandment I give you: love one another; as I love you, so I want you, too, to love one another." (John 13:34. The old commandment on this point is in Leviticus 19:18. Look it up and tell how this one is new). "This is what will prove

to all men you are my disciples," Jesus continues, "your love one for another." (John 13:35)

Why must Jesus leave his disciples? Remember, they have never succeeded in understanding that Jesus must suffer and die, even though he has tried to explain this to them several times. His answer on his need to depart is: "I am going to prepare a place for you . . . then I shall come back and take you home with me. I want you to be where I shall be." (John 14:2-4)

JESUS GOES BACK
SO SPIRIT WILL COME

These followers of his must spend years and years (and you and I our entire lifetimes), living apart from the daily impact of his personality that had changed their lives so completely. How would they be equal to the separation? How will we? He answers that although he is going back to the Father and to his own glory, it is only by going back that the Spirit of truth will be given to them. "And should you ask for anything in my name I will do it, that the Father may be glorified in the Son." (John 14:13-16) This promise sounds like one of those wild promises in a chain letter until you read on a bit and see what type of favor Jesus is interested in granting. His big interest, notice, is that the Father shall be praised by men. This praise or glory will be given *in* the Son. If the friends of Jesus love him, he tells them, they will obey the commandments he gives them. When they do, Jesus will ask the Father, "and he will grant you another Advocate to be with you for all time to come: the Spirit of truth." (John 14:16)

It is in the Spirit that these words of God spoken in the gospel, spoken in the Church by Jesus, head of the Church, go on and on. They are like a brilliant cascade or waterfall. Every droplet, every gushing jet strikes the sun at a new angle and in-

creases the beauty of the whole. *As we grow in God's grace, these phrases in the gospel grow in meaning for us.* They are signs of the never-ending presence of Jesus in our midst as the Church of God. We are his holy people gathered before him. We have the great sacrament of his body and blood, and the other "sacrament" of his spoken word in the gospel. *Neither sign can do its full work of grace in us without the other.*

JESUS COMES BACK FOREVER
IN EUCHARIST AND SCRIPTURE

See, you must love me, Christ says, I who have first loved you. Then prove your love. I am the roadway: walk on me. I am the truth: believe me. I am life: live by me. If you do this my Father will have to love you. He cannot fail to, being a God of love. Then he and I will send the Holy Spirit to be your friend. The Spirit will make everything plain to you and recall to your minds everything I have told you.

"I have told you this that my joy may be yours, and your hearts may be brimful of joy." (John 15:11)

Those who love us and have some authority over us give us advice. When this advice is about a good and holy life it is sometimes called "good counsel." To follow this advice is right, but it should be made very clear that this is not enough. If you want to live a *full Christian life,* you should let the Father speak to you in Jesus Christ's words and follow the "interior Master," the Holy Spirit. That is the way that Father, Son and Holy Spirit will come to you and dwell within you.

Jesus left his friends only so that he could come back to them for all time in those two great signs of grace, his eucharistic body and the holy scriptures.

190

27

The Last Supper: Vow and Remembrance Rite

In the preceding chapter we spoke about Jesus' words of comfort and instruction to his twelve friends at their last supper together, the night before he left them to suffer and die. It was perfectly natural that he should be eating with them in Jerusalem at this time of year. The time was spring, the season of the Passover or great Jewish feast of remembrance. The chief thing the people called to mind on this occasion was the deliverance of Israel by her God, the Lord, centuries earlier (thirteen centuries is about as close as we can come; the event is described in chapter 12 of Exodus, but there are no clear chronological indications there).

LAST SUPPER IS NEW PASCH

From the gospels we cannot learn the exact year of Jesus' crucifixion. The best conclusion is that our Lord's last earthly Passover came in early April of 30 A.D. This date is based on what
little the gospels tell us about the length of Jesus' public life,
and calendar indications which tell us in what year the fourteenth day of Nisan, the day of Passover, fell on Friday. Other
years that have been suggested, in the order of their likelihood,
are: 33, 29, 31, 28 and 32. Complicated, wouldn't you say?

This variety of opinions, however, tells us something important about the gospels. Matthew, Mark, Luke and John—the
four inspired writers—had no interest in such matters as dates,
but they did have a burning interest in how this Passover was
the last and perfect one. They cared greatly that it was a sign of
the deliverance Jesus would be interceding for, at the Father's
right hand, as long as men had need of it.

The gospel account is full of unsolved problems of detail
about the Last Supper. For instance, the meal is nowhere described in so many words as being a Jewish Passover meal. All
the emphasis is on the fact that it is a *new* Pasch (a word taken
from the Greek form of the Hebrew *pesach*, a *sparing* or *ex-
emption*). We must conclude that the only fitting time for Jesus
to celebrate this new and perfect remembrance meal was on the
occasion of the old meal that had pointed to it for so long.

IT WAS A FAMILY MEAL

"When the hour had come," writes Saint Luke, "he took his
place on a couch, and so did the apostles. 'It has been my heart's
desire,' he said to them, 'to eat this paschal supper with you before I suffer. I tell you, I shall not eat it again till it is fulfilled in
the kingdom of God.' " (Luke 22:14-16)

See how anxious Jesus is that this celebration should take

place among them as a family group. Even Judas, the black sheep of the "little flock" (Luke 12:32), is there. Notice, too, the relation between the joyous celebration and the bitter death that will follow it. This is somewhat like the happy Thanksgiving dinner of a condemned man with his family on the night before he is to be hanged. In the gospel case, however, the relation between the two events is not just one of before-and-after, or even of a gathering on the eve of tragedy, arranged to provide a happy memory for family and friends.

THIS SUPPER LOOKS FORWARD
TO THE KINGDOM

No, Jesus' meaning goes much deeper than that. He is saying that this supper has a certain finality about it. It is closely related to the coming of God's kingdom, in the way that a sign is to the thing it stands for. Like a prophet of old, Jesus utters a solemn vow that he will touch no food until something very important happens. Meanwhile, he will drink of *this cup* and eat of *this bread* to hasten the event which he foretells—the coming of the kingdom.

At this point time out should be taken to read the gospel account of the Last Supper; it is almost useless to go on exploring this topic without this background. Luke's account (22:7-38) and Matthew's account (26:20-29) should be read first, then Mark 14:12-25 and I Corinthians 11:23-25.

PREPARATIONS MADE FOR MEAL

What are the main things to single out in this event? There have been preparations made for the meal, of course. On the first of eight days when the Jews ate all of their bread free of yeast— a holdover from an ancient Spring agricultural festival—Peter and John are sent by the Master to get things ready. All over

194

Jerusalem, pilgrims are eating this meal as families or groups of families in dining rooms. Chapter 12 of Exodus gives you a description of how they had to roast the lamb and prepare the yeast-free bread and bitter herbs for the paschal supper.

The upstairs room which Peter and John arranged for is "spacious and well furnished." (Luke 22:12) The thirteen husky men—all outdoor types, at least during the last few years—mount to the dining place, probably by way of an outside stairway. There they "lie down to eat." (Matthew 26:20; Mark 14:17) The Jews had adopted the Greek custom of reclining at the table for banquets.

The most painful part seems to come early in the meal. Jesus has already said clearly that he expects to die before long. (Matthew 26:2; Mark 14:8) Now he makes a direct reference to how it will happen: "Frankly I tell you, one of you will betray me." (Matthew 26:21) The various accounts describe how Jesus told Judas in different ways that he knew he was the guilty one. There must have been a great hubbub of voices at the table. Surely by now the men had heard how the leading priests were sworn to "get" Jesus. Whether all, or Judas only, heard our Lord's words to Judas we cannot tell; but Judas certainly heard them. Saint Matthew makes the direct accusation spoken by Jesus very clear. "It is not I, is it, Rabbi?" Judas asks. (Matthew 26:25) Jesus replies that the words are his, a Jewish way of saying, "Now that you've said it, make of it what you will."

SIGN OF BETRAYAL IS GIVEN

Notice that there is a sign here at the table ("Jesus answered, 'It is he to whom I will give the morsel, after dipping it in the bowl.' So he dipped the morsel, and with his own hand reached it to Judas Iscariot, the son of Simon." John 13:26) There will likewise be a sign later in the garden. ("And when he came, he [Judas] went straight up to him, and said, 'Rabbi!' and kissed

him." Mark 14:45) This time the sign is food shared in common (Matthew 26:23); later it will be a warm embrace. (Luke 22:48) It is especially fitting that a betrayal should have the same signs as a friendship. You cannot describe sin any better than by saying that it is selling out a friend—trading on a close relationship for private gain.

The central event at the supper is the blessing Jesus pronounces over the bread and wine. When we read the account carefully and slowly, we can see that his words are in a fixed form (actually, in four fixed forms). The essentials are there in all four cases. They are very much like the fixed form of words used by the priest at the consecration of the Mass. This should not surprise us. We ought to expect it. Saint Paul says that he learned what Jesus said and did at the supper table "from the Lord" (I Corinthians 11:23), that is to say—as scholars understand him to mean—from the community at Jerusalem whose living tradition is, in fact, the voice of "the Lord."

'TAKE! EAT! THIS IS MY BODY'

Jesus' words and actions seem abrupt and business-like; there is no wasted motion or speech. This is because these phrases are already worn smooth with usage, like the stones in a river bed. They are taken from the community celebration of this sacred meal by Christians in Palestine, Rome and Antioch (where the first three gospels were composed). The eucharistic meal is already decades old when the gospel accounts of it come to be written.

In each account, Jesus takes the bread, speaks a blessing in praise of God over it, breaks it and hands it around: "Take! Eat! This is my body." He does the same with the cup of wine. As he passes this around, his words to his friends are different, naturally: "Drink of it, every one of you; for this is my cove-

196

nant-blood, which is about to be shed for the sake of many, with a view to the forgiveness of sins. I tell you, I shall never drink again of the product of the vine till that day when I drink new wine with you in the kingdom of my Father." (Matthew 26:28-29)

THE NEW BREAD IS JESUS' BODY

We may wonder why Jesus spoke and acted as he did. Did his friends understand him? They were probably mystified, we may surmise, but they had a few clues. First of all, the idea of a sacred meal is as old as the people Israel. The Passover feast was the one best known; but in Jesus' day, pious groups were meeting all the time to take part in holy actions like this. They first said grace—a prayer of thanks to the Creator for his gifts of food and drink. Their thanks was not an ordinary "Thanks," however. Indeed not. The form they used was that of first reciting the marvelous deeds done by God in the past to save his people; then his holy name was blessed in gratitude for these deeds of his.

This is what Jesus did. This is what we do in the Mass. First we review all that God has done for us, in the *preface*. Then we bring that great blessing in praise of God to a climax by the priest's words which change food and drink into our gift to God, the living body and blood of Jesus.

At the last supper, our Lord did exactly what you would expect—up to a point. He presided over a family meal, passing the food around after he blessed it. The chief items that received a blessing were bread and wine, signs for the Jews of all food and drink. Then Jesus indicated that the new Passover bread that they were to eat as an *everlasting* remembrance was the bread of his body, not the yeast-free bread they ate at the old remembrance meal. They were no longer merely to recall the deliverance from Egypt under Moses, but the deliverance from

sin under Jesus. This was a major change. Moses had given them manna, bread from the heavens to keep them from starving. (Exodus 16:8-35) Jesus gave them himself to eat as their food for the same purpose.

JESUS DRAWS UP NEW COVENANT

Secondly, Jesus drew up an agreement with the whole human race and used his blood as the sign of it. This is what Moses had done when he gave the people the Ten Commandments and the Book of the Law. He sprinkled the people with the blood of bulls to prove how faithful God was going to be to the agreement, and how faithful the people ought to be. (Exodus 24:1-8) At the supper, Jesus said that this covenant-blood of his, now no longer wine, was going to be shed as a part of a new and everlasting agreement. It would not only be the *sign* of setting men free from their sins. It would actually *cause* this to happen. They were to be sons of the covenant (*b'nai b'rith*, you would say in Hebrew), sons of this new and eternal agreement between God and all his children. It was sealed not in the blood of bulls and heifers but in the blood of Jesus Christ. (Read chapter 9 of the Epistle to the Hebrews right now. You will find it hard, but when you get to verse 18 it will begin to look familiar).

Once Jesus passes his body and blood around to be eaten and drunk, they chant the final hymn of praise and go out into the night. He is to offer himself to God now, as a victim for men's sins. He will die a painful death, marked by bloodshed. It will come as a result of his perfect love for the Father and for us. The comforting thought about this death is this: *it will make the eucharist—the sign of Christ's love—available to us always.*

CHURCH ACTS AS JESUS DOES

That is why the Church constantly invites us to step forward to the table and eat. She does what Jesus does. Christians are those who follow their bishop, or the priest he sends them, in performing this act of love in the bread and in the cup. To be Catholic is to belong to that worldwide holy communion which the eucharist creates. It is to receive life from Christ's body, remission of sins from his blood.

Might you ever wish to stop taking this meal? You're free to, you know. Judas walked out on it. "And it was night," the gospel says. (John 13:30) Remember that from time to time. You may leave the feast whenever you please; but it is "night."

28

Agony and Trial

"I Am He"

Every man who lives on this earth has to die. This is the price of sin that all of us must pay. Some people die gallantly; others badly. Many die in pain. Some die without any idea that death is overtaking them. Though many die happy deaths, no one can be said to die with pleasure. Peace marks the death of the man with a good conscience who believes that he will rise again. Yet every normal human being shrinks from death because it is an unknown experience.

Jesus shrank from death. He knew he was to overcome death forever within a matter of days. Even so, as he lay outstretched on the ground in prayer, in the olive grove where he went after the Last Supper, he shuddered at the prospect of death.

SINLESS JESUS TO DIE
BECAUSE OF MEN'S SINS

We cannot say that it was death alone that frightened Jesus. He was to die as a result of the evil in his enemies' hearts. That knowledge would have been a shock to someone whose heart was full of love, as his was. Much worse, Jesus was to die under the weight of the sins of all men everywhere. This was a tremendous burden. He must have recoiled at the thought of being so closely associated with sin, he who was without sin.

Or—and this last suggestion is not to be dismissed lightly—being the most intelligent and sensitive of men, Jesus may have been in mortal dread of the pain that lay ahead for him. This wouldn't mean he was not brave—far from it. Rather, it would have required a special bravery for one so sensitive as he to face his brutal death.

It is hard to know Jesus' innermost thoughts, but it is not hard at all to know his words. "Abba" (Aramaic for Father), he said, "You can do all things! Spare me this cup! No, not what I will, but what you will." (Mark 14:36)

The English word *agony* comes from the Greek word for a contest, like that of wrestlers. The agony Jesus suffered in the Garden of Gethsemane was a death-struggle with the forces of evil. He went out to the slope of the Mount of Olives, directly east of Jerusalem, with his friends. There were only eleven of them, now that Judas had deserted. The Passover moon was close to full. Despite its light, this was soon to be the hour of the power of darkness. (See Luke 22:53)

WITHOUT THE SHEPHERD,
THE SHEEP SCATTER

Jesus felt he had to warn his friends about the weakness that would overtake them. "You will all stumble and fall," was the

sense of what he told them. (See Mark 14:27). Then he quoted a prophet of old, Zacharia, to this effect: "I will smite the shepherd, and the sheep will be scattered." (See Zacharia 13:7) Just as the whole nation Israel, made up of twelve tribes, had suffered from lack of leadership many times, so this little group of friends would run like frightened sheep once Jesus was taken from them.

He was right in his prophecy, of course. He knew their anxious hearts—and he knew that the Holy Spirit had not yet come to strengthen them. The eleven were to prove about as spineless and unintelligent as you and I would be if we were to turn away from the leadership of Christ. Have you ever thought of that—what a "nothing" each of us would be on his own, without Jesus as our Head?

Peter—poor, excitable Peter—got all worked up over this. Everybody desert the Teacher? No sir, not he! (See Mark 14:29) Then Jesus had to give Peter the facts about his weakness. Before the hour of 5:30 or 6:00 A.M. (second cockcrow, as they called it), Peter would have proved himself to be a weakling. Three different times he would swear to high heaven that he had never met Jesus. That is what Jesus told Peter would happen, but Peter denied it with all his strength—said he would sooner die than do that.

HIS CLOSEST FRIENDS SLEPT
WHILE JESUS FACED AGONY

All the rest of them said the same thing. In a way, the other ten were right in saying they wouldn't deny him. They didn't stay close enough to Jesus to be heard saying *anything* about him!

Then, the three who were closest to Jesus—Peter, James and John—went to sleep on the job! The Passover meal was a big

one; at least four cups of wine were required as part of it. You've guessed what happened. While Jesus was going through the bitterest struggle his soul had ever faced, his three friends went sound asleep. When he came back and found them, he called Peter by his given name, Simon. Peter was no "rock" now, the meaning of the name Peter (or Kepha, as Jesus would have called him in their own language). He was no better than a handful of pebbles.

Twice more Jesus came back, and twice more he found them dead to the world. Fine thing! Satan could have brought the kingdom of God to the brink of destruction (never destroyed it, of course), and this trio would still be snoring away. The difference between the devil and those who declare themselves friends of God is summed up in this scene, somehow. Satan doesn't sleep. It's a good thing Jesus doesn't either, or we'd have gone under a long time ago, for *we* sleep. Our lives as strong friends at the Master's side can be called one long cat nap.

BETRAYED BY A 'FRIEND,' JESUS SAYS, 'I AM HE'

On his third return to the sleeping disciples, Jesus roused them by saying that the hour had come for the Son of Man to be betrayed. When he used the word *hour,* he did not mean sixty minutes but that period of climax when the world would be saved by his death and resurrection. At the beginning of his career—at Cana, when a sign was asked for—Jesus made it clear that his hour had not yet come. (John 2:4) Now he was equally clear in stating that it had come.

In a darker sense, Judas's hour had come, too. Out he came, at the head of an armed band, to the place of Christ's prayer, a place he knew well.

It is hard to know from the gospel exactly who these armed

men were; probably temple police. It is perfectly clear whom they represented, namely Jesus' sworn enemies among the leading priests and learned men and elders.

"Who is it you are looking for?" Jesus asked.

"Jesus of Nazareth," they answered.

Jesus said to them, "I am he." (John 18:5-6) At that moment, they fell back and dropped to the ground. That "I am" (the exact wording of Jesus' answer) terrified them, for it was the very name that God had used to identify himself when he spoke to Moses at the burning bush. (Exodus 3:14)

JUDAS KISSES JESUS,
THE MOB SEIZES HIM

Almost everyone has heard how our Lord reacted to Judas's warm embrace, the signal that this was the one they were looking for. Jesus called Judas "friend" and asked him what business he had come on. Not that Jesus needed to know. It was the kind of question that was meant to slow down the onrush of evil by getting the sinner to pause and look within himself. But it didn't work. "Rabbi," Judas said, and kissed Jesus. "And they seized him and held him." (Mark 14:45)

Simon Peter put up a brief fight by swinging his sword at a servant of the high priest, a certain Malchus. Peter managed to cut off the servant's right ear. Saint Luke, author of the "gospel of healing" as the third gospel is sometimes called, says that Jesus restored the ear miraculously with a touch. (Luke 22:51)

The Master then looked squarely at this band of hired thugs with their swords and clubs, and spoke to them as his ancestor David had spoken to Goliath. Just as David's confidence had been in the Lord and not in a suit of armor, so Jesus' trust was wholly in his Father. He had no fear whatever of strong-arm tactics. He had taught daily in the temple and in the streets. (Luke 22:53) No one had captured him then. They needed the

204

cover of night for their dirty business. They required the confusion of a busy feast day to mask their deed.

'THEN ALL HIS DISCIPLES LEFT HIM AND FLED'

A verse occurs in Scripture at this point which may be the most pathetic in all the Bible: "Then all his disciples left him and fled." (Mark 14:50)

Life is full of mysteries. One of the greatest is why supposedly religious people fall apart in a time of crisis. It happens all the time. It happened then; it is happening now, in high schools, in the armed forces all over the world, in colleges, in big cities, in residential neighborhoods. Should anyone ask you: "If you were with Jesus then, would you have left him?" your immediate response would be, "Of course not." But isn't that what happens when anyone chooses to leave his Church to marry someone he thinks he can't live without? when he collapses morally while on overseas duty, or takes his first payoff in a job of public trust?

How does this happen? The Catholic cannot say that the Spirit hasn't come upon him as yet, as one can say of the apostles; most have been confirmed, in fact. When individuals do abandon Christ, this shows that the descent of the Spirit upon them hasn't meant much to them. It shows that their confirmation was chiefly a catechism bee, not a being set on fire by the Strengthener of hearts.

Secondly, it's evident that following Jesus has never yet cost these deserters anything. A little inconvenience, perhaps, but no more. When they reach a test, the first real test, and do not choose Christ, it is because he doesn't mean anything to them. Or if he means something, he doesn't mean enough. When Jesus isn't a person in your life whom you know as a friend, turning and running makes sense. Who wants to die, after all, or miss

29

Jesus Dies Because

His Work Is Finished

There is a story told about Marshal Lyautey, the French resident general of Morocco before and after World War I, that describes his hurry to get things done. One morning under the bright North African sun, he told the orderly landscaping his compound that, by noon, he wanted a certain plant moved from one place to another. The orderly was too heavy for light work, so he raised an objection that was a stroke of genius. "What's the hurry, *mon Général?*" he asked. "After all, it's a century plant and it won't bloom for another eighty years." "Then," Lyautey answered, "we haven't a moment to lose!"

JESUS LOST NO TIME IN
ACCOMPLISHING HIS TASK

Jesus of Nazareth, too, went about his public career like a man who hadn't a moment to lose. He was never rushed, never feverish in his activity; yet he lost no time in accomplishing his task. Once when he wanted to go back to Judea, the southern province where Jerusalem lay, his friends objected because they feared for his safety. Earlier he had met his bitterest opposition there. This time, the disciples were afraid that he might not escape with his life. "Rabbi, only recently the Jews [Judeans?] wanted to stone you to death," they said, "and you mean to go back there again?"

Jesus answered: "Are there not twelve hours to the day? As long as a man walks in the day, he does not stumble because he sees the light of this world. But when a man walks in the night he stumbles because he has no light to guide him." (John 11:8-10)

This is Jesus' way of telling us of the importance of an opportunity sent by God. In his case, there is a job to do in saving the world. The Father has appointed the time in which to do it, included the amount of time which Jesus has to accomplish it. Saint John makes an important play on words in this passage. He takes the simple statement of Jesus about daylight and dark (there was no electricity or gas in those days, remember) and reports a powerful reference that Jesus made to himself. Jesus is the Light of this world. The forces of evil and refusal to believe in him are darkness. Not only is Jesus' lifetime before he is captured *his* unique opportunity; it is also the opportunity of *everyone* who would walk in his light. Jesus used this providential time to do the work the Father had sent him to do, and when his hour had come he died on the cross to free us from the guilt of our sins.

CHRIST'S CRUCIFIXION IS ONLY
FIRST STAGE OF REDEMPTION

The image of Christ on the cross, which is used so often to recall this task that Jesus accomplished, might give the impression that Jesus' followers are deeply concerned with torture and bloodshed. Actually, *Christianity is a religion of hope and joy.* If that is so, why is the cross our great sign? The answer is that even though Jesus' death *is only the first stage* of the mystery of our redemption, *it is the part that best reminds us of his love.*

The crucifix wasn't used as a sign of the way God saved us until Christianity was at least five centuries old. The holy eucharist is the oldest and best sign of our salvation. That is why Jesus gave it to us, to act as a sign which would save us.

Before the crucifix gained favor as a sign of our salvation, a cross set with precious stones was used, to show that Jesus is the world's rich treasure. His glorious wounds are like gems to us. (In fact, the custom of covering the crucifix with violet during Passiontide started with the covering of these precious gems—not the image of Christ's body).

JESUS IN HIS GLORY REMINDS
US OF OUR REDEMPTION, TOO

However, an image of Christ standing glorious beside an empty tomb, or ascending to his Father, would remind us of our redemption just as well as the crucifix does. The crucifix especially helps us to recall the *pain* or *cost* of the great mystery of the redemption, whereas picturing Christ's glory following his death aids us in remembering the Father's *acceptance* or *approval* of this redemption of mankind.

A complete reminder of the mystery by which God saves us can be seen in three wood carvings which hang above the altars

of a church dedicated to Saint Pius X in Aurora, Colorado. On the gospel side you see Mary holding up her infant Son, who is wrapped in swaddling bands which are painted silver. The center carving is of Christ crucified; this time he is clad in the loincloth of his last hours. On the epistle side you see Jesus coming forth from his tomb, with his linen gravecloth a silver sheen behind him as he goes heavenward.

JESUS ON CROSS—SATAN VICTOR; JESUS IN GLORY—SATAN CRUSHED

This full story of the redemption is a far better reminder than the devotion of the Way of the Cross, which stops when the story is half over. Indeed, there are special reasons why showing Christ in kingly robes or in priestly vestments is better than showing his naked, bleeding body. Again, that is because we are reminded of the whole mystery when we see Christ in his glory, and not just a part of it as in a crucifixion scene; for Christ is not death to us—but life! His dying on the cross reminds us of our sins, it is true, for Satan is still victorious over Jesus at this point. But when Jesus rises from the dead in priestly glory, he reminds us that he has crushed the serpent's head (defeated Satan) and washed away all the guilt of our sins.

Jesus himself said, when he referred to himself as the good shepherd, that no one could rob him of his life: "I have power to lay it down and power to take it back again." (John 10:18) The Father's will governed when and how this should happen.

At the Last Supper, Jesus raised his eyes to heaven and said, "Father, the hour is come." (John 17:1) Then he prayed, asking God for glory so that he in turn might glorify the Father: "I have glorified you on earth by completing the work you gave me to do . . . I have made your name known to the men whom you singled out from the world and entrusted to me . . .

211

the message you delivered to me I have delivered to them."
(John 17:4, 6, 8) Every word Jesus spoke breathed certainty
that he had faithfully carried out the mission on which he had
been sent. So his death was not untimely, nor a moment too
soon. It came at exactly the right time, because his work was
finished.

PILATE TRIED TO MAKE
THE CROWD PITY JESUS

The way his death came about was swift and sickening. You
must know the story. Pilate had tried hard to excite some pity
in the crowd for Jesus, but it didn't work. He called Jesus
"king of the Jews" at one point. Now this was a bad mistake,
for the Jewish people never used this title because they knew
their own history well enough to realize that only the Lord was
king over Israel. Was Pilate taunting them, they wondered?

Then, when he offered to free either the prisoner Barabbas
or Jesus (as was the custom on religious feasts), Pilate proved
how little he knew about the political situation. Here this thug,
Barabbas, was in prison for murder and revolt against Roman
rule, while Jesus, who proved by his miracles that he had the
power to do something to win Israel's independence, hadn't
raised a finger. For the mob, bent on rebellion against Rome
with the dagger and a curse, this was no choice at all. "Barabbas!" they cried. Give us our own kind, in other words.

Pilate tried one thing more. He had Jesus whipped. (John
19:1) Neither that, nor the cruel game of the soldiers in the
courtyard in which they mocked Jesus as a king, had any effect.
The crowd wanted blood. Pilate had more weakness than pity
in his make-up, so he gave in and turned Jesus over to be crucified.

CALVARY—'PLACE OF THE SKULL'— WHERE JESUS WAS CRUCIFIED

In those days the condemned man had to carry his own cross-beam, a rough-hewn affair, to the place of execution.* Someone helped Jesus on his way to be crucified—a man named Simon. He was "drafted" into helping Jesus, the gospel says. (Mark 15:21) The gospel also says that Jesus met good women on his way who wailed over his death.

He was dragged to the knob of sandstone outside Jerusalem where criminals were put to death in those days. It was called *Golgotha*, "place of the skull." (Matthew 27:33) "Calvary" says the same thing in Latin. Perhaps it was called that because of the remains of other crucifixions at the place. Grisly business!

Have you ever seen a skull at the bottom of a cross? Sometimes the crucifix on a rosary will have one. It goes back to an old Christian legend that Adam was buried where Christ gave his life. That theory isn't much good as history, but as theology it's hard to improve on. What Adam lost for us, Christ regained. The father of death, Adam, lies at the feet of the first Victor over death, Christ Jesus.

CHRIST CRUCIFIED BETWEEN TWO THIEVES FULFILLED A PROPHECY

Jesus was crucified between two robbers. Saint Mark says he was crucified between the "wicked." (Mark 15:28) This is a powerful reference to one of the Servant Songs we spoke of earlier: "And he was counted among the wicked." (Isaia 53:12)

---

* The Greek word for the heavy crossbeam that Jesus had to carry is *stauros*. This is a Christian name in Russia—Stavros; occasionally you read of a Communist diplomat with that name. That is a case of bearing Christ's cross whether you want to or not. There surely ought to be hope for a man like that, or an Anastas, "resurrection"; Vassily, "king"; Nikita, "victory"—all names taken from the mystery of Christ.

The earth grew dark: "It was now the sixth hour, and there was darkness over the whole land until the ninth hour." (Luke 23:44) Men shrieked at Jesus and challenged him to come down: "He saved others, himself he cannot save. If he is the king of Israel, let him come down now from the cross, and we will believe him." (Matthew 27:42) A thief asked forgiveness: "Lord, remember me when you come into your kingdom." (Luke 23:42) Jesus spoke gently to his mother: "Woman, behold, your son." (John 19:26), and we begin to see why he addressed her in this way at Cana. (John 2:4) He gave her, the new Eve, as mother to us all.

Mostly, though, Jesus went on with his dying. He had a work to do. Nothing would keep him from it.

JESUS DIES: 'FATHER, INTO YOUR HANDS I COMMEND MY SPIRIT'

Jesus cried out loudly. All that the crowds could hear was a snatch of a psalm: "O God, my God, look upon me: why have you forsaken me?" (Psalm 21:2. Read it through; it's a wonderful prayer). Then he tasted a bit of cheap wine which someone put to his lips, but did not drink. He cried out clearly, in the madness of that afternoon which we call "good" Friday, that his work was finished: "It is consummated!" (John 19:30) Then he breathed forth his last breath, giving his soul back into his Father's hands: "Father, into your hands I commend my spirit." (Luke 23:46)

Can we hope to do more? Can we hope to do as much? Not saving the world, of course, just finishing our work.

On second thought, what is our work if it is not saving the world, in union with the only Savior?

214

30

Death the Loser in
a Duel with Life

There was a time, at the dawn of the world, when the Lord God walked in the garden in the cool of the day. But Adam, the man in the story, hid himself among the trees. "Where are you?" the Lord called to him, and Adam answered, "I heard you in the garden and I was afraid because I was naked [Adam refers here to his loss of holiness], and I hid." (Genesis 3:10)

JESUS DIDN'T HIDE IN HIS TOMB,
BUT CAME FORTH TO OBEY GOD

Ages later, there was another garden and another Man. This Man did not hide. He who had said to Lazarus, "Come forth!" himself emerged from the tomb that held him and stood in the

light of day. Unlike Adam, he was neither naked nor ashamed. No, this Jesus, son of Joseph the carpenter, as was supposed, was clothed in the many-colored coat of glory which his heavenly Father had given him as a reward for his obedience. In the splendor of his risen body he rivaled the sunlight. The crucified Jesus, now made Lord and Messia, stood forth and said, like Moses at the burning bush, "Here I am" (Exodus 3:4), and like Isaia in the temple, "Lo, here am I, send me." (Isaia 6:8) He stood ready, in other words, to sanctify the world.

Unlike Jesus, Lord and Christ, man often tries to run out on his duties. In an old legend from Catalonia in Spain, we hear how the tiny hero, Padre Pantufet, got lost in the country one day. A kindly ox swallowed him to protect him. When Pantufet heard his parents calling, "Where are you?" he replied, "I am in the belly of the ox where it does not snow and it does not rain." What Pantufet did was run away from life. He made himself as he had been before he was born, in his mother's womb.

The prophet Jona ran away from responsibility in the same way. He didn't want to do the job God has chosen for him: preach to the men of Nineveh. As he fled in fear, a whale swallowed him up. But his luck didn't last. He was thrown up on the shore and had to go to Nineveh anyway. That is the way it is when you oppose God. There's no place to hide.

JESUS BROUGHT THE GOOD NEWS TO SOULS IN LIMBO

Jesus knew the Jona story well. In referring to it, he used it as a sign of himself. "Just as Jona spent three days and three nights in the belly of the sea monster, so the Son of Man will spend three days and three nights in the heart of the earth." (Matthew 12:40) But Jesus did not hide in the heart of the earth. Even in death he was active, "going in the Spirit to bring the Good News to the spirits who were in prison

216

[limbo]." (I Peter 3:19) He did not run, ostrich-like, to a rest-ing place in a cool tomb. No, he went to limbo to free the fathers of Israel. Having done his work there, he came forth to press his advantage over death and hell, both of which he had con-quered. He had a further work to do, and so he rose up to do it.

It was a strange war that Jesus had been through. As the poet, Francis Thompson, explains: "The slain had the gain and the victor had the rout." A smashing victory for Christ the "loser," while Satan, the "winner," was utterly defeated.

CHRIST'S WOUNDS ARE SIGNS
OF HIS VICTORY OVER SATAN

Jesus Christ got his scars "as they wounded all his brow, and they smote him through the side." But because he won his wounds in overthrowing Satan, the prince of this world, the Father gave him "titles that are high—'King of Kings!' are the words, 'Lord of Lords!'" During the Easter Vigil this year, you may remember, we prayed, "By his wounds holy and glorious may he preserve us who is Christ the Lord."

That is the basic message of the resurrection. We look for protection at the hands—the blood-red hands—of Christ, the one who did not run away.

Living in the twentieth century, as we've remarked before, is a far from easy business. All about us there's the attitude that no one is to blame for his own carelessness, his own ignorance, his own wrongdoing. "I blacked out," says the murderer or the rapist, meaning, "I got into one of those passionate rages I've been flying into since I was a kid." The rest of that statement ought to run, "No one ever stopped me before. What's this judge trying to do to me now?"

ARE WE FAST BECOMING
A NATION OF QUITTERS?

Another favorite modern trick is the hit-and-run performance. It happens every day in manslaughter cases. Even creasing someone's fender in a parking lot and driving off is not uncommon. "My brake slipped," is another way of saying, "My sense of decency—which was never very firm—slipped."

This is the era of the best machine-made products, installed by the sloppiest workmanship, in human history; it is the age of firing people by mail or through a secretary because bosses can't look them in the eye and give reasons; it is the era when people get more exercise passing the buck than they do walking. Sometimes it seems that the words that ought to be inscribed on one side of the great seal of the U.S. are, "Am I my brother's keeper?" and on the other, "The woman gave me the fruit . . . and I ate." We are fast becoming a nation of quitters, people who will do anything under the sun sooner than follow through on the consequences of their own actions.

IN SPITE OF MEN'S CRUELTY,
JESUS SAID, 'I WILL SERVE'

Jesus of Nazareth had a task to finish and *he finished it*. His vocation was to be perfectly obedient to his Father's will, even though it meant his death on a cross. He answered this call, never looking to left or right. In spite of the cruelty of evil and thoughtless men, he continued to say to his Father what Satan could not say: "I will serve." When Saint Paul was speaking of this perfect obedience which led to Jesus' humiliation and death, he said, "That is why God has exalted him and given him the name above all names, so that at the name 'Jesus' everyone in heaven, on earth and beneath the earth should bend their knee

and publicly acknowledge to the glory of God the Father that Jesus Christ is Lord." (Philippians 2:9-11)

Let us look at some of the events that led to the acknowledgment and praise of the Lordship of Christ on the morning he rose from the dead. First, several good women who had been his close friends in life (there were three, says Mark; Luke adds a fourth name, but all mention Mary Magdalene as being one of them) went to his tomb early in the morning while it was still dark. They had assisted at his hasty burial before sundown on Friday night. Now they went back armed with many pounds of spices and ointments. The Jews didn't embalm as the Egyptians did, but they used sweet-smelling spices and ointments to lessen the odor of decay. The process of decay would have made steady progress in the nearly forty hours since Jesus' death. At least, it was natural for the women to think so.

WOMEN WERE TERRIFIED TO FIND
TOMB OPENED AND JESUS GONE

When they got to the garden, the huge stone was rolled away from the door of the cave-like tomb. All their worry about how they would get into the outer chamber of the tomb was needless. The stone was already moved—by an earthquake, Saint Matthew says. (Matthew 28:2)

The *details* in the four accounts of the gospel differ in describing what the women found, just as they differ in the case of the Last Supper, or indeed almost any incident reported about Jesus. But the various accounts are quite alike in the *main lines* of the story, as they always are.

The women were terrified at finding the tomb unexpectedly open. They bent low and entered through the small door. Their first discovery was that there was no corpse of Jesus on the sandstone slab where they had laid it. They then discovered a youth (two of them, says Luke), with the appearance of a heav-

enly messenger, in the tomb. The messenger said to them, quite simply, "He is risen. He is not here." (Mark 16:6) By this time, the women were nearly petrified with fright. They bowed their faces to the ground so as not to have to look at the dazzling garments of the stranger who informed them. (Luke 24:4-5)

THE DISCIPLES WERE FIRST
SKEPTICAL, THEN PUZZLED

The mysterious youth (or "angel," as Saint Matthew calls him) assured the women not to be afraid: "For I know that you seek Jesus, who was crucified." (Matthew 28:5) Then, having showed them clearly that his body was not to be found, he directed them to report the event to the disciples. More than that, they were to meet him, the young man said, in Galilee—the scene of Jesus' prophecy that he would be crucified and on the third day rise. (Mark 16:7; Luke 24:6-7)

The women left the tomb area in a joyous state, but also trembling with "fear"—awe, actually, or dread—at how close the mystery of God had come to them. Off they went to report their breathtaking news to the Eleven and all the rest.

During his life, our Lord had told his disciples clearly that he would rise from the dead after his treatment at the hands of sinful men. In spite of this, the "tale seemed to them to be nonsense and they did not believe the women." (Luke 24:11) Two of them ran to the tomb to check for themselves, Peter and another. They stooped low to enter it and found the linen gravecloths neatly folded there. Of Jesus they saw nothing. They believed the evidence of their senses, namely that the tomb was, in fact, empty. But, says the fourth gospel, "They had not as yet understood the Scripture text which says that he must rise from the dead. The disciples then left from home." (John 20:9-10)

JESUS DID NOT MEAN TO MYSTIFY
US; HE MEANT TO GIVE US LIFE

Up to this point, the account of Christ's rising up from the dead is a kind of mystery story. Frank Morison has written a serious book about the events of Easter morning which catches this spirit perfectly. He calls it *Who Moved the Stone?*

Jesus did not rise from death to provide us with a puzzle, however. He meant to give us life—to make us alive in him. You best get the idea of this in the meeting between the risen Jesus and Mary Magdalene in the garden. (John 20:11-18) She sees him but does not know him, for she is weeping. Taking him for a groundskeeper, she pleads for Jesus' body, if he should have it. Our Lord then calls her by name. To his "Mary," she answers "Rabboni—my Master." This is the moment that matters: the instant of recognition. After it, but only after it, she can say, "I have seen the Lord!"

THE RESURRECTION IS AN END—
AND A BEGINNING OF *NEW* LIFE

Those are the events of the first Easter morning. They are an *end* and a *beginning*. An end to grief, to death, to sin that caused the Master's death; a beginning of glory and new life. Notice this, though. As a rumor or report, the resurrection story is meaningless. It signifies nothing to Peter and the other disciples at this point. They have only heard about it. They neither believe nor disbelieve it. They are unchanged.

Mary, however, has seen the risen Jesus, spoken to him. For her, everything is different now. She has acknowledged him as Lord and Master, and this commitment affects her whole way of living.

OUR LIVES ARE CHANGED WHEN
WE MEET THE RISEN CHRIST

That is the way it is with you and me. We either know *about* Christ's resurrection, or we *know* it. Our moment of clear recognition of the person of the risen Christ is chiefly in the eucharist. But, we also meet him when we perform any act of love, for his eucharistic body is the sign of love.

He has called out to you: "Joe," "Helen," "Manuel." Have you heard him? Enough to say, "Master!"?

31

The Forty Days and the Paschal Faith

In the first chapter of this book, we spoke of the strong faith in him that Jesus' disciples had when they first began to proclaim his death and resurrection to the crowds in Jerusalem. By that time, Jesus' followers believed two great things about him: that he was Lord, a title that had the ring of "God" to the pious Jew, and that he was Christ, Israel's Messia. The forward movement of the four accounts of the gospel describes the slow progress Jesus had in getting the seeds of these two ideas across to His friends. Actually, the gospel makes it clear that they didn't really succeed in understanding these ideas during his lifetime.

HOLY SPIRIT GAVE APOSTLES
POWER TO SPREAD GOSPEL

The unfolding of the great mystery of who he was, and the work of saving men that the Father had sent him to do, had to be gone about slowly, very slowly. The disciples' "dullness of heart" (we would call it their "stupidity" or "resistance") got in the way. It was only the Holy Spirit's coming down on the Twelve that gave them the understanding, the courage and the desire to spread the good news (the meaning of the word "gospel") about Christ. The power they received when the Holy Spirit came on them sent them out to be Christ's witnesses in Jerusalem, all Judea and Samaria, and even to the very ends of the earth. (Read Acts 1:7-8).

Yet there was one period in the Savior's earthly stay that greatly helped prepare his followers' hearts for the spread of the gospel. It was, of course, the time of his risen life, the period between his resurrection, and his ascension into heaven. When we spoke in the preceding chapter of Jesus' coming forth from the tomb, we did not describe how it happened. We only spoke of what he said and did *after* he had risen. That is because the gospel does not describe his resurrection as it takes place, but as something that has just *taken* place. There is, in other words, no gospel account of the "rising Christ," but only one of the "risen Christ."

Saint Matthew does tell us that when Jesus sent his disciples to bring word to his brethren to set out for Galilee (a good distance from Jerusalem), some of the guards over Jesus' tomb came into the city to report to the chief priests all that had happened. (Matthew 28:11-15) The leaders bribed the guards to say that Jesus' body had been stolen while they were sleeping. This is the story you hear in Jerusalem "even to the present day," Saint Matthew said, when he wrote his account of the gospel.

JESUS' FRIENDS KNOW
ABOUT HIS RISEN LIFE

But aside from the guards and their employers, who suspect something, the only people who we are sure know about Jesus' risen life are his friends who come to believe in it. He gives them courage by appearing to them and teaching them about the kingdom of God "throughout forty days." (Acts 1:3) He showed himself alive to them, after his passion, "giving many conclusive proofs," says Saint Luke, that he is alive. (Acts 1:3)

The Church's belief in Christ's death and resurrection is known as "the paschal faith." The Church has always had this belief, from the time she first came to be the Church. The roots of this faith are described in the period between the first Easter and the first Pentecost. During this time, that is to say up to his ascension, the Twelve on whom the Spirit descended (Acts 1:13) are visited by Jesus from time to time. He wants to plant this faith deep in their hearts. *Paschal* is a word that comes from the Greek word for *Passover*. Here it means the faith of Christians that Jesus Christ, our passover Lamb, has not only been sacrificed, but has also been raised up in glory. *Paschal faith is the faith of Christians in the fact of the resurrection.*

WE NEED A CLEAR-CUT GOAL
TO MAKE LIFE BEARABLE

We really ought to examine the appearances of the Lord to his friends, one by one, so that we'll know what "conclusive proofs" of his resurrection he gave them. *You and I must have the faith in him as the risen, glorious Christ that the Church has.* If we don't, then we will go through life with only a half-hearted conviction of the "resurrection of the body and life everlasting" which we say we believe, in the Apostles Creed. Life is hard enough. Not having a clear goal in sight can make it unbearable.

"Going-to-heaven-when-I-die" may suit some people, but it is hardly definite enough to suit the Christian.

No sir! The Christian's *complete* faith is that he will be raised up in the glory of a risen body because Christ has first been raised up in glory. "If Christ has not been raised," Saint Paul says, "your faith is groundless." (I Corinthians 15:17) He means that the faith of the Church is that Christ's resurrection is going to be the cause of yours and mine. If our Lord's resurrection didn't take place, Saint Paul says quite logically, we had better look into *that*, for it would mean that our bodies are going to lie in the earth forever.

MAN'S FINAL END IS TO BE WITH GOD—BODY AND SOUL

If Christ didn't rise from the dead, in other words, we actually have nothing to hope for. Living on as a "soul" for all eternity won't do. That state is only a temporary one, to last until Christ returns to earth in glory and raises up the dead. The Church has never believed that living on as a "soul" would be man's final end, because God loves us the way he made us, and that means body and soul. If he means to bring us to himself, he will surely do it by giving us a come-as-you-are invitation. We are to come, not as angels nor as spooks, but as human beings, body and soul. (Read Chapter 15 of Saint Paul's first letter to the Christians at Corinth. It will help you to know clearly what Catholics believe about life after death).

Jesus' first visit that we are told about, after the early morning ones that we examined in the last chapter, took place "that very day" (Luke 24:13), the day Jesus rose from the dead. Saint Mark mentions very briefly that the Lord appeared "in another form" to two disciples as they went into the country (Mark 16:12), but Saint Luke describes it at length.

JESUS APPEARED TO TWO WHO
HAD SHOWN BELIEF IN HIM

Remember, that Sunday was no sacred day in those times, let alone Easter day, as it is for us now. The great Passover Sabbath was ended and it was a business-as-usual morning. Even though the Jews could not eat yeast for a week, in remembrance of their deliverance from slavery in Egypt, they did resume their ordinary tasks. Many of the pilgrims to Jerusalem broke camp, so to say, and went home that morning. Two men who had begun to believe in Jesus were making their way, downcast, to the town of Emmaus, seven miles from Jerusalem, when they were joined by a stranger. They had been talking about the hopes they had placed in Jesus of Nazareth, which had all been crushed by his death.

When the stranger expressed his ignorance of these facts they were surprised. They patiently explained to him that Jesus was a prophet, "mighty in deed and word in the eyes of God and the mass of the people." They went on to say: "We had hoped He might be the man destined to redeem Israel." But, alas, his death had happened three days ago, so now they had nothing to hope for. They *had* heard a story of an empty tomb and a vision of angels to some women (Luke 24:22-24), but they weren't putting much stock in it. They told the stranger that while the empty tomb was evidently a fact, the women had not seen Jesus in person.

At this point, Jesus, who was the stranger (they did not realize this because "their eyes were prevented from recognizing Him," Luke 24:16), finally broke in. He called them dull, and told them they were slow to understand what the prophets had said whenever the prophets' message had to do with the Messia and suffering. "Was it not necessary," he asked, "for the Messia to undergo these sufferings and *thus* enter into his glory?" Time

228

and again, you see, Jesus recalled the Suffering Servant of the Lord, meaning himself. Then he carefully went through the main parts of Israel's holy books with them, from Moses through all the prophets, "explaining the passages which referred to himself in every part of the scriptures." (Luke 24:27)

THE TWO RECOGNIZED JESUS
IN THE BREAKING OF BREAD

When he rose to go, they begged him to stay with them for the evening meal. As he took bread, he said the blessing over it, broke it and offered it to them (the very words used to describe his action at the Last Supper). Then, "their eyes were opened and they recognized him . . . in the breaking of bread." (Luke 24:31, 35) But he vanished from their sight.

The two men raced back to Jerusalem with their news, only to be told that Peter had also seen the Lord. After that, the appearances of Jesus began to multiply. On "that same day, the first of the week" (John 20:19-23), Jesus came to them behind closed doors while the apostle Thomas was absent. He gave them the gift of his peace, and then the gift of the Holy Spirit. As the Father had sent him into the world, so Jesus sent his disciples. He gave them power in the Spirit to forgive or not to forgive sins. This shouldn't surprise us. The whole purpose of his dying and rising was "the forgiveness of sins," as the Apostles' Creed says. Now the work is done, and he is able to give this gift.

Saint Luke tells the story of Jesus breaking in on his startled and panic-stricken friends on the night the two Emmaus disciples returned to Jerusalem. (Luke 24:36-43) He asked for food while he was with them, and ate some broiled fish and a honeycomb. His first efforts to show them he was not a ghost were not proving successful, even though he told them to ex-

amine his hands and feet: "Feel me and convince yourselves," are Jesus' words. (Luke 24:39) The disbelief continued, however, and the Lord scolded them for it. (Mark 16:14)

THOMAS INSISTED ON PROOF
OF JESUS' RESURRECTION

Saint John is the one who tells the famous story of "doubting Thomas." Jesus came to visit his friends one week to the day after his resurrection. Thomas missed him the first time, and he said later, "Unless I see in his hands the print of the nails, and put my finger into the place of the nails, and my hand into his side, I will not believe." (John 20:25) That is exactly what Jesus made him do, however, and Thomas responded in awe and amazement: "My Lord and my God!"

Perhaps the most attractive account of an appearance of Christ is one given by Saint John. (John 21:1-3) He tells how seven of the Twelve had gone back to Galilee and taken up their work again. They were fishing on their familiar lake—probably wondering what the marvelous events they had witnessed could mean—when Jesus joined them at the lakeshore. He cooked a breakfast of fish and bread for them. On this occasion, the Lord gave Peter the special responsibility of taking care of his flock. He did this by putting to him the question "Do you love me?" three times. Lambs and sheep, the Master said, all need feeding, even though this work of feeding them may end by Peter's being dragged off to death. (John 21:19)

MYSTERY OF CHRIST'S GLORY
SHOWS DEATH IS NOT FINAL

The mysteries of Christ's resurrection and of his ascent to his Father are joined in one—the mystery of his "glory." Even though the proofs of the mystery of his glory are several, and, in

230

Saint Luke's phrase, the time of them forty days, the glorification of Jesus by the Father remains a single mystery. The mystery of Jesus' glory should mean a lot to us. This is the great sign that death is not final. This shows us that the body which causes us so much trouble in life, with its needs and demands, is meant to end in an entirely different state from the one it has now. It is meant to end in *glory*.

Jesus controlled his Body by his thoughts and his obedient will. He made it his servant, not his master. The result? No grave could hold him, because he did *perfectly*—in soul and body—what was required of him.

EACH DAY WE MUST CHOOSE
BETWEEN DECAY AND GLORY

Think of that the next time there's a rebellion going on inside of you. There is the stinking decay of the tomb—a sign of hell, because sin causes death—and there is the glory of the man who rises with Christ.

That's the choice. For a whole lifetime you have to make that choice—afresh, each day.

32

Jesus Sends Another
to Sustain Us

Almost every one knows who the Quakers are, that religious
Society of Friends to which William Penn belonged. They were
founded by George Fox, a pious young Englishman of the
1600's, as a "peculiar people" (different, that is) who lived
simply, as the gospel demanded. They were called "in scorn by
their detractors Quakers," Fox wrote, because when the Spirit
of God or Inner Light spoke to their spirit during a "meeting"
they quaked all over. The Shakers are a similar group. (Have
you heard of Shaker Heights, Ohio, named for them?) Their
real name is "The United Society of Believers in Christ's Second Appearing," but because they shook "in holy expectation
before the Lord," people called them Shakers.

Holy Rollers get their name in the same way. So do the

232

"jumper Churches" of the U.S. southland and the islands of the Caribbean. The largest bodies of this sort are the many Pentecostal Churches, some of which are entitled "Assemblies of God." A common sign to be seen in U.S. cities where Puerto Rican and other Spanish-speaking Americans live is one in the form of a cross bearing the words *Iglesia Pentecostal*—Pentecostal Church. People who know a lot about the growth of religious bodies say that these groups (and the Jehovah's Witnesses, who say they aren't a church) are likely to comprise the largest totals of non-Catholic Christians in a hundred years—more numerous than all the Protestants in the world—depending on what happens in Latin America.

THE HOLY SPIRIT GIVES LIFE
TO CHRIST'S BODY, THE CHURCH

It is important to bring this matter up because these believers have a firm grasp on one great Catholic principle at least, namely that the Spirit of God dwells in the Church. They are sound as can be on that, though they may not be so firm on other mysteries of faith. We must try to learn from them. If anyone should say to you, "Where do you Catholics get the right to claim that you are the Church of Jesus Christ?", a good *first* answer would be: "We are a family of charity in whom the Holy Spirit dwells." Later we might tell our questioner certain other things, for example, how the eucharist can be celebrated with a perfect love only where there is a bishop who has complete or Catholic faith; how the Church is composed of all those "made into one" by eucharists like those celebrated in a Catholic "household" (the Greek word is *diocese*) by a bishop or one of his priests, and so on. But the first thing we should say is: "Ours is the faith of Jesus Christ because the Holy Spirit lives in our midst."

233

THE CHRIST-MESSAGE HIDDEN,
EVEN AS IT UNFOLDS

What underlies every chapter in this book is the message of God to men—and that is a serious business. Not a heavy business. Not somber or dull, but joyous. Lively in fact. Nonetheless, a matter of life and death. This message is a Word spoken by God to men in the person of Jesus Christ, and kept alive in our hearts by the Spirit whom he sends from the Father.

There is a possibility you may not have known until reading these chapters, and the parts of the Bible they send you to, how full of mystery Jesus the Lord is. That he is the Son of God and the second person of the blessed Trinity you knew. God has taught this and Catholics believe it. You are a Catholic (well—many who read this are), and you believe it. Simple as ABC, in a way. It is only when you begin to look into the gospels that you see how much lies beneath the statement: "Jesus Christ is true God and true man." The closer you examine the words and actions of this mysterious Person the better you understand him. At the same time, however, you become less sure of yourself and of the tidy little mental picture you had of the Savior up till now.

Close study of the New Testament shows that he was much more fully human than we had supposed, and also much more divine. A better way to express it would be to say that his divine-humanness (or God-man-ness) escapes us farther and farther, the more we get to know Him. God reveals, unfolds, the mystery of himself in Christ. As he does so, something of the hiddenness of God becomes known to us. He is terribly near to us, yet we will never understand him. An infinity sets us apart from him, yet he is our familiar friend. All this grows clearer as we reflect on Jesus' words: "Philip . . . he who sees me sees the Father." (John 14:9)

NO KNOWLEDGE OF CHRIST
WITHOUT THE SPIRIT'S HELP

This should have been a hard book to get through, if you struggled to know the mysteriousness and the friendship of Jesus. If it were easy, it wouldn't have been him at all you were confronting, but only some caricature. His friendship is hard won. The spendor of God himself shines out of those eyes, not that of a Colonel Glenn or a Dr. Tom Dooley. Moreover, it is impossible to know Jesus unless the strong Counselor whom he sends us from the Father gives us light and understanding. If a man can't even say the name "Jesus" in faith without the Holy Spirit's help (so Paul says in 1 Corinthians 12:3), how can he take in the whole *person* of the Lord apart from this help? It is quite impossible, obviously. Something that is very easy, on the other hand, is to study about Jesus on a shallow level and then—without much effort and without the Holy Spirit's guidance—to say that we "know" the Lord. All we would be knowing in that case is our own puny mental image of him. That picture is an easy one to take in because it is so much like us and so much unlike him.

SPEAKING OF PICTURES
OF CHRIST

The whole idea of sacred art can be of great help here. Do you know why the Greek Christians of old used to show Christ with coal-black eyes, a nose like a hawk's beak, and hair the color of tar? Was it because they couldn't paint, or set mosaic-tile, any better than that? Nothing of the sort. They knew they were representing someone who was the great Mystery of God, and that if they portrayed an ordinary man whom you could take in at a glance they had failed in their task.

That is why the sketches done in these pages by "S. Irenita"

(as your bifocals may have informed you) of Jesus, his friends, and his mother, are so rich. There is so much more there than meets the eye. They require study and prayer because they are mystery drawings: they show forth the Mystery of God's love. You do not see Rock Hudson, hair parted in the middle, or that lady-with-a-beard meant to be Christ that you find on the nearest undertaker's calendar—*twelve times!* No, these sketches have been a challenge, just as Jesus is a challenge. If we think in soft and sentimental terms we will tend to *dislike* them. Jesus must be fashioned in *our* image and likeness, we are inclined to say. When he leaves the level of our values, he is of no more use to us. That is the great danger.

But the Jesus who is, the Lord of the New Covenant, is nothing like an image of ourselves. "Then He turned around, and looked full on Peter." (Luke 22:61) "Here He changed His appearance before their eyes . . . then a cloud formed and enveloped them, and a voice rang out in the cloud: 'This is my beloved Son. Listen to Him!' " (Mark 9:3,8) "At this very moment (Stephen speaks), I see the skies opened and the Son of Man standing at the right hand of God." (Acts 7:56) "I saw heaven opened. I saw a white horse, and its rider is called Faithful and True . . . His eyes are like a flame of fire . . . He is clothed in a garment sprinkled with blood, and his name is 'The Word of God' . . . He will rule them with an iron rod . . . on his robe is his name inscribed, 'King of Kings and Lord of Lords.' " (Apocalypse 19:11-16)

A SUMMING-UP:
WHOSE FRIENDS ARE WE?

As this brief volume draws to a close, we ought to be asking ourselves what impact our faith in Jesus Christ is having on those who know us. Can they tell, for example, that the beloved Son of the Father is our intimate friend? That we willingly

serve the faithful and true one who is King of Kings and Lord of Lords? Often, it seems, our acquaintances can not so much as guess this. The friends of Jesus huddle together like frightened sheep, hoping no one will bring up the embarrassing question of religion, particularly *their* religion. They follow the Lamb of God, all right. The Rider on a white horse with eyes like a flame of fire they don't know very well.

"IT HAS SEEMED GOOD TO THE HOLY SPIRIT AND TO US . . ."

Browse in the Acts of the Apostles for a bit to see how the men who first preached about Jesus conducted themselves. They did many wonders and signs (Acts 2:43); they taught the people, and proclaimed in the case of Jesus' resurrection from the dead (4:2); they said they could not keep from speaking of what they had seen and heard. (4:20) Why such boldness on their parts? Because they were filled with the Holy Spirit! (See Acts 2:4; 4:31; 6:5; 8:29; 9:17; 10:44; 13:9) They rejoiced that they had been counted worthy to suffer disgrace for the name of Jesus. Never for a single day did they cease teaching and preaching the good news about him. (5:41-42) You couldn't shut them up.

When St. Paul went spreading the good news he came to Ephesus where he found a group of believers. They had been baptized in the name of the Lord Jesus but had never heard of the Holy Spirit! Paul laid his hands on them, and immediately the Spirit came on them in full measure. (Acts 19:1-7)

A SPIRIT-GOVERNED CHURCH

If you had to describe the life of the infant Church, no phrase would do it better than to say that it was a community impelled and ruled by the Holy Spirit. It had to be that way, of course,

if it really was Christ's Church. "Unless I depart," he had said, "the Advocate will not come to you." (John 16:7) "When the Spirit of truth has come, he will conduct you through the whole range of truth." (V. 13) "He will teach you everything, and refresh your memory on everything I have told you." (John 14:26)

Almost every reader of this book has been confirmed, which means you have the gift of the Holy Spirit. All through these pages you have been reading the good news about Jesus Christ in whom you have been saved. You must let that sacrament do its work in you now. Let the Holy Ghost refresh your memories on all you have learned. You and your family and your friends, all confirmed in the Spirit, must be welded by Him into a holy community which will make men say: "They *have* to be the Church of Jesus Christ. They have the Spirit of Jesus (Acts 16:7), don't they—the Spirit of truth and love?"

It isn't they alone who live. It's—well, actually, it's *Christ* who lives in them.

Date Due

DEMCO NO 295

AUG 12 '65	SANISIUS			
SEP 15 '65	CANISIUS			
JAN 6 '66				
APR 5 '66				
JUL 29 '66				
APR 28 '66 MAY 14 '7?	CANISIUS			

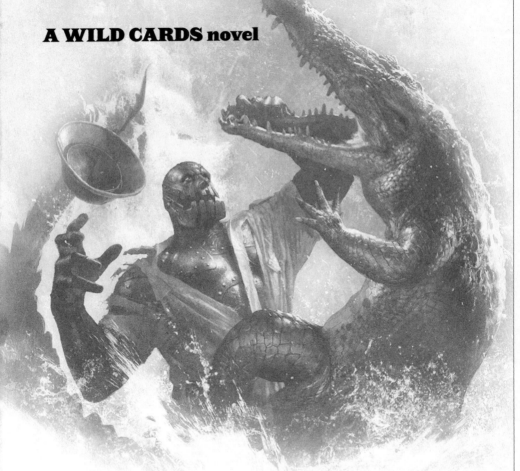

EDITED BY

GEORGE R. R. MARTIN

BUSTED FLUSH

A WILD CARDS
novel

This world-spanning "mosaic novel" interweaves action and adventure with very human stories of ordinary people to whom awesome power comes as both blessing and curse.

"Clever twists on today's political landscape and the unique powers of several new 'aces' will lure back past readers."
—*Publishers Weekly*

tor-forge.com

EDITED BY

GEORGE R. R. MARTIN

Six decades since the release of the
Wild Card virus, a new generation of
aces has taken its place on the world
stage, becoming crucial players in
international events. At the UN,
veteran ace John Fortune has
assembled a team of young aces,
known as the Committee,
to assist at trouble spots
around the world. But their
opponents have their own
aces and jokers ready....

INSIDE STRAIGHT

A WILD CARDS NOVEL

TOR®
tor-forge.com

Like what you've read already?
Make it a full hand!

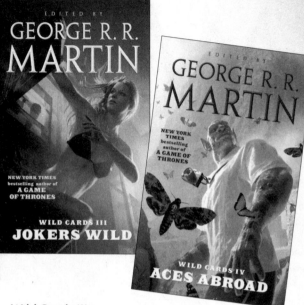

Wild Cards II: Aces High

In book two we trace these heroes and villains through the tumultuous 1980s, in stories from SF and fantasy giants such as George R. R. Martin, Roger Zelazny, Pat Cadigan, Lewis Shiner, Walter Jon Williams, and others.

Wild Cards III: Jokers Wild

The third volume of the Wild Cards series features seven of science fiction's most gifted writers. Join Edward Bryant, Leanne C. Harper, George R. R. Martin, John J. Miller, Lewis Shiner, Walter Simons, and Melinda M. Snodgrass for a journey of wonder and excitement

Wild Cards IV: Aces Abroad

The action-packed alternate fantasy is back for a new generation, featuring fiction from #1 *New York Times* bestselling author George R. R. Martin, Michael Cassutt, Melinda M. Snodgrass, Lewis Shiner, and more— plus two completely new stories from Kevin Andrew Murphy and bestselling author Carrie Vaughn.

"Emotionally powerful. Wild Cards deals up the variety of short fiction without losing the continuity of a novel."
—*Seattle Times*

"The shared-world series known as Wild Cards has had a long and illustrious history of contributors and achievements." —SciFi.com

"Perhaps the most original and provocative of the shared worlds books."
—Peter S. Beagle, author of *The Last Unicorn*

tor-forge.com

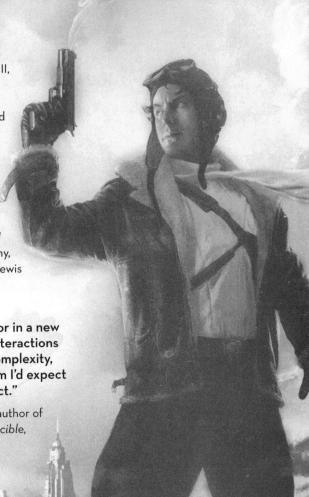